Lost Illusions

Honore De Balzac

Lits © 2011

Printed in the United States.

Balzac, Honore de.
Lost Illusions. Honore de Balzac – 1st ed.

1. Fiction - Classics

CONTENTS

INTRODUCTION

The longest, without exception, of Balzac's books, and one which contains hardly any passage that is not very nearly of his best, *Illusions Perdues* suffers, I think, a little in point of composition from the mixture of the Angouleme scenes of its first and third parts with the purely Parisian interest of *Un Grand Homme de Province*. It is hardly possible to exaggerate the gain in distinctness and lucidity of arrangement derived from putting *Les Deux Poetes* and *Eve et David* (a much better title than that which has been preferred in the *Edition Definitive*) together in one volume, and reserving the greatness and decadence of Lucien de Rubempre for another. It is distinctly awkward that this should be divided, as it is itself an enormous episode, a sort of Herodotean parenthesis, rather than an integral part of the story. And, as a matter of fact, it joins on much more to the *Splendeurs et Miseres des Courtisanes* than to its actual companions. In fact, it is an instance of the somewhat haphazard and arbitrary way in which the actual division of the *Comedie* has worked, that it should, dealing as it does wholly and solely with Parisian life, be put in the *Scenes de la Vie de Province*, and should be separated from its natural conclusion not merely as a matter of volumes, but as a matter of divisions. In making the arrangement, however, it is necessary to remember Balzac's own scheme, especially as the connection of the three parts in other ways is too close to permit the wrenching of them asunder altogether and finally. This caution given, all that is necessary can be done by devoting the first part of the introduction entirely to the first and third or Angouleme parts, and by consecrating the latter part to the egregious Lucien by himself.

There is a double gain in doing this, for, independently of the connection as above referred to, Lucien has little to do except as an opportunity for the display of virtue by his sister and David Sechard; and the parts in which they appear are among the most interesting of Balzac's work. The "Idyllic" charm of this marriage for love, combined as it is with exhibitions of the author's power in more than one of the ways in which he loved best to show it, has never escaped attention from Balzac's most competent critics. He himself had speculated in print and paper before David Sechard was conceived; he himself had for all "maniacs," all men of one idea, the fraternal enthusiasm of a fellow-victim. He could never touch a miser without a sort of shudder of interest; and that singular fancy of his for describing complicated legal and commercial undertakings came in too. Nor did he spare, in this wide-ranging book, to bring in other favorite matters of his, the *hobereau*--or squireen--aristocracy, the tittle-tattle of the country town and so forth.

The result is a book of multifarious interest, not hampered, as some of its fellows are, by an uncertainty on the author's part as to what particular hare he is coursing. Part of the interest, after the description of the printing office and of old Sechard's swindling of his son, is a doubling, it is true, upon that of *La muse du Departement*, and is perhaps a little less amusingly done; but it is blended with better matters. Sixte du Chatelet is a considerable addition to Balzac's gallery of the aristocracy in transition--of the Bonaparte *parvenus* whom perhaps he understood even better than the old nobility, for they were already in his time becoming adulterated and alloyed; or than the new folk of business and finance, for they were but in their earliest stages. Nor is the rest of the society of Madame de Bargeton inferior.

But the real interest both of *Les Deux Poetes*, and still more of *Eve et David*, between which two, be it always remembered, comes in the *Distinguished Provincial*, lies in the characters who gave their name to the last part. In David, the man of one idea, who yet has room for an honest love and an all-deserved friendship, Balzac could not go wrong. David Sechard takes a place by himself among the sheep of the *Comedie*. Some may indeed say that this phrase is unfortunate, that Balzac's sheep have more qualities of the mutton than innocence. It is not quite to be denied. But David is very far indeed from being a good imbecile, like Cesar Birotteau, or a man intoxicated out of common-sense by a passion respectable in itself, like Goriot. His sacrifice of his mania in time is something--nay, it is very much; and his disinterested devotion to his brother-in-law does not quite pass the limits of sense.

But what shall we say of Eve? She is good of course, good as gold, as Eugenie Grandet herself; and the novelist has been kind enough to allow her to be happier. But has he quite interested us in her love for David? Has he even persuaded us that the love existed in a form deserving the name? Did not Eve rather take her husband to protect him, to look after him, than either to love, honor, and obey in the orthodox sense, or to love for love's sake only, as some still take their husbands and wives even at the end of the nineteenth century? This is a question which each reader must answer for himself; but few are likely to refuse assent to the sentence, "Happy the husband who has such a wife as Eve Chardon!"

The central part of *Illusions Perdues*, which in reason stands by itself, and may do so ostensibly with considerably less than the introduction explanatory which Balzac often gives to his own books, is one of the most carefully worked out and diversely important of his novels. It should, of course, be read before *Splendeurs et Miseres des Courtisanes*, which is avowedly its second part, a small piece of *Eve et David* serving as the link between them. But it is almost sufficient by and to itself. *Lucien de Rubempre ou le Journalisme* would be the most straightforward and descriptive title for it, and one which Balzac in some of his moods would have been content enough to use.

The story of it is too continuous and interesting to need elaborate argument, for nobody is likely to miss any important link in it. But Balzac has nowhere excelled in finesse and success of analysis, the double disillusion which introduces itself at once between Madame de Bargeton and Lucien, and which makes any *redintegratio amoris* of a valid kind impossible, because each cannot but be aware that the other has anticipated the rupture. It will not, perhaps, be a matter of such general agreement whether he has or has not exceeded the fair license of the novelist in attributing to Lucien those charms of body and gifts of mind which make him, till his moral weakness and worthlessness are exposed, irresistible, and enable him for a time to repair his faults by a sort of fairy good-luck. The sonnets of *Les Marguerites*, which were given to the author by poetical friends --Gautier, it is said, supplied the "Tulip"--are undoubtedly good and sufficient. But Lucien's first article, which is (according to a practice the rashness of which cannot be too much deprecated) given likewise, is certainly not very wonderful; and the Paris press must have been rather at a low ebb if it made any sensation. As we are not favored with any actual portrait of Lucien, detection is less possible here, but the novelist has perhaps a very little abused the privilege of making a hero, "Like Paris handsome, and like Hector brave," or rather "Like Paris handsome, and like Phoebus clever." There is no doubt, however, that the interest of the book lies partly in the vivid and severe picture of journalism given in it, and partly in the way in which the character of Lucien is adjusted to show up that of the abstract journalist still farther.

How far is the picture true? It must be said, in fairness to Balzac, that a good many persons of some competence in France have pronounced for its truth there; and if that be so, all one can say is, "So much the worse for French journalists." It is also certain that a lesser, but still not inconsiderable number of persons in England--generally persons who, not perhaps with Balzac's genius, have like Balzac published books, and are not satisfied with their reception by the press--agree more or less as to England. For myself, I can only say that I do not believe things have ever been quite so bad in England, and that I am quite sure there never has been any need for them to be. There are, no doubt, spiteful, unprincipled, incompetent practitioners of journalism as of everything else; and it is of course obvious that while advertisements, the favor of the chiefs of parties, and so forth, are temptations to newspaper managers not to hold up a very high standard of honor, anonymity affords to newspaper writers a dangerously easy shield to cover malice or dishonesty. But I can only say that during long practice in every kind of political and literary journalism, I never was seriously asked to write anything I did not think, and never had the slightest difficulty in confining myself to what I did think.

In fact Balzac, like a good many other men of letters who abuse journalism, put himself very much out of court by continually practising it, not merely during his struggling period, but long after he had made his name, indeed almost to the very last. And it is very hard to resist the conclusion that when he charged journalism generally not merely with envy, hatred, malice, and all uncharitableness, but with hopeless and pervading dishonesty, he had little more ground for it than an inability to conceive how any one, except from vile reasons of this kind, could fail to praise Honore de Balzac.

At any rate, either his art by itself, or his art assisted and strengthened by that personal feeling which, as we have seen counted for much with him, has here produced a wonderfully vivid piece of fiction--one, I think, inferior in success to hardly anything he has done. Whether, as at a late period a very well-informed, well-affected, and well-equipped critic hinted, his picture of the Luciens and the Lousteaus did not a little to propagate both is another matter. The seriousness with which Balzac took the accusation perhaps shows a little sense of galling. But putting this aside, *Un Grand Homme de Province a Paris* must be ranked, both for comedy and tragedy, both for scheme and execution, in the first rank of his work.

The bibliography of this long and curious book--almost the only one which contains some verse, some of Balzac's own, some given to him by his more poetical friends--occupies full ten pages of M. de Lovenjoul's record. The first part, which bore the general title, was a book from the beginning, and appeared in 1837 in the *Scenes de la Vie de Province*. It had five chapters, and the original verse it contained had appeared in the *Annalaes Romantiques* ten years earlier with slight variants. The second part, *Un Grand Homme de Province*, likewise appeared as a book, independently published by Souverain in 1839 in two volumes and forty chapters. But two of these chapters had been inserted a few days before the publications in the *Estafette*. Here Canalis was more distinctly identified with Lamartine than in the subsequent texts. The third part, unlike its forerunners, appeared serially in two papers, *L'Etat* and *Le Parisien*, in the year 1843, under the title of *David Sechard, ou les Souffrances d'un Inventeur*, and next year became a book under the first title only. But before this last issue it had been united to the other two parts, and had appeared as *Eve et David* in the first edition of the *Comedie*.

George Saintsbury

DEDICATION

To Monsieur Victor Hugo,

It was your birthright to be, like a Rafael or a Pitt, a great poet at an age when other men are children; it was your fate, the fate of Chateaubriand and of every man of genius, to struggle against jealousy skulking behind the columns of a newspaper, or crouching in the subterranean places of journalism. For this reason I desired that your victorious name should help to win a victory for this work that I inscribe to you, a work which, if some persons are to be believed, is an act of courage as well as a veracious history. If there had been journalists in the time of Moliere, who can doubt but that they, like marquises, financiers, doctors, and lawyers, would have been within the province of the writer of plays? And why should Comedy, *qui castigat ridendo mores*, make an exception in favor of one power, when the Parisian press spares none? I am happy, monsieur, in this opportunity of subscribing myself your sincere admirer and friend,

DE BALZAC.

1

TWO POETS
(Lost Illusions I)

At the time when this story opens, the Stanhope press and the ink-distributing roller were not as yet in general use in small provincial printing establishments. Even at Angouleme, so closely connected through its paper-mills with the art of typography in Paris, the only machinery in use was the primitive wooden invention to which the language owes a figure of speech--"the press groans" was no mere rhetorical expression in those days. Leather ink-balls were still used in old-fashioned printing houses; the pressman dabbed the ink by hand on the characters, and the movable table on which the form of type was placed in readiness for the sheet of paper, being made of marble, literally deserved its name of "impression-stone." Modern machinery has swept all this old-world mechanism into oblivion; the wooden press which, with all its imperfections, turned out such beautiful work for the Elzevirs, Plantin, Aldus, and Didot is so completely forgotten, that something must be said as to the obsolete gear on which Jerome-Nicolas Sechard set an almost superstitious affection, for it plays a part in this chronicle of great small things.

Sechard had been in his time a journeyman pressman, a "bear" in compositors' slang. The continued pacing to and fro of the pressman from ink-table to press, from press to ink-table, no doubt suggested the nickname. The "bears," however, make matters even by calling the compositors monkeys, on account of the nimble industry displayed by those gentlemen in picking out the type from the hundred and fifty-two compartments of the cases.

In the disastrous year 1793, Sechard, being fifty years old and a married man, escaped the great Requisition which swept the bulk of French workmen into the army. The old pressman was the only hand left in the printing-house; and when the master (otherwise the "gaffer") died, leaving a widow, but no children, the business seemed to be on the verge of extinction; for the solitary "bear" was quite incapable of the feat of transformation into a "monkey," and in his quality of pressman had never learned to read or write. Just then, however, a Representative of the People being in a mighty hurry to publish the Decrees of the Convention, bestowed a master printer's license on Sechard, and requisitioned the establishment. Citizen Sechard accepted the dangerous patent, bought the business of his master's widow with his wife's savings, and took over the plant at half its value. But he was not even at the beginning. He was bound to print the Decrees of the Republic without mistakes and without delay.

In this strait Jerome-Nicolas Sechard had the luck to discover a noble Marseillais who had no mind to emigrate and lose his lands, nor yet to show himself openly and lose his head, and consequently was fain to earn a living by some lawful industry. A bargain was struck. M. le Comte de Maucombe, disguised in a provincial printer's jacket, set up, read, and corrected the decrees which forbade citizens to harbor aristocrats under pain of death; while the "bear," now a "gaffer," printed the copies and duly posted them, and the pair remained safe and sound.

In 1795, when the squall of the Terror had passed over, Nicolas Sechard was obliged to look out for another jack-of-all-trades to be compositor, reader, and foreman in one; and an Abbe who declined the oath succeeded the Comte de Maucombe as soon as the First Consul restored public worship. The Abbe became a Bishop at the Restoration, and in after days the Count and the Abbe met and sat together on the same bench of the House of Peers.

In 1795 Jerome-Nicolas had not known how to read or write; in 1802 he had made no progress in either art; but by allowing a handsome margin for "wear and tear" in his estimates, he managed to pay a foreman's wages. The once easy-going journeyman was a terror to his "bears" and "monkeys." Where poverty ceases, avarice begins. From the day when Sechard first caught a glimpse of the possibility of making a fortune, a growing covetousness developed and sharpened in him a certain practical faculty for business--greedy, suspicious, and keen-eyed. He carried on his craft in disdain of theory. In course of time he had learned to estimate at a glance the cost of printing per page or per sheet in every kind of type. He proved to unlettered customers that large type costs more to move; or, if small type was under discussion, that it was more difficult to handle. The setting-up of the type was the one part of his craft of which he knew nothing; and so great was his terror lest he should not charge enough, that he always made a heavy profit. He never took his eyes off his compositors while they were paid by the hour. If he knew that a paper manufacturer was in difficulties, he would buy up his stock at a cheap rate and warehouse the paper. So from this time forward he was his own landlord, and owned the old house which had been a printing office from time immemorial.

He had every sort of luck. He was left a widower with but one son. The boy he sent to the grammar school; he must be educated, not so much for his own sake as to train a successor to the business; and Sechard treated the lad harshly so as to prolong the time of parental rule, making him work at case on holidays, telling him that he must learn to earn his own living, so as to recompense his poor old father, who was slaving his life out to give him an education.

Then the Abbe went, and Sechard promoted one of his four compositors to be foreman, making his choice on the future bishop's recommendation of the man as an honest and intelligent workman. In these ways the worthy printer thought to tide over the time until his son could take a business which was sure to extend in young and clever hands.

David Sechard's school career was a brilliant one. Old Sechard, as a "bear" who had succeeded in life without any education, entertained a very considerable contempt for attainments in book learning; and when he sent his son to Paris to study the higher branches of typography, he recommended the lad so earnestly to save a good round sum in the "working man's paradise" (as he was pleased to call the city), and so distinctly gave the boy to understand that he was not to draw upon the paternal purse, that it seemed as if old Sechard saw some way of gaining private ends of his own by that sojourn in the Land of Sapience. So David learned his trade, and completed his education at the same time, and Didot's foreman became a scholar; and yet when he left Paris at the end of 1819, summoned home by his father to take the helm of business, he had not cost his parent a farthing.

Now Nicolas Sechard's establishment hitherto had enjoyed a monopoly of all the official printing in the department, besides the work of the prefecture and the diocese--three connections which should prove mighty profitable to an active young printer; but precisely at this juncture the firm of Cointet Brothers, paper manufacturers, applied to the authorities for the second printer's license in Angouleme. Hitherto old Sechard had contrived to reduce this license to a dead letter, thanks to the war crisis of the Empire, and consequent atrophy of commercial enterprise; but he had neglected to buy up the right himself, and this piece of parsimony was the ruin of the old business. Sechard thought joyfully when he heard the news that the coming struggle with the Cointets would be fought out by his son and not by himself.

"I should have gone to the wall," he thought, "but a young fellow from the Didots will pull through."

The septuagenarian sighed for the time when he could live at ease in his own fashion. If his knowledge of the higher branches of the craft of printing was scanty, on the other hand, he was supposed to be past master of an art which workmen pleasantly call "tipple-ography," an art held in high esteem by the divine author of *Pantagruel*; though of late, by reason of the persecution of societies yclept of Temperance, the cult has fallen, day by day, into disuse.

Jerome-Nicolas Sechard, bound by the laws of etymology to be a dry subject, suffered from an inextinguishable thirst. His wife, during her lifetime, managed to control within reasonable bounds the passion for the juice of the grape, a taste so natural to the bear that M. de Chateaubriand remarked it among the ursine tribes of the New World. But philosophers inform us that old age is apt to revert to the habits of youth, and Sechard senior is a case in point--the older he grew, the better he loved to drink. The master-passion had given a stamp of originality to an ursine physiognomy; his nose had developed till it reached the proportions of a double great-canon A; his veined cheeks looked like vine-leaves, covered, as they were, with bloated patches of purple, madder red, and often mottled hues; till altogether, the countenance suggested a huge truffle clasped about by autumn vine tendrils. The little gray eyes, peering out from beneath thick eyebrows like bushes covered with snow, were agleam with the cunning of avarice that had extinguished everything else in the man, down to the very instinct of fatherhood. Those eyes never lost their cunning even when disguised in drink. Sechard put you in mind of one of La Fontaine's Franciscan friars, with the fringe of grizzled hair still curling about his bald pate. He was short and corpulent, like one of the old-fashioned lamps for illumination, that burn a vast deal of oil to a very small piece of wick; for excess of any sort confirms the habit of body, and drunkenness, like much study, makes the fat man stouter, and the lean man leaner still.

For thirty years Jerome-Nicolas-Sechard had worn the famous municipal three-cornered hat, which you may still see here and there on the head of the towncrier in out-of-the-way places. His breeches and waistcoat were of greenish velveteen, and he wore an old-fashioned brown greatcoat, gray cotton stockings, and shoes with silver buckles to them. This costume, in which the workman shone through the burgess, was so thoroughly in keeping with the man's character, defects, and way of life, that he might have come ready dressed into the world. You could no more imagine him apart from his clothes than you could think of a bulb without its husk. If the old printer had not long since given the measure of his blind greed, the very nature of the man came out in the manner of his abdication.

Knowing, as he did, that his son must have learned his business pretty thoroughly in the great school of the Didots, he had yet been ruminating for a long while over the bargain that he meant to drive with David. All that the father made, the son, of course, was bound to lose, but in business this worthy knew nothing of father or son. If, in the first instance, he had looked on David as his only child, later he came to regard him as the natural purchaser of the business, whose interests were therefore his own. Sechard meant to sell dear; David, of course, to buy cheap; his son, therefore, was an antagonist, and it was his duty to get the better of him. The transformation of sentiment into self-seeking, ordinarily slow, tortuous, and veiled by hypocrisy in better educated people, was swift and direct in the old "bear," who demonstrated the superiority of shrewd tipple-ography over book-learned typography.

David came home, and the old man received him with all the cordiality which cunning folk can assume with an eye to business. He was as full of thought for him as any lover for his mistress; giving him his arm, telling him where to put his foot down so as to avoid the mud, warming the bed for him, lighting a fire in his room, making his supper ready. The next day, after he had done his best to fluster his son's wits over a sumptuous dinner, Jerome-Nicolas Sechard, after copious potations, began with a "Now for business," a remark so singularly misplaced between two hiccoughs, that David begged his parent to postpone serious matters until the morrow. But the old "bear" was by no means inclined to put off the long-expected battle; he was too well prepared to turn his tipsiness to good account. He had dragged the chain these fifty years, he would not wear it another hour; tomorrow his son should be the "gaffer."

Perhaps a word or two about the business premises may be said here. The printing-house had been established since the reign of Louis XIV. in the angle made by the Rue de Beaulieu and the Place du Murier; it had been devoted to its present purposes for a long time past. The ground floor consisted of a single huge room lighted on the side next the street by an old-fashioned casement, and by a large sash window that gave upon the yard at the back. A passage at the side led to the private office; but in the provinces the processes of typography excite such a lively interest, that customers usually preferred to enter by way of the glass door in the street front, though they at once descended three steps, for the floor of the workshop lay below the level of the street. The gaping newcomer always failed to note the perils of the passage through the shop; and while staring at the sheets of paper strung in groves across the ceiling, ran against the rows of cases, or knocked his hat against the tie-bars that secured the presses in position. Or the customer's eyes would follow the agile movements of a compositor, picking out type from the hundred and fifty-two compartments of his case, reading his copy, verifying the words in the composing-stick, and leading the lines, till a ream of damp paper weighted with heavy slabs, and set down in the middle of the gangway, tripped up the bemused spectator, or he caught his hip against the angle of a bench, to the huge delight of boys, "bears," and "monkeys." No wight had ever been known to reach the further end without accident. A couple of glass-windowed cages had been built out into the yard at the back; the foreman sat in state in the one, the master printer in the other. Out in the yard the walls were agreeably decorated by trellised vines, a tempting bit of color, considering the owner's reputation. On the one side of the space stood the kitchen, on the other the woodshed, and in a ramshackle penthouse against the hall at the back, the paper was trimmed and damped down. Here, too, the forms, or, in ordinary language, the masses of set-up type, were washed. Inky streams issuing thence blended with the ooze from the kitchen sink, and found their way into the kennel in the street outside; till peasants coming into the town of a market day believed that the Devil was taking a wash inside the establishment.

As to the house above the printing office, it consisted of three rooms on the first floor and a couple of attics in the roof. The first room did duty as dining-room and lobby; it was exactly the same length as the passage below, less the space taken up by the old-fashioned wooden staircase; and was lighted by a narrow casement on the street and a bull's-eye window looking into the yard. The chief characteristic of the apartment was a cynic simplicity, due to money-making greed. The bare walls were covered with plain whitewash, the dirty brick floor had never been scoured, the furniture consisted of three rickety chairs, a round table, and a sideboard stationed between the two doors of a bedroom and a sitting-room. Windows and doors alike were dingy with accumulated grime. Reams of blank paper or printed matter usually encumbered the floor, and more frequently than not the remains of Sechard's dinner, empty bottles and plates, were lying about on the packages.

The bedroom was lighted on the side of the yard by a window with leaded panes, and hung with the old-world tapestry that decorated house fronts in provincial towns on Corpus Christi Day. For furniture it boasted a vast four-post bedstead with canopy, valances and quilt of crimson serge, a couple of worm-eaten armchairs, two tapestry-covered chairs in walnut wood, an aged bureau, and a timepiece on the mantel-shelf. The Seigneur Rouzeau, Jerome-Nicolas' master and predecessor, had furnished the homely old-world room; it was just as he had left it.

The sitting-room had been partly modernized by the late Mme. Sechard; the walls were adorned with a wainscot, fearful to behold, painted the color of powder blue. The panels were decorated with wall-paper --Oriental scenes in sepia tint-- and for all furniture, half-a-dozen chairs with lyre-shaped backs and blue leather cushions were ranged round the room. The two clumsy arched windows that gave upon the Place du Murier were curtainless; there was neither clock nor candle sconce nor mirror above the mantel-shelf, for Mme. Sechard had died before she carried out her scheme of decoration; and the "bear," unable to conceive the use of improvements that brought in no return in money, had left it at this point.

Hither, *pede titubante*, Jerome-Nicolas Sechard brought his son, and pointed to a sheet of paper lying on the table--a valuation of plant drawn up by the foreman under his direction.

"Read that, my boy," said Jerome-Nicolas, rolling a drunken eye from the paper to his son, and back to the paper. "You will see what a jewel of a printing-house I am giving you."

"'Three wooden presses, held in position by iron tie-bars, cast-iron plates----'"

"An improvement of my own," put in Sechard senior.

"'----Together with all the implements, ink-tables, balls, benches, et cetera, sixteen hundred francs!' Why, father," cried David, letting the sheet fall, "these presses of yours are old sabots not worth a hundred crowns; they are only fit for firewood."

"Sabots?" cried old Sechard, "*Sabots*? There, take the inventory and let us go downstairs. You will soon see whether your paltry iron-work contrivances will work like these solid old tools, tried and trusty. You will not have the heart after that to slander honest old presses that go like mail coaches, and are good to last you your lifetime without needing repairs of any sort. Sabots! Yes, sabots that are like to hold salt enough to cook your eggs with--sabots that your father has plodded on with these twenty years; they have helped him to make you what you are."

The father, without coming to grief on the way, lurched down the worn, knotty staircase that shook under his tread. In the passage he opened the door of the workshop, flew to the nearest press (artfully oiled and cleaned for the occasion) and pointed out the strong oaken cheeks, polished up by the apprentice.

"Isn't it a love of a press?"

A wedding announcement lay in the press. The old "bear" folded down the frisket upon the tympan, and the tympan upon the form, ran in the carriage, worked the lever, drew out the carriage, and lifted the frisket and tympan, all with as much agility as the youngest of the tribe. The press, handled in this sort, creaked aloud in such fine style that you might have thought some bird had dashed itself against the window pane and flown away again.

"Where is the English press that could go at that pace?" the parent asked of his astonished son.

Old Sechard hurried to the second, and then to the third in order, repeating the manoeuvre with equal dexterity. The third presenting to his wine-troubled eye a patch overlooked by the apprentice, with a notable oath he rubbed it with the skirt of his overcoat, much as a horse-dealer polishes the coat of an animal that he is trying to sell.

"With those three presses, David, you can make your nine thousand francs a year without a foreman. As your future partner, I am opposed to your replacing these presses by your cursed cast-iron machinery, that wears out the type. You in Paris have been making such a to-do over that damned Englishman's invention--a foreigner, an enemy of France who wants to help the ironfounders to a fortune. Oh! you wanted Stanhopes, did you? Thanks for your Stanhopes, that cost two thousand five hundred francs apiece, about twice as much as my three jewels put together, and maul your type to pieces, because there is no give in them. I haven't book-learning like you, but you keep this well in mind, the life of the Stanhope is the death of the type. Those three presses will serve your turn well enough, the printing will be properly done, and folk here in Angouleme won't ask any more of you. You may print with presses made of wood or iron or gold or silver, *they* will never pay you a farthing more."

"'Item,'" pursued David, "'five thousand pounds weight of type from M. Vaflard's foundry----'" Didot's apprentice could not help smiling at the name.

"Laugh away! After twelve years of wear, that type is as good as new. That is what I call a typefounder! M. Vaflard is an honest man, who uses hard metal; and, to my way of thinking, the best typefounder is the one you go to most seldom."

"'----Taken at ten thousand francs,'" continued David. "Ten thousand francs, father! Why, that is two francs a pound, and the Messrs. Didot only ask thirty-six sous for their *Cicero*! These nail-heads of yours will only fetch the price of old metal-- fivepence a pound."

"You call M. Gille's italics, running-hand and round-hand, 'nail-heads,' do you? M. Gille, that used to be printer to the

Emperor! And type that costs six francs a pound! masterpieces of engraving, bought only five years ago. Some of them are as bright yet as when they came from the foundry. Look here!"

Old Sechard pounced upon some packets of unused sorts, and held them out for David to see.

"I am not book-learned; I don't know how to read or write; but, all the same, I know enough to see that M. Gille's sloping letters are the fathers of your Messrs. Didot's English running-hand. Here is the round-hand," he went on, taking up an unused pica type.

David saw that there was no way of coming to terms with his father. It was a case of Yes or No--of taking or leaving it. The very ropes across the ceiling had gone down into the old "bear's" inventory, and not the smallest item was omitted; jobbing chases, wetting-boards, paste-pots, rinsing-trough, and lye-brushes had all been put down and valued separately with miserly exactitude. The total amounted to thirty thousand francs, including the license and the goodwill. David asked himself whether or not this thing was feasible.

Old Sechard grew uneasy over his son's silence; he would rather have had stormy argument than a wordless acceptance of the situation. Chaffering in these sorts of bargains means that a man can look after his interests. "A man who is ready to pay you anything you ask will pay nothing," old Sechard was saying to himself. While he tried to follow his son's train of thought, he went through the list of odds and ends of plant needed by a country business, drawing David now to a hot-press, now to a cutting-press, bragging of its usefulness and sound condition.

"Old tools are always the best tools," said he. "In our line of business they ought to fetch more than the new, like goldbeaters' tools."

Hideous vignettes, representing Hymen and Cupids, skeletons raising the lids of their tombs to describe a V or an M, and huge borders of masks for theatrical posters became in turn objects of tremendous value through old Jerome-Nicolas' vinous eloquence. Old custom, he told his son, was so deeply rooted in the district that he (David) would only waste his pains if he gave them the finest things in life. He himself had tried to sell them a better class of almanac than the *Double Liegeois* on grocers' paper; and what came of it?--the original *Double Liegeois* sold better than the most sumptuous calendars. David would soon see the importance of these old-fashioned things when he found he could get more for them than for the most costly new-fangled articles.

"Aha! my boy, Paris is Paris, and the provinces are the provinces. If a man came in from L'Houmeau with an order for wedding cards, and you were to print them without a Cupid and garlands, he would not believe that he was properly married; you would have them all back again if you sent them out with a plain M on them after the style of your Messrs. Didot. They may be fine printers, but their inventions won't take in the provinces for another hundred years. So there you are."

A generous man is a bad bargain-driver. David's nature was of the sensitive and affectionate type that shrinks from a dispute, and gives way at once if an opponent touches his feelings. His loftiness of feeling, and the fact that the old toper had himself well in hand, put him still further at a disadvantage in a dispute about money matters with his own father, especially as he credited that father with the best intentions, and took his covetous greed for a printer's attachment to his old familiar tools. Still, as Jerome-Nicolas Sechard had taken the whole place over from Rouzeau's widow for ten thousand francs, paid in assignats, it stood to reason that thirty thousand francs in coin at the present day was an exorbitant demand.

"Father, you are cutting my throat!" exclaimed David.

"*I*," cried the old toper, raising his hand to the lines of cord across the ceiling, "I who gave you life? Why, David, what do you suppose the license is worth? Do you know that the sheet of advertisements alone, at fivepence a line, brought in five hundred francs last month? You turn up the books, lad, and see what we make by placards and the registers at the Prefecture, and the work for the mayor's office, and the bishop too. You are a do-nothing that has no mind to get on. You are haggling over the horse that will carry you to some pretty bit of property like Marsac."

Attached to the valuation of plant there was a deed of partnership between Sechard senior and his son. The good father was to let his house and premises to the new firm for twelve hundred francs per annum, reserving one of the two rooms in the roof for himself. So long as David's purchase-money was not paid in full, the profits were to be divided equally; as soon as he paid off his father, he was to be made sole proprietor of the business.

David made a mental calculation of the value of the license, the goodwill, and the stock of paper, leaving the plant out of account. It was just possible, he thought, to clear off the debt. He accepted the conditions. Old Sechard, accustomed to peasants' haggling, knowing nothing of the wider business views of Paris, was amazed at such a prompt conclusion.

"Can he have been putting money by?" he asked himself. "Or is he scheming out, at this moment, some way of not paying me?"

With this notion in his head, he tried to find out whether David had any money with him; he wanted to be paid something on account. The old man's inquisitiveness roused his son's distrust; David remained close buttoned up to the chin.

Next day, old Sechard made the apprentice move all his own household stuff up into the attic until such time as an empty market cart could take it out on the return journey into the country; and David entered into possession of three bare, unfurnished rooms on the day that saw him installed in the printing-house, without one sou wherewith to pay his men's wages. When he asked his father, as a partner, to contribute his share towards the working expenses, the old man pretended not to understand. He had found the printing-house, he said, and he was not bound to find the money too. He had paid his share. Pressed close by his son's reasoning, he answered that when he himself had paid Rouzeau's widow he had not had a penny left. If he, a poor, ignorant working man, had made his way, Didot's apprentice should do still better. Besides, had not David been earning money, thanks to an education paid for by the sweat of his old father's brow? Now surely was the time when the education would come in useful.

"What have you done with your 'polls?'" he asked, returning to the charge. He meant to have light on a problem which his son left unresolved the day before.

"Why, had I not to live?" David asked indignantly, "and books to buy besides?"

"Oh! you bought books, did you? You will make a poor man of business. A man that buys books is hardly fit to print them," retorted the "bear."

Then David endured the most painful of humiliations--the sense of shame for a parent; there was nothing for it but to be passive while his father poured out a flood of reasons--sordid, whining, contemptible, money-getting reasons--in which the niggardly old man wrapped his refusal. David crushed down his pain into the depths of his soul; he saw that he was alone; saw that he had no one to look to but himself; saw, too, that his father was trying to make money out of him; and in a spirit of philosophical curiosity, he tried to find out how far the old man would go. He called old Sechard's attention to the fact that he had never as yet made any inquiry as to his mother's fortune; if that fortune would not buy the printing-house, it might go some ways towards paying the working expenses.

"Your mother's fortune?" echoed old Sechard; "why, it was her beauty and intelligence!"

David understood his father thoroughly after that answer; he understood that only after an interminable, expensive, and disgraceful lawsuit could he obtain any account of the money which by rights was his. The noble heart accepted the heavy burden laid upon it, seeing clearly beforehand how difficult it would be to free himself from the engagements into which he had entered with his father.

"I will work," he said to himself. "After all, if I have a rough time of it, so had the old man; besides, I shall be working for myself, shall I not?"

"I am leaving you a treasure," said Sechard, uneasy at his son's silence.

David asked what the treasure might be.

"Marion!" said his father.

Marion, a big country girl, was an indispensable part of the establishment. It was Marion who damped the paper and cut it to size; Marion did the cooking, washing, and marketing; Marion unloaded the paper carts, collected accounts, and cleaned the ink-balls; and if Marion had but known how to read, old Sechard would have put her to set up type into the bargain.

Old Sechard set out on foot for the country. Delighted as he was with his sale of the business, he was not quite easy in his mind as to the payment. To the throes of the vendor, the agony of uncertainty as to the completion of the purchase inevitably succeeds. Passion of every sort is essentially Jesuitical. Here was a man who thought that education was useless, forcing himself to believe in the influence of education. He was mortgaging thirty thousand francs upon the ideas of honor and conduct which education should have developed in his son; David had received a good training, so David would sweat blood and water to fulfil his engagements; David's knowledge would discover new resources; and David seemed to be full of fine feelings, so--David would pay! Many a parent does in this way, and thinks that he has acted a father's part; old Sechard was quite of that opinion by the time that he had reached his vineyard at Marsac, a hamlet some four leagues out of Angouleme. The previous owner had built a nice little house on the bit of property, and from year to year had added other bits of land to it, until in 1809 the old "bear" bought the whole, and went thither, exchanging the toil of the printing press for the labor of the winepress. As he put it himself, "he had been in that line so long that he ought to know something about it."

During the first twelvemonth of rural retirement, Sechard senior showed a careful countenance among his vine props; for he was always in his vineyard now, just as, in the old days, he had lived in his shop, day in, day out. The prospect of thirty thousand francs was even more intoxicating than sweet wine; already in imagination he fingered the coin. The less the claim to the money, the more eager he grew to pouch it. Not seldom his anxieties sent him hurrying from Marsac to Angouleme; he would climb up the rocky staircases into the old city and walk into his son's workshop to see how business went. There stood the presses in their places; the one apprentice, in a paper cap, was cleaning the ink-balls; there was a creaking of a press over the printing of some trade circular, the old type was still unchanged, and in the dens at the end of the room he saw his son and the foreman reading books, which the "bear" took for proof-sheets. Then he would join David at dinner and go back to Marsac, chewing the cud of uneasy reflection.

Avarice, like love, has the gift of second sight, instinctively guessing at future contingencies, and hugging its presentiments. Sechard senior living at a distance, far from the workshop and the machinery which possessed such a fascination for him, reminding him, as it did, of days when he was making his way, could *feel* that there were disquieting symptoms of inactivity in his son. The name of Cointet Brothers haunted him like a dread; he saw Sechard & Son dropping into the second place. In short, the old man scented misfortune in the wind.

His presentiments were too well founded; disaster was hovering over the house of Sechard. But there is a tutelary deity for misers, and by a chain of unforeseen circumstances that tutelary deity was so ordering matters that the purchase-money of his extortionate bargain was to be tumbled after all into the old toper's pouch.

Indifferent to the religious reaction brought about by the Restoration, indifferent no less to the Liberal movement, David preserved a most unlucky neutrality on the burning questions of the day. In those times provincial men of business were bound to profess political opinions of some sort if they meant to secure custom; they were forced to choose for themselves between the patronage of the Liberals on the one hand or the Royalists on the other. And Love, moreover, had come to David's heart, and with his scientific preoccupation and finer nature he had not room for the dogged greed of which our successful man of business is made; it choked the keen money-getting instinct which would have led him to study the differences between the Paris trade and the business of a provincial printing-house. The shades of opinion so sharply defined in the country are blurred and lost in the great currents of Parisian business life. Cointet Brothers set themselves deliberately to assimilate all shades of monarchical opinion. They let every one know that they fasted of a Friday and kept Lent; they haunted the cathedral; they cultivated the society of the clergy; and in consequence, when books of devotion were once more in demand, Cointet Brothers were the first in this lucrative field. They slandered David, accusing him of Liberalism, Atheism, and what not. How, asked they, could any one employ a man whose father had been a Septembrist, a Bonapartist, and a drunkard to boot? The old man was sure to leave plenty of gold pieces behind him. They themselves were poor men with families to support, while David was a bachelor and could do as he pleased; he would have plenty one of these days; he could afford to take things easily; whereas . . . and so forth and so forth.

Such tales against David, once put into circulation, produced their effect. The monopoly of the prefectorial and diocesan work passed gradually into the hands of Cointet Brothers; and before long David's keen competitors, emboldened by his inaction, started a second local sheet of advertisements and announcements. The older establishment was left at length with the job-printing orders from the town, and the circulation of the *Charente Chronicle* fell off by one-half. Meanwhile the Cointets grew richer; they had made handsome profits on their devotional books; and now they offered to buy Sechard's paper, to have all the trade and judicial announcements of the department in their own hands.

The news of this proposal sent by David to his father brought the old vinegrower from Marsac into the Place du Murier with the swiftness of the raven that scents the corpses on a battlefield.

"Leave me to manage the Cointets," said he to his son; "don't you meddle in this business."

The old man saw what the Cointets meant; and they took alarm at his clearsighted sagacity. His son was making a blunder, he said, and he, Sechard, had come to put a stop to it.

"What was to become of the connection if David gave up the paper? It all depended upon the paper. All the attorneys and solicitors and men of business in L'Houmeau were Liberals to a man. The Cointets had tried to ruin the Sechards by accusing them of Liberalism, and by so doing gave them a plank to cling to--the Sechards should keep the Liberal business. Sell the paper indeed! Why, you might as well sell the stock-in-trade and the license!"

Old Sechard asked the Cointets sixty thousand francs for the printing business, so as not to ruin his son; he was fond of his son; he was taking his son's part. The vinegrower brought his son to the front to gain his point, as a peasant brings in his wife.

His son was unwilling to do this, that, or the other; it varied according to the offers which he wrung one after another from the Cointets, until, not without an effort, he drew them on to give twenty-two thousand francs for the *Charente Chronicle*. But, at the same time, David must pledge himself thenceforward to print no newspaper whatsoever, under a penalty of thirty thousand francs for damages.

That transaction dealt the deathblow to the Sechard establishment; but the old vinegrower did not trouble himself much on that head. Murder usually follows robbery. Our worthy friend intended to pay himself with the ready money. To have the cash in his own hands he would have given in David himself over and above the bargain, and so much the more willingly since that this nuisance of a son could claim one-half of the unexpected windfall. Taking this fact into consideration, therefore, the generous parent consented to abandon his share of the business but not the business premises; and the rental was still maintained at the famous sum of twelve hundred francs per annum.

The old man came into town very seldom after the paper was sold to the Cointets. He pleaded his advanced age, but the truth was that he took little interest in the establishment now that it was his no longer. Still, he could not quite shake off his old kindness for his stock-in-trade; and when business brought him into Angouleme, it would have been hard to say which was the stronger attraction to the old house --his wooden presses or the son whom (as a matter of form) he asked for rent. The old foreman, who had gone over to the rival establishment, knew exactly how much this fatherly generosity was worth; the old fox meant to reserve a right to interfere in his son's affairs, and had taken care to appear in the bankruptcy as a privileged creditor for arrears of rent.

The causes of David's heedlessness throw a light on the character of that young man. Only a few days after his establishment in the paternal printing office, he came across an old school friend in the direst poverty. Lucien Chardon, a young fellow of one-and-twenty or thereabouts, was the son of a surgeon-major who had retired with a wound from the republican army. Nature had meant M. Chardon senior for a chemist; chance opened the way for a retail druggist's business in Angouleme. After many years of scientific research, death cut him off in the midst of his incompleted experiments, and the great discovery that should have brought wealth to the family was never made. Chardon had tried to find a specific for the gout. Gout is a rich man's malady; the rich will pay large sums to recover health when they have lost it, and for this reason the druggist deliberately selected gout as his problem. Halfway between the man of science on the one side and the charlatan on the other, he saw that the scientific method was the one road to assured success, and had studied the causes of the complaint, and based his remedy on a certain general theory of treatment, with modifications in practice for varying temperaments. Then, on a visit to Paris undertaken to solicit the approval of the *Academie des Sciences*, he died, and lost all the fruits of his labors.

It may have been that some presentiment of the end had led the country druggist to do all that in him lay to give his boy and girl a good education; the family had been living up to the income brought in by the business; and now when they were left almost destitute, it was an aggravation of their misfortune that they had been brought up in the expectations of a brilliant future; for these hopes were extinguished by their father's death. The great Desplein, who attended Chardon in his last illness, saw him die in convulsions of rage.

The secret of the army surgeon's ambition lay in his passionate love for his wife, the last survivor of the family of Rubempre, saved as by a miracle from the guillotine in 1793. He had gained time by declaring that she was pregnant, a lie told without the girl's knowledge or consent. Then, when in a manner he had created a claim to call her his wife, he had married her in spite of their common poverty. The children of this marriage, like all children of love, inherited the mother's wonderful beauty, that gift so often fatal when accompanied by poverty. The life of hope and hard work and despair, in all of which Mme. Chardon had shared with such keen sympathy, had left deep traces in her beautiful face, just as the slow decline of a scanty income had changed her ways and habits; but both she and her children confronted evil days bravely enough. She sold the druggist's shop in the Grand' Rue de L'Houmeau, the principal suburb of Angouleme; but it was impossible for even one woman to exist on the three hundred francs of income brought in by the investment of the purchase-money, so the mother and daughter accepted the position, and worked to earn a living. The mother went out as a monthly nurse, and for her gentle manners was preferred to any other among the wealthy houses, where she lived without expense to her children, and earned some seven francs a week. To save her son the embarrassment of seeing his mother reduced to this humble position, she assumed the name of Madame Charlotte; and persons requiring her services were requested to apply to M. Postel, M. Chardon's successor in the business. Lucien's sister worked for a laundress, a decent woman much respected in L'Houmeau, and earned fifteen daily sous. As Mme. Prieur's forewoman she had a certain position in the workroom, which raised her slightly above the class of working-girls.

The two women's slender earnings, together with Mme. Chardon's three hundred francs of *rentes*, amounted to about eight hundred francs a year, and on this sum three persons must be fed, clothed, and lodged. Yet, with all their frugal thrift, the pittance was scarcely sufficient; nearly the whole of it was needed for Lucien. Mme. Chardon and her daughter Eve believed in Lucien as Mahomet's wife believed in her husband; their devotion for his future knew no bounds. Their present landlord was the successor to the business, for M. Postel let them have rooms at the further end of a yard at the back of the laboratory for a very low rent, and Lucien slept in the poor garret above. A father's passion for natural science had stimulated the boy, and at first induced him to follow in the same path. Lucien was one of the most brilliant pupils at the grammar school of Angouleme, and when David Sechard left, his future friend was in the third form.

When chance brought the school-fellows together again, Lucien was weary of drinking from the rude cup of penury, and ready for any of the rash, decisive steps that youth takes at the age of twenty. David's generous offer of forty francs a month if Lucien would come to him and learn the work of a printer's reader came in time; David had no need whatever of a printer's reader, but he saved Lucien from despair. The ties of a school friendship thus renewed were soon drawn closer than ever by the similarity of their lot in life and the dissimilarity of their characters. Both felt high swelling hopes of manifold success; both consciously possessed the high order of intelligence which sets a man on a level with lofty heights, consigned though they were socially to the lowest level. Fate's injustice was a strong bond between them. And then, by different ways, following each his own bent of mind, they had attained to poesy. Lucien, destined for the highest speculative fields of natural science, was aiming with hot enthusiasm at fame through literature; while David, with that meditative temperament which inclines to poetry, was drawn by his tastes towards natural science.

The exchange of roles was the beginning of an intellectual comradeship. Before long, Lucien told David of his own father's farsighted views of the application of science to manufacture, while David pointed out the new ways in literature that Lucien must follow if he meant to succeed. Not many days had passed before the young men's friendship became a passion such as is only known in early manhood. Then it was that David caught a glimpse of Eve's fair face, and loved, as grave and meditative natures can love. The *et nunc et semper et in secula seculorum* of the Liturgy is the device taken by many a sublime unknown poet, whose works consist in magnificent epics conceived and lost between heart and heart. With a lover's insight, David read the secret hopes set by the mother and sister on Lucien's poet's brow; and knowing their blind devotion, it was very sweet to him to draw nearer to his love by sharing her hopes and her self-sacrifice. And in this way Lucien came to be David's chosen brother. As there are ultras who would fain be more Royalist than the King, so David outdid the mother and sister in his belief in Lucien's genius; he spoiled Lucien as a mother spoils her child.

Once, under pressure of the lack of money which tied their hands, the two were ruminating after the manner of young men over ways of promptly realizing a large fortune; and, after fruitless shakings of all the trees already stripped by previous comers, Lucien bethought himself of two of his father's ideas. M. Chardon had talked of a method of refining sugar by a chemical process, which would reduce the cost of production by one-half; and he had another plan for employing an American vegetable fibre for making paper, something after the Chinese fashion, and effecting an enormous saving in the cost of raw material. David, knowing the importance of a question raised already by the Didots, caught at this latter notion, saw a fortune in it, and looked upon Lucien as the benefactor whom he could never repay.

Any one may guess how the ruling thoughts and inner life of this pair of friends unfitted them for carrying on the business of a printing house. So far from making fifteen to twenty thousand francs, like Cointet Brothers, printers and publishers to the diocese, and proprietors of the *Charente Chronicle* (now the only newspaper in the department)--Sechard & Son made a bare three hundred francs per month, out of which the foreman's salary must be paid, as well as Marion's wages and the rent and taxes; so that David himself was scarcely making twelve hundred francs per annum. Active and industrious men of business would have bought new type and new machinery, and made an effort to secure orders for cheap printing from the Paris book trade; but master and foreman, deep in absorbing intellectual interests, were quite content with such orders as came to them from their remaining customers.

In the long length the Cointets had come to understand David's character and habits. They did not slander him now; on the contrary, wise policy required that they should allow the business to flicker on; it was to their interest indeed to maintain it in a small way, lest it should fall into the hands of some more formidable competitor; they made a practice of sending prospectuses and circulars --job-printing, as it is called--to the Sechard's establishment. So it came about that, all unwittingly, David owed his existence, commercially speaking, to the cunning schemes of his competitors. The Cointets, well pleased with his "craze," as they called it, behaved to all appearance both fairly and handsomely; but, as a matter of fact, they were adopting the tactics of the mail-coach owners who set up a sham opposition coach to keep *bona fide* rivals out of the field.

Inside and outside, the condition of the Sechard printing establishment bore testimony to the sordid avarice of the old "bear," who never spent a penny on repairs. The old house had stood in sun and rain, and borne the brunt of the weather, till it looked like some venerable tree trunk set down at the entrance of the alley, so riven it was with seams and cracks of all sorts and sizes. The house front, built of brick and stone, with no pretensions to symmetry, seemed to be bending beneath the weight of a worm-eaten roof covered with the curved pantiles in common use in the South of France. The decrepit casements were fitted with the heavy, unwieldy shutters necessary in that climate, and held in place by massive iron cross bars. It would have puzzled you to find a more dilapidated house in Angouleme; nothing but sheer tenacity of mortar kept it together. Try to picture the workshop, lighted at either end, and dark in the middle; the walls covered with handbills and begrimed by friction of all the workmen who had rubbed past them for thirty years; the cobweb of cordage across the ceiling, the stacks of paper, the old-fashioned presses, the pile of slabs for weighting the damp sheets, the rows of cases, and the two dens in the far corners where the master printer and foreman sat--and you will have some idea of the life led by the two friends.

One day early in May, 1821, David and Lucien were standing together by the window that looked into the yard. It was nearly two o'clock, and the four or five men were going out to dinner. David waited until the apprentice had shut the street door with the bell fastened to it; then he drew Lucien out into the yard as if the smell of paper, ink, and presses and old woodwork had grown intolerable to him, and together they sat down under the vines, keeping the office and the door in view. The sunbeams, playing among the trellised vine-shoots, hovered over the two poets, making, as it were, an aureole about their heads, bringing the contrast between their faces and their characters into a vigorous relief that would have tempted the brush of some great painter.

David's physique was of the kind that Nature gives to the fighter, the man born to struggle in obscurity, or with the eyes of all men turned upon him. The strong shoulders, rising above the broad chest, were in keeping with the full development of his whole frame. With his thick crop of black hair, his fleshy, high-colored, swarthy face, supported by a thick neck, he looked at first sight like one of Boileau's canons: but on a second glance there was that in the lines about the thick lips, in the dimple of the chin, in the turn of the square nostrils, with the broad irregular line of central cleavage, and, above all, in the eyes, with the steady light of an all-absorbing love that burned in them, which revealed the real character of the man--the wisdom of the thinker, the strenuous melancholy of a spirit that discerns the horizon on either side, and sees clearly to the end of winding ways, turning the clear light of analysis upon the joys of fruition, known as yet in idea alone, and quick to turn from them in disgust. You might look for the flash of genius from such a face; you could not miss the ashes of the volcano; hopes extinguished beneath a profound sense of the social annihilation to which lowly birth and lack of fortune condemns so many a loftier mind. And by the side of the poor printer, who loathed a handicraft so closely allied to intellectual work, close to this Silenus, joyless, self-sustained, drinking deep draughts from the cup of knowledge and of poetry that he might forget the cares of his narrow lot in the intoxication of soul and brain, stood Lucien, graceful as some sculptured Indian Bacchus.

For in Lucien's face there was the distinction of line which stamps the beauty of the antique; the Greek profile, with the velvet whiteness of women's faces, and eyes full of love, eyes so blue that they looked dark against a pearly setting, and dewy and fresh as those of a child. Those beautiful eyes looked out from under their long chestnut lashes, beneath eyebrows that might have been traced by a Chinese pencil. The silken down on his cheeks, like his bright curling hair, shone golden in the sunlight. A divine graciousness transfused the white temples that caught that golden gleam; a matchless nobleness had set its seal in the short chin raised, but not abruptly. The smile that hovered about the coral lips, yet redder as they seemed by force of contrast with the even teeth, was the smile of some sorrowing angel. Lucien's hands denoted race; they were shapely hands; hands that men obey at a sign, and women love to kiss. Lucien was slender and of middle height. From a glance at his feet, he might have been taken for a girl in disguise, and this so much the more easily from the feminine contour of the hips, a characteristic of keen-witted, not to say, astute, men. This is a trait which seldom misleads, and in Lucien it was a true indication of character; for when he analyzed the society of today, his restless mind was apt to take its stand on the lower ground of those diplomatists who hold that success justifies the use of any means however base. It is one of the misfortunes attendant upon great intellects that perforce they comprehend all things, both good and evil.

The two young men judged society by the more lofty standard because their social position was at the lowest end of the scale, for unrecognized power is apt to avenge itself for lowly station by viewing the world from a lofty standpoint. Yet it is, nevertheless, true that they grew but the more bitter and hopeless after these swift soaring flights to the upper regions of thought, their world by right. Lucien had read much and compared; David had thought much and deeply. In spite of the young printer's look of robust, country-bred health, his turn of mind was melancholy and somewhat morbid--he lacked confidence in himself; but Lucien, on the other hand, with a boldness little to be expected from his feminine, almost effeminate, figure, graceful though it was, Lucien possessed the Gascon temperament to the highest degree--rash, brave, and adventurous, prone to make the most of the bright side, and as little as possible of the dark; his was the nature that sticks at no crime if there is anything to be gained by it, and laughs at the vice which serves as a stepping-stone. Just now these tendencies of ambition were held in check, partly by the fair illusions of youth, partly by the enthusiasm which led him to prefer the nobler methods, which every man in love with glory tries first of all. Lucien was struggling as yet with himself and his own desires, and not with the difficulties of life; at strife with his own power, and not with the baseness of other men, that fatal exemplar for impressionable minds. The brilliancy of his intellect had a keen attraction for David. David admired his friend, while he kept him out of the scrapes into which he was led by the *furie francaise*.

David, with his well-balanced mind and timid nature at variance with a strong constitution, was by no means wanting in the persistence of the Northern temper; and if he saw all the difficulties before him, none the less he vowed to himself to conquer, never to give way. In him the unswerving virtue of an apostle was softened by pity that sprang from inexhaustible indulgence. In the friendship grown old already, one was the worshiper, and that one was David; Lucien ruled him like a woman sure of love, and David loved to give way. He felt that his friend's physical beauty implied a real superiority, which he accepted, looking upon himself as one made of coarser and commoner human clay.

"The ox for patient labor in the fields, the free life for the bird," he thought to himself. "I will be the ox, and Lucien shall be the eagle."

So for three years these friends had mingled the destinies bright with such glorious promise. Together they read the great works that appeared above the horizon of literature and science since the Peace --the poems of Schiller, Goethe, and Byron, the prose writings of Scott, Jean-Paul, Berzelius, Davy, Cuvier, Lamartine, and many more. They warmed themselves beside these great hearthfires; they tried their powers in abortive creations, in work laid aside and taken up again with new glow of enthusiasm. Incessantly they worked with the unwearied vitality of youth; comrades in poverty, comrades in the consuming love of art and science, till they forgot the hard life of the present, for their minds were wholly bent on laying the foundations of future fame.

"Lucien," said David, "do you know what I have just received from Paris?" He drew a tiny volume from his pocket. "Listen!"

And David read, as a poet can read, first Andre de Chenier's Idyll *Neere*, then *Le Malade*, following on with the Elegy on a Suicide, another elegy in the classic taste, and the last two *Iambes*.

"So that is Andre de Chenier!" Lucien exclaimed again and again. "It fills one with despair!" he cried for the third time, when David surrendered the book to him, unable to read further for emotion.--"A poet rediscovered by a poet!" said Lucien, reading the signature of the preface.

"After Chenier had written those poems, he thought that he had written nothing worth publishing," added David.

Then Lucien in his turn read aloud the fragment of an epic called *L'Aveugle* and two or three of the Elegies, till, when he came upon the line--

If they know not bliss, is there happiness on earth?

He pressed the book to his lips, and tears came to the eyes of either, for the two friends were lovers and fellow-worshipers.

The vine-stems were changing color with the spring; covering the rifted, battered walls of the old house where squalid cracks were spreading in every direction, with fluted columns and knots and bas-reliefs and uncounted masterpieces of I know not what order of architecture, erected by fairy hands. Fancy had scattered flowers and crimson gems over the gloomy little yard, and Chenier's *Camille* became for David the Eve whom he worshiped, for Lucien a great lady to whom he paid his homage. Poetry had shaken out her starry robe above the workshop where the "monkeys" and "bears" were grotesquely busy among types and presses. Five o'clock struck, but the friends felt neither hunger nor thirst; life had turned to a golden dream, and all the treasures of the world lay at their feet. Far away on the horizon lay the blue streak to which Hope points a finger in storm and stress; and a siren voice sounded in their ears, calling, "Come, spread your wings; through that streak of gold or silver or azure lies the sure way of escape from evil fortune!"

Just at that moment the low glass door of the workshop was opened, and out came Cerizet, an apprentice (David had brought the urchin from Paris). This youth introduced a stranger, who saluted the friends politely, and spoke to David.

"This, sir, is a monograph which I am desirous of printing," said he, drawing a huge package of manuscript from his pocket. "Will you oblige me with an estimate?"

"We do not undertake work on such a scale, sir," David answered, without looking at the manuscript. "You had better see the Messieurs Cointet about it."

"Still we have a very pretty type which might suit it," put in Lucien, taking up the roll. "We must ask you to be kind enough, sir, to leave your commission with us and call again tomorrow, and we will give you an estimate."

"Have I the pleasure of addressing M. Lucien Chardon?"

"Yes, sir," said the foreman.

"I am fortunate in this opportunity of meeting with a young poet destined to such greatness," returned the author. "Mme. de Bargeton sent me here."

Lucien flushed red at the name, and stammered out something about gratitude for the interest which Mme. de Bargeton took in him. David noticed his friend's embarrassed flush, and left him in conversation with the country gentleman, the author of a monograph on silkwork cultivation, prompted by vanity to print the effort for the benefit of fellow-members of the local agricultural society.

When the author had gone, David spoke.

"Lucien, are you in love with Mme. de Bargeton?"

"Passionately."

"But social prejudices set you as far apart as if she were living at Pekin and you in Greenland."

"The will of two lovers can rise victorious over all things," said Lucien, lowering his eyes.

"You will forget us," returned the alarmed lover, as Eve's fair face rose before his mind.

"On the contrary, I have perhaps sacrificed my love to you," cried Lucien.

"What do you mean?"

"In spite of my love, in spite of the different motives which bid me obtain a secure footing in her house, I have told her that I will never go thither again unless another is made welcome too, a man whose gifts are greater than mine, a man destined for a brilliant future --David Sechard, my brother, my friend. I shall find an answer waiting when I go home. All the aristocrats may have been asked to hear me read my verses this evening, but I shall not go if the answer is negative, and I will never set foot in Mme. de Bargeton's house again."

David brushed the tears from his eyes, and wrung Lucien's hand. The clock struck six.

"Eve must be anxious; good-bye," Lucien added abruptly.

He hurried away. David stood overcome by the emotion that is only felt to the full at his age, and more especially in such a position as his --the friends were like two young swans with wings unclipped as yet by the experiences of provincial life.

"Heart of gold!" David exclaimed to himself, as his eyes followed Lucien across the workshop.

Lucien went down to L'Houmeau along the broad Promenade de Beaulieu, the Rue du Minage, and Saint-Peter's Gate. It was the longest way round, so you may be sure that Mme. de Bargeton's house lay on the way. So delicious it was to pass under her windows, though she knew nothing of his presence, that for the past two months he had gone round daily by the Palet Gate into L'Houmeau.

Under the trees of Beaulieu he saw how far the suburb lay from the city. The custom of the country, moreover, had raised other barriers harder to surmount than the mere physical difficulty of the steep flights of steps which Lucien was descending. Youth and ambition had thrown the flying-bridge of glory across the gulf between the city and the suburb, yet Lucien was as uneasy in his mind over his lady's answer as any king's favorite who has tried to climb yet higher, and fears that being over-bold he is like to fall. This must seem a dark saying to those who have never studied the manners and customs of cities divided into the upper and lower town; wherefore it is necessary to enter here upon some topographical details, and this so much the more if the reader is to comprehend the position of one of the principal characters in the story--Mme. de Bargeton.

The old city of Angouleme is perched aloft on a crag like a sugar-loaf, overlooking the plain where the Charente winds away through the meadows. The crag is an outlying spur on the Perigord side of a long, low ridge of hill, which terminates abruptly just above the road from Paris to Bordeaux, so that the Rock of Angouleme is a sort of promontory marking out the line of three picturesque valleys. The ramparts and great gateways and ruined fortress on the summit of the crag still remain to bear witness to the importance of this stronghold during the Religious Wars, when Angouleme was a military position coveted alike of Catholics and Calvinists, but its old-world strength is a source of weakness in modern days; Angouleme could not spread down to the Charente, and shut in between its ramparts and the steep sides of the crag, the old town is condemned to stagnation of the most fatal kind.

The Government made an attempt about this very time to extend the town towards Perigord, building a Prefecture, a Naval School, and barracks along the hillside, and opening up roads. But private enterprise had been beforehand elsewhere. For some time past the suburb of L'Houmeau had sprung up, a mushroom growth at the foot of the crag and along the river-side, where the direct road runs from Paris to Bordeaux. Everybody has heard of the great paper-mills of Angouleme, established perforce three hundred years ago on the Charente and its branch streams, where there was a sufficient fall of water. The largest State factory of marine ordnance in France was established at Ruelle, some six miles away. Carriers, wheelwrights, posthouses, and inns, every agency for public conveyance, every industry that lives by road or river, was crowded together in Lower Angouleme, to avoid the difficulty of the ascent of the hill. Naturally, too, tanneries, laundries, and all such waterside trades stood within reach of the Charente; and along the banks of the river lay the stores of brandy and great warehouses full of the water-borne raw material; all the carrying trade of the Charente, in short, had lined the quays with buildings.

So the Faubourg of L'Houmeau grew into a busy and prosperous city, a second Angouleme rivaling the upper town, the residence of the powers that be, the lords spiritual and temporal of Angouleme; though L'Houmeau, with all its business and increasing greatness, was still a mere appendage of the city above. The *noblesse* and officialdom dwelt on the crag, trade and wealth remained below. No love was lost between these two sections of the community all the world over, and in Angouleme it would have been hard to say which of the two camps detested the other the more cordially. Under the Empire the machinery worked fairly smoothly, but the Restoration wrought both sides to the highest pitch of exasperation.

Nearly every house in the upper town of Angouleme is inhabited by noble, or at any rate by old burgher, families, who live independently on their incomes--a sort of autochthonous nation who suffer no aliens to come among them. Possibly, after two hundred years of unbroken residence, and it may be an intermarriage or two with one of the primordial houses, a family from some neighboring district may be adopted, but in the eyes of the aboriginal race they are still newcomers of yesterday.

Prefects, receivers-general, and various administrations that have come and gone during the last forty years, have tried to tame the ancient families perched aloft like wary ravens on their crag; the said families were always willing to accept invitations to dinners and dances; but as to admitting the strangers to their own houses, they were inexorable. Ready to scoff and disparage, jealous and niggardly, marrying only among themselves, the families formed a serried phalanx to keep out intruders. Of modern luxury they had no notion; and as for sending a boy to Paris, it was sending him, they thought to certain ruin. Such sagacity will give a sufficient idea of the old-world manners and customs of this society, suffering from thick-headed Royalism, infected with bigotry rather than zeal, all stagnating together, motionless as their town founded upon a rock. Yet Angouleme enjoyed a great reputation in the provinces round about for its educational advantages, and neighboring towns sent their daughters to its boarding schools and convents.

It is easy to imagine the influence of the class sentiment which held Angouleme aloof from L'Houmeau. The merchant classes are rich, the *noblesse* are usually poor. Each side takes its revenge in scorn of the other. The tradespeople in

Angouleme espouse the quarrel. "He is a man of L'Houmeau!" a shopkeeper of the upper town will tell you, speaking of a merchant in the lower suburb, throwing an accent into the speech which no words can describe. When the Restoration defined the position of the French *noblesse*, holding out hopes to them which could only be realized by a complete and general topsy-turvydom, the distance between Angouleme and L'Houmeau, already more strongly marked than the distance between the hill and plain, was widened yet further. The better families, all devoted as one man to the Government, grew more exclusive here than in any other part of France. "The man of L'Houmeau" became little better than a pariah. Hence the deep, smothered hatred which broke out everywhere with such ugly unanimity in the insurrection of 1830 and destroyed the elements of a durable social system in France. As the overweening haughtiness of the Court nobles detached the provincial *noblesse* from the throne, so did these last alienate the *bourgeoisie* from the royal cause by behavior that galled their vanity in every possible way.

So "a man of L'Houmeau," a druggist's son, in Mme. de Bargeton's house was nothing less than a little revolution. Who was responsible for it? Lamartine and Victor Hugo, Casimir Delavigne and Canalis, Beranger and Chateaubriand. Davrigny, Benjamin Constant and Lamennais, Cousin and Michaud,--all the old and young illustrious names in literature in short, Liberals and Royalists, alike must divide the blame among them. Mme. de Bargeton loved art and letters, eccentric taste on her part, a craze deeply deplored in Angouleme. In justice to the lady, it is necessary to give a sketch of the previous history of a woman born to shine, and left by unlucky circumstances in the shade, a woman whose influence decided Lucien's career.

M. de Bargeton was the great-grandson of an alderman of Bordeaux named Mirault, ennobled under Louis XIII. for long tenure of office. His son, bearing the name of Mirault de Bargeton, became an officer in the household troops of Louis XIV., and married so great a fortune that in the reign of Louis XV. his son dropped the Mirault and was called simply M. de Bargeton. This M. de Bargeton, the alderman's grandson, lived up to his quality so strenuously that he ran through the family property and checked the course of its fortunes. Two of his brothers indeed, great-uncles of the present Bargeton, went into business again, for which reason you will find the name of Mirault among Bordeaux merchants at this day. The lands of Bargeton, in Angoumois in the barony of Rochefoucauld, being entailed, and the house in Angouleme, called the Hotel Bargeton, likewise, the grandson of M. de Bargeton the Waster came in for these hereditaments; though the year 1789 deprived him of all seignorial rights save to the rents paid by his tenants, which amounted to some ten thousand francs per annum. If his grandsire had but walked in the ways of his illustrious progenitors, Bargeton I. and Bargeton II., Bargeton V. (who may be dubbed Bargeton the Mute by way of distinction) should by rights have been born to the title of Marquis of Bargeton; he would have been connected with some great family or other, and in due time he would have been a duke and a peer of France, like many another; whereas, in 1805, he thought himself uncommonly lucky when he married Mlle. Marie-Louise-Anaïs de Negrepelisse, the daughter of a noble long relegated to the obscurity of his manor-house, scion though he was of the younger branch of one of the oldest families in the south of France. There had been a Negrepelisse among the hostages of St. Louis. The head of the elder branch, however, had borne the illustrious name of d'Espard since the reign of Henri Quatre, when the Negrepelisse of that day married an heiress of the d'Espard family. As for M. de Negrepelisse, the younger son of a younger son, he lived upon his wife's property, a small estate in the neighborhood of Barbezieux, farming the land to admiration, selling his corn in the market himself, and distilling his own brandy, laughing at those who ridiculed him, so long as he could pile up silver crowns, and now and again round out his estate with another bit of land.

Circumstances unusual enough in out-of-the-way places in the country had inspired Mme. de Bargeton with a taste for music and reading. During the Revolution one Abbe Niollant, the Abbe Roze's best pupil, found a hiding-place in the old manor-house of Escarbas, and brought with him his baggage of musical compositions. The old country gentleman's hospitality was handsomely repaid, for the Abbe undertook his daughter's education. Anais, or Nais, as she was called must otherwise have been left to herself, or, worse still, to some coarse-minded servant-maid. The Abbe was not only a musician, he was well and widely read, and knew both Italian and German; so Mlle. de Negrepelise received instruction in those tongues, as well as in counterpoint. He explained the great masterpieces of the French, German, and Italian literatures, and deciphered with her the music of the great composers. Finally, as time hung heavy on his hands in the seclusion enforced by political storms, he taught his pupil Latin and Greek and some smatterings of natural science. A mother might have modified the effects of a man's education upon a young girl, whose independent spirit had been fostered in the first place by a country life. The Abbe Niollant, an enthusiast and a poet, possessed the artistic temperament in a peculiarly high degree, a temperament compatible with many estimable qualities, but prone to raise itself above *bourgeois* prejudices by the liberty of its judgments and breadth of view. In society an intellect of this order wins pardon for its boldness by its depth and originality; but in private life it would seem to do positive mischief, by suggesting wanderings from the beaten track. The Abbe was by no means wanting in goodness of heart, and his ideas were therefore the more contagious for this high-spirited girl, in whom they were confirmed by a lonely life. The Abbe Niollant's pupil learned to be fearless in criticism and ready in judgement; it never occurred to her tutor that qualities so necessary in a man are disadvantages in a woman destined for the homely life of a house-mother. And though the Abbe constantly impressed it upon his pupil that it behoved her to be the more modest and gracious with the extent of her attainments, Mlle. de Negrepelisse conceived an excellent opinion of herself and a robust contempt for ordinary humanity. All those about her were her inferiors, or persons who hastened to do her bidding, till she grew to be as haughty as a great lady, with none of the charming blandness and urbanity of a great lady. The instincts of vanity were flattered by the pride that the poor Abbe took in his pupil, the pride of an author who sees himself in his work, and for her misfortune she met no one with whom she could measure herself. Isolation is one of the greatest drawbacks of a country life. We lose the habit of putting ourselves to any inconvenience for the sake of others when there is no one for whom to make the trifling sacrifices of personal effort required by dress and manner. And everything in us shares in the change for the worse; the form and the spirit deteriorate together.

With no social intercourse to compel self-repression, Mlle. de Negrepelisse's bold ideas passed into her manner and the expression of her face. There was a cavalier air about her, a something that seems at first original, but only suited to women of adventurous life. So this education, and the consequent asperities of character, which would have been softened down in a higher social sphere, could only serve to make her ridiculous at Angouleme so soon as her adorers should cease to worship eccentricities that charm only in youth.

As for M. de Negrepelisse, he would have given all his daughter's books to save the life of a sick bullock; and so miserly was he, that he would not have given her two farthings over and above the allowance to which she had a right, even if it had been a question of some indispensable trifle for her education.

In 1802 the Abbe died, before the marriage of his dear child, a marriage which he, doubtless, would never have advised. The old father found his daughter a great care now that the Abbe was gone. The high-spirited girl, with nothing else to do, was sure to break into rebellion against his niggardliness, and he felt quite unequal to the struggle. Like all young women who leave the appointed track of woman's life, Nais had her own opinions about marriage, and had no great inclination thereto. She shrank from submitting herself, body and soul, to the feeble, undignified specimens of mankind whom she had chanced to meet. She wished to rule, marriage meant obedience; and between obedience to coarse caprices and a mind without indulgence for her tastes, and flight with a lover who should please her, she would not have hesitated for a moment.

M. de Negrepelisse maintained sufficient of the tradition of birth to dread a *mesalliance*. Like many another parent, he resolved to marry his daughter, not so much on her account as for his own peace of mind. A noble or a country gentleman was the man for him, somebody not too clever, incapable of haggling over the account of the trust; stupid enough and easy enough to allow Nais to have her own way, and disinterested enough to take her without a dowry. But where to look for a son-in-law to suit father and daughter equally well, was the problem. Such a man would be the phoenix of sons-in-law.

To M. de Negrepelisse pondering over the eligible bachelors of the province with these double requirements in his mind. M. de Bargeton seemed to be the only one who answered to this description. M. de Bargeton, aged forty, considerably shattered by the amorous dissipations of his youth, was generally held to be a man of remarkably feeble intellect; but he had just the exact amount of commonsense required for the management of his fortune, and breeding sufficient to enable him to avoid blunders or blatant follies in society in Angouleme. In the bluntest manner M. de Negrepelisse pointed out the negative virtues of the model husband designed for his daughter, and made her see the way to manage him so as to secure her own happiness. So Nais married the bearer of arms, two hundred years old already, for the Bargeton arms are blazoned thus: *the first or, three attires gules; the second, three ox's heads cabossed, two and one, sable; the third, barry of six, azure and argent, in the first, six shells or, three, two, and one.* Provided with a chaperon, Nais could steer her fortunes as she chose under the style of the firm, and with the help of such connections as her wit and beauty would obtain for her in Paris. Nais was enchanted by the prospect of such liberty. M. de Bargeton was of the opinion that he was making a brilliant marriage, for he expected that in no long while M. de Negrepelisse would leave him the estates which he was rounding out so lovingly; but to an unprejudiced spectator it certainly seemed as though the duty of writing the bridegroom's epitaph might devolve upon his father-in-law.

By this time Mme. de Bargeton was thirty-six years old and her husband fifty-eight. The disparity in age was the more startling since M. de Bargeton looked like a man of seventy, whereas his wife looked scarcely half her age. She could still wear rose-color, and her hair hanging loose upon her shoulders. Although their income did not exceed twelve thousand francs, they ranked among the half-dozen largest fortunes in the old city, merchants and officials excepted; for M. and Mme. de Bargeton were obliged to live in Angouleme until such time as Mme. de Bargeton's inheritance should fall in and they could go to Paris. Meanwhile they were bound to be attentive to old M. de Negrepelisse (who kept them waiting so long that his son-in-law in fact predeceased him), and Nais' brilliant intellectual gifts, and the wealth that lay like undiscovered ore in her nature, profited her nothing, underwent the transforming operation of Time and changed to absurdities. For our absurdities spring, in fact, for the most part, from the good in us, from some faculty or quality abnormally developed. Pride, untempered by intercourse with the great world becomes stiff and starched by contact with petty things; in a loftier moral atmosphere it would have grown to noble magnanimity. Enthusiasm, that virtue within a virtue, forming the saint, inspiring the devotion hidden from all eyes and glowing out upon the world in verse, turns to exaggeration, with the trifles of a narrow existence for its object. Far away from the centres of light shed by great minds, where the air is quick with thought, knowledge stands still, taste is corrupted like stagnant water, and passion dwindles, frittered away upon the infinitely small objects which it strives to exalt. Herein lies the secret of the avarice and tittle-tattle that poison provincial life. The contagion of narrow-mindedness and meanness affects the noblest natures; and in such ways as these, men born to be great, and women who would have been charming if they had fallen under the forming influence of greater minds, are balked of their lives.

Here was Mme. de Bargeton, for instance, smiting the lyre for every trifle, and publishing her emotions indiscriminately to her circle. As a matter of fact, when sensations appeal to an audience of one, it is better to keep them to ourselves. A sunset certainly is a glorious poem; but if a woman describes it, in high-sounding words, for the benefit of matter-of-fact people, is she not ridiculous? There are pleasures which can only be felt to the full when two souls meet, poet and poet, heart and heart. She had a trick of using high-sounding phrases, interlarded with exaggerated expressions, the kind of stuff ingeniously nicknamed *tartines* by the French journalist, who furnishes a daily supply of the commodity for a public that daily performs the difficult feat of swallowing it. She squandered superlatives recklessly in her talk, and the smallest things took giant proportions. It was at this period of her career that she began to type-ize, individualize, synthesize, dramatize, superiorize, analyze, poetize, angelize, neologize, tragedify, prosify, and colossify--you must violate the laws of language to find words to express the new-fangled whimsies in which even women here and there indulge. The heat of her language communicated itself to the brain, and the dithyrambs on her lips were spoken out of the abundance of her heart. She palpitated, swooned, and went into ecstasies over anything and everything, over the devotion of a sister of Charity, and the execution of the brothers Fauchet, over M. d'Arlincourt's *Ipsiboe*, Lewis' *Anaconda*, or the escape of La Valette, or the presence of mind of a lady friend who put burglars to flight by imitating a man's voice. Everything was heroic, extraordinary, strange, wonderful, and divine. She would work herself into a state of excitement, indignation, or depression; she soared to heaven, and sank again, gazed at the sky, or looked to earth; her eyes were always filled with tears. She wore herself out with chronic admiration, and wasted her strength on curious dislikes. Her mind ran on the Pasha of Janina; she would have liked to try conclusions with him in his seraglio, and had a great notion of being sewn in a sack and thrown into the water. She envied that blue-stocking of the desert, Lady Hester Stanhope; she longed to be a sister of Saint Camilla and tend the sick and die of yellow fever in a hospital at Barcelona; 'twas a high, a noble destiny! In short, she thirsted for any draught but the clear spring water of her own life, flowing hidden among green pastures. She adored Byron and Jean-Jacques Rousseau, or anybody else with a picturesque or dramatic career. Her tears were ready to flow for every misfortune; she sang paeans for every victory. She sympathized with the fallen Napoleon, and with Mehemet Ali, massacring the foreign usurpers of Egypt. In short, any kind of genius was accommodated with an aureole, and she was fully persuaded that gifted immortals lived on incense and light.

A good many people looked upon her as a harmless lunatic, but in these extravagances of hers a keener observer surely would have seen the broken fragments of a magnificent edifice that had crumbled into ruin before it was completed, the stones of a heavenly Jerusalem--love, in short, without a lover. And this was indeed the fact.

The story of the first eighteen years of Mme. de Bargeton's married life can be summed up in a few words. For a long while she lived upon herself and distant hopes. Then, when she began to see that their narrow income put the longed-for life in Paris quite out of the question, she looked about her at the people with whom her life must be spent, and shuddered at her loneliness. There was not a single man who could inspire the madness to which women are prone when they despair of a life become stale and unprofitable in the present, and with no outlook for the future. She had nothing to look for, nothing to expect from chance, for there are lives in which chance plays no part. But when the Empire was in the full noonday of glory, and Napoleon was sending the flower of his troops to the Peninsula, her disappointed hopes revived. Natural curiosity prompted her to make an effort to see the heroes who were conquering Europe in obedience to a word from the Emperor in the order of the day; the heroes of a modern time who outdid the mythical feats of paladins of old. The cities of France, however avaricious or refractory, must perforce do honor to the Imperial Guard, and mayors and prefects went out to meet them with set speeches as if the conquerors had been crowned kings. Mme. de Bargeton went to a *ridotto* given to the town by a regiment, and fell in love with an officer of a good family, a sub-lieutenant, to whom the crafty Napoleon had given a glimpse of the baton of a Marshal of France. Love, restrained, greater and nobler than the ties that were made and unmade so easily in those days, was consecrated coldly by the hands of death. On the battlefield of Wagram a shell shattered the only record of Mme. de Bargeton's young beauty, a portrait worn on the heart of the Marquis of Cante-Croix. For long afterwards she wept for the young soldier, the colonel in his second campaign, for the heart hot with love and glory that set a letter from Nais above Imperial favor. The pain of those days cast a veil of sadness over her face, a shadow that only vanished at the terrible age when a woman first discovers with dismay that the best years of her life are over, and she has had no joy of them; when she sees her roses wither, and the longing for love is revived again with the desire to linger yet for a little on the last smiles of youth. Her nobler qualities dealt so many wounds to her soul at the moment when the cold of the provinces seized upon her. She would have died of grief like the ermine if by chance she had been sullied by contact with those men whose thoughts are bent on winning a few sous nightly at cards after a good dinner; pride saved her from the shabby love intrigues of the provinces. A woman so much above the level of those about her, forced to decide between the emptiness of the men whom she meets and the emptiness of her own life, can make but one choice; marriage and society became a cloister for Anais. She lived by poetry as the Carmelite lives by religion. All the famous foreign books published in France for the first time between 1815 and 1821, the great essayists, M. de Bonald and M. de Maistre (those two eagles of thought)--all the lighter French literature, in short, that appeared during that sudden outburst of first vigorous growth might bring delight into her solitary life, but not flexibility of mind or body. She stood strong and straight like some forest tree, lightning-blasted but still erect. Her dignity became a stilted manner, her social supremacy led her into affectation and sentimental over-refinements; she queened it with her foibles, after the usual fashion of those who allow their courtiers to adore them.

This was Mme. de Bargeton's past life, a dreary chronicle which must be given if Lucien's position with regard to the lady is to be comprehensible. Lucien's introduction came about oddly enough. In the previous winter a newcomer had brought some interest into Mme. de Bargeton's monotonous life. The place of controller of excise fell vacant, and M. de Barante appointed a man whose adventurous life was a sufficient passport to the house of the sovereign lady who had her share of feminine curiosity.

M. de Chatelet--he began life as plain Sixte Chatelet, but since 1806 had the wit to adopt the particle--M. du Chatelet was one of the agreeable young men who escaped conscription after conscription by keeping very close to the Imperial sun. He had begun his career as private secretary to an Imperial Highness, a post for which he possessed every qualification. Personable and of a good figure, a clever billiard-player, a passable amateur actor, he danced well, and excelled in most physical exercises; he could, moreover, sing a ballad and applaud a witticism. Supple, envious, never at a loss, there was nothing that he did not know--nothing that he really knew. He knew nothing, for instance, of music, but he could sit down to the piano and accompany, after a fashion, a woman who consented after much pressing to sing a ballad learned by heart in a month of hard practice. Incapable though he was of any feeling for poetry, he would boldly ask permission to retire for ten minutes to compose an impromptu, and return with a quatrain, flat as a pancake, wherein rhyme did duty for reason. M. du Chatelet had besides a very pretty talent for filling in the ground of the Princess' worsted work after the flowers had been begun; he held her skeins of silk with infinite grace, entertained her with dubious nothings more or less transparently veiled. He was ignorant of painting, but he could copy a landscape, sketch a head in profile, or design a costume and color it. He had, in short, all the little talents that a man could turn to such useful account in times when women exercised more influence in public life than most people imagine. Diplomacy he claimed to be his strong point; it usually is with those who have no knowledge, and are profound by reason of their emptiness; and, indeed, this kind of skill possesses one signal advantage, for it can only be displayed in the conduct of the affairs of the great, and when discretion is the quality required, a man who knows nothing can safely say nothing, and take refuge in a mysterious shake of the head; in fact; the cleverest practitioner is he who can swim with the current and keep his head well above the stream of events which he appears to control, a man's fitness for this business varying inversely as his specific gravity. But in this particular art or craft, as in all others, you shall find a thousand mediocrities for one man of genius; and in spite of Chatelet's services, ordinary and extraordinary, Her Imperial Highness could not procure a seat in the Privy Council for her private secretary; not that he would not have made a delightful Master of Requests, like many another, but the Princess was of the opinion that her secretary was better placed with her than anywhere else in the world. He was made a Baron, however, and went to Cassel as envoy-extraordinary, no empty form of words, for he cut a very extraordinary figure there--Napoleon used him as a diplomatic courier in the thick of a European crisis. Just as he had been promised the post of minister to Jerome in Westphalia, the Empire fell to pieces; and balked of his *ambassade de famille* as he called it, he went off in despair to Egypt with General de Montriveau. A strange chapter of accidents separated him from his traveling companion, and for two long years Sixte du Chatelet led a wandering life among the Arab tribes of the desert, who sold and resold their captive--his talents being not of the slightest use to the nomad tribes. At length, about the time that Montriveau reached Tangier, Chatelet found himself in the territory of the Imam of Muscat, had the luck to find an English vessel just about to set sail, and so came back to Paris a year sooner than his sometime companion. Once in Paris, his recent misfortunes, and certain connections of long standing, together with services rendered to great persons now in power, recommended him to the President of the Council, who put him in M. de Barante's department until such time as a controllership should fall vacant. So the part that M. du Chatelet once had played in the history of the Imperial Princess, his reputation for success with women, the strange story of his travels and sufferings, all awakened the interest of the ladies of Angouleme.

M. le Baron Sixte du Chatelet informed himself as to the manners and customs of the upper town, and took his cue accordingly. He appeared on the scene as a jaded man of the world, broken in health, and weary in spirit. He would raise his hand to his forehead at all seasons, as if pain never gave him a moment's respite, a habit that recalled his travels and made him interesting. He was on visiting terms with the authorities--the general in command, the prefect, the receiver-general, and the bishop but in every house he was frigid, polite, and slightly supercilious, like a man out of his proper place awaiting the favors of power. His social talents he left to conjecture, nor did they lose anything in reputation on that account; then when people began to talk about him and wish to know him, and curiosity was still lively; when he had reconnoitred the men and found them nought, and studied the women with the eyes of experience in the cathedral for several Sundays, he saw that Mme. de. Bargeton was the person with whom it would be best to be on intimate terms. Music, he thought, should open the doors of a house where strangers were never received. Surreptitiously he procured one of Miroir's Masses, learned it upon the piano; and one fine Sunday when all Angouleme went to the cathedral, he played the organ, sent those who knew no better into ecstasies over the performance, and stimulated the interest felt in him by allowing his name to slip out through the attendants. As he came out after mass, Mme. de Bargeton complimented him, regretting that she had no opportunity of playing duets with such a musician; and naturally, during an interview of her own seeking, he received the passport, which he could not have obtained if he had asked for it.

So the adroit Baron was admitted to the circle of the queen of Angouleme, and paid her marked attention. The elderly beau--he was forty-five years old--saw that all her youth lay dormant and ready to revive, saw treasures to be turned to account, and possibly a rich widow to wed, to say nothing of expectations; it would be a marriage into the family of Negrepelisse, and for him this meant a family connection with the Marquise d'Espard, and a political career in Paris. Here was a fair tree to cultivate in spite of the ill-omened, unsightly mistletoe that grew thick upon it; he would hang his fortunes upon it, and prune it, and wait till he could gather its golden fruit.

High-born Angouleme shrieked against the introduction of a Giaour into the sanctuary, for Mme. de Bargeton's salon was a kind of holy of holies in a society that kept itself unspotted from the world. The only outsider intimate there was the bishop; the prefect was admitted twice or thrice in a year, the receiver-general was never received at all; Mme. de Bargeton would go to concerts and "at homes" at his house, but she never accepted invitations to dinner. And now, she who had declined to open her doors to the receiver-general, welcomed a mere controller of excise! Here was a novel order of precedence for snubbed authority; such a thing it had never entered their minds to conceive.

Those who by dint of mental effort can understand a kind of pettiness which, for that matter, can be found on any and every social level, will realize the awe with which the *bourgeoisie* of Angouleme regarded the Hotel de Bargeton. The inhabitant of L'Houmeau beheld the grandeur of that miniature Louvre, the glory of the Angoumoisin Hotel de Rambouillet, shining at a solar distance; and yet, within it there was gathered together all the direst intellectual poverty, all the decayed gentility from twenty leagues round about.

Political opinion expanded itself in wordy commonplaces vociferated with emphasis; the *Quotidienne* was comparatively Laodicean in its loyalty, and Louis XVIII. a Jacobin. The women, for the most part, were awkward, silly, insipid, and ill dressed; there was always something amiss that spoiled the whole; nothing in them was complete, toilette or talk, flesh or spirit. But for his designs on Mme. de Bargeton, Chatelet could not have endured the society. And yet the manners and spirit of the noble in his ruined manor-house, the knowledge of the traditions of good breeding,--these things covered a multitude of deficiencies. Nobility of feeling was far more real here than in the lofty world of Paris. You might compare these country Royalists, if the metaphor may be allowed, to old-fashioned silver plate, antiquated and tarnished, but weighty; their attachment to the House of Bourbon as the House of Bourbon did them honor. The very fixity of their political opinions was a sort of faithfulness. The distance that they set between themselves and the *bourgeoisie*, their very exclusiveness, gave them a certain elevation, and enhanced their value. Each noble represented a certain price for the townsmen, as Bambara Negroes, we are told, attach a money value to cowrie shells.

Some of the women, flattered by M. du Chatelet, discerned in him the superior qualities lacking in the men of their own sect, and the insurrection of self-love was pacified. These ladies all hoped to succeed to the Imperial Highness. Purists were of the opinion that you might see the intruder in Mme. de Bargeton's house, but not elsewhere. Du Chatelet was fain to put up with a good deal of insolence, but he held his ground by cultivating the clergy. He encouraged the queen of Angouleme in foibles bred of the soil; he brought her all the newest books; he read aloud the poetry that appeared. Together they went into ecstasies over these poets; she in all sincerity, he with suppressed yawns; but he bore with the Romantics with a patience hardly to be expected of a man of the Imperial school, who scarcely could make out what the young writers meant. Not so Mme. de Bargeton; she waxed enthusiastic over the renaissance, due to the return of the Bourbon Lilies; she loved M. de Chateaubriand for calling Victor Hugo "a sublime child." It depressed her that she could only know genius from afar, she sighed for Paris, where great men live. For these reasons M. du Chatelet thought he had done a wonderfully clever thing when he told the lady that at that moment in Angouleme there was "another sublime child," a young poet, a rising star whose glory surpassed the whole Parisian galaxy, though he knew it not. A great man of the future had been born in L'Houmeau! The headmaster of the school had shown the Baron some admirable verses. The poor and humble lad was a second Chatterton, with none of the political baseness and ferocious hatred of the great ones of earth that led his English prototype to turn pamphleteer and revile his benefactors. Mme. de Bargeton in her little circle of five or six persons, who were supposed to share her tastes for art and letters, because this one scraped a fiddle, and that splashed sheets of white paper, more or less, with sepia, and the other was president of a local agricultural society, or was gifted with a bass voice that rendered *Se fiato in corpo* like a war whoop --Mme. de Bargeton amid these grotesque figures was like a famished actor set down to a stage dinner of pasteboard. No words, therefore, can describe her joy at these tidings. She must see this poet, this angel! She raved about him, went into raptures, talked of him for whole hours together. Before two days were out the sometime diplomatic courier had negotiated (through the headmaster) for Lucien's appearance in the Hotel de Bargeton.

Poor helots of the provinces, for whom the distances between class and class are so far greater than for the Parisian (for whom, indeed, these distances visibly lessen day by day); souls so grievously oppressed by the social barriers behind which all sorts and conditions of men sit crying *Raca!* with mutual anathemas--you, and you alone, will fully comprehend the ferment in Lucien's heart and brain, when his awe-inspiring headmaster told him that the great gates of the Hotel de Bargeton would shortly open and turn upon their hinges at his fame! Lucien and David, walking together of an evening in the Promenade de Beaulieu, had looked up at the house with the old-fashioned gables, and wondered whether their names would ever so much as reach ears inexorably deaf to knowledge that came from a lowly origin; and now he (Lucien) was to be made welcome there!

No one except his sister was in the secret. Eve, like the thrifty housekeeper and divine magician that she was, conjured up a few louis d'or from her savings to buy thin shoes for Lucien of the best shoemaker in Angouleme, and an entirely new suit of clothes from the most renowned tailor. She made a frill for his best shirt, and washed and pleated it with her own hands. And how pleased she was to see him so dressed! How proud she felt of her brother, and what quantities of advice she gave him! Her intuition foresaw countless foolish fears. Lucien had a habit of resting his elbows on the table when he was in deep thought; he would even go so far as to draw a table nearer to lean upon it; Eve told him that he must not forget himself in those aristocratic precincts.

She went with him as far as St. Peter's Gate, and when they were almost opposite the cathedral she stopped, and watched him pass down the Rue de Beaulieu to the Promenade, where M. du Chatelet was waiting for him. And after he was out of sight, she still stood there, poor girl! in a great tremor of emotion, as though some great thing had happened to them. Lucien in Mme. de Bargeton's house!--for Eve it meant the dawn of success. The innocent creature did not suspect that where ambition begins, ingenuous feeling ends.

Externals in the Rue du Minage gave Lucien no sense of surprise. This palace, that loomed so large in his imagination, was a house built of the soft stone of the country, mellowed by time. It looked dismal enough from the street, and inside it was extremely plain; there was the usual provincial courtyard--chilly, prim, and neat; and the house itself was sober, almost convent-like, but in good repair.

Lucien went up the old staircase with the balustrade of chestnut wood (the stone steps ceased after the second floor), crossed a shabby antechamber, and came into the presence in a little wainscoted drawing-room, beyond a dimly-lit salon. The carved woodwork, in the taste of the eighteenth century, had been painted gray. There were monochrome paintings on the frieze panels, and the walls were adorned with crimson damask with a meagre border. The old-fashioned furniture shrank piteously from sight under covers of a red-and-white check pattern. On the sofa, covered with thin mattressed cushions, sat Mme. de Bargeton; the poet beheld her by the light of two wax candles on a sconce with a screen fitted to it, that stood before her on a round table with a green cloth.

The queen did not attempt to rise, but she twisted very gracefully on her seat, smiling on the poet, who was not a little fluttered by the serpentine quiverings; her manner was distinguished, he thought. For Mme. de Bargeton, she was impressed with Lucien's extreme beauty, with his diffidence, with everything about him; for her the poet already was poetry incarnate. Lucien scrutinized his hostess with discreet side glances; she disappointed none of his expectations of a great lady.

Mme. de Bargeton, following a new fashion, wore a coif of slashed black velvet, a head-dress that recalls memories of mediaeval legend to a young imagination, to amplify, as it were, the dignity of womanhood. Her red-gold hair, escaping from under her cap, hung loose; bright golden color in the light, red in the rounded shadow of the curls that only partially hid her neck. Beneath a massive white brow, clean cut and strongly outlined, shone a pair of bright gray eyes encircled by a margin of mother-of-pearl, two blue veins on each side of the nose bringing out the whiteness of that delicate setting. The Bourbon curve of the nose added to the ardent expression of an oval face; it was as if the royal temper of the House of Conde shone conspicuous in this feature. The careless cross-folds of the bodice left a white throat bare, and half revealed the outlines of a still youthful figure and shapely, well placed contours beneath.

With fingers tapering and well-kept, though somewhat too thin, Mme. de Bargeton amiably pointed to a seat by her side, M. du Chatelet ensconced himself in an easy-chair, and Lucien then became aware that there was no one else in the room.

Mme. de Bargeton's words intoxicated the young poet from L'Houmeau. For Lucien those three hours spent in her presence went by like a dream that we would fain have last forever. She was not thin, he thought; she was slender; in love with love, and loverless; and delicate in spite of her strength. Her foibles, exaggerated by her manner, took his fancy; for youth sets out with a love of hyperbole, that infirmity of noble souls. He did not so much as see that her cheeks were faded, that the patches of color on the cheek-bone were faded and hardened to a brick-red by listless days and a certain amount of ailing health. His imagination fastened at once on the glowing eyes, on the dainty curls rippling with light, on the dazzling fairness of her skin, and hovered about those bright points as the moth hovers about the candle flame. For her spirit made such appeal to his that he could no longer see the woman as she was. Her feminine exaltation had carried him away, the energy of her expressions, a little staled in truth by pretty hard and constant wear, but new to Lucien, fascinated him so much the more easily because he was determined to be pleased. He had brought none of his own verses to read, but nothing was said of them; he had purposely left them behind because he meant to return; and Mme. de Bargeton did not ask for them, because she meant that he should come back some future day to read them to her. Was not this a beginning of an understanding?

As for M. Sixte du Chatelet, he was not over well pleased with all this. He perceived rather too late in the day that he had a rival in this handsome young fellow. He went with him as far as the first flight of steps below Beaulieu to try the effect of a little diplomacy; and Lucien was not a little astonished when he heard the controller of excise pluming himself on having effected the introduction, and proceeding in this character to give him (Lucien) the benefit of his advice.

"Heaven send that Lucien might meet with better treatment than he had done," such was the matter of M. du Chatelet's discourse. "The Court was less insolent that this pack of dolts in Angouleme. You were expected to endure deadly insults; the superciliousness you had to put up with was something abominable. If this kind of folk did not alter their behavior, there would be another Revolution of '89. As for himself, if he continued to go to the house, it was because he had found Mme. de Bargeton to his taste; she was the only woman worth troubling about in Angouleme; he had been paying court to her for want of anything better to do, and now he was desperately in love with her. She would be his before very long, she loved him, everything pointed that way. The conquest of this haughty queen of the society would be his one revenge on the whole houseful of booby clodpates."

Chatelet talked of his passion in the tone of a man who would have a rival's life if he crossed his path. The elderly butterfly of the Empire came down with his whole weight on the poor poet, and tried to frighten and crush him by his self-importance. He grew taller as he gave an embellished account of his perilous wanderings; but while he impressed the poet's imagination, the lover was by no means afraid of him.

In spite of the elderly coxcomb, and regardless of his threats and airs of a *bourgeois* bravo, Lucien went back again and again to the house--not too often at first, as became a man of L'Houmeau; but before very long he grew accustomed to the vast condescension, as it had seemed to him at the outset, and came more and more frequently. The druggist's son was a completely insignificant being. If any of the *noblesse*, men or women, calling upon Nais, found Lucien in the room, they met him with the overwhelming graciousness that well-bred people use towards their inferiors. Lucien thought them very kind for a time, and later found out the real reason for their specious amiability. It was not long before he detected a patronizing tone that stirred his gall and confirmed him in his bitter Republicanism, a phase of opinion through which many a would-be patrician passes by way of prelude to his introduction to polite society.

But was there anything that he would not have endured for Nais?--for so he heard her named by the clan. Like Spanish grandees and the old Austrian nobility at Vienna, these folk, men and women alike, called each other by their Christian names, a final shade of distinction in the inmost ring of Angoumoisin aristocracy.

Lucien loved Nais as a young man loves the first woman who flatters him, for Nais prophesied great things and boundless fame for Lucien. She used all her skill to secure her hold upon her poet; not merely did she exalt him beyond measure, but she represented him to himself as a child without fortune whom she meant to start in life; she treated him like a child, to keep him near her; she made him her reader, her secretary, and cared more for him than she would have thought possible after the dreadful calamity that had befallen her.

She was very cruel to herself in those days, telling herself that it would be folly to love a young man of twenty, so far apart from her socially in the first place; and her behavior to him was a bewildering mixture of familiarity and capricious fits of pride arising from her fears and scruples. She was sometimes a lofty patroness, sometimes she was tender and flattered him. At first, while he was overawed by her rank, Lucien experienced the extremes of dread, hope, and despair, the torture of a first love, that is beaten deep into the heart with the hammer strokes of alternate bliss and anguish. For two months Mme. de Bargeton was for him a benefactress who would take a mother's interest in him; but confidences came next. Mme. de Bargeton began to address her poet as "dear Lucien," and then as "dear," without more ado. The poet grew bolder, and addressed the great lady as Nais, and there followed a flash of anger that captivates a boy; she reproached him for calling her by a name in everybody's mouth. The haughty and high-born Negrepelisse offered the fair angel youth that one of her appellations which was unsoiled by use; for him she would be "Louise." Lucien was in the third heaven.

One evening when Lucien came in, he found Mme. de Bargeton looking at a portrait, which she promptly put away. He wished to see it, and to quiet the despair of a first fit of jealousy Louise showed him Cante-Croix's picture, and told with tears the piteous story of a love so stainless, so cruelly cut short. Was she experimenting with herself? Was she trying a first unfaithfulness to the memory of the dead? Or had she taken it into her head to raise up a rival to Lucien in the portrait? Lucien was too much of a boy to analyze his lady-love; he gave way to unfeigned despair when she opened the campaign by entrenching herself behind the more or less skilfully devised scruples which women raise to have them battered down. When a woman begins to talk about her duty, regard for appearances or religion, the objections she raises are so many redoubts which she loves to have carried by storm. But on the guileless Lucien these coquetries were thrown away; he would have advanced of his own accord.

"*I* shall not die for you, I will live for you," he cried audaciously one evening; he meant to have no more of M. de Cante-Croix, and gave Louise a glance which told plainly that a crisis was at hand.

Startled at the progress of this new love in herself and her poet, Louise demanded some verses promised for the first page of her album, looking for a pretext for a quarrel in his tardiness. But what became of her when she read the following stanzas, which, naturally, she considered finer than the finest work of Canalis, the poet of the aristocracy?--

The magic brush, light flying flights of song-- To these, but not to these alone, belong My pages fair; Often to me, my mistress' pencil steals To tell the secret gladness that she feels, The hidden care.

And when her fingers, slowlier at the last, Of a rich Future, now become the Past, Seek count of me, Oh Love, when swift, thick-coming memories rise, I pray of Thee. May they bring visions fair as cloudless skies Of happy voyage o'er a summer sea!

"Was it really I who inspired those lines?" she asked.

The doubt suggested by coquetry to a woman who amused herself by playing with fire brought tears to Lucien's eyes; but her first kiss upon his forehead calmed the storm. Decidedly Lucien was a great man, and she meant to form him; she thought of teaching him Italian and German and perfecting his manners. That would be pretext sufficient for having him constantly with her under the very eyes of her tiresome courtiers. What an interest in her life! She took up music again for her poet's sake, and revealed the world of sound to him, playing grand fragments of Beethoven till she sent him into ecstasy; and, happy in his delight, turned to the half-swooning poet.

"Is not such happiness as this enough?" she asked hypocritically; and poor Lucien was stupid enough to answer, "Yes."

In the previous week things had reached such a point, that Louise had judged it expedient to ask Lucien to dine with M. de Bargeton as a third. But in spite of this precaution, the whole town knew the state of affairs; and so extraordinary did it appear, that no one would believe the truth. The outcry was terrific. Some were of the opinion that society was on the eve of cataclysm. "See what comes of Liberal doctrines!" cried others.

Then it was that the jealous du Chatelet discovered that Madame Charlotte, the monthly nurse, was no other than Mme. Chardon, "the mother of the Chateaubriand of L'Houmeau," as he put it. The remark passed muster as a joke. Mme. de Chandour was the first to hurry to Mme. de Bargeton.

"Nais, dear," she said, "do you know what everybody is talking about in Angouleme? This little rhymster's mother is the Madame Charlotte who nursed my sister-in-law through her confinement two months ago."

"What is there extraordinary in that, my dear?" asked Mme. de Bargeton with her most regal air. "She is a druggist's widow, is she not? A poor fate for a Rubempre. Suppose that you and I had not a penny in the world, what should either of us do for a living? How would you support your children?"

Mme. de Bargeton's presence of mind put an end to the jeremiads of the *noblesse*. Great natures are prone to make a virtue of misfortune; and there is something irresistibly attractive about well-doing when persisted in through evil report; innocence has the piquancy of the forbidden.

Mme. de Bargeton's rooms were crowded that evening with friends who came to remonstrate with her. She brought her most caustic wit into play. She said that as noble families could not produce a Moliere, a Racine, a Rousseau, a Voltaire, a Massillon, a Beaumarchais, or a Diderot, people must make up their minds to it, and accept the fact that great men had upholsterers and clockmakers and cutlers for their fathers. She said that genius was always noble. She railed at boorish squires for understanding their real interests so imperfectly. In short, she talked a good deal of nonsense, which would have let the light into heads less dense, but left her audience agape at her eccentricity. And in these ways she conjured away the storm with her heavy artillery.

When Lucien, obedient to her request, appeared for the first time in the faded great drawing-room, where the whist-tables were set out, she welcomed him graciously, and brought him forward, like a queen who means to be obeyed. She addressed the controller of excise as "M. Chatelet," and left that gentleman thunderstruck by the discovery that she knew about the illegal superfetation of the particle. Lucien was forced upon her circle, and was received as a poisonous element, which every person in it vowed to expel with the antidote of insolence.

Nais had won a victory, but she had lost her supremacy of empire. There was a rumor of insurrection. Amelie, otherwise Mme. de Chandour, harkening to "M. Chatelet's" counsels, determined to erect a rival altar by receiving on Wednesdays. Now Mme. de Bargeton's salon was open every evening; and those who frequented it were so wedded to their ways, so accustomed to meet about the same tables, to play the familiar game of backgammon, to see the same faces and the same candle sconces night after night; and afterwards to cloak and shawl, and put on overshoes and hats in the old corridor, that they were quite as much attached to the steps of the staircase as to the mistress of the house.

"All resigned themselves to endure the songster" (*chardonneret*) "of the sacred grove," said Alexandre de Brebian, which was witticism number two. Finally, the president of the agricultural society put an end to the sedition by remarking judicially that "before the Revolution the greatest nobles admitted men like Dulcos and Grimm and Crebillon to their society--men who were nobodies, like this little poet of L'Houmeau; but one thing they never did, they never received tax-collectors, and, after all, Chatelet is only a tax-collector."

Du Chatelet suffered for Chardon. Every one turned the cold shoulder upon him; and Chatelet was conscious that he was attacked. When Mme. de Bargeton called him "M. Chatelet," he swore to himself that he would possess her; and now he entered into the views of the mistress of the house, came to the support of the young poet, and declared himself Lucien's friend. The great diplomatist, overlooked by the shortsighted Emperor, made much of Lucien, and declared himself his friend! To launch the poet into society, he gave a dinner, and asked all the authorities to meet him--the prefect, the receiver-general, the colonel in command of the garrison, the head of the Naval School, the president of the Court, and so forth. The poet, poor fellow, was feted so magnificently, and so belauded, that anybody but a young man of two-and-twenty would have shrewdly suspected a hoax. After dinner, Chatelet drew his rival on to recite *The Dying Sardanapalus*, the masterpiece of the hour; and the headmaster of the school, a man of a phlegmatic temperament, applauded with both hands, and vowed that Jean-Baptiste Rousseau had done nothing finer. Sixte, Baron du Chatelet, thought in his heart that this slip of a rhymster would wither incontinently in a hothouse of adulation; perhaps he hoped that when the poet's head was turned with brilliant dreams, he would indulge in some impertinence that would promptly consign him to the obscurity from which he had emerged. Pending the decease of genius, Chatelet appeared to offer up his hopes as a sacrifice at Mme. de Bargeton's feet; but with the ingenuity of a rake, he kept his own plan in abeyance, watching the lovers' movements with keenly critical eyes, and waiting for the opportunity of ruining Lucien.

From this time forward, vague rumors reported the existence of a great man in Angoumois. Mme. de Bargeton was praised on all sides for the interest which she took in this young eagle. No sooner was her conduct approved than she tried to win a general sanction. She announced a soiree, with ices, tea, and cakes, a great innovation in a city where tea, as yet, was sold only by druggists as a remedy for indigestion. The flower of Angoumoisin aristocracy was summoned to hear Lucien read his great work. Louise had hidden all the difficulties from her friend, but she let fall a few words touching the social cabal formed against him; she would not have him ignorant of the perils besetting his career as a man of genius, nor of the obstacles insurmountable to weaklings. She drew a lesson from the recent victory. Her white hands pointed him to glory that lay beyond a prolonged martyrdom; she spoke of stakes and flaming pyres; she spread the adjectives thickly on her finest *tartines*, and decorated them with a variety of her most pompous epithets. It was an infringement of the copyright of the passages of declamation that disfigure *Corinne*; but Louise grew so much the greater in her own eyes as she talked, that she loved the Benjamin who inspired her eloquence the more for it. She counseled him to take a bold step and renounce his patronymic for the noble name of Rubempre; he need not mind the little tittle-tattle over a change which the King, for that matter, would authorize. Mme. de Bargeton undertook to procure this favor; she was related to the Marquise d'Espard, who was a Blamont-Chauvry before her marriage, and a *persona grata* at Court. The words "King," "Marquise d'Espard," and "the Court" dazzled Lucien like a blaze of fireworks, and the necessity of the baptism was plain to him.

"Dear child," said Louise, with tender mockery in her tones, "the sooner it is done, the sooner it will be sanctioned."

She went through social strata and showed the poet that this step would raise him many rungs higher in the ladder. Seizing the moment, she persuaded Lucien to forswear the chimerical notions of '89 as to equality; she roused a thirst for social distinction allayed by David's cool commonsense; she pointed out fashionable society as the goal and the only stage for such a talent as his. The rabid Liberal became a Monarchist *in petto*; Lucien set his teeth in the apple of desire of rank, luxury, and fame. He swore to win a crown to lay at his lady's feet, even if there should be blood-stains on the bays. He would conquer at any cost, *quibuscumque viis*. To prove his courage, he told her of his present way of life; Louise had known nothing of its hardships, for there is an indefinable pudency inseparable from strong feeling in youth, a delicacy which shrinks from a display of great qualities; and a young man loves to have the real quality of his nature discerned through the incognito. He described that life, the shackles of poverty borne with pride, his days of work for David, his nights of study. His young ardor recalled memories of the colonel of six-and-twenty; Mme. de Bargeton's eyes grew soft; and Lucien, seeing this weakness in his awe-inspiring mistress, seized a hand that she had abandoned to him, and kissed it with the frenzy of a lover and a poet in his youth. Louise even allowed him to set his eager, quivering lips upon her forehead.

"Oh, child! child! if any one should see us, I should look very ridiculous," she said, shaking off the ecstatic torpor.

In the course of that evening, Mme. de Bargeton's wit made havoc of Lucien's prejudices, as she styled them. Men of genius, according to her doctrine, had neither brothers nor sisters nor father nor mother; the great tasks laid upon them required that they should sacrifice everything that they might grow to their full stature. Perhaps their families might suffer at first from the all-absorbing exactions of a giant brain, but at a later day they were repaid a hundredfold for self-denial of every kind during the early struggles of the kingly intellect with adverse fate; they shared the spoils of victory. Genius was answerable to no man. Genius alone could judge of the means used to an end which no one else could know. It was the duty of a man of genius, therefore, to set himself above law; it was his mission to reconstruct law; the man who is master of his age may take all that he needs, run any risks, for all is his. She quoted instances. Bernard Palissy, Louis XI., Fox, Napoleon, Christopher Columbus, and Julius Caesar,--all these world-famous gamblers had begun life hampered with debt, or as poor men; all of them had been misunderstood, taken for madmen, reviled for bad sons, bad brothers, bad fathers; and yet in after life each one had come to be the pride of his family, of his country, of the civilized world.

Her arguments fell upon fertile soil in the worst of Lucien's nature, and spread corruption in his heart; for him, when his desires were hot, all means were admissible. But--failure is high treason against society; and when the fallen conqueror has run amuck through *bourgeois* virtues, and pulled down the pillars of society, small wonder that society, finding Marius seated among the ruins, should drive him forth in abhorrence. All unconsciously Lucien stood with the palm of genius on the one hand and a shameful ending in the hulks upon the other; and, on high upon the Sinai of the prophets, beheld no Dead Sea covering the cities of the plain--the hideous winding-sheet of Gomorrah.

So well did Louise loosen the swaddling-bands of provincial life that confined the heart and brain of her poet that the said poet determined to try an experiment upon her. He wished to feel certain that this proud conquest was his without laying himself open to the mortification of a rebuff. The forthcoming soiree gave him his opportunity. Ambition blended with his love. He loved, and he meant to rise, a double desire not unnatural in young men with a heart to satisfy and the battle of life to fight. Society, summoning all her children to one banquet, arouses ambition in the very morning of life. Youth is robbed of its charm, and generous thoughts are corrupted by mercenary scheming. The idealist would fain have it otherwise, but intrusive fact too often gives the lie to the fiction which we should like to believe, making it impossible to paint the young man of the nineteenth century other than he is. Lucien imagined that his scheming was entirely prompted by good feeling, and persuaded himself that it was done solely for his friend David's sake.

He wrote a long letter to his Louise; he felt bolder, pen in hand, than face to face. In a dozen sheets, copied out three several times, he told her of his father's genius and blighted hopes and of his grinding poverty. He described his beloved sister as an angel, and David as another Cuvier, a great man of the future, and a father, friend, and brother to him in the present. He should feel himself unworthy of his Louise's love (his proudest distinction) if he did not ask her to do for David all that she had done for him. He would give up everything rather than desert David Sechard; David must witness his success. It was one of those wild letters in which a young man points a pistol at a refusal, letters full of boyish casuistry and the incoherent reasoning of an idealist; a delicious tissue of words embroidered here and there by the naive utterances that women love so well--unconscious revelations of the writer's heart.

Lucien left the letter with the housemaid, went to the office, and spent the day in reading proofs, superintending the execution of orders, and looking after the affairs of the printing-house. He said not a word to David. While youth bears a child's heart, it is capable of sublime reticence. Perhaps, too, Lucien began to dread the Phocion's axe which David could wield when he chose, perhaps he was afraid to meet those clear-sighted eyes that read the depths of his soul. But when he read Chenier's poems with David, his secret rose from his heart to his lips at the sting of a reproach that he felt as the patient feels the probing of a wound.

And now try to understand the thoughts that troubled Lucien's mind as he went down from Angouleme. Was the great lady angry with him? Would she receive David? Had he, Lucien, in his ambition, flung himself headlong back into the depths of L'Houmeau? Before he set that kiss on Louise's forehead, he had had time to measure the distance between a queen and her favorite, so far had he come in five months, and he did not tell himself that David could cross over the same ground in a moment. Yet he did not know how completely the lower orders were excluded from this upper world; he did not so much as suspect that a second experiment of this kind meant ruin for Mme. de Bargeton. Once accused and fairly convicted of a liking for *canaille*, Louise would be driven from the place, her caste would shun her as men shunned a leper in the Middle Ages. Nais might have broken the moral law, and her whole circle, the clergy and the flower of the aristocracy, would have defended her against the world through thick and then; but a breach of another law, the offence of admitting all sorts of people to her house --this was sin without remission. The sins of those in power are always overlooked--once let them abdicate, and they shall pay the penalty. And what was it but abdication to receive David?

But if Lucien did not see these aspects of the question, his aristocratic instinct discerned plenty of difficulties of another kind, and he took alarm. A fine manner is not the invariable outcome of noble feeling; and while no man at court had a nobler air than Racine, Corneille looked very much like a cattle-dealer, and Descartes might have been taken for an honest Dutch merchant; and visitors to La Brede, meeting Montesquieu in a cotton nightcap, carrying a rake over his shoulder, mistook him for a gardener. A knowledge of the world, when it is not sucked in with mother's milk and part of the inheritance of descent, is only acquired by education, supplemented by certain gifts of chance--a graceful figure, distinction of feature, a certain ring in the voice. All these, so important trifles, David lacked, while Nature had bestowed them upon his friend. Of gentle blood on the mother's side, Lucien was a Frank, even down to the high-arched instep. David had inherited the physique of his father the pressman and the flat foot of the Gael. Lucien could hear the shower of jokes at David's expense; he could see Mme. de Bargeton's repressed smile; and at length, without being exactly ashamed of his brother, he made up his mind to disregard his first impulse and to think twice before yielding to it in future.

So, after the hour of poetry and self-sacrifice, after the reading of verse that opened out before the friends the fields of literature in the light of a newly-risen sun, the hour of worldly wisdom and of scheming struck for Lucien.

Down once more in L'Houmeau he wished that he had not written that letter; he wished he could have it back again; for down the vista of the future he caught a glimpse of the inexorable laws of the world. He guessed that nothing succeeds like success, and it cost him something to step down from the first rung of the scaling ladder by which he meant to reach and storm the heights above. Pictures of his quiet and simple life rose before him, pictures fair with the brightest colors of blossoming love. There was David; what a genius David had--David who had helped him so generously, and would die for him at need; he thought of his mother, of how great a lady she was in her lowly lot, and how she thought that he was as good as he was clever; then of his sister so gracious in submission to her fate, of his own innocent childhood and conscience as yet unstained, of budding hopes undespoiled by rough winds, and at these thoughts the past broke into flowers once more for his memory.

Then he told himself that it was a far finer thing to hew his own way through serried hostile mobs of aristocrats or philistines by repeated successful strokes, than to reach the goal through a woman's favor. Sooner or later his genius should shine out; it had been so with the others, his predecessors; they had tamed society. Women would love him when that day came! The example of Napoleon, which, unluckily for this nineteenth century of ours, has filled a great many ordinary persons with aspirations after extraordinary destinies,--the example of Napoleon occurred to Lucien's mind. He flung his schemes to the winds and blamed himself for thinking of them. For Lucien was so made that he went from evil to good, or from good to evil, with the same facility.

Lucien had none of the scholar's love for his retreat; for the past month indeed he had felt something like shame at the sight of the shop front, where you could read--

POSTEL (LATE CHARDON), PHARMACEUTICAL CHEMIST,

in yellow letters on a green ground. It was an offence to him that his father's name should be thus posted up in a place where every carriage passed.

Every evening, when he closed the ugly iron gate and went up to Beaulieu to give his arm to Mme. de Bargeton among the dandies of the upper town, he chafed beyond all reason at the disparity between his lodging and his fortune.

"I love Mme. de Bargeton; perhaps in a few days she will be mine, yet here I live in this rat-hole!" he said to himself this evening, as he went down the narrow passage into the little yard behind the shop. This evening bundles of boiled herbs were spread out along the wall, the apprentice was scouring a caldron, and M. Postel himself, girded about with his laboratory apron, was standing with a retort in his hand, inspecting some chemical product while keeping an eye upon the shop door, or if the eye happened to be engaged, he had at any rate an ear for the bell.

A strong scent of camomile and peppermint pervaded the yard and the poor little dwelling at the side, which you reached by a short ladder, with a rope on either side by way of hand-rail. Lucien's room was an attic just under the roof.

"Good-day, sonny," said M. Postel, that typical, provincial tradesman. "Are you pretty middling? I have just been experimenting on treacle, but it would take a man like your father to find what I am looking for. Ah! he was a famous chemist, he was! If I had only known his gout specific, you and I should be rolling along in our carriage this day."

The little druggist, whose head was as thick as his heart was kind, never let a week pass without some allusion to Chardon senior's unlucky secretiveness as to that discovery, words that Lucien felt like a stab.

"It is a great pity," Lucien answered curtly. He was beginning to think his father's apprentice prodigiously vulgar, though he had blessed the man for his kindness, for honest Postel had helped his master's widow and children more than once.

"Why, what is the matter with you?" M. Postel inquired, putting down his test tube on the laboratory table.

"Is there a letter for me?"

"Yes, a letter that smells like balm! it is lying on the corner near my desk."

Mme. de Bargeton's letter lying among the physic bottles in a druggist's shop! Lucien sprang in to rescue it.

"Be quick, Lucien! your dinner has been waiting an hour for you, it will be cold!" a sweet voice called gently through a half-opened window; but Lucien did not hear.

"That brother of yours has gone crazy, mademoiselle," said Postel, lifting his face.

The old bachelor looked rather like a miniature brandy cask, embellished by a painter's fancy, with a fat, ruddy countenance much pitted with the smallpox; at the sight of Eve his face took a ceremonious and amiable expression, which said plainly that he had thoughts of espousing the daughter of his predecessor, but could not put an end to the strife between love and interest in his heart. He often said to Lucien, with a smile, "Your sister is uncommonly pretty, and you are not so bad looking neither! Your father did everything well."

Eve was tall, dark-haired, dark of complexion, and blue-eyed; but notwithstanding these signs of virile character, she was gentle, tender-hearted, and devoted to those she loved. Her frank innocence, her simplicity, her quiet acceptance of a hard-working life, her character--for her life was above reproach--could not fail to win David Sechard's heart. So, since the first time that these two had met, a repressed and single-hearted love had grown up between them in the German fashion, quietly, with no fervid protestations. In their secret souls they thought of each other as if there were a bar between that kept them apart; as if the thought were an offence against some jealous husband; and hid their feelings from Lucien as though their love in some way did him a wrong. David, moreover, had no confidence in himself, and could not believe that Eve could care for him; Eve was a penniless girl, and therefore shy. A real work-girl would have been bolder; but Eve, gently bred, and fallen into poverty, resigned herself to her dreary lot. Diffident as she seemed, she was in reality proud, and would not make a single advance towards the son of a father said to be rich. People who knew the value of a growing property, said that the vineyard at Marsac was worth more than eighty thousand francs, to say nothing of the traditional bits of land which old Sechard used to buy as they came into the market, for old Sechard had savings--he was lucky with his vintages, and a clever salesman. Perhaps David was the only man in Angouleme who knew nothing of his father's wealth. In David's eyes Marsac was a hovel bought in 1810 for fifteen or sixteen thousand francs, a place that he saw once a year at vintage time when his father walked him up and down among the vines and boasted of an output of wine which the young printer never saw, and he cared nothing about it.

David was a student leading a solitary life; and the love that gained even greater force in solitude, as he dwelt upon the difficulties in the way, was timid, and looked for encouragement; for David stood more in awe of Eve than a simple clerk of some high-born lady. He was awkward and ill at ease in the presence of his idol, and as eager to hurry away as he had been to come. He repressed his passion, and was silent. Often of an evening, on some pretext of consulting Lucien, he would leave the Place du Murier and go down through the Palet Gate as far as L'Houmeau, but at the sight of the green iron railings his heart failed. Perhaps he had come too late, Eve might think him a nuisance; she would be in bed by this time no doubt; and so he turned back. But though his great love had only appeared in trifles, Eve read it clearly; she was proud, without a touch of vanity in her pride, of the deep reverence in David's looks and words and manner towards her, but it was the young printer's enthusiastic belief in Lucien that drew her to him most of all. He had divined the way to win Eve. The mute delights of this love of theirs differed from the transports of stormy passion, as wildflowers in the fields from the brilliant flowers in garden beds. Interchange of glances, delicate and sweet as blue water-flowers on the surface of the stream; a look in either face, vanishing as swiftly as the scent of briar-rose; melancholy, tender as the velvet of moss--these were the blossoms of two rare natures, springing up out of a rich and fruitful soil on foundations of rock. Many a time Eve had seen revelations of the strength that lay below the appearance of weakness, and made such full allowance for all that David left undone, that the slightest word now might bring about a closer union of soul and soul.

Eve opened the door, and Lucien sat down without a word at the little table on an X-shaped trestle. There was no tablecloth; the poor little household boasted but three silver spoons and forks, and Eve had laid them all for the dearly loved brother.

"What have you there?" she asked, when she had set a dish on the table, and put the extinguisher on the portable stove, where it had been kept hot for him.

Lucien did not answer. Eve took up a little plate, daintily garnished with vine-leaves, and set it on the table with a jug full of cream.

"There, Lucien, I have had strawberries for you."

But Lucien was so absorbed in his letter that he did not hear a word. Eve came to sit beside him without a murmur; for in a sister's love for a brother it is an element of great pleasure to be treated without ceremony.

"Oh! what is it?" she cried as she saw tears shining in her brother's eyes.

"Nothing, nothing, Eve," he said, and putting his arm about her waist, he drew her towards him and kissed her forehead, her hair, her throat, with warmth that surprised her.

"You are keeping something from me."

"Well, then--she loves me."

"I knew very well that you kissed me for somebody else," the poor sister pouted, flushing red.

"We shall all be happy," cried Lucien, swallowing great spoonfuls of soup.

"*We*?" echoed Eve. The same presentiment that had crossed David's mind prompted her to add, "You will not care so much about us now."

"How can you think that, if you know me?"

Eve put out her hand and grasped his tightly; then she carried off the empty plate and the brown earthen soup-tureen, and brought the dish that she had made for him. But instead of eating his dinner, Lucien read his letter over again; and Eve, discreet maiden, did not ask another question, respecting her brother's silence. If he wished to tell her about it, she could wait; if he did not, how could she ask him to tell her? She waited. Here is the letter:--

"MY FRIEND,--Why should I refuse to your brother in science the help that I have lent you? All merits have equal rights in my eyes; but you do not know the prejudices of those among whom I live. We shall never make an aristocracy of ignorance understand that intellect ennobles. If I have not sufficient influence to compel them to accept M. David Sechard, I am quite willing to sacrifice the worthless creatures to you. It would be a perfect hecatomb in the antique manner. But, dear friend, you would not, of course, ask me to leave them all in exchange for the society of a person whose character and manner might not please me. I know from your flatteries how easily friendship can be blinded. Will you think the worse of me if I attach a condition to my consent? In the interests of your future I should like to see your friend, and know and decide for myself whether you are not mistaken. What is this but the mother's anxious care of my dear poet, which I am in duty bound to take?

"LOUISE DE NEGREPELISSE."

Lucien had no suspicion of the art with which polite society puts forward a "Yes" on the way to a "No," and a "No" that leads to a "Yes." He took this note for a victory. David should go to Mme. de Bargeton's house! David would shine there in all the majesty of his genius! He raised his head so proudly in the intoxication of a victory which increased his belief in himself and his ascendency over others, his face was so radiant with the brightness of many hopes, that his sister could not help telling him that he looked handsome.

"If that woman has any sense, she must love you! And if so, tonight she will be vexed, for all the ladies will try all sorts of coquetries on you. How handsome you will look when you read your *Saint John in Patmos*! If only I were a mouse, and could just slip in and see it! Come, I have put your clothes out in mother's room."

The mother's room bore witness to self-respecting poverty. There were white curtains to the walnut wood bedstead, and a strip of cheap green carpet at the foot. A chest of drawers with a wooden top, a looking-glass, and a few walnut wood chairs completed the furniture. The clock on the chimney-piece told of the old vanished days of prosperity. White curtains hung in the windows, a gray flowered paper covered the walls, and the tiled floor, colored and waxed by Eve herself, shone with cleanliness. On the little round table in the middle of the room stood a red tray with a pattern of gilt roses, and three cups and a sugar-basin of Limoges porcelain. Eve slept in the little adjoining closet, where there was just room for a narrow bed, an old-fashioned low chair, and a work-table by the window; there was about as much space as there is in a ship's cabin, and the door always stood open for the sake of air. But if all these things spoke of great poverty, the atmosphere was sedate and studious; and for those who knew the mother and children, there was something touchingly appropriate in their surroundings.

Lucien was tying his cravat when David's step sounded outside in the little yard, and in another moment the young printer appeared. From his manner and looks he seemed to have come down in a hurry.

"Well, David!" cried the ambitious poet, "we have gained the day! She loves me! You shall come too."

"No," David said with some confusion, "I came down to thank you for this proof of friendship, but I have been thinking things over seriously. My own life is cut out for me, Lucien. I am David Sechard, printer to His Majesty in Angouleme, with my name at the bottom of the bills posted on every wall. For people of that class, I am an artisan, or I am in business, if you like it better, but I am a craftsman who lives over a shop in the Rue de Beaulieu at the corner of the Place du Murier. I have not the wealth of a Keller just yet, nor the name of a Desplein, two sorts of power that the nobles still try to ignore, and --I am so far agreed with them--this power is nothing without a knowledge of the world and the manners of a gentleman. How am I to prove my claim to this sudden elevation? I should only make myself a laughing-stock for nobles and *bourgeoisie* to boot. As for you, your position is different. A foreman is not committed to anything. You are busy gaining knowledge that will be indispensable by and by; you can explain your present work by your future. And, in any case, you can leave your place tomorrow and begin something else; you might study law or diplomacy, or go into civil service. Nobody had docketed and pigeon-holed *you*, in fact. Take advantage of your social maiden fame to walk alone and grasp honors. Enjoy all pleasures gladly, even frivolous pleasures. I wish you luck, Lucien; I shall enjoy your success; you will be like a second self for me. Yes, in my own thoughts I shall live your life. You shall have the holiday life, in the glare of the world and among the swift working springs of intrigue. I will lead the work-a-day life, the tradesman's life of sober toil, and the patient labor of scientific research.

"You shall be our aristocracy," he went on, looking at Eve as he spoke. "If you totter, you shall have my arm to steady you. If you have reason to complain of the treachery of others, you will find a refuge in our hearts, the love there will never change. And influence and favor and the goodwill of others might fail us if we were two; we should stand in each other's way; go forward, you can tow me after you if it comes to that. So far from envying you, I will dedicate my life to yours. The thing that you have just done for me, when you risked the loss of your benefactress, your love it may be, rather than forsake or disown me, that little thing, so great as it was--ah, well, Lucien, that in itself would bind me to you forever if we were not brothers already. Have no remorse, no concern over seeming to take the larger share. This one-sided bargain is exactly to my taste. And, after all, suppose that you should give me a pang now and again, who knows that I shall not still be your debtor all my life long?"

He looked timidly towards Eve as he spoke; her eyes were full of tears, she saw all that lay below the surface.

"In fact," he went on, turning to Lucien, who stood amazed at this, "you are well made, you have a graceful figure, you wear your clothes with an air, you look like a gentleman in that blue coat of yours with the yellow buttons and the plain nankeen trousers; now I should look like a workingman among those people, I should be awkward and out of my element, I should say foolish things, or say nothing at all; but as for you, you can overcome any prejudice as to names by taking your mother's; you can call yourself Lucien de Rubempre; I am and always shall be David Sechard. In this society that you frequent, everything tells for you, everything would tell against me. You were born to shine in it. Women will worship that angel face of yours; won't they, Eve?"

Lucien sprang up and flung his arms about David. David's humility had made short work of many doubts and plenty of difficulties. Was it possible not to feel twice tenderly towards this friend, who by the way of friendship had come to think the very thoughts that he, Lucien, had reached through ambition? The aspirant for love and honors felt that the way had been made smooth for him; the young man and the comrade felt all his heart go out towards his friend.

It was one of those moments that come very seldom in our lives, when all the forces in us are sweetly strung, and every chord vibrating gives out full resonance.

And yet, this goodness of a noble nature increased Lucien's human tendency to take himself as the centre of things. Do not all of us say more or less, "L'Etat, c'est moi!" with Louis Quatorze? Lucien's mother and sister had concentrated all their tenderness on him, David was his devoted friend; he was accustomed to see the three making every effort for him in secret, and consequently he had all the faults of a spoiled eldest son. The noble is eaten up with the egoism which their unselfishness was fostering in Lucien; and Mme. de Bargeton was doing her best to develop the same fault by inciting him to forget all that he owed to his sister, and mother, and David. He was far from doing so as yet; but was there not ground for the fear that as his sphere of ambition widened, his whole thought perforce would be how he might maintain himself in it?

When emotion had subsided, David had a suggestion to make. He thought that Lucien's poem, *Saint John in Patmos*, was possibly too biblical to be read before an audience but little familiar with apocalyptic poetry. Lucien, making his first appearance before the most exacting public in the Charente, seemed to be nervous. David advised him to take Andre de Chenier and substitute certain pleasure for a dubious delight. Lucien was a perfect reader, the listeners would enjoy listening to him, and his modesty would doubtless serve him well. Like most young people, the pair were endowing the rest of the world with their own intelligence and virtues; for if youth that has not yet gone astray is pitiless for the sins of others, it is ready, on the other hand, to put a magnificent faith in them. It is only, in fact, after a good deal of experience of life that we recognize the truth of Raphael's great saying--"To comprehend is to equal."

The power of appreciating poetry is rare, generally speaking, in France; *esprit* soon dries up the source of the sacred tears of ecstasy; nobody cares to be at the trouble of deciphering the sublime, of plumbing the depths to discover the infinite. Lucien was about to have his first experience of the ignorance and indifference of worldlings. He went round by way of the printing office for David's volume of poetry.

The two lovers were left alone, and David had never felt more embarrassed in his life. Countless terrors seized upon him; he half wished, half feared that Eve would praise him; he longed to run away, for even modesty is not exempt from coquetry. David was afraid to utter a word that might seem to beg for thanks; everything that he could think of put him in some false position, so he held his tongue and looked guilty. Eve, guessing the agony of modesty, was enjoying the pause; but when David twisted his hat as if he meant to go, she looked at him and smiled.

"Monsieur David," she said, "if you are not going to pass the evening at Mme. de Bargeton's, we can spend the time together. It is fine; shall we take a walk along the Charente? We will have a talk about Lucien."

David longed to fling himself at the feet of this delicious girl. Eve had rewarded him beyond his hopes by that tone in her voice; the kindness of her accent had solved the difficulties of the position, her suggestion was something better than praise; it was the first grace given by love.

"But give me time to dress!" she said, as David made as if to go at once.

David went out; he who all his life long had not known one tune from another, was humming to himself; honest Postel hearing him with surprise, conceived a vehement suspicion of Eve's feelings towards the printer.

The most trifling things that happened that evening made a great impression on Lucien, and his character was peculiarly susceptible to first impressions. Like all inexperienced lovers he arrived so early that Louise was not in the drawing-room; but M. de Bargeton was there, alone. Lucien had already begun to serve his apprenticeship in the practice of the small deceits with which the lover of a married woman pays for his happiness--deceits through which, moreover, she learns the extent of her power; but so far Lucien had not met the lady's husband face to face.

M. de Bargeton's intellect was of the limited kind, exactly poised on the border line between harmless vacancy, with some glimmerings of sense, and the excessive stupidity that can neither take in nor give out any idea. He was thoroughly impressed with the idea of doing his duty in society; and, doing his utmost to be agreeable, had adopted the smile of an opera dancer as his sole method of expression. Satisfied, he smiled; dissatisfied, he smiled again. He smiled at good news and evil tidings; with slight modifications the smile did duty on all occasions. If he was positively obliged to express his personal approval, a complacent laugh reinforced the smile; but he never vouchsafed a word until driven to the last extremity. A *tete-a-tete* put him in the one embarrassment of his vegetative existence, for then he was obliged to look for something to say in the vast blank of his vacant interior. He usually got out of the difficulty by a return to the artless ways of childhood; he thought aloud, took you into his confidence concerning the smallest details of his existence, his physical wants, the small sensations which did duty for ideas with him. He never talked about the weather, nor did he indulge in the ordinary commonplaces of conversation--the way of escape provided for weak intellects; he plunged you into the most intimate and personal topics.

"I took veal this morning to please Mme. de Bargeton, who is very fond of veal, and my stomach has been very uneasy since," he would tell you. "I knew how it would be; it never suits me. How do you explain it?" Or, very likely--

"I am just about to ring for a glass of *eau sucree*; will you have some at the same time?"

Or, "I am going to take a ride tomorrow; I am going over to see my father-in-law."

These short observations did not permit of discussion; a "Yes" or "No," extracted from his interlocutor, the conversation dropped dead. Then M. de Bargeton mutely implored his visitor to come to his assistance. Turning westward his old asthmatic pug-dog countenance, he gazed at you with big, lustreless eyes, in a way that said, "You were saying?"

The people whom he loved best were bores anxious to talk about themselves; he listened to them with an unfeigned and delicate interest which so endeared him to the species that all the twaddlers of Angouleme credited M. de Bargeton with more understanding than he chose to show, and were of the opinion that he was underrated. So it happened that when these persons could find nobody else to listen to them, they went off to give M. de Bargeton the benefit of the rest of the story, argument, or what not, sure beforehand of his eulogistic smile. Madame de Bargeton's rooms were always crowded, and generally her husband felt quite at ease. He interested himself in the smallest details; he watched those who came in and bowed and smiled, and brought the new arrivals to his wife; he lay in wait for departing visitors, and went with them to the door, taking leave of them with that eternal smile. When conversation grew lively, and he saw that every one was interested in one thing or another, he stood, happy and mute, planted like a swan on both feet, listening, to all appearance, to a political discussion; or he looked over the card-players' hands without a notion of what it was all about, for he could not play at any game; or he walked about and took snuff to promote digestion. Anais was the bright side of his life; she made it unspeakably pleasant for him. Stretched out at full length in his armchair, he watched admiringly while she did her part as hostess, for she talked for him. It was a pleasure, too, to him to try to see the point in her remarks; and as it was often a good while before he succeeded, his smiles appeared after a delay, like the explosion of a shell which has entered the earth and worked up again. His respect for his wife, moreover, almost amounted to adoration. And so long as we can adore, is there not happiness enough in life? Anais' husband was as docile as a child who asks nothing better than to be told what to do; and, generous and clever woman as she was, she had taken no undue advantage of his weaknesses. She had taken care of him as you take care of a cloak; she kept him brushed, neat, and tidy, looked closely after him, and humored him; and humored, looked after, brushed, kept tidy, and cared for, M. de Bargeton had come to feel an almost dog-like affection for his wife. It is so easy to give happiness that costs nothing! Mme. de Bargeton, knowing that her husband had no pleasure but in good cheer, saw that he had good dinners; she had pity upon him, she had never uttered a word of complaint; indeed, there were people who could not understand that a woman might keep silence through pride, and argued that M. de Bargeton must possess good qualities hidden from public view. Mme. de Bargeton had drilled him into military subordination; he yielded a passive obedience to his wife. "Go and call on Monsieur So-and-So or Madame Such-an-One," she would say, and he went forthwith, like a soldier at the word of command. He stood at attention in her presence, and waited motionless for his orders.

There was some talk about this time of nominating the mute gentleman for a deputy. Lucien as yet had not lifted the veil which hid such an unimaginable character; indeed, he had scarcely frequented the house long enough. M. de Bargeton, spread at full length in his great chair, appeared to see and understand all that was going on; his silence added to his dignity, and his figure inspired Lucien with a prodigious awe. It is the wont of imaginative natures to magnify everything, or to find a soul to inhabit every shape; and Lucien took this gentleman, not for a granite guard-post, but for a formidable sphinx, and thought it necessary to conciliate him.

"I am the first comer," he said, bowing with more respect than people usually showed the worthy man.

"That is natural enough," said M. de Bargeton.

Lucien took the remark for an epigram; the lady's husband was jealous, he thought; he reddened under it, looked in the glass and tried to give himself a countenance.

"You live in L'Houmeau," said M. de Bargeton, "and people who live a long way off always come earlier than those who live near by."

"What is the reason of that?" asked Lucien politely.

"I don't know," answered M. de Bargeton, relapsing into immobility.

"You have not cared to find out," Lucien began again; "any one who could make an observation could discover the cause."

"Ah!" said M. de Bargeton, "final causes! Eh! eh! . . ."

The conversation came to a dead stop; Lucien racked his brains to resuscitate it.

"Mme. de Bargeton is dressing, no doubt," he began, shuddering at the silliness of the question.

"Yes, she is dressing," her husband naturally answered.

Lucien looked up at the ceiling and vainly tried to think of something else to say. As his eyes wandered over the gray painted joists and the spaces of plaster between, he saw, not without qualms, that the little chandelier with the old-fashioned cut-glass pendants had been stripped of its gauze covering and filled with wax candles. All the covers had been removed from the furniture, and the faded flowered silk damask had come to light. These preparations meant something extraordinary. The poet looked at his boots, and misgivings about his costume arose in his mind. Grown stupid with dismay, he turned and fixed his eyes on a Japanese jar standing on a begarlanded console table of the time of Louis Quinze; then, recollecting that he must conciliate Mme. de Bargeton's husband, he tried to find out if the good gentleman had a hobby of any sort in which he might be humored.

"You seldom leave the city, monsieur?" he began, returning to M. de Bargeton.

"Very seldom."

Silence again. M. de Bargeton watched Lucien's slightest movements like a suspicious cat; the young man's presence disturbed him. Each was afraid of the other.

"Can he feel suspicious of my attentions?" thought Lucien; "he seems to be anything but friendly."

Lucien was not a little embarrassed by the uneasy glances that the other gave him as he went to and fro, when luckily for him, the old man-servant (who wore livery for the occasion) announced "M. du Chatelet." The Baron came in, very much at ease, greeted his friend Bargeton, and favored Lucien with the little nod then in vogue, which the poet in his mind called purse-proud impertinence.

Sixte du Chatelet appeared in a pair of dazzling white trousers with invisible straps that kept them in shape. He wore pumps and thread stockings; the black ribbon of his eyeglass meandered over a white waistcoat, and the fashion and elegance of Paris was strikingly apparent in his black coat. He was indeed just the faded beau who might be expected from his antecedents, though advancing years had already endowed him with a certain waist-girth which somewhat exceeded the limits of elegance. He had dyed the hair and whiskers grizzled by his sufferings during his travels, and this gave a hard look to his face. The skin which had once been so delicate had been tanned to the copper-red color of Europeans from India; but in spite of his absurd pretensions to youth, you could still discern traces of the Imperial Highness' charming private secretary in du Chatelet's general appearance. He put up his eyeglass and stared at his rival's nankeen trousers, at his boots, at his waistcoat, at the blue coat made by the Angouleme tailor, he looked him over from head to foot, in short, then he coolly returned his eyeglass to his waistcoat pocket with a gesture that said, "I am satisfied." And Lucien, eclipsed at this moment by the elegance of the inland revenue department, thought that it would be his turn by and by, when he should turn a face lighted up with poetry upon the assembly; but this prospect did not prevent him from feeling the sharp pang that succeeded to the uncomfortable sense of M. de Bargeton's imagined hostility. The Baron seemed to bring all the weight of his fortune to bear upon him, the better to humiliate him in his poverty. M. de Bargeton had counted on having no more to say, and his soul was dismayed by the pause spent by the rivals in mutual survey; he had a question which he kept for desperate emergencies, laid up in his mind, as it were, against a rainy day. Now was the proper time to bring it out.

"Well, monsieur," he said, looking at Chatelet with an important air, "is there anything fresh? anything that people are talking about?"

"Why, the latest thing is M. Chardon," Chatelet said maliciously. "Ask him. Have you brought some charming poet for us?" inquired the vivacious Baron, adjusting the side curl that had gone astray on his temple.

"I should have asked you whether I had succeeded," Lucien answered; "you have been before me in the field of verse."

"Pshaw!" said the other, "a few vaudevilles, well enough in their way, written to oblige, a song now and again to suit some occasion, lines for music, no good without the music, and my long Epistle to a Sister of Bonaparte (ungrateful that he was), will not hand down my name to posterity."

At this moment Mme. de Bargeton appeared in all the glory of an elaborate toilette. She wore a Jewess' turban, enriched with an Eastern clasp. The cameos on her neck gleamed through the gauze scarf gracefully wound about her shoulders; the sleeves of her printed muslin dress were short so as to display a series of bracelets on her shapely white arms. Lucien was charmed with this theatrical style of dress. M. du Chatelet gallantly plied the queen with fulsome compliments, that made her smile with pleasure; she was so glad to be praised in Lucien's hearing. But she scarcely gave her dear poet a glance, and met Chatelet with a mortifying civility that kept him at a distance.

By this time the guests began to arrive. First and foremost appeared the Bishop and his Vicar-General, dignified and reverend figures both, though no two men could well be more unlike, his lordship being tall and attenuated, and his acolyte short and fat. Both churchmen's eyes were bright; but while the Bishop was pallid, his Vicar-General's countenance glowed with high health. Both were impassive, and gesticulated but little; both appeared to be prudent men, and their silence and reserve were supposed to hide great intellectual powers.

Close upon the two ecclesiastics followed Mme. de Chandour and her husband, a couple so extraordinary that those who are unfamiliar with provincial life might be tempted to think that such persons are purely imaginary. Amelie de Chandour posed as the rival queen of Angouleme; her husband, M. de Chandour, known in the circle as Stanislas, was a *ci-devant* young man, slim still at five-and-forty, with a countenance like a sieve. His cravat was always tied so as to present two menacing points--one spike reached the height of his right ear, the other pointed downwards to the red ribbon of his cross. His coat-tails were violently at strife. A cut-away waistcoat displayed the ample, swelling curves of a stiffly-starched shirt fastened by massive gold studs. His dress, in fact, was exaggerated, till he looked almost like a living caricature, which no one could behold for the first time with gravity.

Stanislas looked himself over from top to toe with a kind of satisfaction; he verified the number of his waistcoat buttons, and followed the curving outlines of his tight-fitting trousers with fond glances that came to a standstill at last on the pointed tips of his shoes. When he ceased to contemplate himself in this way, he looked towards the nearest mirror to see if his hair still kept in curl; then, sticking a finger in his waistcoat pocket, he looked about him at the women with happy eyes, flinging his head back in three-quarters profile with all the airs of a king of the poultry-yard, airs which were prodigiously admired by the aristocratic circle of which he was the beau. There was a strain of eighteenth century grossness, as a rule, in his talk; a detestable kind of conversation which procured him some success with women--he made them laugh. M. du Chatelet was beginning to give this gentleman some uneasiness; and, as a matter of fact, since Mme. de Bargeton had taken him up, the lively interest taken by the women in the Byron of Angouleme was distinctly on the increase. His coxcomb superciliousness tickled their curiosity; he posed as the man whom nothing can arouse from his apathy, and his jaded Sultan airs were like a challenge.

Amelie de Chandour, short, plump, fair-complexioned, and dark-haired, was a poor actress; her voice was loud, like everything else about her; her head, with its load of feathers in winter and flowers in summer, was never still for a moment. She had a fine flow of conversation, though she could never bring a sentence to an end without a wheezing accompaniment from an asthma, to which she would not confess.

M. de Saintot, otherwise Astolphe, President of the Agricultural Society, a tall, stout, high-colored personage, usually appeared in the wake of his wife, Elisa, a lady with a countenance like a withered fern, called Lili by her friends--a baby name singularly at variance with its owner's character and demeanor. Mme. de Saintot was a solemn and extremely pious woman, and a very trying partner at a game of cards. Astolphe was supposed to be a scientific man of the first rank. He was as ignorant as a carp, but he had compiled the articles on Sugar and Brandy for a Dictionary of Agriculture by wholesale plunder of newspaper articles and pillage of previous writers. It was believed all over the department that M. Saintot was engaged upon a treatise on modern husbandry; but though he locked himself into his study every morning, he had not written a couple of pages in a dozen years. If anybody called to see him, he always contrived to be discovered rummaging among his papers, hunting for a stray note or mending a pen; but he spent the whole time in his study on puerilities, reading the newspaper through from end to end, cutting figures out of corks with his penknife, and drawing patterns on his blotting-paper. He would turn over the leaves of his Cicero to see if anything applicable to the events of the day might catch his eye, and drag his quotation by the heels into the conversation that evening saying, "There is a passage in Cicero which might have been written to suit modern times," and out came his phrase, to the astonishment of his audience. "Really," they said among themselves, "Astolphe is a well of learning." The interesting fact circulated all over the town, and sustained the general belief in M. de Saintot's abilities.

After this pair came M. de Bartas, known as Adrien among the circle. It was M. de Bartas who boomed out his song in a bass voice, and made prodigious claims to musical knowledge. His self-conceit had taken a stand upon solfeggi; he began by admiring his appearance while he sang, passed thence to talking about music, and finally to talking of nothing else. His musical tastes had become a monomania; he grew animated only on the one subject of music; he was miserable all evening until somebody begged him to sing. When he had bellowed one of his airs, he revived again; strutted about, raised himself on his heels, and received compliments with a deprecating air; but modesty did not prevent him from going from group to group for his meed of praise; and when there was no more to be said about the singer, he returned to the subject of the song, discussing its difficulties or extolling the composer.

M. Alexandre de Brebian performed heroic exploits in sepia; he disfigured the walls of his friends' rooms with a swarm of crude productions, and spoiled all the albums in the department. M. Alexandre de Brebian and M. de Bartas came together, each with his friend's wife on his arm, a cross-cornered arrangement which gossip declared to be carried out to the fullest extent. As for the two women, Mesdames Charlotte de Brebian and Josephine de Bartas, or Lolotte and Fifine, as they were called, both took an equal interest in a scarf, or the trimming of a dress, or the reconciliation of several irreconcilable colors; both were eaten up with a desire to look like Parisiennes, and neglected their homes, where everything went wrong. But if they dressed like dolls in tightly-fitting gowns of home manufacture, and exhibited outrageous combinations of crude colors upon their persons, their husbands availed themselves of the artist's privilege and dressed as they pleased, and curious it was to see the provincial dowdiness of the pair. In their threadbare clothes they looked like the supernumeraries that represent rank and fashion at stage weddings in third-rate theatres.

One of the queerest figures in the rooms was M. le Comte de Senonches, known by the aristocratic name of Jacques, a mighty hunter, lean and sunburned, a haughty gentleman, about as amiable as a wild boar, as suspicious as a Venetian, and jealous as a Moor, who lived on terms of the friendliest and most perfect intimacy with M. du Hautoy, otherwise Francis, the friend of the house.

Madame de Senonches (Zephirine) was a tall, fine-looking woman, though her complexion was spoiled already by pimples due to liver complaint, on which grounds she was said to be exacting. With a slender figure and delicate proportions, she could afford to indulge in languid manners, savoring somewhat of affectation, but revealing passion and the consciousness that every least caprice will be gratified by love.

Francis, the house friend, was rather distinguished-looking. He had given up his consulship in Valence, and sacrificed his diplomatic prospects to live near Zephirine (also known as Zizine) in Angouleme. He had taken the household in charge, he superintended the children's education, taught them foreign languages, and looked after the fortunes of M. and Mme. de Senonches with the most complete devotion. Noble Angouleme, administrative Angouleme, and *bourgeois* Angouleme alike had looked askance for a long while at this phenomenon of the perfect union of three persons; but finally the mysterious conjugal trinity appeared to them so rare and pleasing a spectacle, that if M. du Hautoy had shown any intention of marrying, he would have been thought monstrously immoral. Mme. de Senonches, however, had a lady companion, a goddaughter, and her excessive attachment to this Mlle. de la Haye was beginning to raise surmises of disquieting mysteries; it was thought, in spite of some impossible discrepancies in dates, that Françoise de la Haye bore a striking likeness to Francis du Hautoy.

When "Jacques" was shooting in the neighborhood, people used to inquire after Francis, and Jacques would discourse on his steward's little ailments, and talk of his wife in the second place. So curious did this blindness seem in a man of jealous temper, that his greatest friends used to draw him out on the topic for the amusement of others who did not know of the mystery. M. du Hautoy was a finical dandy whose minute care of himself had degenerated into mincing affectation and childishness. He took an interest in his cough, his appetite, his digestion, his night's rest. Zephirine had succeeded in making a valetudinarian of her factotum; she coddled him and doctored him; she crammed him with delicate fare, as if he had been a fine lady's lap-dog; she embroidered waistcoats for him, and pocket-handkerchiefs and cravats until he became so used to wearing finery that she transformed him into a kind of Japanese idol. Their understanding was perfect. In season and out of season Zizine consulted Francis with a look, and Francis seemed to take his ideas from Zizine's eyes. They frowned and smiled together, and seemingly took counsel of each other before making the simplest commonplace remark.

The largest landowner in the neighborhood, a man whom every one envied, was the Marquis de Pimentel; he and his wife, between them, had an income of forty thousand livres, and spent their winters in Paris. This evening they had driven into Angouleme in their caleche, and had brought their neighbors, the Baron and Baroness de Rastignac and their party, the Baroness' aunt and daughters, two charming young ladies, penniless girls who had been carefully brought up, and were dressed in the simple way that sets off natural loveliness.

These personages, beyond question the first in the company, met with a reception of chilling silence; the respect paid to them was full of jealousy, especially as everybody saw that Mme. de Bargeton paid marked attention to the guests. The two families belonged to the very small minority who hold themselves aloof from provincial gossip, belong to no clique, live quietly in retirement, and maintain a dignified reserve. M. de Pimentel and M. de Rastignac, for instance, were addressed by their names in full, and no length of acquaintance had brought their wives and daughters into the select coterie of Angouleme; both families were too nearly connected with the Court to compromise themselves through provincial follies.

The Prefect and the General in command of the garrison were the last comers, and with them came the country gentleman who had brought the treatise on silkworms to David that very morning. Evidently he was the mayor of some canton or other, and a fine estate was his sufficient title to gentility; but from his appearance, it was plain that he was quite unused to polite society. He looked uneasy in his clothes, he was at a loss to know what to do with his hands, he shifted about from one foot to another as he spoke, and half rose and sat down again when anybody spoke to him. He seemed ready to do some menial service; he was obsequious, nervous, and grave by turns, laughing eagerly at every joke, listening with servility; and occasionally, imagining that people were laughing at him, he assumed a knowing air. His treatise weighed upon his mind; again and again he tried to talk about silkworms; but the luckless wight happened first upon M. de Bartas, who talked music in reply, and next on M. de Saintot, who quoted Cicero to him; and not until the evening was half over did the mayor meet with sympathetic listeners in Mme. and Mlle. du Brossard, a widowed gentlewoman and her daughter.

Mme. and Mlle. du Brossard were not the least interesting persons in the clique, but their story may be told in a single phrase--they were as poor as they were noble. In their dress there was just that tinge of pretension which betrayed carefully hidden penury. The daughter, a big, heavy young woman of seven-and-twenty, was supposed to be a good performer on the piano, and her mother praised her in season and out of season in the clumsiest way. No eligible man had any taste which Camille did not share on her mother's authoritative statement. Mme. du Brossard, in her anxiety to establish her child, was capable of saying that her dear Camille liked nothing so much as a roving life from one garrison to another; and before the evening was out, that she was sure her dear Camille liked a quiet country farmhouse existence of all things. Mother and daughter had the pinched sub-acid dignity characteristic of those who have learned by experience the exact value of expressions of sympathy; they belonged to a class which the world delights to pity; they had been the objects of the benevolent interest of egoism; they had sounded the empty void beneath the consoling formulas with which the world ministers to the necessities of the unfortunate.

M. de Severac was fifty-nine years old, and a childless widower. Mother and daughter listened, therefore, with devout admiration to all that he told them about his silkworm nurseries.

"My daughter has always been fond of animals," said the mother. "And as women are especially interested in the silk which the little creatures produce, I shall ask permission to go over to Severac, so that my Camille may see how the silk is spun. My Camille is so intelligent, she will grasp anything that you tell her in a moment. Did she not understand one day the inverse ratio of the squares of distances!"

This was the remark that brought the conversation between Mme. du Brossard and M. de Severac to a glorious close after Lucien's reading that night.

A few habitues slipped in familiarly among the rest, so did one or two eldest sons; shy, mute young men tricked out in gorgeous jewelry, and highly honored by an invitation to this literary solemnity, the boldest men among them so far shook off the weight of awe as to chatter a good deal with Mlle. de la Haye. The women solemnly arranged themselves in a circle, and the men stood behind them. It was a quaint assemblage of wrinkled countenances and heterogeneous costumes, but none the less it seemed very alarming to Lucien, and his heart beat fast when he felt that every one was looking at him. His assurance bore the ordeal with some difficulty in spite of the encouraging example of Mme. de Bargeton, who welcomed the most illustrious personages of Angouleme with ostentatious courtesy and elaborate graciousness; and the uncomfortable feeling that oppressed him was aggravated by a trifling matter which any one might have foreseen, though it was bound to come as an unpleasant shock to a young man with so little experience of the world. Lucien, all eyes and ears, noticed that no one except Louise, M. de Bargeton, the Bishop, and some few who wished to please the mistress of the house, spoke of him as M. de Rubempre; for his formidable audience he was M. Chardon. Lucien's courage sank under their inquisitive eyes. He could read his plebeian name in the mere movements of their lips, and hear the anticipatory criticisms made in the blunt, provincial fashion that too often borders on rudeness. He had not expected this prolonged ordeal of pin-pricks; it put him still more out of humor with himself. He grew impatient to begin the reading, for then he could assume an attitude which should put an end to his mental torments; but Jacques was giving Mme. de Pimentel the history of his last day's sport; Adrien was holding forth to Mlle. Laure de Rastignac on Rossini, the newly-risen music star, and Astolphe, who had got by heart a newspaper paragraph on a patent plow, was giving the Baron the benefit of the description. Lucien, luckless poet that he was, did not know that there was scarce a soul in the room besides Mme. de Bargeton who could understand poetry. The whole matter-of-fact assembly was there by a misapprehension, nor did they, for the most part, know what they had come out for to see. There are some words that draw a public as unfailingly as the clash of cymbals, the trumpet, or the mountebank's big drum; "beauty," "glory," "poetry," are words that bewitch the coarsest intellect.

When every one had arrived; when the buzz of talk ceased after repeated efforts on the part of M. de Bargeton, who, obedient to his wife, went round the room much as the beadle makes the circle of the church, tapping the pavement with his wand; when silence, in fact, was at last secured, Lucien went to the round table near Mme. de Bargeton. A fierce thrill of excitement ran through him as he did so. He announced in an uncertain voice that, to prevent disappointment, he was about to read the masterpieces of a great poet, discovered only recently (for although Andre de Chenier's poems appeared in 1819, no one in Angouleme had so much as heard of him). Everybody interpreted this announcement in one way--it was a shift of Mme. de Bargeton's, meant to save the poet's self-love and to put the audience at ease.

Lucien began with *Le Malade*, and the poem was received with a murmur of applause; but he followed it with *L'Aveugle*, which proved too great a strain upon the average intellect. None but artists or those endowed with the artistic temperament can understand and sympathize with him in the diabolical torture of that reading. If poetry is to be rendered by the voice, and if the listener is to grasp all that it means, the most devout attention is essential; there should be an intimate alliance between the reader and his audience, or swift and subtle communication of the poet's thought and feeling becomes impossible. Here this close sympathy was lacking, and Lucien in consequence was in the position of an angel who should endeavor to sing of heaven amid the chucklings of hell. An intelligent man in the sphere most stimulating to his faculties can see in every direction, like a snail; he has the keen scent of a dog, the ears of a mole; he can hear, and feel, and see all that is going on around him. A musician or a poet knows at once whether his audience is listening in admiration or fails to follow him, and feels it as the plant that revives or droops under favorable or unfavorable conditions. The men who had come with their wives had fallen to discussing their own affairs; by the acoustic law before mentioned, every murmur rang in Lucien's ear; he saw all the gaps caused by the spasmodic workings of jaws sympathetically affected, the teeth that seemed to grin defiance at him.

When, like the dove in the deluge, he looked round for any spot on which his eyes might rest, he saw nothing but rows of impatient faces. Their owners clearly were waiting for him to make an end; they had come together to discuss questions of practical interest. With the exceptions of Laure de Rastignac, the Bishop, and two or three of the young men, they one and all looked bored. As a matter of fact, those who understand poetry strive to develop the germs of another poetry, quickened within them by the poet's poetry; but this glacial audience, so far from attaining to the spirit of the poet, did not even listen to the letter.

Lucien felt profoundly discouraged; he was damp with chilly perspiration; a glowing glance from Louise, to whom he turned, gave him courage to persevere to the end, but this poet's heart was bleeding from countless wounds.

"Do you find this very amusing, Fifine?" inquired the wizened Lili, who perhaps had expected some kind of gymnastics.

"Don't ask me what I think, dear; I cannot keep my eyes open when any one begins to read aloud."

"I hope that Nais will not give us poetry often in the evenings," said Francis. "If I am obliged to attend while somebody reads aloud after dinner, it upsets my digestion."

"Poor dearie," whispered Zephirine, "take a glass of eau *sucree*."

"It was very well declaimed," said Alexandre, "but I like whist better myself."

After this dictum, which passed muster as a joke from the play on the word "whist," several card-players were of the opinion that the reader's voice needed a rest, and on this pretext one or two couples slipped away into the card-room. But Louise, and the Bishop, and pretty Laure de Rastignac besought Lucien to continue, and this time he caught the attention of his audience with Chenier's spirited reactionary *Iambes*. Several persons, carried away by his impassioned delivery, applauded the reading without understanding the sense. People of this sort are impressed by vociferation, as a coarse palate is ticked by strong spirits.

During the interval, as they partook of ices, Zephirine despatched Francis to examine the volume, and informed her neighbor Amelie that the poetry was in print.

Amelie brightened visibly.

"Why, that is easily explained," said she. "M. de Rubempre works for a printer. It is as if a pretty woman should make her own dresses," she added, looking at Lolotte.

"He printed his poetry himself!" said the women among themselves.

"Then, why does he call himself M. de Rubempre?" inquired Jacques. "If a noble takes a handicraft, he ought to lay his name aside."

"So he did as a matter of fact," said Zizine, "but his name was plebeian, and he took his mother's name, which is noble."

"Well, if his verses are printed, we can read them for ourselves," said Astolphe.

This piece of stupidity complicated the question, until Sixte du Chatelet condescended to inform these unlettered folk that the prefatory announcement was no oratorical flourish, but a statement of fact, and added that the poems had been written by a Royalist brother of Marie-Joseph Chenier, the Revolutionary leader. All Angouleme, except Mme. de Rastignac and her two daughters and the Bishop, who had really felt the grandeur of the poetry, were mystified, and took offence at the hoax. There was a smothered murmur, but Lucien did not heed it. The intoxication of the poetry was upon him; he was far away from the hateful world, striving to render in speech the music that filled his soul, seeing the faces about him through a cloudy haze. He read the sombre Elegy on the Suicide, lines in the taste of a by-gone day, pervaded by sublime melancholy; then he turned to the page where the line occurs, "Thy songs are sweet, I love to say them over," and ended with the delicate idyll *Neere*.

Mme. de Bargeton sat with one hand buried in her curls, heedless of the havoc she wrought among them, gazing before her with unseeing eyes, alone in her drawing-room, lost in delicious dreaming; for the first time in her life she had been transported to the sphere which was hers by right of nature. Judge, therefore, how unpleasantly she was disturbed by Amelie, who took it upon herself to express the general wish.

"Nais," this voice broke in, "we came to hear M. Chardon's poetry, and you are giving us poetry out of a book. The extracts are very nice, but the ladies feel a patriotic preference for the wine of the country; they would rather have it."

"The French language does not lend itself very readily to poetry, does it?" Astolphe remarked to Chatelet. "Cicero's prose is a thousand times more poetical to my way of thinking."

"The true poetry of France is song, lyric verse," Chatelet answered.

"Which proves that our language is eminently adapted for music," said Adrien.

"I should like very much to hear the poetry that has cost Nais her reputation," said Zephirine; "but after receiving Amelie's request in such a way, it is not very likely that she will give us a specimen."

"She ought to have them recited in justice to herself," said Francis. "The little fellow's genius is his sole justification."

"You have been in the diplomatic service," said Amelie to M. du Chatelet, "go and manage it somehow."

"Nothing easier," said the Baron.

The Princess' private secretary, being accustomed to petty manoeuvres of this kind, went to the Bishop and contrived to bring him to the fore. At the Bishop's entreaty, Nais had no choice but to ask Lucien to recite his own verses for them, and the Baron received a languishing smile from Amelie as the reward of his prompt success.

"Decidedly, the Baron is a very clever man," she observed to Lolotte.

But Amelie's previous acidulous remark about women who made their own dresses rankled in Lolotte's mind.

"Since when have you begun to recognize the Emperor's barons?" she asked, smiling.

Lucien had essayed to deify his beloved in an ode, dedicated to her under a title in favor with all lads who write verse after leaving school. This ode, so fondly cherished, so beautiful--since it was the outpouring of all the love in his heart, seemed to him to be the one piece of his own work that could hold its own with Chenier's verse; and with a tolerably fatuous glance at Mme. de Bargeton, he announced "TO HER!" He struck an attitude proudly for the delivery of the ambitious piece, for his author's self-love felt safe and at ease behind Mme. de Bargeton's petticoat. And at the selfsame moment Mme. de Bargeton betrayed her own secret to the women's curious eyes. Although she had always looked down upon this audience from her own loftier intellectual heights, she could not help trembling for Lucien. Her face was troubled, there was a sort of mute appeal for indulgence in her glances, and while the verses were recited she was obliged to lower her eyes and dissemble her pleasure as stanza followed stanza.

TO HER.

Out of the glowing heart of the torrent of glory and light, At the foot of Jehovah's throne where the angels stand afar, Each on a seistron of gold repeating the prayers of the night, Put up for each by his star.

Out from the cherubim choir a bright-haired Angel springs, Veiling the glory of God that dwells on a dazzling brow, Leaving the courts of heaven to sink upon silver wings Down to our world below.

God looked in pity on earth, and the Angel, reading His thought, Came down to lull the pain of the mighty spirit at strife, Reverent bent o'er the maid, and for age left desolate brought Flowers of the springtime of life.

Bringing a dream of hope to solace the mother's fears, Hearkening unto the voice of the tardy repentant cry, Glad as angels are glad, to reckon Earth's pitying tears, Given with alms of a sigh.

One there is, and but one, bright messenger sent from the skies Whom earth like a lover fain would hold from the hea'nward flight; But the angel, weeping, turns and gazes with sad, sweet eyes Up to the heaven of light.

Not by the radiant eyes, not by the kindling glow Of virtue sent from God, did I know the secret sign, Nor read the token sent on a white and dazzling brow Of an origin divine.

Nay, it was Love grown blind and dazed with excess of light, Striving and striving in vain to mingle Earth and Heaven, Helpless and powerless against the invincible armor bright By the dread archangel given.

Ah! be wary, take heed, lest aught should be seen or heard Of the shining seraph band, as they take the heavenward way; Too soon the Angel on Earth will learn the magical word Sung at the close of the day.

Then you shall see afar, rifting the darkness of night, A gleam as of dawn that spread across the starry floor, And the seaman that watch for a sign shall mark the track of their flight, A luminous pathway in Heaven and a beacon for evermore.

"Do you read the riddle?" said Amelie, giving M. du Chatelet a coquettish glance.

"It is the sort of stuff that we all of us wrote more or less after we left school," said the Baron with a bored expression--he was acting his part of arbiter of taste who has seen everything. "We used to deal in Ossianic mists, Malvinas and Fingals and cloudy shapes, and warriors who got out of their tombs with stars above their heads. Nowadays this poetical frippery has been replaced by Jehovah, angels, seistrons, the plumes of seraphim, and all the paraphernalia of paradise freshened up with a few new words such as 'immense, infinite, solitude, intelligence'; you have lakes, and the words of the Almighty, a kind of Christianized Pantheism, enriched with the most extraordinary and unheard-of rhymes. We are in quite another latitude, in fact; we have left the North for the East, but the darkness is just as thick as before."

"If the ode is obscure, the declaration is very clear, it seems to me," said Zephirine.

"And the archangel's armor is a tolerably thin gauze robe," said Francis.

Politeness demanded that the audience should profess to be enchanted with the poem; and the women, furious because they had no poets in their train to extol them as angels, rose, looked bored by the reading, murmuring, "Very nice!" "Charming!" "Perfect!" with frigid coldness.

"If you love me, do not congratulate the poet or his angel," Lolotte laid her commands on her dear Adrien in imperious tones, and Adrien was fain to obey.

"Empty words, after all," Zephirine remarked to Francis, "and love is a poem that we live."

"You have just expressed the very thing that I was thinking, Zizine, but I should not have put it so neatly," said Stanislas, scanning himself from top to toe with loving attention.

"I would give, I don't know how much, to see Nais' pride brought down a bit," said Amelie, addressing Chatelet. "Nais sets up to be an archangel, as if she were better than the rest of us, and mixes us up with low people; his father was an apothecary, and his mother is a nurse; his sister works in a laundry, and he himself is a printer's foreman."

"If his father sold biscuits for worms" (*vers*), said Jacques, "he ought to have made his son take them."

"He is continuing in his father's line of business, for the stuff that he has just been reading to us is a drug in the market, it seems," said Stanislas, striking one of his most killing attitudes. "Drug for drug, I would rather have something else."

Every one apparently combined to humiliate Lucien by various aristocrats' sarcasms. Lili the religious thought it a charitable deed to use any means of enlightening Nais, and Nais was on the brink of a piece of folly. Francis the diplomatist undertook the direction of the silly conspiracy; every one was interested in the progress of the drama; it would be something to talk about tomorrow. The ex-consul, being far from anxious to engage in a duel with a young poet who would fly into a rage at the first hint of insult under his lady's eyes, was wise enough to see that the only way of dealing Lucien his deathblow was by the spiritual arm which was safe from vengeance. He therefore followed the example set by Chatelet the astute, and went to the Bishop. Him he proceeded to mystify.

He told the Bishop that Lucien's mother was a woman of uncommon powers and great modesty, and that it was she who found the subjects for her son's verses. Nothing pleased Lucien so much, according to the guileful Francis, as any recognition of her talents--he worshiped his mother. Then, having inculcated these notions, he left the rest to time. His lordship was sure to bring out the insulting allusion, for which he had been so carefully prepared, in the course of conversation.

When Francis and the Bishop joined the little group where Lucien stood, the circle who gave him the cup of hemlock to drain by little sips watched him with redoubled interest. The poet, luckless young man, being a total stranger, and unaware of the manners and customs of the house, could only look at Mme. de Bargeton and give embarrassed answers to embarrassing questions. He knew neither the names nor condition of the people about him; the women's silly speeches made him blush for them, and he was at his wits' end for a reply. He felt, moreover, how very far removed he was from these divinities of Angouleme when he heard himself addressed sometimes as M. Chardon, sometimes as M. de Rubempre, while they addressed each other as Lolotte, Adrien, Astolphe, Lili and Fifine. His confusion rose to a height when, taking Lili for a man's surname, he addressed the coarse M. de Senonches as M. Lili; that Nimrod broke in upon him with a "*MONSIEUR LULU?*" and Mme. de Bargeton flushed red to the eyes.

"A woman must be blind indeed to bring this little fellow among us!" muttered Senonches.

Zephirine turned to speak to the Marquise de Pimentel--"Do you not see a strong likeness between M. Chardon and M. de Cante-Croix, madame?" she asked in a low but quite audible voice.

"The likeness is ideal," smiled Mme. de Pimentel.

"Glory has a power of attraction to which we can confess," said Mme. de Bargeton, addressing the Marquise. "Some women are as much attracted by greatness as others by littleness," she added, looking at Francis.

The was beyond Zephirine's comprehension; she thought her consul a very great man; but the Marquise laughed, and her laughter ranged her on Nais' side.

"You are very fortunate, monsieur," said the Marquis de Pimentel, addressing Lucien for the purpose of calling him M. de Rubempre, and not M. Chardon, as before; "you should never find time heavy on your hands."

"Do you work quickly?" asked Lolotte, much in the way that she would have asked a joiner "if it took long to make a box."

The bludgeon stroke stunned Lucien, but he raised his head at Mme. de Bargeton's reply--

"My dear, poetry does not grow in M. de Rubempre's head like grass in our courtyards."

"Madame, we cannot feel too reverently towards the noble spirits in whom God has set some ray of this light," said the Bishop, addressing Lolotte. "Yes, poetry is something holy. Poetry implies suffering. How many silent nights those verses that you admire have cost! We should bow in love and reverence before the poet; his life here is almost always a life of sorrow; but God doubtless reserves a place in heaven for him among His prophets. This young man is a poet," he added laying a hand on Lucien's head; "do you not see the sign of Fate set on that high forehead of his?"

Glad to be so generously championed, Lucien made his acknowledgments in a grateful look, not knowing that the worthy prelate was to deal his deathblow.

Mme. de Bargeton's eyes traveled round the hostile circle. Her glances went like arrows to the depths of her rivals' hearts, and left them twice as furious as before.

"Ah, monseigneur," cried Lucien, hoping to break thick heads with his golden sceptre, "but ordinary people have neither your intellect nor your charity. No one heeds our sorrows, our toil is unrecognized. The gold-digger working in the mine does not labor as we to wrest metaphors from the heart of the most ungrateful of all languages. If this is poetry--to give ideas such definite and clear expressions that all the world can see and understand--the poet must continually range through the entire scale of human intellects, so that he can satisfy the demands of all; he must conceal hard thinking and emotion, two antagonistic powers, beneath the most vivid color; he must know how to make one word cover a whole world of thought; he must give the results of whole systems of philosophy in a few picturesque lines; indeed, his songs are like seeds that must break into blossom in other hearts wherever they find the soil prepared by personal experience. How can you express unless you first have felt? And is not passion suffering. Poetry is only brought forth after painful wanderings in the vast regions of thought and life. There are men and women in books, who seem more really alive to us than men and women who have lived and died--Richardson's Clarissa, Chenier's Camille, the Delia of Tibullus, Ariosto's Angelica, Dante's Francesca, Moliere's Alceste, Beaumarchais' Figaro, Scott's Rebecca the Jewess, the Don Quixote of Cervantes,--do we not owe these deathless creations to immortal throes?"

"And what are you going to create for us?" asked Chatelet.

"If I were to announce such conceptions, I should give myself out for a man of genius, should I not?" answered Lucien. "And besides, such sublime creations demand a long experience of the world and a study of human passion and interests which I could not possibly have made; but I have made a beginning," he added, with bitterness in his tone, as he took a vengeful glance round the circle; "the time of gestation is long----"

"Then it will be a case of difficult labor," interrupted M. du Hautoy.

"Your excellent mother might assist you," suggested the Bishop.

The epigram, innocently made by the good prelate, the long-looked-for revenge, kindled a gleam of delight in all eyes. The smile of satisfied caste that traveled from mouth to mouth was aggravated by M. de Bargeton's imbecility; he burst into a laugh, as usual, some moments later.

"Monseigneur, you are talking a little above our heads; these ladies do not understand your meaning," said Mme. de Bargeton, and the words paralyzed the laughter, and drew astonished eyes upon her. "A poet who looks to the Bible for his inspiration has a mother indeed in the Church.--M. de Rubempre, will you recite *Saint John in Patmos* for us, or *Belshazzar's Feast*, so that his lordship may see that Rome is still the *Magna Parens* of Virgil?"

The women exchanged smiles at the Latin words.

The bravest and highest spirits know times of prostration at the outset of life. Lucien had sunk to the depths at the blow, but he struck the bottom with his feet, and rose to the surface again, vowing to subjugate this little world. He rose like a bull, stung to fury by a shower of darts, and prepared to obey Louise by declaiming *Saint John in Patmos*; but by this time the card-tables had claimed their complement of players, who returned to the accustomed groove to find amusement there which poetry had not afforded them. They felt besides that the revenge of so many outraged vanities would be incomplete unless it were followed up by contemptuous indifference; so they showed their tacit disdain for the native product by leaving Lucien and Mme. de Bargeton to themselves. Every one appeared to be absorbed in his own affairs; one chattered with the prefect about a new crossroad, another proposed to vary the pleasures of the evening with a little music. The great world of Angouleme, feeling that it was no judge of poetry, was very anxious, in the first place, to hear the verdict of the Pimentels and the Rastignacs, and formed a little group about them. The great influence wielded in the department by these two families was always felt on every important occasion; every one was jealous of them, every one paid court to them, foreseeing that they might some day need that influence.

"What do you think of our poet and his poetry?" Jacques asked of the Marquise. Jacques used to shoot over the lands belonging to the Pimentel family.

"Why, it is not bad for provincial poetry," she said, smiling; "and besides, such a beautiful poet cannot do anything amiss."

Every one thought the decision admirable; it traveled from lip to lip, gaining malignance by the way. Then Chatelet was called upon to accompany M. du Bartas on the piano while he mangled the great solo from *Figaro*; and the way being opened to music, the audience, as in duty bound listened while Chatelet in turn sang one of Chateaubriand's ballads, a chivalrous ditty made in the time of the Empire. Duets followed, of the kind usually left to boarding-school misses, and rescued from the schoolroom by Mme. du Brossard, who meant to make a brilliant display of her dear Camille's talents for M. de Severac's benefit.

Mme. du Bargeton, hurt by the contempt which every one showed her poet, paid back scorn for scorn by going to her boudoir during these performances. She was followed by the prelate. His Vicar-General had just been explaining the profound irony of the epigram into which he had been entrapped, and the Bishop wished to make amends. Mlle. de Rastignac, fascinated by the poetry, also slipped into the boudoir without her mother's knowledge.

Louise drew Lucien to her mattress-cushioned sofa; and with no one to see or hear, she murmured in his ear, "Dear angel, they did not understand you; but, 'Thy songs are sweet, I love to say them over.'"

And Lucien took comfort from the pretty speech, and forgot his woes for a little.

"Glory is not to be had cheaply," Mme. de Bargeton continued, taking his hand and holding it tightly in her own. "Endure your woes, my friend, you will be great one day; your pain is the price of your immortality. If only I had a hard struggle before me! God preserve you from the enervating life without battles, in which the eagle's wings have no room to spread themselves. I envy you; for if you suffer, at least you live. You will put out your strength, you will feel the hope of victory; your strife will be glorious. And when you shall come to your kingdom, and reach the imperial sphere where great minds are enthroned, then remember the poor creatures disinherited by fate, whose intellects pine in an oppressive moral atmosphere, who die and have never lived, knowing all the while what life might be; think of the piercing eyes that have seen nothing, the delicate senses that have only known the scent of poison flowers. Then tell in your song of plants that wither in the depths of the forest, choked by twining growths and rank, greedy vegetation, plants that have never been kissed by the sunlight, and die, never having put forth a blossom. It would be a terribly gloomy poem, would it not, a fanciful subject? What a sublime poem might be made of the story of some daughter of the desert transported to some cold, western clime, calling for her beloved sun, dying of a grief that none can understand, overcome with cold and longing. It would be an allegory; many lives are like that."

"You would picture the spirit which remembers Heaven," said the Bishop; "some one surely must have written such a poem in the days of old; I like to think that I see a fragment of it in the Song of Songs."

"Take that as your subject," said Laure de Rastignac, expressing her artless belief in Lucien's powers.

"The great sacred poem of France is still unwritten," remarked the Bishop. "Believe me, glory and success await the man of talent who shall work for religion."

"That task will be his," said Mme. de Bargeton rhetorically. "Do you not see the first beginnings of the vision of the poem, like the flame of dawn, in his eyes?"

"Nais is treating us very badly," said Fifine; "what can she be doing?"

"Don't you hear?" said Stanislas. "She is flourishing away, using big words that you cannot make head or tail of."

Amelie, Fifine, Adrien, and Francis appeared in the doorway with Mme. de Rastignac, who came to look for her daughter.

"Nais," cried the two ladies, both delighted to break in upon the quiet chat in the boudoir, "it would be very nice of you to come and play something for us."

"My dear child, M. de Rubempre is just about to recite his *Saint John in Patmos*, a magnificent biblical poem."

"Biblical!" echoed Fifine in amazement.

Amelie and Fifine went back to the drawing-room, taking the word back with them as food for laughter. Lucien pleaded a defective memory and excused himself. When he reappeared, nobody took the slightest notice of him; every one was chatting or busy at the card-tables; the poet's aureole had been plucked away, the landowners had no use for him, the more pretentious sort looked upon him as an enemy to their ignorance, while the women were jealous of Mme. de Bargeton, the Beatrice of this modern Dante, to use the Vicar-General's phrase, and looked at him with cold, scornful eyes.

"So this is society!" Lucien said to himself as he went down to L'Houmeau by the steps of Beaulieu; for there are times when we choose to take the longest way, that the physical exercise of walking may promote the flow of ideas.

So far from being disheartened, the fury of repulsed ambition gave Lucien new strength. Like all those whose instincts bring them to a higher social sphere which they reach before they can hold their own in it, Lucien vowed to make any sacrifice to the end that he might remain on that higher social level. One by one he drew out the poisoned shafts on his way home, talking aloud to himself, scoffing at the fools with whom he had to do, inventing neat answers to their idiotic questions, desperately vexed that the witty responses occurred to him so late in the day. By the time that he reached the Bordeaux road, between the river and the foot of the hill, he thought that he could see Eve and David sitting on a baulk of timber by the river in the moonlight, and went down the footpath towards them.

While Lucien was hastening to the torture in Mme. de Bargeton's rooms, his sister had changed her dress for a gown of pink cambric covered with narrow stripes, a straw hat, and a little silk shawl. The simple costume seemed like a rich toilette on Eve, for she was one of those women whose great nature lends stateliness to the least personal detail; and David felt prodigiously shy of her now that she had changed her working dress. He had made up his mind that he would speak of himself; but now as he gave his arm to this beautiful girl, and they walked through L'Houmeau together, he could find nothing to say to her. Love delights in such reverent awe as redeemed souls know on beholding the glory of

God. So, in silence, the two lovers went across the Bridge of Saint Anne, and followed the left bank of the Charente. Eve felt embarrassed by the pause, and stopped to look along the river; a joyous shaft of sunset had turned the water between the bridge and the new powder mills into a sheet of gold.

"What a beautiful evening it is!" she said, for the sake of saying something; "the air is warm and fresh, and full of the scent of flowers, and there is a wonderful sky."

"Everything speaks to our heart," said David, trying to proceed to love by way of analogy. "Those who love find infinite delight in discovering the poetry of their own inmost souls in every chance effect of the landscape, in the thin, clear air, in the scent of the earth. Nature speaks for them."

"And loosens their tongues, too," Eve said merrily. "You were very silent as we came through L'Houmeau. Do you know, I felt quite uncomfortable----"

"You looked so beautiful, that I could not say anything," David answered candidly.

"Then, just now I am not so beautiful?" inquired she.

"It is not that," he said; "but I was so happy to have this walk alone with you, that----" he stopped short in confusion, and looked at the hillside and the road to Saintes.

"If the walk is any pleasure to you, I am delighted; for I owe you an evening, I think, when you have given up yours for me. When you refused to go to Mme. de Bargeton's, you were quite as generous as Lucien when he made the demand at the risk of vexing her."

"No, not generous, only wise," said David. "And now that we are quite alone under the sky, with no listeners except the bushes and the reeds by the edge of the Charente, let me tell you about my anxiety as to Lucien's present step, dear Eve. After all that I have just said, I hope that you will look on my fears as a refinement of friendship. You and your mother have done all that you could to put him above his social position; but when you stimulated his ambition, did you not unthinkingly condemn him to a hard struggle? How can he maintain himself in the society to which his tastes incline him? I know Lucien; he likes to reap, he does not like toil; it is his nature. Social claims will take up the whole of his time, and for a man who has nothing but his brains, time is capital. He likes to shine; society will stimulate his desires until no money will satisfy them; instead of earning money, he will spend it. You have accustomed him to believe in his great powers, in fact, but the world at large declines to believe in any man's superior intellect until he has achieved some signal success. Now success in literature is only won in solitude and by dogged work. What will Mme. de Bargeton give your brother in return for so many days spent at her feet? Lucien has too much spirit to accept help from her; and he cannot afford, as we know, to cultivate her society, twice ruinous as it is for him. Sooner or later that woman will throw over this dear brother of ours, but not before she has spoiled him for hard work, and given him a taste for luxury and a contempt for our humdrum life. She will develop his love of enjoyment, his inclination for idleness, that debauches a poetic soul. Yes, it makes me tremble to think that this great lady may make a plaything of Lucien. If she cares for him sincerely, he will forget everything else for her; or if she does not love him, she will make him unhappy, for he is wild about her."

"You have sent a chill of dread through my heart," said Eve, stopping as they reached the weir. "But so long as mother is strong enough for her tiring life, so long as I live, we shall earn enough, perhaps, between us to keep Lucien until success comes. My courage will never fail," said Eve, brightening. "There is no hardship in work when we work for one we love; it is not drudgery. It makes me happy to think that I toil so much, if indeed it is toil, for him. Oh, do not be in the least afraid, we will earn money enough to send Lucien into the great world. There lies his road to success."

"And there lies his road to ruin," returned David. "Dear Eve, listen to me. A man needs an independent fortune, or the sublime cynicism of poverty, for the slow execution of great work. Believe me, Lucien's horror of privation is so great, the savor of banquets, the incense of success is so sweet in his nostrils, his self-love has grown so much in Mme. de Bargeton's boudoir, that he will do anything desperate sooner than fall back, and you will never earn enough for his requirements.

"Then you are only a false friend to him!" Eve cried in despair, "or you would not discourage us in this way."

"Eve! Eve!" cried David, "if only I could be a brother to Lucien! You alone can give me that title; he could accept anything from me then; I should claim the right of devoting my life to him with the love that hallows your self-sacrifice, but with some worldly wisdom too. Eve, my darling, give Lucien a store from which he need not blush to draw! His brother's purse will be like his own, will it not? If you only knew all my thoughts about Lucien's position! If he means to go to Mme. de Bargeton's, he must not be my foreman any longer, poor fellow! He ought not to live in L'Houmeau; you ought not to be a working girl; and your mother must give up her employment as well. If you would consent to be my wife, the difficulties will all be smoothed away. Lucien might live on the second floor in the Place du Murier until I can build rooms for him over the shed at the back of the yard (if my father will allow it, that is.). And in that way we would arrange a free and independent life for him. The wish to support Lucien will give me a better will to work than I ever should have had for myself alone; but it rests with you to give me the right to devote myself to him. Some day, perhaps, he will go to Paris, the only place that can bring out all that is in him, and where his talents will be appreciated and rewarded. Living in Paris is expensive, and the earnings of all three of us will be needed for his support. And besides, will not you and your mother need some one to lean upon then? Dear Eve, marry me for love of Lucien; perhaps afterwards you will love me when you see how I shall strive to help him and to make you happy. We are, both of us, equally simple in our tastes; we have few wants; Lucien's welfare shall be the great object of our lives. His heart shall be our treasure-house, we will lay up all our fortune, and think and feel and hope in him."

"Worldly considerations keep us apart," said Eve, moved by this love that tried to explain away its greatness. "You are rich and I am poor. One must love indeed to overcome such a difficulty."

"Then you do not care enough for me?" cried the stricken David.

"But perhaps your father would object----"

"Never mind," said David; "if asking my father is all that is necessary, you will be my wife. Eve, my dear Eve, how you have lightened life for me in a moment; and my heart has been very heavy with thoughts that I could not utter, I did not know how to speak of them. Only tell me that you care for me a little, and I will take courage to tell you the rest."

"Indeed," she said, "you make me quite ashamed; but confidence for confidence, I will tell you this, that I have never thought of any one but you in my life. I looked upon you as one of those men to whom a woman might be proud to belong, and I did not dare to hope so great a thing for myself, a penniless working girl with no prospects."

"That is enough, that is enough," he answered, sitting down on the bar by the weir, for they had gone to and fro like mad creatures over the same length of pathway.

"What is the matter?" she asked, her voice expressing for the first time a woman's sweet anxiety for one who belongs to her.

"Nothing but good," he answered. "It is the sight of a whole lifetime of happiness that dazzles me, as it were; it is overwhelming. Why am I happier than you?" he asked, with a touch of sadness. "For I know that I am happier."

Eve looked at David with mischievous, doubtful eyes that asked an explanation.

"Dear Eve, I am taking more than I give. So I shall always love you more than you love me, because I have more reason to love. You are an angel; I am a man."

"I am not so learned," Eve said, smiling. "I love you----"

"As much as you love Lucien?" he broke in.

"Enough to be your wife, enough to devote myself to you, to try not to add anything to your burdens, for we shall have some struggles; it will not be quite easy at first."

"Dear Eve, have you known that I loved you since the first day I saw you?"

"Where is the woman who does not feel that she is loved?"

"Now let me get rid of your scruples as to my imaginary riches. I am a poor man, dear. Yes, it pleased my father to ruin me; he made a speculation of me, as a good many so-called benefactors do. If I make a fortune, it will be entirely through you. That is not a lover's speech, but sober, serious earnest. I ought to tell you about my faults, for they are exceedingly bad ones in a man who has his way to make. My character and habits and favorite occupations all unfit me for business and money-getting, and yet we can only make money by some kind of industry; if I have some faculty for the discovery of gold-mines, I am singularly ill-adapted for getting the gold out of them. But you who, for your brother's sake, went into the smallest details, with a talent for thrift, and the patient watchfulness of the born man of business, you will reap the harvest that I shall sow. The present state of things, for I have been like one of the family for a long time, weighs so heavily upon me, that I have spent days and nights in search of some way of making a fortune. I know something of chemistry, and a knowledge of commercial requirements has put me on the scent of a discovery that is likely to pay. I can say nothing as yet about it; there will be a long while to wait; perhaps for some years we may have a hard time of it; but I shall find out how to make a commercial article at last. Others are busy making the same researches, and if I am first in the field, we shall have a large fortune. I have said nothing to Lucien, his enthusiastic nature would spoil everything; he would convert my hopes into realities, and begin to live like a lord, and perhaps get into debt. So keep my secret for me. Your sweet and dear companionship will be consolation in itself during the long time of experiment, and the desire to gain wealth for you and Lucien will give me persistence and tenacity----"

"I had guessed this too," Eve said, interrupting him; "I knew that you were one of those inventors, like my poor father, who must have a woman to take care of them."

"Then you love me! Ah! say so without fear to me, who saw a symbol of my love for you in your name. Eve was the one woman in the world; if it was true in the outward world for Adam, it is true again in the inner world of my heart for me. My God! do you love me?"

"Yes," said she, lengthening out the word as if to make it cover the extent of feeling expressed by a single syllable.

"Well, let us sit here," he said, and taking Eve's hand, he went to a great baulk of timber lying below the wheels of a paper-mill. "Let me breathe the evening air, and hear the frogs croak, and watch the moonlight quivering upon the river; let me take all this world about us into my soul, for it seems to me that my happiness is written large over it all; I am seeing it for the first time in all its splendor, lighted up by love, grown fair through you. Eve, dearest, this is the first moment of pure and unmixed joy that fate has given to me! I do not think that Lucien can be as happy as I am."

David felt Eve's hand, damp and quivering in his own, and a tear fell upon it.

"May I not know the secret?" she pleaded coaxingly.

"You have a right to know it, for your father was interested in the matter, and today it is a pressing question, and for this reason. Since the downfall of the Empire, calico has come more and more into use, because it is so much cheaper than linen. At the present moment, paper is made of a mixture of hemp and linen rags, but the raw material is dear, and the expense naturally retards the great advance which the French press is bound to make. Now you cannot increase the output of linen rags, a given population gives a pretty constant result, and it only increases with the birth-rate. To make any perceptible difference in the population for this purpose, it would take a quarter of a century and a great revolution in

60

habits of life, trade, and agriculture. And if the supply of linen rags is not enough to meet one-half nor one-third of the demand, some cheaper material than linen rags must be found for cheap paper. This deduction is based on facts that came under my knowledge here. The Angouleme paper-makers, the last to use pure linen rags, say that the proportion of cotton in the pulp has increased to a frightful extent of late years."

In answer to a question from Eve, who did not know what "pulp" meant, David gave an account of paper-making, which will not be out of place in a volume which owes its existence in book form to the paper industry no less than to the printing-press; but the long digression, doubtless, had best be condensed at first.

Paper, an invention not less marvelous than the other dependent invention of printing, was known in ancient times in China. Thence by the unrecognized channels of commerce the art reached Asia Minor, where paper was made of cotton reduced to pulp and boiled. Parchment had become so extremely dear that a cheap substitute was discovered in an imitation of the cotton paper known in the East as *charta bombycina*. The imitation, made from rags, was first made at Basel, in 1170, by a colony of Greek refugees, according to some authorities; or at Padua, in 1301, by an Italian named Pax, according to others. In these ways the manufacture of paper was perfected slowly and in obscurity; but this much is certain, that so early as the reign of Charles VI., paper pulp for playing-cards was made in Paris.

When those immortals, Faust, Coster, and Gutenberg, invented the Book, craftsmen as obscure as many a great artist of those times appropriated paper to the uses of typography. In the fifteenth century, that naive and vigorous age, names were given to the various formats as well as to the different sizes of type, names that bear the impress of the naivete of the times; and the various sheets came to be known by the different watermarks on their centres; the grapes, the figure of our Saviour, the crown, the shield, or the flower-pot, just as at a later day, the eagle of Napoleon's time gave the name to the "double-eagle" size. And in the same way the types were called Cicero, Saint-Augustine, and Canon type, because they were first used to print the treatises of Cicero and theological and liturgical works. Italics are so called because they were invented in Italy by Aldus of Venice.

Before the invention of machine-made paper, which can be woven in any length, the largest sized sheets were the *grand jesus* and the double columbier (this last being scarcely used now except for atlases or engravings), and the size of paper for printers' use was determined by the dimensions of the impression-stone. When David explained these things to Eve, web-paper was almost undreamed of in France, although, about 1799, Denis Robert d'Essonne had invented a machine for turning out a ribbon of paper, and Didot-Saint-Leger had since tried to perfect it. The vellum paper invented by Ambroise Didot only dates back as far as 1780.

This bird's eye view of the history of the invention shows incontestably that great industrial and intellectual advances are made exceedingly slowly, and little by little, even as Nature herself proceeds. Perhaps articulate speech and the art of writing were gradually developed in the same groping way as typography and paper-making.

"Rag-pickers collect all the rags and old linen of Europe," the printer concluded, "and buy any kind of tissue. The rags are sorted and warehoused by the wholesale rag merchants, who supply the paper-mills. To give you some idea of the extent of the trade, you must know, mademoiselle, that in 1814 Cardon the banker, owner of the pulping troughs of Bruges and Langlee (where Leorier de l'Isle endeavored in 1776 to solve the very problem that occupied your father), Cardon brought an action against one Proust for an error in weights of two millions in a total of ten million pounds' weight of rags, worth about four million francs! The manufacturer washes the rags and reduces them to a thin pulp, which is strained, exactly as a cook strains sauce through a tamis, through an iron frame with a fine wire bottom where the mark which give its name to the size of the paper is woven. The size of this *mould*, as it is called, regulates the size of the sheet.

"When I was with the Messieurs Didot," David continued, "they were very much interested in this question, and they are still interested; for the improvement which your father endeavored to make is a great commercial requirement, and one of the crying needs of the time. And for this reason: although linen lasts so much longer than cotton, that it is in reality cheaper in the end, the poor would rather make the smaller outlay in the first instance, and, by virtue of the law of *Vae victis!* pay enormously more before they have done. The middle classes do the same. So there is a scarcity of linen. In England, where four-fifths of the population use cotton to the exclusion of linen, they make nothing but cotton paper. The cotton paper is very soft and easily creased to begin with, and it has a further defect: it is so soluble that if you seep a book made of cotton paper in water for fifteen minutes, it turns to a pulp, while an old book left in water for a couple of hours is not spoilt. You could dry the old book, and the pages, though yellow and faded, would still be legible, the work would not be destroyed.

"There is a time coming when legislation will equalize our fortunes, and we shall all be poor together; we shall want our linen and our books to be cheap, just as people are beginning to prefer small pictures because they have not wall space enough for large ones. Well, the shirts and the books will not last, that is all; it is the same on all sides, solidity is drying out. So this problem is one of the first importance for literature, science, and politics.

"One day, in my office, there was a hot discussion going on about the material that the Chinese use for making paper. Their paper is far better than ours, because the raw material is better; and a good deal was said about this thin, light Chinese paper, for if it is light and thin, the texture is close, there are no transparent spots in it. In Paris there are learned men among the printers' readers; Fourier and Pierre Leroux are Lachevardiere's readers at this moment; and the Comte de Saint-Simon, who happened to be correcting proofs for us, came in in the middle of the discussion. He told us at once that, according to Kempfer and du Halde, the *Broussonetia* furnishes the substance of the Chinese paper; it is a vegetable substance (like linen or cotton for that matter). Another reader maintained that Chinese paper was principally made of an animal substance, to wit, the silk that is abundant there. They made a bet about it in my presence. The Messieurs Didot are printers to the Institute, so naturally they referred the question to that learned body. M. Marcel, who used to be superintendent of the Royal Printing Establishment, was umpire, and he sent the two readers to M. l'Abbe Grozier, Librarian at the Arsenal. By the Abbe's decision they both lost their wages. The paper was not made of silk nor yet from the *Broussonetia*; the pulp proved to be the triturated fibre of some kind of bamboo. The Abbe Grozier had a Chinese book, an iconographical and technological work, with a great many pictures in it, illustrating all the different processes of paper-making, and he showed us a picture of the workshop with the bamboo stalks lying in a heap in the corner; it was extremely well drawn.

"Lucien told me that your father, with the intuition of a man of talent, had a glimmering of a notion of some way of replacing linen rags with an exceedingly common vegetable product, not previously manufactured, but taken direct from the soil, as the Chinese use vegetable fibre at first hand. I have classified the guesses made by those who came before me, and have begun to study the question. The bamboo is a kind of reed; naturally I began to think of the reeds that grow here in France.

"Labor is very cheap in China, where a workman earns three halfpence a day, and this cheapness of labor enables the Chinese to manipulate each sheet of paper separately. They take it out of the mould, and press it between heated tablets of white porcelain, that is the secret of the surface and consistence, the lightness and satin smoothness of the best paper in the world. Well, here in Europe the work must be done by machinery; machinery must take the place of cheap Chinese labor. If we could but succeed in making a cheap paper of as good a quality, the weight and thickness of printed books would be reduced by more than one-half. A set of Voltaire, printed on our woven paper and bound, weighs about two hundred and fifty pounds; it would only weigh fifty if we used Chinese paper. That surely would be a triumph, for the housing of many books has come to be a difficulty; everything has grown smaller of late; this is not an age of giants; men have shrunk, everything about them shrinks, and house-room into the bargain. Great mansions and great suites of rooms will be abolished sooner or later in Paris, for no one will afford to live in the great houses built by our forefathers. What a disgrace for our age if none of its books should last! Dutch paper--that is, paper made from flax--will be quite unobtainable in ten years' time. Well, your brother told me of this idea of your father's, this plan for using vegetable fibre in paper-making, so you see that if I succeed, you have a right to----"

Lucien came up at that moment and interrupted David's generous assertion.

"I do not know whether you have found the evening pleasant," said he; "it has been a cruel time for me."

"Poor Lucien! what can have happened?" cried Eve, as she saw her brother's excited face.

The poet told the history of his agony, pouring out a flood of clamorous thoughts into those friendly hearts, Eve and David listening in pained silence to a torrent of woes that exhibited such greatness and such pettiness.

"M. de Bargeton is an old dotard. The indigestion will carry him off before long, no doubt," Lucien said, as he made an end, "and then I will look down on these proud people; I will marry Mme. de Bargeton. I read tonight in her eyes a love as great as mine for her. Yes, she felt all that I felt; she comforted me; she is as great and noble as she is gracious and beautiful. She will never give me up."

"It is time that life was made smooth for him, is it not?" murmured David, and for answer Eve pressed his arm without speaking. David guessed her thoughts, and began at once to tell Lucien about his own plans.

If Lucien was full of his troubles, the lovers were quite as full of themselves. So absorbed were they, so eager that Lucien should approve their happiness, that neither Eve nor David so much as noticed his start of surprise at the news. Mme. de Bargeton's lover had been dreaming of a great match for his sister; he would reach a high position first, and then secure himself by an alliance with some family of influence, and here was one more obstacle in his way to success! His hopes were dashed to the ground. "If Mme. de Bargeton consents to be Mme. de Rubempre, she would never care to have David Sechard for a brother-in-law!"

This stated clearly and precisely was the thought that tortured Lucien's inmost mind. "Louise is right!" he thought bitterly. "A man with a career before him is never understood by his family."

If the marriage had not been announced immediately after Lucien's fancy had put M. de Bargeton to death, he would have been radiant with heartfelt delight at the news. If he had thought soberly over the probable future of a beautiful and penniless girl like Eve Chardon, he would have seen that this marriage was a piece of unhoped-for good fortune. But he was living just now in a golden dream; he had soared above all barriers on the wings of an *if*; he had seen a vision of himself, rising above society; and it was painful to drop so suddenly down to hard fact.

Eve and David both thought that their brother was overcome with the sense of such generosity; to them, with their noble natures, the silent consent was a sign of true friendship. David began to describe with kindly and cordial eloquence the happy fortunes in store for them all. Unchecked by protests put in by Eve, he furnished his first floor with a lover's lavishness, built a second floor with boyish good faith for Lucien, and rooms above the shed for Mme. Chardon--he meant to be a son to her. In short, he made the whole family so happy and his brother-in-law so independent, that Lucien fell under the spell of David's voice and Eve's caresses; and as they went through the shadows beside the still Charente, a gleam in the warm, star-lit night, he forgot the sharp crown of thorns that had been pressed upon his head. "M. de Rubempre" discovered David's real nature, in fact. His facile character returned almost at once to the innocent, hard-working burgher life that he knew; he saw it transfigured and free from care. The buzz of the aristocratic world grew more and more remote; and when at length they came upon the paved road of L'Houmeau, the ambitious poet grasped his brother's hand, and made a third in the joy of the happy lovers.

"If only your father makes no objection to the marriage," he said.

"You know how much he troubles himself about me; the old man lives for himself," said David. "But I will go over to Marsac tomorrow and see him, if it is only to ask leave to build."

David went back to the house with the brother and sister, and asked Mme. Chardon's consent to his marriage with the eagerness of a man who would fain have no delay. Eve's mother took her daughter's hand, and gladly laid it in David's; and the lover, grown bolder on this, kissed his fair betrothed on the forehead, and she flushed red, and smiled at him.

"The betrothal of the poor," the mother said, raising her eyes as if to pray for heaven's blessing upon them.--"You are brave, my boy," she added, looking at David, "but we have fallen on evil fortune, and I am afraid lest our bad luck should be infectious."

"We shall be rich and happy," David said earnestly. "To begin with, you must not go out nursing any more, and you must come and live with your daughter and Lucien in Angouleme."

The three began at once to tell the astonished mother all their charming plans, and the family party gave themselves up to the pleasure of chatting and weaving a romance, in which it is so pleasant to enjoy future happiness, and to store the unsown harvest. They had to put David out at the door; he could have wished the evening to last for ever, and it was one o'clock in the morning when Lucien and his future brother-in-law reached the Palet Gate. The unwonted movement made honest Postel uneasy; he opened the window, and looking through the Venetian shutters, he saw a light in Eve's room.

"What can be happening at the Chardons'?" thought he, and seeing Lucien come in, he called out to him--

"What is the matter, sonny? Do you want me to do anything?"

"No, sir," returned the poet; "but as you are our friend, I can tell you about it; my mother has just given her consent to my sister's engagement to David Sechard."

For all answer, Postel shut the window with a bang, in despair that he had not asked for Mlle. Chardon earlier.

David, however, did not go back into Angouleme; he took the road to Marsac instead, and walked through the night the whole way to his father's house. He went along by the side of the croft just as the sun rose, and caught sight of the old "bear's" face under an almond-tree that grew out of the hedge.

"Good day, father," called David.

"Why, is it you, my boy? How come you to be out on the road at this time of day? There is your way in," he added, pointing to a little wicket gate. "My vines have flowered and not a shoot has been frosted. There will be twenty puncheons or more to the acre this year; but then look at all the dung that has been put on the land!"

"Father, I have come on important business."

"Very well; how are your presses doing? You must be making heaps of money as big as yourself."

"I shall some day, father, but I am not very well off just now."

"They all tell me that I ought not to put on so much manure," replied his father. "The gentry, that is M. le Marquis, M. le Comte, and Monsieur What-do-you-call-'em, say that I am letting down the quality of the wine. What is the good of book-learning except to muddle your wits? Just you listen: these gentlemen get seven, or sometimes eight puncheons of wine to the acre, and they sell them for sixty francs apiece, that means four hundred francs per acre at most in a good year. Now, I make twenty puncheons, and get thirty francs apiece for them--that is six hundred francs! And where are they, the fools? Quality, quality, what is quality to me? They can keep their quality for themselves, these Lord Marquises. Quality means hard cash for me, that is what it means, You were saying?----"

"I am going to be married, father, and I have come to ask for----"

64

"Ask me for what? Nothing of the sort, my boy. Marry; I give you my consent, but as for giving you anything else, I haven't a penny to bless myself with. Dressing the soil is the ruin of me. These two years I have been paying money out of pocket for top-dressing, and taxes, and expenses of all kinds; Government eats up everything, nearly all the profit goes to the Government. The poor growers have made nothing these last two seasons. This year things don't look so bad; and, of course, the beggarly puncheons have gone up to eleven francs already. We work to put money into the coopers' pockets. Why, are you going to marry before the vintage?----"

"I only came to ask for your consent, father."

"Oh! that is another thing. And who is the victim, if one may ask?"

"I am going to marry Mlle. Eve Chardon."

"Who may she be? What kind of victual does she eat?"

"She is the daughter of the late M. Chardon, the druggist in L'Houmeau."

"You are going to marry a girl out of L'Houmeau! *you*! a burgess of Angouleme, and printer to His Majesty! This is what comes of book-learning! Send a boy to school, forsooth! Oh! well, then she is very rich, is she, my boy?" and the old vinegrower came up closer with a cajoling manner; "if you are marrying a girl out of L'Houmeau, it must be because she has lots of cash, eh? Good! you will pay me my rent now. There are two years and one-quarter owing, you know, my boy; that is two thousand seven hundred francs altogether; the money will come just in the nick of time to pay the cooper. If it was anybody else, I should have a right to ask for interest; for, after all, business is business, but I will let you off the interest. Well, how much has she?"

"Just as much as my mother had."

The old vinegrower very nearly said, "Then she has only ten thousand francs!" but he recollected just in time that he had declined to give an account of her fortune to her son, and exclaimed, "She has nothing!"

"My mother's fortune was her beauty and intelligence," said David.

"You just go into the market and see what you can get for it! Bless my buttons! what bad luck parents have with their children. David, when I married, I had a paper cap on my head for my whole fortune, and a pair of arms; I was a poor pressman; but with the fine printing-house that I gave you, with your industry, and your education, you might marry a burgess' daughter, a woman with thirty or forty thousand francs. Give up your fancy, and I will find you a wife myself. There is some one about three miles away, a miller's widow, thirty-two years old, with a hundred thousand francs in land. There is your chance! You can add her property to Marsac, for they touch. Ah! what a fine property we should have, and how I would look after it! They say she is going to marry her foreman Courtois, but you are the better man of the two. I would look after the mill, and she should live like a lady up in Angouleme."

"I am engaged, father."

"David, you know nothing of business; you will ruin yourself, I see. Yes, if you marry this girl out of L'Houmeau, I shall square accounts and summons you for the rent, for I see that no good will come of this. Oh! my presses, my poor presses! it took some money to grease you and keep you going. Nothing but a good year can comfort me after this."

"It seems to me, father, that until now I have given you very little trouble----"

"And paid mighty little rent," put in his parent.

"I came to ask you something else besides. Will you build a second floor to your house, and some rooms above the shed?"

"Deuce a bit of it; I have not the cash, and that you know right well. Besides, it would be money thrown clean away, for what would it bring in? Oh! you get up early of a morning to come and ask me to build you a place that would ruin a king,

65

do you? Your name may be David, but I have not got Solomon's treasury. Why, you are mad! or they changed my child at nurse. There is one for you that will have grapes on it," he said, interrupting himself to point out a shoot. "Offspring of this sort don't disappoint their parents; you dung the vines, and they repay you for it. I sent you to school; I spent any amount of money to make a scholar of you; I sent you to the Didots to learn your business; and all this fancy education ends in a daughter-in-law out of L'Houmeau without a penny to her name. If you had not studied books, if I had kept you under my eye, you would have done as I pleased, and you would be marrying a miller's widow this day with a hundred thousand francs in hand, to say nothing of the mill. Oh! your cleverness leads you to imagine that I am going to reward this fine sentiment by building palaces for you, does it? . . . Really, anybody might think that the house that has been a house these two hundred years was nothing but a pigsty, not fit for the girl out of L'Houmeau to sleep in! What next! She is the Queen of France, I suppose."

"Very well, father, I will build the second floor myself; the son will improve his father's property. It is not the usual way, but it happens so sometimes."

"What, my lad! you can find money for building, can you, though you can't find money to pay the rent, eh! You sly dog, to come round your father."

The question thus raised was hard to lay, for the old man was only too delighted to seize an opportunity of posing as a good father without disbursing a penny; and all that David could obtain was his bare consent to the marriage and free leave to do what he liked in the house--at his own expense; the old "bear," that pattern of a thrifty parent, kindly consenting not to demand the rent and drain the savings to which David imprudently owned. David went back again in low spirits. He saw that he could not reckon on his father's help in misfortune.

In Angouleme that day people talked of nothing but the Bishop's epigram and Mme. de Bargeton's reply. Every least thing that happened that evening was so much exaggerated and embellished and twisted out of all knowledge, that the poet became the hero of the hour. While this storm in a teacup raged on high, a few drops fell among the *bourgeoisie*; young men looked enviously after Lucien as he passed on his way through Beaulieu, and he overheard chance phrases that filled him with conceit.

"There is a lucky young fellow!" said an attorney's clerk, named Petit-Claud, a plain-featured youth who had been at school with Lucien, and treated him with small, patronizing airs.

"Yes, he certainly is," answered one of the young men who had been present on the occasion of the reading; "he is a good-looking fellow, he has some brains, and Mme. de Bargeton is quite wild about him."

Lucien had waited impatiently until he could be sure of finding Louise alone. He had to break the tidings of his sister's marriage to the arbitress of his destinies. Perhaps after yesterday's soiree, Louise would be kinder than usual, and her kindness might lead to a moment of happiness. So he thought, and he was not mistaken; Mme. de Bargeton met him with a vehemence of sentiment that seemed like a touching progress of passion to the novice in love. She abandoned her hands, her beautiful golden hair, to the burning kisses of the poet who had passed through such an ordeal.

"If only you could have seen your face whilst you were reading," cried Louise, using the familiar *tu*, the caress of speech, since yesterday, while her white hands wiped the pearls of sweat from the brows on which she set a poet's crown. "There were sparks of fire in those beautiful eyes! From your lips, as I watched them, there fell the golden chains that suspend the hearts of men upon the poet's mouth. You shall read Chenier through to me from beginning to end; he is the lover's poet. You shall not be unhappy any longer; I will not have it. Yes, dear angel, I will make an oasis for you, there you shall live your poet's life, sometimes busy, sometimes languid; indolent, full of work, and musing by turns; but never forget that you owe your laurels to me, let that thought be my noble guerdon for the sufferings which I must endure. Poor love! the world will not spare me any more than it has spared you; the world is avenged on all happiness in which it has no share. Yes, I shall always be a mark for envy--did you not see that last night? The bloodthirsty insects are quick enough to drain every wound that they pierce. But I was happy; I lived. It is so long since all my heartstrings vibrated."

The tears flowed fast, and for all answer Lucien took Louise's hand and gave it a lingering kiss. Every one about him soothed and caressed the poet's vanity; his mother and his sister and David and Louise now did the same. Every one helped to raise the imaginary pedestal on which he had set himself. His friends's kindness and the fury of his enemies combined to establish him more firmly in an ureal world. A young imagination readily falls in with the flattering estimates of others, a handsome young fellow so full of promise finds others eager to help him on every side, and only after one or two sharp and bitter lessons does he begin to see himself as an ordinary mortal.

"My beautiful Louise, do you mean in very truth to be my Beatrice, a Beatrice who condescends to be loved?"

Louise raised the fine eyes, hitherto down-dropped.

"If you show yourself worthy--some day!" she said, with an angelic smile which belied her words. "Are you not happy? To be the sole possessor of a heart, to speak freely at all times, with the certainty of being understood, is not this happiness?"

"Yes," he answered, with a lover's pout of vexation.

"Child!" she exclaimed, laughing at him. "Come, you have something to tell me, have you not? You came in absorbed in thought, my Lucien."

Lucien, in fear and trembling, confided to his beloved that David was in love with his sister Eve, and that his sister Eve was in love with David, and that the two were to be married shortly.

"Poor Lucien!" said Louise, "he was afraid he should be beaten and scolded, as if it was he himself that was going to be married! Why, where is the harm?" she continued, her fingers toying with Lucien's hair. "What is your family to me when you are an exception? Suppose that my father were to marry his cook, would that trouble you much? Dear boy, lovers are for each other their whole family. Have I a greater interest than my Lucien in the world? Be great, find the way to win fame, that is our affair!"

This selfish answer made Lucien the happiest of mortals. But in the middle of the fantastic reasonings, with which Louise convinced him that they two were alone in the world, in came M. de Bargeton. Lucien frowned and seemed to be taken aback, but Louise made him a sign, and asked him to stay to dinner and to read Andre de Chenier aloud to them until people arrived for their evening game at cards.

"You will give her pleasure," said M. de Bargeton, "and me also. Nothing suits me better than listening to reading aloud after dinner."

Cajoled by M. de Bargeton, cajoled by Louise, waited upon with the respect which servants show to a favored guest of the house, Lucien remained in the Hotel de Bargeton, and began to think of the luxuries which he enjoyed for the time being as the rightful accessories of Lucien de Rubempre. He felt his position so strong through Louise's love and M. de Bargeton's weakness, that as the rooms filled, he assumed a lordly air, which that fair lady encouraged. He tasted the delights of despotic sway which Nais had acquired by right of conquest, and liked to share with him; and, in short, that evening he tried to act up to the part of the lion of the little town. A few of those who marked these airs drew their own conclusions from them, and thought that, according to the old expression, he had come to the last term with the lady. Amelie, who had come with M. du Chatelet, was sure of the deplorable fact, in a corner of the drawing-room, where the jealous and envious gathered together.

"Do not think of calling Nais to account for the vanity of a youngster, who is as proud as he can be because he has got into society, where he never expected to set foot," said Chatelet. "Don't you see that this Chardon takes the civility of a woman of the world for an advance? He does not know the difference between the silence of real passion and the patronizing graciousness due to his good looks and youth and talent. It would be too bad if women were blamed for all the desires which they inspire. *He* certainly is in love with her, but as for Nais----"

"Oh! Nais," echoed the perfidious Amelie, "Nais is well enough pleased. A young man's love has so many attractions--at her age. A woman grows young again in his company; she is a girl, and acts a girl's hesitation and manners, and does not dream that she is ridiculous. Just look! Think of a druggist's son giving himself a conqueror's airs with Mme. de Bargeton."

"Love knows nought of high or low degree," hummed Adrien.

There was not a single house in Angouleme next day where the degree of intimacy between M. Chardon (alias de Rubempre) and Mme. de Bargeton was not discussed; and though the utmost extent of their guilt amounted to two or three kisses, the world already chose to believe the worst of both. Mme. de Bargeton paid the penalty of her sovereignty. Among the various eccentricities of society, have you never noticed its erratic judgments and the unaccountable differences in the standard it requires of this or that man or woman? There are some persons who may do anything; they may behave totally irrationally, anything becomes them, and it is who shall be first to justify their conduct; then, on the other hand, there are those on whom the world is unaccountably severe, they must do everything well, they are not allowed to fail nor to make mistakes, at their peril they do anything foolish; you might compare these last to the much-admired statues which must come down at once from their pedestal if the frost chips off a nose or a finger. They are not permitted to be human; they are required to be for ever divine and for ever impeccable. So one glance exchanged between Mme. de Bargeton and Lucien outweighed twelve years of Zizine's connection with Francis in the social balance; and a squeeze of the hand drew down all the thunders of the Charente upon the lovers.

David had brought a little secret hoard back with him from Paris, and it was this sum that he set aside for the expenses of his marriage and for the building of the second floor in his father's house. His father's house it was; but, after all, was he not working for himself? It would all be his again some day, and his father was sixty-eight years old. So David build a timbered second story for Lucien, so as not to put too great a strain on the old rifted house-walls. He took pleasure in making the rooms where the fair Eve was to spend her life as brave as might be.

It was a time of blithe and unmixed happiness for the friends. Lucien was tired of the shabbiness of provincial life, and weary of the sordid frugality that looked on a five-franc piece as a fortune, but he bore the hardships and the pinching thrift without grumbling. His moody looks had been succeeded by an expression of radiant hope. He saw the star shining above his head, he had dreams of a great time to come, and built the fabric of his good fortune on M. de Bargeton's tomb. M. de Bargeton, troubled with indigestion from time to time, cherished the happy delusion that indigestion after dinner was a complaint to be cured by a hearty supper.

By the beginning of September, Lucien had ceased to be a printer's foreman; he was M. de Rubempre, housed sumptuously in comparison with his late quarters in the tumbledown attic with the dormer-window, where "young Chardon" had lived in L'Houmeau; he was not even a "man of L'Houmeau"; he lived in the heights of Angouleme, and dined four times a week with Mme. de Bargeton. A friendship had grown up between M. de Rubempre and the Bishop, and he went to the palace. His occupations put him upon a level with the highest rank; his name would be one day among the great names of France; and, in truth, as he went to and fro in his apartments, the pretty sitting-room, the charming bedroom, and the tastefully furnished study, he might console himself for the thought that he drew thirty francs every month out of his mother's and sister's hard earnings; for he saw the day approaching when *An Archer of Charles IX.*, the historical romance on which he had been at work for two years, and a volume of verse entitled *Marguerites*, should spread his fame through the world of literature, and bring in money enough to repay them all, his mother and sister and David. So, grown great in his own eyes, and giving ear to the echoes of his name in the future, he could accept present sacrifices with noble assurance; he smiled at his poverty, he relished the sense of these last days of penury.

Eve and David had set Lucien's happiness before their own. They had put off their wedding, for it took some time to paper and paint their rooms, and to buy the furniture, and Lucien's affairs had been settled first. No one who knew Lucien could wonder at their devotion. Lucien was so engaging, he had such winning ways, his impatience and his desires were so graciously expressed, that his cause was always won before he opened his mouth to speak. This unlucky gift of fortune, if it is the salvation of some, is the ruin of many more. Lucien and his like find a world predisposed in favor of youth and good looks, and ready to protect those who give it pleasure with the selfish good-nature that flings alms to a beggar, if he appeals to the feelings and awakens emotion; and in this favor many a grown child is content to bask instead of putting it to a profitable use. With mistaken notions as to the significance and the motive of social relations they imagine that they shall always meet with deceptive smiles; and so at last the moment comes for them when the world leaves them bald, stripped bare, without fortune or worth, like an elderly coquette by the door of a salon, or a stray rag in the gutter.

Eve herself had wished for the delay. She meant to establish the little household on the most economical footing, and to buy only strict necessaries; but what could two lovers refuse to a brother who watched his sister at her work, and said in tones that came from the heart, "How I wish I could sew!" The sober, observant David had shared in the devotion; and yet, since Lucien's triumph, David had watched him with misgivings; he was afraid that Lucien would change towards them, afraid that he would look down upon their homely ways. Once or twice, to try his brother, David had made him choose between home pleasures and the great world, and saw that Lucien gave up the delights of vanity for them, and exclaimed to himself, "They will not spoil him for us!" Now and again the three friends and Mme. Chardon arranged picnic parties in provincial fashion--a walk in the woods along the Charente, not far from Angouleme, and dinner out on the grass, David's apprentice bringing the basket of provisions to some place appointed before-hand; and at night they would come back, tired somewhat, but the whole excursion had not cost three francs. On great occasion, when they dined at a *restaurat*, as it is called, a sort of a country inn, a compromise between a provincial wineshop and a Parisian *guinguette*, they would spend as much as five francs, divided between David and the Chardons. David gave his brother infinite credit for forsaking Mme. de Bargeton and grand dinners for these days in the country, and the whole party made much of the great man of Angouleme.

Matters had gone so far, that the new home was very nearly ready, and David had gone over to Marsac to persuade his father to come to the wedding, not without a hope that the old man might relent at the sight of his daughter-in-law, and give something towards the heavy expenses of the alterations, when there befell one of those events which entirely change the face of things in a small town.

Lucien and Louise had a spy in Chatelet, a spy who watched, with the persistence of a hate in which avarice and passion are blended, for an opportunity of making a scandal. Sixte meant that Mme. de Bargeton should compromise herself with Lucien in such a way that she should be "lost," as the saying goes; so he posed as Mme. de Bargeton's humble confidant, admired Lucien in the Rue du Minage, and pulled him to pieces everywhere else. Nais had gradually given him *les petites entrees*, in the language of the court, for the lady no longer mistrusted her elderly admirer; but Chatelet had taken too much for granted--love was still in the Platonic stage, to the great despair of Louise and Lucien.

There are, for that matter, love affairs which start with a good or a bad beginning, as you prefer to take it. Two creatures launch into the tactics of sentiment; they talk when they should be acting, and skirmish in the open instead of settling down to a siege. And so they grow tired of one another, expend their longings in empty space; and, having time for reflection, come to their own conclusions about each other. Many a passion that has taken the field in gorgeous array, with colors flying and an ardor fit to turn the world upside down, has turned home again without a victory, inglorious and crestfallen, cutting but a foolish figure after these vain alarums and excursions. Such mishaps are sometimes due to the diffidence of youth, sometimes to the demurs of an inexperienced woman, for old players at this game seldom end in a fiasco of this kind.

Provincial life, moreover, is singularly well calculated to keep desire unsatisfied and maintain a lover's arguments on the intellectual plane, while, at the same time, the very obstacles placed in the way of the sweet intercourse which binds lovers so closely each to each, hurry ardent souls on towards extreme measures. A system of espionage of the most minute and intricate kind underlies provincial life; every house is transparent, the solace of close friendships which break no moral law is scarcely allowed; and such outrageously scandalous constructions are put upon the most innocent human intercourse, that many a woman's character is taken away without cause. One here and there, weighed down by her unmerited punishment, will regret that she has never known to the full the forbidden felicity for which she is suffering. The world, which blames and criticises with a superficial knowledge of the patent facts in which a long inward struggle ends, is in reality a prime agent in bringing such scandals about; and those whose voices are loudest in condemnation of the alleged misconduct of some slandered woman never give a thought to the immediate provocation of the overt step. That step many a woman only takes after she has been unjustly accused and condemned, and Mme. de Bargeton was now on the verge of this anomalous position.

The obstacles at the outset of a passion of this kind are alarming to inexperience, and those in the way of the two lovers were very like the bonds by which the population of Lilliput throttled Gulliver, a multiplicity of nothings, which made all movement impossible, and baffle the most vehement desires. Mme. de Bargeton, for instance, must always be visible. If she had denied herself to visitors when Lucien was with her, it would have been all over with her; she might as well have run away with him at once. It is true that they sat in the boudoir, now grown so familiar to Lucien that he felt as if he had a right to be there; but the doors stood scrupulously open, and everything was arranged with the utmost propriety. M. de Bargeton pervaded the house like a cockchafer; it never entered his head that his wife could wish to be alone with Lucien. If he had been the only person in the way, Nais could have got rid of him, sent him out of the house, or given him something to do; but he was not the only one; visitors flocked in upon her, and so much the more as curiosity increased, for your provincial has a natural bent for teasing, and delights to thwart a growing passion. The servants came and went about the house promiscuously and without a summons; they had formed the habits with a mistress who had nothing to conceal; any change now made in her household ways was tantamount to a confession, and Angouleme still hung in doubt.

Mme. de Bargeton could not set foot outside her house but the whole town knew whither she was going. To take a walk alone with Lucien out of Angouleme would have been a decided measure, indeed; it would have been less dangerous to shut herself up with him in the house. There would have been comments the next day if Lucien had stayed on till midnight after the rooms were emptied. Within as without her house, Mme. de Bargeton lived in public.

These details describe life in the provinces; an intrigue is either openly avoided or impossible anywhere.

Like all women carried away for the first time by passion, Louise discovered the difficulties of her position one by one. They frightened her, and her terror reacted upon the fond talk that fills the fairest hours which lovers spend alone together. Mme. de Bargeton had no country house whither she could take her beloved poet, after the manner of some women who will forge ingenious pretexts for burying themselves in the wilderness; but, weary of living in public, and

70

pushed to extremities by a tyranny which afforded no pleasures sweet enough to compensate for the heaviness of the yoke, she even thought of Escarbas, and of going to see her aged father--so much irritated was she by these paltry obstacles.

Chatelet did not believe in such innocence. He lay in wait, and watched Lucien into the house, and followed a few minutes later, always taking M. de Chandour, the most indiscreet person in the clique, along with him; and, putting that gentleman first, hoped to find a surprise by such perseverance in pursuit of the chance. His own part was a very difficult one to play, and its success was the more doubtful because he was bound to appear neutral if he was to prompt the other actors who were to play in his drama. So, to give himself a countenance, he had attached himself to the jealous Amelie, the better to lull suspicion in Lucien and in Mme. de Bargeton, who was not without perspicacity. In order to spy upon the pair, he had contrived of late to open up a stock controversy on the point with M. de Chandour. Chatelet said that Mme. de Bargeton was simply amusing herself with Lucien; she was too proud, too high-born, to stoop to the apothecary's son. The role of incredulity was in accordance with the plan which he had laid down, for he wished to appear as Mme. de Bargeton's champion. Stanislas de Chandour held that Mme. de Bargeton had not been cruel to her lover, and Amelie goaded them to argument, for she longed to know the truth. Each stated his case, and (as not unfrequently happens in small country towns) some intimate friends of the house dropped in in the middle of the argument. Stanislas and Chatelet vied with each other in backing up their opinions by observations extremely pertinent. It was hardly to be expected that the champions should not seek to enlist partisans. "What do you yourself think?" they asked, each of his neighbor. These polemics kept Mme. de Bargeton and Lucien well in sight.

At length one day Chatelet called attention to the fact that whenever he went with M. de Chandour to Mme. de Bargeton's and found Lucien there, there was not a sign nor a trace of anything suspicious; the boudoir door stood open, the servants came and went, there was nothing mysterious to betray the sweet crime of love, and so forth and so forth. Stanislas, who did not lack a certain spice of stupidity in his composition, vowed that he would cross the room on tiptoe the next day, and the perfidious Amelie held him to his bargain.

For Lucien that morrow was the day on which a young man tugs out some of the hairs of his head, and inwardly vows that he will give up the foolish business of sighing. He was accustomed to his situation. The poet, who had seated himself so bashfully in the boudoir-sanctuary of the queen of Angouleme, had been transformed into an urgent lover. Six months had been enough to bring him on a level with Louise, and now he would fain be her lord and master. He left home with a settled determination to be extravagant in his behavior; he would say that it was a matter of life or death to him; he would bring all the resources of torrid eloquence into play; he would cry that he had lost his head, that he could not think, could not write a line. The horror that some women feel for premeditation does honor to their delicacy; they would rather surrender upon the impulse of passion, than in fulfilment of a contract. In general, prescribed happiness is not the kind that any of us desire.

Mme. de Bargeton read fixed purpose in Lucien's eyes and forehead, and in the agitation in his face and manner, and proposed to herself to baffle him, urged thereto partly by a spirit of contradiction, partly also by an exalted conception of love. Being given to exaggeration, she set an exaggerated value upon her person. She looked upon herself as a sovereign lady, a Beatrice, a Laura. She enthroned herself, like some dame of the Middle Ages, upon a dais, looking down upon the tourney of literature, and meant that Lucien, as in duty bound, should win her by his prowess in the field; he must eclipse "the sublime child," and Lamartine, and Sir Walter Scott, and Byron. The noble creature regarded her love as a stimulating power; the desire which she had kindled in Lucien should give him the energy to win glory for himself. This feminine Quixotry is a sentiment which hallows love and turns it to worthy uses; it exalts and reverences love. Mme. de Bargeton having made up her mind to play the part of Dulcinea in Lucien's life for seven or eight years to come, desired, like many other provincials, to give herself as the reward of prolonged service, a trial of constancy which should give her time to judge her lover.

Lucien began the strife by a piece of vehement petulence, at which a woman laughs so long as she is heart-free, and saddens only when she loves; whereupon Louise took a lofty tone, and began one of her long orations, interlarded with high-sounding words.

"Was that your promise to me, Lucien?" she said, as she made an end. "Do not sow regrets in the present time, so sweet as it is, to poison my after life. Do not spoil the future, and, I say it with pride, do not spoil the present! Is not my whole heart yours? What more must you have? Can it be that your love is influenced by the clamor of the senses, when it is the noblest privilege of the beloved to silence them? For whom do you take me? Am I not your Beatrice? If I am not something more than a woman for you, I am less than a woman."

"That is just what you might say to a man if you cared nothing at all for him," cried Lucien, frantic with passion.

"If you cannot feel all the sincere love underlying my ideas, you will never be worthy of me."

"You are throwing doubts on my love to dispense yourself from responding to it," cried Lucien, and he flung himself weeping at her feet.

The poor boy cried in earnest at the prospect of remaining so long at the gate of paradise. The tears of the poet, who feels that he is humbled through his strength, were mingled with childish crying for a plaything.

"You have never loved me!" he cried.

"You do not believe what you say," she answered, flattered by his violence.

"Then give me proof that you are mine," said the disheveled poet.

Just at that moment Stanislas came up unheard by either of the pair. He beheld Lucien in tears, half reclining on the floor, with his head on Louise's knee. The attitude was suspicious enough to satisfy Stanislas; he turned sharply round upon Chatelet, who stood at the door of the salon. Mme. de Bargeton sprang up in a moment, but the spies beat a precipate retreat like intruders, and she was not quick enough for them.

"Who came just now?" she asked the servants.

"M. de Chandour and M. du Chatelet," said Gentil, her old footman.

Mme. de Bargeton went back, pale and trembling, to her boudoir.

"If they saw you just now, I am lost," she told Lucien.

"So much the better!" exclaimed the poet, and she smiled to hear the cry, so full of selfish love.

A story of this kind is aggravated in the provinces by the way in which it is told. Everybody knew in a moment that Lucien had been detected at Nais feet. M. de Chandour, elated by the important part he played in the affair, went first to tell the great news at the club, and thence from house to house, Chatelet hastening to say that *he* had seen nothing; but by putting himself out of court, he egged Stanislas on to talk, he drew him on to add fresh details; and Stanislas, thinking himself very witty, added a little to the tale every time that he told it. Every one flocked to Amelie's house that evening, for by that time the most exaggerated versions of the story were in circulation among the Angouleme nobility, every narrator having followed Stanislas' example. Women and men were alike impatient to know the truth; and the women who put their hands before their faces and shrieked the loudest were none other than Mesdames Amelie, Zephirine, Fifine, and Lolotte, all with more or less heavy indictments of illicit love laid to their charge. There were variations in every key upon the painful theme.

"Well, well," said one of the ladies, "poor Nais! have you heard about it? I do not believe it myself; she has a whole blameless record behind her; she is far too proud to be anything but a patroness to M. Chardon. Still, if it is true, I pity her with all my heart."

"She is all the more to be pitied because she is making herself frightfully ridiculous; she is old enough to be M. Lulu's mother, as Jacques called him. The little poet it twenty-two at most; and Nais, between ourselves, is quite forty."

"For my own part," said M. du Chatelet, "I think that M. de Rubempre's position in itself proves Nais' innocence. A man does not go down on his knees to ask for what he has had already."

"That is as may be!" said Francis, with levity that brought Zephirine's disapproving glance down on him.

"Do just tell us how it really was," they besought Stanislas, and formed a small, secret committee in a corner of the salon.

Stanislas, in the long length, had put together a little story full of facetious suggestions, and accompanied it with pantomime, which made the thing prodigiously worse.

"It is incredible!"

"At midday?"

"Nais was the last person whom I should have suspected!"

"What will she do now?"

Then followed more comments, and suppositions without end. Chatelet took Mme. de Bargeton's part; but he defended her so ill, that he stirred the fire of gossip instead of putting it out.

Lili, disconsolate over the fall of the fairest angel in the Angoumoisin hierarchy, went, dissolved in tears, to carry the news to the palace. When the delighted Chatelet was convinced that the whole town was agog, he went off to Mme. de Bargeton's, where, alas! there was but one game of whist that night, and diplomatically asked Nais for a little talk in the boudoir. They sat down on the sofa, and Chatelet began in an undertone--

"You know what Angouleme is talking about, of course?"

"No."

"Very well, I am too much your friend to leave you in ignorance. I am bound to put you in a position to silence slanders, invented, no doubt, by Amelie, who has the overweening audacity to regard herself as your rival. I came to call on you this morning with that monkey of a Stanislas; he was a few paces ahead of me, and he came so far" (pointing to the door of the boudoir); "he says that he *saw* you and M. de Rubempre in such a position that he could not enter; he turned round upon me, quite bewildered as I was, and hurried me away before I had time to think; we were out in Beaulieu before he told me why he had beaten a retreat. If I had known, I would not have stirred out of the house till I had cleared up the matter and exonerated you, but it would have proved nothing to go back again then.

"Now, whether Stanislas' eyes deceived him, or whether he is right, *he must have made a mistake.* Dear Nais, do not let that dolt trifle with your life, your honor, your future; stop his mouth at once. You know my position here. I have need of all these people, but still I am entirely yours. Dispose of a life that belongs to you. You have rejected my prayers, but my heart is always yours; I am ready to prove my love for you at any time and in any way. Yes, I will watch over you like a faithful servant, for no reward, but simply for the sake of the pleasure that it is to me to do anything for you, even if you do not know of it. This morning I have said everywhere that I was at the door of the salon, and had seen nothing. If you are asked to give the name of the person who told you about this gossip, pray make use of me. I should be very proud to be your acknowledged champion; but, between ourselves, M. de Bargeton is the proper person to ask Stanislas for an explanation. . . . Suppose that young Rubempre had behaved foolishly, a woman's character ought not to be at the mercy of the first hare-brained boy who flings himself at her feet. That is what I have been saying."

Nais bowed in acknowledgment, and looked thoughtful. She was weary to disgust of provincial life. Chatelet had scarcely begun before her mind turned to Paris. Meanwhile Mme. de Bargeton's adorer found the silence somewhat awkward.

"Dispose of me, I repeat," he added.

"Thank you," answered the lady.

"What do you think of doing?"

"I shall see."

A prolonged pause.

"Are you so fond of that young Rubempre?"

A proud smile stole over her lips, she folded her arms, and fixed her gaze on the curtains. Chatelet went out; he could not read that high heart.

Later in the evening, when Lucien had taken his leave, and likewise the four old gentlemen who came for their whist, without troubling themselves about ill-founded tittle-tattle, M. de Bargeton was preparing to go to bed, and had opened his mouth to bid his wife good-night, when she stopped him.

"Come here, dear, I have something to say to you," she said, with a certain solemnity.

M. de Bargeton followed her into the boudoir.

"Perhaps I have done wrongly," she said, "to show a warm interest in M. de Rubempre, which he, as well as the stupid people here in the town, has misinterpreted. This morning Lucien threw himself here at my feet with a declaration, and Stanislas happened to come in just as I told the boy to get up again. A woman, under any circumstances, has claims which courtesy prescribes to a gentleman; but in contempt of these, Stanislas has been saying that he came unexpectedly and found us in an equivocal position. I was treating the boy as he deserved. If the young scatterbrain knew of the scandal caused by his folly, he would go, I am convinced, to insult Stanislas, and compel him to fight. That would simply be a public proclamation of his love. I need not tell you that your wife is pure; but if you think, you will see that it is something dishonoring for both you and me if M. de Rubempre defends her. Go at once to Stanislas and ask him to give you satisfaction for his insulting language; and mind, you must not accept any explanation short of a full and public retraction in the presence of witnesses of credit. In this way you will win back the respect of all right-minded people; you will behave like a man of spirit and a gentleman, and you will have a right to my esteem. I shall send Gentil on horseback to the Escarbas; my father must be your second; old as he is, I know that he is the man to trample this puppet under foot that has smirched the reputation of a Negrepelisse. You have the choice of weapons, choose pistols; you are an admirable shot."

"I am going," said M. de Bargeton, and he took his hat and his walking cane.

"Good, that is how I like a man to behave, dear; you are a gentleman," said his wife. She felt touched by his conduct, and made the old man very happy and proud by putting up her forehead for a kiss. She felt something like a maternal affection for the great child; and when the carriage gateway had shut with a clang behind him, the tears came into her eyes in spite of herself.

"How he loves me!" she thought. "He clings to life, poor, dear man, and yet he would give his life for me."

It did not trouble M. de Bargeton that he must stand up and face his man on the morrow, and look coolly into the muzzle of a pistol pointed straight at him; no, only one thing in the business made him feel uncomfortable, and on the way to M. de Chandour's house he quaked inwardly.

"What shall I say?" he thought within himself; "Nais really ought to have told me what to say," and the good gentleman

74

racked his brains to compose a speech that should not be ridiculous.

But people of M. de Bargeton's stamp, who live perforce in silence because their capacity is limited and their outlook circumscribed, often behave at great crises with a ready-made solemnity. If they say little, it naturally follows that they say little that is foolish; their extreme lack of confidence leads them to think a good deal over the remarks that they are obliged to make; and, like Balaam's ass, they speak marvelously to the point if a miracle loosens their tongues. So M. de Bargeton bore himself like a man of uncommon sense and spirit, and justified the opinion of those who held that he was a philosopher of the school of Pythagoras.

He reached Stanislas' house at nine o'clock, bowed silently to Amelie before a whole room full of people, and greeted others in turn with that simple smile of his, which under the present circumstances seemed profoundly ironical. There followed a great silence, like the pause before a storm. Chatelet had made his way back again, and now looked in a very significant fashion from M. de Bargeton to Stanislas, whom the injured gentleman accosted politely.

Chatelet knew what a visit meant at this time of night, when old M. de Bargeton was invariably in his bed. It was evidently Nais who had set the feeble arm in motion. Chatelet was on such a footing in that house that he had some right to interfere in family concerns. He rose to his feet and took M. de Bargeton aside, saying, "Do you wish to speak to Stanislas?"

"Yes," said the old gentleman, well pleased to find a go-between who perhaps might say his say for him.

"Very well; go into Amelie's bedroom," said the controller of excise, likewise well pleased at the prospect of a duel which possibly might make Mme. de Bargeton a widow, while it put a bar between her and Lucien, the cause of the quarrel. Then Chatelet went to M. de Chandour.

"Stanislas," he said, "here comes Bargeton to call you to account, no doubt, for the things you have been saying about Nais. Go into your wife's room, and behave, both of you, like gentlemen. Keep the thing quiet, and make a great show of politeness, behave with phlegmatic British dignity, in short."

In another minute Stanislas and Chatelet went to Bargeton.

"Sir," said the injured husband, "do you say that you discovered Mme. de Bargeton and M. de Rubempre in an equivocal position?"

"M. Chardon," corrected Stanislas, with ironical stress; he did not take Bargeton seriously.

"So be it," answered the other. "If you do not withdraw your assertions at once before the company now in your house, I must ask you to look for a second. My father-in-law, M. de Negrepelisse, will wait upon you at four o'clock tomorrow morning. Both of us may as well make our final arrangements, for the only way out of the affair is the one that I have indicated. I choose pistols, as the insulted party."

This was the speech that M. de Bargeton had ruminated on the way; it was the longest that he had ever made in life. He brought it out without excitement or vehemence, in the simplest way in the world. Stanislas turned pale. "After all, what did I see?" said he to himself.

Put between the shame of eating his words before the whole town, and fear, that caught him by the throat with burning fingers; confronted by this mute personage, who seemed in no humor to stand nonsense, Stanislas chose the more remote peril.

"All right. Tomorrow morning," he said, thinking that the matter might be arranged somehow or other.

The three went back to the room. Everybody scanned their faces as they came in; Chatelet was smiling, M. de Bargeton looked exactly as if he were in his own house, but Stanislas looked ghastly pale. At the sight of his face, some of the women here and there guessed the nature of the conference, and the whisper, "They are going to fight!" circulated from ear to ear. One-half of the room was of the opinion that Stanislas was in the wrong, his white face and his demeanor convicted him of a lie; the other half admired M. de Bargeton's attitude. Chatelet was solemn and mysterious. M. de Bargeton stayed a few minutes, scrutinized people's faces, and retired.

"Have you pistols?" Chatelet asked in a whisper of Stanislas, who shook from head to foot.

Amelie knew what it all meant. She felt ill, and the women flocked about her to take her into her bedroom. There was a terrific sensation; everybody talked at once. The men stopped in the drawing-room, and declared, with one voice, that M. de Bargeton was within his right.

"Would you have thought the old fogy capable of acting like this?" asked M. de Saintot.

"But he was a crack shot when he was young," said the pitiless Jacques. "My father often used to tell me of Bargeton's exploits."

"Pooh! Put them at twenty paces, and they will miss each other if you give them cavalry pistols," said Francis, addressing Chatelet.

Chatelet stayed after the rest had gone to reassure Stanislas and his wife, and to explain that all would go off well. In a duel between a man of sixty and a man of thirty-five, all the advantage lay with the latter.

Early next morning, as Lucien sat at breakfast with David, who had come back alone from Marsac, in came Mme. Chardon with a scared face.

"Well, Lucien," she said, "have you heard the news? Everyone is talking of it, even the people in the market. M. de Bargeton all but killed M. de Chandour this morning in M. Tulloy's meadow; people are making puns on the name. (Tue Poie.) It seems that M. de Chandour said that he found you with Mme. de Bargeton yesterday."

"It is a lie! Mme. de Bargeton is innocent," cried Lucien.

"I heard about the duel from a countryman, who saw it all from his cart. M. de Negrepelisse came over at three o'clock in the morning to be M. de Bargeton's second; he told M. de Chandour that if anything happened to his son-in-law, he should avenge him. A cavalry officer lent the pistols. M. de Negrepelisse tried them over and over again. M. du Chatelet tried to prevent them from practising with the pistols, but they referred the question to the officer; and he said that, unless they meant to behave like children, they ought to have pistols in working order. The seconds put them at twenty-five paces. M. de Bargeton looked as if he had just come out for a walk. He was the first to fire; the ball lodged in M. de Chandour's neck, and he dropped before he could return the shot. The house-surgeon at the hospital has just said that M. de Chandour will have a wry neck for the rest of his days. I came to tell you how it ended, lest you should go to Mme. de Bargeton's or show yourself in Angouleme, for some of M. de Chandour's friends might call you out."

As she spoke, the apprentice brought in Gentil, M. de Bargeton's footman. The man had come with a note for Lucien; it was from Louise.

"You have doubtless heard the news," she wrote, "of the duel between Chandour and my husband. We shall not be at home to any one today. Be careful; do not show yourself. I ask this in the name of the affection you bear me. Do you not think that it would be best to spend this melancholy day in listening to your Beatrice, whose whole life has been changed by this event, who has a thousand things to say to you?"

"Luckily, my marriage is fixed for the day after tomorrow," said David, "and you will have an excuse for not going to see Mme. de Bargeton quite so often."

"Dear David," returned Lucien, "she asks me to go to her today; and I ought to do as she wishes, I think; she knows better than we do how I should act in the present state of things."

"Then is everything ready here?" asked Mme. Chardon.

"Come and see," cried David, delighted to exhibit the transformation of the first floor. Everything there was new and fresh; everything was pervaded by the sweet influences of early married days, still crowned by the wreath of orange blossoms and the bridal veil; days when the springtide of love finds its reflection in material things, and everything is white and spotless and has not lost its bloom.

"Eve's home will be fit for a princess," said the mother, "but you have spent too much, you have been reckless."

David smiled by way of answer. But Mme. Chardon had touched the sore spot in a hidden wound which caused the poor lover cruel pangs. The cost of carrying out his ideas had far exceeded his estimates; he could not afford to build above the shed. His mother-in-law must wait awhile for the home he had meant to make for her. There is nothing more keenly painful to a generous nature than a failure to keep such promises as these; it is like mortification to the little vanities of affection, as they may be styled. David sedulously hid his embarrassment to spare Lucien; he was afraid that Lucien might be overwhelmed by the sacrifices made for his sake.

"Eve and her girl friends have been working very hard, too," said Mme. Chardon. "The wedding clothes and the house linen are all ready. The girls are so fond of her, that, without letting her know about it, they have covered the mattresses with white twill and a rose-colored piping at the edges. So pretty! It makes one wish one were going to be married."

Mother and daughter had spent all their little savings to furnish David's home with the things of which a young bachelor never thinks. They knew that he was furnishing with great splendor, for something had been said about ordering a dinner-service from Limoges, and the two women had striven to make Eve's contributions to the housekeeping worthy of David's. This little emulation in love and generosity could but bring the husband and wife into difficulties at the very outset of their married life, with every sign of homely comfort about them, comfort that might be regarded as positive luxury in a place so behind the times as the Angouleme of those days.

As soon as Lucien saw his mother and David enter the bedroom with the blue-and-white draperies and neat furniture that he knew, he slipped away to Mme. de Bargeton. He found Nais at table with her husband; M. de Bargeton's early morning walk had sharpened his appetite, and he was breakfasting quite unconcernedly after all that had passed. Lucien saw the dignified face of M. de Negrepelisse, the old provincial noble, a relic of the old French *noblesse*, sitting beside Nais.

When Gentil announced M. de Rubempre, the white-headed old man gave him a keen, curious glance; the father was anxious to form his own opinions of this man whom his daughter had singled out for notice. Lucien's extreme beauty made such a vivid impression upon him, that he could not repress an approving glance; but at the same time he seemed to regard the affair as a flirtation, a mere passing fancy on his daughter's part. Breakfast over, Louise could leave her father and M. de Bargeton together; she beckoned Lucien to follow her as she withdrew.

"Dear," she said, and the tones of her voice were half glad, half melancholy, "I am going to Paris, and my father is taking Bargeton back with him to the Escarbas, where he will stay during my absence. Mme. d'Espard (she was a Blamont-Chauvry before her marriage) has great influence herself, and influential relations. The d'Espards are connections of ours; they are the older branch of the Negrepelisses; and if she vouchsafes to acknowledge the relationship, I intend to cultivate her a good deal; she may perhaps procure a place for Bargeton. At my solicitation, it might be desired at Court that he should represent the Charente, and that would be a step towards his election here. If he were a deputy, it would further other steps that I wish to take in Paris. You, my darling, have brought about this change in my life. After this morning's duel, I am obliged to shut up my house for some time; for there will be people who will side with the Chandours against us. In our position, and in a small town, absence is the only way of softening down bad feeling. But I shall either succeed, and never see Angouleme again, or I shall not succeed, and then I mean to wait in Paris until the time comes when I can spend my summers at the Escarbas and the winters in Paris. It is the only life for a woman of quality, and I have waited too long before entering upon it. The one day will be enough for our preparations; tomorrow night I shall set out, and you are coming with me, are you not? You shall start first. I will overtake you between Mansle and Ruffec, and we shall soon be in Paris. There, beloved, is the life for a man who has anything in him. We are only at our ease among our equals; we are uncomfortable in any other society. Paris, besides, is the capital of the intellectual world, the stage on which you will succeed; overleap the gulf that separates us quickly. You must not allow your ideas to grow rancid in the provinces; put yourself into communication at once with the great men who represent the nineteenth century. Try to stand well with the Court and with those in power. No honor, no distinction, comes to seek out the talent that perishes for lack of light in a little town; tell me, if you can, the name of any great work of art executed in the provinces! On the contrary, see how Jean-Jacques, himself sublime in his poverty, felt the irresistible attraction of that sun of the intellectual world, which produces ever-new glories and stimulates the intellect--Paris, where men rub against one another. What is it but your duty to hasten to take your place in the succession of pleiades that rise from generation to generation? You have no idea how it contributes to the success of a clever young man to be brought into a high light, socially speaking. I will introduce you to Mme. d'Espard; it is not easy to get into her set; but you meet all the greatest people at her house, Cabinet ministers and ambassadors, and great orators from the Chamber of Deputies, and peers and men of influence, and wealthy or famous people. A young man with good looks and more than sufficient genius could fail to excite interest only by very bad management.

"There is no pettiness about those who are truly great; they will lend you their support; and when you yourself have a high position, your work will rise immensely in public opinion. The great problem for the artist is the problem of putting himself in evidence. In these ways there will be hundreds of chances of making your way, of sinecures, of a pension from the civil list. The Bourbons are so fond of encouraging letters and the arts, and you therefore must be a religious poet and a Royalist poet at the same time. Not only is it the right course, but it is the way to get on in life. Do the Liberals and the Opposition give places and rewards, and make the fortunes of men of letters? Take the right road and reach the goal of genius. You have my secret, do not breathe a syllable of it, and prepare to follow me.--Would you rather not go?" she added, surprised that her lover made no answer.

To Lucien, listening to the alluring words, and bewildered by the rapid bird's-eye view of Paris which they brought before him, it seemed as if hitherto he had been using only half his brain and suddenly had found the other half, so swiftly his ideas widened. He saw himself stagnating in Angouleme like a frog under a stone in a marsh. Paris and her splendors rose before him; Paris, the Eldorado of provincial imaginings, with golden robes and the royal diadem about her brows, and arms outstretched to talent of every kind. Great men would greet him there as one of their order. Everything smiled upon genius. There, there were no jealous booby-squires to invent stinging gibes and humiliate a man of letters; there was no stupid indifference to poetry in Paris. Paris was the fountain-head of poetry; there the poet was brought into the light and paid for his work. Publishers should no sooner read the opening pages of *An Archer of Charles IX.* than they should open their cash-boxes with "How much do you want?" And besides all this, he understood that this journey with Mme. de Bargeton would virtually give her to him; that they should live together.

So at the words, "Would you rather not go?" tears came into his eyes, he flung his arms about Louise, held her tightly to his heart, and marbled her throat with impassioned kisses. Suddenly he checked himself, as if memory had dealt him a blow.

"Great heavens!" he cried, "my sister is to be married on the day after tomorrow!"

That exclamation was the last expiring cry of noble and single-hearted boyhood. The so-powerful ties that bind young hearts to home, and a first friendship, and all early affections, were to be severed at one ruthless blow.

"Well," cried the haughty Negrepelisse, "and what has your sister's marriage to do with the progress of our love? Have you set your mind so much on being best man at a wedding party of tradespeople and workingmen, that you cannot give up these exalted joys for my sake? A great sacrifice, indeed!" she went on, scornfully. "This morning I sent my husband out to fight in your quarrel. There, sir, go; I am mistaken in you."

She sank fainting upon the sofa. Lucien went to her, entreating her pardon, calling execrations upon his family, his sister, and David.

"I had such faith in you!" she said. "M. de Cante-Croix had an adored mother; but to win a letter from me, and the words, 'I am satisfied,' he fell in the thick of the fight. And now, when I ask you to take a journey with me, you cannot think of giving up a wedding dinner for my sake."

Lucien was ready to kill himself; his desperation was so unfeigned, that Louise forgave him, though at the same time she made him feel that he must redeem his mistake.

"Come, come," she said, "be discreet, and tomorrow at midnight be upon the road, a hundred paces out of Mansle."

Lucien felt the globe shrink under his feet; he went back to David's house, hopes pursuing him as the Furies followed Orestes, for he had glimmerings of endless difficulties, all summed up in the appalling words, "Where is the money to come from?"

He stood in such terror of David's perspicacity, that he locked himself into his pretty new study until he could recover himself, his head was swimming in this new position. So he must leave the rooms just furnished for him at such a cost, and all the sacrifices that had been made for him had been made in vain. Then it occurred to Lucien that his mother might take the rooms and save David the heavy expense of building at the end of the yard, as he had meant to do; his departure would be, in fact, a convenience to the family. He discovered any quantity of urgent reasons for his sudden flight; for there is no such Jesuit as the desire of your heart. He hurried down at once to tell the news to his sister in L'Houmeau and to take counsel with her. As he reached Postel's shop, he bethought himself that if all other means failed, he could borrow enough to live upon for a year from his father's successor.

"Three francs per day will be abundance for me if I live with Louise," he thought; "it is only a thousand francs for a whole year. And in six months' time I shall have plenty of money."

Then, under seal and promise of secrecy, Eve and her mother heard Lucien's confidences. Both the women began to cry as they heard of the ambitious plans; and when he asked the reason of their trouble, they told him that every penny they possessed had been spent on table-linen, house-linen, Eve's wedding clothes, and on a host of things that David had overlooked. They had been so glad to do this, for David had made a marriage-settlement of ten thousand francs on Eve. Lucien then spoke of his idea of a loan, and Mme. Chardon undertook to ask M. Postel to lend them a thousand francs for a twelve-month.

"But, Lucien," said Eve, as a thought clutched at her heart, "you will not be here at my wedding! Oh! come back, I will put it off for a few days. Surely she will give you leave to come back in a fortnight, if only you go with her now? Surely, she would spare you to us for a week, Lucien, when we brought you up for her? We shall have no luck if you are not at the wedding. . . . But will a thousand francs be enough for you?" she asked, suddenly interrupting herself. "Your coat suits you divinely, but you have only that one! You have only two fine shirts, the other six are coarse linen; and three of your white ties are just common muslin, there are only two lawn cravats, and your pocket-handkerchiefs are not good ones. Where

79

will you find a sister in Paris who will get up your linen in one day as you want it? You will want ever so much more. Then you have just the one pair of new nankeen trousers, last year's trousers are tight for you; you will be obliged to have clothes made in Paris, and Paris prices are not like Angouleme prices. You have only two presentable white waistcoats; I have mended the others already. Come, I advise you to take two thousand francs."

David came in as she spoke, and apparently heard the last two words, for he looked at the brother and sister and said nothing.

"Do not keep anything from me," he said at last.

"Well," exclaimed Eve, "he is going away with *her*."

Mme. Chardon came in again, and, not seeing David, began at once:

"Postel is willing to lend you the thousand francs, Lucien," she said, "but only for six months; and even then he wants you to let him have a bill endorsed by your brother-in-law, for he says that you are giving him no security."

She turned and saw David, and there was a deep silence in the room. The Chardons thought how they had abused David's goodness, and felt ashamed. Tears stood in the young printer's eyes.

"Then you will not be here at our wedding," he began. "You are not going to live with us! And here have I been squandering all that I had! Oh! Lucien, as I came along, bringing Eve her little bits of wedding jewelry, I did not think that I should be sorry I spent the money on them." He brushed his hand over his eyes as he drew the little cases from his pocket.

He set down the tiny morocco-covered boxes on the table in front of his mother-in-law.

"Oh! why do you think so much for me?" protested Eve, giving him a divinely sweet smile that belied her words.

"Mamma, dear," said David, "just tell M. Postel that I will put my name to the bill, for I can tell from your face, Lucien, that you have quite made up your mind to go."

Lucien's head sank dejectedly; there was a little pause, then he said, "Do not think hardly of me, my dear, good angels."

He put his arms about Eve and David, and drew them close, and held them tightly to him as he added, "Wait and see what comes of it, and you shall know how much I love you. What is the good of our high thinking, David, if it does not enable us to disregard the petty ceremonial in which the law entangles our affections? Shall I not be with you in spirit, in spite of the distance between us? Shall we not be united in thought? Have I not a destiny to fulfil? Will publishers come here to seek my *Archer of Charles IX.* and the *Marguerites*? A little sooner or a little later I shall be obliged in any case to do as I am doing today, should I not? And shall I ever find a better opportunity than this? Does not my success entirely depend upon my entrance on life in Paris through the Marquise d'Espard's salon?"

"He is right," said Eve; "you yourself were saying, were you not, that he ought to go to Paris at once?"

David took Eve's hand in his, and drew her into the narrow little room where she had slept for seven years.

"Love, you were saying just now that he would want two thousand francs?" he said in her ear. "Postel is only lending one thousand."

Eve gave her betrothed a look, and he read all her anguish in her eyes.

"Listen, my adored Eve, we are making a bad start in life. Yes, my expenses have taken all my capital; I have just two thousand francs left, and half of it will be wanted to carry on the business. If we give your brother the thousand francs, it will mean that we are giving away our bread, that we shall live in anxiety. If I were alone, I know what I should do; but we are two. Decide for us."

Eve, distracted, sprang to her lover's arms, and kissed him tenderly, as she answered through her tears:

"Do as you would do if you were alone; I will work to earn the money."

In spite of the most impassioned kiss ever given and taken by betrothed lovers, David left Eve overcome with trouble, and went out to Lucien.

"Do not worry yourself," he said; "you shall have your two thousand francs."

"Go in to see Postel," said Mme. Chardon, "for you must both give your signatures to the bill."

When Lucien and David came back again unexpectedly, they found Eve and her mother on their knees in prayer. The women felt sure that Lucien's return would bring the realization of many hopes; but at the moment they could only feel how much they were losing in the parting, and the happiness to come seemed too dearly bought by an absence that broke up their life together, and would fill the coming days with innumerable fears for Lucien.

"If you could ever forget this sight," David said in Lucien's ear, "you would be the basest of men."

David, no doubt, thought that these brave words were needed; Mme. de Bargeton's influence seemed to him less to be feared than his friend's unlucky instability of character, Lucien was so easily led for good or evil. Eve soon packed Lucien's clothes; the Fernando Cortez of literature carried but little baggage. He was wearing his best overcoat, his best waistcoat, and one of the two fine shirts. The whole of his linen, the celebrated coat, and his manuscript made up so small a package that to hide it from Mme. de Bargeton, David proposed to send it by coach to a paper merchant with whom he had dealings, and wrote and advised him to that effect, and asked him to keep the parcel until Lucien sent for it.

In spite of Mme. de Bargeton's precautions, Chatelet found out that she was leaving Angouleme; and with a view to discovering whether she was traveling alone or with Lucien, he sent his man to Ruffec with instructions to watch every carriage that changed horses at that stage.

"If she is taking her poet with her," thought he, "I have her now."

Lucien set out before daybreak the next morning. David went with him. David had hired a cabriolet, pretending that he was going to Marsac on business, a little piece of deception which seemed probable under the circumstances. The two friends went to Marsac, and spent part of the day with the old "bear." As evening came on they set out again, and in the beginning of the dawn they waited in the road, on the further side of Mansle, for Mme. de Bargeton. When the seventy-year old traveling carriage, which he had many a time seen in the coach-house, appeared in sight, Lucien felt more deeply moved than he had ever been in his life before; he sprang into David's arms.

"God grant that this may be for your good!" said David, and he climbed into the shabby cabriolet and drove away with a feeling of dread clutching at his heart; he had terrible presentiments of the fate awaiting Lucien in Paris.

ADDENDUM

The following personages appear in other stories of the Human Comedy.

Bargeton, Madame de (see Chatelet, Baronne du)

Cerizet Eve and David A Man of Business Scenes from a Courtesan's Life The Middle Classes

Chardon, Madame (nee Rubempre) Eve and David Scenes from a Courtesan's Life

Chatelet, Sixte, Baron du A Distinguished Provincial at Paris Scenes from a Courtesan's Life The Thirteen

Chatelet, Marie-Louise-Anais de Negrepelisse, Baronne du A Distinguished Provincial at Paris The Government Clerks

Cointet, Boniface Eve and David The Firm of Nucingen The Member for Arcis

Cointet, Jean Eve and David

Courtois Eve and David

Courtois, Madame Eve and David

Desplein The Atheist's Mass Cousin Pons The Thirteen The Government Clerks Pierrette A Bachelor's Establishment The Seamy Side of History Modeste Mignon Scenes from a Courtesan's Life Honorine

Gentil A Distinguished Provincial at Paris

Grozier, Abbe The Commission in Lunacy

Hautoy, Francis du Eve and David

Maucombe, Comte de

Letters of Two Brides

Montriveau, General Marquis Armand de The Thirteen Father Goriot A Distinguished Provincial at Paris Another Study of Woman Pierrette The Member for Arcis

Negrepelisse, De The Commission in Lunacy A Distinguished Provincial at Paris

Petit-Claud Eve and David

Pimentel, Marquis and Marquise de Eve and David

Postel Eve and David

Prieur, Madame Eve and David

Rastignac, Baron and Baronne de (Eugene's parents) Father Goriot

Rastignac, Laure-Rose and Agathe de Father Goriot The Member for Arcis

Rubempre, Lucien-Chardon de Eve and David A Distinguished Provincial at Paris The Government Clerks Ursule Mirouet Scenes from a Courtesan's Life

Sechard, Jerome-Nicolas Eve and David

Sechard, David Eve and David A Distinguished Provincial At Paris Scenes from a Courtesan's Life

Sechard, Madame David Eve and David A Distinguished Provincial At Paris Scenes from a Courtesan's Life

Senonches, Jacques de Eve and David
Senonches, Madame Jacques de Eve and David
Stanhope, Lady Esther The Lily of the Valley

2

A DISTINGUISHED PROVINCIAL AT PARIS
(Lost Illusions II)

PART 1

Mme. de Bargeton and Lucien de Rubempre had left Angouleme behind, and
were traveling together upon the road to Paris. Not one of the party who made that journey alluded to it afterwards; but it may be believed that an infatuated youth who had looked forward to the delights of an elopement, must have found the continual presence of Gentil, the man-servant, and Albertine, the maid, not a little irksome on the way. Lucien, traveling post for the first time in his life, was horrified to see pretty nearly the whole sum on which he meant to live in Paris for a twelvemonth dropped along the road. Like other men who combine great intellectual powers with the charming simplicity of childhood, he openly expressed his surprise at the new and wonderful things which he saw, and thereby made a mistake. A man should study a woman very carefully before he allows her to see his thoughts and emotions as they arise in him. A woman, whose nature is large as her heart is tender, can smile upon childishness, and make allowances; but let her have ever so small a spice of vanity herself, and she cannot forgive childishness, or littleness, or vanity in her lover. Many a woman is so extravagant a worshiper that she must always see the god in her idol; but there are yet others who love a man for his sake and not for their own, and adore his failings with his greater qualities.

Lucien had not guessed as yet that Mme. de Bargeton's love was grafted on pride. He made another mistake when he failed to discern the meaning of certain smiles which flitted over Louise's lips from time to time; and instead of keeping himself to himself, he indulged in the playfulness of the young rat emerging from his hole for the first time.

The travelers were set down before daybreak at the sign of the Gaillard-Bois in the Rue de l'Echelle, both so tired out with the journey that Louise went straight to bed and slept, first bidding Lucien to engage the room immediately overhead. Lucien slept on till four o'clock in the afternoon, when he was awakened by Mme. de Bargeton's servant, and learning the hour, made a hasty toilet and hurried downstairs.

Louise was sitting in the shabby inn sitting-room. Hotel accommodation is a blot on the civilization of Paris; for with all its pretensions to elegance, the city as yet does not boast a single inn where a well-to-do traveler can find the surroundings to which he is accustomed at home. To Lucien's just-awakened, sleep-dimmed eyes, Louise was hardly recognizable in this cheerless, sunless room, with the shabby window-curtains, the comfortless polished floor, the hideous furniture bought second-hand, or much the worse for wear.

Some people no longer look the same when detached from the background of faces, objects, and surroundings which serve as a setting, without which, indeed, they seem to lose something of their intrinsic worth. Personality demands its appropriate atmosphere to bring out its values, just as the figures in Flemish interiors need the arrangement of light and shade in which they are placed by the painter's genius if they are to live for us. This is especially true of provincials. Mme. de Bargeton, moreover, looked more thoughtful and dignified than was necessary now, when no barriers stood between her and happiness.

Gentil and Albertine waited upon them, and while they were present Lucien could not complain. The dinner, sent in from a neighboring restaurant, fell far below the provincial average, both in quantity and quality; the essential goodness of country fare was wanting, and in point of quantity the portions were cut with so strict an eye to business that they savored of short commons. In such small matters Paris does not show its best side to travelers of moderate fortune. Lucien waited till the meal was over. Some change had come over Louise, he thought, but he could not explain it.

And a change had, in fact, taken place. Events had occurred while he slept; for reflection is an event in our inner history, and Mme. de Bargeton had been reflecting.

About two o'clock that afternoon, Sixte du Chatelet made his appearance in the Rue de l'Echelle and asked for Albertine. The sleeping damsel was roused, and to her he expressed his wish to speak with her mistress. Mme. de Bargeton had scarcely time to dress before he came back again. The unaccountable apparition of M. du Chatelet roused the lady's curiosity, for she had kept her journey a profound secret, as she thought. At three o'clock the visitor was admitted.

"I have risked a reprimand from headquarters to follow you," he said, as he greeted her; "I foresaw coming events. But if I lose my post for it, YOU, at any rate, shall not be lost."

"What do you mean?" exclaimed Mme. de Bargeton.

"I can see plainly that you love Lucien," he continued, with an air of tender resignation. "You must love indeed if *you* can act thus recklessly, and disregard the conventions which you know so well. Dear adored Nais, can you really imagine that Mme. d'Espard's salon, or any other salon in Paris, will not be closed to you as soon as it is known that you have fled from Angouleme, as it were, with a young man, especially after the duel between M. de Bargeton and M. de Chandour? The fact that your husband has gone to the Escarbas looks like a separation. Under such circumstances a gentleman fights first and afterwards leaves his wife at liberty. By all means, give M. de Rubempre your love and your countenance; do just as you please; but you must not live in the same house. If anybody here in Paris knew that you had traveled together, the whole world that you have a mind to see would point the finger at you.

"And, Nais, do not make these sacrifices for a young man whom you have as yet compared with no one else; he, on his side, has been put to no proof; he may forsake you for some Parisienne, better able, as he may fancy, to further his ambitions. I mean no harm to the man you love, but you will permit me to put your own interests before his, and to beg you to study him, to be fully aware of the serious nature of this step that you are taking. And, then, if you find all doors closed against you, and that none of the women call upon you, make sure at least that you will feel no regret for all that you have renounced for him. Be very certain first that he for whom you will have given up so much will always be worthy of your sacrifices and appreciate them.

"Just now," continued Chatelet, "Mme. d'Espard is the more prudish and particular because she herself is separated from her husband, nobody knows why. The Navarreins, the Lenoncourts, the Blamont-Chauvrys, and the rest of the relations have all rallied round her; the most strait-laced women are seen at her house, and receive her with respect, and the Marquis d'Espard has been put in the wrong. The first call that you pay will make it clear to you that I am right; indeed, knowing Paris as I do, I can tell you beforehand that you will no sooner enter the Marquise's salon than you will be in despair lest she should find out that you are staying at the Gaillard-Bois with an apothecary's son, though he may wish to be called M. de Rubempre.

"You will have rivals here, women far more astute and shrewd than Amelie; they will not fail to discover who you are, where you are, where you come from, and all that you are doing. You have counted upon your incognito, I see, but you are one of those women for whom an incognito is out of the question. You will meet Angouleme at every turn. There are the deputies from the Charente coming up for the opening of the session; there is the Commandant in Paris on leave. Why, the first man or woman from Angouleme who happens to see you would cut your career short in a strange fashion. You would simply be Lucien's mistress.

"If you need me at any time, I am staying with the Receiver-General in the Rue du Faubourg Saint-Honore, two steps away from Mme. d'Espard's. I am sufficiently acquainted with the Marechale de Carigliano, Mme. de Serizy, and the President of the Council to introduce you to those houses; but you will meet so many people at Mme. d'Espard's, that you are not likely to require me. So far from wishing to gain admittance to this set or that, every one will be longing to make your acquaintance."

Chatelet talked on; Mme. de Bargeton made no interruption. She was struck with his perspicacity. The queen of Angouleme had, in fact, counted upon preserving her incognito.

"You are right, my dear friend," she said at length; "but what am I to do?"

"Allow me to find suitable furnished lodgings for you," suggested Chatelet; "that way of living is less expensive than an inn. You will have a home of your own; and, if you will take my advice, you will sleep in your new rooms this very night."

"But how did you know my address?" queried she.

"Your traveling carriage is easily recognized; and, besides, I was following you. At Sevres your postilion told mine that he had brought you here. Will you permit me to act as your harbinger? I will write as soon as I have found lodgings."

"Very well, do so," said she. And in those seemingly insignificant words, all was said. The Baron du Chatelet had spoken the language of worldly wisdom to a woman of the world. He had made his appearance before her in faultless dress, a neat cab was waiting for him at the door; and Mme. de Bargeton, standing by the window thinking over the position, chanced to see the elderly dandy drive away.

A few moments later Lucien appeared, half awake and hastily dressed. He was handsome, it is true; but his clothes, his last year's nankeen trousers, and his shabby tight jacket were ridiculous. Put Antinous or the Apollo Belvedere himself into a water-carrier's blouse, and how shall you recognize the godlike creature of the Greek or Roman chisel? The eyes note and compare before the heart has time to revise the swift involuntary judgment; and the contrast between Lucien and Chatelet was so abrupt that it could not fail to strike Louise.

Towards six o'clock that evening, when dinner was over, Mme. de Bargeton beckoned Lucien to sit beside her on the shabby sofa, covered with a flowered chintz--a yellow pattern on a red ground.

"Lucien mine," she said, "don't you think that if we have both of us done a foolish thing, suicidal for both our interests, it would only be common sense to set matters right? We ought not to live together in Paris, dear boy, and we must not allow anyone to suspect that we traveled together. Your career depends so much upon my position that I ought to do nothing to spoil it. So, tonight, I am going to remove into lodgings near by. But you will stay on here, we can see each other every day, and nobody can say a word against us."

And Louise explained conventions to Lucien, who opened wide eyes. He had still to learn that when a woman thinks better of her folly, she thinks better of her love; but one thing he understood--he saw that he was no longer the Lucien of Angouleme. Louise talked of herself, of *her* interests, *her* reputation, and of the world; and, to veil her egoism, she tried to make him believe that this was all on his account. He had no claim upon Louise thus suddenly transformed into Mme. de Bargeton, and, more serious still, he had no power over her. He could not keep back the tears that filled his eyes.

"If I am your glory," cried the poet, "you are yet more to me--you are my one hope, my whole future rests with you. I thought that if you meant to make my successes yours, you would surely make my adversity yours also, and here we are going to part already."

"You are judging my conduct," said she; "you do not love me."

Lucien looked at her with such a dolorous expression, that in spite of herself, she said:

"Darling, I will stay if you like. We shall both be ruined, we shall have no one to come to our aid. But when we are both equally wretched, and every one shuts their door upon us both, when failure (for we must look all possibilities in the face), when failure drives us back to the Escarbas, then remember, love, that I foresaw the end, and that at the first I proposed that we should make your way by conforming to established rules."

"Louise," he cried, with his arms around her, "you are wise; you frighten me! Remember that I am a child, that I have given myself up entirely to your dear will. I myself should have preferred to overcome obstacles and win my way among men by the power that is in me; but if I can reach the goal sooner through your aid, I shall be very glad to owe all my success to you. Forgive me! You mean so much to me that I cannot help fearing all kinds of things; and, for me, parting means that desertion is at hand, and desertion is death."

"But, my dear boy, the world's demands are soon satisfied," returned she. "You must sleep here; that is all. All day long you will be with me, and no one can say a word."

A few kisses set Lucien's mind completely at rest. An hour later Gentil brought in a note from Chatelet. He told Mme. de Bargeton that he had found lodgings for her in the Rue Nueve-de-Luxembourg. Mme. de Bargeton informed herself of the exact place, and found that it was not very far from the Rue de l'Echelle. "We shall be neighbors," she told Lucien.

Two hours afterwards Louise stepped into the hired carriage sent by Chatelet for the removal to the new rooms. The apartments were of the class that upholsterers furnish and let to wealthy deputies and persons of consideration on a short visit to Paris--showy and uncomfortable. It was eleven o'clock when Lucien returned to his inn, having seen nothing as yet of Paris except the part of the Rue Saint-Honore which lies between the Rue Neuve-de-Luxembourg and the Rue de l'Echelle. He lay down in his miserable little room, and could not help comparing it in his own mind with Louise's sumptuous apartments.

Just as he came away the Baron du Chatelet came in, gorgeously arrayed in evening dress, fresh from the Minister for Foreign Affairs, to inquire whether Mme. de Bargeton was satisfied with all that he had done on her behalf. Nais was uneasy. The splendor was alarming to her mind. Provincial life had reacted upon her; she was painfully conscientious over her accounts, and economical to a degree that is looked upon as miserly in Paris. She had brought with her twenty thousand francs in the shape of a draft on the Receiver-General, considering that the sum would more than cover the expenses of four years in Paris; she was afraid already lest she should not have enough, and should run into debt; and now Chatelet told her that her rooms would only cost six hundred francs per month.

"A mere trifle," added he, seeing that Nais was startled. "For five hundred francs a month you can have a carriage from a livery stable; fifty louis in all. You need only think of your dress. A woman moving in good society could not well do less; and if you mean to obtain a Receiver-General's appointment for M. de Bargeton, or a post in the Household, you ought not to look poverty-stricken. Here, in Paris, they only give to the rich. It is most fortunate that you brought Gentil to go out with you, and Albertine for your own woman, for servants are enough to ruin you here. But with your introductions you will seldom be home to a meal."

Mme. de Bargeton and the Baron de Chatelet chatted about Paris. Chatelet gave her all the news of the day, the myriad nothings that you are bound to know, under penalty of being a nobody. Before very long the Baron also gave advice as to shopping, recommending Herbault for toques and Juliette for hats and bonnets; he added the address of a fashionable dressmaker to supersede Victorine. In short, he made the lady see the necessity of rubbing off Angouleme. Then he took his leave after a final flash of happy inspiration.

"I expect I shall have a box at one of the theatres tomorrow," he remarked carelessly; "I will call for you and M. de Rubempre, for you must allow me to do the honors of Paris."

"There is more generosity in his character than I thought," said Mme. de Bargeton to herself when Lucien was included in the invitation.

In the month of June ministers are often puzzled to know what to do with boxes at the theatre; ministerialist deputies and their constituents are busy in their vineyards or harvest fields, and their more exacting acquaintances are in the country or traveling about; so it comes to pass that the best seats are filled at this season with heterogeneous theatre-goers, never seen at any other time of year, and the house is apt to look as if it were tapestried with very shabby material. Chatelet had thought already that this was his opportunity of giving Nais the amusements which provincials crave most eagerly, and that with very little expense.

The next morning, the very first morning in Paris, Lucien went to the Rue Nueve-de-Luxembourg and found that Louise had gone out. She had gone to make some indispensable purchases, to take counsel of the mighty and illustrious authorities in the matter of the feminine toilette, pointed out to her by Chatelet, for she had written to tell the Marquise d'Espard of her arrival. Mme. de Bargeton possessed the self-confidence born of a long habit of rule, but she was exceedingly afraid of appearing to be provincial. She had tact enough to know how greatly the relations of women among themselves depend upon first impressions; and though she felt that she was equal to taking her place at once in such a distinguished set as Mme. de d'Espard's, she felt also that she stood in need of goodwill at her first entrance into society, and was resolved, in the first place, that she would leave nothing undone to secure success. So she felt boundlessly thankful to Chatelet for pointing out these ways of putting herself in harmony with the fashionable world.

A singular chance so ordered it that the Marquise was delighted to find an opportunity of being useful to a connection of her husband's family. The Marquis d'Espard had withdrawn himself without apparent reason from society, and ceased to take any active interest in affairs, political or domestic. His wife, thus left mistress of her actions, felt the need of the support of public opinion, and was glad to take the Marquis' place and give her countenance to one of her husband's relations. She meant to be ostentatiously gracious, so as to put her husband more evidently in the wrong; and that very day she wrote, "Mme. de Bargeton *nee* Negrepelisse" a charming billet, one of the prettily worded compositions of which time alone can discover the emptiness.

"She was delighted that circumstances had brought a relative, of whom she had heard, whose acquaintance she had desired to make, into closer connection with her family. Friendships in Paris were not so solid but that she longed to find one more to love on earth; and if this might not be, there would only be one more illusion to bury with the rest. She put herself entirely at her cousin's disposal. She would have called upon her if indisposition had not kept her to the house, and she felt that she lay already under obligations to the cousin who had thought of her."

Lucien, meanwhile, taking his first ramble along the Rue de la Paix and through the Boulevards, like all newcomers, was much more interested in the things that he saw than in the people he met. The general effect of Paris is wholly engrossing at first. The wealth in the shop windows, the high houses, the streams of traffic, the contrast everywhere between the last extremes of luxury and want struck him more than anything else. In his astonishment at the crowds of strange faces, the man of imaginative temper felt as if he himself had shrunk, as it were, immensely. A man of any consequence in his native place, where he cannot go out but he meets with some recognition of his importance at every step, does not readily accustom himself to the sudden and total extinction of his consequence. You are somebody in your own country, in Paris you are nobody. The transition between the first state and the last should be made gradually, for the too abrupt fall is something like annihilation. Paris could not fail to be an appalling wilderness for a young poet, who looked for an echo for all his sentiments, a confidant for all his thoughts, a soul to share his least sensations.

Lucien had not gone in search of his luggage and his best blue coat; and painfully conscious of the shabbiness, to say no worse, of his clothes, he went to Mme. de Bargeton, feeling that she must have returned. He found the Baron du Chatelet, who carried them both off to dinner at the *Rocher de Cancale*. Lucien's head was dizzy with the whirl of Paris, the Baron was in the carriage, he could say nothing to Louise, but he squeezed her hand, and she gave a warm response to the mute confidence.

After dinner Chatelet took his guests to the Vaudeville. Lucien, in his heart, was not over well pleased to see Chatelet again, and cursed the chance that had brought the Baron to Paris. The Baron said that ambition had brought him to town; he had hopes of an appointment as secretary-general to a government department, and meant to take a seat in the Council of State as Master of Requests. He had come to Paris to ask for fulfilment of the promises that had been given him, for a man of his stamp could not be expected to remain a comptroller all his life; he would rather be nothing at all, and offer himself for election as deputy, or re-enter diplomacy. Chatelet grew visibly taller; Lucien dimly began to recognize in this elderly beau the superiority of the man of the world who knows Paris; and, most of all, he felt ashamed to owe his evening's amusement to his rival. And while the poet looked ill at ease and awkward Her Royal Highness' ex-secretary was quite in his element. He smiled at his rival's hesitations, at his astonishment, at the questions he put, at the little mistakes which the latter ignorantly made, much as an old salt laughs at an apprentice who has not found his sea legs; but Lucien's pleasure at seeing a play for the first time in Paris outweighed the annoyance of these small humiliations.

That evening marked an epoch in Lucien's career; he put away a good many of his ideas as to provincial life in the course of it. His horizon widened; society assumed different proportions. There were fair Parisiennes in fresh and elegant toilettes all about him; Mme. de Bargeton's costume, tolerably ambitious though it was, looked dowdy by comparison; the material, like the fashion and the color, was out of date. That way of arranging her hair, so bewitching in Angouleme, looked frightfully ugly here among the daintily devised coiffures which he saw in every direction.

"Will she always look like that?" said he to himself, ignorant that the morning had been spent in preparing a transformation.

In the provinces comparison and choice are out of the question; when a face has grown familiar it comes to possess a certain beauty that is taken for granted. But transport the pretty woman of the provinces to Paris, and no one takes the slightest notice of her; her prettiness is of the comparative degree illustrated by the saying that among the blind the one-eyed are kings. Lucien's eyes were now busy comparing Mme. de Bargeton with other women, just as she herself had contrasted him with Chatelet on the previous day. And Mme. de Bargeton, on her part, permitted herself some strange reflections upon her lover. The poet cut a poor figure notwithstanding his singular beauty. The sleeves of his jacket were too short; with his ill-cut country gloves and a waistcoat too scanty for him, he looked prodigiously ridiculous, compared with the young men in the balcony--"positively pitiable," thought Mme. de Bargeton. Chatelet, interested in her without presumption, taking care of her in a manner that revealed a profound passion; Chatelet, elegant, and as much at home as an actor treading the familiar boards of his theatre, in two days had recovered all the ground lost in the past six months.

Ordinary people will not admit that our sentiments towards each other can totally change in a moment, and yet certain it is, that two lovers not seldom fly apart even more quickly than they drew together. In Mme. de Bargeton and in Lucien a process of disenchantment was at work; Paris was the cause. Life had widened out before the poet's eyes, as society came to wear a new aspect for Louise. Nothing but an accident now was needed to sever finally the bond that united them; nor was that blow, so terrible for Lucien, very long delayed.

Mme. de Bargeton set Lucien down at his inn, and drove home with Chatelet, to the intense vexation of the luckless lover.

"What will they say about me?" he wondered, as he climbed the stairs to his dismal room.

"That poor fellow is uncommonly dull," said Chatelet, with a smile, when the door was closed.

"That is the way with those who have a world of thoughts in their heart and brain. Men who have so much in them to give out in great works long dreamed of, profess a certain contempt for conversation, a commerce in which the intellect spends itself in small change," returned the haughty Negrepelisse. She still had courage to defend Lucien, but less for Lucien's sake than for her own.

"I grant it you willingly," replied the Baron, "but we live with human beings and not with books. There, dear Nais! I see how it is, there is nothing between you yet, and I am delighted that it is so. If you decide to bring an interest of a kind hitherto lacking into your life, let it not be this so-called genius, I implore you. How if you have made a mistake? Suppose that in a few days' time, when you have compared him with men whom you will meet, men of real ability, men who have distinguished themselves in good earnest; suppose that you should discover, dear and fair siren, that it is no lyre-bearer that you have borne into port on your dazzling shoulders, but a little ape, with no manners and no capacity; a presumptuous fool who may be a wit in L'Houmeau, but turns out a very ordinary specimen of a young man in Paris? And, after all, volumes of verse come out every week here, the worst of them better than all M. Chardon's poetry put together. For pity's sake, wait and compare! Tomorrow, Friday, is Opera night," he continued as the carriage turned into the Rue Nueve-de-Luxembourg; "Mme. d'Espard has the box of the First Gentlemen of the Chamber, and will take you, no doubt. I shall go to Mme. de Serizy's box to behold you in your glory. They are giving *Les Danaides*."

"Good-bye," said she.

Next morning Mme. de Bargeton tried to arrange a suitable toilette in which to call on her cousin, Mme. d'Espard. The weather was rather chilly. Looking through the dowdy wardrobe from Angouleme, she found nothing better than a certain green velvet gown, trimmed fantastically enough. Lucien, for his part, felt that he must go at once for his celebrated blue best coat; he felt aghast at the thought of his tight jacket, and determined to be well dressed, lest he should meet the Marquise d'Espard or receive a sudden summons to her house. He must have his luggage at once, so he took a cab, and in two hours' time spent three or four francs, matter for much subsequent reflection on the scale of the cost of living in Paris. Having dressed himself in his best, such as it was, he went to the Rue Nueve-de-Luxembourg, and on the doorstep encountered Gentil in company with a gorgeously be-feathered chasseur.

"I was just going round to you, sir, madame gave me a line for you," said Gentil, ignorant of Parisian forms of respect, and accustomed to homely provincial ways. The chasseur took the poet for a servant.

Lucien tore open the note, and learned that Mme. de Bargeton had gone to spend the day with the Marquise d'Espard. She was going to the Opera in the evening, but she told Lucien to be there to meet her. Her cousin permitted her to give him a seat in her box. The Marquise d'Espard was delighted to procure the young poet that pleasure.

"Then she loves me! my fears were all nonsense!" said Lucien to himself. "She is going to present me to her cousin this very evening."

He jumped for joy. He would spend the day that separated him from the happy evening as joyously as might be. He dashed out in the direction of the Tuileries, dreaming of walking there until it was time to dine at Very's. And now, behold Lucien frisking and skipping, light of foot because light of heart, on his way to the Terrasse des Feuillants to take a look at the people of quality on promenade there. Pretty women walk arm-in-arm with men of fashion, their adorers, couples greet each other with a glance as they pass; how different it is from the terrace at Beaulieu! How far finer the birds on this perch than the Angouleme species! It is as if you beheld all the colors that glow in the plumage of the feathered tribes of India and America, instead of the sober European families.

Those were two wretched hours that Lucien spent in the Garden of the Tuileries. A violent revulsion swept through him, and he sat in judgment upon himself.

In the first place, not a single one of these gilded youths wore a swallow-tail coat. The few exceptions, one or two poor wretches, a clerk here and there, an annuitant from the Marais, could be ruled out on the score of age; and hard upon the discovery of a distinction between morning and evening dress, the poet's quick sensibility and keen eyes saw likewise that his shabby old clothes were not fit to be seen; the defects in his coat branded that garment as ridiculous; the cut was old-fashioned, the color was the wrong shade of blue, the collar outrageously ungainly, the coat tails, by dint of long wear, overlapped each other, the buttons were reddened, and there were fatal white lines along the seams. Then his waistcoat was too short, and so grotesquely provincial, that he hastily buttoned his coat over it; and, finally, no man of any pretension to fashion wore nankeen trousers. Well-dressed men wore charming fancy materials or immaculate white, and every one had straps to his trousers, while the shrunken hems of Lucien's nether garments manifested a violent antipathy for the heels of boots which they wedded with obvious reluctance. Lucien wore a white cravat with embroidered ends; his sister had seen that M. du Hautoy and M. de Chandour wore such things, and hastened to make similar ones for her brother. Here, no one appeared to wear white cravats of a morning except a few grave seniors, elderly capitalists, and austere public functionaries, until, in the street on the other side of the railings, Lucien noticed a grocer's boy walking along the Rue de Rivoli with a basket on his head; him the man of Angouleme detected in the act of sporting a cravat, with both ends adorned by the handiwork of some adored shop-girl. The sight was a stab to Lucien's breast; penetrating straight to that organ as yet undefined, the seat of our sensibility, the region whither, since sentiment has had any existence, the sons of men carry their hands in any excess of joy or anguish. Do not accuse this chronicle of puerility. The rich, to be sure, never having experienced sufferings of this kind, may think them incredibly petty and small; but the agonies of less fortunate mortals are as well worth our attention as crises and vicissitudes in the lives of the mighty and privileged ones of earth. Is not the pain equally great for either? Suffering exalts all things. And, after all, suppose that we change the terms and for a suit of clothes, more or less fine, put instead a ribbon, or a star, or a title; have not brilliant careers been tormented by reason of such apparent trifles as these? Add, moreover, that for those people who must seem to have that which they have not, the question of clothes is of enormous importance, and not unfrequently the appearance of possession is the shortest road to possession at a later day.

A cold sweat broke out over Lucien as he bethought himself that tonight he must make his first appearance before the Marquise in this dress--the Marquise d'Espard, relative of a First Gentleman of the Bedchamber, a woman whose house was frequented by the most illustrious among illustrious men in every field.

"I look like an apothecary's son, a regular shop-drudge," he raged inwardly, watching the youth of the Faubourg Saint-Germain pass under his eyes; graceful, spruce, fashionably dressed, with a certain uniformity of air, a sameness due to a fineness of contour, and a certain dignity of carriage and expression; though, at the same time, each one differed from the rest in the setting by which he had chosen to bring his personal characteristics into prominence. Each one made the most of his personal advantages. Young men in Paris understand the art of presenting themselves quite as well as women. Lucien had inherited from his mother the invaluable physical distinction of race, but the metal was still in the ore, and not set free by the craftsman's hand.

His hair was badly cut. Instead of holding himself upright with an elastic corset, he felt that he was cooped up inside a hideous shirt-collar; he hung his dejected head without resistance on the part of a limp cravat. What woman could guess that a handsome foot was hidden by the clumsy boots which he had brought from Angouleme? What young man could envy him his graceful figure, disguised by the shapeless blue sack which hitherto he had mistakenly believed to be a coat? What bewitching studs he saw on those dazzling white shirt fronts, his own looked dingy by comparison; and how marvelously all these elegant persons were gloved, his own gloves were only fit for a policeman! Yonder was a youth toying with a cane exquisitely mounted; there, another with dainty gold studs in his wristbands. Yet another was twisting a charming riding-whip while he talked with a woman; there were specks of mud on the ample folds of his white trousers, he wore clanking spurs and a tight-fitting jacket, evidently he was about to mount one of the two horses held by a hop-o'-my-thumb of a tiger. A young man who went past drew a watch no thicker than a five-franc piece from his pocket, and looked at it with the air of a person who is either too early or too late for an appointment.

Lucien, seeing these petty trifles, hitherto unimagined, became aware of a whole world of indispensable superfluities, and shuddered to think of the enormous capital needed by a professional pretty fellow! The more he admired these gay and careless beings, the more conscious he grew of his own outlandishness; he knew that he looked like a man who has no idea of the direction of the streets, who stands close to the Palais Royal and cannot find it, and asks his way to the Louvre of a passer-by, who tells him, "Here you are." Lucien saw a great gulf fixed between him and this new world, and asked himself how he might cross over, for he meant to be one of these delicate, slim youths of Paris, these young patricians who bowed before women divinely dressed and divinely fair. For one kiss from one of these, Lucien was ready to be cut in pieces like Count Philip of Konigsmark. Louise's face rose up somewhere in the shadowy background of memory--compared with these queens, she looked like an old woman. He saw women whose names will appear in the history of the nineteenth century, women no less famous than the queens of past times for their wit, their beauty, or their lovers; one who passed was the heroine Mlle. des Touches, so well known as Camille Maupin, the great woman of letters, great by her intellect, great no less by her beauty. He overheard the name pronounced by those who went by.

"Ah!" he thought to himself, "she is Poetry."

What was Mme. de Bargeton in comparison with this angel in all the glory of youth, and hope, and promise of the future, with that sweet smile of hers, and the great dark eyes with all heaven in them, and the glowing light of the sun? She was laughing and chatting with Mme. Firmiani, one of the most charming women in Paris. A voice indeed cried, "Intellect is the lever by which to move the world," but another voice cried no less loudly that money was the fulcrum.

He would not stay any longer on the scene of his collapse and defeat, and went towards the Palais Royal. He did not know the topography of his quarter yet, and was obliged to ask his way. Then he went to Very's and ordered dinner by way of an initiation into the pleasures of Paris, and a solace for his discouragement. A bottle of Bordeaux, oysters from Ostend, a dish of fish, a partridge, a dish of macaroni and dessert,--this was the *ne plus ultra* of his desire. He enjoyed this little debauch, studying the while how to give the Marquise d'Espard proof of his wit, and redeem the shabbiness of his grotesque accoutrements by the display of intellectual riches. The total of the bill drew him down from these dreams, and left him the poorer by fifty of the francs which were to have gone such a long way in Paris. He could have lived in Angouleme for a month on the price of that dinner. Wherefore he closed the door of the palace with awe, thinking as he did so that he should never set foot in it again.

"Eve was right," he said to himself, as he went back under the stone arcading for some more money. "There is a difference between Paris prices and prices in L'Houmeau."

He gazed in at the tailors' windows on the way, and thought of the costumes in the Garden of the Tuileries.

"No," he exclaimed, "I will *not* appear before Mme. d'Espard dressed out as I am."

He fled to his inn, fleet as a stag, rushed up to his room, took out a hundred crowns, and went down again to the Palais Royal, where his future elegance lay scattered over half a score of shops. The first tailor whose door he entered tried as many coats upon him as he would consent to put on, and persuaded his customer that all were in the very latest fashion. Lucien came out the owner of a green coat, a pair of white trousers, and a "fancy waistcoat," for which outfit he gave two hundred francs. Ere long he found a very elegant pair of ready-made shoes that fitted his foot; and, finally, when he had made all necessary purchases, he ordered the tradespeople to send them to his address, and inquired for a hairdresser. At seven o'clock that evening he called a cab and drove away to the Opera, curled like a Saint John of a Procession Day, elegantly waistcoated and gloved, but feeling a little awkward in this kind of sheath in which he found himself for the first time.

In obedience to Mme. de Bargeton's instructions, he asked for the box reserved for the First Gentleman of the Bedchamber. The man at the box office looked at him, and beholding Lucien in all the grandeur assumed for the occasion, in which he looked like a best man at a wedding, asked Lucien for his order.

"I have no order."

"Then you cannot go in," said the man at the box office drily.

"But I belong to Mme. d'Espard's party."

"It is not our business to know that," said the man, who could not help exchanging a barely perceptible smile with his colleague.

A carriage stopped under the peristyle as he spoke. A chasseur, in a livery which Lucien did not recognize, let down the step, and two women in evening dress came out of the brougham. Lucien had no mind to lay himself open to an insolent order to get out of the way from the official. He stepped aside to let the two ladies pass.

"Why, that lady is the Marquise d'Espard, whom you say you know, sir," said the man ironically.

Lucien was so much the more confounded because Mme. de Bargeton did not seem to recognize him in his new plumage; but when he stepped up to her, she smiled at him and said:

"This has fallen out wonderfully--come!"

The functionaries at the box office grew serious again as Lucien followed Mme. de Bargeton. On their way up the great staircase the lady introduced M. de Rubempre to her cousin. The box belonging to the First Gentleman of the Bedchamber is situated in one of the angles at the back of the house, so that its occupants see and are seen all over the theatre. Lucien took his seat on a chair behind Mme. de Bargeton, thankful to be in the shadow.

"M. de Rubempre," said the Marquise with flattering graciousness, "this is your first visit to the Opera, is it not? You must have a view of the house; take this seat, sit in front of the box; we give you permission."

Lucien obeyed as the first act came to an end.

"You have made good use of your time," Louise said in his ear, in her first surprise at the change in his appearance.

Louise was still the same. The near presence of the Marquise d'Espard, a Parisian Mme. de Bargeton, was so damaging to her; the brilliancy of the Parisienne brought out all the defects in her country cousin so clearly by contrast; that Lucien, looking out over the fashionable audience in the superb building, and then at the great lady, was twice enlightened, and saw poor Anais de Negrepelisse as she really was, as Parisians saw her--a tall, lean, withered woman, with a pimpled face and faded complexion; angular, stiff, affected in her manner; pompous and provincial in her speech; and, and above all these things, dowdily dressed. As a matter of fact, the creases in an old dress from Paris still bear witness to good taste, you can tell what the gown was meant for; but an old dress made in the country is inexplicable, it is a thing to provoke laughter. There was neither charm nor freshness about the dress or its wearer; the velvet, like the complexion had seen wear. Lucien felt ashamed to have fallen in love with this cuttle-fish bone, and vowed that he would profit by Louise's next fit of virtue to leave her for good. Having an excellent view of the house, he could see the opera-glasses pointed at the aristocratic box par excellence. The best-dressed women must certainly be scrutinizing Mme. de Bargeton, for they smiled and talked among themselves.

If Mme. d'Espard knew the object of their sarcasms from those feminine smiles and gestures, she was perfectly insensible to them. In the first place, anybody must see that her companion was a poor relation from the country, an affliction with which any Parisian family may be visited. And, in the second, when her cousin had spoken to her of her dress with manifest misgivings, she had reassured Anais, seeing that, when once properly dressed, her relative would very easily acquire the tone of Parisian society. If Mme. de Bargeton needed polish, on the other hand she possessed the native haughtiness of good birth, and that indescribable something which may be called "pedigree." So, on Monday her turn would come. And, moreover, the Marquise knew that as soon as people learned that the stranger was her cousin, they would suspend their banter and look twice before they condemned her.

Lucien did not foresee the change in Louise's appearance shortly to be worked by a scarf about her throat, a pretty dress, an elegant coiffure, and Mme. d'Espard's advice. As they came up the staircase even now, the Marquise told her cousin not to hold her handkerchief unfolded in her hand. Good or bad taste turns upon hundreds of such almost imperceptible shades, which a quick-witted woman discerns at once, while others will never grasp them. Mme. de Bargeton, plentifully apt, was more than clever enough to discover her shortcomings. Mme. d'Espard, sure that her pupil would do her credit, did not decline to form her. In short, the compact between the two women had been confirmed by self-interest on either side.

Mme. de Bargeton, enthralled, dazzled, and fascinated by her cousin's manner, wit, and acquaintances, had suddenly declared herself a votary of the idol of the day. She had discerned the signs of the occult power exerted by the ambitious great lady, and told herself that she could gain her end as the satellite of this star, so she had been outspoken in her admiration. The Marquise was not insensible to the artlessly admitted conquest. She took an interest in her cousin, seeing that she was weak and poor; she was, besides, not indisposed to take a pupil with whom to found a school, and asked nothing better than to have a sort of lady-in-waiting in Mme. de Bargeton, a dependent who would sing her praises, a treasure even more scarce among Parisian women than a staunch and loyal critic among the literary tribe. The flutter of curiosity in the house was too marked to be ignored, however, and Mme. d'Espard politely endeavored to turn her cousin's mind from the truth.

"If any one comes to our box," she said, "perhaps we may discover the cause to which we owe the honor of the interest that these ladies are taking----"

"I have a strong suspicion that it is my old velvet gown and Angoumoisin air which Parisian ladies find amusing," Mme. de Bargeton answered, laughing.

"No, it is not you; it is something that I cannot explain," she added, turning to the poet, and, as she looked at him for the first time, it seemed to strike her that he was singularly dressed.

"There is M. du Chatelet," exclaimed Lucien at that moment, and he pointed a finger towards Mme. de Serizy's box, which the renovated beau had just entered.

Mme. de Bargeton bit her lips with chagrin as she saw that gesture, and saw besides the Marquise's ill-suppressed smile of contemptuous astonishment. "Where does the young man come from?" her look said, and Louise felt humbled through her love, one of the sharpest of all pangs for a Frenchwoman, a mortification for which she cannot forgive her lover.

In these circles where trifles are of such importance, a gesture or a word at the outset is enough to ruin a newcomer. It is the principal merit of fine manners and the highest breeding that they produce the effect of a harmonious whole, in which every element is so blended that nothing is startling or obtrusive. Even those who break the laws of this science, either through ignorance or carried away by some impulse, must comprehend that it is with social intercourse as with music, a single discordant note is a complete negation of the art itself, for the harmony exists only when all its conditions are observed down to the least particular.

"Who is that gentleman?" asked Mme. d'Espard, looking towards Chatelet. "And have you made Mme. de Serizy's acquaintance already?"

"Oh! is that the famous Mme. de Serizy who has had so many adventures and yet goes everywhere?"

"An unheard-of-thing, my dear, explicable but unexplained. The most formidable men are her friends, and why? Nobody dares to fathom the mystery. Then is this person the lion of Angouleme?"

"Well, M. le Baron du Chatelet has been a good deal talked about," answered Mme. de Bargeton, moved by vanity to give her adorer the title which she herself had called in question. "He was M. de Montriveau's traveling companion."

"Ah!" said the Marquise d'Espard, "I never hear that name without thinking of the Duchesse de Langeais, poor thing. She vanished like a falling star.--That is M. de Rastignac with Mme. de Nucingen," she continued, indicating another box; "she is the wife of a contractor, a banker, a city man, a broker on a large scale; he forced his way into society with his money, and they say that he is not very scrupulous as to his methods of making it. He is at endless pains to establish his credit as a staunch upholder of the Bourbons, and has tried already to gain admittance into my set. When his wife took Mme. de Langeais' box, she thought that she could take her charm, her wit, and her success as well. It is the old fable of the jay in the peacock's feathers!"

"How do M. and Mme. de Rastignac manage to keep their son in Paris, when, as we know, their income is under a thousand crowns?" asked Lucien, in his astonishment at Rastignac's elegant and expensive dress.

"It is easy to see that you come from Angouleme," said Mme. d'Espard, ironically enough, as she continued to gaze through her opera-glass.

Her remark was lost upon Lucien; the all-absorbing spectacle of the boxes prevented him from thinking of anything else. He guessed that he himself was an object of no small curiosity. Louise, on the other hand, was exceedingly mortified by the evident slight esteem in which the Marquise held Lucien's beauty.

"He cannot be so handsome as I thought him," she said to herself; and between "not so handsome" and "not so clever as I thought him" there was but one step.

The curtain fell. Chatelet was now paying a visit to the Duchesse de Carigliano in an adjourning box; Mme. de Bargeton acknowledged his bow by a slight inclination of the head. Nothing escapes a woman of the world; Chatelet's air of distinction was not lost upon Mme. d'Espard. Just at that moment four personages, four Parisian celebrities, came into the box, one after another.

The most striking feature of the first comer, M. de Marsay, famous for the passions which he had inspired, was his girlish beauty; but its softness and effeminacy were counteracted by the expression of his eyes, unflinching, steady, untamed, and hard as a tiger's. He was loved and he was feared. Lucien was no less handsome; but Lucien's expression was so gentle, his blue eyes so limpid, that he scarcely seemed to possess the strength and the power which attract women so strongly. Nothing, moreover, so far had brought out the poet's merits; while de Marsay, with his flow of spirits, his confidence in his power to please, and appropriate style of dress, eclipsed every rival by his presence. Judge, therefore, the kind of figure that Lucien, stiff, starched, unbending in clothes as new and unfamiliar as his surroundings, was likely to cut in de Marsay's vicinity. De Marsay with his wit and charm of manner was privileged to be insolent. From Mme. d'Espard's reception of this personage his importance was at once evident to Mme. de Bargeton.

The second comer was a Vandenesse, the cause of the scandal in which Lady Dudley was concerned. Felix de Vandenesse, amiable, intellectual, and modest, had none of the characteristics on which de Marsay prided himself, and owed his success to diametrically opposed qualities. He had been warmly recommended to Mme. d'Espard by her cousin Mme. de Mortsauf.

The third was General de Montriveau, the author of the Duchesse de Langeais' ruin.

The fourth, M. de Canalis, one of the most famous poets of the day, and as yet a newly risen celebrity, was prouder of his birth than of his genius, and dangled in Mme. d'Espard's train by way of concealing his love for the Duchesse de Chaulieu. In spite of his graces and the affectation that spoiled them, it was easy to discern the vast, lurking ambitions that plunged him at a later day into the storms of political life. A face that might be called insignificantly pretty and caressing manners thinly disguised the man's deeply-rooted egoism and habit of continually calculating the chances of a career which at that time looked problematical enough; though his choice of Mme. de Chaulieu (a woman past forty) made interest for him at Court, and brought him the applause of the Faubourg Saint-Germain and the gibes of the Liberal party, who dubbed him "the poet of the sacristy."

Mme. de Bargeton, with these remarkable figures before her, no longer wondered at the slight esteem in which the Marquise held Lucien's good looks. And when conversation began, when intellects so keen, so subtle, were revealed in two-edged words with more meaning and depth in them than Anais de Bargeton heard in a month of talk at Angouleme; and, most of all, when Canalis uttered a sonorous phrase, summing up a materialistic epoch, and gilding it with poetry-- then Anais felt all the truth of Chatelet's dictum of the previous evening. Lucien was nothing to her now. Every one cruelly ignored the unlucky stranger; he was so much like a foreigner listening to an unknown language, that the Marquise d'Espard took pity upon him. She turned to Canalis.

"Permit me to introduce M. de Rubempre," she said. "You rank too high in the world of letters not to welcome a *debutant*. M. de Rubempre is from Angouleme, and will need your influence, no doubt, with the powers that bring genius to light. So far, he has no enemies to help him to success by their attacks upon him. Is there enough originality in the idea of obtaining for him by friendship all that hatred has done for you to tempt you to make the experiment?"

The four newcomers all looked at Lucien while the Marquise was speaking. De Marsay, only a couple of paces away, put up an eyeglass and looked from Lucien to Mme. de Bargeton, and then again at Lucien, coupling them with some mocking thought, cruelly mortifying to both. He scrutinized them as if they had been a pair of strange animals, and then he smiled. The smile was like a stab to the distinguished provincial. Felix de Vandenesse assumed a charitable air. Montriveau looked Lucien through and through.

"Madame," M. de Canalis answered with a bow, "I will obey you, in spite of the selfish instinct which prompts us to show a rival no favor; but you have accustomed us to miracles."

"Very well, do me the pleasure of dining with me on Monday with M. de Rubempre, and you can talk of matters literary at your ease. I will try to enlist some of the tyrants of the world of letters and the great people who protect them, the author of *Ourika*, and one or two young poets with sound views."

"Mme. la Marquise," said de Marsay, "if you give your support to this gentleman for his intellect, I will support him for his good looks. I will give him advice which will put him in a fair way to be the luckiest dandy in Paris. After that, he may be a poet--if he has a mind."

Mme. de Bargeton thanked her cousin by a grateful glance.

"I did not know that you were jealous of intellect," Montriveau said, turning to de Marsay; "good fortune is the death of a poet."

"Is that why your lordship is thinking of marriage?" inquired the dandy, addressing Canalis, and watching Mme. d'Espard to see if the words went home.

Canalis shrugged his shoulders, and Mme. d'Espard, Mme. de Chaulieu's niece, began to laugh. Lucien in his new clothes felt as if he were an Egyptian statue in its narrow sheath; he was ashamed that he had nothing to say for himself all this while. At length he turned to the Marquise.

"After all your kindness, madame, I am pledged to make no failures," he said in those soft tones of his.

Chatelet came in as he spoke; he had seen Montriveau, and by hook or crook snatched at the chance of a good introduction to the Marquise d'Espard through one of the kings of Paris. He bowed to Mme. de Bargeton, and begged Mme. d'Espard to pardon him for the liberty he took in invading her box; he had been separated so long from his traveling companion! Montriveau and Chatelet met for the first time since they parted in the desert.

"To part in the desert, and meet again in the opera-house!" said Lucien.

"Quite a theatrical meeting!" said Canalis.

Montriveau introduced the Baron du Chatelet to the Marquise, and the Marquise received Her Royal Highness' ex-secretary the more graciously because she had seen that he had been very well received in three boxes already. Mme. de Serizy knew none but unexceptionable people, and moreover he was Montriveau's traveling companion. So potent was this last credential, that Mme. de Bargeton saw from the manner of the group that they accepted Chatelet as one of themselves without demur. Chatelet's sultan's airs in Angouleme were suddenly explained.

At length the Baron saw Lucien, and favored him with a cool, disparaging little nod, indicative to men of the world of the recipient's inferior station. A sardonic expression accompanied the greeting, "How does *he* come here?" he seemed to say. This was not lost on those who saw it; for de Marsay leaned towards Montriveau, and said in tones audible to Chatelet:

"Do ask him who the queer-looking young fellow is that looks like a dummy at a tailor's shop-door."

Chatelet spoke a few words in his traveling companion's ear, and while apparently renewing his acquaintance, no doubt cut his rival to pieces.

If Lucien was surprised at the apt wit and the subtlety with which these gentlemen formulated their replies, he felt bewildered with epigram and repartee, and, most of all, by their offhand way of talking and their ease of manner. The material luxury of Paris had alarmed him that morning; at night he saw the same lavish expenditure of intellect. By what mysterious means, he asked himself, did these people make such piquant reflections on the spur of the moment, those repartees which he could only have made after much pondering? And not only were they at ease in their speech, they were at ease in their dress, nothing looked new, nothing looked old, nothing about them was conspicuous, everything attracted the eyes. The fine gentleman of today was the same yesterday, and would be the same tomorrow. Lucien guessed that he himself looked as if he were dressed for the first time in his life.

"My dear fellow," said de Marsay, addressing Felix de Vandenesse, "that young Rastignac is soaring away like a paper-kite. Look at him in the Marquise de Listomere's box; he is making progress, he is putting up his eyeglass at us! He knows this gentleman, no doubt," added the dandy, speaking to Lucien, and looking elsewhere.

"He can scarcely fail to have heard the name of a great man of whom we are proud," said Mme. de Bargeton. "Quite lately his sister was present when M. de Rubempre read us some very fine poetry."

Felix de Vandenesse and de Marsay took leave of the Marquise d'Espard, and went off to Mme. de Listomere,

Vandenesse's sister. The second act began, and the three were left to themselves again. The curious women learned how Mme. de Bargeton came to be there from some of the party, while the others announced the arrival of a poet, and made fun of his costume. Canalis went back to the Duchesse de Chaulieu, and no more was seen of him.

Lucien was glad when the rising of the curtain produced a diversion. All Mme. de Bargeton's misgivings with regard to Lucien were increased by the marked attention which the Marquise d'Espard had shown to Chatelet; her manner towards the Baron was very different from the patronizing affability with which she treated Lucien. Mme. de Listomere's box was full during the second act, and, to all appearance, the talk turned upon Mme. de Bargeton and Lucien. Young Rastignac evidently was entertaining the party; he had raised the laughter that needs fresh fuel every day in Paris, the laughter that seizes upon a topic and exhausts it, and leaves it stale and threadbare in a moment. Mme. d'Espard grew uneasy. She knew that an ill-natured speech is not long in coming to the ears of those whom it will wound, and waited till the end of the act.

After a revulsion of feeling such as had taken place in Mme. de Bargeton and Lucien, strange things come to pass in a brief space of time, and any revolution within us is controlled by laws that work with great swiftness. Chatelet's sage and politic words as to Lucien, spoken on the way home from the Vaudeville, were fresh in Louise's memory. Every phrase was a prophecy, it seemed as if Lucien had set himself to fulfil the predictions one by one. When Lucien and Mme. de Bargeton had parted with their illusions concerning each other, the luckless youth, with a destiny not unlike Rousseau's, went so far in his predecessor's footsteps that he was captivated by the great lady and smitten with Mme. d'Espard at first sight. Young men and men who remember their young emotions can see that this was only what might have been looked for. Mme. d'Espard with her dainty ways, her delicate enunciation, and the refined tones of her voice; the fragile woman so envied, of such high place and high degree, appeared before the poet as Mme. de Bargeton had appeared to him in Angouleme. His fickle nature prompted him to desire influence in that lofty sphere at once, and the surest way to secure such influence was to possess the woman who exerted it, and then everything would be his. He had succeeded at Angouleme, why should he not succeed in Paris?

Involuntarily, and despite the novel counter fascination of the stage, his eyes turned to the Celimene in her splendor; he glanced furtively at her every moment; the longer he looked, the more he desired to look at her. Mme. de Bargeton caught the gleam in Lucien's eyes, and saw that he found the Marquise more interesting than the opera. If Lucien had forsaken her for the fifty daughters of Danaus, she could have borne his desertion with equanimity; but another glance-- bolder, more ardent and unmistakable than any before--revealed the state of Lucien's feelings. She grew jealous, but not so much for the future as for the past.

"He never gave me such a look," she thought. "Dear me! Chatelet was right!"

Then she saw that she had made a mistake; and when a woman once begins to repent of her weaknesses, she sponges out the whole past. Every one of Lucien's glances roused her indignation, but to all outward appearance she was calm. De Marsay came back in the interval, bringing M. de Listomere with him; and that serious person and the young coxcomb soon informed the Marquise that the wedding guest in his holiday suit, whom she had the bad luck to have in her box, had as much right to the appellation of Rubempre as a Jew to a baptismal name. Lucien's father was an apothecary named Chardon. M. de Rastignac, who knew all about Angouleme, had set several boxes laughing already at the mummy whom the Marquise styled her cousin, and at the Marquise's forethought in having an apothecary at hand to sustain an artificial life with drugs. In short, de Marsay brought a selection from the thousand-and-one jokes made by Parisians on the spur of the moment, and no sooner uttered than forgotten. Chatelet was at the back of it all, and the real author of this Punic faith.

Mme. d'Espard turned to Mme. de Bargeton, put up her fan, and said, "My dear, tell me if your protege's name is really M. de Rubempre?"

"He has assumed his mother's name," said Anais, uneasily.

"But who was his father?"

"His father's name was Chardon."

"And what was this Chardon?"

"A druggist."

"My dear friend, I felt quite sure that all Paris could not be laughing at any one whom I took up. I do not care to stay here when wags come in in high glee because there is an apothecary's son in my box. If you will follow my advice, we will leave it, and at once."

Mme. d'Espard's expression was insolent enough; Lucien was at a loss to account for her change of countenance. He thought that his waistcoat was in bad taste, which was true; and that his coat looked like a caricature of the fashion, which was likewise true. He discerned, in bitterness of soul, that he must put himself in the hands of an expert tailor, and vowed that he would go the very next morning to the most celebrated artist in Paris. On Monday he would hold his own with the men in the Marquise's house.

Yet, lost in thought though he was, he saw the third act to an end, and, with his eyes fixed on the gorgeous scene upon the stage, dreamed out his dream of Mme. d'Espard. He was in despair over her sudden coldness; it gave a strange check to the ardent reasoning through which he advanced upon this new love, undismayed by the immense difficulties in the way, difficulties which he saw and resolved to conquer. He roused himself from these deep musings to look once more at his new idol, turned his head, and saw that he was alone; he had heard a faint rustling sound, the door closed--Madame d'Espard had taken her cousin with her. Lucien was surprised to the last degree by the sudden desertion; he did not think long about it, however, simply because it was inexplicable.

When the carriage was rolling along the Rue de Richelieu on the way to the Faubourg Saint-Honore, the Marquise spoke to her cousin in a tone of suppressed irritation.

"My dear child, what are you thinking about? Pray wait till an apothecary's son has made a name for himself before you trouble yourself about him. The Duchesse de Chaulieu does not acknowledge Canalis even now, and he is famous and a man of good family. This young fellow is neither your son nor your lover, I suppose?" added the haughty dame, with a keen, inquisitive glance at her cousin.

"How fortunate for me that I kept the little scapegrace at a distance!" thought Madame de Bargeton.

"Very well," continued the Marquise, taking the expression in her cousin's eyes for an answer, "drop him, I beg of you. Taking an illustrious name in that way!--Why, it is a piece of impudence that will meet with its desserts in society. It is his mother's name, I dare say; but just remember, dear, that the King alone can confer, by a special ordinance, the title of de Rubempre on the son of a daughter of the house. If she made a *mesalliance*, the favor would be enormous, only to be granted to vast wealth, or conspicuous services, or very powerful influence. The young man looks like a shopman in his Sunday suit; evidently he is neither wealthy nor noble; he has a fine head, but he seems to me to be very silly; he has no idea what to do, and has nothing to say for himself; in fact, he has no breeding. How came you to take him up?"

Mme. de Bargeton renounced Lucien as Lucien himself had renounced her; a ghastly fear lest her cousin should learn the manner of her journey shot through her mind.

"Dear cousin, I am in despair that I have compromised you."

"People do not compromise me," Mme. d'Espard said, smiling; "I am only thinking of you."

"But you have asked him to dine with you on Monday."

"I shall be ill," the Marquise said quickly; "you can tell him so, and I shall leave orders that he is not to be admitted under either name."

During the interval Lucien noticed that every one was walking up and down the lobby. He would do the same. In the first place, not one of Mme. d'Espard's visitors recognized him nor paid any attention to him, their conduct seemed nothing less than extraordinary to the provincial poet; and, secondly, Chatelet, on whom he tried to hang, watched him out of the corner of his eye and fought shy of him. Lucien walked to and fro, watching the eddying crowd of men, till he felt convinced that his costume was absurd, and he went back to his box, ensconced himself in a corner, and stayed there till the end. At times he thought of nothing but the magnificent spectacle of the ballet in the great Inferno scene in the fifth act; sometimes the sight of the house absorbed him, sometimes his own thoughts; he had seen society in Paris, and the sight had stirred him to the depths.

"So this is my kingdom," he said to himself; "this is the world that I must conquer."

As he walked home through the streets he thought over all that had been said by Mme. d'Espard's courtiers; memory reproducing with strange faithfulness their demeanor, their gestures, their manner of coming and going.

Next day, towards noon, Lucien betook himself to Staub, the great tailor of that day. Partly by dint of entreaties, and partly by virtue of cash, Lucien succeeded in obtaining a promise that his clothes should be ready in time for the great day. Staub went so far as to give his word that a perfectly elegant coat, a waistcoat, and a pair of trousers should be forthcoming. Lucien then ordered linen and pocket-handkerchiefs, a little outfit, in short, of a linen-draper, and a celebrated bootmaker measured him for shoes and boots. He bought a neat walking cane at Verdier's; he went to Mme. Irlande for gloves and shirt studs; in short, he did his best to reach the climax of dandyism. When he had satisfied all his fancies, he went to the Rue Neuve-de-Luxembourg, and found that Louise had gone out.

"She was dining with Mme. la Marquise d'Espard," her maid said, "and would not be back till late."

Lucien dined for two francs at a restaurant in the Palais Royal, and went to bed early. The next day was Sunday. He went to Louise's lodging at eleven o'clock. Louise had not yet risen. At two o'clock he returned once more.

"Madame cannot see anybody yet," reported Albertine, "but she gave me a line for you."

"Cannot see anybody yet?" repeated Lucien. "But I am not anybody----"

"I do not know," Albertine answered very impertinently; and Lucien, less surprised by Albertine's answer than by a note from Mme. de Bargeton, took the billet, and read the following discouraging lines:--

"Mme. d'Espard is not well; she will not be able to see you on Monday. I am not feeling very well myself, but I am about to dress and go to keep her company. I am in despair over this little disappointment; but your talents reassure me, you will make your way without charlatanism."

"And no signature!" Lucien said to himself. He found himself in the Tuileries before he knew whither he was walking.

With the gift of second-sight which accompanies genius, he began to suspect that the chilly note was but a warning of the catastrophe to come. Lost in thought, he walked on and on, gazing at the monuments in the Place Louis Quinze.

It was a sunny day; a stream of fine carriages went past him on the way to the Champs Elysees. Following the direction of the crowd of strollers, he saw the three or four thousand carriages that turn the Champs Elysees into an improvised Longchamp on Sunday afternoons in summer. The splendid horses, the toilettes, and liveries bewildered him; he went further and further, until he reached the Arc de Triomphe, then unfinished. What were his feelings when, as he returned, he saw Mme. de Bargeton and Mme. d'Espard coming towards him in a wonderfully appointed caleche, with a chasseur behind it in waving plumes and that gold-embroidered green uniform which he knew only too well. There was a block somewhere in the row, and the carriages waited. Lucien beheld Louise transformed beyond recognition. All the colors of her toilette had been carefully subordinated to her complexion; her dress was delicious, her hair gracefully and becomingly arranged, her hat, in exquisite taste, was remarkable even beside Mme. d'Espard, that leader of fashion.

There is something in the art of wearing a hat that escapes definition. Tilted too far to the back of the head, it imparts a bold expression to the face; bring it too far forward, it gives you a sinister look; tipped to one side, it has a jaunty air; a well-dressed woman wears her hat exactly as she means to wear it, and exactly at the right angle. Mme. de Bargeton had solved this curious problem at sight. A dainty girdle outlined her slender waist. She had adopted her cousin's gestures and tricks of manner; and now, as she sat by Mme. d'Espard's side, she played with a tiny scent bottle that dangled by a slender gold chain from one of her fingers, displayed a little well-gloved hand without seeming to do so. She had modeled herself on Mme. d'Espard without mimicking her; the Marquise had found a cousin worthy of her, and seemed to be proud of her pupil.

The men and women on the footways all gazed at the splendid carriage, with the bearings of the d'Espards and Blamont-Chauvrys upon the panels. Lucien was amazed at the number of greetings received by the cousins; he did not know that the "all Paris," which consists in some score of salons, was well aware already of the relationship between the ladies. A little group of young men on horseback accompanied the carriage in the Bois; Lucien could recognize de Marsay and Rastignac among them, and could see from their gestures that the pair of coxcombs were complimenting Mme. de Bargeton upon her transformation. Mme. d'Espard was radiant with health and grace. So her indisposition was simply a pretext for ridding herself of him, for there had been no mention of another day!

The wrathful poet went towards the caleche; he walked slowly, waited till he came in full sight of the two ladies, and made them a bow. Mme. de Bargeton would not see him; but the Marquise put up her eyeglass, and deliberately cut him. He had been disowned by the sovereign lords of Angouleme, but to be disowned by society in Paris was another thing; the booby-squires by doing their utmost to mortify Lucien admitted his power and acknowledged him as a man; for Mme. d'Espard he had positively no existence. This was a sentence, it was a refusal of justice. Poor poet! a deadly cold seized on him when he saw de Marsay eying him through his glass; and when the Parisian lion let that optical instrument fall, it dropped in so singular a fashion that Lucien thought of the knife-blade of the guillotine.

The caleche went by. Rage and a craving for vengeance took possession of his slighted soul. If Mme. de Bargeton had been in his power, he could have cut her throat at that moment; he was a Fouquier-Tinville gloating over the pleasure of sending Mme. d'Espard to the scaffold. If only he could have put de Marsay to the torture with refinements of savage cruelty! Canalis went by on horseback, bowing to the prettiest women, his dress elegant, as became the most dainty of poets.

"Great heavens!" exclaimed Lucien. "Money, money at all costs! money is the one power before which the world bends the knee." ("No!" cried conscience, "not money, but glory; and glory means work! Work! that was what David said.") "Great heavens! what am I doing here? But I will triumph. I will drive along this avenue in a caleche with a chasseur behind me! I will possess a Marquise d'Espard." And flinging out the wrathful words, he went to Hurbain's to dine for two francs.

Next morning, at nine o'clock, he went to the Rue Neuve-de-Luxembourg to upbraid Louise for her barbarity. But Mme. de Bargeton was not at home to him, and not only so, but the porter would not allow him to go up to her rooms; so he stayed outside in the street, watching the house till noon. At twelve o'clock Chatelet came out, looked at Lucien out of the corner of his eye, and avoided him.

Stung to the quick, Lucien hurried after his rival; and Chatelet, finding himself closely pursued, turned and bowed, evidently intending to shake him off by this courtesy.

"Spare me just a moment for pity's sake, sir," said Lucien; "I want just a word or two with you. You have shown me friendship, I now ask the most trifling service of that friendship. You have just come from Mme. de Bargeton; how have I fallen into disgrace with her and Mme. d'Espard?--please explain."

"M. Chardon, do you know why the ladies left you at the Opera that evening?" asked Chatelet, with treacherous good-nature.

"No," said the poor poet.

"Well, it was M. de Rastignac who spoke against you from the beginning. They asked him about you, and the young dandy simply said that your name was Chardon, and not de Rubempre; that your mother was a monthly nurse; that your father, when he was alive, was an apothecary in L'Houmeau, a suburb of Angouleme; and that your sister, a charming girl, gets up shirts to admiration, and is just about to be married to a local printer named Sechard. Such is the world! You no sooner show yourself than it pulls you to pieces.

"M. de Marsay came to Mme. d'Espard to laugh at you with her; so the two ladies, thinking that your presence put them in a false position, went out at once. Do not attempt to go to either house. If Mme. de Bargeton continued to receive your visits, her cousin would have nothing to do with her. You have genius; try to avenge yourself. The world looks down upon you; look down in your turn upon the world. Take refuge in some garret, write your masterpieces, seize on power of any kind, and you will see the world at your feet. Then you can give back the bruises which you have received, and in the very place where they were given. Mme. de Bargeton will be the more distant now because she has been friendly. That is the way with women. But the question now for you is not how to win back Anais' friendship, but how to avoid making an enemy of her. I will tell you of a way. She has written letters to you; send all her letters back to her, she will be sensible that you are acting like a gentleman; and at a later time, if you should need her, she will not be hostile. For my own part, I have so high an opinion of your future, that I have taken your part everywhere; and if I can do anything here for you, you will always find me ready to be of use."

The elderly beau seemed to have grown young again in the atmosphere of Paris. He bowed with frigid politeness; but Lucien, woe-begone, haggard, and undone, forgot to return the salutation. He went back to his inn, and there found the great Staub himself, come in person, not so much to try his customer's clothes as to make inquiries of the landlady with regard to that customer's financial status. The report had been satisfactory. Lucien had traveled post; Mme. de Bargeton brought him back from Vaudeville last Thursday in her carriage. Staub addressed Lucien as "Monsieur le Comte," and called his customer's attention to the artistic skill with which he had brought a charming figure into relief.

"A young man in such a costume has only to walk in the Tuileries," he said, "and he will marry an English heiress within a fortnight."

Lucien brightened a little under the influences of the German tailor's joke, the perfect fit of his new clothes, the fine cloth, and the sight of a graceful figure which met his eyes in the looking-glass. Vaguely he told himself that Paris was the capital of chance, and for the moment he believed in chance. Had he not a volume of poems and a magnificent romance entitled *The Archer of Charles IX.* in manuscript? He had hope for the future. Staub promised the overcoat and the rest of the clothes the next day.

The next day the bootmaker, linen-draper, and tailor all returned armed each with his bill, which Lucien, still under the charm of provincial habits, paid forthwith, not knowing how otherwise to rid himself of them. After he had paid, there remained but three hundred and sixty francs out of the two thousand which he had brought with him from Angouleme, and he had been but one week in Paris! Nevertheless, he dressed and went to take a stroll in the Terrassee des Feuillants. He had his day of triumph. He looked so handsome and so graceful, he was so well dressed, that women looked at him; two or three were so much struck with his beauty, that they turned their heads to look again. Lucien studied the gait and carriage of the young men on the Terrasse, and took a lesson in fine manners while he meditated on his three hundred and sixty francs.

That evening, alone in his chamber, an idea occurred to him which threw a light on the problem of his existence at the Gaillard-Bois, where he lived on the plainest fare, thinking to economize in this way. He asked for his account, as if he meant to leave, and discovered that he was indebted to his landlord to the extent of a hundred francs. The next morning was spent in running around the Latin Quarter, recommended for its cheapness by David. For a long while he looked about till, finally, in the Rue de Cluny, close to the Sorbonne, he discovered a place where he could have a furnished room for such a price as he could afford to pay. He settled with his hostess of the Gaillard-Bois, and took up his quarters in the Rue de Cluny that same day. His removal only cost him the cab fare.

When he had taken possession of his poor room, he made a packet of Mme. de Bargeton's letters, laid them on the table, and sat down to write to her; but before he wrote he fell to thinking over that fatal week. He did not tell himself that he had been the first to be faithless; that for a sudden fancy he had been ready to leave his Louise without knowing what would become of her in Paris. He saw none of his own shortcomings, but he saw his present position, and blamed Mme. de Bargeton for it. She was to have lighted his way; instead she had ruined him. He grew indignant, he grew proud, he worked himself into a paroxysm of rage, and set himself to compose the following epistle:--

"What would you think, madame, of a woman who should take a fancy to some poor and timid child full of the noble superstitions which the grown man calls 'illusions;' and using all the charms of woman's coquetry, all her most delicate ingenuity, should feign a mother's love to lead that child astray? Her fondest promises, the card-castles which raised his wonder, cost her nothing; she leads him on, tightens her hold upon him, sometimes coaxing, sometimes scolding him for his want of confidence, till the child leaves his home and follows her blindly to the shores of a vast sea. Smiling, she lures him into a frail skiff, and sends him forth alone and helpless to face the storm. Standing safe on the rock, she laughs and wishes him luck. You are that woman; I am that child.

"The child has a keepsake in his hands, something which might betray the wrongs done by your beneficence, your kindness in deserting him. You might have to blush if you saw him struggling for life, and chanced to recollect that once you clasped him to your breast. When you read these words the keepsake will be in your own safe keeping; you are free to forget everything.

"Once you pointed out fair hopes to me in the skies, I awake to find reality in the squalid poverty of Paris. While you pass, and others bow before you, on your brilliant path in the great world, I, I whom you deserted on the threshold, shall be shivering in the wretched garret to which you consigned me. Yet some pang may perhaps trouble your mind amid festivals and pleasures; you may think sometimes of the child whom you thrust into the depths. If so, madame, think of him without remorse. Out of the depths of his misery the child offers you the one thing left to him--his forgiveness in a last look. Yes, madame, thanks to you, I have nothing left. Nothing! was not the world created from nothing? Genius should follow the Divine example; I begin with God-like forgiveness, but as yet I know not whether I possess the God-like power. You need only tremble lest I should go astray; for you would be answerable for my sins. Alas! I pity you, for you will have no part in the future towards which I go, with work as my guide."

After penning this rhetorical effusion, full of the sombre dignity which an artist of one-and-twenty is rather apt to overdo,

Lucien's thoughts went back to them at home. He saw the pretty rooms which David had furnished for him, at the cost of part of his little store, and a vision rose before him of quiet, simple pleasures in the past. Shadowy figures came about him; he saw his mother and Eve and David, and heard their sobs over his leave-taking, and at that he began to cry himself, for he felt very lonely in Paris, and friendless and forlorn.

Two or three days later he wrote to his sister:--

"MY DEAR EVE,--When a sister shares the life of a brother who devotes himself to art, it is her sad privilege to take more sorrow than joy into her life; and I am beginning to fear that I shall be a great trouble to you. Have I not abused your goodness already? have not all of you sacrificed yourselves to me? It is the memory of the past, so full of family happiness, that helps me to bear up in my present loneliness. Now that I have tasted the first beginnings of poverty and the treachery of the world of Paris, how my thoughts have flown to you, swift as an eagle back to its eyrie, so that I might be with true affection again. Did you see sparks in the candle? Did a coal pop out of the fire? Did you hear singing in your ears? And did mother say, 'Lucien is thinking of us,' and David answer, 'He is fighting his way in the world?'

"My Eve, I am writing this letter for your eyes only. I cannot tell any one else all that has happened to me, good and bad, blushing for both, as I write, for good here is as rare as evil ought to be. You shall have a great piece of news in a very few words. Mme. de Bargeton was ashamed of me, disowned me, would not see me, and gave me up nine days after we came to Paris. She saw me in the street and looked another way; when, simply to follow her into the society to which she meant to introduce me, I had spent seventeen hundred and sixty francs out of the two thousand I brought from Angouleme, the money so hardly scraped together. 'How did you spend it?' you will ask. Paris is a strange bottomless gulf, my poor sister; you can dine here for less than a franc, yet the simplest dinner at a fashionable restaurant costs fifty francs; there are waistcoats and trousers to be had for four francs and two francs each; but a fashionable tailor never charges less than a hundred francs. You pay for everything; you pay a halfpenny to cross the kennel in the street when it rains; you cannot go the least little way in a cab for less than thirty-two sous.

"I have been staying in one of the best parts of Paris, but now I am living at the Hotel de Cluny, in the Rue de Cluny, one of the poorest and darkest slums, shut in between three churches and the old buildings of the Sorbonne. I have a furnished room on the fourth floor; it is very bare and very dirty, but, all the same, I pay fifteen francs a month for it. For breakfast I spend a penny on a roll and a halfpenny for milk, but I dine very decently for twenty-two sous at a restaurant kept by a man named Flicoteaux in the Place de la Sorbonne itself. My expenses every month will not exceed sixty francs, everything included, until the winter begins --at least I hope not. So my two hundred and forty francs ought to last me for the first four months. Between now and then I shall have sold *The Archer of Charles IX.* and the *Marguerites* no doubt. Do not be in the least uneasy on my account. If the present is cold and bare and poverty-stricken, the blue distant future is rich and splendid; most great men have known the vicissitudes which depress but cannot overwhelm me.

"Plautus, the great comic Latin poet, was once a miller's lad. Machiavelli wrote *The Prince* at night, and by day was a common working-man like any one else; and more than all, the great Cervantes, who lost an arm at the battle of Lepanto, and helped to win that famous day, was called a 'base-born, handless dotard' by the scribblers of his day; there was an interval of ten years between the appearance of the first part and the second of his sublime *Don Quixote* for lack of a publisher. Things are not so bad as that nowadays. Mortifications and want only fall to the lot of unknown writers; as soon as a man's name is known, he grows rich, and I will be rich. And besides, I live within myself, I spend half the day at the Bibliotheque Sainte-Genevieve, learning all that I want to learn; I should not go far unless I knew more than I do. So at this moment I am almost happy. In a few days I have fallen in with my life very gladly. I begin the work that I love with daylight, my subsistence is secure, I think a great deal, and I study. I do not see that I am open to attack at any point, now that I have renounced a world where my vanity might suffer at any moment. The great men of every age are obliged to lead lives apart. What are they but birds in the forest? They sing, nature falls under the spell of their song, and no one should see them. That shall be my lot, always supposing that I can carry out my ambitious plans.

"Mme. de Bargeton I do not regret. A woman who could behave as she behaved does not deserve a thought. Nor am I sorry that I left Angouleme. She did wisely when she flung me into the sea of Paris to sink or swim. This is the place for men of letters and thinkers and poets; here you cultivate glory, and I know how fair the harvest is that we reap in these days. Nowhere else can a writer find the living works of the great dead, the works of art which quicken the imagination in the galleries and museums here; nowhere else will you find great reference libraries always open in which the intellect may find pasture. And lastly, here in Paris there is a spirit which you breathe in the air; it infuses the least details, every literary creation bears traces of its influence. You learn more by talk in a cafe, or at a theatre, in one half hour, than you would learn in ten years in the provinces. Here, in truth, wherever you go, there is always something to see, something to learn, some comparison to make. Extreme cheapness and excessive dearness--there is Paris for you; there is honeycomb here for every bee, every nature finds its own nourishment. So, though life is hard for me just now, I repent of nothing. On the contrary, a fair future spreads out before me, and my heart rejoices though it is saddened for the moment. Good-bye my dear sister. Do not expect letters from me regularly; it is one of the peculiarities of Paris that one really does not know how the time goes. Life is so alarmingly rapid. I kiss the mother and you and David more tenderly than ever.

"LUCIEN."

The name of Flicoteaux is engraved on many memories. Few indeed were the students who lived in the Latin Quarter during the last twelve years of the Restoration and did not frequent that temple sacred to hunger and impecuniosity. There a dinner of three courses, with a quarter bottle of wine or a bottle of beer, could be had for eighteen sous; or for twenty-two sous the quarter bottle becomes a bottle. Flicoteaux, that friend of youth, would beyond a doubt have amassed a colossal fortune but for a line on his bill of fare, a line which rival establishments are wont to print in capital letters, thus--BREAD AT DISCRETION, which, being interpreted, should read "indiscretion."

Flicoteaux has been nursing-father to many an illustrious name. Verily, the heart of more than one great man ought to wax warm with innumerable recollections of inexpressible enjoyment at the sight of the small, square window panes that look upon the Place de la Sorbonne, and the Rue Neuve-de-Richelieu. Flicoteaux II. and Flicoteaux III. respected the old exterior, maintaining the dingy hue and general air of a respectable, old-established house, showing thereby the depth of their contempt for the charlatanism of the shop-front, the kind of advertisement which feasts the eyes at the expense of the stomach, to which your modern restaurant almost always has recourse. Here you beheld no piles of straw-stuffed game never destined to make the acquaintance of the spit, no fantastical fish to justify the mountebank's remark, "I saw a fine carp today; I expect to buy it this day week." Instead of the prime vegetables more fittingly described by the word primeval, artfully displayed in the window for the delectation of the military man and his fellow country-woman the nursemaid, honest Flicoteaux exhibited full salad-bowls adorned with many a rivet, or pyramids of stewed prunes to rejoice the sight of the customer, and assure him that the word "dessert," with which other handbills made too free, was in this case no charter to hoodwink the public. Loaves of six pounds' weight, cut in four quarters, made good the promise of "bread at discretion." Such was the plenty of the establishment, that Moliere would have celebrated it if it had been in existence in his day, so comically appropriate is the name.

Flicoteaux still subsists; so long as students are minded to live, Flicoteaux will make a living. You feed there, neither more nor less; and you feed as you work, with morose or cheerful industry, according to the circumstances and the temperament.

At that time his well-known establishment consisted of two dining-halls, at right angles to each other; long, narrow, low-ceiled rooms, looking respectively on the Rue Neuve-de-Richelieu and the Place de la Sorbonne. The furniture must have come originally from the refectory of some abbey, for there was a monastic look about the lengthy tables, where the serviettes of regular customers, each thrust through a numbered ring of crystallized tin plate, were laid by their places. Flicoteaux I. only changed the serviettes of a Sunday; but Flicoteaux II. changed them twice a week, it is said, under pressure of competition which threatened his dynasty.

Flicoteaux's restaurant is no banqueting-hall, with its refinements and luxuries; it is a workshop where suitable tools are provided, and everybody gets up and goes as soon as he has finished. The coming and going within are swift. There is no dawdling among the waiters; they are all busy; every one of them is wanted.

The fare is not very varied. The potato is a permanent institution; there might not be a single tuber left in Ireland, and prevailing dearth elsewhere, but you would still find potatoes at Flicoteaux's. Not once in thirty years shall you miss its pale gold (the color beloved of Titian), sprinkled with chopped verdure; the potato enjoys a privilege that women might envy; such as you see it in 1814, so shall you find it in 1840. Mutton cutlets and fillet of beef at Flicoteaux's represent black game and fillet of sturgeon at Very's; they are not on the regular bill of fare, that is, and must be ordered beforehand. Beef of the feminine gender there prevails; the young of the bovine species appears in all kinds of ingenious disguises. When the whiting and mackerel abound on our shores, they are likewise seen in large numbers at Flicoteaux's; his whole establishment, indeed, is directly affected by the caprices of the season and the vicissitudes of French agriculture. By eating your dinners at Flicoteaux's you learn a host of things of which the wealthy, the idle, and folk indifferent to the phases of Nature have no suspicion, and the student penned up in the Latin Quarter is kept accurately informed of the state of the weather and good or bad seasons. He knows when it is a good year for peas or French beans, and the kind of salad stuff that is plentiful; when the Great Market is glutted with cabbages, he is at once aware of the fact, and the failure of the beetroot crop is brought home to his mind. A slander, old in circulation in Lucien's time, connected the appearance of beef-steaks with a mortality among horseflesh.

Few Parisian restaurants are so well worth seeing. Every one at Flicoteaux's is young; you see nothing but youth; and although earnest faces and grave, gloomy, anxious faces are not lacking, you see hope and confidence and poverty gaily endured. Dress, as a rule, is careless, and regular comers in decent clothes are marked exceptions. Everybody knows at once that something extraordinary is afoot: a mistress to visit, a theatre party, or some excursion into higher spheres. Here, it is said, friendships have been made among students who became famous men in after days, as will be seen in the course of this narrative; but with the exception of a few knots of young fellows from the same part of France who make a group about the end of a table, the gravity of the diners is hardly relaxed. Perhaps this gravity is due to the catholicity of the wine, which checks good fellowship of any kind.

Flicoteaux's frequenters may recollect certain sombre and mysterious figures enveloped in the gloom of the chilliest penury; these beings would dine there daily for a couple of years and then vanish, and the most inquisitive regular comer could throw no light on the disappearance of such goblins of Paris. Friendships struck up over Flicoteaux's dinners were sealed in neighboring cafes in the flames of heady punch, or by the generous warmth of a small cup of black coffee glorified by a dash of something hotter and stronger.

Lucien, like all neophytes, was modest and regular in his habits in those early days at the Hotel de Cluny. After the first unlucky venture in fashionable life which absorbed his capital, he threw himself into his work with the first earnest enthusiasm, which is frittered away so soon over the difficulties or in the by-paths of every life in Paris. The most luxurious and the very poorest lives are equally beset with temptations which nothing but the fierce energy of genius or the morose persistence of ambition can overcome.

Lucien used to drop in at Flicoteaux's about half-past four, having remarked the advantages of an early arrival; the bill-of-fare was more varied, and there was still some chance of obtaining the dish of your choice. Like all imaginative persons, he had taken a fancy to a particular seat, and showed discrimination in his selection. On the very first day he had noticed a table near the counter, and from the faces of those who sat about it, and chance snatches of their talk, he recognized brothers of the craft. A sort of instinct, moreover, pointed out the table near the counter as a spot whence he could parlay with the owners of the restaurant. In time an acquaintance would grow up, he thought, and then in the day of distress he could no doubt obtain the necessary credit. So he took his place at a small square table close to the desk, intended probably for casual comers, for the two clean serviettes were unadorned with rings. Lucien's opposite neighbor was a thin, pallid youth, to all appearance as poor as himself; his handsome face was somewhat worn, already it told of hopes that had vanished, leaving lines upon his forehead and barren furrows in his soul, where seeds had been sown that had come to nothing. Lucien felt drawn to the stranger by these tokens; his sympathies went out to him with irresistible fervor.

After a week's exchange of small courtesies and remarks, the poet from Angouleme found the first person with whom he could chat. The stranger's name was Etienne Lousteau. Two years ago he had left his native place, a town in Berri, just as Lucien had come from Angouleme. His lively gestures, bright eyes, and occasionally curt speech revealed a bitter apprenticeship to literature. Etienne had come from Sancerre with his tragedy in his pocket, drawn to Paris by the same motives that impelled Lucien--hope of fame and power and money.

Sometimes Etienne Lousteau came for several days together; but in a little while his visits became few and far between, and he would stay away for five or six days in succession. Then he would come back, and Lucien would hope to see his poet next day, only to find a stranger in his place. When two young men meet daily, their talk harks back to their last conversation; but these continual interruptions obliged Lucien to break the ice afresh each time, and further checked an intimacy which made little progress during the first few weeks. On inquiry of the damsel at the counter, Lucien was told that his future friend was on the staff of a small newspaper, and wrote reviews of books and dramatic criticism of pieces played at the Ambigu-Comique, the Gaite, and the Panorama-Dramatique. The young man became a personage all at once in Lucien's eyes. Now, he thought, he would lead the conversation on rather more personal topics, and make some effort to gain a friend so likely to be useful to a beginner. The journalist stayed away for a fortnight. Lucien did not know that Etienne only dined at Flicoteaux's when he was hard up, and hence his gloomy air of disenchantment and the chilly manner, which Lucien met with gracious smiles and amiable remarks. But, after all, the project of a friendship called for mature deliberation. This obscure journalist appeared to lead an expensive life in which *petits verres*, cups of coffee, punch-bowls, sight-seeing, and suppers played a part. In the early days of Lucien's life in the Latin Quarter, he behaved like a poor child bewildered by his first experience of Paris life; so that when he had made a study of prices and weighed his purse, he lacked courage to make advances to Etienne; he was afraid of beginning a fresh series of blunders of which he was still repenting. And he was still under the yoke of provincial creeds; his two guardian angels, Eve and David, rose up before him at the least approach of an evil thought, putting him in mind of all the hopes that were centered on him, of the happiness that he owed to the old mother, of all the promises of his genius.

He spent his mornings in studying history at the Bibliotheque Sainte-Genevieve. His very first researches made him aware of frightful errors in the memoirs of *The Archer of Charles IX*. When the library closed, he went back to his damp, chilly room to correct his work, cutting out whole chapters and piecing it together anew. And after dining at Flicoteaux's, he went down to the Passage du Commerce to see the newspapers at Blosse's reading-room, as well as new books and magazines and poetry, so as to keep himself informed of the movements of the day. And when, towards midnight, he returned to his wretched lodgings, he had used neither fuel nor candle-light. His reading in those days made such an enormous change in his ideas, that he revised the volume of flower-sonnets, his beloved *Marguerites*, working them over to such purpose, that scarce a hundred lines of the original verses were allowed to stand.

So in the beginning Lucien led the honest, innocent life of the country lad who never leaves the Latin Quarter; devoting himself wholly to his work, with thoughts of the future always before him; who finds Flicoteaux's ordinary luxurious after the simple home-fare; and strolls for recreation along the alleys of the Luxembourg, the blood surging back to his heart as he gives timid side glances to the pretty women. But this could not last. Lucien, with his poetic temperament and boundless longings, could not withstand the temptations held out by the play-bills.

The Theatre-Francais, the Vaudeville, the Varietes, the Opera-Comique relieved him of some sixty francs, although he always went to the pit. What student could deny himself the pleasure of seeing Talma in one of his famous roles? Lucien was fascinated by the theatre, that first love of all poetic temperaments; the actors and actresses were awe-inspiring creatures; he did not so much as dream of the possibility of crossing the footlights and meeting them on familiar terms. The men and women who gave him so much pleasure were surely marvelous beings, whom the newspapers treated with as much gravity as matters of national interest. To be a dramatic author, to have a play produced on the stage! What a dream was this to cherish! A dream which a few bold spirits like Casimir Delavigne had actually realized. Thick swarming thoughts like these, and moments of belief in himself, followed by despair gave Lucien no rest, and kept him in the narrow way of toil and frugality, in spite of the smothered grumblings of more than one frenzied desire.

Carrying prudence to an extreme, he made it a rule never to enter the precincts of the Palais Royal, that place of perdition where he had spent fifty francs at Very's in a single day, and nearly five hundred francs on his clothes; and when he yielded to temptation, and saw Fleury, Talma, the two Baptistes, or Michot, he went no further than the murky passage where theatre-goers used to stand in a string from half-past five in the afternoon till the hour when the doors opened, and belated comers were compelled to pay ten sous for a place near the ticket-office. And after waiting for two hours, the cry of "All tickets are sold!" rang not unfrequently in the ears of disappointed students. When the play was over, Lucien went home with downcast eyes, through streets lined with living attractions, and perhaps fell in with one of those commonplace adventures which loom so large in a young and timorous imagination.

One day Lucien counted over his remaining stock of money, and took alarm at the melting of his funds; a cold perspiration broke out upon him when he thought that the time had come when he must find a publisher, and try also to find work for which a publisher would pay him. The young journalist, with whom he had made a one-sided friendship, never came now to Flicoteaux's. Lucien was waiting for a chance--which failed to present itself. In Paris there are no chances except for men with a very wide circle of acquaintance; chances of success of every kind increase with the number of your connections; and, therefore, in this sense also the chances are in favor of the big battalions. Lucien had sufficient provincial foresight still left, and had no mind to wait until only a last few coins remained to him. He resolved to face the publishers.

So one tolerably chilly September morning Lucien went down the Rue de la Harpe, with his two manuscripts under his arm. As he made his way to the Quai des Augustins, and went along, looking into the booksellers' windows on one side and into the Seine on the other, his good genius might have counseled him to pitch himself into the water sooner than plunge into literature. After heart-searching hesitations, after a profound scrutiny of the various countenances, more or less encouraging, soft-hearted, churlish, cheerful, or melancholy, to be seen through the window panes, or in the doorways of the booksellers' establishments, he espied a house where the shopmen were busy packing books at a great rate. Goods were being despatched. The walls were plastered with bills:

JUST OUT.

LE SOLITAIRE, by M. le Vicomte d'Arlincourt. Third edition. LEONIDE, by Victor Ducange; five volumes 12mo, printed on fine paper. 12 francs. INDUCTIONS MORALES, by Keratry.

"They are lucky, that they are!" exclaimed Lucien.

The placard, a new and original idea of the celebrated Ladvocat, was just beginning to blossom out upon the walls. In no long space Paris was to wear motley, thanks to the exertions of his imitators, and the Treasury was to discover a new source of revenue.

Anxiety sent the blood surging to Lucien's heart, as he who had been so great at Angouleme, so insignificant of late in Paris, slipped past the other houses, summoned up all his courage, and at last entered the shop thronged with assistants, customers, and booksellers--"And authors too, perhaps!" thought Lucien.

"I want to speak with M. Vidal or M. Porchon," he said, addressing a shopman. He had read the names on the sign-board-- VIDAL & PORCHON (it ran), *French and foreign booksellers' agents*.

"Both gentlemen are engaged," said the man.

"I will wait."

Left to himself, the poet scrutinized the packages, and amused himself for a couple of hours by scanning the titles of books, looking into them, and reading a page or two here and there. At last, as he stood leaning against a window, he heard voices, and suspecting that the green curtains hid either Vidal or Porchon, he listened to the conversation.

"Will you take five hundred copies of me? If you will, I will let you have them at five francs, and give fourteen to the dozen."

"What does that bring them in at?"

"Sixteen sous less."

"Four francs four sous?" said Vidal or Porchon, whichever it was.

"Yes," said the vendor.

"Credit your account?" inquired the purchaser.

"Old humbug! you would settle with me in eighteen months' time, with bills at a twelvemonth."

"No. Settled at once," returned Vidal or Porchon.

"Bills at nine months?" asked the publisher or author, who evidently was selling his book.

"No, my dear fellow, twelve months," returned one of the firm of booksellers' agents.

There was a pause.

"You are simply cutting my throat!" said the visitor.

"But in a year's time shall we have placed a hundred copies of *Leonide*?" said the other voice. "If books went off as fast as the publishers would like, we should be millionaires, my good sir; but they don't, they go as the public pleases. There is some one now bringing out an edition of Scott's novels at eighteen sous per volume, three livres twelve sous per copy, and you want me to give you more for your stale remainders? No. If you mean me to push this novel of yours, you must make it worth my while.--Vidal!"

A stout man, with a pen behind his ear, came down from his desk.

"How many copies of Ducange did you place last journey?" asked Porchon of his partner.

"Two hundred of *Le Petit Vieillard de Calais*, but to sell them I was obliged to cry down two books which pay in less commission, and uncommonly fine 'nightingales' they are now.

(A "nightingale," as Lucien afterwards learned, is a bookseller's name for books that linger on hand, perched out of sight in the loneliest nooks in the shop.)

"And besides," added Vidal, "Picard is bringing out some novels, as you know. We have been promised twenty per cent on the published price to make the thing a success."

"Very well, at twelve months," the publisher answered in a piteous voice, thunderstruck by Vidal's confidential remark.

"Is it an offer?" Porchon inquired curtly.

"Yes." The stranger went out. After he had gone, Lucien heard Porchon say to Vidal:

"We have three hundred copies on order now. We will keep him waiting for his settlement, sell the *Leonides* for five francs net, settlement in six months, and----"

"And that will be fifteen hundred francs into our pockets," said Vidal.

"Oh, I saw quite well that he was in a fix. He is giving Ducange four thousand francs for two thousand copies."

Lucien cut Vidal short by appearing in the entrance of the den.

"I have the honor of wishing you a good day, gentlemen," he said, addressing both partners. The booksellers nodded slightly.

"I have a French historical romance after the style of Scott. It is called *The Archer of Charles IX.*; I propose to offer it to you----"

Porchon glanced at Lucien with lustreless eyes, and laid his pen down on the desk. Vidal stared rudely at the author.

"We are not publishing booksellers, sir; we are booksellers' agents," he said. "When we bring out a book ourselves, we only deal in well-known names; and we only take serious literature besides--history and epitomes."

"But my book is very serious. It is an attempt to set the struggle between Catholics and Calvinists in its true light; the Catholics were supporters of absolute monarchy, and the Protestants for a republic."

"M. Vidal!" shouted an assistant. Vidal fled.

"I don't say, sir, that your book is not a masterpiece," replied Porchon, with scanty civility, "but we only deal in books that are ready printed. Go and see somebody that buys manuscripts. There is old Doguereau in the Rue du Coq, near the Louvre, he is in the romance line. If you had only spoken sooner, you might have seen Pollet, a competitor of Doguereau and of the publisher in the Wooden Galleries."

"I have a volume of poetry----"

"M. Porchon!" somebody shouted.

"*Poetry*!" Porchon exclaimed angrily. "For what do you take me?" he added, laughing in Lucien's face. And he dived into the regions of the back shop.

Lucien went back across the Pont Neuf absorbed in reflection. From all that he understood of this mercantile dialect, it appeared that books, like cotton nightcaps, were to be regarded as articles of merchandise to be sold dear and bought cheap.

"I have made a mistake," said Lucien to himself; but, all the same, this rough-and-ready practical aspect of literature made an impression upon him.

In the Rue du Coq he stopped in front of a modest-looking shop, which he had passed before. He saw the inscription DOGUEREAU, BOOKSELLER, painted above it in yellow letters on a green ground, and remembered that he had seen the name at the foot of the title-page of several novels at Blosse's reading-room. In he went, not without the inward trepidation which a man of any imagination feels at the prospect of a battle. Inside the shop he discovered an odd-looking old man, one of the queer characters of the trade in the days of the Empire.

Doguereau wore a black coat with vast square skirts, when fashion required swallow-tail coats. His waistcoat was of some cheap material, a checked pattern of many colors; a steel chain, with a copper key attached to it, hung from his fob and dangled down over a roomy pair of black nether garments. The booksellers' watch must have been the size of an onion. Iron-gray ribbed stockings, and shoes with silver buckles completed is costume. The old man's head was bare, and ornamented with a fringe of grizzled locks, quite poetically scanty. "Old Doguereau," as Porchon styled him, was dressed half like a professor of belles-lettres as to his trousers and shoes, half like a tradesman with respect to the variegated waistcoat, the stockings, and the watch; and the same odd mixture appeared in the man himself. He united the magisterial, dogmatic air, and the hollow countenance of the professor of rhetoric with the sharp eyes, suspicious mouth, and vague uneasiness of the bookseller.

"M. Doguereau?" asked Lucien.

"That is my name, sir."

"You are very young," remarked the bookseller.

"My age, sir, has nothing to do with the matter."

"True," and the old bookseller took up the manuscript. "Ah, begad! *The Archer of Charles IX.*, a good title. Let us see now, young man, just tell me your subject in a word or two."

"It is a historical work, sir, in the style of Scott. The character of the struggle between the Protestants and Catholics is depicted as a struggle between two opposed systems of government, in which the throne is seriously endangered. I have taken the Catholic side."

"Eh! but you have ideas, young man. Very well, I will read your book, I promise you. I would rather have had something more in Mrs. Radcliffe's style; but if you are industrious, if you have some notion of style, conceptions, ideas, and the art of telling a story, I don't ask better than to be of use to you. What do we want but good manuscripts?"

"When can I come back?"

"I am going into the country this evening; I shall be back again the day after tomorrow. I shall have read your manuscript by that time; and if it suits me, we might come to terms that very day."

Seeing his acquaintance so easy, Lucien was inspired with the unlucky idea of bringing the *Marguerites* upon the scene.

"I have a volume of poetry as well, sir----" he began.

"Oh! you are a poet! Then I don't want your romance," and the old man handed back the manuscript. "The rhyming fellows come to grief when they try their hands at prose. In prose you can't use words that mean nothing; you absolutely must say something."

"But Sir Walter Scott, sir, wrote poetry as well as----"

"That is true," said Doguereau, relenting. He guessed that the young fellow before him was poor, and kept the manuscript. "Where do you live? I will come and see you."

Lucien, all unsuspicious of the idea at the back of the old man's head, gave his address; he did not see that he had to do with a bookseller of the old school, a survival of the eighteenth century, when booksellers tried to keep Voltaires and Montesquieus starving in garrets under lock and key.

"The Latin Quarter. I am coming back that very way," said Doguereau, when he had read the address.

"Good man!" thought Lucien, as he took his leave. "So I have met with a friend to young authors, a man of taste who knows something. That is the kind of man for me! It is just as I said to David--talent soon makes its way in Paris."

Lucien went home again happy and light of heart; he dreamed of glory. He gave not another thought to the ominous words which fell on his ear as he stood by the counter in Vidal and Porchon's shop; he beheld himself the richer by twelve hundred francs at least. Twelve hundred francs! It meant a year in Paris, a whole year of preparation for the work that he meant to do. What plans he built on that hope! What sweet dreams, what visions of a life established on a basis of work! Mentally he found new quarters, and settled himself in them; it would not have taken much to set him making a purchase or two. He could only stave off impatience by constant reading at Blosse's.

Two days later old Doguereau come to the lodgings of his budding Sir Walter Scott. He was struck with the pains which Lucien had taken with the style of this his first work, delighted with the strong contrasts of character sanctioned by the epoch, and surprised at the spirited imagination which a young writer always displays in the scheming of a first plot--he had not been spoiled, thought old Daddy Doguereau. He had made up his mind to give a thousand francs for *The Archer of Charles IX.*; he would buy the copyright out and out, and bind Lucien by an engagement for several books, but when he came to look at the house, the old fox thought better of it.

"A young fellow that lives here has none but simple tastes," said he to himself; "he is fond of study, fond of work; I need not give more than eight hundred francs."

"Fourth floor," answered the landlady, when he asked for M. Lucien de Rubempre. The old bookseller, peering up, saw nothing but the sky above the fourth floor.

"This young fellow," thought he, "is a good-looking lad; one might go so far as to say that he is very handsome. If he were to make too much money, he would only fall into dissipated ways, and then he would not work. In the interests of us both, I shall only offer six hundred francs, in coin though, not paper."

He climbed the stairs and gave three raps at the door. Lucien came to open it. The room was forlorn in its bareness. A bowl of milk and a penny roll stood on the table. The destitution of genius made an impression on Daddy Doguereau.

"Let him preserve these simple habits of life, this frugality, these modest requirements," thought he.--Aloud he said: "It is a pleasure to me to see you. Thus, sir, lived Jean-Jacques, whom you resemble in more ways than one. Amid such surroundings the fire of genius shines brightly; good work is done in such rooms as these. This is how men of letters should work, instead of living riotously in cafes and restaurants, wasting their time and talent and our money."

He sat down.

"Your romance is not bad, young man. I was a professor of rhetoric once; I know French history, there are some capital things in it. You have a future before you, in fact."

"Oh! sir."

"No; I tell you so. We may do business together. I will buy your romance."

Lucien's heart swelled and throbbed with gladness. He was about to enter the world of literature; he should see himself in print at last.

"I will give you four hundred francs," continued Doguereau in honeyed accents, and he looked at Lucien with an air which seemed to betoken an effort of generosity.

"The volume?" queried Lucien.

"For the romance," said Doguereau, heedless of Lucien's surprise. "In ready money," he added; "and you shall undertake to write two books for me every year for six years. If the first book is out of print in six months, I will give you six hundred francs for the others. So, if you write two books each year, you will be making a hundred francs a month; you will have a sure income, you will be well off. There are some authors whom I only pay three hundred francs for a romance; I give two hundred for translations of English books. Such prices would have been exorbitant in the old days."

"Sir, we cannot possibly come to an understanding. Give me back my manuscript, I beg," said Lucien, in a cold chill.

"Here it is," said the old bookseller. "You know nothing of business, sir. Before an author's first book can appear, a publisher is bound to sink sixteen hundred francs on the paper and the printing of it. It is easier to write a romance than to find all that money. I have a hundred romances in manuscript, and I have not a hundred and sixty thousand francs in my cash box, alas! I have not made so much in all these twenty years that I have been a bookseller. So you don't make a fortune by printing romances, you see. Vidal and Porchon only take them of us on conditions that grow harder and harder day by day. You have only your time to lose, while I am obliged to disburse two thousand francs. If we fail, *habent sua fata libelli*, I lose two thousand francs; while, as for you, you simply hurl an ode at the thick-headed public. When you have thought over this that I have the honor of telling you, you will come back to me.--*You will come back to me*!" he asserted authoritatively, by way of reply to a scornful gesture made involuntarily by Lucien. "So far from finding a publisher obliging enough to risk two thousand francs for an unknown writer, you will not find a publisher's clerk that will trouble himself to look through your screed. Now that I have read it I can point out a good many slips in grammar. You have put *observer* for *faire observer* and *malgre que. Malgre* is a preposition, and requires an object."

Lucien appeared to be humiliated.

"When I see you again, you will have lost a hundred francs," he added. "I shall only give a hundred crowns."

With that he rose and took his leave. On the threshold he said, "If you had not something in you, and a future before you; if I did not take an interest in studious youth, I should not have made you such a handsome offer. A hundred francs per month! Think of it! After all, a romance in a drawer is not eating its head off like a horse in a stable, nor will it find you in victuals either, and that's a fact."

Lucien snatched up his manuscript and dashed it on the floor.

"I would rather burn it, sir!" he exclaimed.

"You have a poet's head," returned his senior.

Lucien devoured his bread and supped his bowl of milk, then he went downstairs. His room was not large enough for him; he was turning round and round in it like a lion in a cage at the Jardin des Plantes.

At the Bibliotheque Saint-Genevieve, whither Lucien was going, he had come to know a stranger by sight; a young man of five-and-twenty or thereabouts, working with the sustained industry which nothing can disturb nor distract, the sign by which your genuine literary worker is known. Evidently the young man had been reading there for some time, for the librarian and attendants all knew him and paid him special attention; the librarian would even allow him to take away books, with which Lucien saw him return in the morning. In the stranger student he recognized a brother in penury and hope.

Pale-faced and slight and thin, with a fine forehead hidden by masses of black, tolerably unkempt hair, there was something about him that attracted indifferent eyes: it was a vague resemblance which he bore to portraits of the young Bonaparte, engraved from Robert Lefebvre's picture. That engraving is a poem of melancholy intensity, of suppressed ambition, of power working below the surface. Study the face carefully, and you will discover genius in it and discretion, and all the subtlety and greatness of the man. The portrait has speaking eyes like a woman's; they look out, greedy of space, craving difficulties to vanquish. Even if the name of Bonaparte were not written beneath it, you would gaze long at that face.

Lucien's young student, the incarnation of this picture, usually wore footed trousers, shoes with thick soles to them, an overcoat of coarse cloth, a black cravat, a waistcoat of some gray-and-white material buttoned to the chin, and a cheap hat. Contempt for superfluity in dress was visible in his whole person. Lucien also discovered that the mysterious stranger with that unmistakable stamp which genius sets upon the forehead of its slaves was one of Flicoteaux's most regular customers; he ate to live, careless of the fare which appeared to be familiar to him, and drank water. Wherever Lucien saw him, at the library or at Flicoteaux's, there was a dignity in his manner, springing doubtless from the consciousness of a purpose that filled his life, a dignity which made him unapproachable. He had the expression of a thinker, meditation dwelt on the fine nobly carved brow. You could tell from the dark bright eyes, so clear-sighted and quick to observe, that their owner was wont to probe to the bottom of things. He gesticulated very little, his demeanor was grave. Lucien felt an involuntary respect for him.

Many times already the pair had looked at each other at the Bibliotheque or at Flicoteaux's; many times they had been on the point of speaking, but neither of them had ventured so far as yet. The silent young man went off to the further end of the library, on the side at right angles to the Place de la Sorbonne, and Lucien had no opportunity of making his acquaintance, although he felt drawn to a worker whom he knew by indescribable tokens for a character of no common order. Both, as they came to know afterwards, were unsophisticated and shy, given to fears which cause a pleasurable emotion to solitary creatures. Perhaps they never would have been brought into communication if they had not come across each other that day of Lucien's disaster; for as Lucien turned into the Rue des Gres, he saw the student coming away from the Bibliotheque Sainte-Genevieve.

"The library is closed; I don't know why, monsieur," said he.

Tears were standing in Lucien's eyes; he expressed his thanks by one of those gestures that speak more eloquently than words, and unlock hearts at once when two men meet in youth. They went together along the Rue des Gres towards the Rue de la Harpe.

"As that is so, I shall go to the Luxembourg for a walk," said Lucien. "When you have come out, it is not easy to settle down to work again."

"No; one's ideas will not flow in the proper current," remarked the stranger. "Something seems to have annoyed you, monsieur?"

"I have just had a queer adventure," said Lucien, and he told the history of his visit to the Quai, and gave an account of his subsequent dealings with the old bookseller. He gave his name and said a word or two of his position. In one month or thereabouts he had spent sixty francs on his board, thirty for lodging, twenty more francs in going to the theatre, and ten at Blosse's reading room--one hundred and twenty francs in all, and now he had just a hundred and twenty francs in hand.

"Your story is mine, monsieur, and the story of ten or twelve hundred young fellows besides who come from the country to Paris every year. There are others even worse off than we are. Do you see that theatre?" he continued, indicating the turrets of the Odeon. "There came one day to lodge in one of the houses in the square a man of talent who had fallen into the lowest depths of poverty. He was married, in addition to the misfortunes which we share with him, to a wife whom he loved; and the poorer or the richer, as you will, by two children. He was burdened with debt, but he put his faith in his pen. He took a comedy in five acts to the Odeon; the comedy was accepted, the management arranged to bring it out, the actors learned their parts, the stage manager urged on the rehearsals. Five several bits of luck, five dramas to be performed in real life, and far harder tasks than the writing of a five-act play. The poor author lodged in a garret; you can see the place from here. He drained his last resources to live until the first representation; his wife pawned her clothes, they all lived on dry bread. On the day of the final rehearsal, the household owed fifty francs in the Quarter to the baker, the milkwoman, and the porter. The author had only the strictly necessary clothes--a coat, a shirt, trousers, a waistcoat, and a pair of boots. He felt sure of his success; he kissed his wife. The end of their troubles was at hand. 'At last! There is nothing against us now,' cried he.--'Yes, there is fire,' said his wife; 'look, the Odeon is on fire!'--The Odeon was on fire, monsieur. So do not you complain. You have clothes, you have neither wife nor child, you have a hundred and twenty francs for emergencies in your pocket, and you owe no one a penny.--Well, the piece went through a hundred and fifty representations at the Theatre Louvois. The King allowed the author a pension. 'Genius is patience,' as Buffon said. And patience after all is a man's nearest approach to Nature's processes of creation. What is Art, monsieur, but Nature concentrated?"

By this time the young men were striding along the walks of the Luxembourg, and in no long time Lucien learned the name of the stranger who was doing his best to administer comfort. That name has since grown famous. Daniel d'Arthez is one of the most illustrious of living men of letters; one of the rare few who show us an example of "a noble gift with a noble nature combined," to quote a poet's fine thought.

"There is no cheap route to greatness," Daniel went on in his kind voice. "The works of Genius are watered with tears. The gift that is in you, like an existence in the physical world, passes through childhood and its maladies. Nature sweeps away sickly or deformed creatures, and Society rejects an imperfectly developed talent. Any man who means to rise above the rest must make ready for a struggle and be undaunted by difficulties. A great writer is a martyr who does not die; that is all.--There is the stamp of genius on your forehead," d'Arthez continued, enveloping Lucien by a glance; "but unless you have within you the will of genius, unless you are gifted with angelic patience, unless, no matter how far the freaks of Fate have set you from your destined goal, you can find the way to your Infinite as the turtles in the Indies find their way to the ocean, you had better give up at once."

"Then do you yourself expect these ordeals?" asked Lucien.

"Trials of every kind, slander and treachery, and effrontery and cunning, the rivals who act unfairly, and the keen competition of the literary market," his companion said resignedly. "What is a first loss, if only your work was good?"

"Will you look at mine and give me your opinion?" asked Lucien.

"So be it," said d'Arthez. "I am living in the Rue des Quatre-Vents. Desplein, one of the most illustrious men of genius in our time, the greatest surgeon that the world has known, once endured the martyrdom of early struggles with the first difficulties of a glorious career in the same house. I think of that every night, and the thought gives me the stock of courage that I need every morning. I am living in the very room where, like Rousseau, he had no Theresa. Come in an hour's time. I shall be in."

The poets grasped each other's hands with a rush of melancholy and tender feeling inexpressible in words, and went their separate ways; Lucien to fetch his manuscript, Daniel d'Arthez to pawn his watch and buy a couple of faggots. The weather was cold, and his new-found friend should find a fire in his room.

Lucien was punctual. He noticed at once that the house was of an even poorer class than the Hotel de Cluny. A staircase gradually became visible at the further end of a dark passage; he mounted to the fifth floor, and found d'Arthez's room.

A bookcase of dark-stained wood, with rows of labeled cardboard cases on the shelves, stood between the two crazy windows. A gaunt, painted wooden bedstead, of the kind seen in school dormitories, a night-table, picked up cheaply somewhere, and a couple of horsehair armchairs, filled the further end of the room. The wall-paper, a Highland plaid pattern, was glazed over with the grime of years. Between the window and the grate stood a long table littered with papers, and opposite the fireplace there was a cheap mahogany chest of drawers. A second-hand carpet covered the floor-

-a necessary luxury, for it saved firing. A common office armchair, cushioned with leather, crimson once, but now hoary with wear, was drawn up to the table. Add half-a-dozen rickety chairs, and you have a complete list of the furniture. Lucien noticed an old-fashioned candle-sconce for a card-table, with an adjustable screen attached, and wondered to see four wax candles in the sockets. D'Arthez explained that he could not endure the smell of tallow, a little trait denoting great delicacy of sense perception, and the exquisite sensibility which accompanies it.

The reading lasted for seven hours. Daniel listened conscientiously, forbearing to interrupt by word or comment--one of the rarest proofs of good taste in a listener.

"Well?" queried Lucien, laying the manuscript on the chimney-piece.

"You have made a good start on the right way," d'Arthez answered judicially, "but you must go over your work again. You must strike out a different style for yourself if you do not mean to ape Sir Walter Scott, for you have taken him for your model. You begin, for instance, as he begins, with long conversations to introduce your characters, and only when they have said their say does description and action follow.

"This opposition, necessary in all work of a dramatic kind, comes last. Just put the terms of the problem the other way round. Give descriptions, to which our language lends itself so admirably, instead of diffuse dialogue, magnificent in Scott's work, but colorless in your own. Lead naturally up to your dialogue. Plunge straight into the action. Treat your subject from different points of view, sometimes in a side-light, sometimes retrospectively; vary your methods, in fact, to diversify your work. You may be original while adapting the Scots novelist's form of dramatic dialogue to French history. There is no passion in Scott's novels; he ignores passion, or perhaps it was interdicted by the hypocritical manners of his country. Woman for him is duty incarnate. His heroines, with possibly one or two exceptions, are all alike; he has drawn them all from the same model, as painters say. They are, every one of them, descended from Clarissa Harlowe. And returning continually, as he did, to the same idea of woman, how could he do otherwise than produce a single type, varied only by degrees of vividness in the coloring? Woman brings confusion into Society through passion. Passion gives infinite possibilities. Therefore depict passion; you have one great resource open to you, foregone by the great genius for the sake of providing family reading for prudish England. In France you have the charming sinner, the brightly-colored life of Catholicism, contrasted with sombre Calvinistic figures on a background of the times when passions ran higher than at any other period of our history.

"Every epoch which has left authentic records since the time of Charles the Great calls for at least one romance. Some require four or five; the periods of Louis XIV., of Henry IV., of Francis I., for instance. You would give us in this way a picturesque history of France, with the costumes and furniture, the houses and their interiors, and domestic life, giving us the spirit of the time instead of a laborious narration of ascertained facts. Then there is further scope for originality. You can remove some of the popular delusions which disfigure the memories of most of our kings. Be bold enough in this first work of yours to rehabilitate the great magnificent figure of Catherine, whom you have sacrificed to the prejudices which still cloud her name. And finally, paint Charles IX. for us as he really was, and not as Protestant writers have made him. Ten years of persistent work, and fame and fortune will be yours."

By this time it was nine o'clock; Lucien followed the example set in secret by his future friend by asking him to dine at Eldon's, and spent twelve francs at that restaurant. During the dinner Daniel admitted Lucien into the secret of his hopes and studies. Daniel d'Arthez would not allow that any writer could attain to a pre-eminent rank without a profound knowledge of metaphysics. He was engaged in ransacking the spoils of ancient and modern philosophy, and in the assimilation of it all; he would be like Moliere, a profound philosopher first, and a writer of comedies afterwards. He was studying the world of books and the living world about him--thought and fact. His friends were learned naturalists, young doctors of medicine, political writers and artists, a number of earnest students full of promise.

D'Arthez earned a living by conscientious and ill-paid work; he wrote articles for encyclopaedias, dictionaries of biography and natural science, doing just enough to enable him to live while he followed his own bent, and neither more nor less. He had a piece of imaginative work on hand, undertaken solely for the sake of studying the resources of language, an important psychological study in the form of a novel, unfinished as yet, for d'Arthez took it up or laid it down as the humor took him, and kept it for days of great distress. D'Arthez's revelations of himself were made very simply, but to Lucien he seemed like an intellectual giant; and by eleven o'clock, when they left the restaurant, he began to feel a sudden, warm friendship for this nature, unconscious of its loftiness, this unostentatious worth.

Lucien took d'Arthez's advice unquestioningly, and followed it out to the letter. The most magnificent palaces of fancy had been suddenly flung open to him by a nobly-gifted mind, matured already by thought and critical examinations undertaken for their own sake, not for publication, but for the solitary thinker's own satisfaction. The burning coal had been laid on the lips of the poet of Angouleme, a word uttered by a hard student in Paris had fallen upon ground prepared to receive it in the provincial. Lucien set about recasting his work.

In his gladness at finding in the wilderness of Paris a nature abounding in generous and sympathetic feeling, the distinguished provincial did, as all young creatures hungering for affection are wont to do; he fastened, like a chronic disease, upon this one friend that he had found. He called for D'Arthez on his way to the Bibliotheque, walked with him on fine days in the Luxembourg Gardens, and went with his friend every evening as far as the door of his lodging-house after sitting next to him at Flicoteaux's. He pressed close to his friend's side as a soldier might keep by a comrade on the frozen Russian plains.

During those early days of his acquaintance, he noticed, not without chagrin, that his presence imposed a certain restraint on the circle of Daniel's intimates. The talk of those superior beings of whom d'Arthez spoke to him with such concentrated enthusiasm kept within the bounds of a reserve but little in keeping with the evident warmth of their friendships. At these times Lucien discreetly took his leave, a feeling of curiosity mingling with the sense of something like pain at the ostracism to which he was subjected by these strangers, who all addressed each other by their Christian names. Each one of them, like d'Arthez, bore the stamp of genius upon his forehead.

After some private opposition, overcome by d'Arthez without Lucien's knowledge, the newcomer was at length judged worthy to make one of the *cenacle* of lofty thinkers. Henceforward he was to be one of a little group of young men who met almost every evening in d'Arthez's room, united by the keenest sympathies and by the earnestness of their intellectual life. They all foresaw a great writer in d'Arthez; they looked upon him as their chief since the loss of one of their number, a mystical genius, one of the most extraordinary intellects of the age. This former leader had gone back to his province for reasons on which it serves no purpose to enter, but Lucien often heard them speak of this absent friend as "Louis." Several of the group were destined to fall by the way; but others, like d'Arthez, have since won all the fame that was their due. A few details as to the circle will readily explain Lucien's strong feeling of interest and curiosity.

One among those who still survive was Horace Bianchon, then a house-student at the Hotel-Dieu; later, a shining light at the Ecole de Paris, and now so well known that it is needless to give any description of his appearance, genius, or character.

Next came Leon Giraud, that profound philosopher and bold theorist, turning all systems inside out, criticising, expressing, and formulating, dragging them all to the feet of his idol--Humanity; great even in his errors, for his honesty ennobled his mistakes. An intrepid toiler, a conscientious scholar, he became the acknowledged head of a school of moralists and politicians. Time alone can pronounce upon the merits of his theories; but if his convictions have drawn him into paths in which none of his old comrades tread, none the less he is still their faithful friend.

Art was represented by Joseph Bridau, one of the best painters among the younger men. But for a too impressionable nature, which made havoc of Joseph's heart, he might have continued the traditions of the great Italian masters, though, for that matter, the last word has not yet been said concerning him. He combines Roman outline with Venetian color; but love is fatal to his work, love not merely transfixes his heart, but sends his arrow through the brain, deranges the course of his life, and sets the victim describing the strangest zigzags. If the mistress of the moment is too kind or too cruel, Joseph will send into the Exhibition sketches where the drawing is clogged with color, or pictures finished under the stress of some imaginary woe, in which he gave his whole attention to the drawing, and left the color to take care of itself. He is a constant disappointment to his friends and the public; yet Hoffmann would have worshiped him for his daring experiments in the realms of art. When Bridau is wholly himself he is admirable, and as praise is sweet to him, his disgust is great when one praises the failures in which he alone discovers all that is lacking in the eyes of the public. He is whimsical to the last degree. His friends have seen him destroy a finished picture because, in his eyes, it looked too smooth. "It is overdone," he would say; "it is niggling work."

With his eccentric, yet lofty nature, with a nervous organization and all that it entails of torment and delight, the craving for perfection becomes morbid. Intellectually he is akin to Sterne, though he is not a literary worker. There is an indescribable piquancy about his epigrams and sallies of thought. He is eloquent, he knows how to love, but the uncertainty that appears in his execution is a part of the very nature of the man. The brotherhood loved him for the very qualities which the philistine would style defects.

Last among the living comes Fulgence Ridal. No writer of our times possesses more of the exuberant spirit of pure comedy than this poet, careless of fame, who will fling his more commonplace productions to theatrical managers, and keep the most charming scenes in the seraglio of his brain for himself and his friends. Of the public he asks just sufficient to secure his independence, and then declines to do anything more. Indolent and prolific as Rossini, compelled, like great poet-comedians, like Moliere and Rabelais, to see both sides of everything, and all that is to be said both for and against, he is a sceptic, ready to laugh at all things. Fulgence Ridal is a great practical philosopher. His worldly wisdom, his genius for observation, his contempt for fame ("fuss," as he calls it) have not seared a kind heart. He is as energetic on behalf of another as he is careless where his own interests are concerned; and if he bestirs himself, it is for a friend. Living up to his Rabelaisian mask, he is no enemy to good cheer, though he never goes out of his way to find it; he is melancholy and gay. His friends dubbed him the "Dog of the Regiment." You could have no better portrait of the man than his nickname.

Three more of the band, at least as remarkable as the friends who have just been sketched in outline, were destined to fall by the way. Of these, Meyraux was the first. Meyraux died after stirring up the famous controversy between Cuvier and Geoffroy Saint-Hilaire, a great question which divided the whole scientific world into two opposite camps, with these two men of equal genius as leaders. This befell some months before the death of the champion of rigorous analytical science as opposed to the pantheism of one who is still living to bear an honored name in Germany. Meyraux was the friend of that "Louis" of whom death was so soon to rob the intellectual world.

With these two, both marked by death, and unknown today in spite of their wide knowledge and their genius, stands a third, Michel Chrestien, the great Republican thinker, who dreamed of European Federation, and had no small share in bringing about the Saint-Simonian movement of 1830. A politician of the calibre of Saint-Just and Danton, but simple, meek as a maid, and brimful of illusions and loving-kindness; the owner of a singing voice which would have sent Mozart, or Weber, or Rossini into ecstasies, for his singing of certain songs of Beranger's could intoxicate the heart in you with poetry, or hope, or love--Michel Chrestien, poor as Lucien, poor as Daniel d'Arthez, as all the rest of his friends, gained a living with the haphazard indifference of a Diogenes. He indexed lengthy works, he drew up prospectuses for booksellers, and kept his doctrines to himself, as the grave keeps the secrets of the dead. Yet the gay bohemian of intellectual life, the great statesman who might have changed the face of the world, fell as a private soldier in the cloister of Saint-Merri; some shopkeeper's bullet struck down one of the noblest creatures that ever trod French soil, and Michel Chrestien died for other doctrines than his own. His Federation scheme was more dangerous to the aristocracy of Europe than the Republican propaganda; it was more feasible and less extravagant than the hideous doctrines of indefinite liberty proclaimed by the young madcaps who assume the character of heirs of the Convention. All who knew the noble plebeian wept for him; there is not one of them but remembers, and often remembers, a great obscure politician.

Esteem and friendship kept the peace between the extremes of hostile opinion and conviction represented in the brotherhood. Daniel d'Arthez came of a good family in Picardy. His belief in the Monarchy was quite as strong as Michel Chrestien's faith in European Federation. Fulgence Ridal scoffed at Leon Giraud's philosophical doctrines, while Giraud himself prophesied for d'Arthez's benefit the approaching end of Christianity and the extinction of the institution of the family. Michel Chrestien, a believer in the religion of Christ, the divine lawgiver, who taught the equality of men, would defend the immortality of the soul from Bianchon's scalpel, for Horace Bianchon was before all things an analyst.

There was plenty of discussion, but no bickering. Vanity was not engaged, for the speakers were also the audience. They would talk over their work among themselves and take counsel of each other with the delightful openness of youth. If the matter in hand was serious, the opponent would leave his own position to enter into his friend's point of view; and being an impartial judge in a matter outside his own sphere, would prove the better helper; envy, the hideous treasure of disappointment, abortive talent, failure, and mortified vanity, was quite unknown among them. All of them, moreover, were going their separate ways. For these reasons, Lucien and others admitted to their society felt at their ease in it. Wherever you find real talent, you will find frank good fellowship and sincerity, and no sort of pretension, the wit that caresses the intellect and never is aimed at self-love.

When the first nervousness, caused by respect, wore off, it was unspeakably pleasant to make one of this elect company of youth. Familiarity did not exclude in each a consciousness of his own value, nor a profound esteem for his neighbor; and finally, as every member of the circle felt that he could afford to receive or to give, no one made a difficulty of accepting. Talk was unflagging, full of charm, and ranging over the most varied topics; words light as arrows sped to the mark. There was a strange contrast between the dire material poverty in which the young men lived and the splendor of their intellectual wealth. They looked upon the practical problems of existence simply as matter for friendly jokes. The cold weather happened to set in early that year. Five of d'Arthez's friends appeared one day, each concealing firewood under his cloak; the same idea had occurred to the five, as it sometimes happens that all the guests at a picnic are inspired with the notion of bringing a pie as their contribution.

All of them were gifted with the moral beauty which reacts upon the physical form, and, no less than work and vigils, overlays a youthful face with a shade of divine gold; purity of life and the fire of thought had brought refinement and regularity into features somewhat pinched and rugged. The poet's amplitude of brow was a striking characteristic common to them all; the bright, sparkling eyes told of cleanliness of life. The hardships of penury, when they were felt at all, were born so gaily and embraced with such enthusiasm, that they had left no trace to mar the serenity peculiar to the faces of the young who have no grave errors laid to their charge as yet, who have not stooped to any of the base compromises wrung from impatience of poverty by the strong desire to succeed. The temptation to use any means to this end is the greater since that men of letters are lenient with bad faith and extend an easy indulgence to treachery.

There is an element in friendship which doubles its charm and renders it indissoluble--a sense of certainty which is lacking in love. These young men were sure of themselves and of each other; the enemy of one was the enemy of all; the most urgent personal considerations would have been shattered if they had clashed with the sacred solidarity of their fellowship. All alike incapable of disloyalty, they could oppose a formidable No to any accusation brought against the absent and defend them with perfect confidence. With a like nobility of nature and strength of feeling, it was possible to think and speak freely on all matters of intellectual or scientific interest; hence the honesty of their friendships, the gaiety of their talk, and with this intellectual freedom of the community there was no fear of being misunderstood; they stood upon no ceremony with each other; they shared their troubles and joys, and gave thought and sympathy from full hearts. The charming delicacy of feeling which makes the tale of *Deux Amis* a treasury for great souls, was the rule of their daily life. It may be imagined, therefore, that their standard of requirements was not an easy one; they were too conscious of their worth, too well aware of their happiness, to care to trouble their life with the admixture of a new and unknown element.

This federation of interests and affection lasted for twenty years without a collision or disappointment. Death alone could thin the numbers of the noble Pleiades, taking first Louis Lambert, later Meyraux and Michel Chrestien.

When Michel Chrestien fell in 1832 his friends went, in spite of the perils of the step, to find his body at Saint-Merri; and Horace Bianchon, Daniel d'Arthez, Leon Giraud, Joseph Bridau, and Fulgence Ridal performed the last duties to the dead, between two political fires. By night they buried their beloved in the cemetery of Pere-Lachaise; Horace Bianchon, undaunted by the difficulties, cleared them away one after another--it was he indeed who besought the authorities for permission to bury the fallen insurgent and confessed to his old friendship with the dead Federalist. The little group of friends present at the funeral with those five great men will never forget that touching scene.

As you walk in the trim cemetery you will see a grave purchased in perpetuity, a grass-covered mound with a dark wooden cross above it, and the name in large red letters--MICHEL CHRESTIEN. There is no other monument like it. The friends thought to pay a tribute to the sternly simple nature of the man by the simplicity of the record of his death.

So, in that chilly garret, the fairest dreams of friendship were realized. These men were brothers leading lives of intellectual effort, loyally helping each other, making no reservations, not even of their worst thoughts; men of vast acquirements, natures tried in the crucible of poverty. Once admitted as an equal among such elect souls, Lucien represented beauty and poetry. They admired the sonnets which he read to them; they would ask him for a sonnet as he would ask Michel Chrestien for a song. And, in the desert of Paris, Lucien found an oasis in the Rue des Quatre-Vents.

At the beginning of October, Lucien had spent the last of his money on a little firewood; he was half-way through the task of recasting his work, the most strenuous of all toil, and he was penniless. As for Daniel d'Arthez, burning blocks of spent tan, and facing poverty like a hero, not a word of complaint came from him; he was as sober as any elderly spinster, and methodical as a miser. This courage called out Lucien's courage; he had only newly come into the circle, and shrank with invincible repugnance from speaking of his straits. One morning he went out, manuscript in hand, and reached the Rue du Coq; he would sell *The Archer of Charles IX.* to Doguereau; but Doguereau was out. Lucien little knew how indulgent great natures can be to the weaknesses of others. Every one of the friends had thought of the peculiar troubles besetting the poetic temperament, of the prostration which follows upon the struggle, when the soul has been overwrought by the contemplation of that nature which it is the task of art to reproduce. And strong as they were to endure their own ills, they felt keenly for Lucien's distress; they guessed that his stock of money was failing; and after all the pleasant evenings spent in friendly talk and deep meditations, after the poetry, the confidences, the bold flights over the fields of thought or into the far future of the nations, yet another trait was to prove how little Lucien had understood these new friends of his.

"Lucien, dear fellow," said Daniel, "you did not dine at Flicoteaux's yesterday, and we know why."

Lucien could not keep back the overflowing tears.

"You showed a want of confidence in us," said Michel Chrestien; "we shall chalk that up over the chimney, and when we have scored ten we will----"

"We have all of us found a bit of extra work," said Bianchon; "for my own part, I have been looking after a rich patient for Desplein; d'Arthez has written an article for the *Revue Encyclopedique*; Chrestien thought of going out to sing in the Champs Elysees of an evening with a pocket-handkerchief and four candles, but he found a pamphlet to write instead for a man who has a mind to go into politics, and gave his employer six hundred francs worth of Machiavelli; Leon Giraud borrowed fifty francs of his publisher, Joseph sold one or two sketches; and Fulgence's piece was given on Sunday, and there was a full house."

"Here are two hundred francs," said Daniel, "and let us say no more about it."

"Why, if he is not going to hug us all as if we had done something extraordinary!" cried Chrestien.

Lucien, meanwhile, had written to the home circle. His letter was a masterpiece of sensibility and goodwill, as well as a sharp cry wrung from him by distress. The answers which he received the next day will give some idea of the delight that Lucien took in this living encyclopedia of angelic spirits, each of whom bore the stamp of the art or science which he followed:--

David Sechard to Lucien.

"MY DEAR LUCIEN,--Enclosed herewith is a bill at ninety days, payable to your order, for two hundred francs. You can draw on M. Metivier, paper merchant, our Paris correspondent in the Rue Serpente. My good Lucien, we have absolutely nothing. Eve has undertaken the charge of the printing-house, and works at her task with such devotion, patience, and industry, that I bless heaven for giving me such an angel for a wife. She herself says that it is impossible to send you the least help. But I think, my friend now that you are started in so promising a way, with such great and noble hearts for your companions, that you can hardly fail to reach the greatness to which you were born, aided as you are by intelligence almost divine in Daniel d'Arthez and Michel Chrestien and Leon Giraud, and counseled by Meyraux and Bianchon and Ridal, whom we have come to know through your dear letter. So I have drawn this bill without Eve's knowledge, and I will contrive somehow to meet it when the time comes. Keep on your way, Lucien; it is rough, but it will be glorious. I can bear anything but the thought of you sinking into the sloughs of Paris, of which I saw so much. Have sufficient strength of mind to do as you are doing, and keep out of scrapes and bad company, wild young fellows and men of letters of a certain stamp, whom I learned to take at their just valuation when I lived in Paris. Be a worthy compeer of the divine spirits whom we have learned to love through you. Your life will soon meet with its reward. Farewell, dearest brother; you have sent transports of joy to my heart. I did not expect such courage of you.

"DAVID."

Eve Sechard to Lucien.

"DEAR,--your letter made all of us cry. As for the noble hearts to whom your good angel surely led you, tell them that a mother and a poor young wife will pray for them night and morning; and if the most fervent prayers can reach the Throne of God, surely they will bring blessings upon you all. Their names are engraved upon my heart. Ah! some day I shall see your friends; I will go to Paris, if I have to walk the whole way, to thank them for their friendship for you, for to me the thought has been like balm to smarting wounds. We are working like day laborers here, dear. This husband of mine, the unknown great man whom I love more and more every day, as I discover moment by moment the wealth of his nature, leaves the printing-house more and more to me. Why, I guess. Our poverty, yours, and ours, and our mother's, is heartbreaking to him. Our adored David is a Prometheus gnawed by a vulture, a haggard, sharp-beaked regret. As for himself, noble fellow, he scarcely thinks of himself; he is hoping to make a fortune for *us*. He spends his whole time in experiments in paper-making; he begged me to take his place and look after the business, and gives me as much help as his preoccupation allows. Alas! I shall be a mother soon. That should have been a crowning joy; but as things are, it saddens me. Poor mother! she has grown young again; she has found strength to go back to her tiring nursing. We should be happy if it were not for these money cares. Old Father Sechard will not give his son a farthing. David went over to see if he could borrow a little for you, for we were in despair over your letter. 'I know Lucien,' David said; 'he will lose his head and do something rash.'--I gave him a good scolding. 'My brother disappoint us in any way!' I told him, 'Lucien knows that I should die of sorrow.'--Mother and I have pawned a few things; David does not know about it, mother will redeem them as soon as she has made a little money. In this way we have managed to put together a hundred francs, which I am sending you by the coach. If I did not answer your last letter, do not remember it against me, dear; we were working all night just then. I have been working like a man. Oh, I had no idea that I was so strong!

"Mme. de Bargeton is a heartless woman; she has no soul; even if she cared for you no longer, she owed it to herself to use her influence for you and to help you when she had torn you from us to plunge you into that dreadful sea of Paris. Only by the special blessing of Heaven could you have met with true friends there among those crowds of men and innumerable interests. She is not worth a regret. I used to wish that there might be some devoted woman always with you, a second myself; but now I know that your friends will take my place, and I am happy. Spread your wings, my dear great genius, you will be our pride as well as our beloved.

"EVE."

"My darling," the mother wrote, "I can only add my blessing to all that your sister says, and assure you that you are more in my thoughts and in my prayers (alas!) than those whom I see daily; for some hearts, the absent are always in the right, and so it is with the heart of your mother."

So two days after the loan was offered so graciously, Lucien repaid it. Perhaps life had never seemed so bright to him as at that moment; but the touch of self-love in his joy did not escape the delicate sensibility and searching eyes of his friends.

"Any one might think that you were afraid to owe us anything," exclaimed Fulgence.

"Oh! the pleasure that he takes in returning the money is a very serious symptom to my mind," said Michel Chrestien. "It confirms some observations of my own. There is a spice of vanity in Lucien."

"He is a poet," said d'Arthez.

"But do you grudge me such a very natural feeling?" asked Lucien.

"We should bear in mind that he did not hide it," said Leon Giraud; "he is still open with us; but I am afraid that he may come to feel shy of us."

"And why?" Lucien asked.

"We can read your thoughts," answered Joseph Bridau.

"There is a diabolical spirit in you that will seek to justify courses which are utterly contrary to our principles. Instead of being a sophist in theory, you will be a sophist in practice."

"Ah! I am afraid of that," said d'Arthez. "You will carry on admirable debates in your own mind, Lucien, and take up a lofty position in theory, and end by blameworthy actions. You will never be at one with yourself."

"What ground have you for these charges?"

"Thy vanity, dear poet, is so great that it intrudes itself even into thy friendships!" cried Fulgence. "All vanity of that sort is a symptom of shocking egoism, and egoism poisons friendship."

"Oh! dear," said Lucien, "you cannot know how much I love you all."

"If you loved us as we love you, would you have been in such a hurry to return the money which we had such pleasure in lending? or have made so much of it?"

"We don't lend here; we give," said Joseph Bridau roughly.

"Don't think us unkind, dear boy," said Michel Chrestien; "we are looking forward. We are afraid lest some day you may prefer a petty revenge to the joys of pure friendship. Read Goethe's *Tasso*, the great master's greatest work, and you will see how the poet-hero loved gorgeous stuffs and banquets and triumph and applause. Very well, be Tasso without his folly. Perhaps the world and its pleasures tempt you? Stay with us. Carry all the cravings of vanity into the world of imagination. Transpose folly. Keep virtue for daily wear, and let imagination run riot, instead of doing, as d'Arthez says, thinking high thoughts and living beneath them."

Lucien hung his head. His friends were right.

"I confess that you are stronger than I," he said, with a charming glance at them. "My back and shoulders are not made to bear the burden of Paris life; I cannot struggle bravely. We are born with different temperaments and faculties, and you know better than I that faults and virtues have their reverse side. I am tired already, I confess."

"We will stand by you," said d'Arthez; "it is just in these ways that a faithful friendship is of use."

"The help that I have just received is precarious, and every one of us is just as poor as another; want will soon overtake me again. Chrestien, at the service of the first that hires him, can do nothing with the publishers; Bianchon is quite out of it; d'Arthez's booksellers only deal in scientific and technical books--they have no connection with publishers of new literature; and as for Horace and Fulgence Ridal and Bridau, their work lies miles away from the booksellers. There is no help for it; I must make up my mind one way or another."

"Stick by us, and make up your mind to it," said Bianchon. "Bear up bravely, and trust in hard work."

"But what is hardship for you is death for me," Lucien put in quickly.

"Before the cock crows thrice," smiled Leon Giraud, "this man will betray the cause of work for an idle life and the vices of Paris."

"Where has work brought you?" asked Lucien, laughing.

"When you start out from Paris for Italy, you don't find Rome half-way," said Joseph Bridau. "You want your pease to grow ready buttered for you."

The conversation ended in a joke, and they changed the subject. Lucien's friends, with their perspicacity and delicacy of heart, tried to efface the memory of the little quarrel; but Lucien knew thenceforward that it was no easy matter to deceive them. He soon fell into despair, which he was careful to hide from such stern mentors as he imagined them to be; and the Southern temper that runs so easily through the whole gamut of mental dispositions, set him making the most contradictory resolutions.

Again and again he talked of making the plunge into journalism; and time after time did his friends reply with a "Mind you do nothing of the sort!"

"It would be the tomb of the beautiful, gracious Lucien whom we love and know," said d'Arthez.

"You would not hold out for long between the two extremes of toil and pleasure which make up a journalist's life, and resistance is the very foundation of virtue. You would be so delighted to exercise your power of life and death over the offspring of the brain, that you would be an out-and-out journalist in two months' time. To be a journalist --that is to turn Herod in the republic of letters. The man who will say anything will end by sticking at nothing. That was Napoleon's maxim, and it explains itself."

"But you would be with me, would you not?" asked Lucien.

"Not by that time," said Fulgence. "If you were a journalist, you would no more think of us than the Opera girl in all her glory, with her adorers and her silk-lined carriage, thinks of the village at home and her cows and her sabots. You could never resist the temptation to pen a witticism, though it should bring tears to a friend's eyes. I come across journalists in theatre lobbies; it makes me shudder to see them. Journalism is an inferno, a bottomless pit of iniquity and treachery and lies; no one can traverse it undefiled, unless, like Dante, he is protected by Virgil's sacred laurel."

But the more the set of friends opposed the idea of journalism, the more Lucien's desire to know its perils grew and tempted him. He began to debate within his own mind; was it not ridiculous to allow want to find him a second time defenceless? He bethought him of the failure of his attempts to dispose of his first novel, and felt but little tempted to begin a second. How, besides, was he to live while he was writing another romance? One month of privation had exhausted his stock of patience. Why should he not do nobly that which journalists did ignobly and without principle? His friends insulted him with their doubts; he would convince them of his strength of mind. Some day, perhaps, he would be of use to them; he would be the herald of their fame!

"And what sort of a friendship is it which recoils from complicity?" demanded he one evening of Michel Chrestien; Lucien and Leon Giraud were walking home with their friend.

"We shrink from nothing," Michel Chrestien made reply. "If you were so unlucky as to kill your mistress, I would help you to hide your crime, and could still respect you; but if you were to turn spy, I should shun you with abhorrence, for a spy is systematically shameless and base. There you have journalism summed up in a sentence. Friendship can pardon error and the hasty impulse of passion; it is bound to be inexorable when a man deliberately traffics in his own soul, and intellect, and opinions."

"Why cannot I turn journalist to sell my volume of poetry and the novel, and then give up at once?"

"Machiavelli might do so, but not Lucien de Rubempre," said Leon Giraud.

"Very well," exclaimed Lucien; "I will show you that I can do as much as Machiavelli."

"Oh!" cried Michel, grasping Leon's hand, "you have done it, Leon. --Lucien," he continued, "you have three hundred francs in hand; you can live comfortably for three months; very well, then, work hard and write another romance. D'Arthez and Fulgence will help you with the plot; you will improve, you will be a novelist. And I, meanwhile, will enter one of those *lupanars* of thought; for three months I will be a journalist. I will sell your books to some bookseller or other by attacking his publications; I will write the articles myself; I will get others for you. We will organize a success; you shall be a great man, and still remain our Lucien."

"You must despise me very much, if you think that I should perish while you escape," said the poet.

"O Lord, forgive him; it is a child!" cried Michel Chrestien.

When Lucien's intellect had been stimulated by the evenings spent in d'Arthez's garret, he had made some study of the jokes and articles in the smaller newspapers. He was at least the equal, he felt, of the wittiest contributors; in private he tried some mental gymnastics of the kind, and went out one morning with the triumphant idea of finding some colonel of such light skirmishers of the press and enlisting in their ranks. He dressed in his best and crossed the bridges, thinking as he went that authors, journalists, and men of letters, his future comrades, in short, would show him rather more kindness and disinterestedness than the two species of booksellers who had so dashed his hopes. He should meet with fellow-feeling, and something of the kindly and grateful affection which he found in the *cenacle* of the Rue des Quatre-Vents. Tormented by emotion, consequent upon the presentiments to which men of imagination cling so fondly, half believing, half battling with their belief in them, he arrived in the Rue Saint-Fiacre off the Boulevard Montmartre. Before a house, occupied by the offices of a small newspaper, he stopped, and at the sight of it his heart began to throb as heavily as the pulses of a youth upon the threshold of some evil haunt.

Nevertheless, upstairs he went, and found the offices in the low *entresol* between the ground floor and the first story. The first room was divided down the middle by a partition, the lower half of solid wood, the upper lattice work to the ceiling. In this apartment Lucien discovered a one-armed pensioner supporting several reams of paper on his head with his remaining hand, while between his teeth he held the passbook which the Inland Revenue Department requires every newspaper to produce with each issue. This ill-favored individual, owner of a yellow countenance covered with red excrescences, to which he owed his nickname of "Coloquinte," indicated a personage behind the lattice as the Cerberus of the paper. This was an elderly officer with a medal on his chest and a silk skull-cap on his head; his nose was almost hidden by a pair of grizzled moustaches, and his person was hidden as completely in an ample blue overcoat as the body of the turtle in its carapace.

"From what date do you wish your subscription to commence, sir?" inquired the Emperor's officer.

"I did not come about a subscription," returned Lucien. Looking about him, he saw a placard fastened on a door, corresponding to the one by which he had entered, and read the words--EDITOR'S OFFICE, and below, in smaller letters, *No admittance except on business*.

"A complaint, I expect?" replied the veteran. "Ah! yes; we have been hard on Mariette. What would you have? I don't know the why and wherefore of it yet.--But if you want satisfaction, I am ready for you," he added, glancing at a collection of small arms and foils stacked in a corner, the armory of the modern warrior.

"That was still further from my intention, sir. I have come to speak to the editor."

"Nobody is ever here before four o'clock."

"Look you here, Giroudeau, old chap," remarked a voice, "I make it eleven columns; eleven columns at five francs apiece is fifty-five francs, and I have only been paid forty; so you owe me another fifteen francs, as I have been telling you."

These words proceeded from a little weasel-face, pallid and semi-transparent as the half-boiled white of an egg; two slits of eyes looked out of it, mild blue in tint, but appallingly malignant in expression; and the owner, an insignificant young man, was completely hidden by the veteran's opaque person. It was a blood-curdling voice, a sound between the mewing of a cat and the wheezy chokings of a hyena.

"Yes, yes, my little militiaman," retorted he of the medal, "but you are counting the headings and white lines. I have Finot's instructions to add up the totals of the lines, and to divide them by the proper number for each column; and after I performed that concentrating operation on your copy, there were three columns less."

"He doesn't pay for the blanks, the Jew! He reckons them in though when he sends up the total of his work to his partner, and he gets paid for them too. I will go and see Etienne Lousteau, Vernou----"

"I cannot go beyond my orders, my boy," said the veteran. "What! do you cry out against your foster-mother for a matter of fifteen francs? you that turn out an article as easily as I smoke a cigar. Fifteen francs! why, you will give a bowl of punch to your friends, or win an extra game of billiards, and there's an end of it!"

"Finot's savings will cost him very dear," said the contributor as he took his departure.

"Now, would not anybody think that he was Rousseau and Voltaire rolled in one?" the cashier remarked to himself as he glanced at Lucien.

"I will come in again at four, sir," said Lucien.

While the argument proceeded, Lucien had been looking about him. He saw upon the walls the portraits of Benjamin Constant, General Foy, and the seventeen illustrious orators of the Left, interspersed with caricatures at the expense of the Government; but he looked more particularly at the door of the sanctuary where, no doubt, the paper was elaborated, the witty paper that amused him daily, and enjoyed the privilege of ridiculing kings and the most portentous events, of calling anything and everything in question with a jest. Then he sauntered along the boulevards. It was an entirely novel amusement; and so agreeable did he find it, that, looking at the turret clocks, he saw the hour hands were pointing to four, and only then remembered that he had not breakfasted.

He went at once in the direction of the Rue Saint-Fiacre, climbed the stair, and opened the door.

The veteran officer was absent; but the old pensioner, sitting on a pile of stamped papers, was munching a crust and acting as sentinel resignedly. Coloquinte was as much accustomed to his work in the office as to the fatigue duty of former days, understanding as much or as little about it as the why and wherefore of forced marches made by the Emperor's orders. Lucien was inspired with the bold idea of deceiving that formidable functionary. He settled his hat on his head, and walked into the editor's office as if he were quite at home.

Looking eagerly about him, he beheld a round table covered with a green cloth, and half-a-dozen cherry-wood chairs, newly reseated with straw. The colored brick floor had not been waxed, but it was clean; so clean that the public, evidently, seldom entered the room. There was a mirror above the chimney-piece, and on the ledge below, amid a sprinkling of visiting-cards, stood a shopkeeper's clock, smothered with dust, and a couple of candlesticks with tallow dips thrust into their sockets. A few antique newspapers lay on the table beside an inkstand containing some black lacquer-like substance, and a collection of quill pens twisted into stars. Sundry dirty scraps of paper, covered with almost undecipherable hieroglyphs, proved to be manuscript articles torn across the top by the compositor to check off the sheets as they were set up. He admired a few rather clever caricatures, sketched on bits of brown paper by somebody who evidently had tried to kill time by killing something else to keep his hand in.

Other works of art were pinned in the cheap sea-green wall-paper. These consisted of nine pen-and-ink illustrations for *Le Solitaire*. The work had attained to such an unheard-of European popularity, that journalists evidently were tired of it.-- "The Solitary makes his first appearance in the provinces; sensation among the women.--The Solitary perused at a chateau.--Effect of the Solitary on domestic animals. --The Solitary explained to savage tribes, with the most brilliant results.--The Solitary translated into Chinese and presented by the author to the Emperor at Pekin.--The Mont Sauvage, Rape of Elodie." --(Lucien though this caricature very shocking, but he could not help laughing at it.)--"The Solitary under a canopy conducted in triumphal procession by the newspapers.--The Solitary breaks the press to splinters, and wounds the printers.--Read backwards, the superior beauties of the Solitary produce a sensation at the Academie."--On a newspaper-wrapper Lucien noticed a sketch of a contributor holding out his hat, and beneath it the words, "Finot! my hundred francs," and a name, since grown more notorious than famous.

Between the window and the chimney-piece stood a writing-table, a mahogany armchair, and a waste-paper basket on a strip of hearth-rug; the dust lay thick on all these objects. There were short curtains in the windows. About a score of new books lay on the writing-table, deposited there apparently during the day, together with prints, music, snuff-boxes of the "Charter" pattern, a copy of the ninth edition of *Le Solitaire* (the great joke of the moment), and some ten unopened letters.

Lucien had taken stock of this strange furniture, and made reflections of the most exhaustive kind upon it, when, the clock striking five, he returned to question the pensioner. Coloquinte had finished his crust, and was waiting with the patience of a commissionaire, for the man of medals, who perhaps was taking an airing on the boulevard.

At this conjuncture the rustle of a dress sounded on the stair, and the light unmistakable footstep of a woman on the threshold. The newcomer was passably pretty. She addressed herself to Lucien.

"Sir," she said, "I know why you cry up Mlle. Virginie's hats so much; and I have come to put down my name for a year's subscription in the first place; but tell me your conditions----"

"I am not connected with the paper, madame."

"Oh!"

"A subscription dating from October?" inquired the pensioner.

"What does the lady want to know?" asked the veteran, reappearing on the scene.

The fair milliner and the retired military man were soon deep in converse; and when Lucien, beginning to lose patience, came back to the first room, he heard the conclusion of the matter.

"Why, I shall be delighted, quite delighted, sir. Mlle. Florentine can come to my shop and choose anything she likes. Ribbons are in my department. So it is all quite settled. You will say no more about Virginie, a botcher that cannot design a new shape, while I have ideas of my own, I have."

Lucien heard a sound as of coins dropping into a cashbox, and the veteran began to make up his books for the day.

"I have been waiting here for an hour, sir," Lucien began, looking not a little annoyed.

"And 'they' have not come yet!" exclaimed Napoleon's veteran, civilly feigning concern. "I am not surprised at that. It is some time since I have seen 'them' here. It is the middle of the month, you see. Those fine fellows only turn up on pay days--the 29th or the 30th."

"And M. Finot?" asked Lucien, having caught the editor's name.

"He is in the Rue Feydeau, that's where he lives. Coloquinte, old chap, just take him everything that has come in today when you go with the paper to the printers."

"Where is the newspaper put together?" Lucien said to himself.

"The newspaper?" repeated the officer, as he received the rest of the stamp money from Coloquinte, "the newspaper?--broum! broum!--(Mind you are round at the printers' by six o'clock tomorrow, old chap, to send off the porters.)--The newspaper, sir, is written in the street, at the writers' houses, in the printing-office between eleven and twelve o'clock at night. In the Emperor's time, sir, these shops for spoiled paper were not known. Oh! he would have cleared them out with four men and a corporal; they would not have come over *him* with their talk. But that is enough of prattling. If my nephew finds it worth his while, and so long as they write for the son of the Other (broum! broum!) ----after all, there is no harm in that. Ah! by the way, subscribers don't seem to me to be advancing in serried columns; I shall leave my post."

"You seem to know all about the newspaper, sir," Lucien began.

"From a business point of view, broum! broum!" coughed the soldier, clearing his throat. "From three to five francs per column, according to ability.--Fifty lines to a column, forty letters to a line; no blanks; there you are! As for the staff, they are queer fish, little youngsters whom I wouldn't take on for the commissariat; and because they make fly tracks on sheets of white paper, they look down, forsooth, on an old Captain of Dragoons of the Guard, that retired with a major's rank after entering every European capital with Napoleon."

The soldier of Napoleon brushed his coat, and made as if he would go out, but Lucien, swept to the door, had courage enough to make a stand.

"I came to be a contributor of the paper," he said. "I am full of respect, I vow and declare, for a captain of the Imperial Guard, those men of bronze----"

"Well said, my little civilian, there are several kinds of contributors; which kind do you wish to be?" replied the trooper, bearing down on Lucien, and descending the stairs. At the foot of the flight he stopped, but it was only to light a cigar at the porter's box.

"If any subscribers come, you see them and take note of them, Mother Chollet.--Simply subscribers, never know anything but subscribers," he added, seeing that Lucien followed him. "Finot is my nephew; he is the only one of my family that has done anything to relieve me in my position. So when anybody comes to pick a quarrel with Finot, he finds old Giroudeau, Captain of the Dragoons of the Guard, that set out as a private in a cavalry regiment in the army of the Sambre-et-Meuse, and was fencing-master for five years to the First Hussars, army of Italy! One, two, and the man that had any complaints to make would be turned off into the dark," he added, making a lunge. "Now writers, my boy, are in different corps; there is the writer who writes and draws his pay; there is the writer who writes and gets nothing (a volunteer we call him); and, lastly, there is the writer who writes nothing, and he is by no means the stupidest, for he makes no mistakes; he gives himself out for a literary man, he is on the paper, he treats us to dinners, he loafs about the theatres, he keeps an actress, he is very well off. What do you mean to be?"

"The man that does good work and gets good pay."

"You are like the recruits. They all want to be marshals of France. Take old Giroudeau's word for it, and turn right about, in double-quick time, and go and pick up nails in the gutter like that good fellow yonder; you can tell by the look of him that he has been in the army.--Isn't it a shame that an old soldier who has walked into the jaws of death hundreds of times should be picking up old iron in the streets of Paris? Ah! God A'mighty! 'twas a shabby trick to desert the Emperor.--Well, my boy, the individual you saw this morning has made his forty francs a month. Are you going to do better? And, according to Finot, he is the cleverest man on the staff."

"When you enlisted in the Sambre-et-Meuse, did they talk about danger?"

"Rather."

"Very well?"

"Very well. Go and see my nephew Finot, a good fellow, as good a fellow as you will find, if you can find him, that is, for he is like a fish, always on the move. In his way of business, there is no writing, you see, it is setting others to write. That sort like gallivanting about with actresses better than scribbling on sheets of paper, it seems. Oh! they are queer customers, they are. Hope I may have the honor of seeing you again."

With that the cashier raised his formidable loaded cane, one of the defenders of Germainicus, and walked off, leaving Lucien in the street, as much bewildered by this picture of the newspaper world as he had formerly been by the practical aspects of literature at Messrs. Vidal and Porchon's establishment.

Ten several times did Lucien repair to the Rue Feydeau in search of Andoche Finot, and ten times he failed to find that gentleman. He went first thing in the morning; Finot had not come in. At noon, Finot had gone out; he was breakfasting at such and such a cafe. At the cafe, in answer to inquiries of the waitress, made after surmounting unspeakable repugnance, Lucien heard that Finot had just left the place. Lucien, at length tired out, began to regard Finot as a mythical and fabulous character; it appeared simpler to waylay Etienne Lousteau at Flicoteaux's. That youthful journalist would, doubtless, explain the mysteries that enveloped the paper for which he wrote.

Since the day, a hundred times blessed, when Lucien made the acquaintance of Daniel d'Arthez, he had taken another seat at Flicoteaux's. The two friends dined side by side, talking in lowered voices of the higher literature, of suggested subjects, and ways of presenting, opening up, and developing them. At the present time Daniel d'Arthez was correcting the manuscript of *The Archer of Charles IX*. He reconstructed whole chapters, and wrote the fine passages found therein, as well as the magnificent preface, which is, perhaps, the best thing in the book, and throws so much light on the work of the young school of literature. One day it so happened that Daniel had been waiting for Lucien, who now sat with his friend's hand in his own, when he saw Etienne Lousteau turn the door-handle. Lucien instantly dropped Daniel's hand, and told the waiter that he would dine at his old place by the counter. D'Arthez gave Lucien a glance of divine kindness, in which reproach was wrapped in forgiveness. The glance cut the poet to the quick; he took Daniel's hand and grasped it anew.

"It is an important question of business for me; I will tell you about it afterwards," said he.

Lucien was in his old place by the time that Lousteau reached the table; as the first comer, he greeted his acquaintance; they soon struck up a conversation, which grew so lively that Lucien went off in search of the manuscript of the *Marguerites*, while Lousteau finished his dinner. He had obtained leave to lay his sonnets before the journalist, and mistook the civility of the latter for willingness to find him a publisher, or a place on the paper. When Lucien came hurrying back again, he saw d'Arthez resting an elbow on the table in a corner of the restaurant, and knew that his friend was watching him with melancholy eyes, but he would not see d'Arthez just then; he felt the sharp pangs of poverty, the goadings of ambition, and followed Lousteau.

In the late afternoon the journalist and the neophyte went to the Luxembourg, and sat down under the trees in that part of the gardens which lies between the broad Avenue de l'Observatoire and the Rue de l'Ouest. The Rue de l'Ouest at that time was a long morass, bounded by planks and market-gardens; the houses were all at the end nearest the Rue de Vaugirard; and the walk through the gardens was so little frequented, that at the hour when Paris dines, two lovers might fall out and exchange the earnest of reconciliation without fear of intruders. The only possible spoil-sport was the pensioner on duty at the little iron gate on the Rue de l'Ouest, if that gray-headed veteran should take it into his head to lengthen his monotonous beat. There, on a bench beneath the lime-trees, Etienne Lousteau sat and listened to sample-sonnets from the *Marguerites*.

Etienne Lousteau, after a two-years' apprenticeship, was on the staff of a newspaper; he had his foot in the stirrup; he reckoned some of the celebrities of the day among his friends; altogether, he was an imposing personage in Lucien's eyes. Wherefore, while Lucien untied the string about the *Marguerites*, he judged it necessary to make some sort of preface.

"The sonnet, monsieur," said he, "is one of the most difficult forms of poetry. It has fallen almost entirely into disuse. No Frenchman can hope to rival Petrarch; for the language in which the Italian wrote, being so infinitely more pliant than French, lends itself to play of thought which our positivism (pardon the use of the expression) rejects. So it seemed to me that a volume of sonnets would be something quite new. Victor Hugo has appropriated the old, Canalis writes lighter verse, Beranger has monopolized songs, Casimir Delavigne has taken tragedy, and Lamartine the poetry of meditation."

"Are you a 'Classic' or a 'Romantic'?" inquired Lousteau.

Lucien's astonishment betrayed such complete ignorance of the state of affairs in the republic of letters, that Lousteau thought it necessary to enlighten him.

"You have come up in the middle of a pitched battle, my dear fellow; you must make your decision at once. Literature is divided, in the first place, into several zones, but our great men are ranged in two hostile camps. The Royalists are 'Romantics,' the Liberals are 'Classics.' The divergence of taste in matters literary and divergence of political opinion coincide; and the result is a war with weapons of every sort, double-edged witticisms, subtle calumnies and nicknames *a outrance*, between the rising and the waning glory, and ink is shed in torrents. The odd part of it is that the Royalist-

129

Romantics are all for liberty in literature, and for repealing laws and conventions; while the Liberal-Classics are for maintaining the unities, the Alexandrine, and the classical theme. So opinions in politics on either side are directly at variance with literary taste. If you are eclectic, you will have no one for you. Which side do you take?"

"Which is the winning side?"

"The Liberal newspapers have far more subscribers than the Royalist and Ministerial journals; still, though Canalis is for Church and King, and patronized by the Court and the clergy, he reaches other readers.--Pshaw! sonnets date back to an epoch before Boileau's time," said Etienne, seeing Lucien's dismay at the prospect of choosing between two banners. "Be a Romantic. The Romantics are young men, and the Classics are pedants; the Romantics will gain the day."

The word "pedant" was the latest epithet taken up by Romantic journalism to heap confusion on the Classical faction.

Lucien began to read, choosing first of all the title-sonnets.

EASTER DAISIES.

The daisies in the meadows, not in vain, In red and white and gold before our eyes, Have written an idyll for man's sympathies, And set his heart's desire in language plain.

Gold stamens set in silver filigrane Reveal the treasures which we idolize; And all the cost of struggle for the prize Is symboled by a secret blood-red stain.

Was it because your petals once uncurled When Jesus rose upon a fairer world, And from wings shaken for a heav'nward flight Shed grace, that still as autumn reappears You bloom again to tell of dead delight, To bring us back the flower of twenty years?

Lucien felt piqued by Lousteau's complete indifference during the reading of the sonnet; he was unfamiliar as yet with the disconcerting impassibility of the professional critic, wearied by much reading of poetry, prose, and plays. Lucien was accustomed to applause. He choked down his disappointment and read another, a favorite with Mme. de Bargeton and with some of his friends in the Rue des Quatre-Vents.

"This one, perhaps, will draw a word from him," he thought.

THE MARGUERITE.

I am the Marguerite, fair and tall I grew In velvet meadows, 'mid the flowers a star. They sought me for my beauty near and far; My dawn, I thought, should be for ever new. But now an all unwished-for gift I rue, A fatal ray of knowledge shed to mar My radiant star-crown grown oracular, For I must speak and give an answer true. An end of silence and of quiet days, The Lover with two words my counsel prays; And when my secret from my heart is reft, When all my silver petals scattered lie, I am the only flower neglected left, Cast down and trodden under foot to die.

At the end, the poet looked up at his Aristarchus. Etienne Lousteau was gazing at the trees in the Pepiniere.

"Well?" asked Lucien.

"Well, my dear fellow, go on! I am listening to you, am I not? That fact in itself is as good as praise in Paris."

"Have you had enough?" Lucien asked.

"Go on," the other answered abruptly enough.

Lucien proceeded to read the following sonnet, but his heart was dead within him; Lousteau's inscrutable composure froze his utterance. If he had come a little further upon the road, he would have known that between writer and writer silence or abrupt speech, under such circumstances, is a betrayal of jealousy, and outspoken admiration means a sense of relief over the discovery that the work is not above the average after all.

THE CAMELLIA.

In Nature's book, if rightly understood, The rose means love, and red for beauty glows; A pure, sweet spirit in the violet blows, And bright the lily gleams in lowlihood.

But this strange bloom, by sun and wind unwooed, Seems to expand and blossom 'mid the snows, A lily sceptreless, a scentless rose, For dainty listlessness of maidenhood.

Yet at the opera house the petals trace For modesty a fitting aureole; An alabaster wreath to lay, methought, In dusky hair o'er some fair woman's face Which kindles ev'n such love within the soul As sculptured marble forms by Phidias wrought.

"What do you think of my poor sonnets?" Lucien asked, coming straight to the point.

"Do you want the truth?"

"I am young enough to like the truth, and so anxious to succeed that I can hear it without taking offence, but not without despair," replied Lucien.

"Well, my dear fellow, the first sonnet, from its involved style, was evidently written at Angouleme; it gave you so much trouble, no doubt, that you cannot give it up. The second and third smack of Paris already; but read us one more sonnet," he added, with a gesture that seemed charming to the provincial.

Encouraged by the request, Lucien read with more confidence, choosing a sonnet which d'Arthez and Bridau liked best, perhaps on account of its color.

THE TULIP.

I am the Tulip from Batavia's shore; The thrifty Fleming for my beauty rare Pays a king's ransom, when that I am fair, And tall, and straight, and pure my petal's core.

And, like some Yolande of the days of yore, My long and amply folded skirts I wear, O'er-painted with the blazon that I bear --Gules, a fess azure; purpure, fretty, or.

The fingers of the Gardener divine Have woven for me my vesture fair and fine, Of threads of sunlight and of purple stain; No flower so glorious in the garden bed, But Nature, woe is me, no fragrance shed Within my cup of Orient porcelain.

"Well?" asked Lucien after a pause, immeasurably long, as it seemed to him.

"My dear fellow," Etienne said, gravely surveying the tips of Lucien's boots (he had brought the pair from Angouleme, and was wearing them out). "My dear fellow, I strongly recommend you to put your ink on your boots to save blacking, and to take your pens for toothpicks, so that when you come away from Flicoteaux's you can swagger along this picturesque alley looking as if you had dined. Get a situation of any sort or description. Run errands for a bailiff if you have the heart, be a shopman if your back is strong enough, enlist if you happen to have a taste for military music. You have the stuff of three poets in you; but before you can reach your public, you will have time to die of starvation six times over, if you intend to live on the proceeds of your poetry, that is. And from your too unsophisticated discourse, it would seem to be your intention to coin money out of your inkstand.

"I say nothing as to your verses; they are a good deal better than all the poetical wares that are cumbering the ground in booksellers' backshops just now. Elegant 'nightingales' of that sort cost a little more than the others, because they are printed on hand-made paper, but they nearly all of them come down at last to the banks of the Seine. You may study their range of notes there any day if you care to make an instructive pilgrimage along the Quais from old Jerome's stall by the Pont Notre Dame to the Pont Royal. You will find them all there --all the *Essays in Verse*, the *Inspirations*, the lofty flights, the hymns, and songs, and ballads, and odes; all the nestfuls hatched during the last seven years, in fact. There lie their muses, thick with dust, bespattered by every passing cab, at the mercy of every profane hand that turns them over to look at the vignette on the title-page.

"You know nobody; you have access to no newspaper, so your *Marguerites* will remain demurely folded as you hold them now. They will never open out to the sun of publicity in fair fields with broad margins enameled with the florets which Dauriat the illustrious, the king of the Wooden Galleries, scatters with a lavish hand for poets known to fame. I came to Paris as you came, poor boy, with a plentiful stock of illusions, impelled by irrepressible longings for glory--and I found the realities of the craft, the practical difficulties of the trade, the hard facts of poverty. In my enthusiasm (it is kept well under control now), my first ebullition of youthful spirits, I did not see the social machinery at work; so I had to learn to see it by bumping against the wheels and bruising myself against the shafts, and chains. Now you are about to learn, as I learned, that between you and all these fair dreamed-of things lies the strife of men, and passions, and necessities.

"Willy-nilly, you must take part in a terrible battle; book against book, man against man, party against party; make war you must, and that systematically, or you will be abandoned by your own party. And they are mean contests; struggles which leave you disenchanted, and wearied, and depraved, and all in pure waste; for it often happens that you put forth all your strength to win laurels for a man whom you despise, and maintain, in spite of yourself, that some second-rate writer is a genius.

"There is a world behind the scenes in the theatre of literature. The public in front sees unexpected or well-deserved success, and applauds; the public does *not* see the preparations, ugly as they always are, the painted supers, the *claqueurs* hired to applaud, the stage carpenters, and all that lies behind the scenes. You are still among the audience. Abdicate, there is still time, before you set your foot on the lowest step of the throne for which so many ambitious spirits are contending, and do not sell your honor, as I do, for a livelihood." Etienne's eyes filled with tears as he spoke.

"Do you know how I make a living?" he continued passionately. "The little stock of money they gave me at home was soon eaten up. A piece of mine was accepted at the Theatre-Francais just as I came to an end of it. At the Theatre-Francais the influence of a first gentleman of the bedchamber, or of a prince of the blood, would not be enough to secure a turn of favor; the actors only make concessions to those who threaten their self-love. If it is in your power to spread a report that the *jeune premier* has the asthma, the leading lady a fistula where you please, and the soubrette has foul breath, then your piece would be played tomorrow. I do not know whether in two years' time, I who speak to you now, shall be in a position to exercise such power. You need so many to back you. And where and how am I to gain my bread meanwhile?

"I tried lots of things; I wrote a novel, anonymously; old Doguereau gave me two hundred francs for it, and he did not make very much out of it himself. Then it grew plain to me that journalism alone could give me a living. The next thing was to find my way into those shops. I will not tell you all the advances I made, nor how often I begged in vain. I will say nothing of the six months I spent as extra hand on a paper, and was told that I scared subscribers away, when as a fact I attracted them. Pass over the insults I put up with. At this moment I am doing the plays at the Boulevard theatres, almost *gratis*, for a paper belonging to Finot, that stout young fellow who breakfasts two or three times a month, even now, at the Cafe Voltaire (but you don't go there). I live by selling tickets that managers give me to bribe a good word in the paper, and reviewers' copies of books. In short, Finot once satisfied, I am allowed to write for and against various commercial articles, and I traffic in tribute paid in kind by various tradesmen. A facetious notice of a Carminative Toilet Lotion, *Pate des Sultanes*, Cephalic Oil, or Brazilian Mixture brings me in twenty or thirty francs.

"I am obliged to dun the publishers when they don't send in a sufficient number of reviewers' copies; Finot, as editor, appropriates two and sells them, and I must have two to sell. If a book of capital importance comes out, and the publisher is stingy with copies, his life is made a burden to him. The craft is vile, but I live by it, and so do scores of others. Do not imagine that things are any better in public life. There is corruption everywhere in both regions; every man is corrupt or corrupts others. If there is any publishing enterprise somewhat larger than usual afoot, the trade will pay me something to buy neutrality. The amount of my income varies, therefore, directly with the prospectuses. When prospectuses break out like a rash, money pours into my pockets; I stand treat all round. When trade is dull, I dine at Flicoteaux's.

"Actresses will pay you likewise for praise, but the wiser among them pay for criticism. To be passed over in silence is what they dread the most; and the very best thing of all, from their point of view, is criticism which draws down a reply; it is far more effectual than bald praise, forgotten as soon as read, and it costs more in consequence. Celebrity, my dear fellow, is based upon controversy. I am a hired bravo; I ply my trade among ideas and reputations, commercial, literary, and dramatic; I make some fifty crowns a month; I can sell a novel for five hundred francs; and I am beginning to be looked upon as a man to be feared. Some day, instead of living with Florine at the expense of a druggist who gives himself the airs of a lord, I shall be in a house of my own; I shall be on the staff of a leading newspaper, I shall have a *feuilleton*; and on that day, my dear fellow, Florine will become a great actress. As for me, I am not sure what I shall be when that time comes, a minister or an honest man--all things are still possible."

He raised his humiliated head, and looked out at the green leaves, with an expression of despairing self-condemnation dreadful to see.

"And I had a great tragedy accepted!" he went on. "And among my papers there is a poem, which will die. And I was a good fellow, and my heart was clean! I used to dream lofty dreams of love for great ladies, queens in the great world; and--my mistress is an actress at the Panorama-Dramatique. And lastly, if a bookseller declines to send a copy of a book to my paper, I will run down work which is good, as I know."

Lucien was moved to tears, and he grasped Etienne's hand in his. The journalist rose to his feet, and the pair went up and down the broad Avenue de l'Observatoire, as if their lungs craved ampler breathing space.

"Outside the world of letters," Etienne Lousteau continued, "not a single creature suspects that every one who succeeds in that world --who has a certain vogue, that is to say, or comes into fashion, or gains reputation, or renown, or fame, or favor with the public (for by these names we know the rungs of the ladder by which we climb to the higher heights above and beyond them),--every one who comes even thus far is the hero of a dreadful Odyssey. Brilliant portents rise above the mental horizon through a combination of a thousand accidents; conditions change so swiftly that no two men have been known to reach success by the same road. Canalis and Nathan are two dissimilar cases; things never fall out in the same way twice. There is d'Arthez, who knocks himself to pieces with work--he will make a famous name by some other chance.

"This so much desired reputation is nearly always crowned prostitution. Yes; the poorest kind of literature is the hapless creature freezing at the street corner; second rate literature is the kept-mistress picked out of the brothels of journalism, and I am her bully; lastly, there is lucky literature, the flaunting, insolent courtesan who has a house of her own and pays taxes, who receives great lords, treating or ill-treating them as she pleases, who has liveried servants and a carriage, and can afford to keep greedy creditors waiting. Ah! and for yet others, for me not so very long ago, for you today--she is a white-robed angel with many-colored wings, bearing a green palm branch in the one hand, and in the other a flaming sword. An angel, something akin to the mythological abstraction which lives at the bottom of a well, and to the poor and honest girl who lives a life of exile in the outskirts of the great city, earning every penny with a noble fortitude and in the full light of virtue, returning to heaven inviolate of body and soul; unless, indeed, she comes to lie at the last, soiled, despoiled, polluted, and forgotten, on a pauper's bier. As for the men whose brains are encompassed with bronze, whose hearts are still warm under the snows of experience, they are found but seldom in the country that lies at our feet," he added, pointing to the great city seething in the late afternoon light.

133

A vision of d'Arthez and his friends flashed upon Lucien's sight, and made appeal to him for a moment; but Lousteau's appalling lamentation carried him away.

"They are very few and far between in that great fermenting vat; rare as love in love-making, rare as fortunes honestly made in business, rare as the journalist whose hands are clean. The experience of the first man who told me all that I am telling you was thrown away upon me, and mine no doubt will be wasted upon you. It is always the same old story year after year; the same eager rush to Paris from the provinces; the same, not to say a growing, number of beardless, ambitious boys, who advance, head erect, and the heart that Princess Tourandocte of the *Mille et un Jours*--each one of them fain to be her Prince Calaf. But never a one of them reads the riddle. One by one they drop, some into the trench where failures lie, some into the mire of journalism, some again into the quagmires of the book-trade.

"They pick up a living, these beggars, what with biographical notices, penny-a-lining, and scraps of news for the papers. They become booksellers' hacks for the clear-headed dealers in printed paper, who would sooner take the rubbish that goes off in a fortnight than a masterpiece which requires time to sell. The life is crushed out of the grubs before they reach the butterfly stage. They live by shame and dishonor. They are ready to write down a rising genius or to praise him to the skies at a word from the pasha of the *Constitutionnel*, the *Quotidienne*, or the *Debats*, at a sign from a publisher, at the request of a jealous comrade, or (as not seldom happens) simply for a dinner. Some surmount the obstacles, and these forget the misery of their early days. I, who am telling you this, have been putting the best that is in me into newspaper articles for six months past for a blackguard who gives them out as his own and has secured a *feuilleton* in another paper on the strength of them. He has not taken me on as his collaborator, he has not give me so much as a five-franc piece, but I hold out a hand to grasp his when we meet; I cannot help myself."

"And why?" Lucien, asked, indignantly.

"I may want to put a dozen lines into his *feuilleton* some day," Lousteau answered coolly. "In short, my dear fellow, in literature you will not make money by hard work, that is not the secret of success; the point is to exploit the work of somebody else. A newspaper proprietor is a contractor, we are the bricklayers. The more mediocre the man, the better his chance of getting on among mediocrities; he can play the toad-eater, put up with any treatment, and flatter all the little base passions of the sultans of literature. There is Hector Merlin, who came from Limoges a short time ago; he is writing political articles already for a Right Centre daily, and he is at work on our little paper as well. I have seen an editor drop his hat and Merlin pick it up. The fellow was careful never to give offence, and slipped into the thick of the fight between rival ambitions. I am sorry for you. It is as if I saw in you the self that I used to be, and sure am I that in one or two years' time you will be what I am now.--You will think that there is some lurking jealousy or personal motive in this bitter counsel, but it is prompted by the despair of a damned soul that can never leave hell.--No one ventures to utter such things as these. You hear the groans of anguish from a man wounded to the heart, crying like a second Job from the ashes, 'Behold my sores!'"

"But whether I fight upon this field or elsewhere, fight I must," said Lucien.

"Then, be sure of this," returned Lousteau, "if you have anything in you, the war will know no truce, the best chance of success lies in an empty head. The austerity of your conscience, clear as yet, will relax when you see that a man holds your future in his two hands, when a word from such a man means life to you, and he will not say that word. For, believe me, the most brutal bookseller in the trade is not so insolent, so hard-hearted to a newcomer as the celebrity of the day. The bookseller sees a possible loss of money, while the writer of books dreads a possible rival; the first shows you the door, the second crushes the life out of you. To do really good work, my boy, means that you will draw out the energy, sap, and tenderness of your nature at every dip of the pen in the ink, to set it forth for the world in passion and sentiment and

134

phrases. Yes; instead of acting, you will write; you will sing songs instead of fighting; you will love and hate and live in your books; and then, after all, when you shall have reserved your riches for your style, your gold and purple for your characters, and you yourself are walking the streets of Paris in rags, rejoicing in that, rivaling the State Register, you have authorized the existence of beings styled Adolphe, Corinne or Clarissa, Rene or Manon; when you shall have spoiled your life and your digestion to give life to that creation, then you shall see it slandered, betrayed, sold, swept away into the back waters of oblivion by journalists, and buried out of sight by your best friends. How can you afford to wait until the day when your creation shall rise again, raised from the dead--how? when? and by whom? Take a magnificent book, the *pianto* of unbelief; *Obermann* is a solitary wanderer in the desert places of booksellers' warehouses, he has been a 'nightingale,' ironically so called, from the very beginning: when will his Easter come? Who knows? Try, to begin with, to find somebody bold enough to print the *Marguerites*; not to pay for them, but simply to print them; and you will see some queer things."

The fierce tirade, delivered in every tone of the passionate feeling which it expressed, fell upon Lucien's spirit like an avalanche, and left a sense of glacial cold. For one moment he stood silent; then, as he felt the terrible stimulating charm of difficulty beginning to work upon him, his courage blazed up. He grasped Lousteau's hand.

"I will triumph!" he cried aloud.

"Good!" said the other, "one more Christian given over to the wild beasts in the arena.--There is a first-night performance at the Panorama-Dramatique, my dear fellow; it doesn't begin till eight, so you can change your coat, come properly dressed in fact, and call for me. I am living on the fourth floor above the Cafe Servel, Rue de la Harpe. We will go to Dauriat's first of all. You still mean to go on, do you not? Very well, I will introduce you to one of the kings of the trade tonight, and to one or two journalists. We will sup with my mistress and several friends after the play, for you cannot count that dinner as a meal. Finot will be there, editor and proprietor of my paper. As Minette says in the Vaudeville (do you remember?), 'Time is a great lean creature.' Well, for the like of us, Chance is a great lean creature, and must be tempted."

"I shall remember this day as long as I live," said Lucien.

"Bring your manuscript with you, and be careful of your dress, not on Florine's account, but for the booksellers' benefit."

The comrade's good-nature, following upon the poet's passionate outcry, as he described the war of letters, moved Lucien quite as deeply as d'Arthez's grave and earnest words on a former occasion. The prospect of entering at once upon the strife with men warmed him. In his youth and inexperience he had no suspicion how real were the moral evils denounced by the journalist. Nor did he know that he was standing at the parting of two distinct ways, between two systems, represented by the brotherhood upon one hand, and journalism upon the other. The first way was long, honorable, and sure; the second beset with hidden dangers, a perilous path, among muddy channels where conscience is inevitably bespattered. The bent of Lucien's character determined for the shorter way, and the apparently pleasanter way, and to snatch at the quickest and promptest means. At this moment he saw no difference between d'Arthez's noble friendship and Lousteau's easy comaraderie; his inconstant mind discerned a new weapon in journalism; he felt that he could wield it, so he wished to take it.

He was dazzled by the offers of this new friend, who had struck a hand in his in an easy way, which charmed Lucien. How should he know that while every man in the army of the press needs friends, every leader needs men. Lousteau, seeing that Lucien was resolute, enlisted him as a recruit, and hoped to attach him to himself. The relative positions of the two were similar--one hoped to become a corporal, the other to enter the ranks.

Lucien went back gaily to his lodgings. He was as careful over his toilet as on that former unlucky occasion when he occupied the Marquise d'Espard's box; but he had learned by this time how to wear his clothes with a better grace. They looked as though they belonged to him. He wore his best tightly-fitting, light-colored trousers, and a dress-coat. His boots, a very elegant pair adorned with tassels, had cost him forty francs. His thick, fine, golden hair was scented and crimped into bright, rippling curls. Self-confidence and belief in his future lighted up his forehead. He paid careful attention to his almost feminine hands, the filbert nails were a spotless pink, and the white contours of his chin were dazzling by contrast with a black satin stock. Never did a more beautiful youth come down from the hills of the Latin Quarter.

Glorious as a Greek god, Lucien took a cab, and reached the Cafe Servel at a quarter to seven. There the portress gave him some tolerably complicated directions for the ascent of four pairs of stairs. Provided with these instructions, he discovered, not without difficulty, an open door at the end of a long, dark passage, and in another moment made the acquaintance of the traditional room of the Latin Quarter.

A young man's poverty follows him wherever he goes--into the Rue de la Harpe as into the Rue de Cluny, into d'Arthez's room, into Chrestien's lodging; yet everywhere no less the poverty has its own peculiar characteristics, due to the idiosyncrasies of the sufferer. Poverty in this case wore a sinister look.

A shabby, cheap carpet lay in wrinkles at the foot of a curtainless walnut-wood bedstead; dingy curtains, begrimed with cigar smoke and fumes from a smoky chimney, hung in the windows; a Carcel lamp, Florine's gift, on the chimney-piece, had so far escaped the pawnbroker. Add a forlorn-looking chest of drawers, and a table littered with papers and disheveled quill pens, and the list of furniture was almost complete. All the books had evidently arrived in the course of the last twenty-four hours; and there was not a single object of any value in the room. In one corner you beheld a collection of crushed and flattened cigars, coiled pocket-handkerchiefs, shirts which had been turned to do double duty, and cravats that had reached a third edition; while a sordid array of old boots stood gaping in another angle of the room among aged socks worn into lace.

The room, in short, was a journalist's bivouac, filled with odds and ends of no value, and the most curiously bare apartment imaginable. A scarlet tinder-box glowed among a pile of books on the nightstand. A brace of pistols, a box of cigars, and a stray razor lay upon the mantel-shelf; a pair of foils, crossed under a wire mask, hung against a panel. Three chairs and a couple of armchairs, scarcely fit for the shabbiest lodging-house in the street, completed the inventory.

The dirty, cheerless room told a tale of a restless life and a want of self-respect; some one came hither to sleep and work at high pressure, staying no longer than he could help, longing, while he remained, to be out and away. What a difference between this cynical disorder and d'Arthez's neat and self-respecting poverty! A warning came with the thought of d'Arthez; but Lucien would not heed it, for Etienne made a joking remark to cover the nakedness of a reckless life.

"This is my kennel; I appear in state in the Rue de Bondy, in the new apartments which our druggist has taken for Florine; we hold the house-warming this evening."

Etienne Lousteau wore black trousers and beautifully-varnished boots; his coat was buttoned up to his chin; he probably meant to change his linen at Florine's house, for his shirt collar was hidden by a velvet stock. He was trying to renovate his hat by an application of the brush.

"Let us go," said Lucien.

"Not yet. I am waiting for a bookseller to bring me some money; I have not a farthing; there will be play, perhaps, and in any case I must have gloves."

As he spoke, the two new friends heard a man's step in the passage outside.

"There he is," said Lousteau. "Now you will see, my dear fellow, the shape that Providence takes when he manifests himself to poets. You are going to behold Dauriat, the fashionable bookseller of the Quai des Augustins, the pawnbroker, the marine store dealer of the trade, the Norman ex-greengrocer.--Come along, old Tartar!" shouted Lousteau.

"Here am I," said a voice like a cracked bell.

"Brought the money with you?"

"Money? There is no money now in the trade," retorted the other, a young man who eyed Lucien curiously.

"*Imprimis*, you owe me fifty francs," Lousteau continued.

"There are two copies of *Travels in Egypt* here, a marvel, so they say, swarming with woodcuts, sure to sell. Finot has been paid for two reviews that I am to write for him. *Item* two works, just out, by Victor Ducange, a novelist highly thought of in the Marais. *Item* a couple of copies of a second work by Paul de Kock, a beginner in the same style. *Item* two copies of *Yseult of Dole*, a charming provincial work. Total, one hundred francs, my little Barbet."

Barbet made a close survey of edges and binding.

"Oh! they are in perfect condition," cried Lousteau. "The *Travels* are uncut, so is the Paul de Kock, so is the Ducange, so is that other thing on the chimney-piece, *Considerations on Symbolism*. I will throw that in; myths weary me to that degree that I will let you have the thing to spare myself the sight of the swarms of mites coming out of it."

"But," asked Lucien, "how are you going to write your reviews?"

Barbet, in profound astonishment, stared at Lucien; then he looked at Etienne and chuckled.

"One can see that the gentleman has not the misfortune to be a literary man," said he.

"No, Barbet--no. He is a poet, a great poet; he is going to cut out Canalis, and Beranger, and Delavigne. He will go a long way if he does not throw himself into the river, and even so he will get as far as the drag-nets at Saint-Cloud."

"If I had any advice to give the gentleman," remarked Barbet, "it would be to give up poetry and take to prose. Poetry is not wanted on the Quais just now."

Barbet's shabby overcoat was fastened by a single button; his collar was greasy; he kept his hat on his head as he spoke; he wore low shoes, an open waistcoat gave glimpses of a homely shirt of coarse linen. Good-nature was not wanting in the round countenance, with its two slits of covetous eyes; but there was likewise the vague uneasiness habitual to those who have money to spend and hear constant applications for it. Yet, to all appearance, he was plain-dealing and easy-natured, his business shrewdness was so well wadded round with fat. He had been an assistant until he took a wretched little shop on the Quai des Augustins two years since, and issued thence on his rounds among journalists, authors, and printers, buying up free copies cheaply, making in such ways some ten or twenty francs daily. Now, he had money saved; he knew instinctively where every man was pressed; he had a keen eye for business. If an author was in difficulties, he would discount a bill given by a publisher at fifteen or twenty per cent; then the next day he would go to the publisher, haggle over the price of some work in demand, and pay him with his own bills instead of cash. Barbet was something of a scholar; he had had just enough education to make him careful to steer clear of modern poetry and modern romances. He had a liking for small speculations, for books of a popular kind which might be bought outright for a thousand francs and exploited at pleasure, such as the *Child's History of France*, *Book-keeping in Twenty Lessons*, and *Botany for Young Ladies*. Two or three times already he had allowed a good book to slip through his fingers; the authors had come and gone a score of times while he hesitated, and could not make up his mind to buy the manuscript. When reproached for his pusillanimity, he was wont to produce the account of a notorious trial taken from the newspapers; it cost him nothing, and had brought him in two or three thousand francs.

Barbet was the type of bookseller that goes in fear and trembling; lives on bread and walnuts; rarely puts his name to a bill; filches little profits on invoices; makes deductions, and hawks his books about himself; heaven only knows where they go, but he sells them somehow, and gets paid for them. Barbet was the terror of printers, who could not tell what to make of him; he paid cash and took off the discount; he nibbled at their invoices whenever he thought they were pressed for money; and when he had fleeced a man once, he never went back to him--he feared to be caught in his turn.

"Well," said Lousteau, "shall we go on with our business?"

"Eh! my boy," returned Barbet in a familiar tone; "I have six thousand volumes of stock on hand at my place, and paper is not gold, as the old bookseller said. Trade is dull."

"If you went into his shop, my dear Lucien," said Etienne, turning to his friend, "you would see an oak counter from some bankrupt wine merchant's sale, and a tallow dip, never snuffed for fear it should burn too quickly, making darkness visible. By that anomalous light you descry rows of empty shelves with some difficulty. An urchin in a blue blouse mounts guard over the emptiness, and blows his fingers, and shuffles his feet, and slaps his chest, like a cabman on the box. Just look about you! there are no more books there than I have here. Nobody could guess what kind of shop he keeps."

"Here is a bill at three months for a hundred francs," said Barbet, and he could not help smiling as he drew it out of his pocket; "I will take your old books off your hands. I can't pay cash any longer, you see; sales are too slow. I thought that you would be wanting me; I had not a penny, and I made a bill simply to oblige you, for I am not fond of giving my signature."

"So you want my thanks and esteem into the bargain, do you?"

"Bills are not met with sentiment," responded Barbet; "but I will accept your esteem, all the same."

"But I want gloves, and the perfumers will be base enough to decline your paper," said Lousteau. "Stop, there is a superb engraving in the top drawer of the chest there, worth eighty francs, proof before letters and after letterpress, for I have written a pretty droll article upon it. There was something to lay hold of in *Hippocrates refusing the Presents of Artaxerxes*. A fine engraving, eh? Just the thing to suit all the doctors, who are refusing the extravagant gifts of Parisian satraps. You will find two or three dozen novels underneath it. Come, now, take the lot and give me forty francs."

"*Forty francs*!" exclaimed the bookseller, emitting a cry like the squall of a frightened fowl. "Twenty at the very most! And then I may never see the money again," he added.

"Where are your twenty francs?" asked Lousteau.

"My word, I don't know that I have them," said Barbet, fumbling in his pockets. "Here they are. You are plundering me; you have an ascendency over me----"

"Come, let us be off," said Lousteau, and taking up Lucien's manuscript, he drew a line upon it in ink under the string.

"Have you anything else?" asked Barbet.

"Nothing, you young Shylock. I am going to put you in the way of a bit of very good business," Etienne continued ("in which you shall lose a thousand crowns, to teach you to rob me in this fashion"), he added for Lucien's ear.

"But how about your reviews?" said Lucien, as they rolled away to the Palais Royal.

"Pooh! you do not know how reviews are knocked off. As for the *Travels in Egypt*, I looked into the book here and there (without cutting the pages), and I found eleven slips in grammar. I shall say that the writer may have mastered the dicky-bird language on the flints that they call 'obelisks' out there in Egypt, but he cannot write in his own, as I will prove to him in a column and a half. I shall say that instead of giving us the natural history and archaeology, he ought to have interested himself in the future of Egypt, in the progress of civilization, and the best method of strengthening the bond between Egypt and France. France has won and lost Egypt, but she may yet attach the country to her interests by gaining

138

a moral ascendency over it. Then some patriotic penny-a-lining, interlarded with diatribes on Marseilles, the Levant and our trade."

"But suppose that he had taken that view, what would you do?"

"Oh well, I should say that instead of boring us with politics, he should have written about art, and described the picturesque aspects of the country and the local color. Then the critic bewails himself. Politics are intruded everywhere; we are weary of politics--politics on all sides. I should regret those charming books of travel that dwelt upon the difficulties of navigation, the fascination of steering between two rocks, the delights of crossing the line, and all the things that those who never will travel ought to know. Mingle this approval with scoffing at the travelers who hail the appearance of a bird or a flying-fish as a great event, who dilate upon fishing, and make transcripts from the log. Where, you ask, is that perfectly unintelligible scientific information, fascinating, like all that is profound, mysterious, and incomprehensible. The reader laughs, that is all that he wants. As for novels, Florine is the greatest novel reader alive; she gives me a synopsis, and I take her opinion and put a review together. When a novelist bores her with 'author's stuff,' as she calls it, I treat the work respectfully, and ask the publisher for another copy, which he sends forthwith, delighted to have a favorable review."

"Goodness! and what of criticism, the critic's sacred office?" cried Lucien, remembering the ideas instilled into him by the brotherhood.

"My dear fellow," said Lousteau, "criticism is a kind of brush which must not be used upon flimsy stuff, or it carries it all away with it. That is enough of the craft, now listen! Do you see that mark?" he continued, pointing to the manuscript of the *Marguerites*. "I have put ink on the string and paper. If Dauriat reads your manuscript, he certainly could not tie the string and leave it just as it was before. So your book is sealed, so to speak. This is not useless to you for the experiment that you propose to make. And another thing: please to observe that you are not arriving quite alone and without a sponsor in the place, like the youngsters who make the round of half-a-score of publishers before they find one that will offer them a chair."

Lucien's experience confirmed the truth of this particular. Lousteau paid the cabman, giving him three francs--a piece of prodigality following upon such impecuniosity astonishing Lucien more than a little. Then the two friends entered the Wooden Galleries, where fashionable literature, as it is called, used to reign in state.

PART 2

The Wooden Galleries of the Palais Royal used to be one of the most

famous sights of Paris. Some description of the squalid bazar will not be out of place; for there are few men of forty who will not take an interest in recollections of a state of things which will seem incredible to a younger generation.

The great dreary, spacious Galerie d'Orleans, that flowerless hothouse, as yet was not; the space upon which it now stands was covered with booths; or, to be more precise, with small, wooden dens, pervious to the weather, and dimly illuminated on the side of the court and the garden by borrowed lights styled windows by courtesy, but more like the filthiest arrangements for obscuring daylight to be found in little wineshops in the suburbs.

The Galleries, parallel passages about twelve feet in height, were formed by a triple row of shops. The centre row, giving back and front upon the Galleries, was filled with the fetid atmosphere of the place, and derived a dubious daylight through the invariably dirty windows of the roof; but so thronged were these hives, that rents were excessively high, and as much as a thousand crowns was paid for a space scarce six feet by eight. The outer rows gave respectively upon the garden and the court, and were covered on that side by a slight trellis-work painted green, to protect the crazy plastered walls from continual friction with the passers-by. In a few square feet of earth at the back of the shops, strange freaks of vegetable life unknown to science grew amid the products of various no less flourishing industries. You beheld a rosebush capped with printed paper in such a sort that the flowers of rhetoric were perfumed by the cankered blossoms of that ill-kept, ill-smelling garden. Handbills and ribbon streamers of every hue flaunted gaily among the leaves; natural flowers competed unsuccessfully for an existence with odds and ends of millinery. You discovered a knot of ribbon adorning a green tuft; the dahlia admired afar proved on a nearer view to be a satin rosette.

The Palais seen from the court or from the garden was a fantastic sight, a grotesque combination of walls of plaster patchwork which had once been whitewashed, of blistered paint, heterogeneous placards, and all the most unaccountable freaks of Parisian squalor; the green trellises were prodigiously the dingier for constant contact with a Parisian public. So, upon either side, the fetid, disreputable approaches might have been there for the express purpose of warning away fastidious people; but fastidious folk no more recoiled before these horrors than the prince in the fairy stories turns tail at sight of the dragon or of the other obstacles put between him and the princess by the wicked fairy.

There was a passage through the centre of the Galleries then as now; and, as at the present day, you entered them through the two peristyles begun before the Revolution, and left unfinished for lack of funds; but in place of the handsome modern arcade leading to the Theatre-Francais, you passed along a narrow, disproportionately lofty passage, so ill-roofed that the rain came through on wet days. All the roofs of the hovels indeed were in very bad repair, and covered here and again with a double thickness of tarpaulin. A famous silk mercer once brought an action against the Orleans family for damages done in the course of a night to his stock of shawls and stuffs, and gained the day and a considerable sum. It was in this last-named passage, called "The Glass Gallery" to distinguish it from the Wooden Galleries, that Chevet laid the foundations of his fortunes.

140

Here, in the Palais, you trod the natural soil of Paris, augmented by importations brought in upon the boots of foot passengers; here, at all seasons, you stumbled among hills and hollows of dried mud swept daily by the shopman's besom, and only after some practice could you walk at your ease. The treacherous mud-heaps, the window-panes incrusted with deposits of dust and rain, the mean-looking hovels covered with ragged placards, the grimy unfinished walls, the general air of a compromise between a gypsy camp, the booths of a country fair, and the temporary structures that we in Paris build round about public monuments that remain unbuilt; the grotesque aspect of the mart as a whole was in keeping with the seething traffic of various kinds carried on within it; for here in this shameless, unblushing haunt, amid wild mirth and a babel of talk, an immense amount of business was transacted between the Revolution of 1789 and the Revolution of 1830.

For twenty years the Bourse stood just opposite, on the ground floor of the Palais. Public opinion was manufactured, and reputations made and ruined here, just as political and financial jobs were arranged. People made appointments to meet in the Galleries before or after 'Change; on showery days the Palais Royal was often crowded with weather-bound capitalists and men of business. The structure which had grown up, no one knew how, about this point was strangely resonant, laughter was multiplied; if two men quarreled, the whole place rang from one end to the other with the dispute. In the daytime milliners and booksellers enjoyed a monopoly of the place; towards nightfall it was filled with women of the town. Here dwelt poetry, politics, and prose, new books and classics, the glories of ancient and modern literature side by side with political intrigue and the tricks of the bookseller's trade. Here all the very latest and newest literature were sold to a public which resolutely decline to buy elsewhere. Sometimes several thousand copies of such and such a pamphlet by Paul-Louis Courier would be sold in a single evening; and people crowded thither to buy *Les aventures de la fille d'un Roi*--that first shot fired by the Orleanists at The Charter promulgated by Louis XVIII.

When Lucien made his first appearance in the Wooden Galleries, some few of the shops boasted proper fronts and handsome windows, but these in every case looked upon the court or the garden. As for the centre row, until the day when the whole strange colony perished under the hammer of Fontaine the architect, every shop was open back and front like a booth in a country fair, so that from within you could look out upon either side through gaps among the goods displayed or through the glass doors. As it was obviously impossible to kindle a fire, the tradesmen were fain to use charcoal chafing-dishes, and formed a sort of brigade for the prevention of fires among themselves; and, indeed, a little carelessness might have set the whole quarter blazing in fifteen minutes, for the plank-built republic, dried by the heat of the sun, and haunted by too inflammable human material, was bedizened with muslin and paper and gauze, and ventilated at times by a thorough draught.

The milliners' windows were full of impossible hats and bonnets, displayed apparently for advertisement rather than for sale, each on a separate iron spit with a knob at the top. The galleries were decked out in all the colors of the rainbow. On what heads would those dusty bonnets end their careers?--for a score of years the problem had puzzled frequenters of the Palais. Saleswomen, usually plain-featured, but vivacious, waylaid the feminine foot passenger with cunning importunities, after the fashion of market-women, and using much the same language; a shop-girl, who made free use of her eyes and tongue, sat outside on a stool and harangued the public with "Buy a pretty bonnet, madame?--Do let me sell you something!"--varying a rich and picturesque vocabulary with inflections of the voice, with glances, and remarks upon the passers-by. Booksellers and milliners lived on terms of mutual understanding.

But it was in the passage known by the pompous title of the "Glass Gallery" that the oddest trades were carried on. Here were ventriloquists and charlatans of every sort, and sights of every description, from the kind where there is nothing to see to panoramas of the globe. One man who has since made seven or eight hundred thousand francs by traveling from fair to fair began here by hanging out a signboard, a revolving sun in a blackboard, and the inscription in red letters: "Here

141

Man may see what God can never see. Admittance, two sous." The showman at the door never admitted one person alone, nor more than two at a time. Once inside, you confronted a great looking-glass; and a voice, which might have terrified Hoffmann of Berlin, suddenly spoke as if some spring had been touched, "You see here, gentlemen, something that God can never see through all eternity, that is to say, your like. God has not His like." And out you went, too shamefaced to confess to your stupidity.

Voices issued from every narrow doorway, crying up the merits of Cosmoramas, views of Constantinople, marionettes, automatic chess-players, and performing dogs who would pick you out the prettiest woman in the company. The ventriloquist Fritz-James flourished here in the Cafe Borel before he went to fight and fall at Montmartre with the young lads from the Ecole polytechnique. Here, too, there were fruit and flower shops, and a famous tailor whose gold-laced uniforms shone like the sun when the shops were lighted at night.

Of a morning the galleries were empty, dark, and deserted; the shopkeepers chatted among themselves. Towards two o'clock in the afternoon the Palais began to fill; at three, men came in from the Bourse, and Paris, generally speaking, crowded the place. Impecunious youth, hungering after literature, took the opportunity of turning over the pages of the books exposed for sale on the stalls outside the booksellers' shops; the men in charge charitably allowed a poor student to pursue his course of free studies; and in this way a duodecimo volume of some two hundred pages, such as *Smarra* or *Pierre Schlemihl*, or *Jean Sbogar* or *Jocko*, might be devoured in a couple of afternoons. There was something very French in this alms given to the young, hungry, starved intellect. Circulating libraries were not as yet; if you wished to read a book, you were obliged to buy it, for which reason novels of the early part of the century were sold in numbers which now seem well-nigh fabulous to us.

But the poetry of this terrible mart appeared in all its splendor at the close of the day. Women of the town, flocking in and out from the neighboring streets, were allowed to make a promenade of the Wooden Galleries. Thither came prostitutes from every quarter of Paris to "do the Palais." The Stone Galleries belonged to privileged houses, which paid for the right of exposing women dressed like princesses under such and such an arch, or in the corresponding space of garden; but the Wooden Galleries were the common ground of women of the streets. This was *the* Palais, a word which used to signify the temple of prostitution. A woman might come and go, taking away her prey whithersoever seemed good to her. So great was the crowd attracted thither at night by the women, that it was impossible to move except at a slow pace, as in a procession or at a masked ball. Nobody objected to the slowness; it facilitated examination. The women dressed in a way that is never seen nowadays. The bodices cut extremely low both back and front; the fantastical head-dresses, designed to attract notice; here a cap from the Pays de Caux, and there a Spanish mantilla; the hair crimped and curled like a poodle's, or smoothed down in bandeaux over the forehead; the close-fitting white stockings and limbs, revealed it would not be easy to say how, but always at the right moment--all this poetry of vice has fled. The license of question and reply, the public cynicism in keeping with the haunt, is now unknown even at masquerades or the famous public balls. It was an appalling, gay scene. The dazzling white flesh of the women's necks and shoulders stood out in magnificent contrast against the men's almost invariably sombre costumes. The murmur of voices, the hum of the crowd, could be heard even in the middle of the garden as a sort of droning bass, interspersed with *fioriture* of shrill laughter or clamor of some rare dispute. You saw gentlemen and celebrities cheek by jowl with gallows-birds. There was something indescribably piquant about the anomalous assemblage; the most insensible of men felt its charm, so much so, that, until the very last moment, Paris came hither to walk up and down on the wooden planks laid over the cellars where men were at work on the new buildings; and when the squalid wooden erections were finally taken down, great and unanimous regret was felt.

Ladvocat the bookseller had opened a shop but a few days since in the angle formed by the central passage which crossed the galleries; and immediately opposite another bookseller, now forgotten, Dauriat, a bold and youthful pioneer, who opened up the paths in which his rival was to shine. Dauriat's shop stood in the row which gave upon the garden; Ladvocat's, on the opposite side, looked out upon the court. Dauriat's establishment was divided into two parts; his shop was simply a great trade warehouse, and the second room was his private office.

Lucien, on this first visit to the Wooden Galleries, was bewildered by a sight which no novice can resist. He soon lost the guide who befriended him.

"If you were as good-looking as yonder young fellow, I would give you your money's worth," a woman said, pointing out Lucien to an old man.

Lucien slunk through the crowd like a blind man's dog, following the stream in a state of stupefaction and excitement difficult to describe. Importuned by glances and white-rounded contours, dazzled by the audacious display of bared throat and bosom, he gripped his roll of manuscript tightly lest somebody should steal it--innocent that he was!

"Well, what is it, sir!" he exclaimed, thinking, when some one caught him by the arm, that his poetry had proved too great a temptation to some author's honesty, and turning, he recognized Lousteau.

"I felt sure that you would find your way here at last," said his friend.

The poet was standing in the doorway of a shop crowded with persons waiting for an audience with the sultan of the publishing trade. Printers, paper-dealers, and designers were catechizing Dauriat's assistants as to present or future business.

Lousteau drew Lucien into the shop. "There! that is Finot who edits my paper," he said; "he is talking with Felicien Vernou, who has abilities, but the little wretch is as dangerous as a hidden disease."

"Well, old boy, there is a first night for you," said Finot, coming up with Vernou. "I have disposed of the box."

"Sold it to Braulard?"

"Well, and if I did, what then? You will get a seat. What do you want with Dauriat? Oh, it is agreed that we are to push Paul de Kock, Dauriat has taken two hundred copies, and Victor Ducange is refusing to give him his next. Dauriat wants to set up another man in the same line, he says. You must rate Paul de Kock above Ducange."

"But I have a piece on with Ducange at the Gaite," said Lousteau.

"Very well, tell him that I wrote the article. It can be supposed that I wrote a slashing review, and you toned it down; and he will owe you thanks."

"Couldn't you get Dauriat's cashier to discount this bit of a bill for a hundred francs?" asked Etienne Lousteau. "We are celebrating Florine's house-warming with a supper tonight, you know."

"Ah! yes, you are treating us all," said Finot, with an apparent effort of memory. "Here, Gabusson," he added, handing Barbet's bill to the cashier, "let me have ninety francs for this individual.--Fill in your name, old man."

Lousteau signed his name while the cashier counted out the money; and Lucien, all eyes and ears, lost not a syllable of the conversation.

"That is not all, my friend," Etienne continued; "I don't thank you, we have sworn an eternal friendship. I have taken it upon myself to introduce this gentleman to Dauriat, and you must incline his ear to listen to us."

"What is on foot?" asked Finot.

"A volume of poetry," said Lucien.

"Oh!" said Finot, with a shrug of the shoulders.

"Your acquaintance cannot have had much to do with publishers, or he would have hidden his manuscript in the loneliest spot in his dwelling," remarked Vernou, looking at Lucien as he spoke.

Just at that moment a good-looking young man came into the shop, gave a hand to Finot and Lousteau, and nodded slightly to Vernou. The newcomer was Emile Blondet, who had made his first appearance in the *Journal des Debats*, with articles revealing capacities of the very highest order.

"Come and have supper with us at midnight, at Florine's," said Lousteau.

"Very good," said the newcomer. "But who is going to be there?"

"Oh, Florine and Matifat the druggist," said Lousteau, "and du Bruel, the author who gave Florine the part in which she is to make her first appearance, a little old fogy named Cardot, and his son-in-law Camusot, and Finot, and----"

"Does your druggist do things properly?"

"He will not give us doctored wine," said Lucien.

"You are very witty, monsieur," Blondet returned gravely. "Is he coming, Lousteau?"

"Yes."

"Then we shall have some fun."

Lucien had flushed red to the tips of his ears. Blondet tapped on the window above Dauriat's desk.

"Is your business likely to keep you long, Dauriat?"

"I am at your service, my friend."

"That's right," said Lousteau, addressing his protege. "That young fellow is hardly any older than you are, and he is on the *Debats*! He is one of the princes of criticism. They are afraid of him, Dauriat will fawn upon him, and then we can put in a word about our business with the pasha of vignettes and type. Otherwise we might have waited till eleven o'clock, and our turn would not have come. The crowd of people waiting to speak with Dauriat is growing bigger every moment."

Lucien and Lousteau followed Blondet, Finot, and Vernou, and stood in a knot at the back of the shop.

"What is he doing?" asked Blondet of the head-clerk, who rose to bid him good-evening.

"He is buying a weekly newspaper. He wants to put new life into it, and set up a rival to the *Minerve* and the *Conservateur*; Eymery has rather too much of his own way in the *Minerve*, and the *Conservateur* is too blindly Romantic."

"Is he going to pay well?"

"Only too much--as usual," said the cashier.

Just as he spoke another young man entered; this was the writer of a magnificent novel which had sold very rapidly and met with the greatest possible success. Dauriat was bringing out a second edition. The appearance of this odd and extraordinary looking being, so unmistakably an artist, made a deep impression on Lucien's mind.

"That is Nathan," Lousteau said in his ear.

Nathan, then in the prime of his youth, came up to the group of journalists, hat in hand; and in spite of his look of fierce pride he was almost humble to Blondet, whom as yet he only knew by sight. Blondet did not remove his hat, neither did Finot.

"Monsieur, I am delighted to avail myself of an opportunity yielded by chance----"

("He is so nervous that he is committing a pleonasm," said Felicien in an aside to Lousteau.)

"----to give expression to my gratitude for the splendid review which you were so good as to give me in the *Journal des Debats*. Half the success of my book is owing to you."

"No, my dear fellow, no," said Blondet, with an air of patronage scarcely masked by good-nature. "You have talent, the

144

deuce you have, and I'm delighted to make your acquaintance."

"Now that your review has appeared, I shall not seem to be courting power; we can feel at ease. Will you do me the honor and the pleasure of dining with me tomorrow? Finot is coming.--Lousteau, old man, you will not refuse me, will you?" added Nathan, shaking Etienne by the hand.--"Ah, you are on the way to a great future, monsieur," he added, turning again to Blondet; "you will carry on the line of Dussaults, Fievees, and Geoffrois! Hoffmann was talking about you to a friend of mine, Claude Vignon, his pupil; he said that he could die in peace, the *Journal des Debats* would live forever. They ought to pay you tremendously well."

"A hundred francs a column," said Blondet. "Poor pay when one is obliged to read the books, and read a hundred before you find one worth interesting yourself in, like yours. Your work gave me pleasure, upon my word."

"And brought him in fifteen hundred francs," said Lousteau for Lucien's benefit.

"But you write political articles, don't you?" asked Nathan.

"Yes; now and again."

Lucien felt like an embryo among these men; he had admired Nathan's book, he had reverenced the author as an immortal; Nathan's abject attitude before this critic, whose name and importance were both unknown to him, stupefied Lucien.

"How if I should come to behave as he does?" he thought. "Is a man obliged to part with his self-respect?--Pray put on your hat again, Nathan; you have written a great book, and the critic has only written a review of it."

These thoughts set the blood tingling in his veins. Scarce a minute passed but some young author, poverty-stricken and shy, came in, asked to speak with Dauriat, looked round the crowded shop despairingly, and went out saying, "I will come back again." Two or three politicians were chatting over the convocation of the Chambers and public business with a group of well-known public men. The weekly newspaper for which Dauriat was in treaty was licensed to treat of matters political, and the number of newspapers suffered to exist was growing smaller and smaller, till a paper was a piece of property as much in demand as a theatre. One of the largest shareholders in the *Constitutionnel* was standing in the midst of the knot of political celebrities. Lousteau performed the part of cicerone to admiration; with every sentence he uttered Dauriat rose higher in Lucien's opinion. Politics and literature seemed to converge in Dauriat's shop. He had seen a great poet prostituting his muse to journalism, humiliating Art, as woman was humiliated and prostituted in those shameless galleries without, and the provincial took a terrible lesson to heart. Money! That was the key to every enigma. Lucien realized the fact that he was unknown and alone, and that the fragile clue of an uncertain friendship was his sole guide to success and fortune. He blamed the kind and loyal little circle for painting the world for him in false colors, for preventing him from plunging into the arena, pen in hand. "I should be a Blondet at this moment!" he exclaimed within himself.

Only a little while ago they had sat looking out over Paris from the Gardens of the Luxembourg, and Lousteau had uttered the cry of a wounded eagle; then Lousteau had been a great man in Lucien's eyes, and now he had shrunk to scarce visible proportions. The really important man for him at this moment was the fashionable bookseller, by whom all these men lived; and the poet, manuscript in hand, felt a nervous tremor that was almost like fear. He noticed a group of busts mounted on wooden pedestals, painted to resemble marble; Byron stood there, and Goethe and M. de Canalis. Dauriat was hoping to publish a volume by the last-named poet, who might see, on his entrance into the shop, the estimation in which he was held by the trade. Unconsciously Lucien's own self-esteem began to shrink, and his courage ebbed. He began to see how large a part this Dauriat would play in his destinies, and waited impatiently for him to appear.

"Well, children," said a voice, and a short, stout man appeared, with a puffy face that suggested a Roman pro-consul's visage, mellowed by an air of good-nature which deceived superficial observers. "Well, children, here am I, the proprietor

145

of the only weekly paper in the market, a paper with two thousand subscribers!"

"Old joker! The registered number is seven hundred, and that is over the mark," said Blondet.

"Twelve thousand, on my sacred word of honor--I said two thousand for the benefit of the printers and paper-dealers yonder," he added, lowering his voice, then raising it again. "I thought you had more tact, my boy," he added.

"Are you going to take any partners?" inquired Finot.

"That depends," said Dauriat. "Will you take a third at forty thousand francs?"

"It's a bargain, if you will take Emile Blondet here on the staff, and Claude Vignon, Scribe, Theodore Leclercq, Felicien Vernou, Jay, Jouy, Lousteau, and----"

"And why not Lucien de Rubempre?" the provincial poet put in boldly.

"----and Nathan," concluded Finot.

"Why not the people out there in the street?" asked Dauriat, scowling at the author of the *Marguerites*.--"To whom have I the honor of speaking?" he added, with an insolent glance.

"One moment, Dauriat," said Lousteau. "I have brought this gentleman to you. Listen to me, while Finot is thinking over your proposals."

Lucien watched this Dauriat, who addressed Finot with the familiar tu, which even Finot did not permit himself to use in reply; who called the redoubtable Blondet "my boy," and extended a hand royally to Nathan with a friendly nod. The provincial poet felt his shirt wet with perspiration when the formidable sultan looked indifferent and ill pleased.

"Another piece of business, my boy!" exclaimed Dauriat. "Why, I have eleven hundred manuscripts on hand, as you know! Yes, gentlemen, I have eleven hundred manuscripts submitted to me at this moment; ask Gabusson. I shall soon be obliged to start a department to keep account of the stock of manuscripts, and a special office for reading them, and a committee to vote on their merits, with numbered counters for those who attend, and a permanent secretary to draw up the minutes for me. It will be a kind of local branch of the Academie, and the Academicians will be better paid in the Wooden Galleries than at the Institut."

"'Tis an idea," said Blondet.

"A bad idea," returned Dauriat. "It is not my business to take stock of the lucubrations of those among you who take to literature because they cannot be capitalists, and there is no opening for them as bootmakers, nor corporals, nor domestic servants, nor officials, nor bailiffs. Nobody comes here until he has made a name for himself! Make a name for yourself, and you will find gold in torrents. I have made three great men in the last two years; and lo and behold three examples of ingratitude! Here is Nathan talking of six thousand francs for the second edition of his book, which cost me three thousand francs in reviews, and has not brought in a thousand yet. I paid a thousand francs for Blondet's two articles, besides a dinner, which cost me five hundred----"

"But if all booksellers talked as you do, sir, how could a man publish his first book at all?" asked Lucien. Blondet had gone down tremendously in his opinion since he had heard the amount given by Dauriat for the articles in the *Debats*.

"That is not my affair," said Dauriat, looking daggers at this handsome young fellow, who was smiling pleasantly at him. "I do not publish books for amusement, nor risk two thousand francs for the sake of seeing my money back again. I speculate in literature, and publish forty volumes of ten thousand copies each, just as Panckouke does and the Baudoins. With my influence and the articles which I secure, I can push a business of a hundred thousand crowns, instead of a single volume involving a couple of thousand francs. It is just as much trouble to bring out a new name and to induce the public to take up an author and his book, as to make a success with the *Theatres etrangers*, *Victoires et Conquetes*, or *Memoires sur la Revolution*, books that bring in a fortune. I am not here as a stepping-stone to future fame, but to make money, and to find it for men with distinguished names. The manuscripts for which I give a hundred thousand francs pay me better than work by an unknown author who asks six hundred. If I am not exactly a Maecenas, I deserve the gratitude of literature; I have doubled the prices of manuscripts. I am giving you this explanation because you are a friend of Lousteau's my boy," added Dauriat, clapping Lucien on the shoulder with odious familiarity. "If I were to talk to all the authors who have a mind that I should be their publisher, I should have to shut up shop; I should pass my time very agreeably no doubt, but the conversations would cost too much. I am not rich enough yet to listen to all the monologues of self-conceit. Nobody does, except in classical tragedies on the stage."

The terrible Dauriat's gorgeous raiment seemed in the provincial poet's eyes to add force to the man's remorseless logic.

"What is it about?" he continued, addressing Lucien's protector.

"It is a volume of magnificent poetry."

At that word, Dauriat turned to Gabusson with a gesture worthy of Talma.

"Gabusson, my friend," he said, "from this day forward, when anybody begins to talk of works in manuscript here--Do you hear that, all of you?" he broke in upon himself; and three assistants at once emerged from among the piles of books at the sound of their employer's wrathful voice. "If anybody comes here with manuscripts," he continued, looking at the finger-nails of a well-kept hand, "ask him whether it is poetry or prose; and if he says poetry, show him the door at once. Verses mean reverses in the booktrade."

"Bravo! well put, Dauriat," cried the chorus of journalists.

"It is true!" cried the bookseller, striding about his shop with Lucien's manuscript in his hand. "You have no idea, gentlemen, of the amount of harm that Byron, Lamartine, Victor Hugo, Casimir Delavigne, Canalis, and Beranger have done by their success. The fame of them has brought down an invasion of barbarians upon us. I know *this*: there are a thousand volumes of manuscript poetry going the round of the publishers at this moment, things that nobody can make head nor tail of, stories in verse that begin in the middle, like *The Corsair* and *Lara*. They set up to be original, forsooth, and indulge in stanzas that nobody can understand, and descriptive poetry after the pattern of the younger men who discovered Delille, and imagine that they are doing something new. Poets have been swarming like cockchafers for two years past. I have lost twenty thousand francs through poetry in the last twelvemonth. You ask Gabusson! There may be immortal poets somewhere in the world; I know of some that are blooming and rosy, and have no beards on their chins as yet," he continued, looking at Lucien; "but in the trade, young man, there are only four poets --Beranger, Casimir Delavigne, Lamartine, and Victor Hugo; as for Canalis--he is a poet made by sheer force of writing him up."

Lucien felt that he lacked the courage to hold up his head and show his spirit before all these influential persons, who were laughing with all their might. He knew very well that he should look hopelessly ridiculous, and yet he felt consumed by a fierce desire to catch the bookseller by the throat, to ruffle the insolent composure of his cravat, to break the gold chain that glittered on the man's chest, trample his watch under his feet, and tear him in pieces. Mortified vanity opened the door to thoughts of vengeance, and inwardly he swore eternal enmity to that bookseller. But he smiled amiably.

"Poetry is like the sun," said Blondet, "giving life alike to primeval forests and to ants and gnats and mosquitoes. There is no virtue but has a vice to match, and literature breeds the publisher."

"And the journalist," said Lousteau.

Dauriat burst out laughing.

"What is this after all?" he asked, holding up the manuscript.

"A volume of sonnets that will put Petrarch to the blush," said Lousteau.

"What do you mean?"

"Just what I say," answered Lousteau, seeing the knowing smile that went round the group. Lucien could not take offence but he chafed inwardly.

"Very well, I will read them," said Dauriat, with a regal gesture that marked the full extent of the concession. "If these sonnets of yours are up to the level of the nineteenth century, I will make a great poet of you, my boy."

"If he has brains to equal his good looks, you will run no great risks," remarked one of the greatest public speakers of the day, a deputy who was chatting with the editor of the *Minerve*, and a writer for the *Constitutionnel*.

"Fame means twelve thousand francs in reviews, and a thousand more for dinners, General," said Dauriat. "If M. Benjamin de Constant means to write a paper on this young poet, it will not be long before I make a bargain with him."

At the title of General, and the distinguished name of Benjamin Constant, the bookseller's shop took the proportions of Olympus for the provincial great man.

"Lousteau, I want a word with you," said Finot; "but I shall see you again later, at the theatre.--Dauriat, I will take your offer, but on conditions. Let us step into your office."

"Come in, my boy," answered Dauriat, allowing Finot to pass before him. Then, intimating to some ten persons still waiting for him that he was engaged, he likewise was about to disappear when Lucien impatiently stopped him.

"You are keeping my manuscript. When shall I have an answer?"

"Oh, come back in three or four days, my little poet, and we will see."

Lousteau hurried Lucien away; he had not time to take leave of Vernou and Blondet and Raoul Nathan, nor to salute General Foy nor Benjamin Constant, whose book on the Hundred Days was just about to appear. Lucien scarcely caught a glimpse of fair hair, a refined oval-shaped face, keen eyes, and the pleasant-looking mouth belonging to the man who had played the part of a Potemkin to Mme. de Stael for twenty years, and now was at war with the Bourbons, as he had been at war with Napoleon. He was destined to win his cause and to die stricken to earth by his victory.

"What a shop!" exclaimed Lucien, as he took his place in the cab beside Lousteau.

"To the Panorama-Dramatique; look sharp, and you shall have thirty sous," Etienne Lousteau called to the cabman.-- "Dauriat is a rascal who sells books to the amount of fifteen or sixteen hundred thousand francs every year. He is a kind of Minister of Literature," Lousteau continued. His self-conceit had been pleasantly tickled, and he was showing off before Lucien. "Dauriat is just as grasping as Barbet, but it is on a wholesale scale. Dauriat can be civil, and he is generous, but he has a great opinion of himself; as for his wit, it consists in a faculty for picking up all that he hears, and his shop is a capital place to frequent. You meet all the best men at Dauriat's. A young fellow learns more there in an hour than by poring over books for half-a-score of years. People talk about articles and concoct subjects; you make the acquaintance of great or influential people who may be useful to you. You must know people if you mean to get on nowadays.--It is all luck, you see. And as for sitting by yourself in a corner alone with your intellect, it is the most dangerous thing of all."

"But what insolence!" said Lucien.

"Pshaw! we all of us laugh at Dauriat," said Etienne. "If you are in need of him, he tramples upon you; if he has need of the *Journal des Debats*, Emile Blondet sets him spinning like a top. Oh, if you take to literature, you will see a good many queer things. Well, what was I telling you, eh?"

"Yes, you were right," said Lucien. "My experience in that shop was even more painful than I expected, after your programme."

"Why do you choose to suffer? You find your subject, you wear out your wits over it with toiling at night, you throw your very life into it: and after all your journeyings in the fields of thought, the monument reared with your life-blood is simply a good or a bad speculation for a publisher. Your work will sell or it will not sell; and therein, for them, lies the whole question. A book means so much capital to risk, and the better the book, the less likely it is to sell. A man of talent rises above the level of ordinary heads; his success varies in direct ratio with the time required for his work to be appreciated. And no publisher wants to wait. Today's book must be sold by tomorrow. Acting on this system, publishers and booksellers do not care to take real literature, books that call for the high praise that comes slowly."

"D'Arthez was right," exclaimed Lucien.

"Do you know d'Arthez?" asked Lousteau. "I know of no more dangerous company than solitary spirits like that fellow yonder, who fancy that they can draw the world after them. All of us begin by thinking that we are capable of great things; and when once a youthful imagination is heated by this superstition, the candidate for posthumous honors makes no attempt to move the world while such moving of the world is both possible and profitable; he lets the time go by. I am for Mahomet's system--if the mountain does not come to me, I am for going to the mountain."

The common-sense so trenchantly put in this sally left Lucien halting between the resignation preached by the brotherhood and Lousteau's militant doctrine. He said not a word till they reached the Boulevard du Temple.

The Panorama-Dramatique no longer exists. A dwelling-house stands on the site of the once charming theatre in the Boulevard du Temple, where two successive managements collapsed without making a single hit; and yet Vignol, who has since fallen heir to some of Potier's popularity, made his *debut* there; and Florine, five years later a celebrated actress, made her first appearance in the theatre opposite the Rue Charlot. Play-houses, like men, have their vicissitudes. The Panorama-Dramatique suffered from competition. The machinations of its rivals, the Ambigu, the Gaite, the Porte Saint-Martin, and the Vaudeville, together with a plethora of restrictions and a scarcity of good plays, combined to bring about the downfall of the house. No dramatic author cared to quarrel with a prosperous theatre for the sake of the Panorama-Dramatique, whose existence was, to say the least, problematical. The management at this moment, however, was counting on the success of a new melodramatic comedy by M. du Bruel, a young author who, after working in collaboration with divers celebrities, had now produced a piece professedly entirely his own. It had been specially composed for the leading lady, a young actress who began her stage career as a supernumerary at the Gaite, and had been promoted to small parts for the last twelvemonth. But though Mlle. Florine's acting had attracted some attention, she obtained no engagement, and the Panorama accordingly had carried her off. Coralie, another actress, was to make her *debut* at the same time.

Lucien was amazed at the power wielded by the press. "This gentleman is with me," said Etienne Lousteau, and the box-office clerks bowed before him as one man.

"You will find it no easy matter to get seats," said the head-clerk. "There is nothing left now but the stage box."

A certain amount of time was wasted in controversies with the box-keepers in the lobbies, when Etienne said, "Let us go behind the scenes; we will speak to the manager, he will take us into the stage-box; and besides, I will introduce you to Florine, the heroine of the evening."

At a sign from Etienne Lousteau, the doorkeeper of the orchestra took out a little key and unlocked a door in the thickness of the wall. Lucien, following his friend, went suddenly out of the lighted corridor into the black darkness of the passage between the house and the wings. A short flight of damp steps surmounted, one of the strangest of all spectacles opened out before the provincial poet's eyes. The height of the roof, the slenderness of the props, the ladders hung with Argand lamps, the atrocious ugliness of scenery beheld at close quarters, the thick paint on the actors' faces, and their outlandish costumes, made of such coarse materials, the stage carpenters in greasy jackets, the firemen, the stage manager strutting about with his hat on his head, the supernumeraries sitting among the hanging back-scenes, the ropes and pulleys, the heterogeneous collection of absurdities, shabby, dirty, hideous, and gaudy, was something so altogether different from the stage seen over the footlights, that Lucien's astonishment knew no bounds. The curtain was just about to fall on a good old-fashioned melodrama entitled *Bertram*, a play adapted from a tragedy by Maturin which Charles Nodier, together with Byron and Sir Walter Scott, held in the highest esteem, though the play was a failure on the stage in Paris.

"Keep a tight hold of my arm, unless you have a mind to fall through a trap-door, or bring down a forest on your head; you will pull down a palace, or carry off a cottage, if you are not careful," said Etienne. --"Is Florine in her dressing-room, my pet?" he added, addressing an actress who stood waiting for her cue.

"Yes, love. Thank you for the things you said about me. You are so much nicer since Florine has come here."

"Come, don't spoil your entry, little one. Quick with you, look sharp, and say, 'Stop, wretched man!' nicely, for there are two thousand francs of takings."

Lucien was struck with amazement when the girl's whole face suddenly changed, and she shrieked, "Stop, wretched man!" a cry that froze the blood in your veins. She was no longer the same creature.

"So this is the stage," he said to Lousteau.

"It is like the bookseller's shop in the Wooden Galleries, or a literary paper," said Etienne Lousteau; "it is a kitchen, neither more nor less."

Nathan appeared at this moment.

"What brings you here?" inquired Lousteau.

"Why, I am doing the minor theatres for the *Gazette* until something better turns up."

"Oh! come to supper with us this evening; speak well of Florine, and I will do as much for you."

"Very much at your service," returned Nathan.

"You know; she is living in the Rue du Bondy now."

"Lousteau, dear boy, who is the handsome young man that you have brought with you?" asked the actress, now returned to the wings.

"A great poet, dear, that will have a famous name one of these days. --M. Nathan, I must introduce M. Lucien de Rubempre to you, as you are to meet again at supper."

"You have a good name, monsieur," said Nathan.

"Lucien, M. Raoul Nathan," continued Etienne.

"I read your book two days ago; and, upon my word, I cannot understand how you, who have written such a book, and such poetry, can be so humble to a journalist."

"Wait till your first book comes out," said Nathan, and a shrewd smile flitted over his face.

"I say! I say! here are Ultras and Liberals actually shaking hands!" cried Vernou, spying the trio.

"In the morning I hold the views of my paper," said Nathan, "in the evening I think as I please; all journalists see double at night."

Felicien Vernou turned to Lousteau.

"Finot is looking for you, Etienne; he came with me, and--here he is!"

"Ah, by the by, there is not a place in the house, is there?" asked Finot.

"You will always find a place in our hearts," said the actress, with the sweetest smile imaginable.

"I say, my little Florville, are you cured already of your fancy? They told me that a Russian prince had carried you off."

"Who carries off women in these days" said Florville (she who had cried, "Stop, wretched man!"). "We stayed at Saint-Mande for ten days, and my prince got off with paying the forfeit money to the management. The manager will go down on his knees to pray for some more Russian princes," Florville continued, laughing; "the forfeit money was so much clear gain."

"And as for you, child," said Finot, turning to a pretty girl in a peasant's costume, "where did you steal these diamond ear-drops? Have you hooked an Indian prince?"

"No, a blacking manufacturer, an Englishman, who has gone off already. It is not everybody who can find millionaire shopkeepers, tired of domestic life, whenever they like, as Florine does and Coralie. Aren't they just lucky?"

"Florville, you will make a bad entry," said Lousteau; "the blacking has gone to your head!"

"If you want a success," said Nathan, "instead of screaming, 'He is saved!' like a Fury, walk on quite quietly, go to the staircase, and say, 'He is saved,' in a chest voice, like Pasta's '*O patria*,' in *Tancreda*.--There, go along!" and he pushed her towards the stage.

"It is too late," said Vernou, "the effect has hung fire."

"What did she do? the house is applauding like mad," asked Lousteau.

"Went down on her knees and showed her bosom; that is her great resource," said the blacking-maker's widow.

"The manager is giving up the stage box to us; you will find me there when you come," said Finot, as Lousteau walked off with Lucien.

At the back of the stage, through a labyrinth of scenery and corridors, the pair climbed several flights of stairs and reached a little room on a third floor, Nathan and Felicien Vernou following them.

"Good-day or good-night, gentlemen," said Florine. Then, turning to a short, stout man standing in a corner, "These gentlemen are the rulers of my destiny," she said, my future is in their hands; but they will be under our table tomorrow morning, I hope, if M. Lousteau has forgotten nothing----"

"Forgotten! You are going to have Blondet of the *Debats*," said Etienne, "the genuine Blondet, the very Blondet--Blondet himself, in short."

"Oh! Lousteau, you dear boy! stop, I must give you a kiss," and she flung her arms about the journalist's neck. Matifat, the stout person in the corner, looked serious at this.

Florine was thin; her beauty, like a bud, gave promise of the flower to come; the girl of sixteen could only delight the eyes of artists who prefer the sketch to the picture. All the quick subtlety of her character was visible in the features of the charming actress, who at that time might have sat for Goethe's Mignon. Matifat, a wealthy druggist of the Rue des Lombards, had imagined that a little Boulevard actress would have no very expensive tastes, but in eleven months Florine had cost him sixty thousand francs. Nothing seemed more extraordinary to Lucien than the sight of an honest and worthy merchant standing like a statue of the god Terminus in the actress' narrow dressing-room, a tiny place some ten feet square, hung with a pretty wall-paper, and adorned with a full-length mirror, a sofa, and two chairs. There was a fireplace in the dressing-closet, a carpet on the floor, and cupboards all round the room. A dresser was putting the finishing touches to a Spanish costume; for Florine was to take the part of a countess in an imbroglio.

"That girl will be the handsomest actress in Paris in five years' time," said Nathan, turning to Felicien Vernou.

"By the by, darlings, you will take care of me tomorrow, won't you?" said Florine, turning to the three journalists. "I have engaged cabs for tonight, for I am going to send you home as tipsy as Shrove Tuesday. Matifat has sent in wines--oh! wines worthy of Louis XVIII., and engaged the Prussian ambassador's cook."

"We expect something enormous from the look of the gentleman," remarked Nathan.

"And he is quite aware that he is treating the most dangerous men in Paris," added Florine.

Matifat was looking uneasily at Lucien; he felt jealous of the young man's good looks.

"But here is some one that I do not know," Florine continued, confronting Lucien. "Which of you has imported the Apollo Belvedere from Florence? He is as charming as one of Girodet's figures."

"He is a poet, mademoiselle, from the provinces. I forgot to present him to you; you are so beautiful tonight that you put the *Complete Guide to Etiquette* out of a man's head----"

"Is he so rich that he can afford to write poetry?" asked Florine.

"Poor as Job," said Lucien.

"It is a great temptation for some of us," said the actress.

Just then the author of the play suddenly entered, and Lucien beheld M. du Bruel, a short, attenuated young man in an overcoat, a composite human blend of the jack-in-office, the owner of house-property, and the stockbroker.

"Florine, child," said this personage, "are you sure of your part, eh? No slips of memory, you know. And mind that scene in the second act, make the irony tell, bring out that subtle touch; say, 'I do not love you,' just as we agreed."

"Why do you take parts in which you have to say such things?" asked Matifat.

The druggist's remark was received with a general shout of laughter.

"What does it matter to you," said Florine, "so long as I don't say such things to you, great stupid?--Oh! his stupidity is the pleasure of my life," she continued, glancing at the journalist. "Upon my word, I would pay him so much for every blunder, if it would not be the ruin of me."

"Yes, but you will look at me when you say it, as you do when you are rehearsing, and it gives me a turn," remonstrated the druggist.

"Very well, then, I will look at my friend Lousteau here."

A bell rang outside in the passage.

"Go out, all of you!" cried Florine; "let me read my part over again and try to understand it."

Lucien and Lousteau were the last to go. Lousteau set a kiss on Florine's shoulder, and Lucien heard her say, "Not tonight. Impossible. That stupid old animal told his wife that he was going out into the country."

"Isn't she charming?" said Etienne, as they came away.

"But--but that Matifat, my dear fellow----"

"Oh! you know nothing of Parisian life, my boy. Some things cannot be helped. Suppose that you fell in love with a married woman, it comes to the same thing. It all depends on the way that you look at it."

Etienne and Lucien entered the stage-box, and found the manager there with Finot. Matifat was in the ground-floor box exactly opposite with a friend of his, a silk-mercer named Camusot (Coralie's protector), and a worthy little old soul, his father-in-law. All three of these city men were polishing their opera-glasses, and anxiously scanning the house; certain symptoms in the pit appeared to disturb them. The usual heterogeneous first-night elements filled the boxes--journalists and their mistresses, *lorettes* and their lovers, a sprinkling of the determined playgoers who never miss a first night if they can help it, and a very few people of fashion who care for this sort of sensation. The first box was occupied by the head of a department, to whom du Bruel, maker of vaudevilles, owed a snug little sinecure in the Treasury.

Lucien had gone from surprise to surprise since the dinner at Flicoteaux's. For two months Literature had meant a life of poverty and want; in Lousteau's room he had seen it at its cynical worst; in the Wooden Galleries he had met Literature abject and Literature insolent. The sharp contrasts of heights and depths; of compromise with conscience; of supreme power and want of principle; of treachery and pleasure; of mental elevation and bondage--all this made his head swim, he seemed to be watching some strange unheard-of drama.

Finot was talking with the manager. "Do you think du Bruel's piece will pay?" he asked.

"Du Bruel has tried to do something in Beaumarchais' style. Boulevard audiences don't care for that kind of thing; they like harrowing sensations; wit is not much appreciated here. Everything depends on Florine and Coralie tonight; they are bewitchingly pretty and graceful, wear very short skirts, and dance a Spanish dance, and possibly they may carry off the piece with the public. The whole affair is a gambling speculation. A few clever notices in the papers, and I may make a hundred thousand crowns, if the play takes."

"Oh! come, it will only be a moderate success, I can see," said Finot.

"Three of the theatres have got up a plot," continued the manager; "they will even hiss the piece, but I have made arrangements to defeat their kind intentions. I have squared the men in their pay; they will make a muddle of it. A couple of city men yonder have taken a hundred tickets apiece to secure a triumph for Florine and Coralie, and given them to acquaintances able and ready to act as chuckers out. The fellows, having been paid twice, will go quietly, and a scene of that sort always makes a good impression on the house."

"Two hundred tickets! What invaluable men!" exclaimed Finot.

"Yes. With two more actresses as handsomely kept as Florine and Coralie, I should make something out of the business."

For the past two hours the word money had been sounding in Lucien's ears as the solution of every difficulty. In the theatre as in the publishing trade, and in the publishing trade as in the newspaper-office--it was everywhere the same; there was not a word of art or of glory. The steady beat of the great pendulum, Money, seemed to fall like hammer-strokes on his heart and brain. And yet while the orchestra played the overture, while the pit was full of noisy tumult of applause and hisses, unconsciously he drew a comparison between this scene and others that came up in his mind. Visions arose before him of David and the printing-office, of the poetry that he came to know in that atmosphere of pure peace, when together they beheld the wonders of Art, the high successes of genius, and visions of glory borne on stainless wings. He thought of the evenings spent with d'Arthez and his friends, and tears glittered in his eyes.

"What is the matter with you?" asked Etienne Lousteau.

"I see poetry fallen into the mire."

"Ah! you have still some illusions left, my dear fellow."

"Is there nothing for it but to cringe and submit to thickheads like Matifat and Camusot, as actresses bow down to journalists, and we ourselves to the booksellers?"

"My boy, do you see that dull-brained fellow?" said Etienne, lowering his voice, and glancing at Finot. "He has neither genius nor cleverness, but he is covetous; he means to make a fortune at all costs, and he is a keen man of business. Didn't you see how he made forty per cent out of me at Dauriat's, and talked as if he were doing me a favor?--Well, he gets letters from not a few unknown men of genius who go down on their knees to him for a hundred francs."

The words recalled the pen-and-ink sketch that lay on the table in the editor's office and the words, "Finot, my hundred francs!" Lucien's inmost soul shrank from the man in disgust.

"I would sooner die," he said.

"Sooner live," retorted Etienne.

The curtain rose, and the stage-manager went off to the wings to give orders. Finot turned to Etienne.

"My dear fellow, Dauriat has passed his word; I am proprietor of one-third of his weekly paper. I have agreed to give thirty thousand francs in cash, on condition that I am to be editor and director. 'Tis a splendid thing. Blondet told me that the Government intends to take restrictive measures against the press; there will be no new papers allowed; in six months' time it will cost a million francs to start a new journal, so I struck a bargain though I have only ten thousand francs in hand. Listen to me. If you can sell one-half of my share, that is one-sixth of the paper, to Matifat for thirty thousand francs, you shall be editor of my little paper with a salary of two hundred and fifty francs per month. I want in any case to have the control of my old paper, and to keep my hold upon it; but nobody need know that, and your name will appear as editor. You will be paid at the rate of five francs per column; you need not pay contributors more than three francs, and you keep the difference. That means another four hundred and fifty francs per month. But, at the same time, I reserve the right to use the paper to attack or defend men or causes, as I please; and you may indulge your own likes and dislikes so long as you do not interfere with my schemes. Perhaps I may be a Ministerialist, perhaps Ultra, I do not know yet; but I mean to keep up my connections with the Liberal party (below the surface). I can speak out with you; you are a good fellow. I might, perhaps, give you the Chambers to do for another paper on which I work; I am afraid I can scarcely keep on with it now. So let Florine do this bit of jockeying; tell her to put the screw on her druggist. If I can't find the money within forty-eight hours, I must cry off my bargain. Dauriat sold another third to his printer and paper-dealer for thirty thousand francs; so he has his own third *gratis*, and ten thousand francs to the good, for he only gave fifty thousand for the whole affair. And in another year's time the magazine will be worth two hundred thousand francs, if the Court buys it up; if the Court has the good sense to suppress newspapers, as they say."

"You are lucky," said Lousteau.

"If you had gone through all that I have endured, you would not say that of me. I had my fill of misery in those days, you see, and there was no help for it. My father is a hatter; he still keeps a shop in the Rue du Coq. Nothing but millions of money or a social cataclysm can open out the way to my goal; and of the two alternatives, I don't know now that the revolution is not the easier. If I bore your friend's name, I should have a chance to get on. Hush, here comes the manager. Good-bye," and Finot rose to his feet, "I am going to the Opera. I shall very likely have a duel on my hands tomorrow, for I have put my initials to a terrific attack on a couple of dancers under the protection of two Generals. I am giving it them hot and strong at the Opera."

"Aha?" said the manager.

"Yes. They are stingy with me," returned Finot, "now cutting off a box, and now declining to take fifty subscriptions. I have sent in my *ultimatum*; I mean to have a hundred subscriptions out of them and a box four times a month. If they take my terms, I shall have eight hundred readers and a thousand paying subscribers, so we shall have twelve hundred with the New Year."

"You will end by ruining us," said the manager.

"*You* are not much hurt with your ten subscriptions. I had two good notices put into the *Constitutionnel*."

"Oh! I am not complaining of you," cried the manager.

"Good-bye till tomorrow evening, Lousteau," said Finot. "You can give me your answer at the Francais; there is a new piece on there; and as I shall not be able to write the notice, you can take my box. I will give you preference; you have worked yourself to death for me, and I am grateful. Felicien Vernou offered twenty thousand francs for a third share of my

154

little paper, and to work without a salary for a twelvemonth; but I want to be absolute master. Good-bye."

"He is not named Finot" (*finaud*, slyboots) "for nothing," said Lucien.

"He is a gallows-bird that will get on in the world," said Etienne, careless whether the wily schemer overheard the remark or not, as he shut the door of the box.

"*He*!" said the manager. "He will be a millionaire; he will enjoy the respect of all who know him; he may perhaps have friends some day----"

"Good heavens! what a den!" said Lucien. "And are you going to drag that excellent creature into such a business?" he continued, looking at Florine, who gave them side glances from the stage.

"She will carry it through too. You do not know the devotion and the wiles of these beloved beings," said Lousteau.

"They redeem their failings and expiate all their sins by boundless love, when they love," said the manager. "A great love is all the grander in an actress by reason of its violent contrast with her surroundings."

"And he who finds it, finds a diamond worthy of the proudest crown lying in the mud," returned Lousteau.

"But Coralie is not attending to her part," remarked the manager. "Coralie is smitten with our friend here, all unsuspicious of his conquest, and Coralie will make a fiasco; she is missing her cues, this is the second time she had not heard the prompter. Pray, go into the corner, monsieur," he continued. "If Coralie is smitten with you, I will go and tell her that you have left the house."

"No! no!" cried Lousteau; "tell Coralie that this gentleman is coming to supper, and that she can do as she likes with him, and she will play like Mlle. Mars."

The manager went, and Lucien turned to Etienne. "What! do you mean to say that you will ask that druggist, through Mlle. Florine, to pay thirty thousand francs for one-half a share, when Finot gave no more for the whole of it? And ask without the slightest scruple?----"

Lousteau interrupted Lucien before he had time to finish his expostulation. "My dear boy, what country can you come from? The druggist is not a man; he is a strong box delivered into our hands by his fancy for an actress."

"How about your conscience?"

"Conscience, my dear fellow, is a stick which every one takes up to beat his neighbor and not for application to his own back. Come, now! who the devil are you angry with? In one day chance has worked a miracle for you, a miracle for which I have been waiting these two years, and you must needs amuse yourself by finding fault with the means? What! you appear to me to possess intelligence; you seem to be in a fair way to reach that freedom from prejudice which is a first necessity to intellectual adventurers in the world we live in; and are you wallowing in scruples worthy of a nun who accuses herself of eating an egg with concupiscence? . . . If Florine succeeds, I shall be editor of a newspaper with a fixed salary of two hundred and fifty francs per month; I shall take the important plays and leave the vaudevilles to Vernou, and you can take my place and do the Boulevard theatres, and so get a foot in the stirrup. You will make three francs per column and write a column a day--thirty columns a month means ninety francs; you will have some sixty francs worth of books to sell to Barbet; and lastly, you can demand ten tickets a month of each of your theatres--that is, forty tickets in all--and sell them for forty francs to a Barbet who deals in them (I will introduce you to the man), so you will have two hundred francs coming in every month. Then if you make yourself useful to Finot, you might get a hundred francs for an article in this new weekly review of his, in which case you would show uncommon talent, for all the articles are signed, and you cannot put in slip-shod work as you can on a small paper. In that case you would be making a hundred crowns a month. Now, my dear boy, there are men of ability, like that poor d'Arthez, who dines at Flicoteaux's every day, who may wait for ten years before they will make a hundred crowns; and you will be making four thousand francs a year by your pen, to say nothing of the books you will write for the trade, if you do work of that kind.

"Now, a sub-prefect's salary only amounts to a thousand crowns, and there he stops in his arrondissement, wearing away time like the rung of a chair. I say nothing of the pleasure of going to the theatre without paying for your seat, for that is a delight which quickly palls; but you can go behind the scenes in four theatres. Be hard and sarcastic for a month or two, and you will be simply overwhelmed with invitations from actresses, and their adorers will pay court to you; you will only dine at Flicoteaux's when you happen to have less than thirty sous in your pocket and no dinner engagement. At the Luxembourg, at five o'clock, you did not know which way to turn; now, you are on the eve of entering a privileged class, you will be one of the hundred persons who tell France what to think. In three days' time, if all goes well, you can, if you choose, make a man's life a curse to him by putting thirty jokes at his expense in print at the rate of three a day; you can, if you choose, draw a revenue of pleasure from the actresses at your theatres; you can wreck a good play and send all Paris running after a bad one. If Dauriat declines to pay you for your *Marguerites*, you can make him come to you, and meekly and humbly implore you to take two thousand francs for them. If you have the ability, and knock off two or three articles that threaten to spoil some of Dauriat's speculations, or to ruin a book on which he counts, you will see him come climbing up your stairs like a clematis, and always at the door of your dwelling. As for your novel, the booksellers who would show you more or less politely to the door at this moment will be standing outside your attic in a string, and the value of the manuscript, which old Doguereau valued at four hundred francs will rise to four thousand. These are the advantages of the journalist's profession. So let us do our best to keep all newcomers out of it. It needs an immense amount of brains to make your way, and a still greater amount of luck. And here are you quibbling over your good fortune! If we had not met today, you see, at Flicoteaux's, you might have danced attendance on the booksellers for another three years, or starved like d'Arthez in a garret. By the time that d'Arthez is as learned as Bayle and as great a writer of prose as Rousseau, we shall have made our fortunes, you and I, and we shall hold his in our hands--wealth and fame to give or to hold. Finot will be a deputy and proprietor of a great newspaper, and we shall be whatever we meant to be--peers of France, or prisoner for debt in Sainte-Pelagie."

"So Finot will sell his paper to the highest bidder among the Ministers, just as he sells favorable notices to Mme. Bastienne and runs down Mlle. Virginie, saying that Mme. Bastienne's bonnets are superior to the millinery which they praised at first!" said Lucien, recollecting that scene in the office.

"My dear fellow, you are a simpleton," Lousteau remarked drily. "Three years ago Finot was walking on the uppers of his boots, dining for eighteen sous at Tabar's, and knocking off a tradesman's prospectus (when he could get it) for ten francs. His clothes hung together by some miracle as mysterious as the Immaculate Conception. *Now*, Finot has a paper of his own, worth about a hundred thousand francs. What with subscribers who pay and take no copies, genuine subscriptions, and indirect taxes levied by his uncle, he is making twenty thousand francs a year. He dines most sumptuously every day; he has set up a cabriolet within the last month; and now, at last, behold him the editor of a weekly review with a sixth share, for which he will not pay a penny, a salary of five hundred francs per month, and another thousand francs for supplying matter which costs him nothing, and for which the firm pays. You yourself, to begin with, if Finot consents to pay you fifty francs per sheet, will be only too glad to let him have two or three articles for nothing. When you are in his position, you can judge Finot; a man can only be tried by his peers. And for you, is there not an immense future opening out before you, if you will blindly minister to his enmity, attack at Finot's bidding, and praise when he gives the word? Suppose that you yourself wish to be revenged upon somebody, you can break a foe or friend on the wheel. You have only to say to me, 'Lousteau, let us put an end to So-and-so,' and we will kill him by a phrase put in the paper morning by morning; and afterwards you can slay the slain with a solemn article in Finot's weekly. Indeed, if it is a matter of capital importance to you, Finot would allow you to bludgeon your man in a big paper with ten or twelve thousand subscribers, *if* you make yourself indispensable to Finot."

"Then are you sure that Florine can bring her druggist to make the bargain?" asked Lucien, dazzled by these prospects.

"Quite sure. Now comes the interval, I will go and tell her everything at once in a word or two; it will be settled tonight. If Florine once has her lesson by heart, she will have all my wit and her own besides."

"And there sits that honest tradesman, gaping with open-mouthed admiration at Florine, little suspecting that you are about to get thirty thousand francs out of him!----"

"More twaddle! Anybody might think that the man was going to be robbed!" cried Lousteau. "Why, my dear boy, if the minister buys the newspaper, the druggist may make twenty thousand francs in six months on an investment of thirty thousand. Matifat is not looking at the newspaper, but at Florine's prospects. As soon as it is known that Matifat and Camusot--(for they will go shares)--that Matifat and Camusot are proprietors of a review, the newspapers will be full of friendly notices of Florine and Coralie. Florine's name will be made; she will perhaps obtain an engagement in another theatre with a salary of twelve thousand francs. In fact, Matifat will save a thousand francs every month in dinners and presents to journalists. You know nothing of men, nor of the way things are managed."

"Poor man!" said Lucien, "he is looking forward to an evening's pleasure."

"And he will be sawn in two with arguments until Florine sees Finot's receipt for a sixth share of the paper. And tomorrow I shall be editor of Finot's paper, and making a thousand francs a month. The end of my troubles is in sight!" cried Florine's lover.

Lousteau went out, and Lucien sat like one bewildered, lost in the infinite of thought, soaring above this everyday world. In the Wooden Galleries he had seen the wires by which the trade in books is moved; he has seen something of the kitchen where great reputations are made; he had been behind the scenes; he had seen the seamy side of life, the consciences of men involved in the machinery of Paris, the mechanism of it all. As he watched Florine on the stage he almost envied Lousteau his good fortune; already, for a few moments he had forgotten Matifat in the background. He was not left alone for long, perhaps for not more than five minutes, but those minutes seemed an eternity.

Thoughts rose within him that set his soul on fire, as the spectacle on the stage had heated his senses. He looked at the women with their wanton eyes, all the brighter for the red paint on their cheeks, at the gleaming bare necks, the luxuriant forms outlined by the lascivious folds of the basquina, the very short skirts, that displayed as much as possible of limbs encased in scarlet stockings with green clocks to them--a disquieting vision for the pit.

A double process of corruption was working within him in parallel lines, like two channels that will spread sooner or later in flood time and make one. That corruption was eating into Lucien's soul, as he leaned back in his corner, staring vacantly at the curtain, one arm resting on the crimson velvet cushion, and his hand drooping over the edge. He felt the fascination of the life that was offered to him, of the gleams of light among its clouds; and this so much the more keenly because it shone out like a blaze of fireworks against the blank darkness of his own obscure, monotonous days of toil.

Suddenly his listless eyes became aware of a burning glance that reached him through a rent in the curtain, and roused him from his lethargy. Those were Coralie's eyes that glowed upon him. He lowered his head and looked across at Camusot, who just then entered the opposite box.

That amateur was a worthy silk-mercer of the Rue des Bourdonnais, stout and substantial, a judge in the commercial court, a father of four children, and the husband of a second wife. At the age of fifty-six, with a cap of gray hair on his head, he had the smug appearance of a man who has his eighty thousand francs of income; and having been forced to put up with a good deal that he did not like in the way of business, has fully made up his mind to enjoy the rest of his life, and not to quit this earth until he has had his share of cakes and ale. A brow the color of fresh butter and florid cheeks like a monk's jowl seemed scarcely big enough to contain his exuberant jubilation. Camusot had left his wife at home, and they were applauding Coralie to the skies. All the rich man's citizen vanity was summed up and gratified in Coralie; in Coralie's lodging he gave himself the airs of a great lord of a bygone day; now, at this moment, he felt that half of her success was his; the knowledge that he had paid for it confirmed him in this idea. Camusot's conduct was sanctioned by the presence of his father-in-law, a little old fogy with powdered hair and leering eyes, highly respected nevertheless.

Again Lucien felt disgust rising within him. He thought of the year when he loved Mme. de Bargeton with an exalted and disinterested love; and at that thought love, as a poet understands it, spread its white wings about him; countless memories drew a circle of distant blue horizon about the great man of Angouleme, and again he fell to dreaming.

Up went the curtain, and there stood Coralie and Florine upon the stage.

"He is thinking about as much of you as of the Grand Turk, my dear girl," Florine said in an aside while Coralie was finishing her speech.

Lucien could not help laughing. He looked at Coralie. She was one of the most charming and captivating actresses in Paris, rivaling Mme. Perrin and Mlle. Fleuriet, and destined likewise to share their fate. Coralie was a woman of a type that exerts at will a power of fascination over men. With an oval face of deep ivory tint, a mouth red as a pomegranate, and a chin subtly delicate in its contour as the edge of a porcelain cup, Coralie was a Jewess of the sublime type. The jet black eyes behind their curving lashes seemed to scorch her eyelids; you could guess how soft they might grow, or how sparks of the heat of the desert might flash from them in response to a summons from within. The circles of olive shadow about them were bounded by thick arching lines of eyebrow. Magnificent mental power, well-nigh amounting to genius, seemed to dwell in the swarthy forehead beneath the double curve of ebony hair that lay upon it like a crown, and gleamed in the light like a varnished surface; but like many another actress, Coralie had little wit in spite of her aptness at greenroom repartee, and scarcely any education in spite of her boudoir experience. Her brain was prompted by her senses, her kindness was the impulsive warm-heartedness of girls of her class. But who could trouble over Coralie's psychology when his eyes were dazzled by those smooth, round arms of hers, the spindle-shaped fingers, the fair white shoulders, and breast celebrated in the Song of Songs, the flexible curving lines of throat, the graciously moulded outlines beneath the scarlet silk stockings? And this beauty, worthy of an Eastern poet, was brought into relief by the conventional Spanish costume of the stage. Coralie was the delight of the pit; all eyes dwelt on the outlines moulded by the clinging folds of her bodice, and lingered over the Andalusian contour of the hips from which her skirt hung, fluttering wantonly with every movement. To Lucien, watching this creature, who played for him alone, caring no more for Camusot than a street-boy in the gallery cares for an apple-paring, there came a moment when he set desire above love, and enjoyment above desire, and the demon of Lust stirred strange thoughts in him.

"I know nothing of the love that wallows in luxury and wine and sensual pleasure," he said within himself. "I have lived more with ideas than with realities. You must pass through all experience if you mean to render all experience. This will be my first great supper, my first orgy in a new and strange world; why should I not know, for once, the delights which the great lords of the eighteenth century sought so eagerly of wantons of the Opera? Must one not first learn of courtesans and actresses the delights, the perfections, the transports, the resources, the subtleties of love, if only to translate them afterwards into the regions of a higher love than this? And what is all this, after all, but the poetry of the senses? Two months ago these women seemed to me to be goddesses guarded by dragons that no one dared approach; I was envying Lousteau just now, but here is another handsomer than Florine; why should I not profit by her fancy, when the greatest nobles buy a night with such women with their richest treasures? When ambassadors set foot in these depths, they fling aside all thought of yesterday or tomorrow. I should be a fool to be more squeamish than princes, especially as I love no one as yet."

Lucien had quite forgotten Camusot. To Lousteau he had expressed the utmost disgust for this most hateful of all partitions, and now he himself had sunk to the same level, and, carried away by the casuistry of his vehement desire, had given the reins to his fancy.

"Coralie is raving about you," said Lousteau as he came in. "Your countenance, worthy of the greatest Greek sculptors, has worked unutterable havoc behind the scenes. You are in luck my dear boy. Coralie is eighteen years old, and in a few days' time she may be making sixty thousand francs a year by her beauty. She is an honest girl still. Since her mother sold her three years ago for sixty thousand francs, she has tried to find happiness, and found nothing but annoyance. She took to the stage in a desperate mood; she has a horror of her first purchaser, de Marsay; and when she came out of the galleys, for the king of dandies soon dropped her, she picked up old Camusot. She does not care much about him, but he is like a father to her, and she endures him and his love. Several times already she has refused the handsomest proposals; she is faithful to Camusot, who lets her live in peace. So you are her first love. The first sight of you went to her heart like a pistol-shot, Florine has gone to her dressing-room to bring the girl to reason. She is crying over your cruelty; she has forgotten her part, the play will go to pieces, and good-day to the engagement at the Gymnase which Camusot had planned for her."

"Pooh! . . . Poor thing!" said Lucien. Every instinct of vanity was tickled by the words; he felt his heart swell high with self-conceit. "More adventures have befallen me in this one evening, my dear fellow, than in all the first eighteen years of my life." And Lucien related the history of his love affairs with Mme. de Bargeton, and of the cordial hatred he bore the Baron du Chatelet.

"Stay though! the newspaper wants a *bete noire*; we will take him up. The Baron is a buck of the Empire and a Ministerialist; he is the man for us; I have seen him many a time at the Opera. I can see your great lady as I sit here; she is often in the Marquise d'Espard's box. The Baron is paying court to your lady love, a cuttlefish bone that she is. Wait! Finot has just sent a special messenger round to say that they are short of copy at the office. Young Hector Merlin has left them in the lurch because they did not pay for white lines. Finot, in despair, is knocking off an article against the Opera. Well now, my dear fellow, you can do this play; listen to it and think it over, and I will go to the manager's office and think out three columns about your man and your disdainful fair one. They will be in no pleasant predicament tomorrow."

"So this is how a newspaper is written?" said Lucien.

"It is always like this," answered Lousteau. "These ten months that I have been a journalist, they have always run short of copy at eight o'clock in the evening."

Manuscript sent to the printer is spoken of as "copy," doubtless because the writers are supposed to send in a fair copy of their work; or possibly the word is ironically derived from the Latin word *copia*, for copy is invariably scarce.

"We always mean to have a few numbers ready in advance, a grand idea that will never be realized," continued Lousteau. "It is ten o'clock, you see, and not a line has been written. I shall ask Vernou and Nathan for a score of epigrams on deputies, or on 'Chancellor Cruzoe,' or on the Ministry, or on friends of ours if it needs must be. A man in this pass would slaughter his parent, just as a privateer will load his guns with silver pieces taken out of the booty sooner than perish. Write a brilliant article, and you will make brilliant progress in Finot's estimation; for Finot has a lively sense of benefits to come, and that sort of gratitude is better than any kind of pledge, pawntickets always excepted, for they invariably represent something solid."

"What kind of men can journalists be? Are you to sit down at a table and be witty to order?"

"Just exactly as a lamp begins to burn when you apply a match--so long as there is any oil in it."

Lousteau's hand was on the lock when du Bruel came in with the manager.

"Permit me, monsieur, to take a message to Coralie; allow me to tell her that you will go home with her after supper, or my play will be ruined. The wretched girl does not know what she is doing or saying; she will cry when she ought to laugh and laugh when she ought to cry. She has been hissed once already. You can still save the piece, and, after all, pleasure is not a misfortune."

"I am not accustomed to rivals, sir," Lucien answered.

"Pray don't tell her that!" cried the manager. "Coralie is just the girl to fling Camusot overboard and ruin herself in good earnest. The proprietor of the *Golden Cocoon*, worthy man, allows her two thousand francs a month, and pays for all her dresses and *claqueurs*."

"As your promise pledges me to nothing, save your play," said Lucien, with a sultan's airs.

"But don't look as if you meant to snub that charming creature," pleaded du Bruel.

"Dear me! am I to write the notice of your play and smile on your heroine as well?" exclaimed the poet.

The author vanished with a signal to Coralie, who began to act forthwith in a marvelous way. Vignol, who played the part of the alcalde, and revealed for the first time his genius as an actor of old men, came forward amid a storm of applause to make an announcement to the house.

"The piece which we have the honor of playing for you this evening, gentlemen, is the work of MM. Raoul and de Cursy."

"Why, Nathan is partly responsible," said Lousteau. "I don't wonder that he looked in."

"Coralie*! Coralie*!" shouted the enraptured house. "Florine, too!" roared a voice of thunder from the opposite box, and other voices took up the cry, "Florine and Coralie!"

The curtain rose, Vignol reappeared between the two actresses; Matifat and Camusot flung wreaths on the stage, and Coralie stooped for her flowers and held them out to Lucien.

For him those two hours spent in the theatre seemed to be a dream. The spell that held him had begun to work when he went behind the scenes; and, in spite of its horrors, the atmosphere of the place, its sensuality and dissolute morals had affected the poet's still untainted nature. A sort of malaria that infects the soul seems to lurk among those dark, filthy passages filled with machinery, and lit with smoky, greasy lamps. The solemnity and reality of life disappear, the most sacred things are matter for a jest, the most impossible things seem to be true. Lucien felt as if he had taken some narcotic, and Coralie had completed the work. He plunged into this joyous intoxication.

The lights in the great chandelier were extinguished; there was no one left in the house except the boxkeepers, busy taking away footstools and shutting doors, the noises echoing strangely through the empty theatre. The footlights, blown out as one candle, sent up a fetid reek of smoke. The curtain rose again, a lantern was lowered from the ceiling, and firemen and stage carpenters departed on their rounds. The fairy scenes of the stage, the rows of fair faces in the boxes, the dazzling lights, the magical illusion of new scenery and costume had all disappeared, and dismal darkness, emptiness, and cold reigned in their stead. It was hideous. Lucien sat on in bewilderment.

"Well! are you coming, my boy?" Lousteau's voice called from the stage. "Jump down."

Lucien sprang over. He scarcely recognized Florine and Coralie in their ordinary quilted paletots and cloaks, with their faces hidden by hats and thick black veils. Two butterflies returned to the chrysalis stage could not be more completely transformed.

"Will you honor me by giving me your arm?" Coralie asked tremulously.

"With pleasure," said Lucien. He could feel the beating of her heart throbbing against his like some snared bird as she nestled closely to his side, with something of the delight of a cat that rubs herself against her master with eager silken caresses.

"So we are supping together!" she said.

The party of four found two cabs waiting for them at the door in the Rue des Fosses-du-Temple. Coralie drew Lucien to one of the two, in which Camusot and his father-in-law old Cardot were seated already. She offered du Bruel a fifth place, and the manager drove off with Florine, Matifat, and Lousteau.

"These hackney cabs are abominable things," said Coralie.

"Why don't you have a carriage?" returned du Bruel.

"*Why*?" she asked pettishly. "I do not like to tell you before M. Cardot's face; for he trained his son-in-law, no doubt. Would you believe it, little and old as he is, M. Cardot only gives Florine five hundred francs a month, just about enough to pay for her rent and her grub and her clothes. The old Marquis de Rochegude offered me a brougham two months ago, and he has six hundred thousand francs a year, but I am an artist and not a common hussy."

"You shall have a carriage the day after tomorrow, miss," said Camusot benignly; "you never asked me for one."

"As if one *asked* for such a thing as that? What! you love a woman and let her paddle about in the mud at the risk of breaking her legs? Nobody but a knight of the yardstick likes to see a draggled skirt hem."

As she uttered the sharp words that cut Camusot to the quick, she groped for Lucien's knee, and pressed it against her own, and clasped her fingers upon his hand. She was silent. All her power to feel seemed to be concentrated upon the ineffable joy of a moment which brings compensation for the whole wretched past of a life such as these poor creatures lead, and develops within their souls a poetry of which other women, happily ignorant of these violent revulsions, know nothing.

"You played like Mlle. Mars herself towards the end," said du Bruel.

"Yes," said Camusot, "something put her out at the beginning; but from the middle of the second act to the very end, she was enough to drive you wild with admiration. Half of the success of your play was due to her."

"And half of her success is due to me," said du Bruel.

"This is all much ado about nothing," said Coralie in an unfamiliar voice. And, seizing an opportunity in the darkness, she carried Lucien's hand to her lips and kissed it and drenched it with tears. Lucien felt thrilled through and through by that touch, for in the humility of the courtesan's love there is a magnificence which might set an example to angels.

"Are you writing the dramatic criticism, monsieur?" said du Bruel, addressing Lucien; "you can write a charming paragraph about our dear Coralie."

"Oh! do us that little service!" pleaded Camusot, down on his knees, metaphorically speaking, before the critic. "You will always find me ready to do you a good turn at any time."

"Do leave him his independence," Coralie exclaimed angrily; "he will write what he pleases. Papa Camusot, buy carriages for me instead of praises."

"You shall have them on very easy terms," Lucien answered politely. "I have never written for newspapers before, so I am not accustomed to their ways, my maiden pen is at your disposal----"

"That is funny," said du Bruel.

"Here we are in the Rue de Bondy," said Cardot. Coralie's sally had quite crushed the little old man.

"If you are giving me the first fruits of your pen, the first love that has sprung up in my heart shall be yours," whispered Coralie in the brief instant that they remained alone together in the cab; then she went up to Florine's bedroom to change her dress for a toilette previously sent.

Lucien had no idea how lavishly a prosperous merchant will spend money upon an actress or a mistress when he means to enjoy a life of pleasure. Matifat was not nearly so rich a man as his friend Camusot, and he had done his part rather shabbily, yet the sight of the dining-room took Lucien by surprise. The walls were hung with green cloth with a border of gilded nails, the whole room was artistically decorated, lighted by handsome lamps, stands full of flowers stood in every direction. The drawing-room was resplendent with the furniture in fashion in those days--a Thomire chandelier, a carpet of Eastern design, and yellow silken hangings relieved by a brown border. The candlesticks, fire-irons, and clock were all in good taste; for Matifat had left everything to Grindot, a rising architect, who was building a house for him, and the young man had taken great pains with the rooms when he knew that Florine was to occupy them.

Matifat, a tradesman to the backbone, went about carefully, afraid to touch the new furniture; he seemed to have the totals of the bills always before his eyes, and to look upon the splendors about him as so much jewelry imprudently withdrawn from the case.

"And I shall be obliged to do as much for Florentine!" old Cardot's eyes seemed to say.

Lucien at once began to understand Lousteau's indifference to the state of his garret. Etienne was the real king of these festivals; Etienne enjoyed the use of all these fine things. He was standing just now on the hearthrug with his back to the fire, as if he were the master of the house, chatting with the manager, who was congratulating du Bruel.

"Copy, copy!" called Finot, coming into the room. "There is nothing in the box; the printers are setting up my article, and they will soon have finished."

"We will manage," said Etienne. "There is a fire burning in Florine's boudoir; there is a table there; and if M. Matifat will find us paper and ink, we will knock off the newspaper while Florine and Coralie are dressing."

Cardot, Camusot, and Matifat disappeared in search of quills, penknives, and everything necessary. Suddenly the door was flung open, and Tullia, one of the prettiest opera-dancers of the day, dashed into the room.

"They agree to take the hundred copies, dear boy!" she cried, addressing Finot; "they won't cost the management anything, for the chorus and the orchestra and the *corps de ballet* are to take them whether they like it or not; but your paper is so clever that nobody will grumble. And you are going to have your boxes. Here is the subscription for the first quarter," she continued, holding out a couple of banknotes; "so don't cut me up!"

"It is all over with me!" groaned Finot; "I must suppress my abominable diatribe, and I haven't another notion in my head."

"What a happy inspiration, divine Lais!" exclaimed Blondet, who had followed the lady upstairs and brought Nathan, Vernou and Claude Vignon with him. "Stop to supper, there is a dear, or I will crush thee, butterfly as thou art. There will be no professional jealousies, as you are a dancer; and as to beauty, you have all of you too much sense to show jealousy in public."

"Oh dear!" cried Finot, "Nathan, Blondet, du Bruel, help friends! I want five columns."

"I can make two of the play," said Lucien.

"I have enough for one," added Lousteau.

"Very well; Nathan, Vernou, and du Bruel will make the jokes at the end; and Blondet, good fellow, surely will vouchsafe a couple of short columns for the first sheet. I will run round to the printer. It is lucky that you brought your carriage, Tullia."

"Yes, but the Duke is waiting below in it, and he has a German Minister with him."

"Ask the Duke and the Minister to come up," said Nathan.

"A German? They are the ones to drink, and they listen too; he shall hear some astonishing things to send home to his Government," cried Blondet.

"Is there any sufficiently serious personage to go down to speak to him?" asked Finot. "Here, du Bruel, you are an official; bring up the Duc de Rhetore and the Minister, and give your arm to Tullia. Dear me! Tullia, how handsome you are tonight!"

"We shall be thirteen at table!" exclaimed Matifat, paling visibly.

"No, fourteen," said a voice in the doorway, and Florentine appeared. "I have come to look after 'milord Cardot,'" she added, speaking with a burlesque English accent.

"And besides," said Lousteau, "Claude Vignon came with Blondet."

"I brought him here to drink," returned Blondet, taking up an inkstand. "Look here, all of you, you must use all your wit before those fifty-six bottles of wine drive it out. And, of all things, stir up du Bruel; he is a vaudevillist, he is capable of making bad jokes if you get him to concert pitch."

And Lucien wrote his first newspaper article at the round table in Florine's boudoir, by the light of the pink candles lighted by Matifat; before such a remarkable audience he was eager to show what he could do.

THE PANORAMA-DRAMATIQUE.

First performance of the *Alcalde in a Fix*, an imbroglio in three acts.--First appearance of Mademoiselle Florine.-- Mademoiselle Coralie.--Vignol.

People are coming and going, walking and talking, everybody is looking for something, nobody finds anything. General hubbub. The Alcalde has lost his daughter and found his cap, but the cap does not fit; it must belong to some thief. Where is the thief? People walk and talk, and come and go more than ever. Finally the Alcalde finds a man without his daughter, and his daughter without the man, which is satisfactory for the magistrate, but not for the audience. Quiet being resorted, the Alcalde tries to examine the man. Behold a venerable Alcalde, sitting in an Alcalde's great armchair, arranging the sleeves of his Alcalde's gown. Only in Spain do Alcaldes cling to their enormous sleeves and wear plaited lawn ruffles about the magisterial throat, a good half of an Alcalde's business on the stage in Paris. This particular Alcalde, wheezing and waddling about like an asthmatic old man, is Vignol, on whom Potier's mantle has fallen; a young actor who personates old age so admirably that the oldest men in the audience cannot help laughing. With that quavering voice of his, that bald forehead, and those spindle shanks trembling under the weight of a senile frame, he may look forward to a long career of decrepitude. There is something alarming about the young actor's old age; he is so very old; you feel nervous lest senility should be infectious. And what an admirable Alcalde he makes! What a delightful, uneasy smile! what pompous stupidity! what wooden dignity! what judicial hesitation! How well the man knows that black may be white, or white black! How eminently well he is fitted to be Minister to a constitutional monarch! The stranger answers every one of his inquiries by a question; Vignol retorts in such a fashion, that the person under examination elicits all the truth from the Alcalde. This piece of pure comedy, with a breath of Moliere throughout, puts the house in good humor. The people on the stage all seemed to understand what they were about, but I am quite unable to clear up the mystery, or to say wherein it lay; for the Alcalde's daughter was there, personified by a living, breathing Andalusian, a Spaniard with a

Spaniard's eyes, a Spaniard's complexion, a Spaniard's gait and figure, a Spaniard from top to toe, with her poniard in her garter, love in her heart, and a cross on the ribbon about her neck. When the act was over, and somebody asked me how the piece was going, I answered, "She wears scarlet stockings with green clocks to them; she has a little foot, no larger than *that*, in her patent leather shoes, and the prettiest pair of ankles in Andalusia!" Oh! that Alcalde's daughter brings your heart into your mouth; she tantalizes you so horribly, that you long to spring upon the stage and offer her your thatched hovel and your heart, or thirty thousand livres per annum and your pen. The Andalusian is the loveliest actress in Paris. Coralie, for she must be called by her real name, can be a countess or a *grisette*, and in which part she would be more charming one cannot tell. She can be anything that she chooses; she is born to achieve all possibilities; can more be said of a boulevard actress?

With the second act, a Parisian Spaniard appeared upon the scene, with her features cut like a cameo and her dangerous eyes. "Where does she come from?" I asked in my turn, and was told that she came from the greenroom, and that she was Mademoiselle Florine; but, upon my word, I could not believe a syllable of it, such spirit was there in her gestures, such frenzy in her love. She is the rival of the Alcalde's daughter, and married to a grandee cut out to wear an Almaviva's cloak, with stuff sufficient in it for a hundred boulevard noblemen. Mlle. Florine wore neither scarlet stockings with green clocks, nor patent leather shoes, but she appeared in a mantilla, a veil which she put to admirable uses, like the great lady that she is! She showed to admiration that the tigress can be a cat. I began to understand, from the sparkling talk between the two, that some drama of jealousy was going on; and just as everything was put right, the Alcalde's stupidity embroiled everybody again. Torchbearers, rich men, footmen, Figaros, grandees, alcaldes, dames, and damsels--the whole company on the stage began to eddy about, and come and go, and look for one another. The plot thickened, again I left it to thicken; for Florine the jealous and the happy Coralie had entangled me once more in the folds of mantilla and basquina, and their little feet were twinkling in my eyes.

I managed, however, to reach the third act without any mishap. The commissary of police was not compelled to interfere, and I did nothing to scandalize the house, wherefore I begin to believe in the influence of that "public and religious morality," about which the Chamber of Deputies is so anxious, that any one might think there was no morality left in France. I even contrived to gather that a man was in love with two women who failed to return his affection, or else that two women were in love with a man who loved neither of them; the man did not love the Alcalde, or the Alcalde had no love for the man, who was nevertheless a gallant gentleman, and in love with somebody, with himself, perhaps, or with heaven, if the worst came to the worst, for he becomes a monk. And if you want to know any more, you can go to the Panorama-Dramatique. You are hereby given fair warning--you must go once to accustom yourself to those irresistible scarlet stockings with the green clocks, to little feet full of promises, to eyes with a ray of sunlight shining through them, to the subtle charm of a Parisienne disguised as an Andalusian girl, and of an Andalusian masquerading as a Parisienne. You must go a second time to enjoy the play, to shed tears over the love-distracted grandee, and die of laughing at the old Alcalde. The play is twice a success. The author, who writes it, it is said, in collaboration with one of the great poets of the day, was called before the curtain, and appeared with a love-distraught damsel on each arm, and fairly brought down the excited house. The two dancers seemed to have more wit in their legs than the author himself; but when once the fair rivals left the stage, the dialogue seemed witty at once, a triumphant proof of the excellence of the piece. The applause and calls for the author caused the architect some anxiety; but M. de Cursy, the author, being accustomed to volcanic eruptions of the reeling Vesuvius beneath the chandelier, felt no tremor. As for the actresses, they danced the famous bolero of Seville, which once found favor in the sight of a council of reverend fathers, and escaped ecclesiastical censure in spite of its wanton dangerous grace. The bolero in itself would be enough to attract old age while there is any lingering heat of youth in the veins, and out of charity I warn these persons to keep the lenses of their opera-glasses well polished.

164

While Lucien was writing a column which was to set a new fashion in journalism and reveal a fresh and original gift, Lousteau indited an article of the kind described as *moeurs*--a sketch of contemporary manners, entitled *The Elderly Beau*.

"The buck of the Empire," he wrote, "is invariably long, slender, and well preserved. He wears a corset and the Cross of the Legion of Honor. His name was originally Potelet, or something very like it; but to stand well with the Court, he conferred a *du* upon himself, and *du* Potelet he is until another revolution. A baron of the Empire, a man of two ends, as his name (*Potelet*, a post) implies, he is paying his court to the Faubourg Saint-Germain, after a youth gloriously and usefully spent as the agreeable trainbearer of a sister of the man whom decency forbids me to mention by name. Du Potelet has forgotten that he was once in waiting upon Her Imperial Highness; but he still sings the songs composed for the benefactress who took such a tender interest in his career," and so forth and so forth. It was a tissue of personalities, silly enough for the most part, such as they used to write in those days. Other papers, and notably the *Figaro*, have brought the art to a curious perfection since. Lousteau compared the Baron to a heron, and introduced Mme. de Bargeton, to whom he was paying his court, as a cuttlefish bone, a burlesque absurdity which amused readers who knew neither of the personages. A tale of the loves of the Heron, who tried in vain to swallow the Cuttlefish bone, which broke into three pieces when he dropped it, was irresistibly ludicrous. Everybody remembers the sensation which the pleasantry made in the Faubourg Saint-Germain; it was the first of a series of similar articles, and was one of the thousand and one causes which provoked the rigorous press legislation of Charles X.

An hour later, Blondet, Lousteau, and Lucien came back to the drawing-room, where the other guests were chatting. The Duke was there and the Minister, the four women, the three merchants, the manager, and Finot. A printer's devil, with a paper cap on his head, was waiting even then for copy.

"The men are just going off, if I have nothing to take them," he said.

"Stay a bit, here are ten francs, and tell them to wait," said Finot.

"If I give them the money, sir, they would take to tippleography, and good-night to the newspaper."

"That boy's common-sense is appalling to me," remarked Finot; and the Minister was in the middle of a prediction of a brilliant future for the urchin, when the three came in. Blondet read aloud an extremely clever article against the Romantics; Lousteau's paragraph drew laughter, and by the Duc de Rhetore's advice an indirect eulogium of Mme. d'Espard was slipped in, lest the whole Faubourg Saint-Germain should take offence.

"What have *you* written?" asked Finot, turning to Lucien.

And Lucien read, quaking for fear, but the room rang with applause when he finished; the actresses embraced the neophyte; and the two merchants, following suit, half choked the breath out of him. There were tears in du Bruel's eyes as he grasped his critic's hand, and the manager invited him to dinner.

"There are no children nowadays," said Blondet. "Since M. de Chateaubriand called Victor Hugo a 'sublime child,' I can only tell you quite simply that you have spirit and taste, and write like a gentleman."

"He is on the newspaper," said Finot, as he thanked Etienne, and gave him a shrewd glance.

"What jokes have you made?" inquired Lousteau, turning to Blondet and du Bruel.

"Here are du Bruel's," said Nathan.

*** "Now, that M. le Vicomte d'A---- is attracting so much attention, they will perhaps let *me* alone," M. le Vicomte Demosthenes was heard to say yesterday.

*** An Ultra, condemning M. Pasquier's speech, said his programme was only a continuation of Decaze's policy. "Yes," said a lady, "but he stands on a Monarchical basis, he has just the kind of leg for a Court suit."

"With such a beginning, I don't ask more of you," said Finot; "it will be all right.--Run round with this," he added, turning to the boy; "the paper is not exactly a genuine article, but it is our best number yet," and he turned to the group of writers. Already Lucien's colleagues were privately taking his measure.

"That fellow has brains," said Blondet.

"His article is well written," said Claude Vignon.

"Supper!" cried Matifat.

The Duke gave his arm to Florine, Coralie went across to Lucien, and Tullia went in to supper between Emile Blondet and the German Minister.

"I cannot understand why you are making an onslaught on Mme. de Bargeton and the Baron du Chatelet; they say that he is prefect-designate of the Charente, and will be Master of Requests some day."

"Mme. de Bargeton showed Lucien the door as if he had been an imposter," said Lousteau.

"Such a fine young fellow!" exclaimed the Minister.

Supper, served with new plate, Sevres porcelain, and white damask, was redolent of opulence. The dishes were from Chevet, the wines from a celebrated merchant on the Quai Saint-Bernard, a personal friend of Matifat's. For the first time Lucien beheld the luxury of Paris displayed; he went from surprise to surprise, but he kept his astonishment to himself, like a man who had spirit and taste and wrote like a gentleman, as Blondet had said.

As they crossed the drawing-room, Coralie bent to Florine, "Make Camusot so drunk that he will be compelled to stop here all night," she whispered.

"So you have hooked your journalist, have you?" returned Florine, using the idiom of women of her class.

"No, dear; I love him," said Coralie, with an adorable little shrug of the shoulders.

Those words rang in Lucien's ears, borne to them by the fifth deadly sin. Coralie was perfectly dressed. Every woman possesses some personal charm in perfection, and Coralie's toilette brought her characteristic beauty into prominence. Her dress, moreover, like Florine's, was of some exquisite stuff, unknown as yet to the public, a *mousseline de soie*, with which Camusot had been supplied a few days before the rest of the world; for, as owner of the *Golden Cocoon*, he was a kind of Providence in Paris to the Lyons silkweavers.

Love and toilet are like color and perfume for a woman, and Coralie in her happiness looked lovelier than ever. A looked-for delight which cannot elude the grasp possesses an immense charm for youth; perhaps in their eyes the secret of the attraction of a house of pleasure lies in the certainty of gratification; perhaps many a long fidelity is attributable to the same cause. Love for love's sake, first love indeed, had blent with one of the strange violent fancies which sometimes possess these poor creatures; and love and admiration of Lucien's great beauty taught Coralie to express the thoughts in her heart.

"I should love you if you were ill and ugly," she whispered as they sat down.

What a saying for a poet! Camusot utterly vanished, Lucien had forgotten his existence, he saw Coralie, and had eyes for nothing else. How should he draw back--this creature, all sensation, all enjoyment of life, tired of the monotony of existence in a country town, weary of poverty, harassed by enforced continence, impatient of the claustral life of the Rue de Cluny, of toiling without reward? The fascination of the under world of Paris was upon him; how should he rise and leave this brilliant gathering? Lucien stood with one foot in Coralie's chamber and the other in the quicksands of Journalism. After so much vain search, and climbing of so many stairs, after standing about and waiting in the Rue de Sentier, he had found Journalism a jolly boon companion, joyous over the wine. His wrongs had just been avenged. There were two for whom he had vainly striven to fill the cup of humiliation and pain which he had been made to drink to the dregs, and now tomorrow they should receive a stab in their very hearts. "Here is a real friend!" he thought, as he looked at Lousteau. It never crossed his mind that Lousteau already regarded him as a dangerous rival. He had made a blunder; he had done his very best when a colorless article would have served him admirably well. Blondet's remark to Finot that it would be better to come to terms with a man of that calibre, had counteracted Lousteau's gnawing jealousy. He reflected that it would be prudent to keep on good terms with Lucien, and, at the same time, to arrange with Finot to exploit this formidable newcomer--he must be kept in poverty. The decision was made in a moment, and the bargain made in a few whispered words.

"He has talent."

"He will want the more."

"Ah?"

"Good!"

"A supper among French journalists always fills me with dread," said the German diplomatist, with serene urbanity; he looked as he spoke at Blondet, whom he had met at the Comtesse de Montcornet's. "It is laid upon you, gentlemen, to fulfil a prophecy of Blucher's."

"What prophecy?" asked Nathan.

"When Blucher and Sacken arrived on the heights of Montmartre in 1814 (pardon me, gentlemen, for recalling a day unfortunate for France), Sacken (a rough brute), remarked, 'Now we will set Paris alight!' --'Take very good care that you don't,' said Blucher. 'France will die of *that*, nothing else can kill her,' and he waved his hand over the glowing, seething city, that lay like a huge canker in the valley of the Seine.--There are no journalists in our country, thank Heaven!" continued the Minister after a pause. "I have not yet recovered from the fright that the little fellow gave me, a boy of ten, in a paper cap, with the sense of an old diplomatist. And tonight I feel as if I were supping with lions and panthers, who graciously sheathe their claws in my honor."

"It is clear," said Blondet, "that we are at liberty to inform Europe that a serpent dropped from your Excellency's lips this evening, and that the venomous creature failed to inoculate Mlle. Tullia, the prettiest dancer in Paris; and to follow up the story with a commentary on Eve, and the Scriptures, and the first and last transgression. But have no fear, you are our guest."

"It would be funny," said Finot.

"We would begin with a scientific treatise on all the serpents found in the human heart and human body, and so proceed to the *corps diplomatique*," said Lousteau.

"And we could exhibit one in spirits, in a bottle of brandied cherries," said Vernou.

"Till you yourself would end by believing in the story," added Vignon, looking at the diplomatist.

"Gentlemen," cried the Duc de Rhetore, "let sleeping claws lie."

"The influence and power of the press is only dawning," said Finot. "Journalism is in its infancy; it will grow. In ten years' time, everything will be brought into publicity. The light of thought will be turned on all subjects, and----"

"The blight of thought will be over it all," corrected Blondet.

"Here is an apothegm," cried Claude Vignon.

"Thought will make kings," said Lousteau.

"And undo monarchs," said the German.

167

"And therefore," said Blondet, "if the press did not exist, it would be necessary to invent it forthwith. But here we have it, and live by it."

"You will die of it," returned the German diplomatist. "Can you not see that if you enlighten the masses, and raise them in the political scale, you make it all the harder for the individual to rise above their level? Can you not see that if you sow the seeds of reasoning among the working-classes, you will reap revolt, and be the first to fall victims? What do they smash in Paris when a riot begins?"

"The street-lamps!" said Nathan; "but we are too modest to fear for ourselves, we only run the risk of cracks."

"As a nation, you have too much mental activity to allow any government to run its course without interference. But for that, you would make the conquest of Europe a second time, and win with the pen all that you failed to keep with the sword."

"Journalism is an evil," said Claude Vignon. "The evil may have its uses, but the present Government is resolved to put it down. There will be a battle over it. Who will give way? That is the question."

"The Government will give way," said Blondet. "I keep telling people that with all my might! Intellectual power is *the* great power in France; and the press has more wit than all men of intellect put together, and the hypocrisy of Tartufe besides."

"Blondet! Blondet! you are going too far!" called Finot. "Subscribers are present."

"You are the proprietor of one of those poison shops; you have reason to be afraid; but I can laugh at the whole business, even if I live by it."

"Blondet is right," said Claude Vignon. "Journalism, so far from being in the hands of a priesthood, came to be first a party weapon, and then a commercial speculation, carried on without conscience or scruple, like other commercial speculations. Every newspaper, as Blondet says, is a shop to which people come for opinions of the right shade. If there were a paper for hunchbacks, it would set forth plainly, morning and evening, in its columns, the beauty, the utility, and necessity of deformity. A newspaper is not supposed to enlighten its readers, but to supply them with congenial opinions. Give any newspaper time enough, and it will be base, hypocritical, shameless, and treacherous; the periodical press will be the death of ideas, systems, and individuals; nay, it will flourish upon their decay. It will take the credit of all creations of the brain; the harm that it does is done anonymously. We, for instance--I, Claude Vignon; you, Blondet; you, Lousteau; and you, Finot--we are all Platos, Aristides, and Catos, Plutarch's men, in short; we are all immaculate; we may wash our hands of all iniquity. Napoleon's sublime aphorism, suggested by his study of the Convention, 'No one individual is responsible for a crime committed collectively,' sums up the whole significance of a phenomenon, moral or immoral, whichever you please. However shamefully a newspaper may behave, the disgrace attaches to no one person."

"The authorities will resort to repressive legislation," interposed du Bruel. "A law is going to be passed, in fact."

"Pooh!" retorted Nathan. "What is the law in France against the spirit in which it is received, the most subtle of all solvents?"

"Ideas and opinions can only be counteracted by opinions and ideas," Vignon continued. "By sheer terror and despotism, and by no other means, can you extinguish the genius of the French nation; for the language lends itself admirably to allusion and ambiguity. Epigram breaks out the more for repressive legislation; it is like steam in an engine without a safety-valve.--The King, for example, does right; if a newspaper is against him, the Minister gets all the credit of the measure, and *vice versa*. A newspaper invents a scandalous libel--it has been misinformed. If the victim complains, the paper gets off with an apology for taking so great a freedom. If the case is taken into court, the editor complains that nobody asked him to rectify the mistake; but ask for redress, and he will laugh in your face and treat his offence as a mere

168

trifle. The paper scoffs if the victim gains the day; and if heavy damages are awarded, the plaintiff is held up as an unpatriotic obscurantist and a menace to the liberties of the country. In the course of an article purporting to explain that Monsieur So-and-so is as honest a man as you will find in the kingdom, you are informed that he is not better than a common thief. The sins of the press? Pooh! mere trifles; the curtailers of its liberties are monsters; and give him time enough, the constant reader is persuaded to believe anything you please. Everything which does not suit the newspaper will be unpatriotic, and the press will be infallible. One religion will be played off against another, and the Charter against the King. The press will hold up the magistracy to scorn for meting out rigorous justice to the press, and applaud its action when it serves the cause of party hatred. The most sensational fictions will be invented to increase the circulation; Journalism will descend to mountebanks' tricks worthy of Bobeche; Journalism would serve up its father with the Attic salt of its own wit sooner than fail to interest or amuse the public; Journalism will outdo the actor who put his son's ashes into the urn to draw real tears from his eyes, or the mistress who sacrifices everything to her lover."

"Journalism is, in fact, the People in folio form," interrupted Blondet.

"The people with hypocrisy added and generosity lacking," said Vignon. "All real ability will be driven out from the ranks of Journalism, as Aristides was driven into exile by the Athenians. We shall see newspapers started in the first instance by men of honor, falling sooner or later into the hands of men of abilities even lower than the average, but endowed with the resistance of flexibility of india-rubber, qualities denied to noble genius; nay, perhaps the future newspaper proprietor will be the tradesman with capital sufficient to buy venal pens. We see such things already indeed, but in ten years' time every little youngster that has left school will take himself for a great man, slash his predecessors from the lofty height of a newspaper column, drag them down by the feet, and take their place.

"Napoleon did wisely when he muzzled the press. I would wager that the Opposition papers would batter down a government of their own setting up, just as they are battering the present government, if any demand was refused. The more they have, the more they will want in the way of concessions. The *parvenu* journalist will be succeeded by the starveling hack. There is no salve for this sore. It is a kind of corruption which grows more and more obtrusive and malignant; the wider it spreads, the more patiently it will be endured, until the day comes when newspapers shall so increase and multiply in the earth that confusion will be the result--a second Babel. We, all of us, such as we are, have reason to know that crowned kings are less ungrateful than kings of our profession; that the most sordid man of business is not so mercenary nor so keen in speculation; that our brains are consumed to furnish their daily supply of poisonous trash. And yet we, all of us, shall continue to write, like men who work in quicksilver mines, knowing that they are doomed to die of their trade.

"Look there," he continued, "at that young man sitting beside Coralie --what is his name? Lucien! He has a beautiful face; he is a poet; and what is more, he is witty--so much the better for him. Well, he will cross the threshold of one of those dens where a man's intellect is prostituted; he will put all his best and finest thought into his work; he will blunt his intellect and sully his soul; he will be guilty of anonymous meannesses which take the place of stratagem, pillage, and ratting to the enemy in the warfare of *condottieri*. And when, like hundreds more, he has squandered his genius in the service of others who find the capital and do no work, those dealers in poisons will leave him to starve if he is thirsty, and to die of thirst if he is starving."

"Thanks," said Finot.

"But, dear me," continued Claude Vignon, "*I* knew all this, yet here am I in the galleys, and the arrival of another convict gives me pleasure. We are cleverer, Blondet and I, than Messieurs This and That, who speculate in our abilities, yet nevertheless we are always exploited by them. We have a heart somewhere beneath the intellect; we have NOT the grim qualities of the man who makes others work for him. We are indolent, we like to look on at the game, we are meditative, and we are fastidious; they will sweat our brains and blame us for improvidence."

"I thought you would be more amusing than this!" said Florine.

"Florine is right," said Blondet; "let us leave the cure of public evils to those quacks the statesmen. As Charlet says, 'Quarrel with my own bread and butter? *Never!*'"

"Do you know what Vignon puts me in mind of?" said Lousteau. "Of one of those fat women in the Rue du Pelican telling a schoolboy, 'My boy, you are too young to come here.'"

A burst of laughter followed the sally, but it pleased Coralie. The merchants meanwhile ate and drank and listened.

"What a nation this is! You see so much good in it and so much evil," said the Minister, addressing the Duc de Rhetore.-- "You are prodigals who cannot ruin yourselves, gentlemen."

And so, by the blessing of chance, Lucien, standing on the brink of the precipice over which he was destined to fall, heard warnings on all sides. D'Arthez had set him on the right road, had shown him the noble method of work, and aroused in him the spirit before which all obstacles disappear. Lousteau himself (partly from selfish motives) had tried to warn him away by describing Journalism and Literature in their practical aspects. Lucien had refused to believe that there could be so much hidden corruption; but now he had heard the journalists themselves crying woe for their hurt, he had seen them at their work, had watched them tearing their foster-mother's heart to read auguries of the future.

That evening he had seen things as they are. He beheld the very heart's core of corruption of that Paris which Blucher so aptly described; and so far from shuddering at the sight, he was intoxicated with enjoyment of the intellectually stimulating society in which he found himself.

These extraordinary men, clad in armor damascened by their vices, these intellects environed by cold and brilliant analysis, seemed so far greater in his eyes than the grave and earnest members of the brotherhood. And besides all this, he was reveling in his first taste of luxury; he had fallen under the spell. His capricious instincts awoke; for the first time in his life he drank exquisite wines, this was his first experience of cookery carried to the pitch of a fine art. A minister, a duke, and an opera-dancer had joined the party of journalists, and wondered at their sinister power. Lucien felt a horrible craving to reign over these kings, and he thought that he had power to win his kingdom. Finally, there was this Coralie, made happy by a few words of his. By the bright light of the wax-candles, through the steam of the dishes and the fumes of wine, she looked sublimely beautiful to his eyes, so fair had she grown with love. She was the loveliest, the most beautiful actress in Paris. The brotherhood, the heaven of noble thoughts, faded away before a temptation that appealed to every fibre of his nature. How could it have been otherwise? Lucien's author's vanity had just been gratified by the praises of those who know; by the appreciation of his future rivals; the success of his articles and his conquest of Coralie might have turned an older head than his.

During the discussion, moreover, every one at table had made a remarkably good supper, and such wines are not met with every day. Lousteau, sitting beside Camusot, furtively poured cherry-brandy several times into his neighbor's wineglass, and challenged him to drink. And Camusot drank, all unsuspicious, for he thought himself, in his own way, a match for a journalist. The jokes became more personal when dessert appeared and the wine began to circulate. The German Minister, a keen-witted man of the world, made a sign to the Duke and Tullia, and the three disappeared with the first symptoms of vociferous nonsense which precede the grotesque scenes of an orgy in its final stage. Coralie and Lucien had been behaving like children all the evening; as soon as the wine was uppermost in Camusot's head, they made good their escape down the staircase and sprang into a cab. Camusot subsided under the table; Matifat, looking round for him, thought that he had gone home with Coralie, left his guests to smoke, laugh, and argue, and followed Florine to her room. Daylight surprised the party, or more accurately, the first dawn of light discovered one man still able to speak, and Blondet, that intrepid champion, was proposing to the assembled sleepers a health to Aurora the rosy-fingered.

Lucien was unaccustomed to orgies of this kind. His head was very tolerably clear as he came down the staircase, but the fresh air was too much for him; he was horribly drunk. When they reached the handsome house in the Rue de Vendome, where the actress lived, Coralie and her waiting-woman were obliged to assist the poet to climb to the first floor. Lucien was ignominiously sick, and very nearly fainted on the staircase.

"Quick, Berenice, some tea! Make some tea," cried Coralie.

"It is nothing; it is the air," Lucien got out, "and I have never taken so much before in my life."

"Poor boy! He is as innocent as a lamb," said Berenice, a stalwart Norman peasant woman as ugly as Coralie was pretty. Lucien, half unconscious, was laid at last in bed. Coralie, with Berenice's assistance, undressed the poet with all a mother's tender care.

"It is nothing," he murmured again and again. "It is the air. Thank you, mamma."

"How charmingly he says 'mamma,'" cried Coralie, putting a kiss on his hair.

"What happiness to love such an angel, mademoiselle! Where did you pick him up? I did not think a man could be as beautiful as you are," said Berenice, when Lucien lay in bed. He was very drowsy; he knew nothing and saw nothing; Coralie made him swallow several cups of tea, and left him to sleep.

"Did the porter see us? Was there anyone else about?" she asked.

"No; I was sitting up for you."

"Does Victoire know anything?"

"Rather not!" returned Berenice.

Ten hours later Lucien awoke to meet Coralie's eyes. She had watched by him as he slept; he knew it, poet that he was. It was almost noon, but she still wore the delicate dress, abominably stained, which she meant to lay up as a relic. Lucien understood all the self-sacrifice and delicacy of love, fain of its reward. He looked into Coralie's eyes. In a moment she had flung off her clothing and slipped like a serpent to Lucien's side.

At five o'clock in the afternoon Lucien was still sleeping, cradled in this voluptuous paradise. He had caught glimpses of Coralie's chamber, an exquisite creation of luxury, a world of rose-color and white. He had admired Florine's apartments, but this surpassed them in its dainty refinement.

Coralie had already risen; for if she was to play her part as the Andalusian, she must be at the theatre by seven o'clock. Yet she had returned to gaze at the unconscious poet, lulled to sleep in bliss; she could not drink too deeply of this love that rose to rapture, drawing close the bond between the heart and the senses, to steep both in ecstasy. For in that apotheosis of human passion, which of those that were twain on earth that they might know bliss to the full creates one soul to rise to love in heaven, lay Coralie's justification. Who, moreover, would not have found excuse in Lucien's more than human beauty? To the actress kneeling by the bedside, happy in love within her, it seemed that she had received love's consecration. Berenice broke in upon Coralie's rapture.

"Here comes Camusot!" cried the maid. "And he knows that you are here."

Lucien sprang up at once. Innate generosity suggested that he was doing Coralie an injury. Berenice drew aside a curtain, and he fled into a dainty dressing-room, whither Coralie and the maid brought his clothes with magical speed.

Camusot appeared, and only then did Coralie's eyes alight on Lucien's boots, warming in the fender. Berenice had privately varnished them, and put them before the fire to dry; and both mistress and maid alike forgot that tell-tale witness. Berenice left the room with a scared glance at Coralie. Coralie flung herself into the depths of a settee, and bade Camusot seat himself in the *gondole*, a round-backed chair that stood opposite. But Coralie's adorer, honest soul, dared not look his mistress in the face; he could not take his eyes off the pair of boots.

"Ought I to make a scene and leave Coralie?" he pondered. "Is it worth while to make a fuss about a trifle? There is a pair of boots wherever you go. These would be more in place in a shop window or taking a walk on the boulevard on somebody's feet; here, however, without a pair of feet in them, they tell a pretty plain tale. I am fifty years old, and that is the truth; I ought to be as blind as Cupid himself."

There was no excuse for this mean-spirited monologue. The boots were not the high-lows at present in vogue, which an unobservant man may be allowed to disregard up to a certain point. They were the unmistakable, uncompromising hessians then prescribed by fashion, a pair of extremely elegant betasseled boots, which shone in glistening contrast against tight-fitting trousers invariably of some light color, and reflected their surroundings like a mirror. The boots stared the honest silk-mercer out of countenance, and, it must be added, they pained his heart.

"What is it?" asked Coralie.

"Nothing."

"Ring the bell," said Coralie, smiling to herself at Camusot's want of spirit.--"Berenice," she said, when the Norman handmaid appeared, "just bring me a button-hook, for I must put on these confounded boots again. Don't forget to bring them to my dressing-room tonight."

"What? . . . *your* boots?" . . . faltered out Camusot, breathing more freely.

"And whose should they be?" she demanded haughtily. "Were you beginning to believe?--great stupid! Oh! and he would believe it too," she went on, addressing Berenice.--"I have a man's part in What's-his-name's piece, and I have never worn a man's clothes in my life before. The bootmaker for the theatre brought me these things to try if I could walk in them, until a pair can be made to measure. He put them on, but they hurt me so much that I have taken them off, and after all I must wear them."

"Don't put them on again if they are uncomfortable," said Camusot. (The boots had made him feel so very uncomfortable himself.)

"Mademoiselle would do better to have a pair made of very thin morocco, sir, instead of torturing herself as she did just now; but the management is so stingy. She was crying, sir; if I was a man and loved a woman, I wouldn't let her shed a tear, I know. You ought to order a pair for her----"

"Yes, yes," said Camusot. "Are you just getting up, Coralie?"

"Just this moment; I only came in at six o'clock after looking for you everywhere. I was obliged to keep the cab for seven hours. So much for your care of me; you forget me for a wine-bottle. I ought to take care of myself now when I am to play every night so long as the *Alcalde* draws. I don't want to fall off after that young man's notice of me."

"That is a handsome boy," said Camusot.

"Do you think so? I don't admire men of that sort; they are too much like women; and they do not understand how to love like you stupid old business men. You are so bored with your own society."

"Is monsieur dining with madame?" inquired Berenice.

"No, my mouth is clammy."

"You were nicely screwed yesterday. Ah! Papa Camusot, I don't like men who drink, I tell you at once----"

"You will give that young man a present, I suppose?" interrupted Camusot.

172

"Oh! yes. I would rather do that than pay as Florine does. There, go away with you, good-for-nothing that one loves; or give me a carriage to save time in future."

"You shall go in your own carriage tomorrow to your manager's dinner at the *Rocher de Cancale*. The new piece will not be given next Sunday."

"Come, I am just going to dine," said Coralie, hurrying Camusot out of the room.

An hour later Berenice came to release Lucien. Berenice, Coralie's companion since her childhood, had a keen and subtle brain in her unwieldy frame.

"Stay here," she said. "Coralie is coming back alone; she even talked of getting rid of Camusot if he is in your way; but you are too much of an angel to ruin her, her heart's darling as you are. She wants to clear out of this, she says; to leave this paradise and go and live in your garret. Oh! there are those that are jealous and envious of you, and they have told her that you haven't a brass farthing, and live in the Latin Quarter; and I should go, too, you see, to do the house-work.--But I have just been comforting her, poor child! I have been telling her that you were too clever to do anything so silly. I was right, wasn't I, sir? Oh! you will see that you are her darling, her love, the god to whom she gives her soul; yonder old fool has nothing but the body.--If you only knew how nice she is when I hear her say her part over! My Coralie, my little pet, she is! She deserved that God in heaven should send her one of His angels. She was sick of the life.--She was so unhappy with her mother that used to beat her, and sold her. Yes, sir, sold her own child! If I had a daughter, I would wait on her hand and foot as I wait on Coralie; she is like my own child to me.--These are the first good times she has seen since I have been with her; the first time that she has been really applauded. You have written something, it seems, and they have got up a famous *claque* for the second performance. Braulard has been going through the play with her while you were asleep."

"Who? Braulard?" asked Lucien; it seemed to him that he had heard the name before.

"He is the head of the *claqueurs*, and she was arranging with him the places where she wished him to look after her. Florine might try to play her some shabby trick, and take all for herself, for all she calls herself her friend. There is such a talk about your article on the Boulevards.--Isn't it a bed fit for a prince," she said, smoothing the lace bed-spread.

She lighted the wax-candles, and to Lucien's bewildered fancy, the house seemed to be some palace in the *Cabinet des Fees*. Camusot had chosen the richest stuffs from the *Golden Cocoon* for the hangings and window-curtains. A carpet fit for a king's palace was spread upon the floor. The carving of the rosewood furniture caught and imprisoned the light that rippled over its surface. Priceless trifles gleamed from the white marble chimney-piece. The rug beside the bed was of swan's skins bordered with sable. A pair of little, black velvet slippers lined with purple silk told of happiness awaiting the poet of *The Marguerites*. A dainty lamp hung from the ceiling draped with silk. The room was full of flowering plants, delicate white heaths and scentless camellias, in stands marvelously wrought. Everything called up associations of innocence. How was it possible in these rooms to see the life that Coralie led in its true colors? Berenice noticed Lucien's bewildered expression.

"Isn't it nice?" she said coaxingly. "You would be more comfortable here, wouldn't you, than in a garret?--You won't let her do anything rash?" she continued, setting a costly stand before him, covered with dishes abstracted from her mistress' dinner-table, lest the cook should suspect that her mistress had a lover in the house.

Lucien made a good dinner. Berenice waiting on him, the dishes were of wrought silver, the painted porcelain plates had cost a louis d'or apiece. The luxury was producing exactly the same effect upon him that the sight of a girl walking the pavement, with her bare flaunting throat and neat ankles, produces upon a schoolboy.

"How lucky Camusot is!" cried he.

"Lucky?" repeated Berenice. "He would willingly give all that he is worth to be in your place; he would be glad to barter his gray hair for your golden head."

She gave Lucien the richest wine that Bordeaux keeps for the wealthiest English purchaser, and persuaded Lucien to go to bed to take a preliminary nap; and Lucien, in truth, was quite willing to sleep on the couch that he had been admiring. Berenice had read his wish, and felt glad for her mistress.

At half-past ten that night Lucien awoke to look into eyes brimming over with love. There stood Coralie in most luxurious night attire. Lucien had been sleeping; Lucien was intoxicated with love, and not with wine. Berenice left the room with the inquiry, "What time tomorrow morning?"

"At eleven o'clock. We will have breakfast in bed. I am not at home to anybody before two o'clock."

At two o'clock in the afternoon Coralie and her lover were sitting together. The poet to all appearance had come to pay a call. Lucien had been bathed and combed and dressed. Coralie had sent to Colliau's for a dozen fine shirts, a dozen cravats and a dozen pocket-handkerchiefs for him, as well as twelve pairs of gloves in a cedar-wood box. When a carriage stopped at the door, they both rushed to the window, and watched Camusot alight from a handsome coupe.

"I would not have believed that one could so hate a man and luxury----"

"I am too poor to allow you to ruin yourself for me," he replied. And thus Lucien passed under the Caudine Forks.

"Poor pet," said Coralie, holding him tightly to her, "do you love me so much?--I persuaded this gentleman to call on me this morning," she continued, indicating Lucien to Camusot, who entered the room. "I thought that we might take a drive in the Champs Elysees to try the carriage."

"Go without me," said Camusot in a melancholy voice; "I shall not dine with you. It is my wife's birthday, I had forgotten that."

"Poor Musot, how badly bored you will be!" she said, putting her arms about his neck.

She was wild with joy at the thought that she and Lucien would handsel this gift together; she would drive with him in the new carriage; and in her happiness, she seemed to love Camusot, she lavished caresses upon him.

"If only I could give you a carriage every day!" said the poor fellow.

"Now, sir, it is two o'clock," she said, turning to Lucien, who stood in distress and confusion, but she comforted him with an adorable gesture.

Down the stairs she went, several steps at a time, drawing Lucien after her; the elderly merchant following in their wake like a seal on land, and quite unable to catch them up.

Lucien enjoyed the most intoxicating of pleasures; happiness had increased Coralie's loveliness to the highest possible degree; she appeared before all eyes an exquisite vision in her dainty toilette. All Paris in the Champs Elysees beheld the lovers.

In an avenue of the Bois de Boulogne they met a caleche; Mme. d'Espard and Mme. de Bargeton looked in surprise at Lucien, and met a scornful glance from the poet. He saw glimpses of a great future before him, and was about to make his power felt. He could fling them back in a glance some of the revengeful thoughts which had gnawed his heart ever since they planted them there. That moment was one of the sweetest in his life, and perhaps decided his fate. Once again the Furies seized on Lucien at the bidding of Pride. He would reappear in the world of Paris; he would take a signal revenge; all the social pettiness hitherto trodden under foot by the worker, the member of the brotherhood, sprang up again afresh in his soul.

Now he understood all that Lousteau's attack had meant. Lousteau had served his passions; while the brotherhood, that collective mentor, had seemed to mortify them in the interests of tiresome virtues and work which began to look useless and hopeless in Lucien's eyes. Work! What is it but death to an eager pleasure-loving nature? And how easy it is for the man of letters to slide into a *far niente* existence of self-indulgence, into the luxurious ways of actresses and women of easy virtues! Lucien felt an overmastering desire to continue the reckless life of the last two days.

The dinner at the *Rocher de Cancale* was exquisite. All Florine's supper guests were there except the Minister, the Duke, and the dancer; Camusot, too, was absent; but these gaps were filled by two famous actors and Hector Merlin and his mistress. This charming woman, who chose to be known as Mme. du Val-Noble, was the handsomest and most fashionable of the class of women now euphemistically styled *lorettes*.

Lucien had spent the forty-eight hours since the success of his article in paradise. He was feted and envied; he gained self-possession; his talk sparkled; he was the brilliant Lucien de Rubempre who shone for a few months in the world of letters and art. Finot, with his infallible instinct for discovering ability, scenting it afar as an ogre might scent human flesh, cajoled Lucien, and did his best to secure a recruit for the squadron under his command. And Coralie watched the manoeuvres of this purveyor of brains, saw that Lucien was nibbling at the bait, and tried to put him on his guard.

"Don't make any engagement, dear boy; wait. They want to exploit you; we will talk of it tonight."

"Pshaw!" said Lucien. "I am sure I am quite as sharp and shrewd as they can be."

Finot and Hector Merlin evidently had not fallen out over that affair of the white lines and spaces in the columns, for it was Finot who introduced Lucien to the journalist. Coralie and Mme. du Val-Noble were overwhelmingly amiable and polite to each other, and Mme. du Val-Noble asked Lucien and Coralie to dine with her.

Hector Merlin, short and thin, with lips always tightly compressed, was the most dangerous journalist present. Unbounded ambition and jealousy smouldered within him; he took pleasure in the pain of others, and fomented strife to turn it to his own account. His abilities were but slender, and he had little force of character, but the natural instinct which draws the upstart towards money and power served him as well as fixity of purpose. Lucien and Merlin at once took a dislike to one another, for reasons not far to seek. Merlin, unfortunately, proclaimed aloud the thoughts that Lucien kept to himself. By the time the dessert was put on the table, the most touching friendship appeared to prevail among the men, each one of whom in his heart thought himself a cleverer fellow than the rest; and Lucien as the newcomer was made much of by them all. They chatted frankly and unrestrainedly. Hector Merlin, alone, did not join in the laughter. Lucien asked the reason of his reserve.

"You are just entering the world of letters, I can see," he said. "You are a journalist with all your illusions left. You believe in friendship. Here we are friends or foes, as it happens; we strike down a friend with the weapon which by rights should only be turned against an enemy. You will find out, before very long, that fine sentiments will do nothing for you. If you are naturally kindly, learn to be ill-natured, to be consistently spiteful. If you have never heard this golden rule before, I give it you now in confidence, and it is no small secret. If you have a mind to be loved, never leave your mistress until you have made her shed a tear or two; and if you mean to make your way in literature, let other people continually feel your teeth; make no exception even of your friends; wound their susceptibilities, and everybody will fawn upon you."

Hector Merlin watched Lucien as he spoke, saw that his words went to the neophyte's heart like a stab, and Hector Merlin was glad. Play followed, Lucien lost all his money, and Coralie brought him away; and he forgot for a while, in the delights of love, the fierce excitement of the gambler, which was to gain so strong a hold upon him.

When he left Coralie in the morning and returned to the Latin Quarter, he took out his purse and found the money he had lost. At first he felt miserable over the discovery, and thought of going back at once to return a gift which humiliated him; but--he had already come as far as the Rue de la Harpe; he would not return now that he had almost reached the Hotel de

Cluny. He pondered over Coralie's forethought as he went, till he saw in it a proof of the maternal love which is blended with passion in women of her stamp. For Coralie and her like, passion includes every human affection. Lucien went from thought to thought, and argued himself into accepting the gift. "I love her," he said; "we shall live together as husband and wife; I will never forsake her!"

What mortal, short of a Diogenes, could fail to understand Lucien's feelings as he climbed the dirty, fetid staircase to his lodging, turned the key that grated in the lock, and entered and looked round at the unswept brick floor, at the cheerless grate, at the ugly poverty and bareness of the room.

A package of manuscript was lying on the table. It was his novel; a note from Daniel d'Arthez lay beside it:--

"Our friends are almost satisfied with your work, dear poet," d'Arthez wrote. "You will be able to present it with more confidence now, they say, to friends and enemies. We saw your charming article on the Panorama-Dramatique; you are sure to excite as much jealousy in the profession as regret among your friends here. DANIEL."

"Regrets! What does he mean?" exclaimed Lucien. The polite tone of the note astonished him. Was he to be henceforth a stranger to the brotherhood? He had learned to set a higher value on the good opinion and the friendship of the circle in the Rue des Quatre-Vents since he had tasted of the delicious fruits offered to him by the Eve of the theatrical underworld. For some moments he stood in deep thought; he saw his present in the garret, and foresaw his future in Coralie's rooms. Honorable resolution struggled with temptation and swayed him now this way, now that. He sat down and began to look through his manuscript, to see in what condition his friends had returned it to him. What was his amazement, as he read chapter after chapter, to find his poverty transmuted into riches by the cunning of the pen, and the devotion of the unknown great men, his friends of the brotherhood. Dialogue, closely packed, nervous, pregnant, terse, and full of the spirit of the age, replaced his conversations, which seemed poor and pointless prattle in comparison. His characters, a little uncertain in the drawing, now stood out in vigorous contrast of color and relief; physiological observations, due no doubt to Horace Bianchon, supplied links of interpretations between human character and the curious phenomena of human life--subtle touches which made his men and women live. His wordy passages of description were condensed and vivid. The misshapen, ill-clad child of his brain had returned to him as a lovely maiden, with white robes and rosy-hued girdle and scarf--an entrancing creation. Night fell and took him by surprise, reading through rising tears, stricken to earth by such greatness of soul, feeling the worth of such a lesson, admiring the alterations, which taught him more of literature and art than all his four years' apprenticeship of study and reading and comparison. A master's correction of a line made upon the study always teaches more than all the theories and criticisms in the world.

"What friends are these! What hearts! How fortunate I am!" he cried, grasping his manuscript tightly.

With the quick impulsiveness of a poetic and mobile temperament, he rushed off to Daniel's lodging. As he climbed the stairs, and thought of these friends, who refused to leave the path of honor, he felt conscious that he was less worthy of them than before. A voice spoke within him, telling him that if d'Arthez had loved Coralie, he would have had her break with Camusot. And, besides this, he knew that the brotherhood held journalism in utter abhorrence, and that he himself was already, to some small extent, a journalist. All of them, except Meyraux, who had just gone out, were in d'Arthez's room when he entered it, and saw that all their faces were full of sorrow and despair.

"What is it?" he cried.

"We have just heard news of a dreadful catastrophe; the greatest thinker of the age, our most loved friend, who was like a light among us for two years----"

"Louis Lambert!"

"Has fallen a victim to catalepsy. There is no hope for him," said Bianchon.

"He will die, his soul wandering in the skies, his body unconscious on earth," said Michel Chrestien solemnly.

"He will die as he lived," said d'Arthez.

"Love fell like a firebrand in the vast empire of his brain and burned him away," said Leon Giraud.

"Yes," said Joseph Bridau, "he has reached a height that we cannot so much as see."

"*We* are to be pitied, not Louis," said Fulgence Ridal.

"Perhaps he will recover," exclaimed Lucien.

"From what Meyraux has been telling us, recovery seems impossible," answered Bianchon. "Medicine has no power over the change that is working in his brain."

"Yet there are physical means," said d'Arthez.

"Yes," said Bianchon; "we might produce imbecility instead of catalepsy."

"Is there no way of offering another head to the spirit of evil? I would give mine to save him!" cried Michel Chrestien.

"And what would become of European federation?" asked d'Arthez.

"Ah! true," replied Michel Chrestien. "Our duty to Humanity comes first; to one man afterwards."

"I came here with a heart full of gratitude to you all," said Lucien. "You have changed my alloy into golden coin."

"Gratitude! For what do you take us?" asked Bianchon.

"We had the pleasure," added Fulgence.

"Well, so you are a journalist, are you?" asked Leon Giraud. "The fame of your first appearance has reached even the Latin Quarter."

"I am not a journalist yet," returned Lucien.

"Aha! So much the better," said Michel Chrestien.

"I told you so!" said d'Arthez. "Lucien knows the value of a clean conscience. When you can say to yourself as you lay your head on the pillow at night, 'I have not sat in judgment on another man's work; I have given pain to no one; I have not used the edge of my wit to deal a stab to some harmless soul; I have sacrificed no one's success to a jest; I have not even troubled the happiness of imbecility; I have not added to the burdens of genius; I have scorned the easy triumphs of epigram; in short, I have not acted against my convictions,' is not this a viaticum that gives one daily strength?"

"But one can say all this, surely, and yet work on a newspaper," said Lucien. "If I had absolutely no other way of earning a living, I should certainly come to this."

"Oh! oh! oh!" cried Fulgence, his voice rising a note each time; "we are capitulating, are we?"

"He will turn journalist," Leon Giraud said gravely. "Oh, Lucien, if you would only stay and work with us! We are about to bring out a periodical in which justice and truth shall never be violated; we will spread doctrines that, perhaps, will be of real service to mankind----"

"You will not have a single subscriber," Lucien broke in with Machiavellian wisdom.

"There will be five hundred of them," asserted Michel Chrestien, "but they will be worth five hundred thousand."

"You will need a lot of capital," continued Lucien.

"No, only devotion," said d'Arthez.

"Anybody might take him for a perfumer's assistant," burst out Michel Chrestien, looking at Lucien's head, and sniffing comically. "You were seen driving about in a very smart turnout with a pair of thoroughbreds, and a mistress for a prince,

Coralie herself."

"Well, and is there any harm in it?"

"You would not say that if you thought that there was no harm in it," said Bianchon.

"I could have wished Lucien a Beatrice," said d'Arthez, "a noble woman, who would have been a help to him in life----"

"But, Daniel," asked Lucien, "love is love wherever you find it, is it not?"

"Ah!" said the republican member, "on that one point I am an aristocrat. I could not bring myself to love a woman who must rub shoulders with all sorts of people in the green-room; whom an actor kisses on stage; she must lower herself before the public, smile on every one, lift her skirts as she dances, and dress like a man, that all the world may see what none should see save I alone. Or if I loved such a woman, she should leave the stage, and my love should cleanse her from the stain of it."

"And if she would not leave the stage?"

"I should die of mortification, jealousy, and all sorts of pain. You cannot pluck love out of your heart as you draw a tooth."

Lucien's face grew dark and thoughtful.

"When they find out that I am tolerating Camusot, how they will despise me," he thought.

"Look here," said the fierce republican, with humorous fierceness, "you can be a great writer, but a little play-actor you shall never be," and he took up his hat and went out.

"He is hard, is Michel Chrestien," commented Lucien.

"Hard and salutary, like the dentist's pincers," said Bianchon. "Michel foresees your future; perhaps in the street, at this moment, he is thinking of you with tears in his eyes."

D'Arthez was kind, and talked comfortingly, and tried to cheer Lucien. The poet spent an hour with his friends, then he went, but his conscience treated him hardly, crying to him, "You will be a journalist--a journalist!" as the witch cried to Macbeth that he should be king hereafter!

Out in the street, he looked up at d'Arthez's windows, and saw a faint light shining in them, and his heart sank. A dim foreboding told him that he had bidden his friends good-bye for the last time.

As he turned out of the Place de la Sorbonne into the Rue de Cluny, he saw a carriage at the door of his lodging. Coralie had driven all the way from the Boulevard du Temple for the sake of a moment with her lover and a "good-night." Lucien found her sobbing in his garret. She would be as wretchedly poor as her poet, she wept, as she arranged his shirts and gloves and handkerchiefs in the crazy chest of drawers. Her distress was so real and so great, that Lucien, but even now chidden for his connection with an actress, saw Coralie as a saint ready to assume the hair-shirt of poverty. The adorable girl's excuse for her visit was an announcement that the firm of Camusot, Coralie, and Lucien meant to invite Matifat, Florine, and Lousteau (the second trio) to supper; had Lucien any invitations to issue to people who might be useful to him? Lucien said that he would take counsel of Lousteau.

A few moments were spent together, and Coralie hurried away. She spared Lucien the knowledge that Camusot was waiting for her below.

Next morning, at eight o'clock, Lucien went to Etienne Lousteau's room, found it empty, and hurried away to Florine. Lousteau and Florine, settled into possession of their new quarters like a married couple, received their friend in the pretty bedroom, and all three breakfasted sumptuously together.

"Why, I should advise you, my boy, to come with me to see Felicien Vernou," said Lousteau, when they sat at table, and Lucien had mentioned Coralie's projected supper; "ask him to be of the party, and keep well with him, if you can keep well with such a rascal. Felicien Vernou does a *feuilleton* for a political paper; he might perhaps introduce you, and you could blossom out into leaders in it at your ease. It is a Liberal paper, like ours; you will be a Liberal, that is the popular party; and besides, if you mean to go over to the Ministerialists, you would do better for yourself if they had reason to be afraid of you. Then there is Hector Merlin and his Mme. du Val-Noble; you meet great people at their house--dukes and dandies and millionaires; didn't they ask you and Coralie to dine with them?"

"Yes," replied Lucien; "you are going too, and so is Florine." Lucien and Etienne were now on familiar terms after Friday's debauch and the dinner at the *Rocher de Cancale*.

"Very well, Merlin is on the paper; we shall come across him pretty often; he is the chap to follow close on Finot's heels. You would do well to pay him attention; ask him and Mme. du Val-Noble to supper. He may be useful to you before long; for rancorous people are always in need of others, and he may do you a good turn if he can reckon on your pen."

"Your beginning has made enough sensation to smooth your way," said Florine; "take advantage of it at once, or you will soon be forgotten."

"The bargain, the great business, is concluded," Lousteau continued. "That Finot, without a spark of talent in him, is to be editor of Dauriat's weekly paper, with a salary of six hundred francs per month, and owner of a sixth share, for which he has not paid one penny. And I, my dear fellow, am now editor of our little paper. Everything went off as I expected; Florine managed superbly, she could give points to Tallyrand himself."

"We have a hold on men through their pleasures," said Florine, "while a diplomatist only works on their self-love. A diplomatist sees a man made up for the occasion; we know him in his moments of folly, so our power is greater."

"And when the thing was settled, Matifat made the first and last joke of his whole druggist's career," put in Lousteau. "He said, 'This affair is quite in my line; I am supplying drugs to the public.'"

"I suspect that Florine put him up to it," cried Lucien.

"And by these means, my little dear, your foot is in the stirrup," continued Lousteau.

"You were born with a silver spoon in your mouth," remarked Florine. "What lots of young fellows wait for years, wait till they are sick of waiting, for a chance to get an article into a paper! You will do like Emile Blondet. In six months' time you will be giving yourself high and mighty airs," she added, with a mocking smile, in the language of her class.

"Haven't I been in Paris for three years?" said Lousteau, "and only yesterday Finot began to pay me a fixed monthly salary of three hundred francs, and a hundred francs per sheet for his paper."

"Well; you are saying nothing!" exclaimed Florine, with her eyes turned on Lucien.

"We shall see," said Lucien.

"My dear boy, if you had been my brother, I could not have done more for you," retorted Lousteau, somewhat nettled, "but I won't answer for Finot. Scores of sharp fellows will besiege Finot for the next two days with offers to work for low pay. I have promised for you, but you can draw back if you like.--You little know how lucky you are," he added after a pause. "All those in our set combine to attack an enemy in various papers, and lend each other a helping hand all round."

"Let us go in the first place to Felicien Vernou," said Lucien. He was eager to conclude an alliance with such formidable birds of prey.

Lousteau sent for a cab, and the pair of friends drove to Vernou's house on the second floor up an alley in the Rue Mandar. To Lucien's great astonishment, the harsh, fastidious, and severe critic's surroundings were vulgar to the last degree. A marbled paper, cheap and shabby, with a meaningless pattern repeated at regular intervals, covered the walls, and a series of aqua tints in gilt frames decorated the apartment, where Vernou sat at table with a woman so plain that she could only be the legitimate mistress of the house, and two very small children perched on high chairs with a bar in front to prevent the infants from tumbling out. Felicien Vernou, in a cotton dressing-gown contrived out of the remains of one of his wife's dresses, was not over well pleased by this invasion.

"Have you breakfasted, Lousteau?" he asked, placing a chair for Lucien.

"We have just left Florine; we have been breakfasting with her."

Lucien could not take his eyes off Mme. Vernou. She looked like a stout, homely cook, with a tolerably fair complexion, but commonplace to the last degree. The lady wore a bandana tied over her night-cap, the strings of the latter article of dress being tied so tightly under the chin that her puffy cheeks stood out on either side. A shapeless, beltless garment, fastened by a single button at the throat, enveloped her from head to foot in such a fashion that a comparison to a milestone at once suggested itself. Her health left no room for hope; her cheeks were almost purple; her fingers looked like sausages. In a moment it dawned upon Lucien how it was that Vernou was always so ill at ease in society; here was the living explanation of his misanthropy. Sick of his marriage, unable to bring himself to abandon his wife and family, he had yet sufficient of the artistic temper to suffer continually from their presence; Vernou was an actor by nature bound never to pardon the success of another, condemned to chronic discontent because he was never content with himself. Lucien began to understand the sour look which seemed to add to the bleak expression of envy on Vernou's face; the acerbity of the epigrams with which his conversation was sown, the journalist's pungent phrases, keen and elaborately wrought as a stiletto, were at once explained.

"Let us go into my study," Vernou said, rising from the table; "you have come on business, no doubt."

"Yes and no," replied Etienne Lousteau. "It is a supper, old chap."

"I have brought a message from Coralie," said Lucien (Mme. Vernou looked up at once at the name), "to ask you to supper tonight at her house to meet the same company as before at Florine's, and a few more besides--Hector Merlin and Mme. du Val-Noble and some others. There will be play afterwards."

"But we are engaged to Mme. Mahoudeau this evening, dear," put in the wife.

"What does that matter?" returned Vernou.

"She will take offence if we don't go; and you are very glad of her when you have a bill to discount."

"This wife of mine, my dear boy, can never be made to understand that a supper engagement for twelve o'clock does not prevent you from going to an evening party that comes to an end at eleven. She is always with me while I work," he added.

"You have so much imagination!" said Lucien, and thereby made a mortal enemy of Vernou.

"Well," continued Lousteau, "you are coming; but that is not all. M. de Rubempre is about to be one of us, so you must push him in your paper. Give him out for a chap that will make a name for himself in literature, so that he can put in at least a couple of articles every month."

"Yes, if he means to be one of us, and will attack our enemies, as we will attack his, I will say a word for him at the Opera tonight," replied Vernou.

"Very well--good-bye till tomorrow, my boy," said Lousteau, shaking hands with every sign of cordiality. "When is your book coming out?"

"That depends on Dauriat; it is ready," said Vernou *pater-familias*.

"Are you satisfied?"

"Yes and no----"

"We will get up a success," said Lousteau, and he rose with a bow to his colleague's wife.

The abrupt departure was necessary indeed; for the two infants, engaged in a noisy quarrel, were fighting with their spoons, and flinging the pap in each other's faces.

"That, my boy, is a woman who all unconsciously will work great havoc in contemporary literature," said Etienne, when they came away. "Poor Vernou cannot forgive us for his wife. He ought to be relieved of her in the interests of the public; and a deluge of blood-thirsty reviews and stinging sarcasms against successful men of every sort would be averted. What is to become of a man with such a wife and that pair of abominable brats? Have you seen Rigaudin in Picard's *La Maison en Loterie*? You have? Well, like Rigaudin, Vernou will not fight himself, but he will set others fighting; he would give an eye to put out both eyes in the head of the best friend he has. You will see him using the bodies of the slain for a stepping-stone, rejoicing over every one's misfortunes, attacking princes, dukes, marquises, and nobles, because he himself is a commoner; reviling the work of unmarried men because he forsooth has a wife; and everlastingly preaching morality, the joys of domestic life, and the duties of the citizen. In short, this very moral critic will spare no one, not even infants of tender age. He lives in the Rue Mandar with a wife who might be the *Mamamouchi* of the *Bourgeois gentilhomme* and a couple of little Vernous as ugly as sin. He tries to sneer at the Faubourg Saint-Germain, where he will never set foot, and makes his duchesses talk like his wife. That is the sort of man to raise a howl at the Jesuits, insult the Court, and credit the Court party with the design of restoring feudal rights and the right of primogeniture--just the one to preach a crusade for Equality, he that thinks himself the equal of no one. If he were a bachelor, he would go into society; if he were in a fair way to be a Royalist poet with a pension and the Cross of the Legion of Honor, he would be an optimist, and journalism offers starting-points by the hundred. Journalism is the giant catapult set in motion by pigmy hatreds. Have you any wish to marry after this? Vernou has none of the milk of human kindness in him, it is all turned to gall; and he is emphatically the Journalist, a tiger with two hands that tears everything to pieces, as if his pen had the hydrophobia."

"It is a case of gunophobia," said Lucien. "Has he ability?"

"He is witty, he is a writer of articles. He incubates articles; he does that all his life and nothing else. The most dogged industry would fail to graft a book on his prose. Felicien is incapable of conceiving a work on a large scale, of broad effects, of fitting characters harmoniously in a plot which develops till it reaches a climax. He has ideas, but he has no knowledge of facts; his heroes are utopian creatures, philosophical or Liberal notions masquerading. He is at pains to write an original style, but his inflated periods would collapse at a pin-prick from a critic; and therefore he goes in terror of reviews, like every one else who can only keep his head above water with the bladders of newspaper puffs."

"What an article you are making out of him!"

"That particular kind, my boy, must be spoken, and never written."

"You are turning editor," said Lucien.

"Where shall I put you down?"

"At Coralie's."

"Ah! we are infatuated," said Lousteau. "What a mistake! Do as I do with Florine, let Coralie be your housekeeper, and take your fling."

"You would send a saint to perdition," laughed Lucien.

"Well, there is no damning a devil," retorted Lousteau.

The flippant tone, the brilliant talk of this new friend, his views of life, his paradoxes, the axioms of Parisian Machiavelism,--all these things impressed Lucien unawares. Theoretically the poet knew that such thoughts were perilous; but he believed them practically useful.

Arrived in the Boulevard du Temple, the friends agreed to meet at the office between four and five o'clock. Hector Merlin would doubtless be there. Lousteau was right. The infatuation of desire was upon Lucien; for the courtesan who loves knows how to grapple her lover to her by every weakness in his nature, fashioning herself with incredible flexibility to his every wish, encouraging the soft, effeminate habits which strengthen her hold. Lucien was thirsting already for enjoyment; he was in love with the easy, luxurious, and expensive life which the actress led.

He found Coralie and Camusot intoxicated with joy. The Gymnase offered Coralie an engagement after Easter on terms for which she had never dared to hope.

"And this great success is owing to you," said Camusot.

"Yes, surely. *The Alcalde* would have fallen flat but for him," cried Coralie; "if there had been no article, I should have been in for another six years of the Boulevard theatres."

She danced up to Lucien and flung her arms round him, putting an indescribable silken softness and sweetness into her enthusiasm. Love had come to Coralie. And Camusot? his eyes fell. Looking down after the wont of mankind in moments of sharp pain, he saw the seam of Lucien's boots, a deep yellow thread used by the best bootmakers of that time, in strong contrast with the glistening leather. The color of that seam had tinged his thoughts during a previous conversation with himself, as he sought to explain the presence of a mysterious pair of hessians in Coralie's fender. He remembered now that he had seen the name of "Gay, Rue de la Michodiere," printed in black letters on the soft white kid lining.

"You have a handsome pair of boots, sir," he said.

"Like everything else about him," said Coralie.

"I should be very glad of your bootmaker's address."

"Oh, how like the Rue des Bourdonnais to ask for a tradesman's address," cried Coralie. "Do *you* intend to patronize a young man's bootmaker? A nice young man you would make! Do keep to your own top-boots; they are the kind for a steady-going man with a wife and family and a mistress."

"Indeed, if you would take off one of your boots, sir, I should be very much obliged," persisted Camusot.

"I could not get it on again without a button-hook," said Lucien, flushing up.

"Berenice will fetch you one; we can do with some here," jeered Camusot.

"Papa Camusot!" said Coralie, looking at him with cruel scorn, "have the courage of your pitiful baseness. Come, speak out! You think that this gentleman's boots are very like mine, do you not?--I forbid you to take off your boots," she added, turning to Lucien.--"Yes, M. Camusot. Yes, you saw some boots lying about in the fender here the other day, and that is the identical pair, and this gentleman was hiding in my dressing-room at the time, waiting for them; and he had passed the night here. That was what you were thinking, *hein*? Think so; I would rather you did. It is the simple truth. I am deceiving you. And if I am? I do it to please myself."

She sat down. There was no anger in her face, no embarrassment; she looked from Camusot to Lucien. The two men avoided each other's eyes.

"I will believe nothing that you do not wish me to believe," said Camusot. "Don't play with me, Coralie; I was wrong----"

"I am either a shameless baggage that has taken a sudden fancy; or a poor, unhappy girl who feels what love really is for the first time, the love that all women long for. And whichever way it is, you must leave me or take me as I am," she said, with a queenly gesture that crushed Camusot.

"Is it really true?" he asked, seeing from their faces that this was no jest, yet begging to be deceived.

"I love mademoiselle," Lucien faltered out.

At that word, Coralie sprang to her poet and held him tightly to her; then, with her arms still about him, she turned to the silk-mercer, as if to bid him see the beautiful picture made by two young lovers.

"Poor Musot, take all that you gave to me back again; I do not want to keep anything of yours; for I love this boy here madly, not for his intellect, but for his beauty. I would rather starve with him than have millions with you."

Camusot sank into a low chair, hid his face in his hands, and said not a word.

"Would you like us to go away?" she asked. There was a note of ferocity in her voice which no words can describe.

Cold chills ran down Lucien's spine; he beheld himself burdened with a woman, an actress, and a household.

"Stay here, Coralie; keep it all," the old tradesman said at last, in a faint, unsteady voice that came from his heart; "I don't want anything back. There is the worth of sixty thousand francs here in the furniture; but I could not bear to think of my Coralie in want. And yet, it will not be long before you come to want. However great this gentleman's talent may be, he can't afford to keep you. We old fellows must expect this sort of thing. Coralie, let me come and see you sometimes; I may be of use to you. And--I confess it; I cannot live without you."

The poor man's gentleness, stripped as he was of his happiness just as happiness had reached its height, touched Lucien deeply. Coralie was quite unsoftened by it.

"Come as often as you wish, poor Musot," she said; "I shall like you all the better when I don't pretend to love you."

Camusot seemed to be resigned to his fate so long as he was not driven out of the earthly paradise, in which his life could not have been all joy; he trusted to the chances of life in Paris and to the temptations that would beset Lucien's path; he would wait a while, and all that had been his should be his again. Sooner or later, thought the wily tradesman, this handsome young fellow would be unfaithful; he would keep a watch on him; and the better to do this and use his opportunity with Coralie, he would be their friend. The persistent passion that could consent to such humiliation terrified Lucien. Camusot's proposal of a dinner at Very's in the Palais Royal was accepted.

"What joy!" cried Coralie, as soon as Camusot had departed. "You will not go back now to your garret in the Latin Quarter; you will live here. We shall always be together. You can take a room in the Rue Charlot for the sake of appearances, and *vogue le galere*!"

She began to dance her Spanish dance, with an excited eagerness that revealed the strength of the passion in her heart.

"If I work hard I may make five hundred francs a month," Lucien said.

"And I shall make as much again at the theatre, without counting extras. Camusot will pay for my dresses as before. He is fond of me! We can live like Croesus on fifteen hundred francs a month."

"And the horses? and the coachman? and the footman?" inquired Berenice.

"I will get into debt," said Coralie. And she began to dance with Lucien.

"I must close with Finot after this," Lucien exclaimed.

"There!" said Coralie, "I will dress and take you to your office. I will wait outside in the boulevard for you with the carriage."

Lucien sat down on the sofa and made some very sober reflections as he watched Coralie at her toilet. It would have been wiser to leave Coralie free than to start all at once with such an establishment; but Coralie was there before his eyes, and Coralie was so lovely, so graceful, so bewitching, that the more picturesque aspects of bohemia were in evidence; and he flung down the gauntlet to fortune.

Berenice was ordered to superintend Lucien's removal and installation; and Coralie, triumphant, radiant, and happy, carried off her love, her poet, and must needs go all over Paris on the way to the Rue Saint-Fiacre. Lucien sprang lightly up the staircase, and entered the office with an air of being quite at home. Coloquinte was there with the stamped paper still on his head; and old Giroudeau told him again, hypocritically enough, that no one had yet come in.

"But the editor and contributors *must* meet somewhere or other to arrange about the journal," said Lucien.

"Very likely; but I have nothing to do with the writing of the paper," said the Emperor's captain, resuming his occupation of checking off wrappers with his eternal broum! broum!

Was it lucky or unlucky? Finot chanced to come in at that very moment to announce his sham abdication and to bid Giroudeau watch over his interests.

"No shilly-shally with this gentleman; he is on the staff," Finot added for his uncle's benefit, as he grasped Lucien by the hand.

"Oh! is he on the paper?" exclaimed Giroudeau, much surprised at this friendliness. "Well, sir, you came on without much difficulty."

"I want to make things snug for you here, lest Etienne should bamboozle you," continued Finot, looking knowingly at Lucien. "This gentleman will be paid three francs per column all round, including theatres."

"You have never taken any one on such terms before," said Giroudeau, opening his eyes.

"And he will take the four Boulevard theatres. See that nobody sneaks his boxes, and that he gets his share of tickets.--I should advise you, nevertheless, to have them sent to your address," he added, turning to Lucien.--"And he agrees to write besides ten miscellaneous articles of two columns each, for fifty francs per month, for one year. Does that suit you?"

"Yes," said Lucien. Circumstances had forced his hand.

"Draw up the agreement, uncle, and we will sign it when we come downstairs."

"Who is the gentleman?" inquired Giroudeau, rising and taking off his black silk skull-cap.

"M. Lucien de Rubempre, who wrote the article on *The Alcalde*."

"Young man, you have a gold mine *there*," said the old soldier, tapping Lucien on the forehead. "I am not literary myself, but I read that article of yours, and I liked it. That is the kind of thing! There's gaiety for you! 'That will bring us new subscribers,' says I to myself. And so it did. We sold fifty more numbers."

"Is my agreement with Lousteau made out in duplicate and ready to sign?" asked Finot, speaking aside.

"Yes."

"Then ante-date this gentleman's agreement by one day, so that Lousteau will be bound by the previous contract."

Finot took his new contributor's arm with a friendliness that charmed Lucien, and drew him out on the landing to say:--

"Your position is made for you. I will introduce you to *my* staff myself, and tonight Lousteau will go round with you to the theatres. You can make a hundred and fifty francs per month on this little paper of ours with Lousteau as its editor, so try to keep well with him. The rogue bears a grudge against me as it is, for tying his hands so far as you are concerned; but you have ability, and I don't choose that you shall be subjected to the whims of the editor. You might let me have a couple of sheets every month for my review, and I will pay you two hundred francs. This is between ourselves, don't mention it to anybody else; I should be laid open to the spite of every one whose vanity is mortified by your good fortune. Write four articles, fill your two sheets, sign two with your own name, and two with a pseudonym, so that you may not seem to be taking the bread out of anybody else's mouth. You owe your position to Blondet and Vignon; they think that you have a future before you. So keep out of scrapes, and, above all things, be on your guard against your friends. As for me, we shall

184

always get on well together, you and I. Help me, and I will help you. You have forty francs' worth of boxes and tickets to sell, and sixty francs' worth of books to convert into cash. With that and your work on the paper, you will be making four hundred and fifty francs every month. If you use your wits, you will find ways of making another two hundred francs at least among the publishers; they will pay you for reviews and prospectuses. But you are mine, are you not? I can count upon you."

Lucien squeezed Finot's hand in transports of joy which no words can express.

"Don't let any one see that anything has passed between us," said Finot in his ear, and he flung open a door of a room in the roof at the end of a long passage on the fifth floor.

A table covered with a green cloth was drawn up to a blazing fire, and seated in various chairs and lounges Lucien discovered Lousteau, Felicien Vernou, Hector Merlin, and two others unknown to him, all laughing or smoking. A real inkstand, full of ink this time, stood on the table among a great litter of papers; while a collection of pens, the worse for wear, but still serviceable for journalists, told the new contributor very plainly that the mighty enterprise was carried on in this apartment.

"Gentlemen," said Finot, "the object of this gathering is the installation of our friend Lousteau in my place as editor of the newspaper which I am compelled to relinquish. But although my opinions will necessarily undergo a transformation when I accept the editorship of a review of which the politics are known to you, my *convictions* remain the same, and we shall be friends as before. I am quite at your service, and you likewise will be ready to do anything for me. Circumstances change; principles are fixed. Principles are the pivot on which the hands of the political barometer turn."

There was an instant shout of laughter.

"Who put that into your mouth?" asked Lousteau.

"Blondet!" said Finot.

"Windy, showery, stormy, settled fair," said Merlin; "we will all row in the same boat."

"In short," continued Finot, "not to muddle our wits with metaphors, any one who has an article or two for me will always find Finot.--This gentleman," turning to Lucien, "will be one of you.--I have arranged with him, Lousteau."

Every one congratulated Finot on his advance and new prospects.

"So there you are, mounted on our shoulders," said a contributor whom Lucien did not know. "You will be the Janus of Journal----"

"So long as he isn't the Janot," put in Vernou.

"Are you going to allow us to make attacks on our *betes noires*?"

"Any one you like."

"Ah, yes!" said Lousteau; "but the paper must keep on its lines. M. Chatelet is very wroth; we shall not let him off for a week yet."

"What has happened?" asked Lucien.

"He came here to ask for an explanation," said Vernou. "The Imperial buck found old Giroudeau at home; and old Giroudeau told him, with all the coolness in the world, that Philippe Bridau wrote the article. Philippe asked the Baron to mention the time and the weapons, and there it ended. We are engaged at this moment in offering excuses to the Baron in tomorrow's issue. Every phrase is a stab for him."

"Keep your teeth in him and he will come round to me," said Finot; "and it will look as if I were obliging him by appeasing you. He can say a word to the Ministry, and we can get something or other out of him--an assistant schoolmaster's place, or a tobacconist's license. It is a lucky thing for us that we flicked him on the raw. Does anybody here care to take a serious article on Nathan for my new paper?"

"Give it to Lucien," said Lousteau. "Hector and Vernou will write articles in their papers at the same time."

"Good-day, gentlemen; we shall meet each other face to face at Barbin's," said Finot, laughing.

Lucien received some congratulations on his admission to the mighty army of journalists, and Lousteau explained that they could be sure of him. "Lucien wants you all to sup in a body at the house of the fair Coralie."

"Coralie is going on at the Gymnase," said Lucien.

"Very well, gentlemen; it is understood that we push Coralie, eh? Put a few lines about her new engagement in your papers, and say something about her talent. Credit the management of the Gymnase with tack and discernment; will it do to say intelligence?"

"Yes, say intelligence," said Merlin; "Frederic has something of Scribe's."

"Oh! Well, then, the manager of the Gymnase is the most perspicacious and far-sighted of men of business," said Vernou.

"Look here! don't write your articles on Nathan until we have come to an understanding; you shall hear why," said Etienne Lousteau. "We ought to do something for our new comrade. Lucien here has two books to bring out--a volume of sonnets and a novel. The power of the paragraph should make him a great poet due in three months; and we will make use of his sonnets (*Marguerites* is the title) to run down odes, ballads, and reveries, and all the Romantic poetry."

"It would be a droll thing if the sonnets were no good after all," said Vernou.--"What do you yourself think of your sonnets, Lucien?"

"Yes, what do you think of them?" asked one of the two whom Lucien did not know.

"They are all right, gentlemen; I give you my word," said Lousteau.

"Very well, that will do for me," said Vernou; "I will heave your book at the poets of the sacristy; I am tired of them."

"If Dauriat declines to take the *Marguerites* this evening, we will attack him by pitching into Nathan."

"But what will Nathan say?" cried Lucien.

His five colleagues burst out laughing.

"Oh! he will be delighted," said Vernou. "You will see how we manage these things."

"So he is one of us?" said one of the two journalists.

"Yes, yes, Frederic; no tricks.--We are all working for you, Lucien, you see; you must stand by us when your turn comes. We are all friends of Nathan's, and we are attacking him. Now, let us divide Alexander's empire.--Frederic, will you take the Francais and the Odeon?"

"If these gentlemen are willing," returned the person addressed as Frederic. The others nodded assent, but Lucien saw a gleam of jealousy here and there.

"I am keeping the Opera, the Italiens, and the Opera-Comique," put in Vernou.

"And how about me? Am I to have no theatres at all?" asked the second stranger.

"Oh well, Hector can let you have the Varietes, and Lucien can spare you the Porte Saint-Martin.--Let him have the Porte Saint-Martin, Lucien, he is wild about Fanny Beaupre; and you can take the Cirque-Olympique in exchange. I shall have Bobino and the Funambules and Madame Saqui. Now, what have we for tomorrow?"

"Nothing."

"Nothing?"

"Nothing."

"Gentlemen, be brilliant for my first number. The Baron du Chatelet and his cuttlefish bone will not last for a week, and the writer of *Le Solitaire* is worn out."

"And 'Sosthenes-Demosthenes' is stale too," said Vernou; "everybody has taken it up."

"The fact is, we want a new set of ninepins," said Frederic.

"Suppose that we take the virtuous representatives of the Right?" suggested Lousteau. "We might say that M. de Bonald has sweaty feet."

"Let us begin a series of sketches of Ministerialist orators," suggested Hector Merlin.

"You do that, youngster; you know them; they are your own party," said Lousteau; "you could indulge any little private grudges of your own. Pitch into Beugnot and Syrieys de Mayrinhac and the rest. You might have the sketches ready in advance, and we shall have something to fall back upon."

"How if we invented one or two cases of refusal of burial with aggravating circumstances?" asked Hector.

"Do not follow in the tracks of the big Constitutional papers; they have pigeon-holes full of ecclesiastical *canards*," retorted Vernou.

"*Canards*?" repeated Lucien.

"That is our word for a scrap of fiction told for true, put in to enliven the column of morning news when it is flat. We owe the discovery to Benjamin Franklin, the inventor of the lightning conductor and the republic. That journalist completely deceived the Encyclopaedists by his transatlantic *canards*. Raynal gives two of them for facts in his *Histoire philosophique des Indes*."

"I did not know that," said Vernou. "What were the stories?"

"One was a tale about an Englishman and a negress who helped him to escape; he sold the woman for a slave after getting her with child himself to enhance her value. The other was the eloquent defence of a young woman brought before the authorities for bearing a child out of wedlock. Franklin owned to the fraud in Necker's house when he came to Paris, much to the confusion of French philosophism. Behold how the New World twice set a bad example to the Old!"

"In journalism," said Lousteau, "everything that is probable is true. That is an axiom."

"Criminal procedure is based on the same rule," said Vernou.

"Very well, we meet here at nine o'clock," and with that they rose, and the sitting broke up with the most affecting demonstrations of intimacy and good-will.

"What have you done to Finot, Lucien, that he should make a special arrangement with you? You are the only one that he has bound to himself," said Etienne Lousteau, as they came downstairs.

"I? Nothing. It was his own proposal," said Lucien.

"As a matter of fact, if you should make your own terms with him, I should be delighted; we should, both of us, be the better for it."

On the ground floor they found Finot. He stepped across to Lousteau and asked him into the so-called private office. Giroudeau immediately put a couple of stamped agreements before Lucien.

"Sign your agreement," he said, "and the new editor will think the whole thing was arranged yesterday."

Lucien, reading the document, overheard fragments of a tolerably warm dispute within as to the line of conduct and profits of the paper. Etienne Lousteau wanted his share of the blackmail levied by Giroudeau; and, in all probability, the matter was compromised, for the pair came out perfectly good friends.

"We will meet at Dauriat's, Lucien, in the Wooden Galleries at eight o'clock," said Etienne Lousteau.

A young man appeared, meanwhile, in search of employment, wearing the same nervous shy look with which Lucien himself had come to the office so short a while ago; and in his secret soul Lucien felt amused as he watched Giroudeau playing off the same tactics with which the old campaigner had previously foiled him. Self-interest opened his eyes to the necessity of the manoeuvres which raised well-nigh insurmountable barriers between beginners and the upper room where the elect were gathered together.

"Contributors don't get very much as it is," he said, addressing Giroudeau.

"If there were more of you, there would be so much less," retorted the captain. "So there!"

The old campaigner swung his loaded cane, and went down coughing as usual. Out in the street he was amazed to see a handsome carriage waiting on the boulevard for Lucien.

"*You* are the army nowadays," he said, "and we are the civilians."

"Upon my word," said Lucien, as he drove away with Coralie, "these young writers seem to me to be the best fellows alive. Here am I a journalist, sure of making six hundred francs a month if I work like a horse. But I shall find a publisher for my two books, and I will write others; for my friends will insure a success. And so, Coralie, '*vogue le galere!*' as you say."

"You will make your way, dear boy; but you must not be as good-natured as you are good-looking; it would be the ruin of you. Be ill-natured, that is the proper thing."

Coralie and Lucien drove in the Bois de Boulogne, and again they met the Marquise d'Espard, Mme. de Bargeton and the Baron du Chatelet. Mme. de Bargeton gave Lucien a languishing glance which might be taken as a greeting. Camusot had ordered the best possible dinner; and Coralie, feeling that she was rid of her adorer, was more charming to the poor silk-mercer than she had ever been in the fourteen months during which their connection lasted; he had never seen her so kindly, so enchantingly lovely.

"Come," he thought, "let us keep near her anyhow!"

In consequence, Camusot made secret overtures. He promised Coralie an income of six thousand livres; he would transfer the stock in the funds into her name (his wife knew nothing about the investment) if only she would consent to be his mistress still. He would shut his eyes to her lover.

"And betray such an angel? . . . Why, just look at him, you old fossil, and look at yourself!" and her eyes turned to her poet. Camusot had pressed Lucien to drink till the poet's head was rather cloudy.

There was no help for it; Camusot made up his mind to wait till sheer want should give him this woman a second time.

"Then I can only be your friend," he said, as he kissed her on the forehead.

Lucien went from Coralie and Camusot to the Wooden Galleries. What a change had been wrought in his mind by his initiation into Journalism! He mixed fearlessly now with the crowd which surged to and fro in the buildings; he even swaggered a little because he had a mistress; and he walked into Dauriat's shop in an offhand manner because he was a journalist.

He found himself among distinguished men; gave a hand to Blondet and Nathan and Finot, and to all the coterie with whom he had been fraternizing for a week. He was a personage, he thought, and he flattered himself that he surpassed his comrades. That little flick of the wine did him admirable service; he was witty, he showed that he could "howl with the wolves."

And yet, the tacit approval, the praises spoken and unspoken on which he had counted, were not forthcoming. He noticed the first stirrings of jealousy among a group, less curious, perhaps, than anxious to know the place which this newcomer might take, and the exact portion of the sum-total of profits which he would probably secure and swallow. Lucien only saw smiles on two faces--Finot, who regarded him as a mine to be exploited, and Lousteau, who considered that he had proprietary rights in the poet, looked glad to see him. Lousteau had begun already to assume the airs of an editor; he tapped sharply on the window-panes of Dauriat's private office.

"One moment, my friend," cried a voice within as the publisher's face appeared above the green curtains.

The moment lasted an hour, and finally Lucien and Etienne were admitted into the sanctum.

"Well, have you thought over our friend's proposal?" asked Etienne Lousteau, now an editor.

"To be sure," said Dauriat, lolling like a sultan in his chair. "I have read the volume. And I submitted it to a man of taste, a good judge; for I don't pretend to understand these things myself. I myself, my friend, buy reputations ready-made, as the Englishman bought his love affairs.--You are as great as a poet as you are handsome as a man, my boy," pronounced Dauriat. "Upon my word and honor (I don't tell you that as a publisher, mind), your sonnets are magnificent; no sign of effort about them, as is natural when a man writes with inspiration and verve. You know your craft, in fact, one of the good points of the new school. Your volume of *Marguerites* is a fine book, but there is no business in it, and it is not worth my while to meddle with anything but a very big affair. In conscience, I won't take your sonnets. It would be impossible to push them; there is not enough in the thing to pay the expenses of a big success. You will not keep to poetry besides; this book of yours will be your first and last attempt of the kind. You are young; you bring me the everlasting volume of early verse which every man of letters writes when he leaves school, he thinks a lot of it at the time, and laughs at it later on. Lousteau, your friend, has a poem put away somewhere among his old socks, I'll warrant. Haven't you a poem that you thought a good deal of once, Lousteau?" inquired Dauriat, with a knowing glance at the other.

"How should I be writing prose otherwise, eh?" asked Lousteau.

"There, you see! He has never said a word to me about it, for our friend understands business and the trade," continued Dauriat. "For me the question is not whether you are a great poet, I know that," he added, stroking down Lucien's pride; "you have a great deal, a very great deal of merit; if I were only just starting in business, I should make the mistake of publishing your book. But in the first place, my sleeping partners and those at the back of me are cutting off my supplies; I dropped twenty thousand francs over poetry last year, and that is enough for them; they will not hear of any more just now, and they are my masters. Nevertheless, that is not the question. I admit that you may be a great poet, but will you be a prolific writer? Will you hatch sonnets regularly? Will you run into ten volumes? Is there business in it? Of course not. You will be a delightful prose writer; you have too much sense to spoil your style with tagging rhymes together. You have a chance to make thirty thousand francs per annum by writing for the papers, and you will not exchange that chance for three thousand francs made with difficulty by your hemistiches and strophes and tomfoolery----"

"You know that he is on the paper, Dauriat?" put in Lousteau.

"Yes," Dauriat answered. "Yes, I saw his article, and in his own interests I decline the *Marguerites*. Yes, sir, in six months' time I shall have paid you more money for the articles that I shall ask you to write than for your poetry that will not sell."

"And fame?" said Lucien.

Dauriat and Lousteau laughed.

"Oh dear!" said Lousteau, "there be illusions left."

"Fame means ten years of sticking to work, and a hundred thousand francs lost or made in the publishing trade. If you find anybody mad enough to print your poetry for you, you will feel some respect for me in another twelvemonth, when

189

you have had time to see the outcome of the transaction"

"Have you the manuscript here?" Lucien asked coldly.

"Here it is, my friend," said Dauriat. The publisher's manner towards Lucien had sweetened singularly.

Lucien took up the roll without looking at the string, so sure he felt that Dauriat had read his *Marguerites*. He went out with Lousteau, seemingly neither disconcerted nor dissatisfied. Dauriat went with them into the shop, talking of his newspaper and Lousteau's daily, while Lucien played with the manuscript of the *Marguerites*.

"Do you suppose that Dauriat has read your sonnets or sent them to any one else?" Etienne Lousteau snatched an opportunity to whisper.

"Yes," said Lucien.

"Look at the string." Lucien looked down at the blot of ink, and saw that the mark on the string still coincided; he turned white with rage.

"Which of the sonnets was it that you particularly liked?" he asked, turning to the publisher.

"They are all of them remarkable, my friend; but the sonnet on the *Marguerite* is delightful, the closing thought is fine, and exquisitely expressed. I felt sure from that sonnet that your prose work would command a success, and I spoke to Finot about you at once. Write articles for us, and we will pay you well for them. Fame is a very fine thing, you see, but don't forget the practical and solid, and take every chance that turns up. When you have made money, you can write poetry."

The poet dashed out of the shop to avoid an explosion. He was furious. Lousteau followed.

"Well, my boy, pray keep cool. Take men as they are--for means to an end. Do you wish for revenge?"

"At any price," muttered the poet.

"Here is a copy of Nathan's book. Dauriat has just given it to me. The second edition is coming out tomorrow; read the book again, and knock off an article demolishing it. Felicien Vernou cannot endure Nathan, for he thinks that Nathan's success will injure his own forthcoming book. It is a craze with these little minds to fancy that there is not room for two successes under the sun; so he will see that your article finds a place in the big paper for which he writes."

"But what is there to be said against the book; it is good work!" cried Lucien.

"Oh, I say! you must learn your trade," said Lousteau, laughing. "Given that the book was a masterpiece, under the stroke of your pen it must turn to dull trash, dangerous and unwholesome stuff."

"But how?"

"You turn all the good points into bad ones."

"I am incapable of such a juggler's feat."

"My dear boy, a journalist is a juggler; a man must make up his mind to the drawbacks of the calling. Look here! I am not a bad fellow; this is the way *I* should set to work myself. Attention! You might begin by praising the book, and amuse yourself a while by saying what you really think. 'Good,' says the reader, 'this critic is not jealous; he will be impartial, no doubt,' and from that point your public will think that your criticism is a piece of conscientious work. Then, when you have won your reader's confidence, you will regret that you must blame the tendency and influence of such work upon French literature. 'Does not France,' you will say, 'sway the whole intellectual world? French writers have kept Europe in the path of analysis and philosophical criticism from age to age by their powerful style and the original turn given by them to ideas.' Here, for the benefit of the philistine, insert a panegyric on Voltaire, Rousseau, Diderot, Montesquieu, and Buffon. Hold forth upon the inexorable French language; show how it spreads a varnish, as it were, over thought. Let fall a few aphorisms, such as--'A great writer in France is invariably a great man; he writes in a language which compels him to think; it is otherwise in other countries'--and so on, and so on. Then, to prove your case, draw a comparison between Rabener, the German satirical moralist, and La Bruyere. Nothing gives a critic such an air as an apparent familiarity with foreign literature. Kant is Cousin's pedestal.

"Once on that ground you bring out a word which sums up the French men of genius of the eighteenth century for the benefit of simpletons--you call that literature the 'literature of ideas.' Armed with this expression, you fling all the mighty dead at the heads of the illustrious living. You explain that in the present day a new form of literature has sprung up; that dialogue (the easiest form of writing) is overdone, and description dispenses with any need for thinking on the part of the author or reader. You bring up the fiction of Voltaire, Diderot, Sterne, and Le Sage, so trenchant, so compact of the stuff of life; and turn from them to the modern novel, composed of scenery and word-pictures and metaphor and the dramatic situations, of which Scott is full. Invention may be displayed in such work, but there is no room for anything else. 'The romance after the manner of Scott is a mere passing fashion in literature,' you will say, and fulminate against the fatal way in which ideas are diluted and beaten thin; cry out against a style within the reach of any intellect, for any one can commence author at small expense in a way of literature, which you can nickname the 'literature of imagery.'

"Then you fall upon Nathan with your argument, and establish it beyound cavil that he is a mere imitator with an appearance of genius. The concise grand style of the eighteenth century is lacking; you show that the author substitutes events for sentiments. Action and stir is not life; he gives you pictures, but no ideas.

"Come out with such phrases, and people will take them up.--In spite of the merits of the work, it seems to you to be a dangerous, nay, a fatal precedent. It throws open the gates of the temple of Fame to the crowd; and in the distance you descry a legion of petty authors hastening to imitate this novel and easy style of writing.

"Here you launch out into resounding lamentations over the decadence and decline of taste, and slip in eulogies of Messieurs Etienne Jouy, Tissot, Gosse, Duval, Jay, Benjamin Constant, Aignan, Baour-Lormian, Villemain, and the whole Liberal-Bonapartist chorus who patronize Vernou's paper. Next you draw a picture of that glorious phalanx of writers repelling the invasion of the Romantics; these are the upholders of ideas and style as against metaphor and balderdash; the modern representatives of the school of Voltaire as opposed to the English and German schools, even as the seventeen heroic deputies of the Left fought the battle for the nation against the Ultras of the Right.

"And then, under cover of names respected by the immense majority of Frenchmen (who will always be against the Government), you can crush Nathan; for although his work is far above the average, it confirms the bourgeois taste for literature without ideas. And after that, you understand, it is no longer a question of Nathan and his book, but of France and the glory of France. It is the duty of all honest and courageous pens to make strenuous opposition to these foreign importations. And with that you flatter your readers. Shrewd French mother-wit is not easily caught napping. If publishers, by ways which you do not choose to specify, have stolen a success, the reading public very soon judges for itself, and corrects the mistakes made by some five hundred fools, who always rush to the fore.

"Say that the publisher who sold a first edition of the book is audacious indeed to issue a second, and express regret that so clever a man does not know the taste of the country better. There is the gist of it. Just a sprinkle of the salt of wit and a dash of vinegar to bring out the flavor, and Dauriat will be done to a turn. But mind that you end with seeming to pity Nathan for a mistake, and speak of him as of a man from whom contemporary literature may look for great things if he renounces these ways."

Lucien was amazed at this talk from Lousteau. As the journalist spoke, the scales fell from his eyes; he beheld new truths of which he had never before caught so much as a glimpse.

"But all this that you are saying is quite true and just," said he.

"If it were not, how could you make it tell against Nathan's book?" asked Lousteau. "That is the first manner of demolishing a book, my boy; it is the pickaxe style of criticism. But there are plenty of other ways. Your education will complete itself in time. When you are absolutely obliged to speak of a man whom you do not like, for proprietors and editors are sometimes under compulsion, you bring out a neutral special article. You put the title of the book at the head of it, and begin with general remarks, on the Greeks and the Romans if you like, and wind up with--'and this brings us to Mr. So-and-so's book, which will form the subject of a second article.' The second article never appears, and in this way you snuff out the book between two promises. But in this case you are writing down, not Nathan, but Dauriat; he needs the pickaxe style. If the book is really good, the pickaxe does no harm; but it goes to the core of it if it is bad. In the first case, no one but the publisher is any the worse; in the second, you do the public a service. Both methods, moreover, are equally serviceable in political criticism."

Etienne Lousteau's cruel lesson opened up possibilities for Lucien's imagination. He understood this craft to admiration.

"Let us go to the office," said Lousteau; "we shall find our friends there, and we will agree among ourselves to charge at Nathan; they will laugh, you will see."

Arrived in the Rue Saint-Fiacre, they went up to the room in the roof where the paper was made up, and Lucien was surprised and gratified no less to see the alacrity with which his comrades proceeded to demolish Nathan's book. Hector Merlin took up a piece of paper and wrote a few lines for his own newspaper.--

"A second edition of M. Nathan's book is announced. We had intended to keep silence with regard to that work, but its apparent success obliges us to publish an article, not so much upon the book itself as upon certain tendencies of the new school of literature."

At the head of the "Facetiae" in the morning's paper, Lousteau inserted the following note:--

"M. Dauriat is bringing out a second edition of M. Nathan's book. Evidently he does not know the legal maxim, *Non bis in idem*. All honor to rash courage."

Lousteau's words had been like a torch for burning; Lucien's hot desire to be revenged on Dauriat took the place of conscience and inspiration. For three days he never left Coralie's room; he sat at work by the fire, waited upon by Berenice; petted, in moments of weariness, by the silent and attentive Coralie; till, at the end of that time, he had made a fair copy of about three columns of criticism, and an astonishingly good piece of work.

It was nine o'clock in the evening when he ran round to the office, found his associates, and read over his work to an attentive audience. Felicien said not a syllable. He took up the manuscript, and made off with it pell-mell down the staircase.

"What has come to him?" cried Lucien.

"He has taken your article straight to the printer," said Hector Merlin. "'Tis a masterpiece; not a line to add, nor a word to take out."

"There was no need to do more than show you the way," said Lousteau.

"I should like to see Nathan's face when he reads this tomorrow," said another contributor, beaming with gentle satisfaction.

"It is as well to have you for a friend," remarked Hector Merlin.

"Then it will do?" Lucien asked quickly.

"Blondet and Vignon will feel bad," said Lousteau.

"Here is a short article which I have knocked together for you," began Lucien; "if it takes, I could write you a series."

"Read it over," said Lousteau, and Lucien read the first of the delightful short papers which made the fortune of the little newspaper; a series of sketches of Paris life, a portrait, a type, an ordinary event, or some of the oddities of the great city. This specimen--"The Man in the Street"--was written in a way that was fresh and original; the thoughts were struck out by the shock of the words, the sounding ring of the adverbs and adjectives caught the reader's ear. The paper was as different from the serious and profound article on Nathan as the *Lettres persanes* from the *Esprit des lois*.

"You are a born journalist," said Lousteau. "It shall go in tomorrow. Do as much of this sort of thing as you like."

"Ah, by the by," said Merlin, "Dauriat is furious about those two bombshells hurled into his magazine. I have just come from him. He was hurling imprecations, and in such a rage with Finot, who told him that he had sold his paper to you. As for me, I took him aside and just said a word in his ear. 'The *Marguerites* will cost you dear,' I told him. 'A man of talent comes to you, you turn the cold shoulder on him, and send him into the arms of the newspapers.'"

"Dauriat will be dumfounded by the article on Nathan," said Lousteau. "Do you see now what journalism is, Lucien? Your revenge is beginning to tell. The Baron Chatelet came here this morning for your address. There was a cutting article upon him in this morning's issue; he is a weakling, that buck of the Empire, and he has lost his head. Have you seen the paper? It is a funny article. Look, 'Funeral of the Heron, and the Cuttlefish-bone's lament.' Mme. de Bargeton is called the Cuttlefish-bone now, and no mistake, and Chatelet is known everywhere as Baron Heron."

Lucien took up the paper, and could not help laughing at Vernou's extremely clever skit.

"They will capitulate soon," said Hector Merlin.

Lucien merrily assisted at the manufacture of epigrams and jokes at the end of the paper; and the associates smoked and chatted over the day's adventures, over the foibles of some among their number, or some new bit of personal gossip. From their witty, malicious, bantering talk, Lucien gained a knowledge of the inner life of literature, and of the manners and customs of the craft.

"While they are setting up the paper, I will go round with you and introduce you to the managers of your theatres, and take you behind the scenes," said Lousteau. "And then we will go to the Panorama-Dramatique, and have a frolic in their dressing-rooms."

Arm-in-arm, they went from theatre to theatre. Lucien was introduced to this one and that, and enthroned as a dramatic critic. Managers complimented him, actresses flung him side glances; for every one of them knew that this was the critic who, by a single article, had gained an engagement at the Gymnase, with twelve thousand francs a year, for Coralie, and another for Florine at the Panorama-Dramatique with eight thousand francs. Lucien was a man of importance. The little ovations raised Lucien in his own eyes, and taught him to know his power. At eleven o'clock the pair arrived at the Panorama-Dramatique; Lucien with a careless air that worked wonders. Nathan was there. Nathan held out a hand, which Lucien squeezed.

"Ah! my masters, so you have a mind to floor me, have you?" said Nathan, looking from one to the other.

"Just you wait till tomorrow, my dear fellow, and you shall see how Lucien has taken you in hand. Upon my word, you will be pleased. A piece of serious criticism like that is sure to do a book good."

Lucien reddened with confusion.

"Is it severe?" inquired Nathan.

"It is serious," said Lousteau.

"Then there is no harm done," Nathan rejoined. "Hector Merlin in the greenroom of the Vaudeville was saying that I had

193

been cut up."

"Let him talk, and wait," cried Lucien, and took refuge in Coralie's dressing-room. Coralie, in her alluring costume, had just come off the stage.

Next morning, as Lucien and Coralie sat at breakfast, a carriage drove along the Rue de Vendome. The street was quiet enough, so that they could hear the light sound made by an elegant cabriolet; and there was that in the pace of the horse, and the manner of pulling up at the door, which tells unmistakably of a thoroughbred. Lucien went to the window, and there, in fact, beheld a splendid English horse, and no less a person than Dauriat flinging the reins to his man as he stepped down.

"'Tis the publisher, Coralie," said Lucien.

"Let him wait, Berenice," Coralie said at once.

Lucien smiled at her presence of mind, and kissed her with a great rush of tenderness. This mere girl had made his interests hers in a wonderful way; she was quick-witted where he was concerned. The apparition of the insolent publisher, the sudden and complete collapse of that prince of charlatans, was due to circumstances almost entirely forgotten, so utterly has the book trade changed during the last fifteen years.

From 1816 to 1827, when newspaper reading-rooms were only just beginning to lend new books, the fiscal law pressed more heavily than ever upon periodical publications, and necessity created the invention of advertisements. Paragraphs and articles in the newspapers were the only means of advertisement known in those days; and French newspapers before the year 1822 were so small, that the largest sheet of those times was not so large as the smallest daily paper of ours. Dauriat and Ladvocat, the first publishers to make a stand against the tyranny of journalists, were also the first to use the placards which caught the attention of Paris by strange type, striking colors, vignettes, and (at a later time) by lithograph illustrations, till a placard became a fairy-tale for the eyes, and not unfrequently a snare for the purse of the amateur. So much originality indeed was expended on placards in Paris, that one of that peculiar kind of maniacs, known as a collector, possesses a complete series.

At first the placard was confined to the shop-windows and stalls upon the Boulevards in Paris; afterwards it spread all over France, till it was supplanted to some extent by a return to advertisements in the newspapers. But the placard, nevertheless, which continues to strike the eye, after the advertisement and the book which is advertised are both forgotten, will always be among us; it took a new lease of life when walls were plastered with posters.

Newspaper advertising, the offspring of heavy stamp duties, a high rate of postage, and the heavy deposits of caution-money required by the government as security for good behavior, is within the reach of all who care to pay for it, and has turned the fourth page of every journal into a harvest field alike for the speculator and the Inland Revenue Department. The press restrictions were invented in the time of M. de Villele, who had a chance, if he had but known it, of destroying the power of journalism by allowing newspapers to multiply till no one took any notice of them; but he missed his opportunity, and a sort of privilege was created, as it were, by the almost insuperable difficulties put in the way of starting a new venture. So, in 1821, the periodical press might be said to have power of life and death over the creations of the brain and the publishing trade. A few lines among the items of news cost a fearful amount. Intrigues were multiplied in newspaper offices; and of a night when the columns were divided up, and this or that article was put in or left out to suit the space, the printing-room became a sort of battlefield; so much so, that the largest publishing firms had writers in their pay to insert short articles in which many ideas are put in little space. Obscure journalists of this stamp were only paid after the insertion of the items, and not unfrequently spent the night in the printing-office to make sure that their contributions were not omitted; sometimes putting in a long article, obtained heaven knows how, sometimes a few lines of a puff.

The manners and customs of journalism and of the publishing houses have since changed so much, that many people nowadays will not believe what immense efforts were made by writers and publishers of books to secure a newspaper puff; the martyrs of glory, and all those who are condemned to the penal servitude of a life-long success, were reduced to such shifts, and stooped to depths of bribery and corruption as seem fabulous today. Every kind of persuasion was brought to bear on journalists--dinners, flattery, and presents. The following story will throw more light on the close connection between the critic and the publisher than any quantity of flat assertions.

There was once upon a time an editor of an important paper, a clever writer with a prospect of becoming a statesman; he was young in those days, and fond of pleasure, and he became the favorite of a well-known publishing house. One Sunday the wealthy head of the firm was entertaining several of the foremost journalists of the time in the country, and the mistress of the house, then a young and pretty woman, went to walk in her park with the illustrious visitor. The head-clerk of the firm, a cool, steady, methodical German with nothing but business in his head, was discussing a project with one of the journalists, and as they chatted they walked on into the woods beyond the park. In among the thickets the German thought he caught a glimpse of his hostess, put up his eyeglass, made a sign to his young companion to be silent, and turned back, stepping softly.--"What did you see?" asked the journalist.--"Nothing particular," said the clerk. "Our affair of the long article is settled. Tomorrow we shall have at least three columns in the *Debats*."

Another anecdote will show the influence of a single article.

A book of M. de Chateaubriand's on the last of the Stuarts was for some time a "nightingale" on the bookseller's shelves. A single article in the *Journal des Debats* sold the work in a week. In those days, when there were no lending libraries, a publisher would sell an edition of ten thousand copies of a book by a Liberal if it was well reviewed by the Opposition papers; but then the Belgian pirated editions were not as yet.

The preparatory attacks made by Lucien's friends, followed up by his article on Nathan, proved efficacious; they stopped the sale of his book. Nathan escaped with the mortification; he had been paid; he had nothing to lose; but Dauriat was like to lose thirty thousand francs. The trade in new books may, in fact, be summed up much on this wise. A ream of blank paper costs fifteen francs, a ream of printed paper is worth anything between a hundred sous and a hundred crowns, according to its success; a favorable or unfavorable review at a critical time often decides the question; and Dauriat having five hundred reams of printed paper on hand, hurried to make terms with Lucien. The sultan was now the slave.

After waiting for some time, fidgeting and making as much noise as he could while parleying with Berenice, he at last obtained speech of Lucien; and, arrogant publisher though he was, he came in with the radiant air of a courtier in the royal presence, mingled, however, with a certain self-sufficiency and easy good humor.

"Don't disturb yourselves, my little dears! How nice they look, just like a pair of turtle-doves! Who would think now, mademoiselle, that he, with that girl's face of his, could be a tiger with claws of steel, ready to tear a reputation to rags, just as he tears your wrappers, I'll be bound, when you are not quick enough to unfasten them," and he laughed before he had finished his jest.

"My dear boy----" he began, sitting down beside Lucien. --"Mademoiselle, I am Dauriat," he said, interrupting himself. He judged it expedient to fire his name at her like a pistol shot, for he considered that Coralie was less cordial than she should have been.

"Have you breakfasted, monsieur; will you keep us company?" asked Coralie.

"Why, yes; it is easier to talk at table," said Dauriat. "Besides, by accepting your invitation I shall have a right to expect you to dine with my friend Lucien here, for we must be close friends now, hand and glove!"

"Berenice! Bring oysters, lemons, fresh butter, and champagne," said Coralie.

"You are too clever not to know what has brought me here," said Dauriat, fixing his eyes on Lucien.

"You have come to buy my sonnets."

"Precisely. First of all, let us lay down our arms on both sides." As he spoke he took out a neat pocketbook, drew from it three bills for a thousand francs each, and laid them before Lucien with a suppliant air. "Is monsieur content?" asked he.

"Yes," said the poet. A sense of beatitude, for which no words exist, flooded his soul at the sight of that unhoped wealth. He controlled himself, but he longed to sing aloud, to jump for joy; he was ready to believe in Aladdin's lamp and in enchantment; he believed in his own genius, in short.

"Then the *Marguerites* are mine," continued Dauriat; "but you will undertake not to attack my publications, won't you?"

"The *Marguerites* are yours, but I cannot pledge my pen; it is at the service of my friends, as theirs are mine."

"But you are one of my authors now. All my authors are my friends. So you won't spoil my business without warning me beforehand, so that I am prepared, will you?"

"I agree to that."

"To your fame!" and Dauriat raised his glass.

"I see that you have read the *Marguerites*," said Lucien.

Dauriat was not disconcerted.

"My boy, a publisher cannot pay a greater compliment than by buying your *Marguerites* unread. In six months' time you will be a great poet. You will be written up; people are afraid of you; I shall have no difficulty in selling your book. I am the same man of business that I was four days ago. It is not I who have changed; it is *you*. Last week your sonnets were so many cabbage leaves for me; today your position has ranked them beside Delavigne."

"Ah well," said Lucien, "if you have not read my sonnets, you have read my article." With the sultan's pleasure of possessing a fair mistress, and the certainty of success, he had grown satirical and adorably impertinent of late.

"Yes, my friend; do you think I should have come here in such a hurry but for that? That terrible article of yours is very well written, worse luck. Oh! you have a very great gift, my boy. Take my advice and make the most of your vogue," he added, with good humor, which masked the extreme insolence of the speech. "But have you yourself a copy of the paper? Have you seen your article in print?"

"Not yet," said Lucien, "though this is the first long piece of prose which I have published; but Hector will have sent a copy to my address in the Rue Charlot."

"Here--read!" . . . cried Dauriat, copying Talma's gesture in *Manlius*.

Lucien took the paper but Coralie snatched it from him.

"The first-fruits of your pen belong to me, as you well know," she laughed.

Dauriat was unwontedly courtier-like and complimentary. He was afraid of Lucien, and therefore he asked him to a great dinner which he was giving to a party of journalists towards the end of the week, and Coralie was included in the invitation. He took the *Marguerites* away with him when he went, asking *his* poet to look in when he pleased in the Wooden Galleries, and the agreement should be ready for his signature. Dauriat never forgot the royal airs with which he endeavored to overawe superficial observers, and to impress them with the notion that he was a Maecenas rather than a publisher; at this moment he left the three thousand francs, waving away in lordly fashion the receipt which Lucien offered, kissed Coralie's hand, and took his departure.

"Well, dear love, would you have seen many of these bits of paper if you had stopped in your hole in the Rue de Cluny, prowling about among the musty old books in the Bibliotheque de Sainte-Genevieve?" asked Coralie, for she knew the whole story of Lucien's life by this time. "Those little friends of yours in the Rue des Quatre-Vents are great ninnies, it seems to me."

His brothers of the *cenacle*! And Lucien could hear the verdict and laugh.

He had seen himself in print; he had just experienced the ineffable joy of the author, that first pleasurable thrill of gratified vanity which comes but once. The full import and bearing of his article became apparent to him as he read and re-read it. The garb of print is to manuscript as the stage is to women; it brings beauties and defects to light, killing and giving life; the fine thoughts and the faults alike stare you in the face.

Lucien, in his excitement and rapture, gave not another thought to Nathan. Nathan was a stepping-stone for him--that was all; and he (Lucien) was happy exceedingly--he thought himself rich. The money brought by Dauriat was a very Potosi for the lad who used to go about unnoticed through the streets of Angouleme and down the steep path into L'Houmeau to Postel's garret, where his whole family had lived upon an income of twelve hundred francs. The pleasures of his life in Paris must inevitably dim the memories of those days; but so keen were they, that, as yet, he seemed to be back again in the Place du Murier. He thought of Eve, his beautiful, noble sister, of David his friend, and of his poor mother, and he sent Berenice out to change one of the notes. While she went he wrote a few lines to his family, and on the maid's return he sent her to the coach-office with a packet of five hundred francs addressed to his mother. He could not trust himself; he wanted to sent the money at once; later he might not be able to do it. Both Lucien and Coralie looked upon this restitution as a meritorious action. Coralie put her arms about her lover and kissed him, and thought him a model son and brother; she could not make enough of him, for generosity is a trait of character which delights these kindly creatures, who always carry their hearts in their hands.

"We have a dinner now every day for a week," she said; "we will make a little carnival; you have worked quite hard enough."

Coralie, fain to delight in the beauty of a man whom all other women should envy her, took Lucien back to Staub. He was not dressed finely enough for her. Thence the lovers went to drive in the Bois de Boulogne, and came back to dine at Mme. du Val-Noble's. Rastignac, Bixiou, des Lupeaulx, Finot, Blondet, Vignon, the Baron de Nucingen, Beaudenord, Philippe Bridau, Conti, the great musician, all the artists and speculators, all the men who seek for violent sensations as a relief from immense labors, gave Lucien a welcome among them. And Lucien had gained confidence; he gave himself out in talk as though he had not to live by his wit, and was pronounced to be a "clever fellow" in the slang of the coterie of semi-comrades.

"Oh! we must wait and see what he has in him," said Theodore Gaillard, a poet patronized by the Court, who thought of starting a Royalist paper to be entitled the *Reveil* at a later day.

After dinner, Merlin and Lucien, Coralie and Mme. du Val-Noble, went to the Opera, where Merlin had a box. The whole party adjourned thither, and Lucien triumphant reappeared upon the scene of his first serious check.

He walked in the lobby, arm in arm with Merlin and Blondet, looking the dandies who had once made merry at his expense between the eyes. Chatelet was under his feet. He clashed glances with de Marsay, Vandenesse, and Manerville, the bucks of that day. And indeed Lucien, beautiful and elegantly arrayed, had caused a discussion in the Marquise d'Espard's box; Rastignac had paid a long visit, and the Marquise and Mme. de Bargeton put up their opera-glasses at

Coralie. Did the sight of Lucien send a pang of regret through Mme. de Bargeton's heart? This thought was uppermost in the poet's mind. The longing for revenge aroused in him by the sight of the Corinne of Angouleme was as fierce as on that day when the lady and her cousin had cut him in the Champs-Elysees.

"Did you bring an amulet with you from the provinces?"--It was Blondet who made this inquiry some few days later, when he called at eleven o'clock in the morning and found that Lucien was not yet risen.--"His good looks are making ravages from cellar to garret, high and low," continued Blondet, kissing Coralie on the forehead. "I have come to enlist you, dear fellow," he continued, grasping Lucien by the hand. "Yesterday, at the Italiens, the Comtesse de Montcornet asked me to bring you to her house. You will not give a refusal to a charming woman? You meet people of the first fashion there."

"If Lucien is nice, he will not go to see your Countess," put in Coralie. "What call is there for him to show his face in fine society? He would only be bored there."

"Have you a vested interest in him? Are you jealous of fine ladies?"

"Yes," cried Coralie. "They are worse than we are."

"How do you know that, my pet?" asked Blondet.

"From their husbands," retorted she. "You are forgetting that I once had six months of de Marsay."

"Do you suppose, child, that *I* am particularly anxious to take such a handsome fellow as your poet to Mme. de Montcornet's house? If you object, let us consider that nothing has been said. But I don't fancy that the women are so much in question as a poor devil that Lucien pilloried in his newspaper; he is begging for mercy and peace. The Baron du Chatelet is imbecile enough to take the thing seriously. The Marquise d'Espard, Mme. de Bargeton, and Mme. de Montcornet's set have taken up the Heron's cause; and I have undertaken to reconcile Petrarch and his Laura--Mme. de Bargeton and Lucien."

"Aha!" cried Lucien, the glow of the intoxication of revenge throbbing full-pulsed through every vein. "Aha! so my foot is on their necks! You make me adore my pen, worship my friends, bow down to the fate-dispensing power of the press. I have not written a single sentence as yet upon the Heron and the Cuttlefish-bone.--I will go with you, my boy," he cried, catching Blondet by the waist; "yes, I will go; but first, the couple shall feel the weight of *this*, for so light as it is." He flourished the pen which had written the article upon Nathan.

"Tomorrow," he cried, "I will hurl a couple of columns at their heads. Then, we shall see. Don't be frightened, Coralie, it is not love but revenge; revenge! And I will have it to the full!"

"What a man it is!" said Blondet. "If you but knew, Lucien, how rare such explosions are in this jaded Paris, you might appreciate yourself. You will be a precious scamp" (the actual expression was a trifle stronger); "you are in a fair way to be a power in the land."

"He will get on," said Coralie.

"Well, he has come a good way already in six weeks."

"And if he should climb so high that he can reach a sceptre by treading over a corpse, he shall have Coralie's body for a stepping-stone," said the girl.

"You are a pair of lovers of the Golden Age," said Blondet.--"I congratulate you on your big article," he added, turning to Lucien. "There were a lot of new things in it. You are past master!"

Lousteau called with Hector Merlin and Vernou. Lucien was immensely flattered by this attention. Felicien Vernou brought a hundred francs for Lucien's article; it was felt that such a contributor must be well paid to attach him to the

198

paper.

Coralie, looking round at the chapter of journalists, ordered in a breakfast from the *Cadran bleu*, the nearest restaurant, and asked her visitors to adjourn to her handsomely furnished dining-room when Berenice announced that the meal was ready. In the middle of the repast, when the champagne had gone to all heads, the motive of the visit came out.

"You do not mean to make an enemy of Nathan, do you?" asked Lousteau. "Nathan is a journalist, and he has friends; he might play you an ugly trick with your first book. You have your *Archer of Charles IX.* to sell, have you not? We went round to Nathan this morning; he is in a terrible way. But you will set about another article, and puff praise in his face."

"What! After my article against his book, would you have me say----" began Lucien.

The whole party cut him short with a shout of laughter.

"Did you ask him to supper here the day after tomorrow?" asked Blondet.

"You article was not signed," added Lousteau. "Felicien, not being quite such a new hand as you are, was careful to put an initial C at the bottom. You can do that now with all your articles in his paper, which is pure unadulterated Left. We are all of us in the Opposition. Felicien was tactful enough not to compromise your future opinions. Hector's shop is Right Centre; you might sign your work on it with an L. If you cut a man up, you do it anonymously; if you praise him, it is just as well to put your name to your article."

"It is not the signatures that trouble me," returned Lucien, "but I cannot see anything to be said in favor of the book."

"Then did you really think as you wrote?" asked Hector.

"Yes."

"Oh! I thought you were cleverer than that, youngster," said Blondet. "No. Upon my word, as I looked at that forehead of yours, I credited you with the omnipotence of the great mind--the power of seeing both sides of everything. In literature, my boy, every idea is reversible, and no man can take upon himself to decide which is the right or wrong side. Everything is bi-lateral in the domain of thought. Ideas are binary. Janus is a fable signifying criticism and the symbol of Genius. The Almighty alone is triform. What raises Moliere and Corneille above the rest of us but the faculty of saying one thing with an Alceste or an Octave, and another with a Philinte or a Cinna? Rousseau wrote a letter against dueling in the *Nouvelle Heloise*, and another in favor of it. Which of the two represented his own opinion? will you venture to take it upon yourself to decide? Which of us could give judgement for Clarissa or Lovelace, Hector or Achilles? Who was Homer's hero? What did Richardson himself think? It is the function of criticism to look at a man's work in all its aspects. We draw up our case, in short."

"Do you really stick to your written opinions?" asked Vernou, with a satirical expression. "Why, we are retailers of phrases; that is how we make a livelihood. When you try to do a good piece of work--to write a book, in short--you can put your thoughts, yourself into it, and cling to it, and fight for it; but as for newspaper articles, read today and forgotten tomorrow, they are worth nothing in my eyes but the money that is paid for them. If you attach any importance to such drivel, you might as well make the sign of the Cross and invoke heaven when you sit down to write a tradesman's circular."

Every one apparently was astonished at Lucien's scruples. The last rags of the boyish conscience were torn away, and he was invested with the *toga virilis* of journalism.

"Do you know what Nathan said by way of comforting himself after your criticism?" asked Lousteau.

"How should I know?"

"Nathan exclaimed, 'Paragraphs pass away; but a great work lives!' He will be here to supper in two days, and he will be sure to fall flat at your feet, and kiss your claws, and swear that you are a great man."

"That would be a funny thing," was Lucien's comment.

"*Funny*" repeated Blondet. "He can't help himself."

"I am quite willing, my friends," said Lucien, on whom the wine had begun to take effect. "But what am I to say?"

"Oh well, refute yourself in three good columns in Merlin's paper. We have been enjoying the sight of Nathan's wrath; we have just been telling him that he owes us no little gratitude for getting up a hot controversy that will sell his second edition in a week. In his eyes at this present moment you are a spy, a scoundrel, a caitiff wretch; the day after tomorrow you will be a genius, an uncommonly clever fellow, one of Plutarch's men. Nathan will hug you and call you his best friend. Dauriat has been to see you; you have your three thousand francs; you have worked the trick! Now you want Nathan's respect and esteem. Nobody ought to be let in except the publisher. We must not immolate any one but an enemy. We should not talk like this if it were a question of some outsider, some inconvenient person who had made a name for himself without us and was not wanted; but Nathan is one of us. Blondet got some one to attack him in the *Mercure* for the pleasure of replying in the *Debats*. For which reason the first edition went off at once."

"My friends, upon my word and honor, I cannot write two words in praise of that book----"

"You will have another hundred francs," interrupted Merlin. "Nathan will have brought you in ten louis d'or, to say nothing of an article that you might put in Finot's paper; you would get a hundred francs for writing that, and another hundred francs from Dauriat--total, twenty louis."

"But what am I to say?"

"Here is your way out of the difficulty," said Blondet, after some thought. "Say that the envy that fastens on all good work, like wasps on ripe fruit, has attempted to set its fangs in this production. The captious critic, trying his best to find fault, has been obliged to invent theories for that purpose, and has drawn a distinction between two kinds of literature--'the literature of ideas and the literature of imagery,' as he calls them. On the heads of that, youngster, say that to give expression to ideas through imagery is the highest form of art. Try to show that all poetry is summed up in that, and lament that there is so little poetry in French; quote foreign criticisms on the unimaginative precision of our style, and then extol M. de Canalis and Nathan for the services they have done France by infusing a less prosaic spirit into the language. Knock your previous argument to pieces by calling attention to the fact that we have made progress since the eighteenth century. (Discover the 'progress,' a beautiful word to mystify the bourgeois public.) Say that the new methods in literature concentrate all styles, comedy and tragedy, description, character-drawing and dialogues, in a series of pictures set in the brilliant frame of a plot which holds the reader's interest. The Novel, which demands sentiment, style, and imagery, is the greatest creation of modern days; it is the successor of stage comedy grown obsolete with its restrictions. Facts and ideas are all within the province of fiction. The intellect of an incisive moralist, like La Bruyere, the power of treating character as Moliere could treat it, the grand machinery of a Shakespeare, together with the portrayal of the most subtle shades of passion (the one treasury left untouched by our predecessors)--for all this the modern novel affords free scope. How far superior is all this to the cut-and-dried logic-chopping, the cold analysis to the eighteenth century!--'The Novel,' say sententiously, 'is the Epic grown amusing.' Instance *Corinne*, bring Mme. de Stael up to support your argument. The eighteenth century called all things in question; it is the task of the nineteenth to conclude and speak the last word; and the last word of the nineteenth century has been for realities--realities which live however and move. Passion, in short, an element unknown in Voltaire's philosophy, has been brought into play. Here a diatribe against Voltaire, and as for Rousseau, his characters are polemics and systems masquerading. Julie and Claire are entelechies--informing spirit awaiting flesh and bones.

"You might slip off on a side issue at this, and say that we owe a new and original literature to the Peace and the Restoration of the Bourbons, for you are writing for a Right Centre paper.

"Scoff at Founders of Systems. And cry with a glow of fine enthusiasm, 'Here are errors and misleading statements in abundance in our contemporary's work, and to what end? To depreciate a fine work, to deceive the public, and to arrive at this conclusion--"A book that sells, does not sell."' *Proh pudor*! (Mind you put *Proh pudor*! 'tis a harmless expletive that stimulates the reader's interest.) Foresee the approaching decadence of criticism, in fact. Moral--'There is but one kind of literature, the literature which aims to please. Nathan has started upon a new way; he understands his epoch and fulfils the requirements of his age--the demand for drama, the natural demand of a century in which the political stage has become a permanent puppet show. Have we not seen four dramas in a score of years--the Revolution, the Directory, the Empire, and the Restoration?' With that, wallow in dithyramb and eulogy, and the second edition shall vanish like smoke. This is the way to do it. Next Saturday put a review in our magazine, and sign it 'de Rubempre,' out in full.

"In that final article say that 'fine work always brings about abundant controversy. This week such and such a paper contained such and such an article on Nathan's book, and such another paper made a vigorous reply.' Then you criticise the critics 'C' and 'L'; pay me a passing compliment on the first article in the *Debats*, and end by averring that Nathan's work is the great book of the epoch; which is all as if you said nothing at all; they say the same of everything that comes out.

"And so," continued Blondet, "you will have made four hundred francs in a week, to say nothing of the pleasure of now and again saying what you really think. A discerning public will maintain that either C or L or Rubempre is in the right of it, or mayhap all the three. Mythology, beyond doubt one of the grandest inventions of the human brain, places Truth at the bottom of a well; and what are we to do without buckets? You will have supplied the public with three for one. There you are, my boy, Go ahead!"

Lucien's head was swimming with bewilderment. Blondet kissed him on both cheeks.

"I am going to my shop," said he. And every man likewise departed to his shop. For these "*hommes forts*," a newspaper office was nothing but a shop.

They were to meet again in the evening at the Wooden Galleries, and Lucien would sign his treaty of peace with Dauriat. Florine and Lousteau, Lucien and Coralie, Blondet and Finot, were to dine at the Palais-Royal; du Bruel was giving the manager of the Panorama-Dramatique a dinner.

"They are right," exclaimed Lucien, when he was alone with Coralie. "Men are made to be tools in the hands of stronger spirits. Four hundred francs for three articles! Doguereau would scarcely give me as much for a book which cost me two years of work."

"Write criticism," said Coralie, "have a good time! Look at me, I am an Andalusian girl tonight, tomorrow I may be a gypsy, and a man the night after. Do as I do, give them grimaces for their money, and let us live happily."

Lucien, smitten with love of Paradox, set himself to mount and ride that unruly hybrid product of Pegasus and Balaam's ass; started out at a gallop over the fields of thought while he took a turn in the Bois, and discovered new possibilities in Blondet's outline.

He dined as happy people dine, and signed away all his rights in the *Marguerites*. It never occurred to him that any trouble might arise from that transaction in the future. He took a turn of work at the office, wrote off a couple of columns, and came back to the Rue de Vendome. Next morning he found the germs of yesterday's ideas had sprung up and developed in his brain, as ideas develop while the intellect is yet unjaded and the sap is rising; and thoroughly did he enjoy the projection of this new article. He threw himself into it with enthusiasm. At the summons of the spirit of contradiction, new charms met beneath his pen. He was witty and satirical, he rose to yet new views of sentiment, of ideas and imagery in literature. With subtle ingenuity, he went back to his own first impressions of Nathan's work, when he read it in the newsroom of the Cour du Commerce; and the ruthless, bloodthirsty critic, the lively mocker, became a poet in the final phrases which rose and fell with majestic rhythm like the swaying censer before the altar.

"One hundred francs, Coralie!" cried he, holding up eight sheets of paper covered with writing while she dressed.

The mood was upon him; he went on to indite, stroke by stroke, the promised terrible article on Chatelet and Mme. de Bargeton. That morning he experienced one of the keenest personal pleasures of journalism; he knew what it was to forge the epigram, to whet and polish the cold blade to be sheathed in a victim's heart, to make of the hilt a cunning piece of workmanship for the reader to admire. For the public admires the handle, the delicate work of the brain, while the cruelty is not apparent; how should the public know that the steel of the epigram, tempered in the fire of revenge, has been plunged deftly, to rankle in the very quick of a victim's vanity, and is reeking from wounds innumerable which it has inflicted? It is a hideous joy, that grim, solitary pleasure, relished without witnesses; it is like a duel with an absent enemy, slain at a distance by a quill; a journalist might really possess the magical power of talismans in Eastern tales. Epigram is distilled rancor, the quintessence of a hate derived from all the worst passions of man, even as love concentrates all that is best in human nature. The man does not exist who cannot be witty to avenge himself; and, by the same rule, there is not one to whom love does not bring delight. Cheap and easy as this kind of wit may be in France, it is always relished. Lucien's article was destined to raise the previous reputation of the paper for venomous spite and evil-speaking. His article probed two hearts to the depths; it dealt a grievous wound to Mme. de Bargeton, his Laura of old days, as well as to his rival, the Baron du Chatelet.

"Well, let us go for a drive in the Bois," said Coralie, "the horses are fidgeting. There is no need to kill yourself."

"We will take the article on Nathan to Hector. Journalism is really very much like Achilles' lance, it salves the wounds that it makes," said Lucien, correcting a phrase here and there.

The lovers started forth in splendor to show themselves to the Paris which had but lately given Lucien the cold shoulder, and now was beginning to talk about him. To have Paris talking of you! and this after you have learned how large the great city is, how hard it is to be anybody there--it was this thought that turned Lucien's head with exultation.

"Let us go by way of your tailor's, dear boy, and tell him to be quick with your clothes, or try them on if they are ready. If you are going to your fine ladies' houses, you shall eclipse that monster of a de Marsay and young Rastignac and any Ajuda-Pinto or Maxime de Trailles or Vandenesse of them all. Remember that your mistress is Coralie! But you will not play me any tricks, eh?"

Two days afterwards, on the eve of the supper-party at Coralie's house, there was a new play at the Ambigu, and it fell to Lucien to write the dramatic criticism. Lucien and Coralie walked together after dinner from the Rue de Vendome to the Panorama-Dramatique, going along the Cafe Turc side of the Boulevard du Temple, a lounge much frequented at that time. People wondered at his luck, and praised Coralie's beauty. Chance remarks reached his ears; some said that Coralie was the finest woman in Paris, others that Lucien was a match for her. The romantic youth felt that he was in his atmosphere. This was the life for him. The brotherhood was so far away that it was almost out of sight. Only two months ago, how he had looked up to those lofty great natures; now he asked himself if they were not just a trifle ridiculous with their notions and their Puritanism. Coralie's careless words had lodged in Lucien's mind, and begun already to bear fruit. He took Coralie to her dressing-room, and strolled about like a sultan behind the scenes; the actresses gave him burning glances and flattering speeches.

"I must go to the Ambigu and attend to business," said he.

At the Ambigu the house was full; there was not a seat left for him. Indignant complaints behind the scenes brought no redress; the box-office keeper, who did not know him as yet, said that they had sent orders for two boxes to his paper, and sent him about his business.

"I shall speak of the play as I find it," said Lucien, nettled at this.

"What a dunce you are!" said the leading lady, addressing the box-office keeper, "that is Coralie's adorer."

The box-office keeper turned round immediately at this. "I will speak to the manager at once, sir," he said.

In all these small details Lucien saw the immense power wielded by the press. His vanity was gratified. The manager appeared to say that the Duc de Rhetore and Tullia the opera-dancer were in the stage-box, and they had consented to allow Lucien to join them.

"You have driven two people to distraction," remarked the young Duke, mentioning the names of the Baron du Chatelet and Mme. de Bargeton.

"Distraction? What will it be tomorrow?" said Lucien. "So far, my friends have been mere skirmishers, but I have given them red-hot shot tonight. Tomorrow you will know why we are making game of 'Potelet.' The article is called 'Potelet from 1811 to 1821.' Chatelet will be a byword, a name for the type of courtiers who deny their benefactor and rally to the Bourbons. When I have done with him, I am going to Mme. de Montcornet's."

Lucien's talk was sparkling. He was eager that this great personage should see how gross a mistake Mesdames d'Espard and de Bargeton had made when they slighted Lucien de Rubempre. But he showed the tip of his ear when he asserted his right to bear the name of Rubempre, the Duc de Rhetore having purposely addressed him as Chardon.

"You should go over to the Royalists," said the Duke. "You have proved yourself a man of ability; now show your good sense. The one way of obtaining a patent of nobility and the right to bear the title of your mother's family, is by asking for it in return for services to be rendered to the Court. The Liberals will never make a count of you. The Restoration will get the better of the press, you see, in the long run, and the press is the only formidable power. They have borne with it too long as it is; the press is sure to be muzzled. Take advantage of the last moments of liberty to make yourself formidable, and you will have everything--intellect, nobility, and good looks; nothing will be out of your reach. So if you are a Liberal, let it be simply for the moment, so that you can make a better bargain for your Royalism."

With that the Duke entreated Lucien to accept an invitation to dinner, which the German Minister (of Florine's supper-party) was about to send. Lucien fell under the charm of the noble peer's arguments; the salons from which he had been exiled for ever, as he thought, but a few months ago, would shortly open their doors for him! He was delighted. He marveled at the power of the press; Intellect and the Press, these then were the real powers in society. Another thought shaped itself in his mind--Was Etienne Lousteau sorry that he had opened the gate of the temple to a newcomer? Even now he (Lucien) felt on his own account that it was strongly advisable to put difficulties in the way of eager and ambitious recruits from the provinces. If a poet should come to him as he had flung himself into Etienne's arms, he dared not think of the reception that he would give him.

The youthful Duke meanwhile saw that Lucien was deep in thought, and made a pretty good guess at the matter of his meditations. He himself had opened out wide horizons of public life before an ambitious poet, with a vacillating will, it is true, but not without aspirations; and the journalists had already shown the neophyte, from a pinnacle of the temple, all the kingdoms of the world of letters and its riches.

Lucien himself had no suspicion of a little plot that was being woven, nor did he imagine that M. de Rhetore had a hand in it. M. de Rhetore had spoken of Lucien's cleverness, and Mme. d'Espard's set had taken alarm. Mme. de Bargeton had commissioned the Duke to sound Lucien, and with that object in view, the noble youth had come to the Ambigu-

Comique.

Do not believe in stories of elaborate treachery. Neither the great world nor the world of journalists laid any deep schemes; definite plans are not made by either; their Machiavelism lives from hand to mouth, so to speak, and consists, for the most part, in being always on the spot, always on the alert to turn everything to account, always on the watch for the moment when a man's ruling passion shall deliver him into the hands of his enemies. The young Duke had seen through Lucien at Florine's supper-party; he had just touched his vain susceptibilities; and now he was trying his first efforts in diplomacy upon the living subject.

Lucien hurried to the Rue Saint-Fiacre after the play to write his article. It was a piece of savage and bitter criticism, written in pure wantonness; he was amusing himself by trying his power. The melodrama, as a matter of fact, was a better piece than the *Alcalde*; but Lucien wished to see whether he could damn a good play and send everybody to see a bad one, as his associates had said.

He unfolded the sheet at breakfast next morning, telling Coralie as he did so that he had cut up the Ambigu-Comique; and not a little astonished was he to find below his paper on Mme. de Bargeton and Chatelet a notice of the Ambigu, so mellowed and softened in the course of the night, that although the witty analysis was still preserved, the judgment was favorable. The article was more likely to fill the house than to empty it. No words can describe his wrath. He determined to have a word or two with Lousteau. He had already begun to think himself an indespensable man, and he vowed that he would not submit to be tyrannized over and treated like a fool. To establish his power beyond cavil, he wrote the article for Dauriat's review, summing up and weighing all the various opinions concerning Nathan's book; and while he was in the humor, he hit off another of his short sketches for Lousteau's newspaper. Inexperienced journalists, in the first effervescence of youth, make a labor of love of ephemeral work, and lavish their best thought unthriftily thereon.

The manager of the Panorama-Dramatique gave a first performance of a vaudeville that night, so that Florine and Coralie might be free for the evening. There were to be cards before supper. Lousteau came for the short notice of the vaudeville; it had been written beforehand after the general rehearsal, for Etienne wished to have the paper off his mind. Lucien read over one of the charming sketches of Parisian whimsicalities which made the fortune of the paper, and Lousteau kissed him on both eyelids, and called him the providence of journalism.

"Then why do you amuse yourself by turning my article inside out?" asked Lucien. He had written his brilliant sketch simply and solely to give emphasis to his grievance.

"*I?*" exclaimed Lousteau.

"Well, who else can have altered my article?"

"You do not know all the ins and outs yet, dear fellow. The Ambigu pays for thirty copies, and only takes nine for the manager and box office-keeper and their mistresses, and for the three lessees of the theatre. Every one of the Boulevard theatres pays eight hundred francs in this way to the paper; and there is quite as much again in boxes and orders for Finot, to say nothing of the contributions of the company. And if the minor theatres do this, you may imagine what the big ones do! Now you understand? We are bound to show a good deal of indulgence."

"I understand this, that I am not at liberty to write as I think----"

"Eh! what does that matter, so long as you turn an honest penny?" cried Lousteau. "Besides, my boy, what grudge had you against the theatre? You must have had some reason for it, or you would not have cut up the play as you did. If you slash for the sake of slashing, the paper will get into trouble, and when there is good reason for hitting hard it will not tell. Did the manager leave you out in the cold?"

"He had not kept a place for me."

204

"Good," said Lousteau. "I shall let him see your article, and tell him that I softened it down; you will find it serves you better than if it had appeared in print. Go and ask him for tickets tomorrow, and he will sign forty blank orders every month. I know a man who can get rid of them for you; I will introduce you to him, and he will buy them all up at half-price. There is a trade done in theatre tickets, just as Barbet trades in reviewers' copies. This is another Barbet, the leader of the *claque*. He lives near by; come and see him, there is time enough."

"But, my dear fellow, it is a scandalous thing that Finot should levy blackmail in matters intellectual. Sooner or later----"

"Really!" cried Lousteau, "where do you come from? For what do you take Finot? Beneath his pretence of good-nature, his ignorance and stupidity, and those Turcaret's airs of his, there is all the cunning of his father the hatter. Did you notice an old soldier of the Empire in the den at the office? That is Finot's uncle. The uncle is not only one of the right sort, he has the luck to be taken for a fool; and he takes all that kind of business upon his shoulders. An ambitious man in Paris is well off indeed if he has a willing scapegoat at hand. In public life, as in journalism, there are hosts of emergencies in which the chiefs cannot afford to appear. If Finot should enter on a political career, his uncle would be his secretary, and receive all the contributions levied in his department on big affairs. Anybody would take Giroudeau for a fool at first sight, but he has just enough shrewdness to be an inscrutable old file. He is on picket duty; he sees that we are not pestered with hubbub, beginners wanting a job, or advertisements. No other paper has his equal, I think."

"He plays his part well," said Lucien; "I saw him at work."

Etienne and Lucien reached a handsome house in the Rue du Faubourg-du-Temple.

"Is M. Braulard in?" Etienne asked of the porter.

"*Monsieur*?" said Lucien. "Then, is the leader of the *claque* 'Monsieur'?"

"My dear boy, Braulard has twenty thousand francs of income. All the dramatic authors of the Boulevards are in his clutches, and have a standing account with him as if he were a banker. Orders and complimentary tickets are sold here. Braulard knows where to get rid of such merchandise. Now for a turn at statistics, a useful science enough in its way. At the rate of fifty complimentary tickets every evening for each theatre, you have two hundred and fifty tickets daily. Suppose, taking one with another, that they are worth a couple of francs apiece, Braulard pays a hundred and twenty-five francs daily for them, and takes his chance of making cent per cent. In this way authors' tickets alone bring him in about four thousand francs every month, or forty-eight thousand francs per annum. Allow twenty thousand francs for loss, for he cannot always place all his tickets----"

"Why not?"

"Oh! the people who pay at the door go in with the holders of complimentary tickets for unreserved seats, and the theatre reserves the right of admitting those who pay. There are fine warm evenings to be reckoned with besides, and poor plays. Braulard makes, perhaps, thirty thousand francs every year in this way, and he has his *claqueurs* besides, another industry. Florine and Coralie pay tribute to him; if they did not, there would be no applause when they come on or go off."

Lousteau gave this explanation in a low voice as they went up the stair.

"Paris is a queer place," said Lucien; it seemed to him that he saw self-interest squatting in every corner.

A smart maid-servant opened the door. At the sight of Etienne Lousteau, the dealer in orders and tickets rose from a sturdy chair before a large cylinder desk, and Lucien beheld the leader of the *claque*, Braulard himself, dressed in a gray molleton jacket, footed trousers, and red slippers; for all the world like a doctor or a solicitor. He was a typical self-made man, Lucien thought--a vulgar-looking face with a pair of exceedingly cunning gray eyes, hands made for hired applause, a complexion over which hard living had passed like rain over a roof, grizzled hair, and a somewhat husky voice.

"You have come from Mlle. Florine, no doubt, sir, and this gentleman for Mlle. Coralie," said Braulard; "I know you very well by sight. Don't trouble yourself, sir," he continued, addressing Lucien; "I am buying the Gymnase connection, I will look after your lady, and I will give her notice of any tricks they may try to play on her."

"That is not an offer to be refused, my dear Braulard, but we have come about the press orders for the Boulevard theatres--I as editor, and this gentleman as dramatic critic."

"Oh!--ah, yes! Finot has sold his paper. I heard about it. He is getting on, is Finot. I have asked him to dine with me at the end of the week; if you will do me the honor and pleasure of coming, you may bring your ladies, and there will be a grand jollification. Adele Dupuis is coming, and Ducange, and Frederic du Petit-Mere, and Mlle. Millot, my mistress. We shall have good fun and better liquor."

"Ducange must be in difficulties. He has lost his lawsuit."

"I have lent him ten thousand francs; if *Calas* succeeds, it will repay the loan, so I have been organizing a success. Ducange is a clever man; he has brains----"

Lucien fancied that he must be dreaming when he heard a *claqueur* appraising a writer's value.

"Coralie has improved," continued Braulard, with the air of a competent critic. "If she is a good girl, I will take her part, for they have got up a cabal against her at the Gymnase. This is how I mean to do it. I will have a few well-dressed men in the balconies to smile and make a little murmur, and the applause will follow. That is a dodge which makes a position for an actress. I have a liking for Coralie, and you ought to be satisfied, for she has feeling. Aha! I can hiss any one on the stage if I like."

"But let us settle this business about the tickets," put in Lousteau.

"Very well, I will come to this gentleman's lodging for them at the beginning of the month. He is a friend of yours, and I will treat him as I do you. You have five theatres; you will get thirty tickets--that will be something like seventy-five francs a month. Perhaps you will be wanting an advance?" added Braulard, lifting a cash-box full of coin out of his desk.

"No, no," said Lousteau; "we will keep that shift against a rainy day."

"I will work with Coralie, sir, and we will come to an understanding," said Braulard, addressing Lucien, who was looking about him, not without profound astonishment. There was a bookcase in Braulard's study, there were framed engravings and good furniture; and as they passed through the drawing room, he noticed that the fittings were neither too luxurious nor yet mean. The dining-room seemed to be the best ordered room, he remarked on this jokingly.

"But Braulard is an epicure," said Lousteau; "his dinners are famous in dramatic literature, and they are what you might expect from his cash-box."

"I have good wine," Braulard replied modestly.--"Ah! here are my lamplighters," he added, as a sound of hoarse voices and strange footsteps came up from the staircase.

Lucien on his way down saw a march past of *claqueurs* and retailers of tickets. It was an ill smelling squad, attired in caps, seedy trousers, and threadbare overcoats; a flock of gallows-birds with bluish and greenish tints in their faces, neglected beards, and a strange mixture of savagery and subservience in their eyes. A horrible population lives and swarms upon the Paris boulevards; selling watch guards and brass jewelry in the streets by day, applauding under the chandeliers of the theatre at night, and ready to lend themselves to any dirty business in the great city.

"Behold the Romans!" laughed Lousteau; "behold fame incarnate for actresses and dramatic authors. It is no prettier than our own when you come to look at it close."

"It is difficult to keep illusions on any subject in Paris," answered Lucien as they turned in at his door. "There is a tax upon

206

everything --everything has its price, and anything can be made to order--even success."

Thirty guests were assembled that evening in Coralie's rooms, her dining room would not hold more. Lucien had asked Dauriat and the manager of the Panorama-Dramatique, Matifat and Florine, Camusot, Lousteau, Finot, Nathan, Hector Merlin and Mme. du Val-Noble, Felicien Vernou, Blondet, Vignon, Philippe Bridau, Mariette, Giroudeau, Cardot and Florentine, and Bixiou. He had also asked all his friends of the Rue des Quatre-Vents. Tullia the dancer, who was not unkind, said gossip, to du Bruel, had come without her duke. The proprietors of the newspapers, for whom most of the journalists wrote, were also of the party.

At eight o'clock, when the lights of the candles in the chandeliers shone over the furniture, the hangings, and the flowers, the rooms wore the festal air that gives to Parisian luxury the appearance of a dream; and Lucien felt indefinable stirrings of hope and gratified vanity and pleasure at the thought that he was the master of the house. But how and by whom the magic wand had been waved he no longer sought to remember. Florine and Coralie, dressed with the fanciful extravagance and magnificent artistic effect of the stage, smiled on the poet like two fairies at the gates of the Palace of Dreams. And Lucien was almost in a dream.

His life had been changed so suddenly during the last few months; he had gone so swiftly from the depths of penury to the last extreme of luxury, that at moments he felt as uncomfortable as a dreaming man who knows that he is asleep. And yet, he looked round at the fair reality about him with a confidence to which envious minds might have given the name of fatuity.

Lucien himself had changed. He had grown paler during these days of continual enjoyment; languor had lent a humid look to his eyes; in short, to use Mme. d'Espard's expression, he looked like a man who is loved. He was the handsomer for it. Consciousness of his powers and his strength was visible in his face, enlightened as it was by love and experience. Looking out over the world of letters and of men, it seemed to him that he might go to and fro as lord of it all. Sober reflection never entered his romantic head unless it was driven in by the pressure of adversity, and just now the present held not a care for him. The breath of praise swelled the sails of his skiff; all the instruments of success lay there to his hand; he had an establishment, a mistress whom all Paris envied him, a carriage, and untold wealth in his inkstand. Heart and soul and brain were alike transformed within him; why should he care to be over nice about the means, when the great results were visibly there before his eyes.

As such a style of living will seem, and with good reason, to be anything but secure to economists who have any experience of Paris, it will not be superfluous to give a glance to the foundation, uncertain as it was, upon which the prosperity of the pair was based.

Camusot had given Coralie's tradesmen instructions to grant her credit for three months at least, and this had been done without her knowledge. During those three months, therefore, horses and servants, like everything else, waited as if by enchantment at the bidding of two children, eager for enjoyment, and enjoying to their hearts' content.

Coralie had taken Lucien's hand and given him a glimpse of the transformation scene in the dining-room, of the splendidly appointed table, of chandeliers, each fitted with forty wax-lights, of the royally luxurious dessert, and a menu of Chevet's. Lucien kissed her on the forehead and held her closely to his heart.

"I shall succeed, child," he said, "and then I will repay you for such love and devotion."

"Pshaw!" said Coralie. "Are you satisfied?"

"I should be very hard to please if I were not."

"Very well, then, that smile of yours pays for everything," she said, and with a serpentine movement she raised her head and laid her lips against his.

When they went back to the others, Florine, Lousteau, Matifat, and Camusot were setting out the card-tables. Lucien's friends began to arrive, for already these folk began to call themselves "Lucien's friends"; and they sat over the cards from nine o'clock till midnight. Lucien was unacquainted with a single game, but Lousteau lost a thousand francs, and Lucien could not refuse to lend him the money when he asked for it.

Michel, Fulgence, and Joseph appeared about ten o'clock; and Lucien, chatting with them in a corner, saw that they looked sober and serious enough, not to say ill at ease. D'Arthez could not come, he was finishing his book; Leon Giraud was busy with the first number of his review; so the brotherhood had sent three artists among their number, thinking that they would feel less out of their element in an uproarious supper party than the rest.

"Well, my dear fellows," said Lucien, assuming a slightly patronizing tone, "the 'comical fellow' may become a great public character yet, you see."

"I wish I may be mistaken; I don't ask better," said Michel.

"Are you living with Coralie until you can do better?" asked Fulgence.

"Yes," said Lucien, trying to look unconscious. "Coralie had an elderly adorer, a merchant, and she showed him the door, poor fellow. I am better off than your brother Philippe," he added, addressing Joseph Bridau; "he does not know how to manage Mariette."

"You are a man like another now; in short, you will make your way," said Fulgence.

"A man that will always be the same for you, under all circumstances," returned Lucien.

Michel and Fulgence exchanged incredulous scornful smiles at this. Lucien saw the absurdity of his remark.

"Coralie is wonderfully beautiful," exclaimed Joseph Bridau. "What a magnificent portrait she would make!"

"Beautiful and good," said Lucien; "she is an angel, upon my word. And you shall paint her portrait; she shall sit to you if you like for your Venetian lady brought by the old woman to the senator."

"All women who love are angelic," said Michel Chrestien.

Just at that moment Raoul Nathan flew upon Lucien, and grasped both his hands and shook them in a sudden access of violent friendship.

"Oh, my good friend, you are something more than a great man, you have a heart," cried he, "a much rarer thing than genius in these days. You are a devoted friend. I am yours, in short, through thick and thin; I shall never forget all that you have done for me this week."

Lucien's joy had reached the highest point; to be thus caressed by a man of whom everyone was talking! He looked at his three friends of the brotherhood with something like a superior air. Nathan's appearance upon the scene was the result of an overture from Merlin, who sent him a proof of the favorable review to appear in tomorrow's issue.

"I only consented to write the attack on condition that I should be allowed to reply to it myself," Lucien said in Nathan's ear. "I am one of you." This incident was opportune; it justified the remark which amused Fulgence. Lucien was radiant.

"When d'Arthez's book comes out," he said, turning to the three, "I am in a position to be useful to him. That thought in itself would induce me to remain a journalist."

"Can you do as you like?" Michel asked quickly.

"So far as one can when one is indispensable," said Lucien modestly.

It was almost midnight when they sat down to supper, and the fun grew fast and furious. Talk was less restrained in Lucien's house than at Matifat's, for no one suspected that the representatives of the brotherhood and the newspaper writers held divergent opinions. Young intellects, depraved by arguing for either side, now came into conflict with each other, and fearful axioms of the journalistic jurisprudence, then in its infancy, hurtled to and fro. Claude Vignon, upholding the dignity of criticism, inveighed against the tendency of the smaller newspapers, saying that the writers of personalities lowered themselves in the end. Lousteau, Merlin, and Finot took up the cudgels for the system known by the name of *blague*; puffery, gossip, and humbug, said they, was the test of talent, and set the hall-mark, as it were, upon it.

"Any man who can stand that test has real power," said Lousteau.

"Besides," cried Merlin, "when a great man receives ovations, there ought to be a chorus in insults to balance, as in a Roman triumph."

"Oho!" put in Lucien; "then every one held up to ridicule in print will fancy that he has made a success."

"Any one would think that the question interested you," exclaimed Finot.

"And how about our sonnets," said Michel Chrestien; "is that the way they will win us the fame of a second Petrarch?"

"Laura already counts for something in his fame," said Dauriat, a pun [Laure (l'or)] received with acclamations.

"*Faciamus experimentum in anima vili,*" retorted Lucien with a smile.

"And woe unto him whom reviewers shall spare, flinging him crowns at his first appearance, for he shall be shelved like the saints in their shrines, and no man shall pay him the slightest attention," said Vernou.

"People will say, 'Look elsewhere, simpleton; you have had your due already,' as Champcenetz said to the Marquis de Genlis, who was looking too fondly at his wife," added Blondet.

"Success is the ruin of a man in France," said Finot. "We are so jealous of one another that we try to forget, and to make others forget, the triumphs of yesterday."

"Contradiction is the life of literature, in fact," said Claude Vignon.

"In art as in nature, there are two principles everywhere at strife," exclaimed Fulgence; "and victory for either means death."

"So it is with politics," added Michel Chrestien.

"We have a case in point," said Lousteau. "Dauriat will sell a couple of thousand copies of Nathan's book in the coming week. And why? Because the book that was cleverly attacked will be ably defended."

Merlin took up the proof of tomorrow's paper. "How can such an article fail to sell an edition?" he asked.

"Read the article," said Dauriat. "I am a publisher wherever I am, even at supper."

Merlin read Lucien's triumphant refutation aloud, and the whole party applauded.

"How could that article have been written unless the attack had preceded it?" asked Lousteau.

Dauriat drew the proof of the third article from his pocket and read it over, Finot listening closely; for it was to appear in the second number of his own review, and as editor he exaggerated his enthusiasm.

"Gentlemen," said he, "so and not otherwise would Bossuet have written if he had lived in our day."

"I am sure of it," said Merlin. "Bossuet would have been a journalist today."

"To Bossuet the Second!" cried Claude Vignon, raising his glass with an ironical bow.

"To my Christopher Columbus!" returned Lucien, drinking a health to Dauriat.

"Bravo!" cried Nathan.

"Is it a nickname?" Merlin inquired, looking maliciously from Finot to Lucien.

"If you go on at this pace, you will be quite beyond us," said Dauriat; "these gentlemen" (indicating Camusot and Matifat) "cannot follow you as it is. A joke is like a bit of thread; if it is spun too fine, it breaks, as Bonaparte said."

"Gentlemen," said Lousteau, "we have been eye-witnesses of a strange, portentous, unheard-of, and truly surprising phenomenon. Admire the rapidity with which our friend here has been transformed from a provincial into a journalist!"

"He is a born journalist," said Dauriat.

"Children!" called Finot, rising to his feet, "all of us here present have encouraged and protected our amphitryon in his entrance upon a career in which he has already surpassed our hopes. In two months he has shown us what he can do in a series of excellent articles known to us all. I propose to baptize him in form as a journalist."

"A crown of roses! to signalize a double conquest," cried Bixiou, glancing at Coralie.

Coralie made a sign to Berenice. That portly handmaid went to Coralie's dressing-room and brought back a box of tumbled artificial flowers. The more incapable members of the party were grotesquely tricked out in these blossoms, and a crown of roses was soon woven. Finot, as high priest, sprinkled a few drops of champagne on Lucien's golden curls, pronouncing with delicious gravity the words--"In the name of the Government Stamp, the Caution-money, and the Fine, I baptize thee, Journalist. May thy articles sit lightly on thee!"

"And may they be paid for, including white lines!" cried Merlin.

Just at that moment Lucien caught sight of three melancholy faces. Michel Chrestien, Joseph Bridau, and Fulgence Ridal took up their hats and went out amid a storm of invective.

"Queer customers!" said Merlin.

"Fulgence used to be a good fellow," added Lousteau, "before they perverted his morals."

"Who are 'they'?" asked Claude Vignon.

"Some very serious young men," said Blondet, "who meet at a philosophico-religious symposium in the Rue des Quatre-Vents, and worry themselves about the meaning of human life----"

"Oh! oh!"

"They are trying to find out whether it goes round in a circle, or makes some progress," continued Blondet. "They were very hard put to it between the straight line and the curve; the triangle, warranted by Scripture, seemed to them to be nonsense, when, lo! there arose among them some prophet or other who declared for the spiral."

"Men might meet to invent more dangerous nonsense than that!" exclaimed Lucien, making a faint attempt to champion the brotherhood.

"You take theories of that sort for idle words," said Felicien Vernou; "but a time comes when the arguments take the form of gunshot and the guillotine."

"They have not come to that yet," said Bixiou; "they have only come as far as the designs of Providence in the invention of champagne, the humanitarian significance of breeches, and the blind deity who keeps the world going. They pick up fallen great men like Vico, Saint-Simon, and Fourier. I am much afraid that they will turn poor Joseph Bridau's head among them."

"Bianchon, my old schoolfellow, gives me the cold shoulder now," said Lousteau; "it is all their doing----"

"Do they give lectures on orthopedy and intellectual gymnastics?" asked Merlin.

"Very likely," answered Finot, "if Bianchon has any hand in their theories."

"Pshaw!" said Lousteau; "he will be a great physician anyhow."

"Isn't d'Arthez their visible head?" asked Nathan, "a little youngster that is going to swallow all of us up."

"He is a genius!" cried Lucien.

"Genius, is he! Well, give me a glass of sherry!" said Claude Vignon, smiling.

Every one, thereupon, began to explain his character for the benefit of his neighbor; and when a clever man feels a pressing need of explaining himself, and of unlocking his heart, it is pretty clear that wine has got the upper hand. An hour later, all the men in the company were the best friends in the world, addressing each other as great men and bold spirits, who held the future in their hands. Lucien, in his quality of host, was sufficiently clearheaded to apprehend the meaning of the sophistries which impressed him and completed his demoralization.

"The Liberal party," announced Finot, "is compelled to stir up discussion somehow. There is no fault to find with the action of the Government, and you may imagine what a fix the Opposition is in. Which of you now cares to write a pamphlet in favor of the system of primogeniture, and raise a cry against the secret designs of the Court? The pamphlet will be paid for handsomely."

"I will write it," said Hector Merlin. "It is my own point of view."

"Your party will complain that you are compromising them," said Finot. "Felicien, you must undertake it; Dauriat will bring it out, and we will keep the secret."

"How much shall I get?"

"Six hundred francs. Sign it 'Le Comte C, three stars.'"

"It's a bargain," said Felicien Vernou.

"So you are introducing the *canard* to the political world," remarked Lousteau.

"It is simply the Chabot affair carried into the region of abstract ideas," said Finot. "Fasten intentions on the Government, and then let loose public opinion."

"How a Government can leave the control of ideas to such a pack of scamps as we are, is matter for perpetual and profound astonishment to me," said Claude Vignon.

"If the Ministry blunders so far as to come down into the arena, we can give them a drubbing. If they are nettled by it, the thing will rankle in people's minds, and the Government will lose its hold on the masses. The newspaper risks nothing, and the authorities have everything to lose."

"France will be a cipher until newspapers are abolished by law," said Claude Vignon. "You are making progress hourly," he added, addressing Finot. "You are a modern order of Jesuits, lacking the creed, the fixed idea, the discipline, and the union."

They went back to the card-tables; and before long the light of the candles grew feeble in the dawn.

"Lucien, your friends from the Rue des Quatre-Vents looked as dismal as criminals going to be hanged," said Coralie.

"They were the judges, not the criminals," replied the poet.

"Judges are more amusing than *that*," said Coralie.

For a month Lucien's whole time was taken up with supper parties, dinner engagements, breakfasts, and evening parties; he was swept away by an irresistible current into a vortex of dissipation and easy work. He no longer thought of the future. The power of calculation amid the complications of life is the sign of a strong will which poets, weaklings, and men who live a purely intellectual life can never counterfeit. Lucien was living from hand to mouth, spending his money as fast as he made it, like many another journalist; nor did he give so much as a thought to those periodically recurrent days of reckoning which chequer the life of the bohemian in Paris so sadly.

In dress and figure he was a rival for the great dandies of the day. Coralie, like all zealots, loved to adorn her idol. She ruined herself to give her beloved poet the accoutrements which had so stirred his envy in the Garden of the Tuileries. Lucien had wonderful canes, and a charming eyeglass; he had diamond studs, and scarf-rings, and signet-rings, besides an assortment of waistcoats marvelous to behold, and in sufficient number to match every color in a variety of costumes. His transition to the estate of dandy swiftly followed. When he went to the German Minister's dinner, all the young men regarded him with suppressed envy; yet de Marsay, Vandenesse, Ajuda-Pinto, Maxime de Trailles, Rastignac, Beaudenord, Manerville, and the Duc de Maufrigneuse gave place to none in the kingdom of fashion. Men of fashion are as jealous among themselves as women, and in the same way. Lucien was placed between Mme. de Montcornet and Mme. d'Espard, in whose honor the dinner was given; both ladies overwhelmed him with flatteries.

"Why did you turn your back on society when you would have been so well received?" asked the Marquise. "Every one was prepared to make much of you. And I have a quarrel with you too. You owed me a call--I am still waiting to receive it. I saw you at the Opera the other day, and you would not deign to come to see me nor to take any notice of me."

"Your cousin, madame, so unmistakably dismissed me--"

"Oh! you do not know women," the Marquise d'Espard broke in upon him. "You have wounded the most angelic heart, the noblest nature that I know. You do not know all that Louise was trying to do for you, nor how tactfully she laid her plans for you.--Oh! and she would have succeeded," the Marquise continued, replying to Lucien's mute incredulity. "Her husband is dead now; died, as he was bound to die, of an indigestion; could you doubt that she would be free sooner or later? And can you suppose that she would like to be Madame Chardon? It was worth while to take some trouble to gain the title of Comtesse de Rubempre. Love, you see, is a great vanity, which requires the lesser vanities to be in harmony with itself--especially in marriage. I might love you to madness--which is to say, sufficiently to marry you--and yet I should find it very unpleasant to be called Madame Chardon. You can see that. And now that you understand the difficulties of Paris life, you will know how many roundabout ways you must take to reach your end; very well, then, you must admit that Louise was aspiring to an all but impossible piece of Court favor; she was quite unknown, she is not rich, and therefore she could not afford to neglect any means of success.

"You are clever," the Marquise d'Espard continued; "but we women, when we love, are cleverer than the cleverest man. My cousin tried to make that absurd Chatelet useful--Oh!" she broke off, "I owe not a little amusement to you; your articles on Chatelet made me laugh heartily."

Lucien knew not what to think of all this. Of the treachery and bad faith of journalism he had had some experience; but in spite of his perspicacity, he scarcely expected to find bad faith or treachery in society. There were some sharp lessons in store for him.

"But, madame," he objected, for her words aroused a lively curiosity, "is not the Heron under your protection?"

"One is obliged to be civil to one's worst enemies in society," protested she; "one may be bored, but one must look as if the talk was amusing, and not seldom one seems to sacrifice friends the better to serve them. Are you still a novice? You mean to write, and yet you know nothing of current deceit? My cousin apparently sacrificed you to the Heron, but how could she dispense with his influence for you? Our friend stands well with the present ministry; and we have made him see that your attacks will do him service--up to a certain point, for we want you to make it up again some of these days. Chatelet has received compensations for his troubles; for, as des Lupeaulx said, 'While the newspapers are making Chatelet ridiculous, they will leave the Ministry in peace.'"

There was a pause; the Marquise left Lucien to his own reflections.

"M. Blondet led me to hope that I should have the pleasure of seeing you in my house," said the Comtesse de Montcornet. "You will meet a few artists and men of letters, and some one else who has the keenest desire to become acquainted with you--Mlle. des Touches, the owner of talents rare among our sex. You will go to her house, no doubt. Mlle. de Touches (or Camille Maupin, if you prefer it) is prodigiously rich, and presides over one of the most remarkable salons in Paris. She has heard that you are as handsome as you are clever, and is dying to meet you."

Lucien could only pour out incoherent thanks and glance enviously at Emile Blondet. There was as great a difference between a great lady like Mme. de Montcornet and Coralie as between Coralie and a girl out of the streets. The Countess was young and witty and beautiful, with the very white fairness of women of the north. Her mother was the Princess Scherbellof, and the Minister before dinner had paid her the most respectful attention.

By this time the Marquise had made an end of trifling disdainfully with the wing of a chicken.

"My poor Louise felt so much affection for you," she said. "She took me into her confidence; I knew her dreams of a great career for you. She would have borne a great deal, but what scorn you showed her when you sent back her letters! Cruelty we can forgive; those who hurt us must have still some faith in us; but indifference! Indifference is like polar snows, it extinguishes all life. So, you must see that you have lost a precious affection through your own fault. Why break with her? Even if she had scorned you, you had your way to make, had you not?--your name to win back? Louise thought of all that."

"Then why was she silent?"

"*Eh! mon Dieu!*" cried the Marquise, "it was I myself who advised her not to take you into her confidence. Between ourselves, you know, you seemed so little used to the ways of the world, that I took alarm. I was afraid that your inexperience and rash ardor might wreck our carefully-made schemes. Can you recollect yourself as you were then? You must admit that if you could see your double today, you would say the same yourself. You are not like the same man. That was our mistake. But would one man in a thousand combine such intellectual gifts with such wonderful aptitude for taking the tone of society? I did not think that you would be such an astonishing exception. You were transformed so quickly, you acquired the manner of Paris so easily, that I did not recognize you in the Bois de Boulogne a month ago."

Lucien heard the great lady with inexpressible pleasure; the flatteries were spoken with such a petulant, childlike, confiding air, and she seemed to take such a deep interest in him, that he thought of his first evening at the Panorama-Dramatique, and began to fancy that some such miracle was about to take place a second time. Everything had smiled upon him since that happy evening; his youth, he thought, was the talisman that worked this change. He would prove this great lady; she should not take him unawares.

"Then, what were these schemes which have turned to chimeras, madame?" asked he.

"Louise meant to obtain a royal patent permitting you to bear the name and title of Rubempre. She wished to put Chardon out of sight. Your opinions have put that out of the question now, but *then* it would not have been so hard to manage, and a title would mean a fortune for you.

"You will look on these things as trifles and visionary ideas," she continued; "but we know something of life, and we know, too, all the solid advantages of a Count's title when it is borne by a fashionable and extremely charming young man. Announce 'M. Chardon' and 'M. le Comte de Rubempre' before heiresses or English girls with a million to their fortune, and note the difference of the effect. The Count might be in debt, but he would find open hearts; his good looks, brought into relief by his title, would be like a diamond in a rich setting; M. Chardon would not be so much as noticed. WE have not invented these notions; they are everywhere in the world, even among the burgeois. You are turning your back on fortune at this minute. Do you see that good-looking young man? He is the Vicomte Felix de Vandenesse, one of the

213

King's private secretaries. The King is fond enough of young men of talent, and Vandenesse came from the provinces with baggage nearly as light as yours. You are a thousand times cleverer than he; but do you belong to a great family, have you a name? You know des Lupeaulx; his name is very much like yours, for he was born a Chardin; well, he would not sell his little farm of Lupeaulx for a million, he will be Comte des Lupeaulx some day, and perhaps his grandson may be a duke. -- You have made a false start; and if you continue in that way, it will be all over with you. See how much wiser M. Emile Blondet has been! He is engaged on a Government newspaper; he is well looked on by those in authority; he can afford to mix with Liberals, for he holds sound opinions; and soon or later he will succeed. But then he understood how to choose his opinions and his protectors.

"Your charming neighbor" (Mme. d'Espard glanced at Mme. de Montcornet) "was a Troisville; there are two peers of France in the family and two deputies. She made a wealthy marriage with her name; she sees a great deal of society at her house; she has influence, she will move the political world for young M. Blondet. Where will a Coralie take you? In a few years' time you will be hopelessly in debt and weary of pleasure. You have chosen badly in love, and you are arranging your life ill. The woman whom you delight to wound was at the Opera the other night, and this was how she spoke of you. She deplored the way in which you were throwing away your talent and the prime of youth; she was thinking of you, and not of herself, all the while."

"Ah! if you were only telling me the truth, madame!" cried Lucien.

"What object should I have in telling lies?" returned the Marquise, with a glance of cold disdain which annihilated him. He was so dashed by it, that the conversation dropped, for the Marquise was offended, and said no more.

Lucien was nettled by her silence, but he felt that it was due to his own clumsiness, and promised himself that he would repair his error. He turned to Mme. de Montcornet and talked to her of Blondet, extolling that young writer for her benefit. The Countess was gracious to him, and asked him (at a sign from Mme. d'Espard) to spend an evening at her house. It was to be a small and quiet gathering to which only friends were invited--Mme. de Bargeton would be there in spite of her mourning; Lucien would be pleased, she was sure, to meet Mme. de Bargeton.

"Mme. la Marquise says that all the wrong is on my side," said Lucien; "so surely it rests with her cousin, does it not, to decide whether she will meet me?"

"Put an end to those ridiculous attacks, which only couple her name with the name of a man for whom she does not care at all, and you will soon sign a treaty of peace. You thought that she had used you ill, I am told, but I myself have seen her in sadness because you had forsaken her. Is it true that she left the provinces on your account?"

Lucien smiled; he did not venture to make any other reply.

"Oh! how could you doubt the woman who made such sacrifices for you? Beautiful and intellectual as she is, she deserves besides to be loved for her own sake; and Mme. de Bargeton cared less for you than for your talents. Believe me, women value intellect more than good looks," added the Countess, stealing a glance at Emile Blondet.

In the Minister's hotel Lucien could see the differences between the great world and that other world beyond the pale in which he had lately been living. There was no sort of resemblance between the two kinds of splendor, no single point in common. The loftiness and disposition of the rooms in one of the handsomest houses in the Faubourg Saint-Germain, the ancient gilding, the breadth of decorative style, the subdued richness of the accessories, all this was strange and new to him; but Lucien had learned very quickly to take luxury for granted, and he showed no surprise. His behavior was as far removed from assurance or fatuity on the one hand as from complacency and servility upon the other. His manner was good; he found favor in the eyes of all who were not prepared to be hostile, like the younger men, who resented his sudden intrusion into the great world, and felt jealous of his good looks and his success.

When they rose from table, he offered his arm to Mme. d'Espard, and was not refused. Rastignac, watching him, saw that the Marquise was gracious to Lucien, and came in the character of a fellow-countryman to remind the poet that they had met once before at Mme. du Val-Noble's. The young patrician seemed anxious to find an ally in the great man from his own province, asked Lucien to breakfast with him some morning, and offered to introduce him to some young men of fashion. Lucien was nothing loath.

"The dear Blondet is coming," said Rastignac.

The two were standing near the Marquis de Ronquerolles, the Duc de Rhetore, de Marsay, and General Montriveau. The Minister came across to join the group.

"Well," said he, addressing Lucien with a bluff German heartiness that concealed his dangerous subtlety; "well, so you have made your peace with Mme. d'Espard; she is delighted with you, and we all know," he added, looking round the group, "how difficult it is to please her."

"Yes, but she adores intellect," said Rastignac, "and my illustrious fellow-countryman has wit enough to sell."

"He will soon find out that he is not doing well for himself," Blondet put in briskly. "He will come over; he will soon be one of us."

Those who stood about Lucien rang the changes on this theme; the older and responsible men laid down the law with one or two profound remarks; the younger ones made merry at the expense of the Liberals.

"He simply tossed up head or tails for Right or Left, I am sure," remarked Blondet, "but now he will choose for himself."

Lucien burst out laughing; he thought of his talk with Lousteau that evening in the Luxembourg Gardens.

"He has taken on a bear-leader," continued Blondet, "one Etienne Lousteau, a newspaper hack who sees a five-franc piece in a column. Lousteau's politics consist in a belief that Napoleon will return, and (and this seems to me to be still more simple) in a confidence in the gratitude and patriotism of their worships the gentlemen of the Left. As a Rubempre, Lucien's sympathies should lean towards the aristocracy; as a journalist, he ought to be for authority, or he will never be either Rubempre or a secretary-general."

The Minister now asked Lucien to take a hand at whist; but, to the great astonishment of those present, he declared that he did not know the game.

"Come early to me on the day of that breakfast affair," Rastignac whispered, "and I will teach you to play. You are a discredit to the royal city of Angouleme; and, to repeat M. de Talleyrand's saying, you are laying up an unhappy old age for yourself."

Des Lupeaulx was announced. He remembered Lucien, whom he had met at Mme. du Val-Noble's, and bowed with a semblance of friendliness which the poet could not doubt. Des Lupeaulx was in favor, he was a Master of Requests, and did the Ministry secret services; he was, moreover, cunning and ambitious, slipping himself in everywhere; he was everybody's friend, for he never knew whom he might need. He saw plainly that this was a young journalist whose social success would probably equal his success in literature; saw, too, that the poet was ambitious, and overwhelmed him with protestations and expressions of friendship and interest, till Lucien felt as if they were old friends already, and took his promises and speeches for more than their worth. Des Lupeaulx made a point of knowing a man thoroughly well if he wanted to get rid of him or feared him as a rival. So, to all appearance, Lucien was well received. He knew that much of his success was owing to the Duc de Rhetore, the Minister, Mme. d'Espard, and Mme. de Montcornet, and went to spend a few moments with the two ladies before taking leave, and talked his very best for them.

"What a coxcomb!" said des Lupeaulx, turning to the Marquise when he had gone.

"He will be rotten before he is ripe," de Marsay added, smiling. "You must have private reasons of your own, madame, for turning his head in this way."

When Lucien stepped into the carriage in the courtyard, he found Coralie waiting for him. She had come to fetch him. The little attention touched him; he told her the history of his evening; and, to his no small astonishment, the new notions which even now were running in his head met with Coralie's approval. She strongly advised him to enlist under the ministerial banner.

"You have nothing to expect from the Liberals but hard knocks," she said. "They plot and conspire; they murdered the Duc de Berri. Will they upset the Government? Never! You will never come to anything through them, while you will be Comte de Rubempre if you throw in your lot with the other side. You might render services to the State, and be a peer of France, and marry an heiress. Be an Ultra. It is the proper thing besides," she added, this being the last word with her on all subjects. "I dined with the Val-Noble; she told me that Theodore Gaillard is really going to start his little Royalist *Revue*, so as to reply to your witticisms and the jokes in the *Miroir*. To hear them talk, M. Villele's party will be in office before the year is out. Try to turn the change to account before they come to power; and say nothing to Etienne and your friends, for they are quite equal to playing you some ill turn."

A week later, Lucien went to Mme. de Montcornet's house, and saw the woman whom he had so loved, whom later he had stabbed to the heart with a jest. He felt the most violent agitation at the sight of her, for Louise also had undergone a transformation. She was the Louise that she would always have been but for her detention in the provinces --she was a great lady. There was a grace and refinement in her mourning dress which told that she was a happy widow; Lucien fancied that this coquetry was aimed in some degree at him, and he was right; but, like an ogre, he had tasted flesh, and all that evening he vacillated between Coralie's warm, voluptuous beauty and the dried-up, haughty, cruel Louise. He could not make up his mind to sacrifice the actress to the great lady; and Mme. de Bargeton--all the old feeling reviving in her at the sight of Lucien, Lucien's beauty, Lucien's cleverness--was waiting and expecting that sacrifice all evening; and after all her insinuating speeches and her fascinations, she had her trouble for her pains. She left the room with a fixed determination to be revenged.

"Well, dear Lucien," she had said, and in her kindness there was both generosity and Parisian grace; "well, dear Lucien, so you, that were to have been my pride, took me for your first victim; and I forgave you, my dear, for I felt that in such a revenge there was a trace of love still left."

With that speech, and the queenly way in which it was uttered, Mme. de Bargeton recovered her position. Lucien, convinced that he was a thousand times in the right, felt that he had been put in the wrong. Not one word of the causes of the rupture! not one syllable of the terrible farewell letter! A woman of the world has a wonderful genius for diminishing her faults by laughing at them; she can obliterate them all with a smile or a question of feigned surprise, and she knows this. She remembers nothing, she can explain everything; she is amazed, asks questions, comments, amplifies, and quarrels with you, till in the end her sins disappear like stains on the application of a little soap and water; black as ink you knew them to be; and lo! in a moment, you behold immaculate white innocence, and lucky are you if you do not find that you yourself have sinned in some way beyond redemption.

In a moment old illusions regained their power over Lucien and Louise; they talked like friends, as before; but when the lady, with a hesitating sigh, put the question, "Are you happy?" Lucien was not ready with a prompt, decided answer; he was intoxicated with gratified vanity; Coralie, who (let us admit it) had made life easy for him, had turned his head. A melancholy "No" would have made his fortune, but he must needs begin to explain his position with regard to Coralie. He said that he was loved for his own sake; he said a good many foolish things that a man will say when he is smitten with a tender passion, and thought the while that he was doing a clever thing.

Mme. de Bargeton bit her lips. There was no more to be said. Mme. d'Espard brought Mme. de Montcornet to her cousin, and Lucien became the hero of the evening, so to speak. He was flattered, petted, and made much of by the three women; he was entangled with art which no words can describe. His social success in this fine and brilliant circle was at least as great as his triumphs in journalism. Beautiful Mlle. des Touches, so well known as "Camille Maupin," asked him to one of her Wednesday dinners; his beauty, now so justly famous, seemed to have made an impression upon her. Lucien exerted himself to show that his wit equaled his good looks, and Mlle. des Touches expressed her admiration with a playful outspokenness and a pretty fervor of friendship which deceives those who do not know life in Paris to its depths, nor suspect how continual enjoyment whets the appetite for novelty.

"If she should like me as much as I like her, we might abridge the romance," said Lucien, addressing de Marsay and Rastignac.

"You both of you write romances too well to care to live them," returned Rastignac. "Can men and women who write ever fall in love with each other? A time is sure to come when they begin to make little cutting remarks."

"It would not be a bad dream for you," laughed de Marsay. "The charming young lady is thirty years old, it is true, but she has an income of eighty thousand livres. She is adorably capricious, and her style of beauty wears well. Coralie is a silly little fool, my dear boy, well enough for a start, for a young spark must have a mistress; but unless you make some great conquest in the great world, an actress will do you harm in the long run. Now, my boy, go and cut out Conti. Here he is, just about to sing with Camille Maupin. Poetry has taken precedence of music ever since time began."

But when Lucien heard Mlle. des Touches' voice blending with Conti's, his hopes fled.

"Conti sings too well," he told des Lupeaulx; and he went back to Mme. de Bargeton, who carried him off to Mme. d'Espard in another room.

"Well, will you not interest yourself in him?" asked Mme. de Bargeton.

The Marquise spoke with an air half kindly, half insolent. "Let M. Chardon first put himself in such a position that he will not compromise those who take an interest in him," she said. "If he wishes to drop his patronymic and to bear his mother's name, he should at any rate be on the right side, should he not?"

"In less than two months I will arrange everything," said Lucien.

"Very well," returned Mme. d'Espard. "I will speak to my father and uncle; they are in waiting, they will speak to the Chancellor for you."

The diplomatist and the two women had very soon discovered Lucien's weak side. The poet's head was turned by the glory of the aristocracy; every man who entered the rooms bore a sounding name mounted in a glittering title, and he himself was plain Chardon. Unspeakable mortification filled him at the sound of it. Wherever he had been during the last few days, that pang had been constantly present with him. He felt, moreover, a sensation quite as unpleasant when he went back to his desk after an evening spent in the great world, in which he made a tolerable figure, thanks to Coralie's carriage and Coralie's servants.

He learned to ride, in order to escort Mme. d'Espard, Mlle. des Touches, and the Comtesse de Montcornet when they drove in the Bois, a privilege which he had envied other young men so greatly when he first came to Paris. Finot was delighted to give his right-hand man an order for the Opera, so Lucien wasted many an evening there, and thenceforward he was among the exquisites of the day.

The poet asked Rastignac and his new associates to a breakfast, and made the blunder of giving it in Coralie's rooms in the Rue de Vendome; he was too young, too much of a poet, too self-confident, to discern certain shades and distinctions in conduct; and how should an actress, a good-hearted but uneducated girl, teach him life? His guests were anything but charitably disposed towards him; it was clearly proven to their minds that Lucien the critic and the actress were in collusion for their mutual interests, and all of the young men were jealous of an arrangement which all of them stigmatized. The most pitiless of those who laughed that evening at Lucien's expense was Rastignac himself. Rastignac had made and held his position by very similar means; but so careful had he been of appearances, that he could afford to treat scandal as slander.

Lucien proved an apt pupil at whist. Play became a passion with him; and so far from disapproving, Coralie encouraged his extravagance with the peculiar short-sightedness of an all-absorbing love, which sees nothing beyond the moment, and is ready to sacrifice anything, even the future, to the present enjoyment. Coralie looked on cards as a safe-guard against rivals. A great love has much in common with childhood--a child's heedless, careless, spendthrift ways, a child's laughter and tears.

In those days there lived and flourished a set of young men, some of them rich, some poor, and all of them idle, called "free-livers" (*viveurs*); and, indeed, they lived with incredible insolence --unabashed and unproductive consumers, and yet more intrepid drinkers. These spendthrifts mingled the roughest practical jokes with a life not so much reckless as suicidal; they drew back from no impossibility, and gloried in pranks which, nevertheless, were confined within certain limits; and as they showed the most original wit in their escapades, it was impossible not to pardon them.

No sign of the times more plainly discovered the helotism to which the Restoration had condemned the young manhood of the epoch. The younger men, being at a loss to know what to do with themselves, were compelled to find other outlets for their superabundant energy besides journalism, or conspiracy, or art, or letters. They squandered their strength in the wildest excesses, such sap and luxuriant power was there in young France. The hard workers among these gilded youths wanted power and pleasure; the artists wished for money; the idle sought to stimulate their appetites or wished for excitement; one and all of them wanted a place, and one and all were shut out from politics and public life. Nearly all the "free-livers" were men of unusual mental powers; some held out against the enervating life, others were ruined by it. The most celebrated and the cleverest among them was Eugene Rastignac, who entered, with de Marsay's help, upon a political career, in which he has since distinguished himself. The practical jokes, in which the set indulged became so famous, that not a few vaudevilles have been founded upon them.

Blondet introduced Lucien to this society of prodigals, of which he became a brilliant ornament, ranking next to Bixiou, one of the most mischievous and untiring scoffing wits of his time. All through that winter Lucien's life was one long fit of intoxication, with intervals of easy work. He continued his series of sketches of contemporary life, and very occasionally made great efforts to write a few pages of serious criticism, on which he brought his utmost power of thought to bear. But study was the exception, not the rule, and only undertaken at the bidding of necessity; dinners and breakfasts, parties of pleasure and play, took up most of his time, and Coralie absorbed all that was left. He would not think of the morrow. He saw besides that his so-called friends were leading the same life, earning money easily by writing publishers' prospectuses and articles paid for by speculators; all of them lived beyond their incomes, none of them thought seriously of the future.

Lucien had been admitted into the ranks of journalism and of literature on terms of equality; he foresaw immense difficulties in the way if he should try to rise above the rest. Every one was willing to look upon him as an equal; no one would have him for a superior. Unconsciously he gave up the idea of winning fame in literature, for it seemed easier to gain success in politics.

"Intrigue raises less opposition than talent," du Chatelet had said one day (for Lucien and the Baron had made up their quarrel); "a plot below the surface rouses no one's attention. Intrigue, moreover, is superior to talent, for it makes something out of nothing; while, for the most part, the immense resources of talent only injure a man."

So Lucien never lost sight of his principal idea; and though tomorrow, following close upon the heels of today in the midst of an orgy, never found the promised work accomplished, Lucien was assiduous in society. He paid court to Mme. de Bargeton, the Marquise d'Espard, and the Comtesse de Montcornet; he never missed a single party given by Mlle. des Touches, appearing in society after a dinner given by authors or publishers, and leaving the salons for a supper given in consequence of a bet. The demands of conversation and the excitement of play absorbed all the ideas and energy left by excess. The poet had lost the lucidity of judgment and coolness of head which must be preserved if a man is to see all that is going on around him, and never to lose the exquisite tact which the *parvenu* needs at every moment. How should he know how many a time Mme. de Bargeton left him with wounded susceptibilities, how often she forgave him or added one more condemnation to the rest?

Chatelet saw that his rival had still a chance left, so he became Lucien's friend. He encouraged the poet in dissipation that wasted his energies. Rastignac, jealous of his fellow-countryman, and thinking, besides, that Chatelet would be a surer and more useful ally than Lucien, had taken up the Baron's cause. So, some few days after the meeting of the Petrarch and Laura of Angouleme, Rastignac brought about the reconciliation between the poet and the elderly beau at a sumptuous supper given at the *Rocher de Cancale*. Lucien never returned home till morning, and rose in the middle of the day; Coralie was always at his side, he could not forego a single pleasure. Sometimes he saw his real position, and made good resolutions, but they came to nothing in his idle, easy life; and the mainspring of will grew slack, and only responded to the heaviest pressure of necessity.

Coralie had been glad that Lucien should amuse himself; she had encouraged him in this reckless expenditure, because she thought that the cravings which she fostered would bind her lover to her. But tender-hearted and loving as she was, she found courage to advise Lucien not to forget his work, and once or twice was obliged to remind him that he had earned very little during the month. Their debts were growing frightfully fast. The fifteen hundred francs which remained from the purchase-money of the *Marguerites* had been swallowed up at once, together with Lucien's first five hundred livres. In three months he had only made a thousand francs, yet he felt as though he had been working tremendously hard. But by this time Lucien had adopted the "free-livers" pleasant theory of debts.

Debts are becoming to a young man, but after the age of five-and-twenty they are inexcusable. It should be observed that there are certain natures in which a really poetic temper is united with a weakened will; and these while absorbed in feeling, that they may transmute personal experience, sensation, or impression into some permanent form are essentially deficient in the moral sense which should accompany all observation. Poets prefer rather to receive their own impressions than to enter into the souls of others to study the mechanism of their feelings and thoughts. So Lucien neither asked his associates what became of those who disappeared from among them, nor looked into the futures of his so-called friends. Some of them were heirs to property, others had definite expectations; yet others either possessed names that were known in the world, or a most robust belief in their destiny and a fixed resolution to circumvent the law. Lucien, too, believed in his future on the strength of various profound axiomatic sayings of Blondet's: "Everything comes out all right at last--If a man has nothing, his affairs cannot be embarrassed--We have nothing to lose but the fortune that we seek--Swim with the stream; it will take you somewhere--A clever man with a footing in society can make a fortune whenever he pleases."

That winter, filled as it was with so many pleasures and dissipations, was a necessary interval employed in finding capital for the new Royalist paper; Theodore Gaillard and Hector Merlin only brought out the first number of the *Reveil* in March 1822. The affair had been settled at Mme. du Val-Noble's house. Mme. du val-Noble exercised a certain influence over the great personages, Royalist writers, and bankers who met in her splendid rooms--"fit for a tale out of the *Arabian Nights*," as the elegant and clever courtesan herself used to say--to transact business which could not be arranged elsewhere. The editorship had been promised to Hector Merlin. Lucien, Merlin's intimate, was pretty certain to be his right-hand man, and a *feuilleton* in a Ministerial paper had been promised to him besides. All through the dissipations of that winter Lucien had been secretly making ready for this change of front. Child as he was, he fancied that he was a deep politician because he concealed the preparation for the approaching transformation-scene, while he was counting upon Ministerial largesses to extricate himself from embarrassment and to lighten Coralie's secret cares. Coralie said nothing of her distress; she smiled now, as always; but Berenice was bolder, she kept Lucien informed of their difficulties; and the budding great man, moved, after the fashion of poets, by the tale of disasters, would vow that he would begin to work in earnest, and then forget his resolution, and drown his fleeting cares in excess. One day Coralie saw the poetic brow overcast, and scolded Berenice, and told her lover that everything would be settled.

Mme. d'Espard and Mme. de Bargeton were waiting for Lucien's profession of his new creed, so they said, before applying through Chatelet for the patent which should permit Lucien to bear the so-much desired name. Lucien had proposed to dedicate the *Marguerites* to Mme. d'Espard, and the Marquise seemed to be not a little flattered by a compliment which authors have been somewhat chary of paying since they became a power in the land; but when Lucien went to Dauriat and asked after his book, that worthy publisher met him with excellent reasons for the delay in its appearance. Dauriat had this and that in hand, which took up all his time; a new volume by Canalis was coming out, and he did not want the two books to clash; M. de Lamartine's second series of *Meditations* was in the press, and two important collections of poetry ought not to appear together.

By this time, however, Lucien's needs were so pressing that he had recourse to Finot, and received an advance on his work. When, at a supper-party that evening, the poet journalist explained his position to his friends in the fast set, they drowned his scruples in champagne, iced with pleasantries. Debts! There was never yet a man of any power without debts! Debts represented satisfied cravings, clamorous vices. A man only succeeds under the pressure of the iron hand of necessity. Debts forsooth!

"Why, the one pledge of which a great man can be sure, is given him by his friend the pawnbroker," cried Blondet.

"If you want everything, you must owe for everything," called Bixiou.

"No," corrected des Lupeaulx, "if you owe for everything, you have had everything."

The party contrived to convince the novice that his debts were a golden spur to urge on the horses of the chariot of his fortunes. There is always the stock example of Julius Caesar with his debt of forty millions, and Friedrich II. on an allowance of one ducat a month, and a host of other great men whose failings are held up for the corruption of youth, while not a word is said of their wide-reaching ideas, their courage equal to all odds.

Creditors seized Coralie's horses, carriage, and furniture at last, for an amount of four thousand francs. Lucien went to Lousteau and asked his friend to meet his bill for the thousand francs lent to pay gaming debts; but Lousteau showed him certain pieces of stamped paper, which proved that Florine was in much the same case. Lousteau was grateful, however, and offered to take the necessary steps for the sale of Lucien's *Archer of Charles IX*.

"How came Florine to be in this plight?" asked Lucien.

"The Matifat took alarm," said Lousteau. "We have lost him; but if Florine chooses, she can make him pay dear for his treachery. I will tell you all about it."

Three days after this bootless errand, Lucien and Coralie were breakfasting in melancholy spirits beside the fire in their pretty bedroom. Berenice had cooked a dish of eggs for them over the grate; for the cook had gone, and the coachman and servants had taken leave. They could not sell the furniture, for it had been attached; there was not a single object of any value in the house. A goodly collection of pawntickets, forming a very instructive octavo volume, represented all the gold, silver, and jewelry. Berenice had kept back a couple of spoons and forks, that was all.

Lousteau's newspaper was of service now to Coralie and Lucien, little as they suspected it; for the tailor, dressmaker, and milliner were afraid to meddle with a journalist who was quite capable of writing down their establishments.

Etienne Lousteau broke in upon their breakfast with a shout of "Hurrah! Long live *The Archer of Charles IX*.! And I have converted a hundred francs worth of books into cash, children. We will go halves."

He handed fifty francs to Coralie, and sent Berenice out in quest of a more substantial breakfast.

"Hector Merlin and I went to a booksellers' trade dinner yesterday, and prepared the way for your romance with cunning insinuations. Dauriat is in treaty, but Dauriat is haggling over it; he won't give more than four thousand francs for two thousand copies, and you want six thousand francs. We made you out twice as great as Sir Walter Scott! Oh! you have such novels as never were in the inwards of you. It is not a mere book for sale, it is a big business; you are not simply the writer of one more or less ingenious novel, you are going to write a whole series. The word 'series' did it! So, mind you, don't forget that you have a great historical series on hand--*La Grande Mademoiselle*, or *The France of Louis Quatorze*; *Cotillon I.*, or *The Early Days of Louis Quinze*; *The Queen and the Cardinal*, or *Paris and the Fronde*; *The Son of the Concini*, or *Richelieu's Intrigue*. These novels will be announced on the wrapper of the book. We call this manoeuvre 'giving a success a toss in the coverlet,' for the titles are all to appear on the cover, till you will be better known for the books that you have not written than for the work you have done. And 'In the Press' is a way of gaining credit in advance for work that you will do. Come, now, let us have a little fun! Here comes the champagne. You can understand, Lucien, that our men opened eyes as big as saucers. By the by, I see that you have saucers still left."

"They are attached," explained Coralie.

"I understand, and I resume. Show a publisher one manuscript volume and he will believe in all the rest. A publisher asks to see your manuscript, and gives you to understand that he is going to read it. Why disturb his harmless vanity? They never read a manuscript; they would not publish so many if they did. Well, Hector and I allowed it to leak out that you might consider an offer of five thousand francs for three thousand copies, in two editions. Let me have your *Archer*; the day after tomorrow we are to breakfast with the publishers, and we will get the upper hand of them."

"Who are they?" asked Lucien.

"Two partners named Fendant and Cavalier; they are two good fellows, pretty straightforward in business. One of them used to be with Vidal and Porchon, the other is the cleverest hand on the Quai des Augustins. They only started in business last year, and have lost a little on translations of English novels; so now my gentlemen have a mind to exploit the native product. There is a rumor current that those dealers in spoiled white paper are trading on other people's capital; but I don't think it matters very much to you who finds the money, so long as you are paid."

Two days later, the pair went to a breakfast in the Rue Serpente, in Lucien's old quarter of Paris. Lousteau still kept his room in the Rue de la Harpe; and it was in the same state as before, but this time Lucien felt no surprise; he had been initiated into the life of journalism; he knew all its ups and downs. Since that evening of his introduction to the Wooden Galleries, he had been paid for many an article, and gambled away the money along with the desire to write. He had filled columns, not once but many times, in the ingenious ways described by Lousteau on that memorable evening as they went to the Palais Royal. He was dependent upon Barbet and Braulard; he trafficked in books and theatre-tickets; he shrank no longer from any attack, from writing any panegyric; and at this moment he was in some sort rejoicing to make all he could out of Lousteau before turning his back on the Liberals. His intimate knowledge of the party would stand him in good stead in future. And Lousteau, on his side, was privately receiving five hundred francs of purchase-money, under the name of commission, from Fendant and Cavalier for introducing the future Sir Walter Scott to two enterprising tradesmen in search of a French Author of "Waverley."

The firm of Fendant and Cavalier had started in business without any capital whatsoever. A great many publishing houses were established at that time in the same way, and are likely to be established so long as papermakers and printers will give credit for the time required to play some seven or eight of the games of chance called "new publications." At that time, as at present, the author's copyright was paid for in bills at six, nine, and twelve months--a method of payment determined by the custom of the trade, for booksellers settle accounts between themselves by bills at even longer dates. Papermakers and printers are paid in the same way, so that in practice the publisher-bookseller has a dozen or a score of works on sale for a twelvemonth before he pays for them. Even if only two or three of these hit the public taste, the profitable speculations pay for the bad, and the publisher pays his way by grafting, as it were, one book upon another. But if all of them turn out badly; or if, for his misfortune, the publisher-bookseller happens to bring out some really good literature which stays on hand until the right public discovers and appreciates it; or if it costs too much to discount the paper that he receives, then, resignedly, he files his schedule, and becomes a bankrupt with an untroubled mind. He was prepared all along for something of the kind. So, all the chances being in favor of the publishers, they staked other people's money, not their own upon the gaming-table of business speculation.

This was the case with Fendant and Cavalier. Cavalier brought his experience, Fendant his industry; the capital was a joint-stock affair, and very accurately described by that word, for it consisted in a few thousand francs scraped together with difficulty by the mistresses of the pair. Out of this fund they allowed each other a fairly handsome salary, and scrupulously spent it all in dinners to journalists and authors, or at the theatre, where their business was transacted, as they said. This questionably honest couple were both supposed to be clever men of business, but Fendant was more slippery than Cavalier. Cavalier, true to his name, traveled about, Fendant looked after business in Paris. A partnership between two publishers is always more or less of a duel, and so it was with Fendant and Cavalier.

They had brought out plenty of romances already, such as the *Tour du Nord*, *Le Marchand de Benares*, *La Fontaine du Sepulcre*, and *Tekeli*, translations of the works of Galt, an English novelist who never attained much popularity in France. The success of translations of Scott had called the attention of the trade to English novels. The race of publishers, all agog for a second Norman conquest, were seeking industriously for a second Scott, just as at a rather later day every one must needs look for asphalt in stony soil, or bitumen in marshes, and speculate in projected railways. The stupidity of the Paris commercial world is conspicuous in these attempts to do the same thing twice, for success lies in contraries; and in Paris, of all places in the world, success spoils success. So beneath the title of *Strelitz, or Russia a Hundred Years Ago*, Fendant and Cavalier rashly added in big letters the words, "In the style of Scott."

Fendant and Cavalier were in great need of a success. A single good book might float their sunken bales, they thought; and there was the alluring prospect besides of articles in the newspapers, the great way of promoting sales in those days. A book is very seldom bought and sold for its just value, and purchases are determined by considerations quite other than the merits of the work. So Fendant and Cavalier thought of Lucien as a journalist, and of his book as a salable article, which would help them to tide over their monthly settlement.

The partners occupied the ground floor of one of the great old-fashioned houses in the Rue Serpente; their private office had been contrived at the further end of a suite of large drawing-rooms, now converted into warehouses for books. Lucien and Etienne found the publishers in their office, the agreement drawn up, and the bills ready. Lucien wondered at such prompt action.

Fendant was short and thin, and by no means reassuring of aspect. With his low, narrow forehead, sunken nose, and hard mouth, he looked like a Kalmuck Tartar; a pair of small, wide-awake black eyes, the crabbed irregular outline of his countenance, a voice like a cracked bell--the man's whole appearance, in fact, combined to give the impression that this was a consummate rascal. A honeyed tongue compensated for these disadvantages, and he gained his ends by talk. Cavalier, a stout, thick-set young fellow, looked more like the driver of a mail coach than a publisher; he had hair of a sandy color, a fiery red countenance, and the heavy build and untiring tongue of a commercial traveler.

"There is no need to discuss this affair," said Fendant, addressing Lucien and Lousteau. "I have read the work, it is very literary, and so exactly the kind of thing we want, that I have sent it off as it is to the printer. The agreement is drawn on the lines laid down, and besides, we always make the same stipulations in all cases. The bills fall due in six, nine, and twelve months respectively; you will meet with no difficulty in discounting them, and we will refund you the discount. We have reserved the right of giving a new title to the book. We don't care for *The Archer of Charles IX.*; it doesn't tickle the reader's curiosity sufficiently; there were several kings of that name, you see, and there were so many archers in the Middle Ages. If you had only called it the *Soldier of Napoleon*, now! But *The Archer of Charles IX.*!--why, Cavalier would have to give a course of history lessons before he could place a copy anywhere in the provinces."

"If you but knew the class of people that we have to do with!" exclaimed Cavalier.

"*Saint Bartholomew* would suit better," continued Fendant.

"*Catherine de' Medici, or France under Charles IX.*, would sound more like one of Scott's novels," added Cavalier.

"We will settle it when the work is printed," said Fendant.

"Do as you please, so long as I approve your title," said Lucien.

The agreement was read over, signed in duplicate, and each of the contracting parties took their copy. Lucien put the bills in his pocket with unequaled satisfaction, and the four repaired to Fendant's abode, where they breakfasted on beefsteaks and oysters, kidneys in champagne, and Brie cheese; but if the fare was something of the homeliest, the wines were exquisite; Cavalier had an acquaintance a traveler in the wine trade. Just as they sat down to table the printer appeared, to Lucien's surprise, with the first two proof-sheets.

"We want to get on with it," Fendant said; "we are counting on your book; we want a success confoundedly badly."

The breakfast, begun at noon, lasted till five o'clock.

"Where shall we get cash for these things?" asked Lucien as they came away, somewhat heated and flushed with the wine.

"We might try Barbet," suggested Etienne, and they turned down to the Quai des Augustins.

"Coralie is astonished to the highest degree over Florine's loss. Florine only told her about it yesterday; she seemed to lay the blame of it on you, and was so vexed, that she was ready to throw you over."

"That's true," said Lousteau. Wine had got the better of prudence, and he unbosomed himself to Lucien, ending up with: "My friend--for you are my friend, Lucien; you lent me a thousand francs, and you have only once asked me for the money--shun play! If I had never touched a card, I should be a happy man. I owe money all round. At this moment I have the bailiffs at my heels; indeed, when I go to the Palais Royal, I have dangerous capes to double."

In the language of the fast set, doubling a cape meant dodging a creditor, or keeping out of his way. Lucien had not heard the expression before, but he was familiar with the practice by this time.

"Are your debts so heavy?"

"A mere trifle," said Lousteau. "A thousand crowns would pull me through. I have resolved to turn steady and give up play, and I have done a little 'chantage' to pay my debts."

"What is 'chantage'?" asked Lucien.

"It is an English invention recently imported. A 'chanteur' is a man who can manage to put a paragraph in the papers-- never an editor nor a responsible man, for they are not supposed to know anything about it, and there is always a Giroudeau or a Philippe Bridau to be found. A bravo of this stamp finds up somebody who has his own reasons for not wanting to be talked about. Plenty of people have a few peccadilloes, or some more or less original sin, upon their consciences; there are plenty of fortunes made in ways that would not bear looking into; sometimes a man has kept the letter of the law, and sometimes he has not; and in either case, there is a tidbit of tattle for the inquirer, as, for instance, that tale of Fouche's police surrounding the spies of the Prefect of Police, who, not being in the secret of the fabrication of forged English banknotes, were just about to pounce on the clandestine printers employed by the Minister, or there is the story of Prince Galathionne's diamonds, the Maubreuile affair, or the Pombreton will case. The 'chanteur' gets possession of some compromising letter, asks for an interview; and if the man that made the money does not buy silence, the 'chanteur' draws a picture of the press ready to take the matter up and unravel his private affairs. The rich man is frightened, he comes down with the money, and the trick succeeds.

"You are committed to some risky venture, which might easily be written down in a series of articles; a 'chanteur' waits upon you, and offers to withdraw the articles--for a consideration. 'Chanteurs' are sent to men in office, who will bargain that their acts and not their private characters are to be attacked, or they are heedless of their characters, and anxious only to shield the woman they love. One of your acquaintance, that charming Master of Requests des Lupeaulx, is a kind of agent for affairs of this sort. The rascal has made a position for himself in the most marvelous way in the very centre of power; he is the middle-man of the press and the ambassador of the Ministers; he works upon a man's self-love; he bribes newspapers to pass over a loan in silence, or to make no comment on a contract which was never put up for public tender, and the jackals of Liberal bankers get a share out of it. That was a bit of 'chantage' that you did with Dauriat; he gave you a thousand crowns to let Nathan alone. In the eighteenth century, when journalism was still in its infancy, this kind of blackmail was levied by pamphleteers in the pay of favorites and great lords. The original inventor was Pietro Aretino, a great Italian. Kings went in fear of him, as stage-players go in fear of a newspaper today."

"What did you do to the Matifat to make the thousand crowns?"

"I attacked Florine in half a dozen papers. Florine complained to Matifat. Matifat went to Braulard to find out what the attacks meant. I did my 'chantage' for Finot's benefit, and Finot put Braulard on the wrong scent; Braulard told the man of drugs that *you* were demolishing Florine in Coralie's interest. Then Giroudeau went round to Matifat and told him (in confidence) that the whole business could be accommodated if he (Matifat) would consent to sell his sixth share in Finot's review for ten thousand francs. Finot was to give me a thousand crowns if the dodge succeeded. Well, Matifat was only too glad to get back ten thousand francs out of the thirty thousand invested in a risky speculation, as he thought, for Florine had been telling him for several days past that Finot's review was doing badly; and, instead of paying a dividend, something was said of calling up more capital. So Matifat was just about to close with the offer, when the manager of the Panorama-Dramatique comes to him with some accommodation bills that he wanted to negotiate before filing his schedule. To induce Matifat to take them of him, he let out a word of Finot's trick. Matifat, being a shrewd man of business, took the hint, held tight to his sixth, and is laughing in his sleeve at us. Finot and I are howling with despair. We

224

have been so misguided as to attack a man who has no affection for his mistress, a heartless, soulless wretch. Unluckily, too, for us, Matifat's business is not amenable to the jurisdiction of the press, and he cannot be made to smart for it through his interests. A druggist is not like a hatter or a milliner, or a theatre or a work of art; he is above criticism; you can't run down his opium and dyewoods, nor cocoa beans, paint, and pepper. Florine is at her wits' end; the Panorama closes tomorrow, and what will become of her she does not know."

"Coralie's engagement at the Gymnase begins in a few days," said Lucien; "she might do something for Florine."

"Not she!" said Lousteau. "Coralie is not clever, but she is not quite simple enough to help herself to a rival. We are in a mess with a vengeance. And Finot is in such a hurry to buy back his sixth----"

"Why?"

"It is a capital bit of business, my dear fellow. There is a chance of selling the paper for three hundred thousand francs; Finot would have one-third, and his partners besides are going to pay him a commission, which he will share with des Lupeaulx. So I propose to do another turn of 'chantage.'"

"'Chantage' seems to mean your money or your life?"

"It is better than that," said Lousteau; "it is your money or your character. A short time ago the proprietor of a minor newspaper was refused credit. The day before yesterday it was announced in his columns that a gold repeater set with diamonds belonging to a certain notability had found its way in a curious fashion into the hands of a private soldier in the Guards; the story promised to the readers might have come from the *Arabian Nights*. The notability lost no time in asking that editor to dine with him; the editor was distinctly a gainer by the transaction, and contemporary history has lost an anecdote. Whenever the press makes vehement onslaughts upon some one in power, you may be sure that there is some refusal to do a service behind it. Blackmailing with regard to private life is the terror of the richest Englishman, and a great source of wealth to the press in England, which is infinitely more corrupt than ours. We are children in comparison! In England they will pay five or six thousand francs for a compromising letter to sell again."

"Then how can you lay hold of Matifat?" asked Lucien.

"My dear boy, that low tradesman wrote the queerest letters to Florine; the spelling, style, and matter of them is ludicrous to the last degree. We can strike him in the very midst of his Lares and Penates, where he feels himself safest, without so much as mentioning his name; and he cannot complain, for he lives in fear and terror of his wife. Imagine his wrath when he sees the first number of a little serial entitled the *Amours of a Druggist*, and is given fair warning that his love-letters have fallen into the hands of certain journalists. He talks about the 'little god Cupid,' he tells Florine that she enables him to cross the desert of life (which looks as if he took her for a camel), and spells 'never' with two v's. There is enough in that immensely funny correspondence to bring an influx of subscribers for a fortnight. He will shake in his shoes lest an anonymous letter should supply his wife with the key to the riddle. The question is whether Florine will consent to appear to persecute Matifat. She has some principles, which is to say, some hopes, still left. Perhaps she means to keep the letters and make something for herself out of them. She is cunning, as befits my pupil. But as soon as she finds out that a bailiff is no laughing matter, or Finot gives her a suitable present or hopes of an engagement, she will give me the letters, and I will sell them to Finot. Finot will put the correspondence in his uncle's hands, and Giroudeau will bring Matifat to terms."

These confidences sobered Lucien. His first thought was that he had some extremely dangerous friends; his second, that it would be impolitic to break with them; for if Mme. d'Espard, Mme. de Bargeton, and Chatelet should fail to keep their word with him, he might need their terrible power yet. By this time Etienne and Lucien had reached Barbet's miserable bookshop on the Quai. Etienne addressed Barbet:

"We have five thousand francs' worth of bills at six, nine, and twelve months, given by Fendant and Cavalier. Are you

225

willing to discount them for us?"

"I will give you three thousand francs for them," said Barbet with imperturbable coolness.

"Three thousand francs!" echoed Lucien.

"Nobody else will give you as much," rejoined the bookseller. "The firm will go bankrupt before three months are out; but I happen to know that they have some good books that are hanging on hand; they cannot afford to wait, so I shall buy their stock for cash and pay them with their own bills, and get the books at a reduction of two thousand francs. That's how it is."

"Do you mind losing a couple of thousand francs, Lucien?" asked Lousteau.

"Yes!" Lucien answered vehemently. He was dismayed by this first rebuff.

"You are making a mistake," said Etienne.

"You won't find any one that will take their paper," said Barbet. "Your book is their last stake, sir. The printer will not trust them; they are obliged to leave the copies in pawn with him. If they make a hit now, it will only stave off bankruptcy for another six months, sooner or later they will have to go. They are cleverer at tippling than at bookselling. In my own case, their bills mean business; and that being so, I can afford to give more than a professional discounter who simply looks at the signatures. It is a bill-discounter's business to know whether the three names on a bill are each good for thirty per cent in case of bankruptcy. And here at the outset you only offer two signatures, and neither of them worth ten per cent."

The two journalists exchanged glances in surprise. Here was a little scrub of a bookseller putting the essence of the art and mystery of bill-discounting in these few words.

"That will do, Barbet," said Lousteau. "Can you tell us of a bill-broker that will look at us?"

"There is Daddy Chaboisseau, on the Quai Saint-Michel, you know. He tided Fendant over his last monthly settlement. If you won't listen to my offer, you might go and see what he says to you; but you would only come back to me, and then I shall offer you two thousand francs instead of three."

Etienne and Lucien betook themselves to the Quai Saint-Michel, and found Chaboisseau in a little house with a passage entry. Chaboisseau, a bill-discounter, whose dealings were principally with the book trade, lived in a second-floor lodging furnished in the most eccentric manner. A brevet-rank banker and millionaire to boot, he had a taste for the classical style. The cornice was in the classical style; the bedstead, in the purest classical taste, dated from the time of the Empire, when such things were in fashion; the purple hangings fell over the wall like the classic draperies in the background of one of David's pictures. Chairs and tables, lamps and sconces, and every least detail had evidently been sought with patient care in furniture warehouses. There was the elegance of antiquity about the classic revival as well as its fragile and somewhat arid grace. The man himself, like his manner of life, was in grotesque contrast with the airy mythological look of his rooms; and it may be remarked that the most eccentric characters are found among men who give their whole energies to money-making.

Men of this stamp are, in a certain sense, intellectual libertines. Everything is within their reach, consequently their fancy is jaded, and they will make immense efforts to shake off their indifference. The student of human nature can always discover some hobby, some accessible weakness and sensitive spot in their heart. Chaboisseau might have entrenched himself in antiquity as in an impregnable camp.

"The man will be an antique to match, no doubt," said Etienne, smiling.

Chaboisseau, a little old person with powdered hair, wore a greenish coat and snuff-brown waistcoat; he was tricked out besides in black small-clothes, ribbed stockings, and shoes that creaked as he came forward to take the bills. After a short

226

scrutiny, he returned them to Lucien with a serious countenance.

"MM Fendant and Cavalier are delightful young fellows; they have plenty of intelligence; but, I have no money," he said blandly.

"My friend here would be willing to meet you in the matter of discount----" Etienne began.

"I would not take the bills on any consideration," returned the little broker. The words slid down upon Lousteau's suggestion like the blade of the guillotine on a man's neck.

The two friends withdrew; but as Chaboisseau went prudently out with them across the ante-chamber, Lucien noticed a pile of second-hand books. Chaboisseau had been in the trade, and this was a recent purchase. Shining conspicuous among them, he noticed a copy of a work by the architect Ducereau, which gives exceedingly accurate plans of various royal palaces and chateaux in France.

"Could you let me have that book?" he asked.

"Yes," said Chaboisseau, transformed into a bookseller.

"How much?"

"Fifty francs."

"It is dear, but I want it. And I can only pay you with one of the bills which you refuse to take."

"You have a bill there for five hundred francs at six months; I will take that one of you," said Chaboisseau.

Apparently at the last statement of accounts, there had been a balance of five hundred francs in favor of Fendant and Cavalier.

They went back to the classical department. Chaboisseau made out a little memorandum, interest so much and commission so much, total deduction thirty francs, then he subtracted fifty francs for Ducerceau's book; finally, from a cash-box full of coin, he took four hundred and twenty francs.

"Look here, though, M. Chaboisseau, the bills are either all of them good, or all bad alike; why don't you take the rest?"

"This is not discounting; I am paying myself for a sale," said the old man.

Etienne and Lucien were still laughing at Chaboisseau, without understanding him, when they reached Dauriat's shop, and Etienne asked Gabusson to give them the name of a bill-broker. Gabusson thus appealed to gave them a letter of introduction to a broker in the Boulevard Poissonniere, telling them at the same time that this was the "oddest and queerest party" (to use his own expression) that he, Gabusson, had come across. The friends took a cab by the hour, and went to the address.

"If Samanon won't take your bills," Gabusson had said, "nobody else will look at them."

A second-hand bookseller on the ground floor, a second-hand clothes-dealer on the first story, and a seller of indecent prints on the second, Samanon carried on a fourth business--he was a money-lender into the bargain. No character in Hoffmann's romances, no sinister-brooding miser of Scott's, can compare with this freak of human and Parisian nature (always admitting that Samanon was human). In spite of himself, Lucien shuddered at the sight of the dried-up little old creature, whose bones seemed to be cutting a leather skin, spotted with all sorts of little green and yellow patches, like a portrait by Titian or Veronese when you look at it closely. One of Samanon's eyes was fixed and glassy, the other lively and bright; he seemed to keep that dead eye for the bill-discounting part of his profession, and the other for the trade in the pornographic curiosities upstairs. A few stray white hairs escaping from under a small, sleek, rusty black wig, stood erect above a sallow forehead with a suggestion of menace about it; a hollow trench in either cheek defined the outline of the jaws; while a set of projecting teeth, still white, seemed to stretch the skin of the lips with the effect of an equine yawn.

The contrast between the ill-assorted eyes and grinning mouth gave Samanon a passably ferocious air; and the very bristles on the man's chin looked stiff and sharp as pins.

Nor was there the slightest sign about him of any desire to redeem a sinister appearance by attention to the toilet; his threadbare jacket was all but dropping to pieces; a cravat, which had once been black, was frayed by contact with a stubble chin, and left on exhibition a throat as wrinkled as a turkey-gobbler's.

This was the individual whom Etienne and Lucien discovered in his filthy counting-house, busily affixing tickets to the backs of a parcel of books from a recent sale. In a glance, the friends exchanged the innumerable questions raised by the existence of such a creature; then they presented Gabusson's introduction and Fendant and Cavalier's bills. Samanon was still reading the note when a third comer entered, the wearer of a short jacket, which seemed in the dimly-lighted shop to be cut out of a piece of zinc roofing, so solid was it by reason of alloy with all kinds of foreign matter. Oddly attired as he was, the man was an artist of no small intellectual power, and ten years later he was destined to assist in the inauguration of the great but ill-founded Saint-Simonian system.

"I want my coat, my black trousers, and satin waistcoat," said this person, pressing a numbered ticket on Samanon's attention. Samanon touched the brass button of a bell-pull, and a woman came down from some upper region, a Normande apparently, to judge by her rich, fresh complexion.

"Let the gentleman have his clothes," said Samanon, holding out a hand to the newcomer. "It's a pleasure to do business with you, sir; but that youngster whom one of your friends introduced to me took me in most abominably."

"Took *him* in!" chuckled the newcomer, pointing out Samanon to the two journalists with an extremely comical gesture. The great man dropped thirty sous into the money-lender's yellow, wrinkled hand; like the Neapolitan *lazzaroni*, he was taking his best clothes out of pawn for a state occasion. The coins dropped jingling into the till.

"What queer business are you up to?" asked Lousteau of the artist, an opium-eater who dwelt among visions of enchanted palaces till he either could not or would not create.

"*He* lends you a good deal more than an ordinary pawnbroker on anything you pledge; and, besides, he is so awfully charitable, he allows you to take your clothes out when you must have something to wear. I am going to dine with the Kellers and my mistress tonight," he continued; "and to me it is easier to find thirty sous than two hundred francs, so I keep my wardrobe here. It has brought the charitable usurer a hundred francs in the last six months. Samanon has devoured my library already, volume by volume" (*livre a livre*).

"And sou by sou," Lousteau said with a laugh.

"I will let you have fifteen hundred francs," said Samanon, looking up.

Lucien started, as if the bill-broker had thrust a red-hot skewer through his heart. Samanon was subjecting the bills and their dates to a close scrutiny.

"And even then," he added, "I must see Fendant first. He ought to deposit some books with me. You aren't worth much" (turning to Lucien); "you are living with Coralie, and your furniture has been attached."

Lousteau, watching Lucien, saw him take up his bills, and dash out into the street. "He is the devil himself!" exclaimed the poet. For several seconds he stood outside gazing at the shop front. The whole place was so pitiful, that a passer-by could not see it without smiling at the sight, and wondering what kind of business a man could do among those mean, dirty shelves of ticketed books.

A very few moments later, the great man, in incognito, came out, very well dressed, smiled at his friends, and turned to go with them in the direction of the Passage des Panoramas, where he meant to complete his toilet by the polishing of his boots.

"If you see Samanon in a bookseller's shop, or calling on a paper-merchant or a printer, you may know that it is all over with that man," said the artist. "Samanon is the undertaker come to take the measurements for a coffin."

"You won't discount your bills now, Lucien," said Etienne.

"If Samanon will not take them, nobody else will; he is the *ultima ratio*," said the stranger. "He is one of Gigonnet's lambs, a spy for Palma, Werbrust, Gobseck, and the rest of those crocodiles who swim in the Paris money-market. Every man with a fortune to make, or unmake, is sure to come across one of them sooner or later."

"If you cannot discount your bills at fifty per cent," remarked Lousteau, "you must exchange them for hard cash."

"How?"

"Give them to Coralie; Camusot will cash them for her.--You are disgusted," added Lousteau, as Lucien cut him short with a start. "What nonsense! How can you allow such a silly scruple to turn the scale, when your future is in the balance?"

"I shall take this money to Coralie in any case," began Lucien.

"Here is more folly!" cried Lousteau. "You will not keep your creditors quiet with four hundred francs when you must have four thousand. Let us keep a little and get drunk on it, if we lose the rest at *rouge et noir*."

"That is sound advice," said the great man.

Those words, spoken not four paces from Frascati's, were magnetic in their effect. The friends dismissed their cab and went up to the gaming-table.

At the outset they won three thousand francs, then they lost and fell to five hundred; again they won three thousand seven hundred francs, and again they lost all but a five-franc piece. After another turn of luck they staked two thousand francs on an even number to double the stake at a stroke; an even number had not turned up for five times in succession, and this was the sixth time. They punted the whole sum, and an odd number turned up once more.

After two hours of all-absorbing, frenzied excitement, the two dashed down the staircase with the hundred francs kept back for the dinner. Upon the steps, between two pillars which support the little sheet-iron veranda to which so many eyes have been upturned in longing or despair, Lousteau stopped and looked into Lucien's flushed, excited face.

"Let us just try fifty francs," he said.

And up the stairs again they went. An hour later they owned a thousand crowns. Black had turned up for the fifth consecutive time; they trusted that their previous luck would not repeat itself, and put the whole sum on the red--black turned up for the sixth time. They had lost. It was now six o'clock.

"Let us just try twenty-five francs," said Lucien.

The new venture was soon made--and lost. The twenty-five francs went in five stakes. Then Lucien, in a frenzy, flung down his last twenty-five francs on the number of his age, and won. No words can describe how his hands trembled as he raked in the coins which the bank paid him one by one. He handed ten louis to Lousteau.

"Fly!" he cried; "take it to Very's."

Lousteau took the hint and went to order dinner. Lucien, left alone, laid his thirty louis on the red and won. Emboldened by the inner voice which a gambler always hears, he staked the whole again on the red, and again he won. He felt as if there were a furnace within him. Without heeding the voice, he laid a hundred and twenty louis on the black and lost. Then to the torturing excitement of suspense succeeded the delicious feeling of relief known to the gambler who has nothing left to lose, and must perforce leave the palace of fire in which his dreams melt and vanish.

He found Lousteau at Very's, and flung himself upon the cookery (to make use of Lafontaine's expression), and drowned his cares in wine. By nine o'clock his ideas were so confused that he could not imagine why the portress in the Rue de Vendome persisted in sending him to the Rue de la Lune.

"Mlle. Coralie has gone," said the woman. "She has taken lodgings elsewhere. She left her address with me on this scrap of paper."

Lucien was too far gone to be surprised at anything. He went back to the cab which had brought him, and was driven to the Rue de la Lune, making puns to himself on the name of the street as he went.

The news of the failure of the Panorama-Dramatique had come like a thunder-clap. Coralie, taking alarm, made haste to sell her furniture (with the consent of her creditors) to little old Cardot, who installed Florentine in the rooms at once. The tradition of the house remained unbroken. Coralie paid her creditors and satisfied the landlord, proceeding with her "washing-day," as she called it, while Berenice bought the absolutely indispensable necessaries to furnish a fourth-floor lodging in the Rue de la Lune, a few doors from the Gymnase. Here Coralie was waiting for Lucien's return. She had brought her love unsullied out of the shipwreck and twelve hundred francs.

Lucien, more than half intoxicated, poured out his woes to Coralie and Berenice.

"You did quite right, my angel," said Coralie, with her arms about his neck. "Berenice can easily negotiate your bills with Braulard."

The next morning Lucien awoke to an enchanted world of happiness made about him by Coralie. She was more loving and tender in those days than she had ever been; perhaps she thought that the wealth of love in her heart should make him amends for the poverty of their lodging. She looked bewitchingly charming, with the loose hair straying from under the crushed white silk handkerchief about her head; there was soft laughter in her eyes; her words were as bright as the first rays of sunrise that shone in through the windows, pouring a flood of gold upon such charming poverty.

Not that the room was squalid. The walls were covered with a sea-green paper, bordered with red; there was one mirror over the chimney-piece, and a second above the chest of drawers. The bare boards were covered with a cheap carpet, which Berenice had bought in spite of Coralie's orders, and paid for out of her own little store. A wardrobe, with a glass door and a chest, held the lovers' clothing, the mahogany chairs were covered with blue cotton stuff, and Berenice had managed to save a clock and a couple of china vases from the catastrophe, as well as four spoons and forks and half-a-dozen little spoons. The bedroom was entered from the dining-room, which might have belonged to a clerk with an income of twelve hundred francs. The kitchen was next the landing, and Berenice slept above in an attic. The rent was not more than a hundred crowns.

The dismal house boasted a sham carriage entrance, the porter's box being contrived behind one of the useless leaves of the gate, and lighted by a peephole through which that personage watched the comings and goings of seventeen families, for this hive was a "good-paying property," in auctioneer's phrase.

Lucien, looking round the room, discovered a desk, an easy-chair, paper, pens, and ink. The sight of Berenice in high spirits (she was building hopes on Coralie's *debut* at the Gymnase), and of Coralie herself conning her part with a knot of blue ribbon tied about it, drove all cares and anxieties from the sobered poet's mind.

"So long as nobody in society hears of this sudden comedown, we shall pull through," he said. "After all, we have four thousand five hundred francs before us. I will turn my new position in Royalist journalism to account. Tomorrow we shall start the *Reveil*; I am an old hand now, and I will make something out."

And Coralie, seeing nothing but love in the words, kissed the lips that uttered them. By this time Berenice had set the table near the fire and served a modest breakfast of scrambled eggs, a couple of cutlets, coffee, and cream. Just then there came a knock at the door, and Lucien, to his astonishment, beheld three of his loyal friends of old days--d'Arthez, Leon Giraud, and Michel Chrestien. He was deeply touched, and asked them to share the breakfast.

"No; we have come on more serious business than condolence," said d'Arthez; "we know the whole story, we have just come from the Rue de Vendome. You know my opinions, Lucien. Under any other circumstances I should be glad to hear that you had adopted my political convictions; but situated as you are with regard to the Liberal Press, it is impossible for you to go over to the Ultras. Your life will be sullied, your character blighted for ever. We have come to entreat you in the name of our friendship, weakened though it may be, not to soil yourself in this way. You have been prominent in attacking the Romantics, the Right, and the Government; you cannot now declare for the Government; the Right, and the Romantics."

"My reasons for the change are based on lofty grounds; the end will justify the means," said Lucien.

"Perhaps you do not fully comprehend our position on the side of the Government," said Leon Giraud. "The Government, the Court, the Bourbons, the Absolutist Party, or to sum up in the general expression, the whole system opposed to the constitutional system, may be divided upon the question of the best means of extinguishing the Revolution, but is unanimous as to the advisability of extinguishing the newspapers. The *Reveil*, the *Foudre*, and the *Drapeau Blanc* have all been founded for the express purpose of replying to the slander, gibes, and railing of the Liberal press. I cannot approve them, for it is precisely this failure to recognize the grandeur of our priesthood that has led us to bring out a serious and self-respecting paper; which perhaps," he added parenthetically, "may exercise a worthy influence before very long, and win respect, and carry weight; but this Royalist artillery is destined for a first attempt at reprisals, the Liberals are to be paid back in their own coin--shaft for shaft, wound for wound.

"What can come of it Lucien? The majority of newspaper readers incline for the Left; and in the press, as in warfare, the victory is with the big battalions. You will be blackguards, liars, enemies of the people; the other side will be defenders of their country, martyrs, men to be held in honor, though they may be even more hypocritical and slippery than their opponents. In these ways the pernicious influence of the press will be increased, while the most odious form of journalism will receive sanction. Insult and personalities will become a recognized privilege of the press; newspapers have taken this tone in the subscribers' interests; and when both sides have recourse to the same weapons, the standard is set and the general tone of journalism taken for granted. When the evil is developed to its fullest extent, restrictive laws will be followed by prohibitions; there will be a return of the censorship of the press imposed after the assassination of the Duc de Berri, and repealed since the opening of the Chambers. And do you know what the nation will conclude from the debate? The people will believe the insinuations of the Liberal press; they will think that the Bourbons mean to attack the rights of property acquired by the Revolution, and some fine day they will rise and shake off the Bourbons. You are not only soiling your life, Lucien, you are going over to the losing side. You are too young, too lately a journalist, too little initiated into the secret springs of motive and the tricks of the craft, you have aroused too much jealousy, not to fall a victim to the general hue and cry that will be raised against you in the Liberal newspapers. You will be drawn into the fray by party spirit now still at fever-heat; though the fever, which spent itself in violence in 1815 and 1816, now appears in debates in the Chamber and polemics in the papers."

"I am not quite a featherhead, my friends," said Lucien, "though you may choose to see a poet in me. Whatever may happen, I shall gain one solid advantage which no Liberal victory can give me. By the time your victory is won, I shall have gained my end."

"We will cut off--your hair," said Michel Chrestien, with a laugh.

"I shall have my children by that time," said Lucien; "and if you cut off my head, it will not matter."

The three could make nothing of Lucien. Intercourse with the great world had developed in him the pride of caste, the vanities of the aristocrat. The poet thought, and not without reason, that there was a fortune in his good looks and intellect, accompanied by the name and title of Rubempre. Mme. d'Espard and Mme. de Bargeton held him fast by this clue, as a child holds a cockchafer by a string. Lucien's flight was circumscribed. The words, "He is one of us, he is sound," accidentally overheard but three days ago in Mlle. de Touches' salon, had turned his head. The Duc de Lenoncourt, the Duc de Navarreins, the Duc de Grandlieu, Rastignac, Blondet, the lovely Duchesse de Maufrigneuse, the Comte d'Escrignon, and des Lupeaulx, all the most influential people at Court in fact, had congratulated him on his conversion, and completed his intoxication.

"Then there is no more to be said," d'Arthez rejoined. "You, of all men, will find it hard to keep clean hands and self-respect. I know you, Lucien; you will feel it acutely when you are despised by the very men to whom you offer yourself."

The three took leave, and not one of them gave him a friendly handshake. Lucien was thoughtful and sad for a few minutes.

"Oh! never mind those ninnies," cried Coralie, springing upon his knee and putting her beautiful arms about his neck. "They take life seriously, and life is a joke. Besides, you are going to be Count Lucien de Rubempre. I will wheedle the *Chancellerie* if there is no other way. I know how to come round that rake of a des Lupeaulx, who will sign your patent. Did I not tell you, Lucien, that at the last you should have Coralie's dead body for a stepping stone?"

Next day Lucien allowed his name to appear in the list of contributors to the *Reveil*. His name was announced in the prospectus with a flourish of trumpets, and the Ministry took care that a hundred thousand copies should be scattered abroad far and wide. There was a dinner at Robert's, two doors away from Frascati's, to celebrate the inauguration, and the whole band of Royalist writers for the press were present. Martainville was there, and Auger and Destains, and a host of others, still living, who "did Monarchy and religion," to use the familiar expression coined for them. Nathan had also enlisted under the banner, for he was thinking of starting a theatre, and not unreasonably held that it was better to have the licensing authorities for him than against him.

"We will pay the Liberals out," cried Merlin.

"Gentlemen," said Nathan, "if we are for war, let us have war in earnest; we must not carry it on with pop-guns. Let us fall upon all Classicals and Liberals without distinction of age or sex, and put them all to the sword with ridicule. There must be no quarter."

"We must act honorably; there must be no bribing with copies of books or presents; no taking money of publishers. We must inaugurate a Restoration of Journalism."

"Good!" said Martainville. "*Justum et tenacem propositi virum*! Let us be implacable and virulent. I will give out La Fayette for the prince of harlequins that he is!"

"And I will undertake the heroes of the *Constitutionnel*," added Lucien; "Sergeant Mercier, M. Jouy's Complete Works, and 'the illustrious orators of the Left.'"

A war of extermination was unanimously resolved upon, and by one o'clock in the morning all shades of opinion were merged and drowned, together with every glimmer of sense, in a flaming bowl of punch.

"We have had a fine Monarchical and Religious jollification," remarked an illustrious reveler in the doorway as he went.

That comment appeared in the next day's issue of the *Miroir* through the good offices of a publisher among the guests, and became historic. Lucien was supposed to be the traitor who blabbed. His defection gave the signal for a terrific hubbub in the Liberal camp; Lucien was the butt of the Opposition newspapers, and ridiculed unmercifully. The whole history of his sonnets was given to the public. Dauriat was said to prefer a first loss of a thousand crowns to the risk of publishing the verses; Lucien was called "the Poet sans Sonnets;" and one morning, in that very paper in which he had so brilliant a beginning, he read the following lines, significant enough for him, but barely intelligible to other readers:

*** "If M. Dauriat persistently withholds the Sonnets of the future Petrarch from publication, we will act like generous foes. We will open our own columns to his poems, which must be piquant indeed, to judge by the following specimen obligingly communicated by a friend of the author."

And close upon that ominous preface followed a sonnet entitled "The Thistle" (*le Chardon*):

A chance-come seedling, springing up one day Among the flowers in a garden fair, Made boast that splendid colors bright and rare Its claims to lofty lineage should display.

So for a while they suffered it to stay; But with such insolence it flourished there, That, out of patience with its braggart's air, They bade it prove its claims without delay.

It bloomed forthwith; but ne'er was blundering clown Upon the boards more promptly hooted down; The sister flowers began to jeer and laugh.

The owner flung it out. At close of day A solitary jackass came to bray-- A common Thistle's fitting epitaph.

Lucien read the words through scalding tears.

Vernou touched elsewhere on Lucien's gambling propensities, and spoke of the forthcoming *Archer of Charles IX.* as "anti-national" in its tendency, the writer siding with Catholic cut-throats against their Calvinist victims.

Another week found the quarrel embittered. Lucien had counted upon his friend Etienne; Etienne owed him a thousand francs, and there had been besides a private understanding between them; but Etienne Lousteau during the interval became his sworn foe, and this was the manner of it.

For the past three months Nathan had been smitten with Florine's charms, and much at a loss how to rid himself of Lousteau his rival, who was in fact dependent upon the actress. And now came Nathan's opportunity, when Florine was frantic with distress over the failure of the Panorama-Dramatique, which left her without an engagement. He went as Lucien's colleague to beg Coralie to ask for a part for Florine in a play of his which was about to be produced at the Gymnase. Then Nathan went to Florine and made capital with her out of the service done by the promise of a conditional engagement. Ambition turned Florine's head; she did not hesitate. She had had time to gauge Lousteau pretty thoroughly. Lousteau's courses were weakening his will, and here was Nathan with his ambitions in politics and literature, and energies strong as his cravings. Florine proposed to reappear on the stage with renewed eclat, so she handed over Matifat's correspondence to Nathan. Nathan drove a bargain for them with Matifat, and took the sixth share of Finot's review in exchange for the compromising billets. After this, Florine was installed in sumptuously furnished apartments in the Rue Hauteville, where she took Nathan for her protector in the face of the theatrical and journalistic world.

Lousteau was terribly overcome. He wept (towards the close of a dinner given by his friends to console him in his affliction). In the course of that banquet it was decided that Nathan had not acted unfairly; several writers present--Finot and Vernou, for instance,--knew of Florine's fervid admiration for dramatic literature; but they all agreed that Lucien had behaved very ill when he arranged that business at the Gymnase; he had indeed broken the most sacred laws of friendship. Party-spirit and zeal to serve his new friends had led the Royalist poet on to sin beyond forgiveness.

"Nathan was carried away by passion," pronounced Bixiou, "while this 'distinguished provincial,' as Blondet calls him, is simply scheming for his own selfish ends."

And so it came to pass that deep plots were laid by all parties alike to rid themselves of this little upstart intruder of a poet who wanted to eat everybody up. Vernou bore Lucien a personal grudge, and undertook to keep a tight hand on him; and Finot declared that Lucien had betrayed the secret of the combination against Matifat, and thereby swindled him (Finot) out of fifty thousand francs. Nathan, acting on Florine's advice, gained Finot's support by selling him the sixth share for fifteen thousand francs, and Lousteau consequently lost his commission. His thousand crowns had vanished away; he could not forgive Lucien for this treacherous blow (as he supposed it) dealt to his interests. The wounds of vanity refuse to heal if oxide of silver gets into them.

No words, no amount of description, can depict the wrath of an author in a paroxysm of mortified vanity, nor the energy which he discovers when stung by the poisoned darts of sarcasm; but, on the other hand, the man that is roused to fighting-fury by a personal attack usually subsides very promptly. The more phlegmatic race, who take these things quietly, lay their account with the oblivion which speedily overtakes the spiteful article. These are the truly courageous men of letters; and if the weaklings seem at first to be the strong men, they cannot hold out for any length of time.

During that first fortnight, while the fury was upon him, Lucien poured a perfect hailstorm of articles into the Royalist papers, in which he shared the responsibilities of criticism with Hector Merlin. He was always in the breach, pounding away with all his might in the *Reveil*, backed up by Martainville, the only one among his associates who stood by him without an afterthought. Martainville was not in the secret of certain understandings made and ratified amid after-dinner jokes, or at Dauriat's in the Wooden Galleries, or behind the scenes at the Vaudeville, when journalists of either side met on neutral ground.

When Lucien went to the greenroom of the Vaudeville, he met with no welcome; the men of his own party held out a hand to shake, the others cut him; and all the while Hector Merlin and Theodore Gaillard fraternized unblushingly with Finot, Lousteau, and Vernou, and the rest of the journalists who were known for "good fellows."

The greenroom of the Vaudeville in those days was a hotbed of gossip, as well as a neutral ground where men of every shade of opinion could meet; so much so that the President of a court of law, after reproving a learned brother in a certain council chamber for "sweeping the greenroom with his gown," met the subject of his strictures, gown to gown, in the greenroom of the Vaudeville. Lousteau, in time, shook hands again with Nathan; Finot came thither almost every evening; and Lucien, whenever he could spare the time, went to the Vaudeville to watch the enemies, who showed no sign of relenting towards the unfortunate boy.

In the time of the Restoration party hatred was far more bitter than in our day. Intensity of feeling is diminished in our high-pressure age. The critic cuts a book to pieces and shakes hands with the author afterwards, and the victim must keep on good terms with his slaughterer, or run the gantlet of innumerable jokes at his expense. If he refuses, he is unsociable, eaten up with self-love, he is sulky and rancorous, he bears malice, he is a bad bed-fellow. Today let an author receive a treacherous stab in the back, let him avoid the snares set for him with base hypocrisy, and endure the most unhandsome treatment, he must still exchange greetings with his assassin, who, for that matter, claims the esteem and friendship of his victim. Everything can be excused and justified in an age which has transformed vice into virtue and virtue into vice. Good-fellowship has come to be the most sacred of our liberties; the representatives of the most opposite opinions courteously blunt the edge of their words, and fence with buttoned foils. But in those almost forgotten days the same theatre could scarcely hold certain Royalist and Liberal journalists; the most malignant provocation was offered, glances were like pistol-shots, the least spark produced an explosion of quarrel. Who has not heard his neighbor's half-smothered oath on the entrance of some man in the forefront of the battle on the opposing side? There were but two parties-- Royalists and Liberals, Classics and Romantics. You found the same hatred masquerading in either form, and no longer wondered at the scaffolds of the Convention.

Lucien had been a Liberal and a hot Voltairean; now he was a rabid Royalist and a Romantic. Martainville, the only one among his colleagues who really liked him and stood by him loyally, was more hated by the Liberals than any man on the Royalist side, and this fact drew down all the hate of the Liberals on Lucien's head. Martainville's staunch friendship injured Lucien. Political parties show scanty gratitude to outpost sentinels, and leave leaders of forlorn hopes to their fate; 'tis a rule of warfare which holds equally good in matters political, to keep with the main body of the army if you mean to succeed. The spite of the small Liberal papers fastened at once on the opportunity of coupling the two names, and flung them into each other's arms. Their friendship, real or imaginary, brought down upon them both a series of articles written by pens dipped in gall. Felicien Vernou was furious with jealousy of Lucien's social success; and believed, like all his old associates, in the poet's approaching elevation.

The fiction of Lucien's treason was embellished with every kind of aggravating circumstance; he was called Judas the Less, Martainville being Judas the Great, for Martainville was supposed (rightly or wrongly) to have given up the Bridge of Pecq to the foreign invaders. Lucien said jestingly to des Lupeaulx that he himself, surely, had given up the Asses' Bridge.

Lucien's luxurious life, hollow though it was, and founded on expectations, had estranged his friends. They could not forgive him for the carriage which he had put down--for them he was still rolling about in it--nor yet for the splendors of the Rue de Vendome which he had left. All of them felt instinctively that nothing was beyond the reach of this young and handsome poet, with intellect enough and to spare; they themselves had trained him in corruption; and, therefore, they left no stone unturned to ruin him.

Some few days before Coralie's first appearance at the Gymnase, Lucien and Hector Merlin went arm-in-arm to the Vaudeville. Merlin was scolding his friend for giving a helping hand to Nathan in Florine's affair.

"You then and there made two mortal enemies of Lousteau and Nathan," he said. "I gave you good advice, and you took no notice of it. You gave praise, you did them a good turn--you will be well punished for your kindness. Florine and Coralie will never live in peace on the same stage; both will wish to be first. You can only defend Coralie in our papers; and Nathan not only has a pull as a dramatic author, he can control the dramatic criticism in the Liberal newspapers. He has been a journalist a little longer than you!"

The words responded to Lucien's inward misgivings. Neither Nathan nor Gaillard was treating him with the frankness which he had a right to expect, but so new a convert could hardly complain. Gaillard utterly confounded Lucien by saying roundly that newcomers must give proofs of their sincerity for some time before their party could trust them. There was more jealousy than he had imagined in the inner circles of Royalist and Ministerial journalism. The jealousy of curs fighting for a bone is apt to appear in the human species when there is a loaf to divide; there is the same growling and showing of teeth, the same characteristics come out.

In every possible way these writers of articles tried to injure each other with those in power; they brought reciprocal accusations of lukewarm zeal; they invented the most treacherous ways of getting rid of a rival. There had been none of this internecine warfare among the Liberals; they were too far from power, too hopelessly out of favor; and Lucien, amid the inextricable tangle of ambitions, had neither the courage to draw sword and cut the knot, or the patience to unravel it. He could not be the Beaumarchais, the Aretino, the Freron of his epoch; he was not made of such stuff; he thought of nothing but his one desire, the patent of nobility; for he saw clearly that for him such a restoration meant a wealthy marriage, and, the title once secured, chance and his good looks would do the rest. This was all his plan, and Etienne Lousteau, who had confided so much to him, knew his secret, knew how to deal a deathblow to the poet of Angouleme. That very night, as Lucien and Merlin went to the Vaudeville, Etienne had laid a terrible trap, into which an inexperienced boy could not but fall.

"Here is our handsome Lucien," said Finot, drawing des Lupeaulx in the direction of the poet, and shaking hands with feline amiability. "I cannot think of another example of such rapid success," continued Finot, looking from des Lupeaulx to Lucien. "There are two sorts of success in Paris: there is a fortune in solid cash, which any one can amass, and there is the intangible fortune of connections, position, or a footing in certain circles inaccessible for certain persons, however rich they may be. Now my friend here----"

"Our friend," interposed des Lupeaulx, smiling blandly.

"Our friend," repeated Finot, patting Lucien's hand, "has made a brilliant success from this point of view. Truth to tell, Lucien has more in him, more gift, more wit than the rest of us that envy him, and he is enchantingly handsome besides; his old friends cannot forgive him for his success--they call it luck."

"Luck of that sort never comes to fools or incapables," said des Lupeaulx. "Can you call Bonaparte's fortune luck, eh? There were a score of applicants for the command of the army in Italy, just as there are a hundred young men at this moment who would like to have an entrance to Mlle. des Touches' house; people are coupling her name with yours already in society, my dear boy," said des Lupeaulx, clapping Lucien on the shoulder. "Ah! you are in high favor. Mme. d'Espard, Mme. de Bargeton, and Mme. de Montcornet are wild about you. You are going to Mme. Firmiani's party tonight, are you not, and to the Duchesse de Grandlieu's rout tomorrow?"

"Yes," said Lucien.

"Allow me to introduce a young banker to you, a M. du Tillet; you ought to be acquainted, he has contrived to make a great fortune in a short time."

Lucien and du Tillet bowed, and entered into conversation, and the banker asked Lucien to dinner. Finot and des Lupeaulx, a well-matched pair, knew each other well enough to keep upon good terms; they turned away to continue their chat on one of the sofas in the greenroom, and left Lucien with du Tillet, Merlin, and Nathan.

"By the way, my friend," said Finot, "tell me how things stand. Is there really somebody behind Lucien? For he is the *bete noire* of my staff; and before allowing them to plot against him, I thought I should like to know whether, in your opinion, it would be better to baffle them and keep well with him."

The Master of Requests and Finot looked at each other very closely for a moment or two.

"My dear fellow," said des Lupeaulx, "how can you imagine that the Marquise d'Espard, or Chatelet, or Mme. de Bargeton--who has procured the Baron's nomination to the prefecture and the title of Count, so as to return in triumph to Angouleme--how can you suppose that any of them will forgive Lucien for his attacks on them? They dropped him down in the Royalist ranks to crush him out of existence. At this moment they are looking round for any excuse for not fulfilling the promises they made to that boy. Help them to some; you will do the greatest possible service to the two women, and some day or other they will remember it. I am in their secrets; I was surprised to find how much they hated the little fellow. This Lucien might have rid himself of his bitterest enemy (Mme. de Bargeton) by desisting from his attacks on terms which a woman loves to grant--do you take me? He is young and handsome, he should have drowned her hate in torrents of love, he would be Comte de Rubempre by this time; the Cuttlefish-bone would have obtained some sinecure for him, some post in the Royal Household. Lucien would have made a very pretty reader to Louis XVIII.; he might have been librarian somewhere or other, Master of Requests for a joke, Master of Revels, what you please. The young fool has missed his chance. Perhaps that is his unpardonable sin. Instead of imposing his conditions, he has accepted them. When Lucien was caught with the bait of the patent of nobility, the Baron Chatelet made a great step. Coralie has been the ruin of that boy. If he had not had the actress for his mistress, he would have turned again to the Cuttlefish-bone; and he

236

would have had her too."

"Then we can knock him over?"

"How?" des Lupeaulx asked carelessly. He saw a way of gaining credit with the Marquise d'Espard for this service.

"He is under contract to write for Lousteau's paper, and we can the better hold him to his agreement because he has not a sou. If we tickle up the Keeper of the Seals with a facetious article, and prove that Lucien wrote it, he will consider that Lucien is unworthy of the King's favor. We have a plot on hand besides. Coralie will be ruined, and our distinguished provincial will lose his head when his mistress is hissed off the stage and left without an engagement. When once the patent is suspended, we will laugh at the victim's aristocratic pretensions, and allude to his mother the nurse and his father the apothecary. Lucien's courage is only skindeep, he will collapse; we will send him back to his provinces. Nathan made Florine sell me Matifat's sixth share of the review, I was able to buy; Dauriat and I are the only proprietors now; we might come to an understanding, you and I, and the review might be taken over for the benefit of the Court. I stipulated for the restitution of my sixth before I undertook to protect Nathan and Florine; they let me have it, and I must help them; but I wished to know first how Lucien stood----"

"You deserve your name," said des Lupeaulx. "I like a man of your sort----"

"Very well. Then can you arrange a definite engagement for Florine?" asked Finot.

"Yes, but rid us of Lucien, for Rastignac and de Marsay never wish to hear of him again."

"Sleep in peace," returned Finot. "Nathan and Merlin will always have articles ready for Gaillard, who will promise to take them; Lucien will never get a line into the paper. We will cut off his supplies. There is only Martainville's paper left him in which to defend himself and Coralie; what can a single paper do against so many?"

"I will let you know the weak points of the Ministry; but get Lucien to write that article and hand over the manuscript," said des Lupeaulx, who refrained carefully from informing Finot that Lucien's promised patent was nothing but a joke.

When des Lupeaulx had gone, Finot went to Lucien, and taking the good-natured tone which deceives so many victims, he explained that he could not possibly afford to lose his contributor, and at the same time he shrank from taking proceedings which might ruin him with his friends of the other side. Finot himself liked a man who was strong enough to change his opinions. They were pretty sure to come across one another, he and Lucien, and might be mutually helpful in a thousand little ways. Lucien, besides, needed a sure man in the Liberal party to attack the Ultras and men in office who might refuse to help him.

"Suppose that they play you false, what will you do?" Finot ended. "Suppose that some Minister fancies that he has you fast by the halter of your apostasy, and turns the cold shoulder on you? You will be glad to set on a few dogs to snap at his legs, will you not? Very well. But you have made a deadly enemy of Lousteau; he is thirsting for your blood. You and Felicien are not on speaking terms. I only remain to you. It is a rule of the craft to keep a good understanding with every man of real ability. In the world which you are about to enter you can do me services in return for mine with the press. But business first. Let me have purely literary articles; they will not compromise you, and we shall have executed our agreement."

Lucien saw nothing but good-fellowship and a shrewd eye to business in Finot's offer; Finot and des Lupeaulx had flattered him, and he was in a good humor. He actually thanked Finot!

Ambitious men, like all those who can only make their way by the help of others and of circumstances, are bound to lay their plans very carefully and to adhere very closely to the course of conduct on which they determine; it is a cruel moment in the lives of such aspirants when some unknown power brings the fabric of their fortunes to some severe test and everything gives way at once; threads are snapped or entangled, and misfortune appears on every side. Let a man lose his head in the confusion, it is all over with him; but if he can resist this first revolt of circumstances, if he can stand erect until the tempest passes over, or make a supreme effort and reach the serene sphere about the storm--then he is really strong. To every man, unless he is born rich, there comes sooner or later "his fatal week," as it must be called. For Napoleon, for instance, that week was the Retreat from Moscow. It had begun now for Lucien.

Social and literary success had come to him too easily; he had had such luck that he was bound to know reverses and to see men and circumstances turn against him.

The first blow was the heaviest and the most keenly felt, for it touched Lucien where he thought himself invulnerable--in his heart and his love. Coralie might not be clever, but hers was a noble nature, and she possessed the great actress' faculty of suddenly standing aloof from self. This strange phenomenon is subject, until it degenerates into a habit with long practice, to the caprices of character, and not seldom to an admirable delicacy of feeling in actresses who are still young. Coralie, to all appearance bold and wanton, as the part required, was in reality girlish and timid, and love had wrought in her a revulsion of her woman's heart against the comedian's mask. Art, the supreme art of feigning passion and feeling, had not yet triumphed over nature in her; she shrank before a great audience from the utterance that belongs to Love alone; and Coralie suffered besides from another true woman's weakness--she needed success, born stage queen though she was. She could not confront an audience with which she was out of sympathy; she was nervous when she appeared on the stage, a cold reception paralyzed her. Each new part gave her the terrible sensations of a first appearance. Applause produced a sort of intoxication which gave her encouragement without flattering her vanity; at a murmur of dissatisfaction or before a silent house, she flagged; but a great audience following attentively, admiringly, willing to be pleased, electrified Coralie. She felt at once in communication with the nobler qualities of all those listeners; she felt that she possessed the power of stirring their souls and carrying them with her. But if this action and reaction of the audience upon the actress reveals the nervous organization of genius, it shows no less clearly the poor child's sensitiveness and delicacy. Lucien had discovered the treasures of her nature; had learned in the past months that this woman who loved him was still so much of a girl. And Coralie was unskilled in the wiles of an actress --she could not fight her own battles nor protect herself against the machinations of jealousy behind the scenes. Florine was jealous of her, and Florine was as dangerous and depraved as Coralie was simple and generous. Roles must come to find Coralie; she was too proud to implore authors or to submit to dishonoring conditions; she would not give herself to the first journalist who persecuted her with his advances and threatened her with his pen. Genius is rare enough in the extraordinary art of the stage; but genius is only one condition of success among many, and is positively hurtful unless it is accompanied by a genius for intrigue in which Coralie was utterly lacking.

Lucien knew how much his friend would suffer on her first appearance at the Gymnase, and was anxious at all costs to obtain a success for her; but all the money remaining from the sale of the furniture and all Lucien's earnings had been sunk in costumes, in the furniture of a dressing-room, and the expenses of a first appearance.

A few days later, Lucien made up his mind to a humiliating step for love's sake. He took Fendant and Cavalier's bills, and went to the *Golden Cocoon* in the Rue des Bourdonnais. He would ask Camusot to discount them. The poet had not fallen so low that he could make this attempt quite coolly. There had been many a sharp struggle first, and the way to that decision had been paved with many dreadful thoughts. Nevertheless, he arrived at last in the dark, cheerless little private office that looked out upon a yard, and found Camusot seated gravely there; this was not Coralie's infatuated adorer, not the easy-natured, indolent, incredulous libertine whom he had known hitherto as Camusot, but a heavy father of a family, a merchant grown old in shrewd expedients of business and respectable virtues, wearing a magistrate's mask of judicial prudery; this Camusot was the cool, business-like head of the firm surrounded by clerks, green cardboard boxes, pigeonholes, invoices, and samples, and fortified by the presence of a wife and a plainly-dressed daughter. Lucien trembled from head to foot as he approached; for the worthy merchant, like the money-lenders, turned cool, indifferent eyes upon him.

"Here are two or three bills, monsieur," he said, standing beside the merchant, who did not rise from his desk. "If you will take them of me, you will oblige me extremely."

"You have taken something of *me*, monsieur," said Camusot; "I do not forget it."

On this, Lucien explained Coralie's predicament. He spoke in a low voice, bending to murmur his explanation, so that Camusot could hear the heavy throbbing of the humiliated poet's heart. It was no part of Camusot's plans that Coralie should suffer a check. He listened, smiling to himself over the signatures on the bills (for, as a judge at the Tribunal of Commerce, he knew how the booksellers stood), but in the end he gave Lucien four thousand five hundred francs for them, stipulating that he should add the formula "For value received in silks."

Lucien went straight to Braulard, and made arrangements for a good reception. Braulard promised to come to the dress-rehearsal, to determine on the points where his "Romans" should work their fleshy clappers to bring down the house in applause. Lucien gave the rest of the money to Coralie (he did not tell her how he had come by it), and allayed her anxieties and the fears of Berenice, who was sorely troubled over their daily expenses.

Martainville came several times to hear Coralie rehearse, and he knew more of the stage than most men of his time; several Royalist writers had promised favorable articles; Lucien had not a suspicion of the impending disaster.

A fatal event occurred on the evening before Coralie's *debut*. D'Arthez's book had appeared; and the editor of Merlin's paper, considering Lucien to be the best qualified man on the staff, gave him the book to review. He owed his unlucky reputation to those articles on Nathan's work. There were several men in the office at the time, for all the staff had been summoned; Martainville was explaining that the party warfare with the Liberals must be waged on certain lines. Nathan, Merlin, all the contributors, in fact, were talking of Leon Giraud's paper, and remarking that its influence was the more pernicious because the language was guarded, cool, moderate. People were beginning to speak of the circle in the Rue des Quatre-Vents as a second Convention. It had been decided that the Royalist papers were to wage a systematic war of extermination against these dangerous opponents, who, indeed, at a later day, were destined to sow the doctrines that drove the Bourbons into exile; but that was only after the most brilliant of Royalist writers had joined them for the sake of a mean revenge.

D'Arthez's absolutist opinions were not known; it was taken for granted that he shared the views of his clique, he fell under the same anathema, and he was to be the first victim. His book was to be honored with "a slashing article," to use the consecrated formula. Lucien refused to write the article. Great was the commotion among the leading Royalist writers thus met in conclave. Lucien was told plainly that a renegade could not do as he pleased; if it did not suit his views to take the side of the Monarchy and Religion, he could go back to the other camp. Merlin and Martainville took him aside and begged him, as his friends, to remember that he would simply hand Coralie over to the tender mercies of the Liberal papers, for she would find no champions on the Royalist and Ministerial side. Her acting was certain to provoke a hot battle, and the kind of discussion which every actress longs to arouse.

"You don't understand it in the least," said Martainville; "if she plays for three months amid a cross-fire of criticism, she will make thirty thousand francs when she goes on tour in the provinces at the end of the season; and here are you about to sacrifice Coralie and your own future, and to quarrel with your own bread and butter, all for a scruple that will always stand in your way, and ought to be got rid of at once."

Lucien was forced to choose between d'Arthez and Coralie. His mistress would be ruined unless he dealt his friend a death-blow in the *Reveil* and the great newspaper. Poor poet! He went home with death in his soul; and by the fireside he sat and read that finest production of modern literature. Tears fell fast over it as the pages turned. For a long while he hesitated, but at last he took up the pen and wrote a sarcastic article of the kind that he understood so well, taking the book as children might take some bright bird to strip it of its plumage and torture it. His sardonic jests were sure to tell. Again he turned to the book, and as he read it over a second time, his better self awoke. In the dead of night he hurried across Paris, and stood outside d'Arthez's house. He looked up at the windows and saw the faint pure gleam of light in the panes, as he had so often seen it, with a feeling of admiration for the noble steadfastness of that truly great nature. For some moments he stood irresolute on the curbstone; he had not courage to go further; but his good angel urged him on. He tapped at the door and opened, and found d'Arthez sitting reading in a fireless room.

"What has happened?" asked d'Arthez, for news of some dreadful kind was visible in Lucien's ghastly face.

"Your book is sublime, d'Arthez," said Lucien, with tears in his eyes, "and they have ordered me to write an attack upon it."

"Poor boy! the bread that they give you is hard indeed!" said d'Arthez

"I only ask for one favor, keep my visit a secret and leave me to my hell, to the occupations of the damned. Perhaps it is impossible to attain to success until the heart is seared and callous in every most sensitive spot."

"The same as ever!" cried d'Arthez.

"Do you think me a base poltroon? No, d'Arthez; no, I am a boy half crazed with love," and he told his story.

"Let us look at the article," said d'Arthez, touched by all that Lucien said of Coralie.

Lucien held out the manuscript; d'Arthez read, and could not help smiling.

"Oh, what a fatal waste of intellect!" he began. But at the sight of Lucien overcome with grief in the opposite armchair, he checked himself.

"Will you leave it with me to correct? I will let you have it again tomorrow," he went on. "Flippancy depreciates a work; serious and conscientious criticism is sometimes praise in itself. I know a way to make your article more honorable both for yourself and for me. Besides, I know my faults well enough."

"When you climb a hot, shadowless hillside, you sometimes find fruit to quench your torturing thirst; and I have found it here and now," said Lucien, as he sprang sobbing to d'Arthez's arms and kissed his friend on the forehead. "It seems to me that I am leaving my conscience in your keeping; some day I will come to you and ask for it again."

"I look upon a periodical repentance as great hypocrisy," d'Arthez said solemnly; "repentance becomes a sort of indemnity for wrongdoing. Repentance is virginity of the soul, which we must keep for God; a man who repents twice is a horrible sycophant. I am afraid that you regard repentance as absolution."

Lucien went slowly back to the Rue de la Lune, stricken dumb by those words.

Next morning d'Arthez sent back his article, recast throughout, and Lucien sent it in to the review; but from that day melancholy preyed upon him, and he could not always disguise his mood. That evening, when the theatre was full, he experienced for the first time the paroxysm of nervous terror caused by a *debut*; terror aggravated in his case by all the strength of his love. Vanity of every kind was involved. He looked over the rows of faces as a criminal eyes the judges and the jury on whom his life depends. A murmur would have set him quivering; any slight incident upon the stage, Coralie's exits and entrances, the slightest modulation of the tones of her voice, would perturb him beyond all reason.

The play in which Coralie made her first appearance at the Gymnase was a piece of the kind which sometimes falls flat at first, and afterwards has immense success. It fell flat that night. Coralie was not applauded when she came on, and the chilly reception reacted upon her. The only applause came from Camusot's box, and various persons posted in the balcony and galleries silenced Camusot with repeated cries of "Hush!" The galleries even silenced the *claqueurs* when they led off with exaggerated salvos. Martainville applauded bravely; Nathan, Merlin, and the treacherous Florine followed his example; but it was clear that the piece was a failure. A crowd gathered in Coralie's dressing-room and consoled her, till she had no courage left. She went home in despair, less for her own sake than for Lucien's.

"Braulard has betrayed us," Lucien said.

Coralie was heartstricken. The next day found her in a high fever, utterly unfit to play, face to face with the thought that she had been cut short in her career. Lucien hid the papers from her, and looked them over in the dining-room. The reviewers one and all attributed the failure of the piece to Coralie; she had overestimated her strength; she might be the delight of a boulevard audience, but she was out of her element at the Gymnase; she had been inspired by a laudable ambition, but she had not taken her powers into account; she had chosen a part to which she was quite unequal. Lucien read on through a pile of penny-a-lining, put together on the same system as his attack upon Nathan. Milo of Crotona, when he found his hands fast in the oak which he himself had cleft, was not more furious than Lucien. He grew haggard with rage. His friends gave Coralie the most treacherous advice, in the language of kindly counsel and friendly interest. She should play (according to these authorities) all kind of roles, which the treacherous writers of these unblushing *feuilletons* knew to be utterly unsuited to her genius. And these were the Royalist papers, led off by Nathan. As for the Liberal press, all the weapons which Lucien had used were now turned against him.

Coralie heard a sob, followed by another and another. She sprang out of bed to find Lucien, and saw the papers. Nothing would satisfy her but she must read them all; and when she had read them, she went back to bed, and lay there in silence.

Florine was in the plot; she had foreseen the outcome; she had studied Coralie's part, and was ready to take her place. The management, unwilling to give up the piece, was ready to take Florine in Coralie's stead. When the manager came, he found poor Coralie sobbing and exhausted on her bed; but when he began to say, in Lucien's presence, that Florine knew the part, and that the play must be given that evening, Coralie sprang up at once.

"I will play!" she cried, and sank fainting on the floor.

So Florine took the part, and made her reputation in it; for the piece succeeded, the newspapers all sang her praises, and from that time forth Florine was the great actress whom we all know. Florine's success exasperated Lucien to the highest degree.

"A wretched girl, whom you helped to earn her bread! If the Gymnase prefers to do so, let the management pay you to cancel your engagement. I shall be the Comte de Rubempre; I will make my fortune, and you shall be my wife."

"What nonsense!" said Coralie, looking at him with wan eyes.

"Nonsense!" repeated he. "Very well, wait a few days, and you shall live in a fine house, you shall have a carriage, and I will write a part for you!"

He took two thousand francs and hurried to Frascati's. For seven hours the unhappy victim of the Furies watched his varying luck, and outwardly seemed cool and self-contained. He experienced both extremes of fortune during that day and part of the night that followed; at one time he possessed as much as thirty thousand francs, and he came out at last without a sou. In the Rue de la Lune he found Finot waiting for him with a request for one of his short articles. Lucien so far forgot himself, that he complained.

"Oh, it is not all rosy," returned Finot. "You made your right-about-face in such a way that you were bound to lose the support of the Liberal press, and the Liberals are far stronger in print than all the Ministerialist and Royalist papers put together. A man should never leave one camp for another until he has made a comfortable berth for himself, by way of consolation for the losses that he must expect; and in any case, a prudent politician will see his friends first, and give them his reasons for going over, and take their opinions. You can still act together; they sympathize with you, and you agree to give mutual help. Nathan and Merlin did that before they went over. Hawks don't pike out hawks' eyes. You were as innocent as a lamb; you will be forced to show your teeth to your new party to make anything out of them. You have been necessarily sacrificed to Nathan. I cannot conceal from you that your article on d'Arthez has roused a terrific hubbub. Marat is a saint compared with you. You will be attacked, and your book will be a failure. How far have things gone with your romance?"

"These are the last proof sheets."

"All the anonymous articles against that young d'Arthez in the Ministerialist and Ultra papers are set down to you. The *Reveil* is poking fun at the set in the Rue des Quatre-Vents, and the hits are the more telling because they are funny. There is a whole serious political coterie at the back of Leon Giraud's paper; they will come into power too, sooner or later."

"I have not written a line in the *Reveil* this week past."

"Very well. Keep my short articles in mind. Write fifty of them straight off, and I will pay you for them in a lump; but they must be of the same color as the paper." And Finot, with seeming carelessness, gave Lucien an edifying anecdote of the Keeper of the Seals, a piece of current gossip, he said, for the subject of one of the papers.

Eager to retrieve his losses at play, Lucien shook off his dejection, summoned up his energy and youthful force, and wrote thirty articles of two columns each. These finished, he went to Dauriat's, partly because he felt sure of meeting Finot there, and he wished to give the articles to Finot in person; partly because he wished for an explanation of the non-appearance of the *Marguerites*. He found the bookseller's shop full of his enemies. All the talk immediately ceased as he entered. Put under the ban of journalism, his courage rose, and once more he said to himself, as he had said in the alley at the Luxembourg, "I will triumph."

Dauriat was neither amiable or inclined to patronize; he was sarcastic in tone, and determined not to bate an inch of his rights. The *Marguerites* should appear when it suited his purpose; he should wait until Lucien was in a position to secure the success of the book; it was his, he had bought it outright. When Lucien asserted that Dauriat was bound to publish the *Marguerites* by the very nature of the contract, and the relative positions of the parties to the agreement, Dauriat flatly contradicted him, said that no publisher could be compelled by law to publish at a loss, and that he himself was the best judge of the expediency of producing the book. There was, besides, a remedy open to Lucien, as any court of law would admit--the poet was quite welcome to take his verses to a Royalist publisher upon the repayment of the thousand crowns.

Lucien went away. Dauriat's moderate tone had exasperated him even more than his previous arrogance at their first interview. So the *Marguerites* would not appear until Lucien had found a host of formidable supporters, or grown formidable himself! He walked home slowly, so oppressed and out of heart that he felt ready for suicide. Coralie lay in bed, looking white and ill.

"She must have a part, or she will die," said Berenice, as Lucien dressed for a great evening party at Mlle. des Touches' house in the Rue du Mont Blanc. Des Lupeaulx and Vignon and Blondet were to be there, as well as Mme. d'Espard and Mme. de Bargeton.

The party was given in honor of Conti, the great composer, owner likewise of one of the most famous voices off the stage, Cinti, Pasta, Garcia, Levasseur, and two or three celebrated amateurs in society not excepted. Lucien saw the Marquise, her cousin, and Mme. de Montcornet sitting together, and made one of the party. The unhappy young fellow to all appearances was light-hearted, happy, and content; he jested, he was the Lucien de Rubempre of his days of splendor, he would not seem to need help from any one. He dwelt on his services to the Royalist party, and cited the hue and cry raised after him by the Liberal press as a proof of his zeal.

"And you will be well rewarded, my friend," said Mme. de Bargeton, with a gracious smile. "Go to the *Chancellerie* the day after tomorrow with 'the Heron' and des Lupeaulx, and you will find your patent signed by His Majesty. The Keeper of the Seals will take it tomorrow to the Tuileries, but there is to be a meeting of the Council, and he will not come back till late. Still, if I hear the result tomorrow evening, I will let you know. Where are you living?"

"I will come to you," said Lucien, ashamed to confess that he was living in the Rue de la Lune.

"The Duc de Lenoncourt and the Duc de Navarreins have made mention of you to the King," added the Marquise; "they praised your absolute and entire devotion, and said that some distinction ought to avenge your treatment in the Liberal press. The name and title of Rubempre, to which you have a claim through your mother, would become illustrious through you, they said. The King gave his lordship instructions that evening to prepare a patent authorizing the Sieur Lucien Chardon to bear the arms and title of the Comtes de Rubempre, as grandson of the last Count by the mother's side. 'Let us favor the songsters' (*chardonnerets*) 'of Pindus,' said his Majesty, after reading your sonnet on the Lily, which my cousin luckily remembered to give the Duke.--'Especially when the King can work miracles, and change the song-bird into an eagle,' M. de Navarreins replied."

Lucien's expansion of feeling would have softened the heart of any woman less deeply wounded than Louise d'Espard de Negrepelisse; but her thirst for vengeance was only increased by Lucien's graciousness. Des Lupeaulx was right; Lucien was wanting in tact. It never crossed his mind that this history of the patent was one of the mystifications at which Mme. d'Espard was an adept. Emboldened with success and the flattering distinction shown to him by Mlle. des Touches, he stayed till two o'clock in the morning for a word in private with his hostess. Lucien had learned in Royalist newspaper offices that Mlle. des Touches was the author of a play in which *La petite Fay*, the marvel of the moment was about to appear. As the rooms emptied, he drew Mlle. des Touches to a sofa in the boudoir, and told the story of Coralie's misfortune and his own so touchingly, that Mlle. des Touches promised to give the heroine's part to his friend.

That promise put new life into Coralie. But the next day, as they breakfasted together, Lucien opened Lousteau's newspaper, and found that unlucky anecdote of the Keeper of the Seals and his wife. The story was full of the blackest malice lurking in the most caustic wit. Louis XVIII. was brought into the story in a masterly fashion, and held up to ridicule in such a way that prosecution was impossible. Here is the substance of a fiction for which the Liberal party attempted to win credence, though they only succeeded in adding one more to the tale of their ingenious calumnies.

The King's passion for pink-scented notes and a correspondence full of madrigals and sparkling wit was declared to be the last phase of the tender passion; love had reached the Doctrinaire stage; or had passed, in other words, from the concrete to the abstract. The illustrious lady, so cruelly ridiculed under the name of Octavie by Beranger, had conceived (so it was said) the gravest fears. The correspondence was languishing. The more Octavie displayed her wit, the cooler grew the royal lover. At last Octavie discovered the cause of her decline; her power was threatened by the novelty and piquancy of a correspondence between the august scribe and the wife of his Keeper of the Seals. That excellent woman was believed to be incapable of writing a note; she was simply and solely godmother to the efforts of audacious ambition. Who could be hidden behind her petticoats? Octavie decided, after making observations of her own, that the King was corresponding with his Minister.

She laid her plans. With the help of a faithful friend, she arranged that a stormy debate should detain the Minister at the Chamber; then she contrived to secure a *tete-a-tete*, and to convince outraged Majesty of the fraud. Louis XVIII. flew into a royal and truly Bourbon passion, but the tempest broke on Octavie's head. He would not believe her. Octavie offered immediate proof, begging the King to write a note which must be answered at once. The unlucky wife of the Keeper of the Seals sent to the Chamber for her husband; but precautions had been taken, and at that moment the Minister was on his legs addressing the Chamber. The lady racked her brains and replied to the note with such intellect as she could improvise.

"Your Chancellor will supply the rest," cried Octavie, laughing at the King's chagrin.

There was not a word of truth in the story; but it struck home to three persons--the Keeper of the Seals, his wife, and the King. It was said that des Lupeaulx had invented the tale, but Finot always kept his counsel. The article was caustic and clever, the Liberal papers and the Orleanists were delighted with it, and Lucien himself laughed, and thought of it merely as a very amusing *canard*.

He called next day for des Lupeaulx and the Baron du Chatelet. The Baron had just been to thank his lordship. The Sieur Chatelet, newly appointed Councillor Extraordinary, was now Comte du Chatelet, with a promise of the prefecture of the Charente so soon as the present prefect should have completed the term of office necessary to receive the maximum retiring pension. The Comte *du* Chatelet (for the *du* had been inserted in the patent) drove with Lucien to the *Chancellerie*, and treated his companion as an equal. But for Lucien's articles, he said, his patent would not have been granted so soon; Liberal persecution had been a stepping-stone to advancement. Des Lupeaulx was waiting for them in the Secretary-General's office. That functionary started with surprise when Lucien appeared and looked at des Lupeaulx.

"What!" he exclaimed, to Lucien's utter bewilderment. "Do you dare to come here, sir? Your patent was made out, but his lordship has torn it up. Here it is!" (the Secretary-General caught up the first torn sheet that came to hand). "The Minister wished to discover the author of yesterday's atrocious article, and here is the manuscript," added the speaker, holding out the sheets of Lucien's article. "You call yourself a Royalist, sir, and you are on the staff of that detestable paper which turns the Minister's hair gray, harasses the Centre, and is dragging the country headlong to ruin? You breakfast on the *Corsair*, the *Miroir*, the *Constitutionnel*, and the *Courier*; you dine on the *Quotidienne* and the *Reveil*, and then sup with Martainville, the worst enemy of the Government! Martainville urges the Government on to Absolutist measures; he is more likely to bring on another Revolution than if he had gone over to the extreme Left. You are a very clever journalist, but you will never make a politician. The Minister denounced you to the King, and the King was so angry that he scolded M. le Duc de Navarreins, his First Gentleman of the Bedchamber. Your enemies will be all the more formidable because they have hitherto been your friends. Conduct that one expects from an enemy is atrocious in a friend."

"Why, really, my dear fellow, are you a child?" said des Lupeaulx. "You have compromised me. Mme. d'Espard, Mme. de Bargeton, and Mme. de Montcornet, who were responsible for you, must be furious. The Duke is sure to have handed on his annoyance to the Marquise, and the Marquise will have scolded her cousin. Keep away from them and wait."

"Here comes his lordship--go!" said the Secretary-General.

Lucien went out into the Place Vendome; he was stunned by this bludgeon blow. He walked home along the Boulevards trying to think over his position. He saw himself a plaything in the hands of envy, treachery, and greed. What was he in this world of contending ambitions? A child sacrificing everything to the pursuit of pleasure and the gratification of vanity; a poet whose thoughts never went beyond the moment, a moth flitting from one bright gleaming object to another. He had no definite aim; he was the slave of circumstance --meaning well, doing ill. Conscience tortured him remorselessly. And to crown it all, he was penniless and exhausted with work and emotion. His articles could not compare with Merlin's or Nathan's work.

He walked at random, absorbed in these thoughts. As he passed some of the reading-rooms which were already lending books as well as newspapers, a placard caught his eyes. It was an advertisement of a book with a grotesque title, but beneath the announcement he saw his name in brilliant letters--"By Lucien Chardon de Rubempre." So his book had come out, and he had heard nothing of it! All the newspapers were silent. He stood motionless before the placard, his arms hanging at his sides. He did not notice a little knot of acquaintances --Rastignac and de Marsay and some other fashionable young men; nor did he see that Michel Chrestien and Leon Giraud were coming towards him.

"Are you M. Chardon?" It was Michel who spoke, and there was that in the sound of his voice that set Lucien's heartstrings vibrating.

"Do you not know me?" he asked, turning very pale.

Michel spat in his face.

"Take that as your wages for your article against d'Arthez. If everybody would do as I do on his own or his friend's behalf, the press would be as it ought to be--a self-respecting and respected priesthood."

Lucien staggered back and caught hold of Rastignac.

"Gentlemen," he said, addressing Rastignac and de Marsay, "you will not refuse to act as my seconds. But first, I wish to make matters even and apology impossible."

He struck Michel a sudden, unexpected blow in the face. The rest rushed in between the Republican and Royalist, to prevent a street brawl. Rastignac dragged Lucien off to the Rue Taitbout, only a few steps away from the Boulevard de Gand, where this scene took place. It was the hour of dinner, or a crowd would have assembled at once. De Marsay came to find Lucien, and the pair insisted that he should dine with them at the Cafe Anglais, where they drank and made merry.

"Are you a good swordsman?" inquired de Marsay.

"I have never had a foil in my hands."

"A good shot?"

"Never fired a pistol in my life."

"Then you have luck on your side. You are a formidable antagonist to stand up to; you may kill your man," said de Marsay.

Fortunately, Lucien found Coralie in bed and asleep.

She had played without rehearsal in a one-act play, and taken her revenge. She had met with genuine applause. Her enemies had not been prepared for this step on her part, and her success had determined the manager to give her the heroine's part in Camille Maupin's play. He had discovered the cause of her apparent failure, and was indignant with Florine and Nathan. Coralie should have the protection of the management.

At five o'clock that morning, Rastignac came for Lucien.

"The name of your street my dear fellow, is particularly appropriate for your lodgings; you are up in the sky," he said, by way of greeting. "Let us be first upon the ground on the road to Clignancourt; it is good form, and we ought to set them an example."

"Here is the programme," said de Marsay, as the cab rattled through the Faubourg Saint-Denis: "You stand up at twenty-five paces, coming nearer, till you are only fifteen apart. You have, each of you, five paces to take and three shots to fire-- no more. Whatever happens, that must be the end of it. We load for your antagonist, and his seconds load for you. The weapons were chosen by the four seconds at a gunmaker's. We helped you to a chance, I will promise you; horse pistols are to be the weapons."

For Lucien, life had become a bad dream. He did not care whether he lived or died. The courage of suicide helped him in some sort to carry things off with a dash of bravado before the spectators. He stood in his place; he would not take a step, a piece of recklessness which the others took for deliberate calculation. They thought the poet an uncommonly cool hand.

Michel Chrestien came as far as his limit; both fired twice and at the same time, for either party was considered to be equally insulted. Michel's first bullet grazed Lucien's chin; Lucien's passed ten feet above Chrestien's head. The second shot hit Lucien's coat collar, but the buckram lining fortunately saved its wearer. The third bullet struck him in the chest, and he dropped.

"Is he dead?" asked Michel Chrestien.

"No," said the surgeon, "he will pull through."

"So much the worse," answered Michel.

"Yes; so much the worse," said Lucien, as his tears fell fast.

By noon the unhappy boy lay in bed in his own room. With untold pains they had managed to remove him, but it had taken five hours to bring him to the Rue de la Lune. His condition was not dangerous, but precautions were necessary lest fever should set in and bring about troublesome complications. Coralie choked down her grief and anguish. She sat up with him at night through the anxious weeks of his illness, studying her parts by his bedside. Lucien was in danger for two long months; and often at the theatre Coralie acted her frivolous role with one thought in her heart, "Perhaps he is dying at this moment."

Lucien owed his life to the skill and devotion of a friend whom he had grievously hurt. Bianchon had come to tend him after hearing the story of the attack from d'Arthez, who told it in confidence, and excused the unhappy poet. Bianchon suspected that d'Arthez was generously trying to screen the renegade; but on questioning Lucien during a lucid interval in the dangerous nervous fever, he learned that his patient was only responsible for the one serious article in Hector Merlin's paper.

Before the first month was out, the firm of Fendant and Cavalier filed their schedule. Bianchon told Coralie that Lucien must on no account hear the news. The famous *Archer of Charles IX.*, brought out with an absurd title, had been a complete failure. Fendant, being anxious to realize a little ready money before going into bankruptcy, had sold the whole edition (without Cavalier's knowledge) to dealers in printed paper. These, in their turn, had disposed of it at a cheap rate to hawkers, and Lucien's book at that moment was adorning the bookstalls along the Quays. The booksellers on the Quai des Augustins, who had previously taken a quantity of copies, now discovered that after this sudden reduction of the price they were like to lose heavily on their purchases; the four duodecimo volumes, for which they had paid four francs fifty centimes, were being given away for fifty sous. Great was the outcry in the trade; but the newspapers preserved a profound silence. Barbet had not foreseen this "clearance;" he had a belief in Lucien's abilities; for once he had broken his rule and taken two hundred copies. The prospect of a loss drove him frantic; the things he said of Lucien were fearful to hear. Then Barbet took a heroic resolution. He stocked his copies in a corner of his shop, with the obstinacy of greed, and left his competitors to sell their wares at a loss. Two years afterwards, when d'Arthez's fine preface, the merits of the book, and one or two articles by Leon Giraud had raised the value of the book, Barbet sold his copies, one by one, at ten francs each.

Lucien knew nothing of all this, but Berenice and Coralie could not refuse to allow Hector Merlin to see his dying comrade, and Hector Merlin made him drink, drop by drop, the whole of the bitter draught brewed by the failure of Fendant and Cavalier, made bankrupts by his first ill-fated book. Martainville, the one friend who stood by Lucien through thick and thin, had written a magnificent article on his work; but so great was the general exasperation against the editor of *L'Aristarque*, *L'Oriflamme*, and *Le Drapeau Blanc*, that his championship only injured Lucien. In vain did the athlete return the Liberal insults tenfold, not a newspaper took up the challenge in spite of all his attacks.

Coralie, Berenice, and Bianchon might shut the door on Lucien's so-called friends, who raised a great outcry, but it was impossible to keep out creditors and writs. After the failure of Fendant and Cavalier, their bills were taken into bankruptcy according to that provision of the Code of Commerce most inimical to the claims of third parties, who in this way lose the benefit of delay.

Lucien discovered that Camusot was proceeding against him with great energy. When Coralie heard the name, and for the first time learned the dreadful and humiliating step which her poet had taken for her sake, the angelic creature loved him ten times more than before, and would not approach Camusot. The bailiff bringing the warrant of arrest shrank back from the idea of dragging his prisoner out of bed, and went back to Camusot before applying to the President of the Tribunal of Commerce for an order to remove the debtor to a private hospital. Camusot hurried at once to the Rue de la Lune, and Coralie went down to him.

When she came up again she held the warrants, in which Lucien was described as a tradesman, in her hand. How had she obtained those papers from Camusot? What promise had she given? Coralie kept a sad, gloomy silence, but when she returned she looked as if all the life had gone out of her. She played in Camille Maupin's play, and contributed not a little to the success of that illustrious literary hermaphrodite; but the creation of this character was the last flicker of a bright, dying lamp. On the twentieth night, when Lucien had so far recovered that he had regained his appetite and could walk abroad, and talked of getting to work again, Coralie broke down; a secret trouble was weighing upon her. Berenice always believed that she had promised to go back to Camusot to save Lucien.

Another mortification followed. Coralie was obliged to see her part given to Florine. Nathan had threatened the Gymnase with war if the management refused to give the vacant place to Coralie's rival. Coralie had persisted till she could play no longer, knowing that Florine was waiting to step into her place. She had overtasked her strength. The Gymnase had advanced sums during Lucien's illness, she had no money to draw; Lucien, eager to work though he was, was not yet strong enough to write, and he helped besides to nurse Coralie and to relieve Berenice. From poverty they had come to utter distress; but in Bianchon they found a skilful and devoted doctor, who obtained credit for them of the druggist. The landlord of the house and the tradespeople knew by this time how matters stood. The furniture was attached. The tailor and dressmaker no longer stood in awe of the journalist, and proceeded to extremes; and at last no one, with the exception of the pork-butcher and the druggist, gave the two unlucky children credit. For a week or more all three of them--Lucien, Berenice, and the invalid--were obliged to live on the various ingenious preparations sold by the pork-butcher; the inflammatory diet was little suited to the sick girl, and Coralie grew worse. Sheer want compelled Lucien to ask Lousteau for a return of the loan of a thousand francs lost at play by the friend who had deserted him in his hour of need. Perhaps, amid all his troubles, this step cost him most cruel suffering.

Lousteau was not to be found in the Rue de la Harpe. Hunted down like a hare, he was lodging now with this friend, now with that. Lucien found him at last at Flicoteaux's; he was sitting at the very table at which Lucien had found him that evening when, for his misfortune, he forsook d'Arthez for journalism. Lousteau offered him dinner, and Lucien accepted the offer.

As they came out of Flicoteaux's with Claude Vignon (who happened to be dining there that day) and the great man in obscurity, who kept his wardrobe at Samanon's, the four among them could not produce enough specie to pay for a cup of coffee at the Cafe Voltaire. They lounged about the Luxembourg in the hope of meeting with a publisher; and, as it fell out, they met with one of the most famous printers of the day. Lousteau borrowed forty francs of him, and divided the money into four equal parts.

Misery had brought down Lucien's pride and extinguished sentiment; he shed tears as he told the story of his troubles, but each one of his comrades had a tale as cruel as his own; and when the three versions had been given, it seemed to the poet that he was the least unfortunate among the four. All of them craved a respite from remembrance and thoughts which made trouble doubly hard to bear.

Lousteau hurried to the Palais Royal to gamble with his remaining nine francs. The great man unknown to fame, though he had a divine mistress, must needs hie him to a low haunt of vice to wallow in perilous pleasure. Vignon betook himself to the *Rocher de Cancale* to drown memory and thought in a couple of bottles of Bordeaux; Lucien parted company with him on the threshold, declining to share that supper. When he shook hands with the one journalist who had not been hostile to him, it was with a cruel pang in his heart.

"What shall I do?" he asked aloud.

"One must do as one can," the great critic said. "Your book is good, but it excited jealousy, and your struggle will be hard and long. Genius is a cruel disease. Every writer carries a canker in his heart, a devouring monster, like the tapeworm in the stomach, which destroys all feeling as it arises in him. Which is the stronger? The man or the disease? One has need be a great man, truly, to keep the balance between genius and character. The talent grows, the heart withers. Unless a man is a giant, unless he has the thews of a Hercules, he must be content either to lose his gift or to live without a heart. You are slender and fragile, you will give way," he added, as he turned into the restaurant.

Lucien returned home, thinking over that terrible verdict. He beheld the life of literature by the light of the profound truths uttered by Vignon.

"Money! money!" a voice cried in his ears.

Then he drew three bills of a thousand francs each, due respectively in one, two, and three months, imitating the handwriting of his brother-in-law, David Sechard, with admirable skill. He endorsed the bills, and took them next morning to Metivier, the paper-dealer in the Rue Serpente, who made no difficulty about taking them. Lucien wrote a few lines to give his brother-in-law notice of this assault upon his cash-box, promising, as usual in such cases, to be ready to meet the bills as they fell due.

When all debts, his own and Coralie's, were paid, he put the three hundred francs which remained into Berenice's hands, bidding her to refuse him money if he asked her for it. He was afraid of a return of the gambler's frenzy. Lucien worked away gloomily in a sort of cold, speechless fury, putting forth all his powers into witty articles, written by the light of the lamp at Coralie's bedside. Whenever he looked up in search of ideas, his eyes fell on that beloved face, white as porcelain, fair with the beauty that belongs to the dying, and he saw a smile on her pale lips, and her eyes, grown bright with a more consuming pain than physical suffering, always turned on his face.

Lucien sent in his work, but he could not leave the house to worry editors, and his articles did not appear. When he at last made up his mind to go to the office, he met with a cool reception from Theodore Gaillard, who had advanced him money, and turned his literary diamonds to good account afterwards.

"Take care, my dear fellow, you are falling off," he said. "You must not let yourself down, your work wants inspiration!"

"That little Lucien has written himself out with his romance and his first articles," cried Felicien Vernou, Merlin, and the whole chorus of his enemies, whenever his name came up at Dauriat's or the Vaudeville. "The work he is sending us is pitiable."

"To have written oneself out" (in the slang of journalism), is a verdict very hard to live down. It passed everywhere from mouth to mouth, ruining Lucien, all unsuspicious as he was. And, indeed, his burdens were too heavy for his strength. In the midst of a heavy strain of work, he was sued for the bills which he had drawn in David Sechard's name. He had recourse to Camusot's experience, and Coralie's sometime adorer was generous enough to assist the man she loved. The intolerable situation lasted for two whole months; the days being diversified by stamped papers handed over to

Desroches, a friend of Bixiou, Blondet, and des Lupeaulx.

Early in August, Bianchon told them that Coralie's condition was hopeless--she had only a few days to live. Those days were spent in tears by Berenice and Lucien; they could not hide their grief from the dying girl, and she was broken-hearted for Lucien's sake.

Some strange change was working in Coralie. She would have Lucien bring a priest; she must be reconciled to the Church and die in peace. Coralie died as a Christian; her repentance was sincere. Her agony and death took all energy and heart out of Lucien. He sank into a low chair at the foot of the bed, and never took his eyes off her till Death brought the end of her suffering. It was five o'clock in the morning. Some singing-bird lighting upon a flower-pot on the window-sill, twittered a few notes. Berenice, kneeling by the bedside, was covering a hand fast growing cold with kisses and tears. On the chimney-piece there lay eleven sous.

Lucien went out. Despair made him beg for money to lay Coralie in her grave. He had wild thoughts of flinging himself at the Marquise d'Espard's feet, of entreating the Comte du Chatelet, Mme. de Bargeton, Mlle. des Touches, nay, that terrible dandy of a de Marsay. All his pride had gone with his strength. He would have enlisted as a common soldier at that moment for money. He walked on with a slouching, feverish gait known to all the unhappy, reached Camille Maupin's house, entered, careless of his disordered dress, and sent in a message. He entreated Mlle. des Touches to see him for a moment.

"Mademoiselle only went to bed at three o'clock this morning," said the servant, "and no one would dare to disturb her until she rings."

"When does she ring?"

"Never before ten o'clock."

Then Lucien wrote one of those harrowing appeals in which the well-dressed beggar flings all pride and self-respect to the winds. One evening, not so very long ago, when Lousteau had told him of the abject begging letters which Finot received, Lucien had thought it impossible that any creature would sink so low; and now, carried away by his pen, he had gone further, it may be, than other unlucky wretches upon the same road. He did not suspect, in his fever and imbecility, that he had just written a masterpiece of pathos. On his way home along the Boulevards, he met Barbet.

"Barbet!" he begged, holding out his hand. "Five hundred francs!"

"No. Two hundred," returned the other.

"Ah! then you have a heart."

"Yes; but I am a man of business as well. I have lost a lot of money through you," he concluded, after giving the history of the failure of Fendant and Cavalier, "will you put me in the way of making some?"

Lucien quivered.

"You are a poet. You ought to understand all kinds of poetry," continued the little publisher. "I want a few rollicking songs at this moment to put along with some more by different authors, or they will be down upon me over the copyright. I want to have a good collection to sell on the streets at ten sous. If you care to let me have ten good drinking-songs by tomorrow morning, or something spicy,--you know the sort of thing, eh!--I will pay you two hundred francs."

When Lucien returned home, he found Coralie stretched out straight and stiff on a pallet-bed; Berenice, with many tears, had wrapped her in a coarse linen sheet, and put lighted candles at the four corners of the bed. Coralie's face had taken that strange, delicate beauty of death which so vividly impresses the living with the idea of absolute calm; she looked like some white girl in a decline; it seemed as if those pale, crimson lips must open and murmur the name which had blended

249

with the name of God in the last words that she uttered before she died.

Lucien told Berenice to order a funeral which should not cost more than two hundred francs, including the service at the shabby little church of the Bonne-Nouvelle. As soon as she had gone out, he sat down to a table, and beside the dead body of his love he composed ten rollicking songs to fit popular airs. The effort cost him untold anguish, but at last the brain began to work at the bidding of Necessity, as if suffering were not; and already Lucien had learned to put Claude Vignon's terrible maxims in practice, and to raise a barrier between heart and brain. What a night the poor boy spent over those drinking songs, writing by the light of the tall wax candles while the priest recited the prayers for the dead!

Morning broke before the last song was finished. Lucien tried it over to a street-song of the day, to the consternation of Berenice and the priest, who thought that he was mad:--

Lads, 'tis tedious waste of time To mingle song and reason; Folly calls for laughing rhyme, Sense is out of season. Let Apollo be forgot When Bacchus fills the drinking-cup; Any catch is good, I wot, If good fellows take it up. Let philosophers protest, Let us laugh, And quaff, And a fig for the rest!

As Hippocrates has said, Every jolly fellow, When a century has sped, Still is fit and mellow. No more following of a lass With the palsy in your legs? --While your hand can hold a glass, You can drain it to the dregs, With an undiminished zest. Let us laugh, And quaff, And a fig for the rest!

Whence we come we know full well. Whiter are we going? Ne'er a one of us can tell, 'Tis a thing past knowing. Faith! what does it signify, Take the good that Heaven sends; It is certain that we die, Certain that we live, my friends. Life is nothing but a jest. Let us laugh, And quaff, And a fig for the rest!

He was shouting the reckless refrain when d'Arthez and Bianchon arrived, to find him in a paroxysm of despair and exhaustion, utterly unable to make a fair copy of his verses. A torrent of tears followed; and when, amid his sobs, he had told his story, he saw the tears standing in his friends' eyes.

"This wipes out many sins," said d'Arthez.

"Happy are they who suffer for their sins in this world," the priest said solemnly.

At the sight of the fair, dead face smiling at Eternity, while Coralie's lover wrote tavern-catches to buy a grave for her, and Barbet paid for the coffin--of the four candles lighted about the dead body of her who had thrilled a great audience as she stood behind the footlights in her Spanish basquina and scarlet green-clocked stockings; while beyond in the doorway, stood the priest who had reconciled the dying actress with God, now about to return to the church to say a mass for the soul of her who had "loved much,"--all the grandeur and the sordid aspects of the scene, all that sorrow crushed under by Necessity, froze the blood of the great writer and the great doctor. They sat down; neither of them could utter a word.

Just at that moment a servant in livery announced Mlle. des Touches. That beautiful and noble woman understood everything at once. She stepped quickly across the room to Lucien, and slipped two thousand-franc notes into his hand as she grasped it.

"It is too late," he said, looking up at her with dull, hopeless eyes.

The three stayed with Lucien, trying to soothe his despair with comforting words; but every spring seemed to be broken. At noon all the brotherhood, with the exception of Michel Chrestien (who, however, had learned the truth as to Lucien's treachery), was assembled in the poor little church of the Bonne-Nouvelle; Mlle. de Touches was present, and Berenice and Coralie's dresser from the theatre, with a couple of supernumeraries and the disconsolate Camusot. All the men accompanied the actress to her last resting-place in Pere Lachaise. Camusot, shedding hot tears, had solemnly promised Lucien to buy the grave in perpetuity, and to put a headstone above it with the words:

CORALIE

AGED NINETEEN YEARS

August, 1822

Lucien stayed there, on the sloping ground that looks out over Paris, until the sun had set.

"Who will love me now?" he thought. "My truest friends despise me. Whatever I might have done, she who lies here would have thought me wholly noble and good. I have no one left to me now but my sister and mother and David. And what do they think of me at home?"

Poor distinguished provincial! He went back to the Rue de la Lune; but the sight of the rooms was so acutely painful, that he could not stay in them, and he took a cheap lodging elsewhere in the same street. Mlle. des Touches' two thousand francs and the sale of the furniture paid the debts.

Berenice had two hundred francs left, on which they lived for two months. Lucien was prostrate; he could neither write nor think; he gave way to morbid grief. Berenice took pity upon him.

"Suppose that you were to go back to your own country, how are you to get there?" she asked one day, by way of reply to an exclamation of Lucien's.

"On foot."

"But even so, you must live and sleep on the way. Even if you walk twelve leagues a day, you will want twenty francs at least."

"I will get them together," he said.

He took his clothes and his best linen, keeping nothing but strict necessaries, and went to Samanon, who offered fifty francs for his entire wardrobe. In vain he begged the money-lender to let him have enough to pay his fare by the coach; Samanon was inexorable. In a paroxysm of fury, Lucien rushed to Frascati's, staked the proceeds of the sale, and lost every farthing. Back once more in the wretched room in the Rue de la Lune, he asked Berenice for Coralie's shawl. The good girl looked at him, and knew in a moment what he meant to do. He had confessed to his loss at the gaming-table; and now he was going to hang himself.

"Are you mad, sir? Go out for a walk, and come back again at midnight. I will get the money for you; but keep to the Boulevards, do not go towards the Quais."

Lucien paced up and down the Boulevards. He was stupid with grief. He watched the passers-by and the stream of traffic, and felt that he was alone, and a very small atom in this seething whirlpool of Paris, churned by the strife of innumerable interests. His thoughts went back to the banks of his Charente; a craving for happiness and home awoke in him; and with the craving, came one of the sudden febrile bursts of energy which half-feminine natures like his mistake for strength. He would not give up until he had poured out his heart to David Sechard, and taken counsel of the three good angels still left to him on earth.

As he lounged along, he caught sight of Berenice--Berenice in her Sunday clothes, speaking to a stranger at the corner of the Rue de la Lune and the filthy Boulevard Bonne-Nouvelle, where she had taken her stand.

"What are you doing?" asked Lucien, dismayed by a sudden suspicion.

"Here are your twenty francs," said the girl, slipping four five-franc pieces into the poet's hand. "They may cost dear yet; but you can go," and she had fled before Lucien could see the way she went; for, in justice to him, it must be said that the money burned his hand, he wanted to return it, but he was forced to keep it as the final brand set upon him by life in Paris.

ADDENDUM

The following personages appear in other stories of the Human Comedy.

Barbet A Man of Business The Seamy Side of History The Middle Classes

Beaudenord, Godefroid de The Ball at Sceaux The Firm of Nucingen

Berenice Lost Illusions

Bianchon, Horace Father Goriot The Atheist's Mass Cesar Birotteau The Commission in Lunacy Lost Illusions A Bachelor's Establishment The Secrets of a Princess The Government Clerks Pierrette A Study of Woman Scenes from a Courtesan's Life Honorine The Seamy Side of History The Magic Skin A Second Home A Prince of Bohemia Letters of Two Brides The Muse of the Department The Imaginary Mistress The Middle Classes Cousin Betty The Country Parson In addition, M. Bianchon narrated the following: Another Study of Woman La Grande Breteche

Blondet, Emile Jealousies of a Country Town Scenes from a Courtesan's Life Modeste Mignon Another Study of Woman The Secrets of a Princess A Daughter of Eve The Firm of Nucingen The Peasantry

Blondet, Virginie Jealousies of a Country Town The Secrets of a Princess The Peasantry Another Study of Woman The Member for Arcis A Daughter of Eve

Braulard Cousin Betty Cousin Pons

Bridau, Joseph The Purse A Bachelor's Establishment A Start in Life Modeste Mignon Another Study of Woman Pierre Grassou Letters of Two Brides Cousin Betty The Member for Arcis

Bruel, Jean Francois du A Bachelor's Establishment The Government Clerks A Start in Life A Prince of Bohemia The Middle Classes A Daughter of Eve

Bruel, Claudine Chaffaroux, Madame du A Bachelor's Establishment A Prince of Bohemia Letters of Two Brides The Middle Classes

Cabirolle, Agathe-Florentine A Start in Life Lost Illusions A Bachelor's Establishment

Camusot A Bachelor's Establishment Cousin Pons The Muse of the Department Cesar Birotteau At the Sign of the Cat and Racket

Canalis, Constant-Cyr-Melchior, Baron de Letters of Two Brides Modeste Mignon The Magic Skin Another Study of Woman A Start in Life Beatrix The Unconscious Humorists The Member for Arcis

Cardot, Jean-Jerome-Severin A Start in Life Lost Illusions

A Bachelor's Establishment At the Sign of the Cat and Racket Cesar Birotteau

Carigliano, Duchesse de At the Sign of the Cat and Racket The Peasantry The Member for Arcis

Cavalier The Seamy Side of History

Chaboisseau The Government Clerks A Man of Business

Chatelet, Sixte, Baron du Lost Illusions Scenes from a Courtesan's Life The Thirteen

Chatelet, Marie-Louise-Anais de Negrepelisse, Baronne du Lost Illusions The Government Clerks

Chrestien, Michel A Bachelor's Establishment The Secrets of a Princess

Collin, Jacques Father Goriot Lost Illusions Scenes from a Courtesan's Life The Member for Arcis

Coloquinte A Bachelor's Establishment

Coralie, Mademoiselle A Start in Life A Bachelor's Establishment

Dauriat Scenes from a Courtesan's Life Modeste Mignon

Desroches (son) A Bachelor's Establishment Colonel Chabert A Start in Life A Woman of Thirty The Commission in Lunacy The Government Clerks Scenes from a Courtesan's Life The Firm of Nucingen A Man of Business The Middle Classes

Arthez, Daniel d' Letters of Two Brides The Member for Arcis The Secrets of a Princess

Espard, Jeanne-Clementine-Athenais de Blamont-Chauvry, Marquise d' The Commission in Lunacy Scenes from a Courtesan's Life Letters of Two Brides Another Study of Woman The Gondreville Mystery The Secrets of a Princess A Daughter of Eve Beatrix

Finot, Andoche Cesar Birotteau A Bachelor's Establishment Scenes from a Courtesan's Life The Government Clerks A Start in Life Gaudissart the Great The Firm of Nucingen

Foy, Maximilien-Sebastien Cesar Birotteau

Gaillard, Theodore Beatrix Scenes from a Courtesan's Life The Unconscious Humorists

Gaillard, Madame Theodore Jealousies of a Country Town A Bachelor's Establishment Scenes from a Courtesan's Life Beatrix The Unconscious Humorists

Galathionne, Prince and Princess (both not in each story) The Secrets of a Princess The Middle Classes Father Goriot A Daughter of Eve Beatrix

Gentil Lost Illusions

Giraud, Leon A Bachelor's Establishment The Secrets of a Princess The Unconscious Humorists

Giroudeau A Start in Life A Bachelor's Establishment

Grindot Cesar Birotteau Lost Illusions A Start in Life Scenes from a Courtesan's Life Beatrix The Middle Classes Cousin Betty

Lambert, Louis Louis Lambert A Seaside Tragedy

Listomere, Marquis de The Lily of the Valley A Study of Woman

Listomere, Marquise de The Lily of the Valley Lost Illusions A Study of Woman A Daughter of Eve

Lousteau, Etienne A Bachelor's Establishment Scenes from a Courtesan's Life A Daughter of Eve Beatrix The Muse of the Department Cousin Betty A Prince of Bohemia A Man of Business The Middle Classes The Unconscious Humorists

Lupeaulx, Clement Chardin des The Muse of the Department Eugenie Grandet A Bachelor's Establishment The Government Clerks Scenes from a Courtesan's Life Ursule Mirouet

Manerville, Paul Francois-Joseph, Comte de The Thirteen The Ball at Sceaux Lost Illusions A Marriage Settlement

Marsay, Henri de The Thirteen The Unconscious Humorists Another Study of Woman The Lily of the Valley Father Goriot Jealousies of a Country Town Ursule Mirouet A Marriage Settlement Lost Illusions Letters of Two Brides The Ball at Sceaux Modeste Mignon The Secrets of a Princess The Gondreville Mystery A Daughter of Eve

Matifat (wealthy druggist) Cesar Birotteau A Bachelor's Establishment Lost Illusions The Firm of Nucingen Cousin Pons

Meyraux Louis Lambert

Montcornet, Marechal, Comte de Domestic Peace Lost Illusions

3

EVE AND DAVID
(Lost Illusions III)

Lucien had gone to Paris; and David Sechard, with the courage and intelligence of the ox which painters give the Evangelist for accompanying symbol, set himself to make the large fortune for which he had wished that evening down by the Charente, when he sat with Eve by the weir, and she gave him her hand and her heart. He wanted to make the money quickly, and less for himself than for Eve's sake and Lucien's. He would place his wife amid the elegant and comfortable surroundings that were hers by right, and his strong arm should sustain her brother's ambitions--this was the programme that he saw before his eyes in letters of fire.

Journalism and politics, the immense development of the book trade, of literature and of the sciences; the increase of public interest in matters touching the various industries in the country; in fact, the whole social tendency of the epoch following the establishment of the Restoration produced an enormous increase in the demand for paper. The supply required was almost ten times as large as the quantity in which the celebrated Ouvrard speculated at the outset of the Revolution. Then Ouvrard could buy up first the entire stock of paper and then the manufacturers; but in the year 1821 there were so many paper-mills in France, that no one could hope to repeat his success; and David had neither audacity enough nor capital enough for such speculation. Machinery for producing paper in any length was just coming into use in England. It was one of the most urgent needs of the time, therefore, that the paper trade should keep pace with the requirements of the French system of civil government, a system by which the right of discussion was to be extended to every man, and the whole fabric based upon continual expression of individual opinion; a grave misfortune, for the nation that deliberates is but little wont to act.

So, strange coincidence! while Lucien was drawn into the great machinery of journalism, where he was like to leave his honor and his intelligence torn to shreds, David Sechard, at the back of his printing-house, foresaw all the practical consequences of the increased activity of the periodical press. He saw the direction in which the spirit of the age was tending, and sought to find means to the required end. He saw also that there was a fortune awaiting the discoverer of cheap paper, and the event has justified his clearsightedness. Within the last fifteen years, the Patent Office has received more than a hundred applications from persons claiming to have discovered cheap substances to be employed in the manufacture of paper. David felt more than ever convinced that this would be no brilliant triumph, it is true, but a useful and immensely profitable discovery; and after his brother-in-law went to Paris, he became more and more absorbed in the problem which he had set himself to solve.

The expenses of his marriage and of Lucien's journey to Paris had exhausted all his resources; he confronted the extreme of poverty at the very outset of married life. He had kept one thousand francs for the working expenses of the business, and owed a like sum, for which he had given a bill to Postel the druggist. So here was a double problem for this deep thinker; he must invent a method of making cheap paper, and that quickly; he must make the discovery, in fact, in order to apply the proceeds to the needs of the household and of the business. What words can describe the brain that can forget the cruel preoccupations caused by hidden want, by the daily needs of a family and the daily drudgery of a printer's business, which requires such minute, painstaking care; and soar, with the enthusiasm and intoxication of the man of science, into the regions of the unknown in quest of a secret which daily eludes the most subtle experiment? And the inventor, alas! as will shortly be seen, has plenty of woes to endure, besides the ingratitude of the many; idle folk that can do nothing themselves tell them, "Such a one is a born inventor; he could not do otherwise. He no more deserves credit for his invention than a prince for being born to rule! He is simply exercising his natural faculties, and his work is its own reward," and the people believe them.

Marriage brings profound mental and physical perturbations into a girl's life; and if she marries under the ordinary conditions of lower middle-class life, she must moreover begin to study totally new interests and initiate herself in the intricacies of business. With marriage, therefore, she enters upon a phase of her existence when she is necessarily on the watch before she can act. Unfortunately, David's love for his wife retarded this training; he dared not tell her the real state of affairs on the day after their wedding, nor for some time afterwards. His father's avarice condemned him to the most grinding poverty, but he could not bring himself to spoil the honeymoon by beginning his wife's commercial education and prosaic apprenticeship to his laborious craft. So it came to pass that housekeeping, no less than working expenses, ate up the thousand francs, his whole fortune. For four months David gave no thought to the future, and his wife remained in ignorance. The awakening was terrible! Postel's bill fell due; there was no money to meet it, and Eve knew enough of the debt and its cause to give up her bridal trinkets and silver.

That evening Eve tried to induce David to talk of their affairs, for she had noticed that he was giving less attention to the business and more to the problem of which he had once spoken to her. Since the first few weeks of married life, in fact, David spent most of his time in the shed in the backyard, in the little room where he was wont to mould his ink-rollers. Three months after his return to Angouleme, he had replaced the old fashioned round ink-balls by rollers made of strong glue and treacle, and an ink-table, on which the ink was evenly distributed, an improvement so obvious that Cointet Brothers no sooner saw it than they adopted the plan themselves.

By the partition wall of this kitchen, as it were, David had set up a little furnace with a copper pan, ostensibly to save the cost of fuel over the recasting of his rollers, though the moulds had not been used twice, and hung there rusting upon the wall. Nor was this all; a solid oak door had been put in by his orders, and the walls were lined with sheet-iron; he even replaced the dirty window sash by panes of ribbed glass, so that no one without could watch him at his work.

When Eve began to speak about the future, he looked uneasily at her, and cut her short at the first word by saying, "I know all that you must think, child, when you see that the workshop is left to itself, and that I am dead, as it were, to all business interests; but see," he continued, bringing her to the window, and pointing to the mysterious shed, "there lies our fortune. For some months yet we must endure our lot, but let us bear it patiently; leave me to solve the problem of which I told you, and all our troubles will be at an end."

David was so good, his devotion was so thoroughly to be taken upon his word, that the poor wife, with a wife's anxiety as to daily expenses, determined to spare her husband the household cares and to take the burden upon herself. So she came down from the pretty blue-and-white room, where she sewed and talked contentedly with her mother, took possession of one of the two dens at the back of the printing-room, and set herself to learn the business routine of typography. Was it not heroism in a wife who expected ere long to be a mother?

During the past few months David's workmen had left him one by one; there was not enough work for them to do. Cointet Brothers, on the other hand, were overwhelmed with orders; they were employing all the workmen of the department;

256

the alluring prospect of high wages even brought them a few from Bordeaux, more especially apprentices, who thought themselves sufficiently expert to cancel their articles and go elsewhere. When Eve came to look into the affairs of Sechard's printing works, she discovered that he employed three persons in all.

First in order stood Cerizet, an apprentice of Didot's, whom David had chosen to train. Most foremen have some one favorite among the great numbers of workers under them, and David had brought Cerizet to Angouleme, where he had been learning more of the business. Marion, as much attached to the house as a watch-dog, was the second; and the third was Kolb, an Alsacien, at one time a porter in the employ of the Messrs. Didot. Kolb had been drawn for military service, chance brought him to Angouleme, and David recognized the man's face at a review just as his time was about to expire. Kolb came to see David, and was smitten forthwith by the charms of the portly Marion; she possessed all the qualities which a man of his class looks for in a wife--the robust health that bronzes the cheeks, the strength of a man (Marion could lift a form of type with ease), the scrupulous honesty on which an Alsacien sets such store, the faithful service which bespeaks a sterling character, and finally, the thrift which had saved a little sum of a thousand francs, besides a stock of clothing and linen, neat and clean, as country linen can be. Marion herself, a big, stout woman of thirty-six, felt sufficiently flattered by the admiration of a cuirassier, who stood five feet seven in his stockings, a well-built warrior, strong as a bastion, and not unnaturally suggested that he should become a printer. So, by the time Kolb received his full discharge, Marion and David between them had transformed him into a tolerably creditable "bear," though their pupil could neither read nor write.

Job printing, as it is called, was not so abundant at this season but that Cerizet could manage it without help. Cerizet, compositor, clicker, and foreman, realized in his person the "phenomenal triplicity" of Kant; he set up type, read proof, took orders, and made out invoices; but the most part of the time he had nothing to do, and used to read novels in his den at the back of the workshop while he waited for an order for a bill-head or a trade circular. Marion, trained by old Sechard, prepared and wetted down the paper, helped Kolb with the printing, hung the sheets to dry, and cut them to size; yet cooked the dinner, none the less, and did her marketing very early of a morning.

Eve told Cerizet to draw out a balance-sheet for the last six months, and found that the gross receipts amounted to eight hundred francs. On the other hand, wages at the rate of three francs per day--two francs to Cerizet, and one to Kolb-- reached a total of six hundred francs; and as the goods supplied for the work printed and delivered amounted to some hundred odd francs, it was clear to Eve that David had been carrying on business at a loss during the first half-year of their married life. There was nothing to show for rent, nothing for Marion's wages, nor for the interest on capital represented by the plant, the license, and the ink; nothing, finally, by way of allowance for the host of things included in the technical expression "wear and tear," a word which owes its origin to the cloths and silks which are used to moderate the force of the impression, and to save wear to the type; a square of stuff (the *blanket*) being placed between the platen and the sheet of paper in the press.

Eve made a rough calculation of the resources of the printing office and of the output, and saw how little hope there was for a business drained dry by the all-devouring activity of the brothers Cointet; for by this time the Cointets were not only contract printers to the town and the prefecture, and printers to the Diocese by special appointment --they were paper- makers and proprietors of a newspaper to boot. That newspaper, sold two years ago by the Sechards, father and son, for twenty-two thousand francs, was now bringing in eighteen thousand francs per annum. Eve began to understand the motives lurking beneath the apparent generosity of the brothers Cointet; they were leaving the Sechard establishment just sufficient work to gain a pittance, but not enough to establish a rival house.

When Eve took the management of the business, she began by taking stock. She set Kolb and Marion and Cerizet to work, and the workshop was put to rights, cleaned out, and set in order. Then one evening when David came in from a country excursion, followed by an old woman with a huge bundle tied up in a cloth, Eve asked counsel of him as to the best way of turning to profit the odds and ends left them by old Sechard, promising that she herself would look after the business. Acting upon her husband's advice, Mme. Sechard sorted all the remnants of paper which she found, and printed old popular legends in double columns upon a single sheet, such as peasants paste on their walls, the histories of *The Wandering Jew*, *Robert the Devil*, *La Belle Maguelonne* and sundry miracles. Eve sent Kolb out as a hawker.

Cerizet had not a moment to spare now; he was composing the naive pages, with the rough cuts that adorned them, from morning to night; Marion was able to manage the taking off; and all domestic cares fell to Mme. Chardon, for Eve was busy coloring the prints. Thanks to Kolb's activity and honesty, Eve sold three thousand broad sheets at a penny apiece, and made three hundred francs in all at a cost of thirty francs.

But when every peasant's hut and every little wine-shop for twenty leagues round was papered with these legends, a fresh speculation must be discovered; the Alsacien could not go beyond the limits of the department. Eve, turning over everything in the whole printing house, had found a collection of figures for printing a "Shepherd's Calendar," a kind of almanac meant for those who cannot read, letterpress being replaced by symbols, signs, and pictures in colored inks, red, black and blue. Old Sechard, who could neither read nor write himself, had made a good deal of money at one time by bringing out an almanac in hieroglyph. It was in book form, a single sheet folded to make one hundred and twenty-eight pages.

Thoroughly satisfied with the success of the broad sheets, a piece of business only undertaken by country printing offices, Mme. Sechard invested all the proceeds in the *Shepherd's Calendar*, and began it upon a large scale. Millions of copies of this work are sold annually in France. It is printed upon even coarser paper than the *Almanac of Liege*, a ream (five hundred sheets) costing in the first instance about four francs; while the printed sheets sell at the rate of a halfpenny apiece--twenty-five francs per ream.

Mme. Sechard determined to use one hundred reams for the first impression; fifty thousand copies would bring in two thousand francs. A man so deeply absorbed in his work as David in his researches is seldom observant; yet David, taking a look round his workshop, was astonished to hear the groaning of a press and to see Cerizet always on his feet, setting up type under Mme. Sechard's direction. There was a pretty triumph for Eve on the day when David came in to see what she was doing, and praised the idea, and thought the calendar an excellent stroke of business. Furthermore, David promised to give advice in the matter of colored inks, for an almanac meant to appeal to the eye; and finally, he resolved to recast the ink-rollers himself in his mysterious workshop, so as to help his wife as far as he could in her important little enterprise.

But just as the work began with strenuous industry, there came letters from Lucien in Paris, heart-sinking letters that told his mother and sister and brother-in-law of his failure and distress; and when Eve, Mme. Chardon, and David each secretly sent money to their poet, it must be plain to the reader that the three hundred francs they sent were like their very blood. The overwhelming news, the disheartening sense that work as bravely as she might, she made so little, left Eve looking forward with a certain dread to an event which fills the cup of happiness to the full. The time was coming very near now, and to herself she said, "If my dear David has not reached the end of his researches before my confinement, what will become of us? And who will look after our poor printing office and the business that is growing up?"

The *Shepherd's Calendar* ought by rights to have been ready before the 1st of January, but Cerizet was working unaccountably slowly; all the work of composing fell to him; and Mme. Sechard, knowing so little, could not find fault, and was fain to content herself with watching the young Parisian.

Cerizet came from the great Foundling Hospital in Paris. He had been apprenticed to the MM. Didot, and between the ages of fourteen and seventeen he was David Sechard's fanatical worshiper. David put him under one of the cleverest workmen, and took him for his copy-holder, his page. Cerizet's intelligence naturally interested David; he won the lad's affection by procuring amusements now and again for him, and comforts from which he was cut off by poverty. Nature had endowed Cerizet with an insignificant, rather pretty little countenance, red hair, and a pair of dull blue eyes; he had come to Angouleme and brought the manners of the Parisian street-boy with him. He was formidable by reason of a quick, sarcastic turn and a spiteful disposition. Perhaps David looked less strictly after him in Angouleme; or, perhaps, as the lad grew older, his mentor put more trust in him, or in the sobering influences of a country town; but be that as it may, Cerizet (all unknown to his sponsor) was going completely to the bad, and the printer's apprentice was acting the part of a Don Juan among little work girls. His morality, learned in Paris drinking-saloons, laid down the law of self-interest as the sole rule of guidance; he knew, moreover, that next year he would be "drawn for a soldier," to use the popular expression, saw that he had no prospects, and ran into debt, thinking that soon he should be in the army, and none of his creditors would run after him. David still possessed some ascendency over the young fellow, due not to his position as master, nor yet to the interest that he had taken in his pupil, but to the great intellectual power which the sometime street-boy fully recognized.

Before long Cerizet began to fraternize with the Cointets' workpeople, drawn to them by the mutual attraction of blouse and jacket, and the class feeling, which is, perhaps, strongest of all in the lowest ranks of society. In their company Cerizet forgot the little good doctrine which David had managed to instil into him; but, nevertheless, when the others joked the boy about the presses in his workshop ("old sabots," as the "bears" contemptuously called them), and showed him the magnificent machines, twelve in number, now at work in the Cointets' great printing office, where the single wooden press was only used for experiments, Cerizet would stand up for David and fling out at the braggarts.

"My gaffer will go farther with his 'sabots' than yours with their cast-iron contrivances that turn out mass books all day long," he would boast. "He is trying to find out a secret that will lick all the printing offices in France and Navarre."

"And meantime you take your orders from a washer-woman, you snip of a foreman, on two francs a day."

"She is pretty though," retorted Cerizet; "it is better to have her to look at than the phizes of your gaffers."

"And do you live by looking at his wife?"

From the region of the wineshop, or from the door of the printing office, where these bickerings took place, a dim light began to break in upon the brothers Cointet as to the real state of things in the Sechard establishment. They came to hear of Eve's experiment, and held it expedient to stop these flights at once, lest the business should begin to prosper under the poor young wife's management.

"Let us give her a rap over the knuckles, and disgust her with the business," said the brothers Cointet.

One of the pair, the practical printer, spoke to Cerizet, and asked him to do the proof-reading for them by piecework, to relieve their reader, who had more than he could manage. So it came to pass that Cerizet earned more by a few hours' work of an evening for the brothers Cointet than by a whole day's work for David Sechard. Other transactions followed; the Cointets seeing no small aptitude in Cerizet, he was told that it was a pity that he should be in a position so little favorable to his interests.

"You might be foreman some day in a big printing office, making six francs a day," said one of the Cointets one day, "and with your intelligence you might come to have a share in the business."

"Where is the use of my being a good foreman?" returned Cerizet. "I am an orphan, I shall be drawn for the army next year, and if I get a bad number who is there to pay some one else to take my place?"

"If you make yourself useful," said the well-to-do printer, "why should not somebody advance the money?"

"It won't be my gaffer in any case!" said Cerizet.

"Pooh! Perhaps by that time he will have found out the secret."

The words were spoken in a way that could not but rouse the worst thoughts in the listener; and Cerizet gave the papermaker and printer a very searching look.

"I do not know what he is busy about," he began prudently, as the master said nothing, "but he is not the kind of man to look for capitals in the lower case!"

"Look here, my friend," said the printer, taking up half-a-dozen sheets of the diocesan prayer-book and holding them out to Cerizet, "if you can correct these for us by tomorrow, you shall have eighteen francs tomorrow for them. We are not shabby here; we put our competitor's foreman in the way of making money. As a matter of fact, we might let Mme. Sechard go too far to draw back with her *Shepherd's Calendar*, and ruin her; very well, we give you permission to tell her that we are bringing out a *Shepherd's Calendar* of our own, and to call her attention too to the fact that she will not be the first in the field."

Cerizet's motive for working so slowly on the composition of the almanac should be clear enough by this time.

When Eve heard that the Cointets meant to spoil her poor little speculation, dread seized upon her; at first she tried to see a proof of attachment in Cerizet's hypocritical warning of competition; but before long she saw signs of an over-keen curiosity in her sole compositor--the curiosity of youth, she tried to think.

"Cerizet," she said one morning, "you stand about on the threshold, and wait for M. Sechard in the passage, to pry into his private affairs; when he comes out into the yard to melt down the rollers, you are there looking at him, instead of getting on with the almanac. These things are not right, especially when you see that I, his wife, respect his secrets, and take so much trouble on myself to leave him free to give himself up to his work. If you had not wasted time, the almanac would be finished by now, and Kolb would be selling it, and the Cointets could have done us no harm."

"Eh! madame," answered Cerizet. "Here am I doing five francs' worth of composing for two francs a day, and don't you think that that is enough? Why, if I did not read proofs of an evening for the Cointets, I might feed myself on husks."

"You are turning ungrateful early," said Eve, deeply hurt, not so much by Cerizet's grumbling as by his coarse tone, threatening attitude, and aggressive stare; "you will get on in life."

"Not with a woman to order me about though, for it is not often that the month has thirty days in it then."

Feeling wounded in her womanly dignity, Eve gave Cerizet a withering look and went upstairs again. At dinner-time she spoke to David.

"Are you sure, dear, of that little rogue Cerizet?"

"Cerizet!" said David. "Why, he was my youngster; I trained him, I took him on as my copy-holder. I put him to composing; anything that he is he owes to me, in fact! You might as well ask a father if he is sure of his child."

Upon this, Eve told her husband that Cerizet was reading proofs for the Cointets.

"Poor fellow! he must live," said David, humbled by the consciousness that he had not done his duty as a master.

"Yes, but there is a difference, dear, between Kolb and Cerizet--Kolb tramps about twenty leagues every day, spends fifteen or twenty sous, and brings us back seven and eight and sometimes nine francs of sales; and when his expenses are paid, he never asks for more than his wages. Kolb would sooner cut off his hand than work a lever for the Cointets; Kolb would not peer among the things that you throw out into the yard if people offered him a thousand crowns to do it; but Cerizet picks them up and looks at them."

It is hard for noble natures to think evil, to believe in ingratitude; only through rough experience do they learn the extent of human corruption; and even when there is nothing left them to learn in this kind, they rise to an indulgence which is the last degree of contempt.

"Pooh! pure Paris street-boy's curiosity," cried David.

"Very well, dear, do me the pleasure to step downstairs and look at the work done by this boy of yours, and tell me then whether he ought not to have finished our almanac this month."

David went into the workshop after dinner, and saw that the calendar should have been set up in a week. Then, when he heard that the Cointets were bringing out a similar almanac, he came to the rescue. He took command of the printing office, Kolb helped at home instead of selling broadsheets. Kolb and Marion pulled off the impressions from one form while David worked another press with Cerizet, and superintended the printing in various inks. Every sheet must be printed four separate times, for which reason none but small houses will attempt to produce a *Shepherd's Calendar*, and that only in the country where labor is cheap, and the amount of capital employed in the business is so small that the interest amounts to little. Wherefore, a press which turns out beautiful work cannot compete in the printing of such sheets, coarse though they may be.

So, for the first time since old Sechard retired, two presses were at work in the old house. The calendar was, in its way, a masterpiece; but Eve was obliged to sell it for less than a halfpenny, for the Cointets were supplying hawkers at the rate of three centimes per copy. Eve made no loss on the copies sold to hawkers; on Kolb's sales, made directly, she gained; but her little speculation was spoiled. Cerizet saw that his fair employer distrusted him; in his own conscience he posed as the accuser, and said to himself, "You suspect me, do you? I will have my revenge," for the Paris street-boy is made on this wise. Cerizet accordingly took pay out of all proportion to the work of proof-reading done for the Cointets, going to their office every evening for the sheets, and returning them in the morning. He came to be on familiar terms with them through the daily chat, and at length saw a chance of escaping the military service, a bait held out to him by the brothers. So far from requiring prompting from the Cointets, he was the first to propose the espionage and exploitation of David's researches.

Eve saw how little she could depend upon Cerizet, and to find another Kolb was simply impossible; she made up her mind to dismiss her one compositor, for the insight of a woman who loves told her that Cerizet was a traitor; but as this meant a deathblow to the business, she took a man's resolution. She wrote to M. Metivier, with whom David and the Cointets and almost every papermaker in the department had business relations, and asked him to put the following advertisement into a trade paper:

"FOR SALE, as a going concern, a Printing Office, with License and Plant; situated at Angouleme. Apply for particulars to M. Metivier, Rue Serpente."

The Cointets saw the advertisement. "That little woman has a head on her shoulders," they said. "It is time that we took her business under our own control, by giving her enough work to live upon; we might find a real competitor in David's successor; it is in our interest to keep an eye upon that workshop."

The Cointets went to speak to David Sechard, moved thereto by this thought. Eve saw them, knew that her stratagem had succeeded at once, and felt a thrill of the keenest joy. They stated their proposal. They had more work than they could undertake, their presses could not keep pace with the work, would M. Sechard print for them? They had sent to Bordeaux for workmen, and could find enough to give full employment to David's three presses.

"Gentlemen," said Eve, while Cerizet went across to David's workshop to announce the two printers, "while my husband was with the MM. Didot he came to know of excellent workers, honest and industrious men; he will choose his successor, no doubt, from among the best of them. If he sold his business outright for some twenty thousand francs, it might bring us in a thousand francs per annum; that would be better than losing a thousand yearly over such trade as you leave us. Why did you envy us the poor little almanac speculation, especially as we have always brought it out?"

"Oh, why did you not give us notice, madame? We would not have interfered with you," one of the brothers answered blandly (he was known as the "tall Cointet").

"Oh, come gentlemen! you only began your almanac after Cerizet told you that I was bringing out mine."

She spoke briskly, looking full at "the tall Cointet" as she spoke. He lowered his eyes; Cerizet's treachery was proven to her.

This brother managed the business and the paper-mill; he was by far the cleverer man of business of the two. Jean showed no small ability in the conduct of the printing establishment, but in intellectual capacity he might be said to take colonel's rank, while Boniface was a general. Jean left the command to Boniface. This latter was thin and spare in person; his face, sallow as an altar candle, was mottled with reddish patches; his lips were pinched; there was something in his eyes that reminded you of a cat's eyes. Boniface Cointet never excited himself; he would listen to the grossest insults with the serenity of a bigot, and reply in a smooth voice. He went to mass, he went to confession, he took the sacrament. Beneath his caressing manners, beneath an almost spiritless look, lurked the tenacity and ambition of the priest, and the greed of the man of business consumed with a thirst for riches and honors. In the year 1820 "tall Cointet" wanted all that the *bourgeoisie* finally obtained by the Revolution of 1830. In his heart he hated the aristocrats, and in religion he was indifferent; he was as much or as little of a bigot as Bonaparte was a member of the Mountain; yet his vertebral column bent with a flexibility wonderful to behold before the noblesse and the official hierarchy; for the powers that be, he humbled himself, he was meek and obsequious. One final characteristic will describe him for those who are accustomed to dealings with all kinds of men, and can appreciate its value--Cointet concealed the expression of his eyes by wearing colored glasses, ostensibly to preserve his sight from the reflection of the sunlight on the white buildings in the streets; for Angouleme, being set upon a hill, is exposed to the full glare of the sun. Tall Cointet was really scarcely above middle height; he looked much taller than he actually was by reason of the thinness, which told of overwork and a brain in continual ferment. His lank, sleek gray hair, cut in somewhat ecclesiastical fashion; the black trousers, black stockings, black waistcoat, and long puce-colored greatcoat (styled a *levite* in the south), all completed his resemblance to a Jesuit.

Boniface was called "tall Cointet" to distinguish him from his brother, "fat Cointet," and the nicknames expressed a difference in character as well as a physical difference between a pair of equally redoubtable personages. As for Jean Cointet, a jolly, stout fellow, with a face from a Flemish interior, colored by the southern sun of Angouleme, thick-set, short and paunchy as Sancho Panza; with a smile on his lips and a pair of sturdy shoulders, he was a striking contrast to his older brother. Nor was the difference only physical and intellectual. Jean might almost be called Liberal in politics; he belonged to the Left Centre, only went to mass on Sundays, and lived on a remarkably good understanding with the Liberal men of business. There were those in L'Houmeau who said that this divergence between the brothers was more apparent than real. Tall Cointet turned his brother's seeming good nature to advantage very skilfully. Jean was his bludgeon. It was Jean who gave all the hard words; it was Jean who conducted the executions which little beseemed the elder brother's benevolence. Jean took the storms department; he would fly into a rage, and propose terms that nobody would think of accepting, to pave the way for his brother's less unreasonable propositions. And by such policy the pair attained their ends, sooner or later.

Eve, with a woman's tact, had soon divined the characters of the two brothers; she was on her guard with foes so formidable. David, informed beforehand of everything by his wife, lent a profoundly inattentive mind to his enemies'

262

proposals.

"Come to an understanding with my wife," he said, as he left the Cointets in the office and went back to his laboratory. "Mme. Sechard knows more about the business than I do myself. I am interested in something that will pay better than this poor place; I hope to find a way to retrieve the losses that I have made through you----"

"And how?" asked the fat Cointet, chuckling.

Eve gave her husband a look that meant, "Be careful!"

"You will be my tributaries," said David, "and all other consumers of papers besides."

"Then what are you investigating?" asked the hypocritical Boniface Cointet.

Boniface's question slipped out smoothly and insinuatingly, and again Eve's eyes implored her husband to give an answer that was no answer, or to say nothing at all.

"I am trying to produce paper at fifty per cent less than the present cost price," and he went. He did not see the glances exchanged between the brothers. "That is an inventor, a man of his build cannot sit with his hands before him.--Let us exploit him," said Boniface's eyes. "How can we do it?" said Jean's.

Mme. Sechard spoke. "David treats me just in the same way," she said. "If I show any curiosity, he feels suspicious of my name, no doubt, and out comes that remark of his; it is only a formula, after all."

"If your husband can work out the formula, he will certainly make a fortune more quickly than by printing; I am not surprised that he leaves the business to itself," said Boniface, looking across the empty workshop, where Kolb, seated upon a wetting-board, was rubbing his bread with a clove of garlic; "but it would not suit our views to see this place in the hands of an energetic, pushing, ambitious competitor," he continued, "and perhaps it might be possible to arrive at an understanding. Suppose, for instance, that you consented for a consideration to allow us to put in one of our own men to work your presses for our benefit, but nominally for you; the thing is sometimes done in Paris. We would find the fellow work enough to enable him to rent your place and pay you well, and yet make a profit for himself."

"It depends on the amount," said Eve Sechard. "What is your offer?" she added, looking at Boniface to let him see that she understood his scheme perfectly well.

"What is your own idea?" Jean Cointet put in briskly.

"Three thousand francs for six months," said she.

"Why, my dear young lady, you were proposing to sell the place outright for twenty thousand francs," said Boniface with much suavity. "The interest on twenty thousand francs is only twelve hundred francs per annum at six per cent."

For a moment Eve was thrown into confusion; she saw the need for discretion in matters of business.

"You wish to use our presses and our name as well," she said; "and, as I have already shown you, I can still do a little business. And then we pay rent to M. Sechard senior, who does not load us with presents."

After two hours of debate, Eve obtained two thousand francs for six months, one thousand to be paid in advance. When everything was concluded, the brothers informed her that they meant to put in Cerizet as lessee of the premises. In spite of herself, Eve started with surprise.

"Isn't it better to have somebody who knows the workshop?" asked the fat Cointet.

Eve made no reply; she took leave of the brothers, vowing inwardly to look after Cerizet.

"Well, here are our enemies in the place!" laughed David, when Eve brought out the papers for his signature at dinner-time.

"Pshaw!" said she, "I will answer for Kolb and Marion; they alone would look after things. Besides, we shall be making an income of four thousand francs from the workshop, which only costs us money as it is; and looking forward, I see a year in which you may realize your hopes."

"You were born to be the wife of a scientific worker, as you said by the weir," said David, grasping her hand tenderly.

But though the Sechard household had money sufficient that winter, they were none the less subjected to Cerizet's espionage, and all unconsciously became dependent upon Boniface Cointet.

"We have them now!" the manager of the paper-mill had exclaimed as he left the house with his brother the printer. "They will begin to regard the rent as regular income; they will count upon it and run themselves into debt. In six months' time we will decline to renew the agreement, and then we shall see what this man of genius has at the bottom of his mind; we will offer to help him out of his difficulty by taking him into partnership and exploiting his discovery."

Any shrewd man of business who should have seen tall Cointet's face as he uttered those words, "taking him into partnership," would have known that it behooves a man to be even more careful in the selection of the partner whom he takes before the Tribunal of Commerce than in the choice of the wife whom he weds at the Mayor's office. Was it not enough already, and more than enough, that the ruthless hunters were on the track of the quarry? How should David and his wife, with Kolb and Marion to help them, escape the toils of a Boniface Cointet?

A draft for five hundred francs came from Lucien, and this, with Cerizet's second payment, enabled them to meet all the expenses of Mme. Sechard's confinement. Eve and the mother and David had thought that Lucien had forgotten them, and rejoiced over this token of remembrance as they rejoiced over his success, for his first exploits in journalism made even more noise in Angouleme than in Paris.

But David, thus lulled into a false security, was to receive a staggering blow, a cruel letter from Lucien:--

Lucien to David.

"MY DEAR DAVID,--I have drawn three bills on you, and negotiated them with Metivier; they fall due in one, two, and three months' time. I took this hateful course, which I know will burden you heavily, because the one alternative was suicide. I will explain my necessity some time, and I will try besides to send the amounts as the bills fall due.

"Burn this letter; say nothing to my mother and sister; for, I confess it, I have counted upon you, upon the heroism known so well to your despairing brother,

"LUCIEN DE RUBEMPRE."

By this time Eve had recovered from her confinement.

"Your brother, poor fellow, is in desperate straits," David told her. "I have sent him three bills for a thousand francs at one, two, and three months; just make a note of them," and he went out into the fields to escape his wife's questionings.

But Eve had felt very uneasy already. It was six months since Lucien had written to them. She talked over the news with her mother till her forebodings grew so dark that she made up her mind to dissipate them. She would take a bold step in her despair.

Young M. de Rastignac had come to spend a few days with his family. He had spoken of Lucien in terms that set Paris gossip circulating in Angouleme, till at last it reached the journalist's mother and sister. Eve went to Mme. de Rastignac, asked the favor of an interview with her son, spoke of all her fears, and asked him for the truth. In a moment Eve heard of her brother's connection with the actress Coralie, of his duel with Michel Chrestien, arising out of his own treacherous behavior to Daniel d'Arthez; she received, in short, a version of Lucien's history, colored by the personal feeling of a clever and envious dandy. Rastignac expressed sincere admiration for the abilities so terribly compromised, and a patriotic fear for the future of a native genius; spite and jealousy masqueraded as pity and friendliness. He spoke of Lucien's blunders. It seemed that Lucien had forfeited the favor of a very great person, and that a patent conferring the right to bear the name and arms of Rubempre had actually been made out and subsequently torn up.

"If your brother, madame, had been well advised, he would have been on the way to honors, and Mme. de Bargeton's husband by this time; but what can you expect? He deserted her and insulted her. She is now Mme. la Comtesse Sixte du Chatelet, to her own great regret, for she loved Lucien."

"Is it possible!" exclaimed Mme. Sechard.

"Your brother is like a young eagle, blinded by the first rays of glory and luxury. When an eagle falls, who can tell how far he may sink before he drops to the bottom of some precipice? The fall of a great man is always proportionately great."

Eve came away with a great dread in her heart; those last words pierced her like an arrow. She had been wounded to the quick. She said not a word to anybody, but again and again a tear rolled down her cheeks, and fell upon the child at her breast. So hard is it to give up illusions sanctioned by family feeling, illusions that have grown with our growth, that Eve had doubted Eugene de Rastignac. She would rather hear a true friend's account of her brother. Lucien had given them d'Arthez's address in the days when he was full of enthusiasm for the brotherhood; she wrote a pathetic letter to d'Arthez, and received the following reply:--

D'Arthez to Mme. Sechard.

"MADAME,--You ask me to tell you the truth about the life that your brother is leading in Paris; you are anxious for enlightenment as to his prospects; and to encourage a frank answer on my part, you repeat certain things that M. de Rastignac has told you, asking me if they are true. With regard to the purely personal matter, madame, M. de Rastignac's confidences must be corrected in Lucien's favor. Your brother wrote a criticism of my book, and brought it to me in remorse, telling me that he could not bring himself to publish it, although obedience to the orders of his party might endanger one who was very dear to him. Alas! madame, a man of letters must needs comprehend all passions, since it is his pride to express them; I understood that where a mistress and a friend are involved, the friend is inevitably sacrificed. I smoothed your brother's way; I corrected his murderous article myself, and gave it my full approval.

"You ask whether Lucien has kept my friendship and esteem; to this it is difficult to make an answer. Your brother is on a road that leads him to ruin. At this moment I still feel sorry for him; before long I shall have forgotten him, of set purpose, not so much on account of what he has done already as for that which he inevitably will do. Your Lucien is not a poet, he has the poetic temper; he dreams, he does not think; he spends himself in emotion, he does not create. He is, in fact-- permit me to say it --a womanish creature that loves to shine, the Frenchman's great failing. Lucien will always sacrifice his best friend for the pleasure of displaying his own wit. He would not hesitate to sign a pact with the Devil tomorrow if so he might secure a few years of luxurious and glorious life. Nay, has he not done worse already? He has bartered his future for the short-lived delights of living openly with an actress. So far, he has not seen the dangers of his position; the girl's youth and beauty and devotion (for she worships him) have closed his eyes to the truth; he cannot see that no glory or success or fortune can induce the world to accept the position. Very well, as it is now, so it will be with each new temptation--your brother will not look beyond the enjoyment of the moment. Do not be alarmed: Lucien will never go so far as a crime, he has not the strength of character; but he would take the fruits of a crime, he would share the benefit but not the risk--a thing that seems abhorrent to the whole world, even to scoundrels. Oh, he would despise himself, he would repent; but bring him once more to the test, and he would fail again; for he is weak of will, he cannot resist the allurements of pleasure, nor forego the least of his ambitions. He is indolent, like all who would fain be poets; he thinks it clever to juggle with the difficulties of life instead of facing and overcoming them. He will be brave at one time, cowardly at another, and deserves neither credit for his courage, nor blame for his cowardice. Lucien is like a harp with strings that are slackened or tightened by the atmosphere. He might write a great book in a glad or angry mood, and care nothing for the success that he had desired for so long.

"When he first came to Paris he fell under the influence of an unprincipled young fellow, and was dazzled by his companion's adroitness and experience in the difficulties of a literary life. This juggler completely bewitched Lucien; he dragged him into a life which a man cannot lead and respect himself, and, unluckily for Lucien, love shed its magic over the path. The admiration that is given too readily is a sign of want of judgment; a poet ought not to be paid in the same coin as a dancer on the tight-rope. We all felt hurt when intrigue and literary rascality were preferred to the courage and honor of those who counseled Lucien rather to face the battle than to filch success, to spring down into the arena rather than become a trumpet in the orchestra.

"Society, madame, oddly enough, shows plentiful indulgence to young men of Lucien's stamp; they are popular, the world is fascinated by their external gifts and good looks. Nothing is asked of them, all their sins are forgiven; they are treated like perfect natures, others are blind to their defects, they are the world's spoiled children. And, on the other hand, the world is stern beyond measure to strong and complete natures. Perhaps in this apparently flagrant injustice society acts sublimely, taking a harlequin at his just worth, asking nothing of him but amusement, promptly forgetting him; and asking divine great deeds of those before whom she bends the knee. Everything is judged by laws of its being; the diamond must be flawless; the ephemeral creation of fashion may be flimsy, bizarre, inconsequent. So Lucien may perhaps succeed to admiration in spite of his mistakes; he has only to profit by some happy vein or to be among good companions; but if an evil angel crosses his path, he will go to the very depths of hell. 'Tis a brilliant assemblage of good qualities embroidered upon too slight a tissue; time wears the flowers away till nothing but the web is left; and if that is poor stuff, you behold a rag at the last. So long as Lucien is young, people will like him; but where will he be as a man of thirty? That is the question which those who love him sincerely are bound to ask themselves. If I alone had come to think in this way of Lucien, I might perhaps have spared you the pain which my plain speaking will give you; but to evade the questions put by your anxiety, and to answer a cry of anguish like your letter with commonplaces, seemed to me alike unworthy of you and of me, whom you esteem too highly; and besides, those of my friends who knew Lucien are unanimous in their judgment. So it appeared to me to be a duty to put the truth before you, terrible though it may be. Anything may be expected of Lucien, anything good or evil. That is our opinion, and this letter is summed up in that sentence. If the vicissitudes of his present way of life (a very wretched and slippery one) should bring the poet back to you, use all your influence to keep him among you; for until his character has acquired stability, Paris will not be safe for him. He used to speak of you, you and your husband, as his guardian angels; he has forgotten you, no doubt; but he will remember you again when tossed by tempest, with no refuge left to him but his home. Keep your heart for him, madame; he will need it.

"Permit me, madame, to convey to you the expression of the sincere respect of a man to whom your rare qualities are known, a man who honors your mother's fears so much, that he desires to style himself your devoted servant,
"D'ARTHEZ."

Two days after the letter came, Eve was obliged to find a wet-nurse; her milk had dried up. She had made a god of her brother; now, in her eyes, he was depraved through the exercise of his noblest faculties; he was wallowing in the mire. She, noble creature that she was, was incapable of swerving from honesty and scrupulous delicacy, from all the pious traditions of the hearth, which still burns so clearly and sheds its light abroad in quiet country homes. Then David had been right in his forecasts! The leaden hues of grief overspread Eve's white brow. She told her husband her secret in one of

266

the pellucid talks in which married lovers tell everything to each other. The tones of David's voice brought comfort. Though the tears stood in his eyes when he knew that grief had dried his wife's fair breast, and knew Eve's despair that she could not fulfil a mother's duties, he held out reassuring hopes.

"Your brother's imagination has let him astray, you see, child. It is so natural that a poet should wish for blue and purple robes, and hurry as eagerly after festivals as he does. It is a bird that loves glitter and luxury with such simple sincerity, that God forgives him if man condemns him for it."

"But he is draining our lives!" exclaimed poor Eve.

"He is draining our lives just now, but only a few months ago he saved us by sending us the first fruits of his earnings," said the good David. He had the sense to see that his wife was in despair, was going beyond the limit, and that love for Lucien would very soon come back. "Fifty years ago, or thereabouts, Mercier said in his *Tableau de Paris* that a man cannot live by literature, poetry, letters, or science, by the creatures of his brain, in short; and Lucien, poet that he is, would not believe the experience of five centuries. The harvests that are watered with ink are only reaped ten or twelve years after the sowing, if indeed there is any harvest after all. Lucien has taken the green wheat for the sheaves. He will have learned something of life, at any rate. He was the dupe of a woman at the outset; he was sure to be duped afterwards by the world and false friends. He has bought his experience dear, that is all. Our ancestors used to say, 'If the son of the house brings back his two ears and his honor safe, all is well----'"

"Honor!" poor Eve broke in. "Oh, but Lucien has fallen in so many ways! Writing against his conscience! Attacking his best friend! Living upon an actress! Showing himself in public with her. Bringing us to lie on straw----"

"Oh, that is nothing----!" cried David, and suddenly stopped short. The secret of Lucien's forgery had nearly escaped him, and, unluckily, his start left a vague, uneasy impression on Eve.

"What do you mean by nothing?" she answered. "And where shall we find the money to meet bills for three thousand francs?"

"We shall be obliged to renew the lease with Cerizet, to begin with," said David. "The Cointets have been allowing him fifteen per cent on the work done for them, and in that way alone he has made six hundred francs, besides contriving to make five hundred francs by job printing."

"If the Cointets know that, perhaps they will not renew the lease. They will be afraid of him, for Cerizet is a dangerous man."

"Eh! what is that to me!" cried David, "we shall be rich in a very little while. When Lucien is rich, dear angel, he will have nothing but good qualities."

"Oh! David, my dear, my dear; what is this that you have said unthinkingly? Then Lucien fallen into the clutches of poverty would not have the force of character to resist evil? And you think just as M. d'Arthez thinks! No one is great unless he has strength of character, and Lucien is weak. An angel must not be tempted--what is that?"

"What but a nature that is noble only in its own region, its own sphere, its heaven? I will spare him the struggle; Lucien is not meant for it. Look here! I am so near the end now that I can talk to you about the means."

He drew several sheets of white paper from his pocket, brandished them in triumph, and laid them on his wife's lap.

"A ream of this paper, royal size, would cost five francs at the most," he added, while Eve handled the specimens with almost childish surprise.

"Why, how did you make these sample bits?" she asked.

"With an old kitchen sieve of Marion's."

"And are you not satisfied yet?" asked Eve.

"The problem does not lie in the manufacturing process; it is a question of the first cost of the pulp. Alas, child, I am only a late comer in a difficult path. As long ago as 1794, Mme. Masson tried to use printed paper a second time; she succeeded, but what a price it cost! The Marquis of Salisbury tried to use straw as a material in 1800, and the same idea occurred to Seguin in France in 1801. Those sheets in your hand are made from the common rush, the *arundo phragmites*, but I shall try nettles and thistles; for if the material is to continue to be cheap, one must look for something that will grow in marshes and waste lands where nothing else can be grown. The whole secret lies in the preparation of the stems. At present my method is not quite simple enough. Still, in spite of this difficulty, I feel sure that I can give the French paper trade the privilege of our literature; papermaking will be for France what coal and iron and coarse potter's clay are for England--a monopoly. I mean to be the Jacquart of the trade."

Eve rose to her feet. David's simple-mindedness had roused her to enthusiasm, to admiration; she held out her arms to him and held him tightly to her, while she laid her head upon his shoulder.

"You give me my reward as if I had succeeded already," he said.

For all answer, Eve held up her sweet face, wet with tears, to his, and for a moment she could not speak.

"The kiss was not for the man of genius," she said, "but for my comforter. Here is a rising glory for the glory that has set; and, in the midst of my grief for the brother that has fallen so low, my husband's greatness is revealed to me.--Yes, you will be great, great like the Graindorges, the Rouvets, and Van Robais, and the Persian who discovered madder, like all the men you have told me about; great men whom nobody remembers, because their good deeds were obscure industrial triumphs."

"What are they doing just now?"

It was Boniface Cointet who spoke. He was walking up and down outside in the Place du Murier with Cerizet watching the silhouettes of the husband and wife on the blinds. He always came at midnight for a chat with Cerizet, for the latter played the spy upon his former master's every movement.

"He is showing her the paper he made this morning, no doubt," said Cerizet.

"What is it made of?" asked the paper manufacturer.

"Impossible to guess," answered Cerizet; "I made a hole in the roof and scrambled up and watched the gaffer; he was boiling pulp in a copper pan all last night. There was a heap of stuff in a corner, but I could make nothing of it; it looked like a heap of tow, as near as I could make out."

"Go no farther," said Boniface Cointet in unctuous tones; "it would not be right. Mme. Sechard will offer to renew your lease; tell her that you are thinking of setting up for yourself. Offer her half the value of the plant and license, and, if she takes the bid, come to me. In any case, spin the matter out. . . . Have they no money?"

"Not a sou," said Cerizet.

"Not a sou," repeated tall Cointet.--"I have them now," said he to himself.

Metivier, paper manufacturers' wholesale agent, and Cointet Brothers, printers and paper manufacturers, were also bankers in all but name. This surreptitious banking system defies all the ingenuity of the Inland Revenue Department. Every banker is required to take out a license which, in Paris, costs five hundred francs; but no hitherto devised method of controlling commerce can detect the delinquents, or compel them to pay their due to the Government. And though Metivier and the Cointets were "outside brokers," in the language of the Stock Exchange, none the less among them they could set some hundreds of thousands of francs moving every three months in the markets of Paris, Bordeaux, and Angouleme. Now it so fell out that that very evening Cointet Brothers had received Lucien's forged bills in the course of business. Upon this debt, tall Cointet forthwith erected a formidable engine, pointed, as will presently be seen, against the poor, patient inventor.

By seven o'clock next morning, Boniface Cointet was taking a walk by the mill stream that turned the wheels in his big factory; the sound of the water covered his talk, for he was talking with a companion, a young man of nine-and-twenty, who had been appointed attorney to the Court of First Instance in Angouleme some six weeks ago. The young man's name was Pierre Petit-Claud.

"You are a schoolfellow of David Sechard's, are you not?" asked tall Cointet by way of greeting to the young attorney. Petit-Claud had lost no time in answering the wealthy manufacturer's summons.

"Yes, sir," said Petit-Claud, keeping step with tall Cointet.

"Have you renewed the acquaintance?"

"We have met once or twice at most since he came back. It could hardly have been otherwise. In Paris I was buried away in the office or at the courts on week-days, and on Sundays and holidays I was hard at work studying, for I had only myself to look to." (Tall Cointet nodded approvingly.) "When we met again, David and I, he asked me what I had done with myself. I told him that after I had finished my time at Poitiers, I had risen to be Maitre Olivet's head-clerk, and that some time or other I hoped to make a bid for his berth. I know a good deal more of Lucien Chardon (de Rubempre he calls himself now), he was Mme. de Bargeton's lover, our great poet, David Sechard's brother-in-law, in fact."

"Then you can go and tell David of your appointment, and offer him your services," said tall Cointet.

"One can't do that," said the young attorney.

"He has never had a lawsuit, and he has no attorney, so one can do that," said Cointet, scanning the other narrowly from behind his colored spectacles.

A certain quantity of gall mingled with the blood in Pierre Petit-Claud's veins; his father was a tailor in L'Houmeau, and his schoolfellows had looked down upon him. His complexion was of the muddy and unwholesome kind which tells a tale of bad health, late hours and penury, and almost always of a bad disposition. The best description of him may be given in two familiar expressions--he was sharp and snappish. His cracked voice suited his sour face, meagre look, and magpie eyes of no particular color. A magpie eye, according to Napoleon, is a sure sign of dishonesty. "Look at So-and-so," he said to Las Cases at Saint Helena, alluding to a confidential servant whom he had been obliged to dismiss for malversation. "I do not know how I could have been deceived in him for so long, he has a magpie eye." Tall Cointet, surveying the weedy little lawyer, noted his face pitted with smallpox, the thin hair, and the forehead, bald already, receding towards a bald cranium; saw, too, the confession of weakness in his attitude with the hand on the hip. "Here is my man," said he to himself.

As a matter of fact, this Petit-Claud, who had drunk scorn like water, was eaten up with a strong desire to succeed in life; he had no money, but nevertheless he had the audacity to buy his employer's connection for thirty thousand francs, reckoning upon a rich marriage to clear off the debt, and looking to his employer, after the usual custom, to find him a wife, for an attorney always has an interest in marrying his successor, because he is the sooner paid off. But if Petit-Claud counted upon his employer, he counted yet more upon himself. He had more than average ability, and that of a kind not often found in the provinces, and rancor was the mainspring of his power. A mighty hatred makes a mighty effort.

There is a great difference between a country attorney and an attorney in Paris; tall Cointet was too clever not to know this, and to turn the meaner passions that move a pettifogging lawyer to good account. An eminent attorney in Paris, and there are many who may be so qualified, is bound to possess to some extent the diplomate's qualities; he had so much business to transact, business in which large interests are involved; questions of such wide interest are submitted to him that he does not look upon procedure as machinery for bringing money into his pocket, but as a weapon of attack and defence. A country attorney, on the other hand, cultivates the science of costs, *broutille*, as it is called in Paris, a host of small items that swell lawyers' bills and require stamped paper. These weighty matters of the law completely fill the country attorney's mind; he has a bill of costs always before his eyes, whereas his brother of Paris thinks of nothing but his fees. The fee is a honorarium paid by a client over and above the bill of costs, for the more or less skilful conduct of his case. One-half of the bill of costs goes to the Treasury, whereas the entire fee belongs to the attorney. Let us admit frankly that the fees received are seldom as large as the fees demanded and deserved by a clever lawyer. Wherefore, in Paris, attorneys, doctors, and barristers, like courtesans with a chance-come lover, take very considerable precautions against the gratitude of clients. The client before and after the lawsuit would furnish a subject worthy of Meissonier; there would be brisk bidding among attorneys for the possession of two such admirable bits of genre.

There is yet another difference between the Parisian and the country attorney. An attorney in Paris very seldom appears in court, though he is sometimes called upon to act as arbitrator (*refere*). Barristers, at the present day, swarm in the provinces; but in 1822 the country attorney very often united the functions of solicitor and counsel. As a result of this double life, the attorney acquired the peculiar intellectual defects of the barrister, and retained the heavy responsibilities of the attorney. He grew talkative and fluent, and lost his lucidity of judgment, the first necessity for the conduct of affairs. If a man of more than ordinary ability tries to do the work of two men, he is apt to find that the two men are mediocrities. The Paris attorney never spends himself in forensic eloquence; and as he seldom attempts to argue for and against, he has some hope of preserving his mental rectitude. It is true that he brings the balista of the law to work, and looks for the weapons in the armory of judicial contradictions, but he keeps his own convictions as to the case, while he does his best to gain the day. In a word, a man loses his head not so much by thinking as by uttering thoughts. The spoken word convinces the utterer; but a man can act against his own bad judgment without warping it, and contrive to win in a bad cause without maintaining that it is a good one, like the barrister. Perhaps for this very reason an old attorney is the more likely of the two to make a good judge.

A country attorney, as we have seen, has plenty of excuses for his mediocrity; he takes up the cause of petty passions, he undertakes pettifogging business, he lives by charging expenses, he strains the Code of procedure and pleads in court. In a word, his weak points are legion; and if by chance you come across a remarkable man practising as a country attorney, he is indeed above the average level.

"I thought, sir, that you sent for me on your own affairs," said Petit-Claud, and a glance that put an edge on his words fell upon tall Cointet's impenetrable blue spectacles.

"Let us have no beating about the bush," returned Boniface Cointet. "Listen to me."

After that beginning, big with mysterious import, Cointet set himself down upon a bench, and beckoned Petit-Claud to do likewise.

"When M. du Hautoy came to Angouleme in 1804, on his way to his consulship at Valence, he made the acquaintance of Mme. de Senonches, then Mlle. Zephirine, and had a daughter by her," added Cointet for the attorney's ear----"Yes," he continued, as Petit-Claud gave a start; "yes, and Mlle. Zephirine's marriage with M. de Senoches soon followed the birth of the child. The girl was brought up in my mother's house; she is the Mlle. Francoise de la Haye in whom Mme. de Senoches takes an interest; she is her godmother in the usual style. Now, my mother farmed land belonging to old Mme. de Cardanet, Mlle. Zephirine's grandmother; and as she knew the secret of the sole heiress of the Cardanets and the

Senonches of the older branch, they made me trustee for the little sum which M. Francois du Hautoy meant for the girl's fortune. I made my own fortune with those ten thousand francs, which amount to thirty thousand at the present day. Mme. de Senonches is sure to give the wedding clothes, and some plate and furniture to her goddaughter. Now, I can put you in the way of marrying the girl, my lad," said Cointet, slapping Petit-Claud on the knee; "and when you marry Francoise de la Haye, you will have a large number of the aristocracy of Angouleme as your clients. This understanding between us (under the rose) will open up magnificent prospects for you. Your position will be as much as any one could want; in fact, they don't ask better, I know."

"What is to be done?" Petit-Claud asked eagerly. "You have an attorney, Maitre Cachan----"

"And, moreover, I shall not leave Cachan at once for you; I shall only be your client later on," said Cointet significantly. "What is to be done, do you ask, my friend? Eh! why, David Sechard's business. The poor devil has three thousand francs' worth of bills to meet; he will not meet them; you will stave off legal proceedings in such a way as to increase the expenses enormously. Don't trouble yourself; go on, pile on items. Doublon, my process-server, will act under Cachan's directions, and he will lay on like a blacksmith. A word to the wise is sufficient. Now, young man?----"

An eloquent pause followed, and the two men looked at each other.

"We have never seen each other," Cointet resumed; "I have not said a syllable to you; you know nothing about M. du Hautoy, nor Mme. de Senonches, nor Mlle. de la Haye; only, when the time comes, two months hence, you will propose for the young lady. If we should want to see each other, you will come here after dark. Let us have nothing in writing."

"Then you mean to ruin Sechard?" asked Petit-Claud.

"Not exactly; but he must be in jail for some time----"

"And what is the object?"

"Do you think that I am noodle enough to tell you that? If you have wit enough to find out, you will have sense enough to hold your tongue."

"Old Sechard has plenty of money," said Petit-Claud. He was beginning already to enter into Boniface Cointet's notions, and foresaw a possible cause of failure.

"So long as the father lives, he will not give his son a farthing; and the old printer has no mind as yet to send in an order for his funeral cards."

"Agreed!" said Petit-Claud, promptly making up his mind. "I don't ask you for guarantees; I am an attorney. If any one plays me a trick, there will be an account to settle between us."

"The rogue will go far," thought Cointet; he bade Petit-Claud good-morning.

The day after this conference was the 30th of April, and the Cointets presented the first of the three bills forged by Lucien. Unluckily, the bill was brought to poor Mme. Sechard; and she, seeing at once that the signature was not in her husband's handwriting, sent for David and asked him point-blank:

"You did not put your name to that bill, did you?"

"No," said he; "your brother was so pressed for time that he signed for me."

Eve returned the bill to the bank messenger sent by the Cointets.

"We cannot meet it," she said; then, feeling that her strength was failing, she went up to her room. David followed her.

"Go quickly to the Cointets, dear," Eve said faintly; "they will have some consideration for you; beg them to wait; and call their attention besides to the fact that when Cerizet's lease is renewed, they will owe you a thousand francs."

David went forthwith to his enemies. Now, any foreman may become a master printer, but there are not always the makings of a good man of business in a skilled typographer; David knew very little of business; when, therefore, with a heavily-beating heart and a sensation of throttling, David had put his excuses badly enough and formulated his request, the answer--"This is nothing to do with us; the bill has been passed on to us by Metivier; Metivier will pay us. Apply to M. Metivier"--cut him short at once.

"Oh!" cried Eve when she heard the result, "as soon as the bill is returned to M. Metivier, we may be easy."

At two o'clock the next day, Victor-Ange-Hermenegilde Doublon, bailiff, made protest for non-payment at two o'clock, a time when the Place du Murier is full of people; so that though Doublon was careful to stand and chat at the back door with Marion and Kolb, the news of the protest was known all over the business world of Angouleme that evening. Tall Cointet had enjoined it upon Master Doublon to show the Sechards the greatest consideration; but when all was said and done, could the bailiff's hypocritical regard for appearances save Eve and David from the disgrace of a suspension of payment? Let each judge for himself. A tolerably long digression of this kind will seem all too short; and ninety out of every hundred readers shall seize with avidity upon details that possess all the piquancy of novelty, thus establishing yet once again the trust of the well-known axiom, that there is nothing so little known as that which everybody is supposed to know--the Law of the Land, to wit.

And of a truth, for the immense majority of Frenchmen, a minute description of some part of the machinery of banking will be as interesting as any chapter of foreign travel. When a tradesman living in one town gives a bill to another tradesman elsewhere (as David was supposed to have done for Lucien's benefit), the transaction ceases to be a simple promissory note, given in the way of business by one tradesman to another in the same place, and becomes in some sort a letter of exchange. When, therefore, Metivier accepted Lucien's three bills, he was obliged to send them for collection to his correspondents in Angouleme--to Cointet Brothers, that is to say. Hence, likewise, a certain initial loss for Lucien in exchange on Angouleme, taking the practical shape of an abatement of so much per cent over and above the discount. In this way Sechard's bills had passed into circulation in the bank. You would not believe how greatly the quality of banker, united with the august title of creditor, changes the debtor's position. For instance, when a bill has been passed through the bank (please note that expression), and transferred from the money market in Paris to the financial world of Angouleme, if that bill is protested, then the bankers in Angouleme must draw up a detailed account of the expenses of protest and return; 'tis a duty which they owe to themselves. Joking apart, no account of the most romantic adventure could be more mildly improbable than this of the journey made by a bill. Behold a certain article in the Code of commerce authorizing the most ingenious pleasantries after Mascarille's manner, and the interpretation thereof shall make apparent manifold atrocities lurking beneath the formidable word "legal."

Master Doublon registered the protest and went himself with it to MM. Cointet Brothers. The firm had a standing account with their bailiff; he gave them six months' credit; and the lynxes of Angouleme practically took a twelvemonth, though tall Cointet would say month by month to the lynxes' jackal, "Do you want any money, Doublon?" Nor was this all. Doublon gave the influential house a rebate upon every transaction; it was the merest trifle, one franc fifty centimes on a protest, for instance.

Tall Cointet quietly sat himself down at his desk and took out a small sheet of paper with a thirty-five centime stamp upon it, chatting as he did so with Doublon as to the standing of some of the local tradesmen.

"Well, are you satisfied with young Gannerac?"

"He is not doing badly. Lord, a carrier drives a trade----"

"Drives a trade, yes; but, as a matter of fact, his expenses are a heavy pull on him; his wife spends a good deal, so they tell me----"

"Of *his* money?" asked Doublon, with a knowing look.

The lynx meanwhile had finished ruling his sheet of paper, and now proceeded to trace the ominous words at the head of the following account in bold characters:--

ACCOUNT OF EXPENSES OF PROTEST AND RETURN.

To one bill for one thousand francs, *bearing date of February the tenth, eighteen hundred and twenty-two, drawn by* Sechard junior *of Angouleme, to order of* Lucien Chardon, *otherwise* de Rubempre, *endorsed to order of* Metivier, *and finally to our order, matured the thirtieth of April last, protested by* Doublon, *process-server, on the first of May, eighteen hundred and twenty-two.* fr. c. Principal . . . . 1000 -- Expenses of Protest. . . . . 12 35 Bank charges, one-half per cent. . . . . . . 5 -- Brokerage, one-quarter per cent. . . . . . . 2 50 Stamp on re-draft and present account. . . . 1 35 Interest and postage . . . . 3 -- ___ __ *1024 20 Exchange at the rate of one and a quarter per cent on 1024 fr. 20 c.*. . . . . *13 25* ___ ___ *Total.* *1037 45*

One thousand and thirty-seven francs forty-five centimes, for which we repay ourselves by our draft at sight upon M. Metivier, Rue Serpente, Paris, payable to order of M. Gannerac of L'Houmeau.

ANGOULEME, May 2, 1822 COINTET BROTHERS.

At the foot of this little memorandum, drafted with the ease that comes of long practice (for the writer chatted with Doublon as he wrote), there appeared the subjoined form of declaration:--

"We, the undersigned, Postel of L'Houmeau, pharmaceutical chemist, and Gannerac, forwarding agent, merchant of this town, hereby certify that the present rate of exchange on Paris is one and a quarter per cent.

"ANGOULEME, May 2, 1822."

"Here, Doublon, be so good as to step round and ask Postel and Gannerac to put their names to this declaration, and bring it back with you tomorrow morning."

And Doublon, quite accustomed as he was to these instruments of torture, forthwith went, as if it were the simplest thing in the world. Evidently the protest might have been sent in an envelope, as in Paris, and even so all Angouleme was sure to hear of the poor Sechards' unlucky predicament. How they all blamed his want of business energy! His excessive fondness for his wife had been the ruin of him, according to some; others maintained that it was his affection for his brother-in-law; and what shocking conclusions did they not draw from these premises! A man ought never to embrace the interests of his kith and kin. Old Sechard's hard-hearted conduct met with approval, and people admired him for his treatment of his son!

And now, all you who for any reason whatsoever should forget to "honor your engagements," look well into the methods of the banking business, by which one thousand francs may be made to pay interest at the rate of twenty-eight francs in ten minutes, without breaking the law of the land.

The thousand francs, the one incontestable item in the account, comes first.

The second item is shared between the bailiff and the Inland Revenue Department. The six francs due to the State for providing a piece of stamped paper, and putting the debtor's mortification on record, will probably ensure a long life to this abuse; and as you already know, one franc fifty centimes from this item found its way into the banker's pockets in the shape of Doublon's rebate.

"Bank charges one-half per cent," runs the third item, which appears upon the ingenious plea that if a banker has not received payment, he has for all practical purposes discounted a bill. And although the contrary may be the case, if you fail to receive a thousand francs, it seems to be very much the same thing as if you had paid them away. Everybody who has discounted a bill

knows that he has to pay more than the six per cent fixed by law; for a small percentage appears under the humble title of "charges," representing a premium on the financial genius and skill with which the capitalist puts his money out to interest. The more money he makes out of you, the more he asks. Wherefore it would be undoubtedly cheaper to discount a bill with a fool, if fools there be in the profession of bill-discounting.

The law requires the banker to obtain a stock-broker's certificate for the rate of exchange. When a place is so unlucky as to boast no stock exchange, two merchants act instead. This is the significance of the item "brokerage"; it is a fixed charge of a quarter per cent on the amount of the protested bill. The custom is to consider the amount as paid to the merchants who act for the stock-broker, and the banker quietly puts the money into his cash-box. So much for the third item in this delightful account.

The fourth includes the cost of the piece of stamped paper on which the account itself appears, as well as the cost of the stamp for re-draft, as it is ingeniously named, viz., the banker's draft upon his colleague in Paris.

The fifth is a charge for postage and the legal interest due upon the amount for the time that it may happen to be absent from the banker's strong box.

The final item, the exchange, is the object for which the bank exists, which is to say, for the transmission of sums of money from one place to another.

Now, sift this account thoroughly, and what do you find? The method of calculation closely resembles Polichinelle's arithmetic in Lablache's Neapolitan song, "fifteen and five make twenty-two." The signatures of Messieurs Postel and Gannerac were obviously given to oblige in the way of business; the Cointets would act at need for Gannerac as Gannerac acted for the Cointets. It was a practical application of the well-known proverb, "Reach me the rhubarb and I will pass you the senna." Cointet Brothers, moreover, kept a standing account with Metivier; there was no need of a re-draft, and no re-draft was made. A returned bill between the two firms simply meant a debit or credit entry and another line in a ledger.

This highly-colored account, therefore, is reduced to the one thousand francs, with an additional thirteen francs for expenses of protest, and half per cent for a month's delay, one thousand and eighteen francs it may be in all.

Suppose that in a large banking-house a bill for a thousand francs is daily protested on an average, then the banker receives twenty-eight francs a day by the grace of God and the constitution of the banking system, that all powerful invention due to the Jewish intellect of the Middle Ages, which after six centuries still controls monarchs and peoples. In other words, a thousand francs would bring such a house twenty-eight francs per day, or ten thousand two hundred and twenty francs per annum. Triple the average of protests, and consequently of expenses, and you shall derive an income of thirty thousand francs per annum, interest upon purely fictitious capital. For which reason, nothing is more lovingly cultivated than these little "accounts of expenses."

If David Sechard had come to pay his bill on the 3rd of May, that is, the day after it was protested, MM. Cointet Brothers would have met him at once with, "We have returned your bill to M. Metivier," although, as a matter of fact, the document would have been lying upon the desk. A banker has a right to make out the account of expenses on the evening of the day when the bill is protested, and he uses the right to "sweat the silver crowns," in the country banker's phrase.

The Kellers, with correspondents all over the world, make twenty thousand francs per annum by charges for postage alone; accounts of expenses of protest pay for Mme. la Baronne de Nucingen's dresses, opera box, and carriage. The charge for postage is a more shocking swindle, because a house will settle ten matters of business in as many lines of a single letter. And of the tithe wrung from misfortune, the Government, strange to say! takes its share, and the national revenue is swelled by a tax on commercial failure. And the Bank? from the august height of a counting-house she flings an observation, full of commonsense, at the debtor, "How is it?" asks she, "that you cannot meet your bill?" and, unluckily, there is no reply to the question. Wherefore, the "account of expenses" is an account bristling with dreadful fictions, fit to cause any debtor, who henceforth shall reflect upon this instructive page, a salutary shudder.

On the 4th of May, Metivier received the account from Cointet Brothers, with instructions to proceed against M. Lucien Chardon, otherwise de Rubempre, with the utmost rigor of the law.

Eve also wrote to M. Metivier, and a few days later received an answer which reassured her completely:--

To M. Sechard, Junior, Printer, Angouleme.

"I have duly received your esteemed favor of the 5th instant. From your explanation of the bill due on April 30th, I understand that you have obliged your brother-in-law, M. de Rubempre, who is spending so much that it will be doing you a service to summons him. His present position is such that he is likely to delay payment for long. If your brother-in-law should refuse payment, I shall rely upon the credit of your old-established house.--I sign myself now, as ever, your obedient servant, "Metivier."

"Well," said Eve, commenting upon the letter to David, "Lucien will know when they summons him that we could not pay."

What a change wrought in Eve those few words meant! The love that grew deeper as she came to know her husband's character better and better, was taking the place of love for her brother in her heart. But to how many illusions had she not bade farewell?

And now let us trace out the whole history of the bill and the account of expenses in the business world of Paris. The law enacts that the third holder, the technical expression for the third party into whose hands the bill passes, is at liberty to proceed for the whole amount against any one of the various endorsers who appears to him to be most likely to make prompt payment. M. Metivier, using this discretion, served a summons upon Lucien. Behold the successive stages of the proceedings, all of them perfectly futile. Metivier, with the Cointets behind him, knew that Lucien was not in a position to pay, but insolvency in fact is not insolvency in law until it has been formally proved.

Formal proof of Lucien's inability to pay was obtained in the following manner:

On the 5th of May, Metivier's process-server gave Lucien notice of the protest and an account of the expense thereof, and summoned him to appear before the Tribunal of Commerce, or County Court, of Paris, to hear a vast number of things: this, among others, that he was liable to imprisonment as a merchant. By the time that Lucien, hard pressed and hunted down on all sides, read this jargon, he received notice of judgment against him by default. Coralie, his mistress, ignorant of the whole matter, imagined that Lucien had obliged his brother-in-law, and handed him all the documents together--too late. An actress sees so much of bailiffs, duns, and writs, upon the stage, that she looks on all stamped paper as a farce.

Tears filled Lucien's eyes; he was unhappy on Sechard's account, he was ashamed of the forgery, he wished to pay, he desired to gain time. Naturally he took counsel of his friends. But by the time Lousteau, Blondet, Bixiou, and Nathan had told the poet to snap his fingers at a court only established for tradesmen, Lucien was already in the clutches of the law. He beheld upon his door the little yellow placard which leaves its reflection on the porter's countenance, and exercises a most astringent influence upon credit; striking terror into the heart of the smallest tradesman, and freezing the blood in the veins of a poet susceptible enough to care about the bits of wood, silken rags, dyed woolen stuffs, and multifarious gimcracks entitled furniture.

When the broker's men came for Coralie's furniture, the author of the Marguerites fled to a friend of Bixiou's, one Desroches, a barrister, who burst out laughing at the sight of Lucien in such a state about nothing at all.

"That is nothing, my dear fellow. Do you want to gain time?"

"Yes, as much possible."

"Very well, apply for stay of execution. Go and look up Masson, he is a solicitor in the Commercial Court, and a friend of mine.

Take your documents to him. He will make a second application for you, and give notice of objection to the jurisdiction of the court. There is not the least difficulty; you are a journalist, your name is well known enough. If they summons you before a civil court, come to me about it, that will be my affair; I engage to send anybody who offers to annoy the fair Coralie about his business."

On the 28th of May, Lucien's case came on in the civil court, and judgment was given before Desroches expected it. Lucien's creditor was pushing on the proceedings against him. A second execution was put in, and again Coralie's pilasters were gilded with placards. Desroches felt rather foolish; a colleague had "caught him napping," to use his own expression. He demurred, not without reason, that the furniture belonged to Mlle. Coralie, with whom Lucien was living, and demanded an order for inquiry. Thereupon the judge referred the matter to the registrar for inquiry, the furniture was proved to belong to the actress, and judgment was entered accordingly. Metivier appealed, and judgment was confirmed on appeal on the 30th of June.

On the 7th of August, Maitre Cachan received by the coach a bulky package endorsed, "Metivier *versus* Sechard and Lucien Chardon."

The first document was a neat little bill, of which a copy (accuracy guaranteed) is here given for the reader's benefit:--

To Bill due the last day of April, drawn by *Sechard, junior,* to order of *Lucien de Rubempre,* together with expenses of fr. c. protest and return . . . . *1037 45 May 5th--Serving notice of protest and summons to appear before the Tribunal of Commerce in Paris, May 7th* . . . . *8 75 " 7th--Judgment by default and warrant of arrest.* . . . . *35 -- "* 10th--Notification of judgment . . . . *8 50 " 12th--Warrant of execution* . . . . *5 50 " 14th--Inventory and appraisement previous to execution.* . . . . *16 -- " 18th--Expenses of affixing placards.* . . . . . . *15 25 " 19th--Registration* . . . . *4 -- " 24th--Verification of inventory, and application for stay of execution on the part of the said Lucien de Rubempre, objecting to the jurisdiction of the Court.* . . . . . . *12 -- " 27th--Order of the Court upon application duly repeated, and transfer of of case to the Civil Court.* . . . . *35 -- ___ ___ Carried forward.* *1177 45*

fr. c. Brought forward 1177 45 May 28th--Notice of summary proceedings in the Civil Court at the instance of Metivier, represented by counsel . . . . *6 50 June 2nd--Judgment, after hearing both parties, condemning Lucien for expenses of protest and return; the plaintiff to bear costs of proceedings in the Commercial Court.* . . . . *150 -- " 6th--Notification of judgment.* . . . . *10 --*

" 15th--Warrant of execution. . . . . *5 50 " 19th--Inventory and appraisement preparatory to execution; interpleader summons by the Demoiselle Coralie, claiming goods and chattels taken in execution; demand for immediate special inquiry before further proceedings be taken* . . . . *20 -- " " --Judge's order referring matter to registrar for immediate special inquiry.* . *40 -- " " --Judgment in favor of the said Mademoiselle Coralie* . . . . *250 -- " 20th--Appeal by Metivier* . . . . *17 -- " 30th--Confirmation of judgment* . . . . *250 -- ___ ___ Total* . . . . *1926 45* _____

Bill matured May 31st, with expenses of fr. c. protest and return. . . . . *1037 45 Serving notice of protest.* . . . . *8 75 ___ ___ Total* *1046 20*

Bill matured June 30th, with expenses of protest and return. . . . . *1037 45 Serving notice of protest.* . . . . *8 75 ___ ___ Total* . . . . *1046 20* _____

This document was accompanied by a letter from Metivier, instructing Maitre Cachan, notary of Angouleme, to prosecute David Sechard with the utmost rigor of the law. Wherefore Maitre Victor-Ange-Hermenegilde Doublon summoned David Sechard before the Tribunal of Commerce in Angouleme for the sum-total of four thousand and eighteen francs eighty-five centimes, the amount of the three bills and expenses already incurred. On the morning of the very day when Doublon served the writ upon Eve, requiring her to pay a sum so enormous in her eyes, there came a letter like a thunderbolt from Metivier:--

To Monsieur Sechard, Junior, Printer, Angouleme.

"SIR,--Your brother-in-law, M. Chardon, is so shamelessly dishonest, that he declares his furniture to be the property of an actress with whom he is living. You ought to have informed me candidly of these circumstances, and not have allowed me to go to useless expense over law proceedings. I have received no answer to my letter of the 10th of May last. You must not, therefore, take it amiss if I ask for immediate repayment of the three bills and the expenses to which I have been put.--Yours, etc., "METIVIER."

Eve had heard nothing during these months, and supposed, in her ignorance of commercial law, that her brother had made reparation for his sins by meeting the forged bills.

"Be quick, and go at once to Petit-Claud, dear," she said; "tell him about it, and ask his advice."

David hurried to his schoolfellow's office.

"When you came to tell me of your appointment and offered me your services, I did not think that I should need them so soon," he said.

Petit-Claud studied the fine face of this man who sat opposite him in the office chair, and scarcely listened to the details of the case, for he knew more of them already than the speaker. As soon as he saw Sechard's anxiety, he said to himself, "The trick has succeeded."

This kind of comedy is often played in an attorney's office. "Why are the Cointets persecuting him?" Petit-Claud wondered within himself, for the attorney can use his wit to read his clients' thoughts as clearly as the ideas of their opponents, and it is his business to see both sides of the judicial web.

"You want to gain time," he said at last, when Sechard had come to an end. "How long do you want? Something like three or four months?"

"Oh! four months! that would be my salvation," exclaimed David. Petit-Claud appeared to him as an angel.

"Very well. No one shall lay hands on any of your furniture, and no one shall arrest you for four months----But it will cost you a great deal," said Petit-Claud.

"Eh! what does that matter to me?" cried Sechard.

"You are expecting some money to come in; but are you sure of it?" asked Petit-Claud, astonished at the way in which his client walked into the toils.

"In three months' time I shall have plenty of money," said the inventor, with an inventor's hopeful confidence.

"Your father is still above ground," suggested Petit-Claud; "he is in no hurry to leave his vines."

"Do you think that I am counting on my father's death?" returned David. "I am on the track of a trade secret, the secret of making a sheet of paper as strong as Dutch paper, without a thread of cotton in it, and at a cost of fifty per cent less than cotton pulp."

"There is a fortune in that!" exclaimed Petit-Claud. He knew now what the tall Cointet meant.

"A large fortune, my friend, for in ten years' time the demand for paper will be ten times larger than it is today. Journalism will be the craze of our day."

"Nobody knows your secret?"

"Nobody except my wife."

"You have not told any one what you mean to do--the Cointets, for example?"

"I did say something about it, but in general terms, I think."

A sudden spark of generosity flashed through Petit-Claud's rancorous soul; he tried to reconcile Sechard's interests with the

Cointet's projects and his own.

"Listen, David, we are old schoolfellows, you and I; I will fight your case; but understand this clearly--the defence, in the teeth of the law, will cost you five or six thousand francs! Do not compromise your prospects. I think you will be compelled to share the profits of your invention with some one of our paper manufacturers. Let us see now. You will think twice before you buy or build a paper mill; and there is the cost of the patent besides. All this means time, and money too. The servers of writs will be down upon you too soon, perhaps, although we are going to give them the slip----"

"I have my secret," said David, with the simplicity of the man of books.

"Well and good, your secret will be your plank of safety," said Petit-Claud; his first loyal intention of avoiding a lawsuit by a compromise was frustrated. "I do not wish to know it; but mind this that I tell you. Work in the bowels of the earth if you can, so that no one may watch you and gain a hint from your ways of working, or your plank will be stolen from under your feet. An inventor and a simpleton often live in the same skin. Your mind runs so much on your secrets that you cannot think of everything. People will begin to have their suspicions at last, and the place is full of paper manufacturers. So many manufacturers, so many enemies for you! You are like a beaver with the hunters about you; do not give them your skin----"

"Thank you, dear fellow, I have told myself all this," exclaimed Sechard, "but I am obliged to you for showing so much concern for me and for your forethought. It does not really matter to me myself. An income of twelve hundred francs would be enough for me, and my father ought by rights to leave me three times as much some day. Love and thought make up my life--a divine life. I am working for Lucien's sake and for my wife's."

"Come, give me this power of attorney, and think of nothing but your discovery. If there should be any danger of arrest, I will let you know in time, for we must think of all possibilities. And let me tell you again to allow no one of whom you are not so sure as you are of yourself to come into your place."

"Cerizet did not care to continue the lease of the plant and premises, hence our little money difficulties. We have no one at home now but Marion and Kolb, an Alsacien as trusty as a dog, and my wife and her mother----"

"One word," said Petit-Claud, "don't trust that dog----"

"You do not know him," exclaimed David; "he is like a second self."

"May I try him?"

"Yes," said Sechard.

"There, good-bye, but send Mme. Sechard to me; I must have a power of attorney from your wife. And bear in mind, my friend, that there is a fire burning in your affairs," said Petit-Claud, by way of warning of all the troubles gathering in the law courts to burst upon David's head.

"Here am I with one foot in Burgundy and the other in Champagne," he added to himself as he closed the office door on David.

Harassed by money difficulties, beset with fears for his wife's health, stung to the quick by Lucien's disgrace, David had worked on at his problem. He had been trying to find a single process to replace the various operations of pounding and maceration to which all flax or cotton or rags, any vegetable fibre, in fact, must be subjected; and as he went to Petit-Claud's office, he abstractedly chewed a bit of nettle stalk that had been steeping in water. On his way home, tolerably satisfied with his interview, he felt a little pellet sticking between his teeth. He laid it on his hand, flattened it out, and saw that the pulp was far superior to any previous result. The want of cohesion is the great drawback of all vegetable fibre; straw, for instance, yields a very brittle paper, which may almost be called metallic and resonant. These chances only befall bold inquirers into Nature's methods!

"Now," said he to himself, "I must contrive to do by machinery and some chemical agency the thing that I myself have done *unconsciously."*

When his wife saw him, his face was radiant with belief in victory. There were traces of tears in Eve's face.

"Oh! my darling, do not trouble yourself; Petit-Claud will guarantee that we shall not be molested for several months to come. There will be a good deal of expense over it; but, as Petit-Claud said when he came to the door with me, 'A Frenchman has a right to keep his creditors waiting, provided he repays them capital, interest, and costs.'--Very well, then, we shall do that----"

"And live meanwhile?" asked poor Eve, who thought of everything.

"Ah! that is true," said David, carrying his hand to his ear after the unaccountable fashion of most perplexed mortals.

"Mother will look after little Lucien, and I can go back to work again," said she.

"Eve! oh, my Eve!" cried David, holding his wife closely to him.--"At Saintes, not very far from here, in the sixteenth century, there lived one of the very greatest of Frenchmen, for he was not merely the inventor of glaze, he was the glorious precursor of Buffon and Cuvier besides; he was the first geologist, good, simple soul that he was. Bernard Palissy endured the martyrdom appointed for all seekers into secrets but his wife and children and all his neighbors were against him. His wife used to sell his tools; nobody understood him, he wandered about the countryside, he was hunted down, they jeered at him. But I--am loved----"

"Dearly loved!" said Eve, with the quiet serenity of the love that is sure of itself.

"And so may well endure all that poor Bernard Palissy suffered --Bernard Palissy, the discoverer of Ecouen ware, the Huguenot excepted by Charles IX. on the day of Saint-Bartholomew. He lived to be rich and honored in his old age, and lectured on the 'Science of Earths,' as he called it, in the face of Europe."

"So long as my fingers can hold an iron, you shall want for nothing," cried the poor wife, in tones that told of the deepest devotion. "When I was Mme. Prieur's forewoman I had a friend among the girls, Basine Clerget, a cousin of Postel's, a very good child; well, Basine told me the other day when she brought back the linen, that she was taking Mme. Prieur's business; I will work for her."

"Ah! you shall not work there for long," said David; "I have found out----"

Eve, watching his face, saw the sublime belief in success which sustains the inventor, the belief that gives him courage to go forth into the virgin forests of the country of Discovery; and, for the first time in her life, she answered that confident look with a half-sad smile. David bent his head mournfully.

"Oh! my dear! I am not laughing! I did not doubt! It was not a sneer!" cried Eve, on her knees before her husband. "But I see plainly now that you were right to tell me nothing about your experiments and your hopes. Ah! yes, dear, an inventor should endure the long painful travail of a great idea alone, he should not utter a word of it even to his wife. . . . A woman is a woman still. This Eve of yours could not help smiling when she heard you say, 'I have found out,' for the seventeenth time this month."

David burst out laughing so heartily at his own expense that Eve caught his hand in hers and kissed it reverently. It was a delicious moment for them both, one of those roses of love and tenderness that grow beside the desert paths of the bitterest poverty, nay, at times in yet darker depths.

As the storm of misfortune grew, Eve's courage redoubled; the greatness of her husband's nature, his inventor's simplicity, the tears that now and again she saw in the eyes of this dreamer of dreams with the tender heart,--all these things aroused in her an unsuspected energy of resistance. Once again she tried the plan that had succeeded so well already. She wrote to M. Metivier, reminding him that the printing office was for sale, offered to pay him out of the proceeds, and begged him not to ruin David with needless costs. Metivier received the heroic letter, and shammed dead. His head-clerk replied that in the absence of M. Metivier he could not take it upon himself to stay proceedings, for his employer had made it a rule to let the law take its course. Eve wrote again, offering this time to renew the bills and pay all the costs hitherto incurred. To this the clerk consented, provided that Sechard senior guaranteed payment. So Eve walked over to Marsac, taking Kolb and her mother with her. She braved the old vinedresser, and so charming was she, that the old man's face relaxed, and the puckers smoothed out at the sight of her; but when, with inward quakings, she came to speak of a guarantee, she beheld a sudden and complete change of the tippleographic countenance.

"If I allowed my son to put his hand to the lips of my cash box whenever he had a mind, he would plunge it deep into the vitals, he would take all I have!" cried old Sechard. "That is the way with children; they eat up their parents' purse. What did I do myself, eh? I never cost my parents a farthing. Your printing office is standing idle. The rats and the mice do all the printing that is done in it. . . . You have a pretty face; I am very fond of you; you are a careful, hard-working woman; but that son of mine!--Do you know what David is? I'll tell you--he is a scholar that will never do a stroke of work! If I had reared him, as I was reared myself, without knowing his letters, and if I had made a 'bear' of him, like his father before him, he would have money saved and put out to interest by now. . . . Oh! he is my cross, that fellow is, look you! And, unluckily, he is all the family I have, for there is never like to be a later edition. And when he makes you unhappy----"

Eve protested with a vehement gesture of denial.

"Yes, he does," affirmed old Sechard; "you had to find a wet-nurse for the child. Come, come, I know all about it, you are in the county court, and the whole town is talking about you. I was only a 'bear,' I have no book learning, I was not foreman at the Didots', the first printers in the world; but yet I never set eyes on a bit of stamped paper. Do you know what I say to myself as I go to and fro among my vines, looking after them and getting in my vintage, and doing my bits of business?--I say to myself, 'You are taking a lot of trouble, poor old chap; working to pile one silver crown on another, you will leave a fine property behind you, and the bailiffs and the lawyers will get it all; . . . or else it will go in nonsensical notions and crotchets.'--Look you here, child; you are the mother of yonder little lad; it seemed to me as I held him at the font with Mme. Chardon that I could see his old grandfather's copper nose on his face; very well, think less of Sechard and more of that little rascal. I can trust no one but you; you will prevent him from squandering my property--my poor property."

"But, dear papa Sechard, your son will be a credit to you, you will see; he will make money and be a rich man one of these days, and wear the Cross of the Legion of Honor at his buttonhole."

"What is he going to do to get it?"

"You will see. But, meanwhile, would a thousand crowns ruin you? A thousand crowns would put an end to the proceedings. Well, if you cannot trust him, lend the money to me; I will pay it back; you could make it a charge on my portion, on my earnings----"

"Then has some one brought David into a court of law?" cried the vinedresser, amazed to find that the gossip was really true. "See what comes of knowing how to write your name! And how about my rent! Oh! little girl, I must go to Angouleme at once and ask Cachan's advice, and see that I am straight. You did right well to come over. Forewarned is forearmed."

After two hours of argument Eve was fain to go, defeated by the unanswerable dictum, "Women never understand business." She had come with a faint hope, she went back again almost heartbroken, and reached home just in time to receive notice of judgment; Sechard must pay Metivier in full. The appearance of a bailiff at a house door is an event in a country town, and Doublon had come far too often of late. The whole neighborhood was talking about the Sechards. Eve dared not leave her house; she dreaded to hear the whispers as she passed.

"Oh! my brother, my brother!" cried poor Eve, as she hurried into the passage and up the stairs, "I can never forgive you, unless it was----"

"Alas! it was that, or suicide," said David, who had followed her.

"Let us say no more about it," she said quietly. "The woman who dragged him down into the depths of Paris has much to answer for; and your father, my David, is quite inexorable! Let us bear it in silence."

A discreet rapping at the door cut short some word of love on David's lips. Marion appeared, towing the big, burly Kolb after her across the outer room.

"Madame," said Marion, "we have known, Kolb and I, that you and the master were very much put about; and as we have eleven hundred francs of savings between us, we thought we could not do better than put them in the mistress' hands----"

"Die misdress," echoed Kolb fervently.

"Kolb," cried David, "you and I will never part. Pay a thousand francs on account to Maitre Cachan, and take a receipt for it; we will keep the rest. And, Kolb, no power on earth must extract a word from you as to my work, or my absences from home, or the things you may see me bring back; and if I send you to look for plants for me, you know, no human being must set eyes on you. They will try to corrupt you, my good Kolb; they will offer you thousands, perhaps tens of thousands of francs, to tell----"

"Dey may offer me millions," cried Kolb, "but not ein vort from me shall dey traw. Haf I not peen in der army, and know my orders?"

"Well, you are warned. March, and ask M. Petit-Claud to go with you as witness."

"Yes," said the Alsacien. "Some tay I hope to be rich enough to dust der chacket of dat man of law. I don't like his gountenance."

"Kolb is a good man, madame," said Big Marion; "he is as strong as a Turk, and as meek as a lamb. Just the one that would make a woman happy. It was his notion, too, to invest our savings this way --'safings,' as he calls them. Poor man, if he doesn't speak right, he thinks right, and I understand him all the same. He has a notion of working for somebody else, so as to save us his keep----"

"Surely we shall be rich, if it is only to repay these good folk," said David, looking at his wife.

Eve thought it quite simple; it was no surprise to her to find other natures on a level with her own. The dullest--nay, the most indifferent--observer could have seen all the beauty of her nature in her way of receiving this service.

"You will be rich some day, dear master," said Marion; "your bread is ready baked. Your father has just bought another farm, he is putting by money for you; that he is."

And under the circumstances, did not Marion show an exquisite delicacy of feeling by belittling, as it were, her kindness in this way?

French procedure, like all things human, has its defects; nevertheless, the sword of justice, being a two-edged weapon, is excellently adapted alike for attack or defence. Procedure, moreover, has its amusing side; for when opposed, lawyers arrive at an understanding, as they well may do, without exchanging a word; through their manner of conducting their case, a suit becomes a kind of war waged on the lines laid down by the first Marshal Biron, who, at the siege of Rouen, it may be remembered, received his son's project for taking the city in two days with the remark, "You must be in a great hurry to go and plant cabbages!" Let two commanders-in-chief spare their troops as much as possible, let them imitate the Austrian generals who give the men time to eat their soup though they fail to effect a juncture, and escape reprimand from the Aulic Council; let them avoid all decisive measures, and they shall carry on a war for ever. Maitre Cachan, Petit-Claud, and Doublon, did better than the Austrian generals; they took for their example Quintus Fabius Cunctator--the Austrian of antiquity.

Petit-Claud, malignant as a mule, was not long in finding out all the advantages of his position. No sooner had Boniface Cointet guaranteed his costs than he vowed to lead Cachan a dance, and to dazzle the paper manufacturer with a brilliant display of genius in the creation of items to be charged to Metivier. Unluckily for the fame of the young forensic Figaro, the writer of this history is obliged to pass over the scene of his exploits in as great a hurry as if he trod on burning coals; but a single bill of costs, in the shape of the specimen sent from Paris, will no doubt suffice for the student of contemporary manners. Let us follow the example set us by the Bulletins of the Grande Armee, and give a summary of Petit-Claud's valiant feats and exploits in the province of pure law; they will be the better appreciated for concise treatment.

David Sechard was summoned before the Tribunal of Commerce at Angouleme for the 3rd of July, made default, and notice of judgment was served on the 8th. On the 10th, Doublon obtained an execution warrant, and attempted to put in an execution on the 12th. On this Petit-Claud applied for an interpleader summons, and served notice on Metivier for that day fortnight. Metivier made application for a hearing without delay, and on the 19th, Sechard's application was dismissed. Hard upon this followed notice of judgment, authorizing the issue of an execution warrant on the 22nd, a warrant of arrest on the 23rd, and bailiff's inventory previous to the execution on the 24th. Metivier, Doublon, Cachan & Company were proceeding at this furious pace, when Petit-Claud suddenly pulled them up, and stayed execution by lodging notice of appeal on the Court-Royal. Notice of appeal, duly reiterated on the 25th of July, drew Metivier off to Poitiers.

"Come!" said Petit-Claud to himself, "there we are likely to stop for some time to come."

No sooner was the storm passed over to Poitiers, and an attorney practising in the Court-Royal instructed to defend the case, than Petit-Claud, a champion facing both ways, made application in Mme. Sechard's name for the immediate separation of her estate from her husband's; using "all diligence" (in legal language) to such purpose, that he obtained an order from the court on the 28th, and inserted notice at once in the Charente Courier. Now David the lover had settled ten thousand francs upon his wife in the marriage contract, making over to her as security the fixtures of the printing office and the household furniture; and Petit-Claud therefore constituted Mme. Sechard her husband's creditor for that small amount, drawing up a statement of her claims on the estate in the presence of a notary on the 1st of August.

While Petit-Claud was busy securing the household property of his clients, he gained the day at Poitiers on the point of law on which the demurrer and appeals were based. He held that, as the court of the Seine had ordered the plaintiff to pay costs of proceedings in the Paris commercial court, David was so much the less liable for expenses of litigation incurred upon Lucien's account. The Court-Royal took this view of the case, and judgment was entered accordingly. David Sechard was ordered to pay the amount in dispute in the Angouleme Court, less the law expenses incurred in Paris; these Metivier must pay, and each side must bear its own costs in the appeal to the Court-Royal.

David Sechard was duly notified of the result on the 17th of August. On the 18th the judgment took the practical shape of an order to pay capital, interest, and costs, followed up by notice of an execution for the morrow. Upon this Petit-Claud intervened and put in a claim for the furniture as the wife's property duly separated from her husband's; and what was more, Petit-Claud produced Sechard senior upon the scene of action. The old vinegrower had become his client on this wise. He came to Angouleme on the day after Eve's visit, and went to Maitre Cachan for advice. His son owed him arrears of rent; how could he come by this rent in the scrimmage in which his son was engaged?

"I am engaged by the other side," pronounced Cachan, "and I cannot appear for the father when I am suing the son; but go to Petit-Claud, he is very clever, he may perhaps do even better for you than I should do."

Cachan and Petit-Claud met at the Court.

"I have sent you Sechard senior," said Cachan; "take the case for me in exchange." Lawyers do each other services of this kind in country towns as well as in Paris.

The day after Sechard senior gave Petit-Claud his confidence, the tall Cointet paid a visit to his confederate.

"Try to give old Sechard a lesson," he said. "He is the kind of man that will never forgive his son for costing him a thousand francs or so; the outlay will dry up any generous thoughts in his mind, if he ever has any."

"Go back to your vines," said Petit-Claud to his new client. "Your son is not very well off; do not eat him out of house and home. I will send for you when the time comes."

On behalf of Sechard senior, therefore, Petit-Claud claimed that the presses, being fixtures, were so much the more to be regarded as tools and implements of trade, and the less liable to seizure, in that the house had been a printing office since the reign of Louis XIV. Cachan, on Metivier's account, waxed indignant at this. In Paris Lucien's furniture had belonged to Coralie, and here again in Angouleme David's goods and chattels all belonged to his wife or his father; pretty things were said in court. Father and son were summoned; such claims could not be allowed to stand.

"We mean to unmask the frauds intrenched behind bad faith of the most formidable kind; here is the defence of dishonesty bristling with the plainest and most innocent articles of the Code, and why?--to avoid repayment of three thousand francs; obtained how?--from poor Metivier's cash box! And yet there are those who dare to say a word against bill-discounters! What times we live in! . . . Now, I put it to you--what is this but taking your neighbor's money? . . . You will surely not sanction a claim which would bring immorality to the very core of justice!"

Cachan's eloquence produced an effect on the court. A divided judgment was given in favor of Mme. Sechard, the house furniture being held to be her property; and against Sechard senior, who was ordered to pay costs--four hundred and thirty-four francs, sixty-five centimes.

"It is kind of old Sechard," laughed the lawyers; "he would have a finger in the pie, so let him pay!"

Notice of judgment was given on the 26th of August; the presses and plant could be seized on the 28th. Placards were posted. Application was made for an order empowering them to sell on the spot. Announcements of the sale appeared in the papers, and Doublon flattered himself that the inventory should be verified and the auction take place on the 2nd of September.

By this time David Sechard owed Metivier five thousand two hundred and seventy-five francs, twenty-five centimes (to say nothing of interest), by formal judgment confirmed by appeal, the bill of costs having been duly taxed. Likewise to Petit-Claud he owed twelve hundred francs, exclusive of the fees, which were left to David's generosity with the generous confidence displayed by the hackney coachman who has driven you so quickly over the road on which you desire to go.

Mme. Sechard owed Petit-Claud something like three hundred and fifty francs and fees besides; and of old Sechard, besides four hundred and thirty-four francs, sixty-five centimes, the little attorney demanded a hundred crowns by way of fee. Altogether, the Sechard family owed about ten thousand francs. This is what is called "putting fire into the bed straw."

Apart from the utility of these documents to other nations who thus may behold the battery of French law in action, the French legislator ought to know the lengths to which the abuse of procedure may be carried, always supposing that the said legislator can find time for reading. Surely some sort of regulation might be devised, some way of forbidding lawyers to carry on a case until the sum in dispute is more than eaten up in costs? Is there not something ludicrous in the idea of submitting a square yard of soil and an estate of thousands of acres to the same legal formalities? These bare outlines of the history of the various stages of procedure should open the eyes of Frenchmen to the meaning of the words "legal formalities, justice, and costs," little as the immense majority of the nations know about them.

Five thousand pounds' weight of type in the printing office were worth two thousand francs as old metal; the three presses were valued at six hundred francs; the rest of the plant would fetch the price of old iron and firewood. The household furniture would have brought in a thousand francs at most. The whole personal property of Sechard junior therefore represented the sum of four thousand francs; and Cachan and Petit-Claud made claims for seven thousand francs in costs already incurred, to say nothing of expenses to come, for the blossom gave promise of fine fruits enough, as the reader will shortly see. Surely the lawyers of France and Navarre, nay, even of Normandy herself, will not refuse Petit-Claud his meed of admiration and respect? Surely, too, kind hearts will give Marion and Kolb a tear of sympathy?

All through the war Kolb sat on a chair in the doorway, acting as watch-dog, when David had nothing else for him to do. It was Kolb who received all the notifications, and a clerk of Petit-Claud's kept watch over Kolb. No sooner were the placards announcing the auction put up on the premises than Kolb tore them down; he hurried round the town after the bill-poster, tearing the placards from the walls.

"Ah, scountrels!" he cried, "to dorment so goot a man; and they calls it chustice!"

Marion made half a franc a day by working half time in a paper mill as a machine tender, and her wages contributed to the support of the household. Mme. Chardon went back uncomplainingly to her old occupation, sitting up night after night, and bringing home her wages at the end of the week. Poor Mme. Chardon! Twice already she had made a nine days' prayer for those she loved, wondering that God should be deaf to her petitions, and blind to the light of the candles on His altar.

On the 2nd of September, a letter came from Lucien, the first since the letter of the winter, which David had kept from his wife's knowledge--the announcement of the three bills which bore David's signature. This time Lucien wrote to Eve.

"The third since he left us!" she said. Poor sister, she was afraid to open the envelope that covered the fatal sheet.

She was feeding the little one when the post came in; they could not afford a wet-nurse now, and the child was being brought up by hand. Her state of mind may be imagined, and David's also, when he had been roused to read the letter, for David had been at work all night, and only lay down at daybreak.

Lucien to Eve.

"PARIS, August 29th.

"MY DEAR SISTER,--Two days ago, at five o'clock in the morning, one of God's noblest creatures breathed her last in my arms; she was the one woman on earth capable of loving me as you and mother and David love me, giving me besides that unselfish affection, something that neither mother nor sister can give--the utmost bliss of love. Poor Coralie, after giving up everything for my sake, may perhaps have died for me--for me, who at this moment have not the wherewithal to bury her. She could have solaced my life; you, and you alone, my dear good angels, can console me for her death. God has forgiven her, I think, the innocent girl, for she died like a Christian. Oh, this Paris! Eve, Paris is the glory and the shame of France. Many illusions I have lost here already, and I have others yet to lose, when I begin to beg for the little money needed before I can lay the body of my angel in consecrated earth. "Your unhappy brother, "Lucien."

"P. S. I must have given you much trouble by my heedlessness; some day you will know all, and you will forgive me. You must be quite easy now; a worthy merchant, a M. Camusot, to whom I once caused cruel pangs, promised to arrange everything, seeing that Coralie and I were so much distressed."

"The sheet is still moist with his tears," said Eve, looking at the letter with a heart so full of sympathy that something of the old love for Lucien shone in her eyes.

"Poor fellow, he must have suffered cruelly if he has been loved as he says!" exclaimed Eve's husband, happy in his love; and these two forgot all their own troubles at this cry of a supreme sorrow. Just at that moment Marion rushed in.

"Madame," she panted, "here they are! Here they are!"

"Who is here?"

"Doublon and his men, bad luck to them! Kolb will not let them come in; they have come to sell us up."

"No, no, they are not going to sell you up, never fear," cried a voice in the next room, and Petit-Claud appeared upon the scene. "I have just lodged notice of appeal. We ought not to sit down under a judgment that attaches a stigma of bad faith to us. I did not think it worth while to fight the case here. I let Cachan talk to gain time for you; I am sure of gaining the day at

Poitiers----"

"But how much will it cost to win the day?" asked Mme. Sechard.

"Fees if you win, one thousand francs if we lose our case."

"Oh, dear!" cried poor Eve; "why, the remedy is worse than the disease!"

Petit-Claud was not a little confused at this cry of innocence enlightened by the progress of the flames of litigation. It struck him too that Eve was a very beautiful woman. In the middle of the discussion old Sechard arrived, summoned by Petit-Claud. The old man's presence in the chamber where his little grandson in the cradle lay smiling at misfortune completed the scene. The young attorney at once addressed the newcomer with:

"You owe me seven hundred francs for the interpleader, Papa Sechard; but you can charge the amount to your son in addition to the arrears of rent."

The vinedresser felt the sting of the sarcasm conveyed by Petit-Claud's tone and manner.

"It would have cost you less to give security for the debt at first," said Eve, leaving the cradle to greet her father-in-law with a kiss.

David, quite overcome by the sight of the crowd outside the house (for Kolb's resistance to Doublon's men had collected a knot of people), could only hold out a hand to his father; he did not say a word.

"And how, pray, do I come to owe you seven hundred francs?" the old man asked, looking at Petit-Claud.

"Why, in the first place, I am engaged by you. Your rent is in question; so, as far as I am concerned, you and our debtor are one and the same person. If your son does not pay my costs in the case, you must pay them yourself.--But this is nothing. In a few hours David will be put in prison; will you allow him to go?"

"What does he owe?"

"Something like five or six thousand francs, besides the amounts owing to you and to his wife."

The speech roused all the old man's suspicions at once. He looked round the little blue-and-white bedroom at the touching scene before his eyes--at a beautiful woman weeping over a cradle, at David bowed down by anxieties, and then again at the lawyer. This was a trap set for him by that lawyer; perhaps they wanted to work upon his paternal feelings, to get money out of him? That was what it all meant. He took alarm. He went over to the cradle and fondled the child, who held out both little arms to him. No heir to an English peerage could be more tenderly cared for than this little one in that house of trouble; his little embroidered cap was lined with pale pink.

"Eh! let David get out of it as best he may. I am thinking of this child here," cried the old grandfather, "and the child's mother will approve of that. David that knows so much must know how to pay his debts."

"Now I will just put your meaning into plain language," said Petit-Claud ironically. "Look here, Papa Sechard, you are jealous of your son. Hear the truth! you put David into his present position by selling the business to him for three times its value. You ruined him to make an extortionate bargain! Yes, don't you shake your head; you sold the newspaper to the Cointets and pocketed all the proceeds, and that was as much as the whole business was worth. You bear David a grudge, not merely because you have plundered him, but because, also, your own son is a man far above yourself. You profess to be prodigiously fond of your grandson, to cloak your want of feeling for your son and his wife, because you ought to pay down money hic et nuncfor them, while you need only show a posthumous affection for your grandson. You pretend to be fond of the little fellow, lest you should be taxed with want of feeling for your own flesh and blood. That is the bottom of it, Papa Sechard."

"Did you fetch me over to hear this?" asked the old man, glowering at his lawyer, his daughter-in-law, and his son in turn.

"Monsieur!" protested poor Eve, turning to Petit-Claud, "have you vowed to ruin us? My husband had never uttered a word

against his father." (Here the old man looked cunningly at her.) "David has told me scores of times that you loved him in your way," she added, looking at her father-in-law, and understanding his suspicions.

Petit-Claud was only following out the tall Cointet's instructions. He was widening the breach between the father and son, lest Sechard senior should extricate David from his intolerable position. "The day that David Sechard goes to prison shall be the day of your introduction to Mme. de Senonches," the "tall Cointet" had said no longer ago than yesterday.

Mme. Sechard, with the quick insight of love, had divined Petit-Claud's mercenary hostility, even as she had once before felt instinctively that Cerizet was a traitor. As for David, his astonishment may be imagined; he could not understand how Petit-Claud came to know so much of his father's nature and his own history. Upright and honorable as he was, he did not dream of the relations between his lawyer and the Cointets; nor, for that matter, did he know that the Cointets were at work behind Metivier. Meanwhile old Sechard took his son's silence as an insult, and Petit-Claud, taking advantage of his client's bewilderment, beat a retreat.

"Good-bye, my dear David; you have had warning, notice of appeal doesn't invalidate the warrant for arrest. It is the only course left open to your creditors, and it will not be long before they take it. So, go away at once----Or, rather, if you will take my advice, go to the Cointets and see them about it. They have capital. If your invention is perfected and answers the purpose, go into partnership with them. After all, they are very good fellows----"

"Your invention?" broke in old Sechard.

"Why, do you suppose that your son is fool enough to let his business slip away from him without thinking of something else?" exclaimed the attorney. "He is on the brink of the discovery of a way of making paper at a cost of three francs per ream, instead of ten, he tells me."

"One more dodge for taking me in! You are all as thick as thieves in a fair. If David has found out such a plan, he has no need of me--he is a millionaire! Good-bye, my dears, and a good-day to you all," and the old man disappeared down the staircase.

"Find some way of hiding yourself," was Petit-Claud's parting word to David, and with that he hurried out to exasperate old Sechard still further. He found the vinegrower growling to himself outside in the Place du Murier, went with him as far as L'Houmeau, and there left him with a threat of putting in an execution for the costs due to him unless they were paid before the week was out.

"I will pay you if you will show me how to disinherit my son without injuring my daughter-in-law or the boy," said old Sechard, and they parted forthwith.

"How well the 'tall Cointet' knows the folk he is dealing with! It is just as he said; those seven hundred francs will prevent the father from paying seven thousand," the little lawyer thought within himself as he climbed the path to Angouleme. "Still, that old slyboots of a paper-maker must not overreach us; it is time to ask him for something besides promises."

"Well, David dear, what do you mean to do?" asked Eve, when the lawyer had followed her father-in-law.

"Marion, put your biggest pot on the fire!" called David; "I have my secret fast."

At this Eve put on her bonnet and shawl and walking shoes with feverish haste.

"Kolb, my friend, get ready to go out," she said, "and come with me; if there is any way out of this hell, I must find it."

When Eve had gone out, Marion spoke to David. "Do be sensible, sir," she said, "or the mistress will fret herself to death. Make some money to pay off your debts, and then you can try to find treasure at your ease----"

"Don't talk, Marion," said David; "I am going to overcome my last difficulty, and then I can apply for the patent and the improvement on the patent at the same time."

This "improvement on the patent" is the curse of the French patentee. A man may spend ten years of his life in working out some obscure industrial problem; and when he has invented some piece of machinery, or made a discovery of some kind, he takes out a patent and imagines that he has a right to his own invention; then there comes a competitor; and unless the first inventor has foreseen all possible contingencies, the second comer makes an "improvement on the patent" with a screw or a nut, and takes the whole thing out of his hands. The discovery of a cheap material for paper pulp, therefore, is by no means the conclusion of the whole matter. David Sechard was anxiously looking ahead on all sides lest the fortune sought in the teeth of such difficulties should be snatched out of his hands at the last. Dutch paper as flax paper is still called, though it is no longer made in Holland, is slightly sized; but every sheet is sized separately by hand, and this increases the cost of production. If it were possible to discover some way of sizing the paper in the pulping-trough, with some inexpensive glue, like that in use today (though even now it is not quite perfect), there would be no "improvement on the patent" to fear. For the past month, accordingly, David had been making experiments in sizing pulp. He had two discoveries before him.

Eve went to see her mother. Fortunately, it so happened that Mme. Chardon was nursing the deputy-magistrate's wife, who had just given the Milauds of Nevers an heir presumptive; and Eve, in her distrust of all attorneys and notaries, took into her head to apply for advice to the legal guardian of widows and orphans. She wanted to know if she could relieve David from his embarrassments by taking them upon herself and selling her claims upon the estate, and besides, she had some hope of discovering the truth as to Petit-Claud's unaccountable conduct. The official, struck with Mme. Sechard's beauty, received her not only with the respect due to a woman but with a sort of courtesy to which Eve was not accustomed. She saw in the magistrate's face an expression which, since her marriage, she had seen in no eyes but Kolb's; and for a beautiful woman like Eve, this expression is the criterion by which men are judged. When passion, or self-interest, or age dims that spark of unquestioning fealty that gleams in a young man's eyes, a woman feels a certain mistrust of him, and begins to observe him critically. The Cointets, Cerizet, and Petit-Claud--all the men whom Eve felt instinctively to be her enemies--had turned hard, indifferent eyes on her; with the deputy-magistrate, therefore, she felt at ease, although, in spite of his kindly courtesy, he swept all her hopes away by his first words.

"It is not certain, madame, that the Court-Royal will reverse the judgment of the court restricting your lien on your husband's property, for payment of moneys due to you by the terms of your marriage-contract, to household goods and chattels. Your privilege ought not to be used to defraud the other creditors. But in any case, you will be allowed to take your share of the proceeds with the other creditors, and your father-in-law likewise, as a privileged creditor, for arrears of rent. When the court has given the order, other points may be raised as to the 'contribution,' as we call it, when a schedule of the debts is drawn up, and the creditors are paid a dividend in proportion to their claims."

"Then M. Petit-Claud is bringing us to bankruptcy," she cried.

"Petit-Claud is carrying out your husband's instructions," said the magistrate; "he is anxious to gain time, so his attorney says. In my opinion, you would perhaps do better to waive the appeal and buy in at the sale the indispensable implements for carrying on the business; you and your father-in-law together might do this, you to the extent of your claim through your marriage contract, and he for his arrears of rent. But that would be bringing the matter to an end too soon perhaps. The lawyers are making a good thing out of your case."

"But then I should be entirely in M. Sechard's father's hands. I should owe him the hire of the machinery as well as the house-rent; and my husband would still be open to further proceedings from M. Metivier, for M. Metivier would have had almost nothing."

"That is true, madame."

"Very well, then we should be even worse off than we are."

"The arm of the law, madame, is at the creditor's disposal. You have received three thousand francs, and you must of necessity repay the money."

"Oh, sir, can you think that we are capable----" Eve suddenly came to a stop. She saw that her justification might injure her brother.

"Oh! I know quite well that it is an obscure affair, that the debtors on the one side are honest, scrupulous, and even behaving handsomely; and the creditor, on the other, is only a cat's-paw----"

Eve, aghast, looked at him with bewildered eyes.

"You can understand," he continued, with a look full of homely shrewdness, "that we on the bench have plenty of time to think over all that goes on under our eyes, while the gentlemen in court are arguing with each other."

Eve went home in despair over her useless effort. That evening at seven o'clock, Doublon came with the notification of imprisonment for debt. The proceedings had reached the acute stage.

"After this, I can only go out after nightfall," said David.

Eve and Mme. Chardon burst into tears. To be in hiding was for them a shameful thing. As for Kolb and Marion, they were more alarmed for David because they had long since made up their minds that there was no guile in their master's nature; so frightened were they on his account, that they came upstairs under pretence of asking whether they could do anything, and found Eve and Mme. Chardon in tears; the three whose life had been so straightforward hitherto were overcome by the thought that David must go into hiding. And how, moreover, could they hope to escape the invisible spies who henceforth would dog every least movement of a man, unluckily so absent-minded?

"Gif montame vill vait ein liddle kvarter hour, she can regonnoitre der enemy's camp," put in Kolb. "You shall see dot I oonderstand mein pizness; for gif I look like ein German, I am ein drue Vrenchman, and vat is more, I am ver' conning."

"Oh! madame, do let him go," begged Marion. "He is only thinking of saving his master; he hasn't another thought in his head. Kolb is not an Alsacien, he is--eh! well--a regular Newfoundland dog for rescuing folk."

"Go, my good Kolb," said David; "we have still time to do something."

Kolb hurried off to pay a visit to the bailiff; and it so fell out that David's enemies were in Doublon's office, holding a council as to the best way of securing him.

The arrest of a debtor is an unheard-of thing in the country, an abnormal proceeding if ever there was one. Everybody, in the first place, knows everybody else, and creditor and debtor being bound to meet each other daily all their lives long, nobody likes to take this odious course. When a defaulter--to use the provincial term for a debtor, for they do not mince their words in the provinces when speaking of this legalized method of helping yourself to another man's goods--when a defaulter plans a failure on a large scale, he takes sanctuary in Paris. Paris is a kind of City of Refuge for provincial bankrupts, an almost impenetrable retreat; the writ of the pursuing bailiff has no force beyond the limits of his jurisdiction, and there are other obstacles rendering it almost invalid. Wherefore the Paris bailiff is empowered to enter the house of a third party to seize the person of the debtor, while for the bailiff of the provinces the domicile is absolutely inviolable. The law probably makes this exception as to Paris, because there it is the rule for two or more families to live under the same roof; but in the provinces the bailiff who wishes to make forcible entry must have an order from the Justice of the Peace; and so wide a discretion is allowed the Justice of the Peace, that he is practically able to give or withhold assistance to the bailiffs. To the honor of the Justices, it should be said, that they dislike the office, and are by no means anxious to assist blind passions or revenge.

There are, besides, other and no less serious difficulties in the way of arrest for debt--difficulties which tend to temper the severity of legislation, and public opinion not infrequently makes a dead letter of the law. In great cities there are poor or degraded wretches enough; poverty and vice know no scruples, and consent to play the spy, but in a little country town, people know each other too well to earn wages of the bailiff; the meanest creature who should lend himself to dirty work of this kind would be forced to leave the place. In the absence of recognized machinery, therefore, the arrest of a debtor is a problem presenting no small difficulty; it becomes a kind of strife of ingenuity between the bailiff and the debtor, and matter for many pleasant stories in the newspapers.

Cointet the elder did not choose to appear in the affair; but the fat Cointet openly said that he was acting for Metivier, and went to Doublon, taking Cerizet with him. Cerizet was his foreman now, and had promised his co-operation in return for a thousand-franc note. Doublon could reckon upon two of his understrappers, and thus the Cointets had four bloodhounds already on the victim's track. At the actual time of arrest, Doublon could furthermore count upon the police force, who are bound, if required, to assist a bailiff in the performance of his duty. The two men, Doublon himself, and the visitors were all closeted together in the private office, beyond the public office, on the ground floor.

A tolerably wide-paved lobby, a kind of passage-way, led to the public office. The gilded scutcheons of the court, with the word "Bailiff" printed thereon in large black letters, hung outside on the house wall on either side the door. Both office windows gave upon the street, and were protected by heavy iron bars; but the private office looked into the garden at the back, wherein Doublon, an adorer of Pomona, grew espaliers with marked success. Opposite the office door you beheld the door of the kitchen, and, beyond the kitchen, the staircase that ascended to the first story. The house was situated in a narrow street at the back of the new Law Courts, then in process of construction, and only finished after 1830.--These details are necessary if Kolb's adventures are to be intelligible to the reader.

It was Kolb's idea to go to the bailiff, to pretend to be willing to betray his master, and in this way to discover the traps which would be laid for David. Kolb told the servant who opened the door that he wanted to speak to M. Doublon on business. The servant was busy washing up her plates and dishes, and not very well pleased at Kolb's interruption; she pushed open the door of the outer office, and bade him wait there till her master was at liberty; then, as he was a stranger to her, she told the master in the private office that "a man" wanted to speak to him. Now, "a man" so invariably means "a peasant," that Doublon said, "Tell him to wait," and Kolb took a seat close to the door of the private office. There were voices talking within.

"Ah, by the by, how do you mean to set about it? For, if we can catch him tomorrow, it will be so much time saved." It was the fat Cointet who spoke.

"Nothing easier; the gaffer has come fairly by his nickname," said Cerizet.

At the sound of the fat Cointet's voice, Kolb guessed at once that they were talking about his master, especially as the sense of the words began to dawn upon him; but, when he recognized Cerizet's tones, his astonishment grew more and more.

"Und dat fellow haf eaten his pread!" he thought, horror-stricken.

"We must do it in this way, boys," said Doublon. "We will post our men, at good long intervals, about the Rue de Beaulieu and the Place du Murier in every direction, so that we can follow the gaffer (I like that word) without his knowledge. We will not lose sight of him until he is safe inside the house where he means to lie in hiding (as he thinks); there we will leave him in peace for awhile; then some fine day we will come across him before sunrise or sunset."

"But what is he doing now, at this moment? He may be slipping through our fingers," said the fat Cointet.

"He is in his house," answered Doublon; "if he left it, I should know. I have one witness posted in the Place du Murier, another at the corner of the Law Courts, and another thirty paces from the house. If our man came out, they would whistle; he could not make three paces from his door but I should know of it at once from the signal."

(Bailiffs speak of their understrappers by the polite title of "witnesses.")

Here was better hap than Kolb had expected! He went noiselessly out of the office, and spoke to the maid in the kitchen.

"Meestair Touplon ees encaged for som time to kom," he said; "I vill kom back early tomorrow morning."

A sudden idea had struck the Alsacien, and he proceeded to put it into execution. Kolb had served in a cavalry regiment; he hurried off to see a livery stable-keeper, an acquaintance of his, picked out a horse, had it saddled, and rushed back to the Place du Murier. He found Madame Eve in the lowest depths of despondency.

"What is it, Kolb?" asked David, when the Alsacien's face looked in upon them, scared but radiant.

"You have scountrels all arount you. De safest way ees to hide de master. Haf montame thought of hiding the master anywheres?"

When Kolb, honest fellow, had explained the whole history of Cerizet's treachery, of the circle traced about the house, and of the fat Cointet's interest in the affair, and given the family some inkling of the schemes set on foot by the Cointets against the master,--then David's real position gradually became fatally clear.

"It is the Cointet's doing!" cried poor Eve, aghast at the news; "they are proceeding against you! that accounts for Metivier's hardness. . . . They are paper-makers--David! they want your secret!"

"But what can we do to escape them?" exclaimed Mme. Chardon.

"If de misdress had some liddle blace vere the master could pe hidden," said Kolb; "I bromise to take him dere so dot nopody shall know."

"Wait till nightfall, and go to Basine Clerget," said Eve. "I will go now and arrange it all with her. In this case, Basine will be like another self to me."

"Spies will follow you," David said at last, recovering some presence of mind. "How can we find a way of communicating with Basine if none of us can go to her?"

"Montame kan go," said Kolb. "Here ees my scheme--I go out mit der master, ve draws der vischtlers on our drack. Montame kan go to Montemoiselle Clerchet; nopody vill vollow her. I haf a horse; I take de master oop behint; und der teufel is in it if they katches us."

"Very well; good-bye, dear," said poor Eve, springing to her husband's arms; "none of us can go to see you, the risk is too great. We must say good-bye for the whole time that your imprisonment lasts. We will write to each other; Basine will post your letters, and I will write under cover to her."

No sooner did David and Kolb come out of the house than they heard a sharp whistle, and were followed to the livery stable. Once there, Kolb took his master up behind him, with a caution to keep tight hold.

"Veestle avay, mind goot vriends! I care not von rap," cried Kolb. "You vill not datch an old trooper," and the old cavalry man clapped both spurs to his horse, and was out into the country and the darkness not merely before the spies could follow, but before they had time to discover the direction that he took.

Eve meanwhile went out on the tolerably ingenious pretext of asking advise of Postel, sat awhile enduring the insulting pity that spends itself in words, left the Postel family, and stole away unseen to Basine Clerget, told her troubles, and asked for help and shelter. Basine, for greater safety, had brought Eve into her bedroom, and now she opened the door of a little closet, lighted only by a skylight in such a way that prying eyes could not see into it. The two friends unstopped the flue which opened into the chimney of the stove in the workroom, where the girls heated their irons. Eve and Basine spread ragged coverlets over the brick floor to deaden any sound that David might make, put in a truckle bed, a stove for his experiments, and a table and a chair. Basine promised to bring food in the night; and as no one had occasion to enter her room, David might defy his enemies one and all, or even detectives.

"At last!" Eve said, with her arms about her friend, "at last he is in safety."

Eve went back to Postel to submit a fresh doubt that had occurred to her, she said. She would like the opinion of such an experienced member of the Chamber of Commerce; she so managed that he escorted her home, and listened patiently to his commiseration.

"Would this have happened if you had married me?"--all the little druggist's remarks were pitched in this key.

Then he went home again to find Mme. Postel jealous of Mme. Sechard, and furious with her spouse for his polite attention to that beautiful woman. The apothecary advanced the opinion that little red-haired women were preferable to tall, dark women, who, like fine horses, were always in the stable, he said. He gave proofs of his sincerity, no doubt, for Mme. Postel was very sweet to him next day.

"We may be easy," Eve said to her mother and Marion, whom she found still "in a taking," in the latter's phrase.

"Oh! they are gone," said Marion, when Eve looked unthinkingly round the room.

One league out of Angouleme on the main road to Paris, Kolb stopped.

"Vere shall we go?"

"To Marsac," said David; "since we are on the way already, I will try once more to soften my father's heart."

"I would rader mount to der assault of a pattery," said Kolb, "your resbected fader haf no heart whatefer."

The ex-pressman had no belief in his son; he judged him from the outside point of view, and waited for results. He had no idea, to begin with, that he had plundered David, nor did he make allowance for the very different circumstances under which they had begun life; he said to himself, "I set him up with a printing-house, just as I found it myself; and he, knowing a thousand times more than I did, cannot keep it going." He was mentally incapable of understanding his son; he laid the blame of failure upon him, and even prided himself, as it were on his superiority to a far greater intellect than his own, with the thought, "I am securing his bread for him."

Moralists will never succeed in making us comprehend the full extent of the influence of sentiment upon self-interest, an influence every whit as strong as the action of interest upon our sentiments; for every law of our nature works in two ways, and acts and reacts upon us.

David, on his side, understood his father, and in his sublime charity forgave him. Kolb and David reached Marsac at eight o'clock, and suddenly came in upon the old man as he was finishing his dinner, which, by force of circumstances, came very near bedtime.

"I see you because there is no help for it," said old Sechard with a sour smile.

"Und how should you and mein master meet? He soars in der shkies, and you are always mit your vines! You bay for him, that's vot you are a fader for----"

"Come, Kolb, off with you. Put up the horse at Mme. Courtois' so as to save inconvenience here; fathers are always in the right, remember that."

Kolb went off, growling like a chidden dog, obedient but protesting; and David proposed to give his father indisputable proof of his discovery, while reserving his secret. He offered to give him an interest in the affair in return for money paid down; a sufficient sum to release him from his present difficulties, with or without a further amount of capital to be employed in developing the invention.

"And how are you going to prove to me that you can make good paper that costs nothing out of nothing, eh?" asked the ex-printer, giving his son a glance, vinous, it may be, but keen, inquisitive, and covetous; a look like a flash of lightning from a sodden cloud; for the old "bear," faithful to his traditions, never went to bed without a nightcap, consisting of a couple of bottles of excellent old wine, which he "tippled down" of an evening, to use his own expression.

"Nothing simpler," said David; "I have none of the paper about me, for I came here to be out of Doublon's way; and having come so far, I thought I might as well come to you at Marsac as borrow of a money-lender. I have nothing on me but my clothes. Shut me up somewhere on the premises, so that nobody can come in and see me at work, and----"

"What? you will not let me see you at your work then?" asked the old man, with an ugly look at his son.

"You have given me to understand plainly, father, that in matters of business there is no question of father and son----"

"Ah! you distrust the father that gave you life!"

"No; the other father who took away the means of earning a livelihood."

"Each for himself, you are right!" said the old man. "Very good, I will put you in the cellar."

"I will go down there with Kolb. You must let me have a large pot for my pulp," said David; then he continued, without noticing the quick look his father gave him,--"and you must find artichoke and asparagus stalks for me, and nettles, and the reeds that you cut by the stream side, and tomorrow morning I will come out of your cellar with some splendid paper."

"If you can do that," hiccoughed the "bear," "I will let you have, perhaps--I will see, that is, if I can let you have--pshaw! twenty-five thousand francs. On condition, mind, that you make as much for me every year."

"Put me to the proof, I am quite willing," cried David. "Kolb! take the horse and go to Mansle, quick, buy a large hair sieve for me of a cooper, and some glue of the grocer, and come back again as soon as you can."

"There! drink," said old Sechard, putting down a bottle of wine, a loaf, and the cold remains of the dinner. "You will need your strength. I will go and look for your bits of green stuff; green rags you use for your pulp, and a trifle too green, I am afraid."

Two hours later, towards eleven o'clock that night, David and Kolb took up their quarters in a little out-house against the cellar wall; they found the floor paved with runnel tiles, and all the apparatus used in Angoumois for the manufacture of Cognac brandy.

"Pans and firewood! Why, it is as good as a factory made on purpose!" cried David.

"Very well, good-night," said old Sechard; "I shall lock you in, and let both the dogs loose; nobody will bring you any paper, I am sure. You show me those sheets tomorrow, and I give you my word I will be your partner and the business will be straightforward and properly managed."

David and Kolb, locked into the distillery, spent nearly two hours in macerating the stems, using a couple of logs for mallets. The fire blazed up, the water boiled. About two o'clock in the morning, Kolb heard a sound which David was too busy to notice, a kind of deep breath like a suppressed hiccough. Snatching up one of the two lighted dips, he looked round the walls, and beheld old Sechard's empurpled countenance filling up a square opening above a door hitherto hidden by a pile of empty casks in the cellar itself. The cunning old man had brought David and Kolb into his underground distillery by the outer door, through which the casks were rolled when full. The inner door had been made so that he could roll his puncheons straight from the cellar into the distillery, instead of taking them round through the yard.

"Aha! thees eies not fair blay, you vant to shvindle your son!" cried the Alsacien. "Do you kow vot you do ven you trink ein pottle of vine? You gif goot trink to ein bad scountrel."

"Oh, father!" cried David.

"I came to see if you wanted anything," said old Sechard, half sobered by this time.

"Und it was for de inderest vot you take in us dot you brought der liddle ladder!" commented Kolb, as he pushed the casks aside and flung open the door; and there, in fact, on a short step-ladder, the old man stood in his shirt.

292

"Risking your health!" said David.

"I think I must be walking in my sleep," said old Sechard, coming down in confusion. "Your want of confidence in your father set me dreaming; I dreamed you were making a pact with the Devil to do impossible things."

"Der teufel," said Kolb; "dot is your own bassion for de liddle goldfinches."

"Go back to bed again, father," said David; "lock us in if you will, but you may save yourself the trouble of coming down again. Kolb will mount guard."

At four o'clock in the morning David came out of the distillery; he had been careful to leave no sign of his occupation behind him; but he brought out some thirty sheets of paper that left nothing to be desired in fineness, whiteness, toughness, and strength, all of them bearing by way of water-mark the impress of the uneven hairs of the sieve. The old man took up the samples and put his tongue to them, the lifelong habit of the pressman, who tests papers in this way. He felt it between his thumb and finger, crumpled and creased it, put it through all the trials by which a printer assays the quality of a sample submitted to him, and when it was found wanting in no respect, he still would not allow that he was beaten.

"We have yet to know how it takes an impression," he said, to avoid praising his son.

"Funny man!" exclaimed Kolb.

The old man was cool enough now. He cloaked his feigned hesitation with paternal dignity.

"I wish to tell you in fairness, father, that even now it seems to me that paper costs more than it ought to do; I want to solve the problem of sizing it in the pulping-trough. I have just that one improvement to make."

"Oho! so you are trying to trick me!"

"Well, shall I tell you? I can size the pulp as it is, but so far I cannot do it evenly, and the surface is as rough as a burr!"

"Very good, size your pulp in the trough, and you shall have my money."

"Mein master will nefer see de golor of your money," declared Kolb.

"Father," he began, "I have never borne you any grudge for making over the business to me at such an exorbitant valuation; I have seen the father through it all. I have said to myself--'The old man has worked very hard, and he certainly gave me a better bringing up than I had a right to expect; let him enjoy the fruits of his toil in peace, and in his own way.--I even gave up my mother's money to you. I began encumbered with debt, and bore all the burdens that you put upon me without a murmur. Well, harassed for debts that were not of my making, with no bread in the house, and my feet held to the flames, I have found out the secret. I have struggled on patiently till my strength is exhausted. It is perhaps your duty to help me, but do not give me a thought; think of a woman and a little one" (David could not keep back the tears at this); "think of them, and give them help and protection.--Kolb and Marion have given me their savings; will you do less?" he cried at last, seeing that his father was as cold as the impression-stone.

"And that was not enough for you," said the old man, without the slightest sense of shame; "why, you would waste the wealth of the Indies! Good-night! I am too ignorant to lend a hand in schemes got up on purpose to exploit me. A monkey will never gobble down a bear" (alluding to the workshop nicknames); "I am a vinegrower, I am not a banker. And what is more, look you, business between father and son never turns out well. Stay and eat your dinner here; you shan't say that you came for nothing."

There are some deep-hearted natures that can force their own pain down into inner depths unsuspected by those dearest to them; and with them, when anguish forces its way to the surface and is visible, it is only after a mighty upheaval. David's nature was one of these. Eve had thoroughly understood the noble character of the man. But now that the depths had been stirred, David's father took the wave of anguish that passed over his son's features for a child's trick, an attempt to "get round" his father, and his bitter grief for mortification over the failure of the attempt. Father and son parted in anger.

David and Kolb reached Angouleme on the stroke of midnight. They came back on foot, and steathily, like burglars. Before one o'clock in the morning David was installed in the impenetrable hiding-place prepared by his wife in Basine Clerget's house. No one saw him enter it, and the pity that henceforth should shelter David was the most resourceful pity of all--the pity of a work-girl.

Kolb bragged that day that he had saved his master on horseback, and only left him in a carrier's van well on the way to Limoges. A sufficient provision of raw material had been laid up in Basine's cellar, and Kolb, Marion, Mme. Sechard, and her mother had no communication with the house.

Two days after the scene at Marsac, old Sechard came hurrying to Angouleme and his daughter-in-law. Covetousness had brought him. There were three clear weeks ahead before the vintage began, and he thought he would be on the look-out for squalls, to use his own expression. To this end he took up his quarters in one of the attics which he had reserved by the terms of the lease, wilfully shutting his eyes to the bareness and want that made his son's home desolate. If they owed him rent, they could well afford to keep him. He ate his food from a tinned iron plate, and made no marvel at it. "I began in the same way," he told his daughter-in-law, when she apologized for the absence of silver spoons.

Marion was obliged to run into debt for necessaries for them all. Kolb was earning a franc for daily wage as a brick-layer's laborer; and at last poor Eve, who, for the sake of her husband and child, had sacrificed her last resources to entertain David's father, saw that she had only ten francs left. She had hoped to the last to soften the old miser's heart by her affectionate respect, and patience, and pretty attentions; but old Sechard was obdurate as ever. When she saw him turn the same cold eyes on her, the same look that the Cointets had given her, and Petit-Claud and Cerizet, she tried to watch and guess old Sechard's intentions. Trouble thrown away! Old Sechard, never sober, never drunk, was inscrutable; intoxication is a double veil. If the old man's tipsiness was sometimes real, it was quite often feigned for the purpose of extracting David's secret from his wife. Sometimes he coaxed, sometimes he frightened his daughter-in-law.

"I will drink up my property; I will buy an annuity," he would threaten when Eve told him that she knew nothing.

The humiliating struggle was wearing her out; she kept silence at last, lest she should show disrespect to her husband's father.

"But, father," she said one day when driven to extremity, "there is a very simple way of finding out everything. Pay David's debts; he will come home, and you can settle it between you."

"Ha! that is what you want to get out of me, is it?" he cried. "It is as well to know!"

But if Sechard had no belief in his son, he had plenty of faith in the Cointets. He went to consult them, and the Cointets dazzled him of set purpose, telling him that his son's experiments might mean millions of francs.

"If David can prove that he has succeeded, I shall not hesitate to go into partnership with him, and reckon his discovery as half the capital," the tall Cointet told him.

The suspicious old man learned a good deal over nips of brandy with the work-people, and something more by questioning Petit-Claud and feigning stupidity; and at length he felt convinced that the Cointets were the real movers behind Metivier; they were plotting to ruin Sechard's printing establishment, and to lure him (Sechard) on to pay his son's debts by holding out the discovery as a bait. The old man of the people did not suspect that Petit-Claud was in the plot, nor had he any idea of the toils woven to ensnare the great secret. A day came at last when he grew angry and out of patience with the daughter-in-law who would not so much as tell him where David was hiding; he determined to force the laboratory door, for he had discovered that David was wont to make his experiments in the workshop where the rollers were melted down.

He came downstairs very early one morning and set to work upon the lock.

294

"Hey! Papa Sechard, what are you doing there?" Marion called out. (She had risen at daybreak to go to her papermill, and now she sprang across to the workshop.)

"I am in my own house, am I not?" said the old man, in some confusion.

"Oh, indeed, are you turning thief in your old age? You are not drunk this time either----I shall go straight to the mistress and tell her."

"Hold your tongue, Marion," said Sechard, drawing two crowns of six francs each from his pocket. "There----"

"I will hold my tongue, but don't you do it again," said Marion, shaking her finger at him, "or all Angouleme shall hear of it."

The old man had scarcely gone out, however, when Marion went up to her mistress.

"Look, madame," she said, "I have had twelve francs out of your father-in-law, and here they are----"

"How did you do it?"

"What was he wanting to do but to take a look at the master's pots and pans and stuff, to find out the secret, forsooth. I knew quite well that there was nothing in the little place, but I frightened him and talked as if he were setting about robbing his son, and he gave me twelve francs to say nothing about it."

Just at that moment Basine came in radiant, and with a letter for her friend, a letter from David written on magnificent paper, which she handed over when they were alone.

"MY ADORED EVE,--I am writing to you the first letter on my first sheet of paper made by the new process. I have solved the problem of sizing the pulp in the trough at last. A pound of pulp costs five sous, even supposing that the raw material is grown on good soil with special culture; three francs' worth of sized pulp will make a ream of paper, at twelve pounds to the ream. I am quite sure that I can lessen the weight of books by one-half. The envelope, the letter, and samples enclosed are all manufactured in different ways. I kiss you; you shall have wealth now to add to our happiness, everything else we had before."

"There!" said Eve, handing the samples to her father-in-law, "when the vintage is over let your son have the money, give him a chance to make his fortune, and you shall be repaid ten times over; he has succeeded at last!"

Old Sechard hurried at once to the Cointets. Every sample was tested and minutely examined; the prices, from three to ten francs per ream, were noted on each separate slip; some were sized, others unsized; some were of almost metallic purity, others soft as Japanese paper; in color there was every possible shade of white. If old Sechard and the two Cointets had been Jews examining diamonds, their eyes could not have glistened more eagerly.

"Your son is on the right track," the fat Cointet said at length.

"Very well, pay his debts," returned old Sechard.

"By all means, if he will take us into partnership," said the tall Cointet.

"You are extortioners!" cried old Sechard. "You have been suing him under Metivier's name, and you mean me to buy you off; that is the long and the short of it. Not such a fool, gentlemen----"

The brothers looked at one another, but they contrived to hide their surprise at the old miser's shrewdness.

"We are not millionaires," said fat Cointet; "we do not discount bills for amusement. We should think ourselves well off if we could pay ready money for our bits of accounts for rags, and we still give bills to our dealer."

"The experiment ought to be tried first on a much larger scale," the tall Cointet said coldly; "sometimes you try a thing with a saucepan and succeed, and fail utterly when you experiment with bulk. You should help your son out of difficulties."

"Yes; but when my son is at liberty, would he take me as his partner?"

"That is no business of ours," said the fat Cointet. "My good man, do you suppose that when you have paid some ten thousand francs for your son, that there is an end of it? It will cost two thousand francs to take out a patent; there will be journeys to Paris; and before going to any expense, it would be prudent to do as my brother suggests, and make a thousand reams or so; to try several whole batches to make sure. You see, there is nothing you must be so much on your guard against as an inventor."

"I have a liking for bread ready buttered myself," added the tall Cointet.

All through that night the old man ruminated over this dilemma--"If I pay David's debts, he will be set at liberty, and once set at liberty, he need not share his fortune with me unless he chooses. He knows very well that I cheated him over the first partnership, and he will not care to try a second; so it is to my interest to keep him shut up, the wretched boy."

The Cointets knew enough of Sechard senior to see that they should hunt in couples. All three said to themselves-- "Experiments must be tried before the discovery can take any practical shape. David Sechard must be set at liberty before those experiments can be made; and David Sechard, set at liberty, will slip through our fingers."

Everybody involved, moreover, had his own little afterthought.

Petit-Claud, for instance, said, "As soon as I am married, I will slip my neck out of the Cointets' yoke; but till then I shall hold on."

The tall Cointet thought, "I would rather have David under lock and key, and then I should be master of the situation."

Old Sechard, too, thought, "If I pay my son's debts, he will repay me with a 'Thank you!'"

Eve, hard pressed (for the old man threatened now to turn her out of the house), would neither reveal her husband's hiding-place, nor even send proposals of a safe-conduct. She could not feel sure of finding so safe a refuge a second time.

"Set your son at liberty," she told her father-in-law, "and then you shall know everything."

The four interested persons sat, as it were, with a banquet spread before them, none of them daring to begin, each one suspicious and watchful of his neighbor. A few days after David went into hiding, Petit-Claud went to the mill to see the tall Cointet.

"I have done my best," he said; "David has gone into prison of his own accord somewhere or other; he is working out some improvement there in peace. It is no fault of mine if you have not gained your end; are you going to keep your promise?"

"Yes, if we succeed," said the tall Cointet. "Old Sechard was here only a day or two ago; he came to ask us some questions as to paper-making. The old miser has got wind of his son's invention; he wants to turn it to his own account, so there is some hope of a partnership. You are with the father and the son----"

"Be the third person in the trinity and give them up," smiled Petit-Claud.

"Yes," said Cointet. "When you have David in prison, or bound to us by a deed of partnership, you shall marry Mlle. de la Haye."

"Is that your ultimatum?"

"My sine qua non," said Cointet, "since we are speaking in foreign languages."

"Then here is mine in plain language," Petit-Claud said drily.

"Ah! let us have it," answered Cointet, with some curiosity.

"You will present me tomorrow to Mme. de Sononches, and do something definite for me; you will keep your word, in short; or I will clear off Sechard's debts myself, sell my practice, and go into partnership with him. I will not be duped. You have spoken out, and I am doing the same. I have given proof, give me proof of your sincerity. You have all, and I have nothing. If you won't

296

do fairly by me, I know your cards, and I shall play for my own hand."

The tall Cointet took his hat and umbrella, his face at the same time taking its Jesuitical expression, and out he went, bidding Petit-Claud come with him.

"You shall see, my friend, whether I have prepared your way for you," said he.

The shrewd paper-manufacturer saw his danger at a glance; and saw, too, that with a man like Petit-Claud it was better to play above board. Partly to be prepared for contingencies, partly to satisfy his conscience, he had dropped a word or two to the point in the ear of the ex-consul-general, under the pretext of putting Mlle. de la Haye's financial position before that gentleman.

"I have the man for Francoise," he had said; "for with thirty thousand francs of dot, a girl must not expect too much nowadays."

"We will talk it over later on," answered Francis du Hautoy, ex-consul-general. "Mme. de Senonches' positon has altered very much since Mme. de Bargeton went away; we very likely might marry Francoise to some elderly country gentleman."

"She would disgrace herself if you did," Cointet returned in his dry way. "Better marry her to some capable, ambitious young man; you could help him with your influence, and he would make a good position for his wife."

"We shall see," said Francis du Hautoy; "her godmother ought to be consulted first, in any case."

When M. de Bargeton died, his wife sold the great house in the Rue du Minage. Mme. de Senonches, finding her own house scarcely large enough, persuaded M. de Senonches to buy the Hotel de Bargeton, the cradle of Lucien Chardon's ambitions, the scene of the earliest events in his career. Zephirine de Senonches had it in mind to succeed to Mme. de Bargeton; she, too, would be a kind of queen in Angouleme; she would have "a salon," and be a great lady, in short. There was a schism in Angouleme, a strife dating from the late M. de Bargeton's duel with M. de Chandour. Some maintained that Louise de Negrepelisse was blameless, others believed in Stanislas de Chandour's scandals. Mme. de Senonches declared for the Bargetons, and began by winning over that faction. Many frequenters of the Hotel de Bargeton had been so accustomed for years to their nightly game of cards in the house that they could not leave it, and Mme. de Senonches turned this fact to account. She received every evening, and certainly gained all the ground lost by Amelie de Chandour, who set up for a rival.

Francis du Hautoy, living in the inmost circle of nobility in Angouleme, went so far as to think of marrying Francoise to old M. de Severac, Mme. du Brossard having totally failed to capture that gentleman for her daughter; and when Mme. de Bargeton reappeared as the prefect's wife, Zephirine's hopes for her dear goddaughter waxed high, indeed. The Comtesse du Chatelet, so she argued, would be sure to use her influence for her champion.

Boniface Cointet had Angouleme at his fingers' ends; he saw all the difficulties at a glance, and resolved to sweep them out of the way by a bold stroke that only a Tartuffe's brain could invent. The puny lawyer was not a little amused to find his fellow-conspirator keeping his word with him; not a word did Petit-Claud utter; he respected the musings of his companion, and they walked the whole way from the paper-mill to the Rue du Minage in silence.

"Monsieur and madame are at breakfast"--this announcement met the ill-timed visitors on the steps.

"Take in our names, all the same," said the tall Cointet; and feeling sure of his position, he followed immediately behind the servant and introduced his companion to the elaborately-affected Zephirine, who was breakfasting in company with M. Francis du Hautoy and Mlle. de la Haye. M. de Senonches had gone, as usual, for a day's shooting over M. de Pimentel's land.

"M. Petit-Claud is the young lawyer of whom I spoke to you, madame; he will go through the trust accounts when your fair ward comes of age."

The ex-diplomatist made a quick scrutiny of Petit-Claud, who, for his part, was looking furtively at the "fair ward." As for

Zephirine, who heard of the matter for the first time, her surprise was so great that she dropped her fork.

Mlle. de la Haye, a shrewish young woman with an ill-tempered face, a waist that could scarcely be called slender, a thin figure, and colorless, fair hair, in spite of a certain little air that she had, was by no means easy to marry. The "parentage unknown" on her birth certificate was the real bar to her entrance into the sphere where her godmother's affection stove to establish her. Mlle. de la Haye, ignorant of her real position, was very hard to please; the richest merchant in L'Houmeau had found no favor in her sight. Cointet saw the sufficiently significant expression of the young lady's face at the sight of the little lawyer, and turning, beheld a precisely similar grimace on Petit-Claud's countenance. Mme. de Senonches and Francis looked at each other, as if in search of an excuse for getting rid of the visitors. All this Cointet saw. He asked M. du Hautoy for the favor of a few minutes' speech with him, and the pair went together into the drawing-room.

"Fatherly affection is blinding you, sir," he said bluntly. "You will not find it an easy thing to marry your daughter; and, acting in your interest throughout, I have put you in a position from which you cannot draw back; for I am fond of Francoise, she is my ward. Now --Petit-Claud knows everything! His overweening ambition is a guarantee for our dear child's happiness; for, in the first place, Francoise will do as she likes with her husband; and, in the second, he wants your influence. You can ask the new prefect for the post of crown attorney for him in the court here. M. Milaud is definitely appointed to Nevers, Petit-Claud will sell his practice, you will have no difficulty in obtaining a deputy public prosecutor's place for him; and it will not be long before he becomes attorney for the crown, president of the court, deputy, what you will."

Francis went back to the dining-room and behaved charmingly to his daughter's suitor. He gave Mme. de Senonches a look, and brought the scene to a close with an invitation to dine with them on the morrow; Petit-Claud must come and discuss the business in hand. He even went downstairs and as far as the corner with the visitors, telling Petit-Claud that after Cointet's recommendation, both he and Mme. de Senonches were disposed to approve all that Mlle. de la Haye's trustee had arranged for the welfare of that little angel.

"Oh!" cried Petit-Claud, as they came away, "what a plain girl! I have been taken in----"

"She looks a lady-like girl," returned Cointet, "and besides, if she were a beauty, would they give her to you? Eh! my dear fellow, thirty thousand francs and the influence of Mme. de Senonches and the Comtesse du Chatelet! Many a small landowner would be wonderfully glad of the chance, and all the more so since M. Francis du Hautoy is never likely to marry, and all that he has will go to the girl. Your marriage is as good as settled."

"How?"

"That is what I am just going to tell you," returned Cointet, and he gave his companion an account of his recent bold stroke. "M. Milaud is just about to be appointed attorney for the crown at Nevers, my dear fellow," he continued; "sell your practice, and in ten years' time you will be Keeper of the Seals. You are not the kind of a man to draw back from any service required of you by the Court."

"Very well," said Petit-Claud, his zeal stirred by the prospect of such a career, "very well, be in the Place du Murier tomorrow at half-past four; I will see old Sechard in the meantime; we will have a deed of partnership drawn up, and the father and the son shall be bound thereby, and delivered to the third person of the trinity --Cointet, to wit."

To return to Lucien in Paris. On the morrow of the loss announced in his letter, he obtained a visa for his passport, bought a stout holly stick, and went to the Rue d'Enfer to take a place in the little market van, which took him as far as Longjumeau for half a franc. He was going home to Angouleme. At the end of the first day's tramp he slept in a cowshed, two leagues from Arpajon. He had come no farther than Orleans before he was very weary, and almost ready to break down, but there he found a boatman willing to bring him as far as Tours for three francs, and food during the journey cost him but forty sous. Five days of walking brought him from Tours to Poitiers, and left him with but five francs in his pockets, but he summoned up all his remaining strength for the journey before him.

He was overtaken by night in the open country, and had made up his mind to sleep out of doors, when a traveling carriage passed by, slowly climbing the hillside, and, all unknown to the postilion, the occupants, and the servant, he managed to slip in among the luggage, crouching in between two trunks lest he should be shaken off by the jolting of the carriage--and so he slept.

He awoke with the sun shining into his eyes, and the sound of voices in his ears. The carriage had come to a standstill. Looking about him, he knew that he was at Mansle, the little town where he had waited for Mme. de Bargeton eighteen months before, when his heart was full of hope and love and joy. A group of post-boys eyed him curiously and suspiciously, covered with dust as he was, wedged in among the luggage. Lucien jumped down, but before he could speak two travelers stepped out of the caleche, and the words died away on his lips; for there stood the new Prefect of the Charente, Sixte du Chatelet, and his wife, Louise de Negrepelisse.

"Chance gave us a traveling-companion, if we had but known!" said the Countess. "Come in with us, monsieur."

Lucien gave the couple a distant bow and a half-humbled half-defiant glance; then he turned away into a cross-country road in search of some farmhouse, where he might make a breakfast on milk and bread, and rest awhile, and think quietly over the future. He still had three francs left. On and on he walked with the hurrying pace of fever, noticing as he went, down by the riverside, that the country grew more and more picturesque. It was near mid-day when he came upon a sheet of water with willows growing about the margin, and stopped for awhile to rest his eyes on the cool, thick-growing leaves; and something of the grace of the fields entered into his soul.

In among the crests of the willows, he caught a glimpse of a mill near-by on a branch stream, and of the thatched roof of the mill-house where the house-leeks were growing. For all ornament, the quaint cottage was covered with jessamine and honeysuckle and climbing hops, and the garden about it was gay with phloxes and tall, juicy-leaved plants. Nets lay drying in the sun along a paved causeway raised above the highest flood level, and secured by massive piles. Ducks were swimming in the clear mill-pond below the currents of water roaring over the wheel. As the poet came nearer he heard the clack of the mill, and saw the good-natured, homely woman of the house knitting on a garden bench, and keeping an eye upon a little one who was chasing the hens about.

Lucien came forward. "My good woman," he said, "I am tired out; I have a fever on me, and I have only three francs; will you undertake to give me brown bread and milk, and let me sleep in the barn for a week? I shall have time to write to my people, and they will either come to fetch me or send me money."

"I am quite willing, always supposing that my husband has no objection.--Hey! little man!"

The miller came up, gave Lucien a look over, and took his pipe out of his mouth to remark, "Three francs for a weeks board? You might as well pay nothing at all."

"Perhaps I shall end as a miller's man," thought the poet, as his eyes wandered over the lovely country. Then the miller's wife made a bed ready for him, and Lucien lay down and slept so long that his hostess was frightened.

"Courtois," she said, next day at noon, "just go in and see whether that young man is dead or alive; he has been lying there these fourteen hours."

The miller was busy spreading out his fishing-nets and lines. "It is my belief," he said, "that the pretty fellow yonder is some starveling play-actor without a brass farthing to bless himself with."

"What makes you think that, little man?" asked the mistress of the mill.

"Lord, he is not a prince, nor a lord, nor a member of parliament, nor a bishop; why are his hands as white as if he did nothing?"

"Then it is very strange that he does not feel hungry and wake up," retorted the miller's wife; she had just prepared breakfast for yesterday's chance guest. "A play-actor, is he?" she continued. "Where will he be going? It is too early yet for the fair at Angouleme."

But neither the miller nor his wife suspected that (actors, princes, and bishops apart) there is a kind of being who is both prince and actor, and invested besides with a magnificent order of priesthood --that the Poet seems to do nothing, yet reigns over all humanity when he can paint humanity.

"What can he be?" Courtois asked of his wife.

"Suppose it should be dangerous to take him in?" queried she.

"Pooh! thieves look more alive than that; we should have been robbed by this time," returned her spouse.

"I am neither a prince nor a thief, nor a bishop nor an actor," Lucien said wearily; he must have overheard the colloquy through the window, and now he suddenly appeared. "I am poor, I am tired out, I have come on foot from Paris. My name is Lucien de Rubempre, and my father was M. Chardon, who used to have Postel's business in L'Houmeau. My sister married David Sechard, the printer in the Place du Murier at Angouleme."

"Stop a bit," said the miller, "that printer is the son of the old skinflint who farms his own land at Marsac, isn't he?"

"The very same," said Lucien.

"He is a queer kind of father, he is!" Courtois continued. "He is worth two hundred thousand francs and more, without counting his money-box, and he has sold his son up, they say."

When body and soul have been broken by a prolonged painful struggle, there comes a crisis when a strong nature braces itself for greater effort; but those who give way under the strain either die or sink into unconsciousness like death. That hour of crisis had struck for Lucien; at the vague rumor of the catastrophe that had befallen David he seemed almost ready to succumb. "Oh! my sister!" he cried. "Oh, God! what have I done? Base wretch that I am!"

He dropped down on the wooden bench, looking white and powerless as a dying man; the miller's wife brought out a bowl of milk and made him drink, but he begged the miller to help him back to his bed, and asked to be forgiven for bringing a dying man into their house. He thought his last hour had come. With the shadow of death, thoughts of religion crossed a brain so quick to conceive picturesque fancies; he would see the cure, he would confess and receive the last sacraments. The moan, uttered in the faint voice by a young man with such a comely face and figure, went to Mme. Courtois' heart.

"I say, little man, just take the horse and go to Marsac and ask Dr. Marron to come and see this young man; he is in a very bad way, it seems to me, and you might bring the cure as well. Perhaps they may know more about that printer in the Place du Murier than you do, for Postel married M. Marron's daughter."

Courtois departed. The miller's wife tried to make Lucien take food; like all country-bred folk, she was full of the idea that sick folk must be made to eat. He took no notice of her, but gave way to a violent storm of remorseful grief, a kind of mental process of counter-irritation, which relieved him.

The Courtois' mill lies a league away from Marsac, the town of the district, and the half-way between Mansle and Angouleme; so it was not long before the good miller came back with the doctor and the cure. Both functionaries had heard rumors coupling Lucien's name with the name of Mme. de Bargeton; and now when the whole department was talking of the lady's marriage to the new Prefect and her return to Angouleme as the Comtesse du Chatelet, both cure and doctor were consumed with a violent curiosity to know why M. de Bargeton's widow had not married the young poet with whom she had left

Angouleme. And when they heard, furthermore, that Lucien was at the mill, they were eager to know whether the poet had come to the rescue of his brother-in-law. Curiosity and humanity alike prompted them to go at once to the dying man. Two hours after Courtois set out, Lucien heard the rattle of old iron over the stony causeway, the country doctor's ramshackle chaise came up to the door, and out stepped MM. Marron, for the cure was the doctor's uncle. Lucien's bedside visitors were as intimate with David's father as country neighbors usually are in a small vine-growing township. The doctor looked at the dying man, felt his pulse, and examined his tongue; then he looked at the miller's wife, and smiled reassuringly.

"Mme. Courtois," said he, "if, as I do not doubt, you have a bottle of good wine somewhere in the cellar, and a fat eel in your fish-pond, put them before your patient, it is only exhaustion; there is nothing the matter with him. Our great man will be on his feet again directly."

"Ah! monsieur," said Lucien, "it is not the body, it is the mind that ails. These good people have told me tidings that nearly killed me; I have just heard the bad news of my sister, Mme. Sechard. Mme. Courtois says that your daughter is married to Postel, monsieur, so you must know something of David Sechard's affairs; oh, for heaven's sake, monsieur, tell me what you know!"

"Why, he must be in prison," began the doctor; "his father would not help him----"

"In prison!" repeated Lucien, "and why?"

"Because some bills came from Paris; he had overlooked them, no doubt, for he does not pay much attention to his business, they say," said Dr. Marron.

"Pray leave me with M. le Cure," said the poet, with a visible change of countenance. The doctor and the miller and his wife went out of the room, and Lucien was left alone with the old priest.

"Sir," he said, "I feel that death is near, and I deserve to die. I am a very miserable wretch; I can only cast myself into the arms of religion. I, sir, I have brought all these troubles on my sister and brother, for David Sechard has been a brother to me. I drew those bills that David could not meet! . . . I have ruined him. In my terrible misery, I forgot the crime. A millionaire put an end to the proceedings, and I quite believed that he had met the bills; but nothing of the kind has been done, it seems." And Lucien told the tale of his sorrows. The story, as he told it in his feverish excitement, was worthy of the poet. He besought the cure to go to Angouleme and to ask for news of Eve and his mother, Mme. Chardon, and to let him know the truth, and whether it was still possible to repair the evil.

"I shall live till you come back, sir," he added, as the hot tears fell. "If my mother, and sister, and David do not cast me off, I shall not die."

Lucien's remorse was terrible to see, the tears, the eloquence, the young white face with the heartbroken, despairing look, the tales of sorrow upon sorrow till human strength could no more endure, all these things aroused the cure's pity and interest.

"In the provinces, as in Paris," he said, "you must believe only half of all that you hear. Do not alarm yourself; a piece of hearsay, three leagues away from Angouleme, is sure to be far from the truth. Old Sechard, our neighbor, left Marsac some days ago; very likely he is busy settling his son's difficulties. I am going to Angouleme; I will come back and tell you whether you can return home; your confessions and repentance will help to plead your cause."

The cure did not know that Lucien had repented so many times during the last eighteen months, that penitence, however impassioned, had come to be a kind of drama with him, played to perfection, played so far in all good faith, but none the less a drama. To the cure succeeded the doctor. He saw that the patient was passing through a nervous crisis, and the danger was beginning to subside. The doctor-nephew spoke as comfortably as the cure-uncle, and at length the patient was persuaded to take nourishment.

Meanwhile the cure, knowing the manners and customs of the countryside, had gone to Mansle; the coach from Ruffec to Angouleme was due to pass about that time, and he found a vacant place in it. He would go to his grand-nephew Postel in L'Houmeau (David's former rival) and make inquiries of him. From the assiduity with which the little druggist assisted his venerable relative to alight from the abominable cage which did duty as a coach between Ruffec and Angouleme, it was apparent to the meanest understanding that M. and Mme. Postel founded their hopes of future ease upon the old cure's will.

"Have you breakfasted? Will you take something? We did not in the least expect you! This is a pleasant surprise!" Out came questions innumerable in a breath.

Mme. Postel might have been born to be the wife of an apothecary in L'Houmeau. She was a common-looking woman, about the same height as little Postel himself, such good looks as she possessed being entirely due to youth and health. Her florid auburn hair grew very low upon her forehead. Her demeanor and language were in keeping with homely features, a round countenance, the red cheeks of a country damsel, and eyes that might almost be described as yellow. Everything about her said plainly enough that she had been married for expectations of money. After a year of married life, therefore, she ruled the house; and Postel, only too happy to have discovered the heiress, meekly submitted to his wife. Mme. Leonie Postel, nee *Marron, was nursing her first child, the darling of the old cure, the doctor, and Postel, a repulsive infant, with a strong likeness to both parents.*

"Well, uncle," said Leonie, "what has brought you to Angouleme, since you will not take anything, and no sooner come in than you talk of going?"

But when the venerable ecclesiastic brought out the names of David Sechard and Eve, little Postel grew very red, and Leonie, his wife, felt it incumbent upon her to give him a jealous glance--the glance that a wife never fails to give when she is perfectly sure of her husband, and gives a look into the past by way of a caution for the future.

"What have yonder folk done to you, uncle, that you should mix yourself up in their affairs?" inquired Leonie, with very perceptible tartness.

"They are in trouble, my girl," said the cure, and he told the Postels about Lucien at the Courtois' mill.

"Oh! so that is the way he came back from Paris, is it?" exclaimed Postel. "Yet he had some brains, poor fellow, and he was ambitious, too. He went out to look for wool, and comes home shorn. But what does he want here? His sister is frightfully poor; for all these geniuses, David and Lucien alike, know very little about business. There was some talk of him at the Tribunal, and, as judge, I was obliged to sign the warrant of execution. It was a painful duty. I do not know whether the sister's circumstances are such that Lucien can go to her; but in any case the little room that he used to occupy here is at liberty, and I shall be pleased to offer it to him."

"That is right, Postel," said the priest; he bestowed a kiss on the infant slumbering in Leonie's arms, and, adjusting his cocked hat, prepared to walk out of the shop.

"You will dine with us, uncle, of course," said Mme. Postel; "if once you meddle in these people's affairs, it will be some time before you have done. My husband will drive you back again in his little pony-cart."

Husband and wife stood watching their valued, aged relative on his way into Angouleme. "He carries himself well for his age, all the same," remarked the druggist.

By this time David had been in hiding for eleven days in a house only two doors away from the druggist's shop, which the worthy ecclesiastic had just quitted to climb the steep path into Angouleme with the news of Lucien's present condition.

When the Abbe Marron debouched upon the Place du Murier he found three men, each one remarkable in his own way, and all of them bearing with their whole weight upon the present and future of the hapless voluntary prisoner. There stood old

Sechard, the tall Cointet, and his confederate, the puny limb of the law, three men representing three phases of greed as widely different as the outward forms of the speakers. The first had it in his mind to sell his own son; the second, to betray his client; and the third, while bargaining for both iniquities, was inwardly resolved to pay for neither. It was nearly five o'clock. Passers-by on their way home to dinner stopped a moment to look at the group.

"What the devil can old Sechard and the tall Cointet have to say to each other?" asked the more curious.

"There was something on foot concerning that miserable wretch that leaves his wife and child and mother-in-law to starve," suggested some.

"Talk of sending a boy to Paris to learn his trade!" said a provincial oracle.

"M. le Cure, what brings you here, eh?" exclaimed old Sechard, catching sight of the Abbe as soon as he appeared.

"I have come on account of your family," answered the old man.

"Here is another of my son's notions!" exclaimed old Sechard.

"It would not cost you much to make everybody happy all round," said the priest, looking at the windows of the printing-house. Mme. Sechard's beautiful face appeared at that moment between the curtains; she was hushing her child's cries by tossing him in her arms and singing to him.

"Are you bringing news of my son?" asked old Sechard, "or what is more to the purpose--money?"

"No," answered M. Marron, "I am bringing the sister news of her brother."

"Of Lucien?" cried Petit-Claud.

"Yes. He walked all the way from Paris, poor young man. I found him at the Courtois' house; he was worn out with misery and fatigue. Oh! he is very much to be pitied."

Petit-Claud took the tall Cointet by the arm, saying aloud, "If we are going to dine with Mme. de Senonches, it is time to dress." When they had come away a few paces, he added, for his companion's benefit, "Catch the cub, and you will soon have the dam; we have David now----"

"I have found you a wife, find me a partner," said the tall Cointet with a treacherous smile.

"Lucien is an old school-fellow of mine; we used to be chums. I shall be sure to hear something from him in a week's time. Have the banns put up, and I will engage to put David in prison. When he is on the jailer's register I shall have done my part."

"Ah!" exclaimed the tall Cointet under his breath, "we might have the patent taken out in our name; that would be the thing!"

A shiver ran through the meagre little attorney when he heard those words.

Meanwhile Eve beheld her father-in-law enter with the Abbe Marron, who had let fall a word which unfolded the whole tragedy.

"Here is our cure, Mme. Sechard," the old man said, addressing his daughter-in-law, "and pretty tales about your brother he has to tell us, no doubt!"

"Oh!" cried poor Eve, cut to the heart; "what can have happened now?"

The cry told so unmistakably of many sorrows, of great dread on so many grounds, that the Abbe Marron made haste to say, "Reassure yourself, madame; he is living."

Eve turned to the vinegrower.

"Father," she said, "perhaps you will be good enough to go to my mother; she must hear all that this gentleman has to tell us of Lucien."

The old man went in search of Mme. Chardon, and addressed her in this wise:

"Go and have it out with the Abbe Marron; he is a good sort, priest though he is. Dinner will be late, no doubt. I shall come back again in an hour," and the old man went out. Insensible as he was to everything but the clink of money and the glitter of gold, he left Mme. Chardon without caring to notice the effect of the shock that he had given her.

Mme. Chardon had changed so greatly during the last eighteen months, that in that short time she no longer looked like the same woman. The troubles hanging over both of her children, her abortive hopes for Lucien, the unexpected deterioration in one in whose powers and honesty she had for so long believed,--all these things had told heavily upon her. Mme. Chardon was not only noble by birth, she was noble by nature; she idolized her children; consequently, during the last six months she had suffered as never before since her widowhood. Lucien might have borne the name of Lucien de Rubempre by royal letters patent; he might have founded the family anew, revived the title, and borne the arms; he might have made a great name--he had thrown the chance away; nay, he had fallen into the mire!

For Mme. Chardon the mother was a harder judge than Eve the sister. When she heard of the bills, she looked upon Lucien as lost. A mother is often fain to shut her eyes, but she always knows the child that she held at her breast, the child that has been always with her in the house; and so when Eve and David discussed Lucien's chances of success in Paris, and Lucien's mother to all appearance shared Eve's illusions, in her inmost heart there was a tremor of fear lest David should be right, for a mother's consciousness bore a witness to the truth of his words. So well did she know Eve's sensitive nature, that she could not bring herself to speak of her fears; she was obliged to choke them down and keep such silence as mothers alone can keep when they know how to love their children.

And Eve, on her side, had watched her mother, and saw the ravages of hidden grief with a feeling of dread; her mother was not growing old, she was failing from day to day. Mother and daughter lived a live of generous deception, and neither was deceived. The brutal old vinegrower's speech was the last drop that filled the cup of affliction to overflowing. The words struck a chill to Mme. Chardon's heart.

"Here is my mother, monsieur," said Eve, and the Abbe, looking up, saw a white-haired woman with a face as thin and worn as the features of some aged nun, and yet grown beautiful with the calm and sweet expression that devout submission gives to the faces of women who walk by the will of God, as the saying is. Then the Abbe understood the lives of the mother and daughter, and had no more sympathy left for Lucien; he shuddered to think of all that the victims had endured.

"Mother," said Eve, drying her eyes as she spoke, "poor Lucien is not very far away, he is at Marsac."

"And why is he not here?" asked Mme. Chardon.

Then the Abbe told the whole story as Lucien had told it to him--the misery of the journey, the troubles of the last days in Paris. He described the poet's agony of mind when he heard of the havoc wrought at home by his imprudence, and his apprehension as to the reception awaiting him at Angouleme.

"He has doubts of us; has it come to this?" said Mme. Chardon.

"The unhappy young man has come back to you on foot, enduring the most terrible hardships by the way; he is prepared to enter the humblest walks in life--if so he may make reparation."

"Monsieur," Lucien's sister said, "in spite of the wrong he has done us, I love my brother still, as we love the dead body when the soul has left it; and even so, I love him more than many sisters love their brothers. He has made us poor indeed; but let him come to us, he shall share the last crust of bread, anything indeed that he has left us. Oh, if he had never left us, monsieur, we should not have lost our heart's treasure."

"And the woman who took him from us brought him back on her carriage!" exclaimed Mme. Chardon. "He went away sitting by Mme. de Bargeton's side in her caleche, and he came back behind it."

"Can I do anything for you?" asked the good cure, seeking an opportunity to take leave.

"A wound in the purse is not fatal, they say, monsieur," said Mme. Chardon, "but the patient must be his own doctor."

"If you have sufficient influence with my father-in-law to induce him to help his son, you would save a whole family," said Eve.

"He has no belief in you, and he seemed to me to be very much exasperated against your husband," answered the old cure. He retained an impression, from the ex-pressman's rambling talk, that the Sechards' affairs were a kind of wasps' nest with which it was imprudent to meddle, and his mission being fulfilled, he went to dine with his nephew Postel. That worthy, like the rest of Angouleme, maintained that the father was in the right, and soon dissipated any little benevolence that the old gentleman was disposed to feel towards the son and his family.

"With those that squander money something may be done," concluded little Postel, "but those that make experiments are the ruin of you."

The cure went home; his curiosity was thoroughly satisfied, and this is the end and object of the exceeding interest taken in other people's business in the provinces. In the course of the evening the poet was duly informed of all that had passed in the Sechard family, and the journey was represented as a pilgrimage undertaken from motives of the purest charity.

"You have run your brother-in-law and sister into debt to the amount of ten or twelve thousand francs," said the Abbe as he drew to an end, "and nobody hereabouts has that trifling amount to lend a neighbor, my dear sir. We are not rich in Angoumois. When you spoke to me of your bills, I thought that a much smaller amount was involved."

Lucien thanked the old man for his good offices. "The promise of forgiveness which you have brought is for me a priceless gift."

Very early the next morning Lucien set out from Marsac, and reached Angouleme towards nine o'clock. He carried nothing but his walking-stick; the short jacket that he wore was considerably the worst for his journey, his black trousers were whitened with dust, and a pair of worn boots told sufficiently plainly that their owner belonged to the hapless tribe of tramps. He knew well enough that the contrast between his departure and return was bound to strike his fellow-townsmen; he did not try to hide the fact from himself. But just then, with his heart swelling beneath the oppression of remorse awakened in him by the old cure's story, he accepted his punishment for the moment, and made up his mind to brave the eyes of his acquaintances. Within himself he said, "I am behaving heroically."

Poetic temperaments of this stamp begin as their own dupes. He walked up through L'Houmeau, shame at the manner of his return struggling with the charm of old associations as he went. His heart beat quickly as he passed Postel's shop; but, very luckily for him, the only persons inside it were Leonie and her child. And yet, vanity was still so strong in him, that he could feel glad that his father's name had been painted out on the shop-front; for Postel, since his marriage, had redecorated his abode, and the word "Pharmacy" now alone appeared there, in the Paris fashion, in big letters.

When Lucien reached the steps by the Palet Gate, he felt the influence of his native air, his misfortunes no longer weighed upon him. "I shall see them again!" he said to himself, with a thrill of delight.

He reached the Place du Murier, and had not met a soul, a piece of luck that he scarcely hoped for, he who once had gone about his native place with a conqueror's air. Marion and Kolb, on guard at the door, flew out upon the steps, crying out, "Here he is!"

Lucien saw the familiar workshop and courtyard, and on the staircase met his mother and sister, and for a moment, while their arms were about him, all three almost forgot their troubles. In family life we almost always compound with our misfortunes; we make a sort of bed to rest upon; and, if it is hard, hope to make it tolerable. If Lucien looked the picture of despair, poetic charm was not wanting to the picture. His face had been tanned by the sunlight of the open road, and the deep sadness visible in his features overshadowed his poet's brow. The change in him told so plainly of sufferings endured, his face was so worn by sharp misery, that no one could help pitying him. Imagination had fared forth into the world and found sad reality at the home-coming. Eve was smiling in the midst of her joy, as the saints smile upon martyrdom. The face of a young and very fair woman grows sublimely beautiful at the touch of grief; Lucien remembered the innocent girlish face that he saw last before he went to Paris, and the look of gravity that had come over it spoke so eloquently that he could not but feel a painful impression. The first quick, natural outpouring of affection was followed at once by a reaction on either side; they were afraid to speak; and when Lucien almost involuntarily looked round for another who should have been there, Eve burst into tears, and Lucien did the same, but Mme. Chardon's haggard face showed no sign of emotion. Eve rose to her feet and went downstairs, partly to spare her brother a word of reproach, partly to speak to Marion.

"Lucien is so fond of strawberries, child, we must find some strawberries for him."

"Oh, I was sure that you would want to welcome M. Lucien; you shall have a nice little breakfast and a good dinner, too."

"Lucien," said Mme. Chardon when the mother and son were left alone, "you have a great deal to repair here. You went away that we all might be proud of you; you have plunged us into want. You have all but destroyed your brother's opportunity of making a fortune that he only cared to win for the sake of his new family. Nor is this all that you have destroyed----" said the mother.

There was a dreadful pause; Lucien took his mother's reproaches in silence.

"Now begin to work," Mme. Chardon went on more gently. "You tried to revive the noble family of whom I come; I do not blame you for it. But the man who undertakes such a task needs money above all things, and must bear a high heart in him; both were wanting in your case. We believed in you once, our belief has been shaken. This was a hard-working, contented household, making its way with difficulty; you have troubled their peace. The first offence may be forgiven, but it must be the last. We are in a very difficult position here; you must be careful, and take your sister's advice, Lucien. The school of trouble is a very hard one, but Eve has learned much by her lessons; she has grown grave and thoughtful, she is a mother. In her devotion to our dear David she has taken all the family burdens upon herself; indeed, through your wrongdoing she has come to be my only comfort."

"You might be still more severe, my mother," Lucien said, as he kissed her. "I accept your forgiveness, for I will not need it a second time."

Eve came into the room, saw her brother's humble attitude, and knew that he had been forgiven. Her kindness brought a smile for him to her lips, and Lucien answered with tear-filled eyes. A living presence acts like a charm, changing the most hostile positions of lovers or of families, no matter how just the resentment. Is it that affection finds out the ways of the heart, and we love to fall into them again? Does the phenomenon come within the province of the science of magnetism? Or is it reason that tells us that we must either forgive or never see each other again? Whether the cause be referred to mental, physical, or spiritual conditions, everyone knows the effect; every one has felt that the looks, the actions or gestures of the beloved awaken some vestige of tenderness in those most deeply sinned against and grievously wronged. Though it is hard for the mind to forget, though we still smart under the injury, the heart returns to its allegiance in spite of all. Poor Eve listened to her brother's confidences until breakfast-time; and whenever she looked at him she was no longer mistress of her eyes; in that intimate talk she could not control her voice. And with the comprehension of the conditions of literary life in Paris, she understood that the struggle had been too much for Lucien's strength. The poet's delight as he caressed his sister's child, his deep grief over David's absence, mingled with joy at seeing his country and his own folk again, the melancholy words that he let fall,--all these things combined to make that day a festival. When Marion brought in the strawberries, he was touched to see that Eve had remembered his taste in spite of her distress, and she, his sister, must make ready a room for the prodigal

306

brother and busy herself for Lucien. It was a truce, as it were, to misery. Old Sechard himself assisted to bring about this revulsion of feeling in the two women--"You are making as much of him as if he were bringing you any amount of money!"

"And what has my brother done that we should not make much of him?" cried Eve, jealously screening Lucien.

Nevertheless, when the first expansion was over, shades of truth came out. It was not long before Lucien felt the difference between the old affection and the new. Eve respected David from the depths of her heart; Lucien was beloved for his own sake, as we love a mistress still in spite of the disasters she causes. Esteem, the very foundation on which affection is based, is the solid stuff to which affection owes I know not what of certainty and security by which we live; and this was lacking between Mme. Chardon and her son, between the sister and the brother. Mother and daughter did not put entire confidence in him, as they would have done if he had not lost his honor; and he felt this. The opinion expressed in d'Arthez's letter was Eve's own estimate of her brother; unconsciously she revealed it by her manner, tones, and gestures. Oh! Lucien was pitied, that was true; but as for all that he had been, the pride of the household, the great man of the family, the hero of the fireside,--all this, like their fair hopes of him, was gone, never to return. They were so afraid of his heedlessness that he was not told where David was hidden. Lucien wanted to see his brother; but this Eve, insensible to the caresses which accompanied his curious questionings, was not the Eve of L'Houmeau, for whom a glance from him had been an order that must be obeyed. When Lucien spoke of making reparation, and talked as though he could rescue David, Eve only answered:

"Do not interfere; we have enemies of the most treacherous and dangerous kind."

Lucien tossed his head, as one who should say, "I have measured myself against Parisians," and the look in his sister's eyes said unmistakably, "Yes, but you were defeated."

"Nobody cares for me now," Lucien thought. "In the home circle, as in the world without, success is a necessity."

The poet tried to explain their lack of confidence in him; he had not been at home two days before a feeling of vexation rather than of angry bitterness gained hold on him. He applied Parisian standards to the quiet, temperate existence of the provinces, quite forgetting that the narrow, patient life of the household was the result of his own misdoings.

"They are bourgeoises, they cannot understand me," he said, setting himself apart from his sister and mother and David, now that they could no longer be deceived as to his real character and his future.

Many troubles and shocks of fortune had quickened the intuitive sense in both the women. Eve and Mme. Chardon guessed the thoughts in Lucien's inmost soul; they felt that he misjudged them; they saw him mentally isolating himself.

"Paris has changed him very much," they said between themselves. They were indeed reaping the harvest of egoism which they themselves had fostered.

It was inevitable but that the leaven should work in all three; and this most of all in Lucien, because he felt that he was so heavily to blame. As for Eve, she was just the kind of sister to beg an erring brother to "Forgive me for your trespasses;" but when the union of two souls had been as perfect since life's very beginnings, as it had been with Eve and Lucien, any blow dealt to that fair ideal is fatal. Scoundrels can draw knives on each other and make it up again afterwards, while a look or a word is enough to sunder two lovers for ever. In the recollection of an almost perfect life of heart and heart lies the secret of many an estrangement that none can explain. Two may live together without full trust in their hearts if only their past holds no memories of complete and unclouded love; but for those who once have known that intimate life, it becomes intolerable to keep perpetual watch over looks and words. Great poets know this; Paul and Virginie die before youth is over; can we think of Paul and Virginie estranged? Let us know that, to the honor of Lucien and Eve, the grave injury done was not the source of the pain; it was entirely a matter of feeling upon either side, for the poet in fault, as for the sister who was in no way to blame. Things had reached the point when the slightest misunderstanding, or little quarrel, or a fresh disappointment in Lucien would end in final estrangement. Money difficulties may be arranged, but feelings are inexorable.

Next day Lucien received a copy of the local paper. He turned pale with pleasure when he saw his name at the head of one of the first "leaders" in that highly respectable sheet, which like the provincial academies that Voltaire compared to a well-bred miss, was never talked about.

"Let Franche-Comte boast of giving the light to Victor Hugo, to Charles Nodier, and Cuvier," ran the article, "Brittany of producing a Chateaubriand and a Lammenais, Normandy of Casimir Delavigne, and Touraine of the author of Eloa; Angoumois that gave birth, in the days of Louis XIII., to our illustrious fellow-countryman Guez, better known under the name of Balzac, our Angoumois need no longer envy Limousin her Dupuytren, nor Auvergne, the country of Montlosier, nor Bordeaux, birthplace of so many great men; for we too have our poet!--The writer of the beautiful sonnets entitled the Marguerites unites his poet's fame to the distinction of a prose writer, for to him we also owe the magnificent romance of The Archer of Charles IX. Some day our nephews will be proud to be the fellow-townsmen of Lucien Chardon, a rival of Petrarch!!!"

(The country newspapers of those days were sown with notes of admiration, as reports of English election speeches are studded with "cheers" in brackets.)

"In spite of his brilliant success in Paris, our young poet has not forgotten the Hotel de Bargeton, the cradle of his triumphs; nor the fact that the wife of M. le Comte du Chatelet, our Prefect, encouraged his early footsteps in the pathway of the Muses. He has come back among us once more! All L'Houmeau was thrown into excitement yesterday by the appearance of our Lucien de Rubempre. The news of his return produced a profound sensation throughout the town. Angouleme certainly will not allow L'Houmeau to be beforehand in doing honor to the poet who in journalism and literature has so gloriously represented our town in Paris. Lucien de Rubempre, a religious and Royalist poet, has braved the fury of parties; he has come home, it is said, for repose after the fatigue of a struggle which would try the strength of an even greater intellectual athlete than a poet and a dreamer.

"There is some talk of restoring our great poet to the title of the illustrious house of de Rubempre, of which his mother, Madame Chardon, is the last survivor, and it is added that Mme. la Comtesse du Chatelet was the first to think of this eminently politic idea. The revival of an ancient and almost extinct family by young talent and newly won fame is another proof that the immortal author of the Charter still cherishes the desire expressed by the words 'Union and oblivion.'

"Our poet is staying with his sister, Mme. Sechard."

Under the heading "Angouleme" followed some items of news:--

"Our Prefect, M. le Comte du Chatelet, Gentleman in Ordinary to His Majesty, has just been appointed Extraordinary Councillor of State.

"All the authorities called yesterday on M. le Prefet.

"Mme. la Comtesse du Chatelet will receive on Thursdays.

"The Mayor of Escarbas, M. de Negrepelisse, the representative of the younger branch of the d'Espard family, and father of Mme. du Chatelet, recently raised to the rank of a Count and Peer of France and a Commander of the Royal Order of St. Louis, has been nominated for the presidency of the electoral college of Angouleme at the forthcoming elections."

"There!" said Lucien, taking the paper to his sister. Eve read the article with attention, and returned with the sheet with a thoughtful air.

"What do you say to that?" asked he, surprised at a reserve that seemed so like indifference.

"The Cointets are proprietors of that paper, dear," she said; "they put in exactly what they please, and it is not at all likely that the prefecture or the palace have forced their hands. Can you imagine that your old rival the prefect would be generous enough to sing your praises? Have you forgotten that the Cointets are suing us under Metivier's name? and that they are

308

trying to turn David's discovery to their own advantage? I do not know the source of this paragraph, but it makes me uneasy. You used to rouse nothing but envious feeling and hatred here; a prophet has no honor in his own country, and they slandered you, and now in a moment it is all changed----"

"You do not know the vanity of country towns," said Lucien. "A whole little town in the south turned out not so long ago to welcome a young man that had won the first prize in some competition; they looked on him as a budding great man."

"Listen, dear Lucien; I do not want to preach to you, I will say everything in a very few words--you must suspect every little thing here."

"You are right," said Lucien, but he was surprised at his sister's lack of enthusiasm. He himself was full of delight to find his humiliating and shame-stricken return to Angouleme changed into a triumph in this way.

"You have no belief in the little fame that has cost so dear!" he said again after a long silence. Something like a storm had been gathering in his heart during the past hour. For all answer Eve gave him a look, and Lucien felt ashamed of his accusation.

Dinner was scarcely over when a messenger came from the prefecture with a note addressed to M. Chardon. That note appeared to decide the day for the poet's vanity; the world contending against the family for him had won.

"M. le Comte Sixte du Chatelet and Mme. la Comtesse du Chatelet request the honor of M. Lucien Chardon's company at dinner on the fifteenth of September. R. S. V. P."

Enclosed with the invitation there was a card--

LE COMTE SIXTE DU CHATELET, Gentleman of the Bedchamber, Prefect of the Charente, Councillor of State.

"You are in favor," said old Sechard; "they are talking about you in the town as if you were somebody! Angouleme and L'Houmeau are disputing as to which shall twist wreaths for you."

"Eve, dear," Lucien whispered to his sister, "I am exactly in the same condition as I was before in L'Houmeau when Mme. de Bargeton sent me the first invitation--I have not a dress suit for the prefect's dinner-party."

"Do you really mean to accept the invitation?" Eve asked in alarm, and a dispute sprang up between the brother and sister. Eve's provincial good sense told her that if you appear in society, it must be with a smiling face and faultless costume. "What will come of the prefect's dinner?" she wondered. "What has Lucien to do with the great people of Angouleme? Are they plotting something against him?" but she kept these thoughts to herself.

Lucien spoke the last word at bedtime: "You do not know my influence. The prefect's wife stands in fear of a journalist; and besides, Louise de Negrepelisse lives on in the Comtesse du Chatelet, and a woman with her influence can rescue David. I am going to tell her about my brother's invention, and it would be a mere nothing to her to obtain a subsidy of ten thousand francs from the Government for him."

At eleven o'clock that night the whole household was awakened by the town band, reinforced by the military band from the barracks. The Place du Murier was full of people. The young men of Angouleme were giving Lucien Chardon de Rubempre a serenade. Lucien went to his sister's window and made a speech after the last performance.

"I thank my fellow-townsmen for the honor that they do me," he said in the midst of a great silence; "I will strive to be worthy of it; they will pardon me if I say no more; I am so much moved by this incident that I cannot speak."

"Hurrah for the writer of The Archer of Charles IX.! . . . Hurrah for the poet of the Marguerites! . . . Long live Lucien de Rubempre!"

After these three salvos, taken up by some few voices, three crowns and a quantity of bouquets were adroitly flung into the room through the open window. Ten minutes later the Place du Murier was empty, and silence prevailed in the streets.

"I would rather have ten thousand francs," said old Sechard, fingering the bouquets and garlands with a satirical expression.

"You gave them daisies, and they give you posies in return; you deal in flowers."

"So that is your opinion of the honors shown me by my fellow-townsmen, is it?" asked Lucien. All his melancholy had left him, his face was radiant with good humor. "If you knew mankind, Papa Sechard, you would see that no moment in one's life comes twice. Such a triumph as this can only be due to genuine enthusiasm! . . . My dear mother, my good sister, this wipes out many mortifications."

Lucien kissed them; for when joy overflows like a torrent flood, we are fain to pour it out into a friend's heart. "When an author is intoxicated with success, he will hug his porter if there is nobody else on hand," according to Bixiou.

"Why, darling, why are you crying?" he said, looking into Eve's face. "Ah! I know, you are crying for joy!"

"Oh me!" said her mother, shaking her head as she spoke. "Lucien has forgotten everything already; not merely his own troubles, but ours as well."

Mother and daughter separated, and neither dared to utter all her thoughts.

In a country eaten up with the kind of social insubordination disguised by the word Equality, a triumph of any kind whatsoever is a sort of miracle which requires, like some other miracles for that matter, the co-operation of skilled labor. Out of ten ovations offered to ten living men, selected for this distinction by a grateful country, you may be quite sure that nine are given from considerations connected as remotely as possible with the conspicuous merits of the renowned recipient. What was Voltaire's apotheosis at the Theatre-Francais but the triumph of eighteenth century philosophy? A triumph in France means that everybody else feels that he is adorning his own temples with the crown that he sets on the idol's head.

The women's presentiments proved correct. The distinguished provincial's reception was antipathetic to Angoumoisin immobility; it was too evidently got up by some interested persons or by enthusiastic stage mechanics, a suspicious combination. Eve, moreover, like most of her sex, was distrustful by instinct, even when reason failed to justify her suspicions to herself. "Who can be so fond of Lucien that he could rouse the town for him?" she wondered as she fell asleep. "The Marguerites are not published yet; how can they compliment him on a future success?"

The ovation was, in fact, the work of Petit-Claud.

Petit-Claud had dined with Mme. de Senonches, for the first time, on the evening of the day that brought the cure of Marsac to Angouleme with the news of Lucien's return. That same evening he made formal application for the hand of Mlle. de la Haye. It was a family dinner, one of the solemn occasions marked not so much by the number of the guests as by the splendor of their toilettes. Consciousness of the performance weighs upon the family party, and every countenance looks significant. Francoise was on exhibition. Mme. de Senonches had sported her most elaborate costume for the occasion; M. du Hautoy wore a black coat; M. de Senonches had returned from his visit to the Pimentels on the receipt of a note from his wife, informing him that Mme. du Chatelet was to appear at their house for the first time since her arrival, and that a suitor in form for Francoise would appear on the scenes. Boniface Cointet also was there, in his best maroon coat of clerical cut, with a diamond pin worth six thousand francs displayed in his shirt frill--the revenge of the rich merchant upon a poverty-stricken aristocracy.

Petit-Claud himself, scoured and combed, had carefully removed his gray hairs, but he could not rid himself of his wizened air. The puny little man of law, tightly buttoned into his clothes, reminded you of a torpid viper; for if hope had brought a spark of life into his magpie eyes, his face was icily rigid, and so well did he assume an air of gravity, that an ambitious public prosecutor could not have been more dignified.

Mme. de Senonches had told her intimate friends that her ward would meet her betrothed that evening, and that Mme. du Chatelet would appear at the Hotel de Senonches for the first time; and having particularly requested them to keep these matters secret, she expected to find her rooms crowded. The Comte and Comtesse du Chatelet had left cards everywhere

310

officially, but they meant the honor of a personal visit to play a part in their policy. So aristocratic Angouleme was in such a prodigious ferment of curiosity, that certain of the Chandour camp proposed to go to the Hotel de Bargeton that evening. (They persistently declined to call the house by its new name.)

Proofs of the Countess' influence had stirred up ambition in many quarters; and not only so, it was said that the lady had changed so much for the better that everybody wished to see and judge for himself. Petit-Claud learned great news on the way to the house; Cointet told him that Zephirine had asked leave to present her dear Francoise's betrothed to the Countess, and that the Countess had granted the favor. Petit-Claud had seen at once that Lucien's return put Louise de Negrepelisse in a false position; and now, in a moment, he flattered himself that he saw a way to take advantage of it.

M. and Mme. de Senonches had undertaken such heavy engagements when they bought the house, that, in provincial fashion, they thought it imprudent to make any changes in it. So when Madame du Chatelet was announced, Zephirine went up to her with--"Look, dear Louise, you are still in your old home!" indicating, as she spoke, the little chandelier, the paneled wainscot, and the furniture, which once had dazzled Lucien.

"I wish least of all to remember it, dear," Madame la Prefete answered graciously, looking round on the assemblage.

Every one admitted that Louise de Negrepelisse was not like the same woman. If the provincial had undergone a change, the woman herself had been transformed by those eighteen months in Paris, by the first happiness of a still recent second marriage, and the kind of dignity that power confers. The Comtesse du Chatelet bore the same resemblance to Mme. de Bargeton that a girl of twenty bears to her mother.

She wore a charming cap of lace and flowers, fastened by a diamond-headed pin; the ringlets that half hid the contours of her face added to her look of youth, and suited her style of beauty. Her foulard gown, designed by the celebrated Victorine, with a pointed bodice, exquisitely fringed, set off her figure to advantage; and a silken lace scarf, adroitly thrown about a too long neck, partly concealed her shoulders. She played with the dainty scent-bottle, hung by a chain from her bracelet; she carried her fan and her handkerchief with ease--pretty trifles, as dangerous as a sunken reef for the provincial dame. The refined taste shown in the least details, the carriage and manner modeled upon Mme. d'Espard, revealed a profound study of the Faubourg Saint-Germain.

As for the elderly beau of the Empire, he seemed since his marriage to have followed the example of the species of melon that turns from green to yellow in a night. All the youth that Sixte had lost seemed to appear in his wife's radiant countenance; provincial pleasantries passed from ear to ear, circulating the more readily because the women were furious at the new superiority of the sometime queen of Angouleme; and the persistent intruder paid the penalty of his wife's offence.

The rooms were almost as full as on that memorable evening of Lucien's readings from Chenier. Some faces were missing: M. de Chandour and Amelie, M. de Pimental and the Rastignacs--and M. de Bargeton was no longer there; but the Bishop came, as before, with his vicars-general in his train. Petit-Claud was much impressed by the sight of the great world of Angouleme. Four months ago he had no hope of entering the circle, today he felt his detestation of "the classes" sensibly diminished. He thought the Comtesse du Chatelet a most fascinating woman. "It is she who can procure me the appointment of deputy public prosecutor," he said to himself.

Louise chatted for an equal length of time with each of the women; her tone varied with the importance of the person addressed and the position taken up by the latter with regard to her journey to Paris with Lucien. The evening was half over when she withdrew to the boudoir with the Bishop. Zephirine came over to Petit-Claud, and laid her hand on his arm. His heart beat fast as his hostess brought him to the room where Lucien's troubles first began, and were now about to come to a crisis.

"This is M. Petit-Claud, dear; I recommend him to you the more warmly because anything that you may do for him will *doubtless benefit my ward."*

"You are an attorney, are you not, monsieur?" said the august Negrepelisse, scanning Petit-Claud.

"Alas! yes, Madame la Comtesse." (The son of the tailor in L'Houmeau had never once had occasion to use those three words in his life before, and his mouth was full of them.) "But it rests with you, Madame la Comtesse, whether or no I shall act for the Crown. M. Milaud is going to Nevers, it is said----"

"But a man is usually second deputy and then first deputy, is he not?" broke in the Countess. "I should like to see you in the first deputy's place at once. But I should like first to have some assurance of your devotion to the cause of our legitimate sovereigns, to religion, and more especially to M. de Villele, if I am to interest myself on your behalf to obtain the favor."

Petit-Claud came nearer. "Madame," he said in her ear, "I am the man to yield the King absolute obedience."

"That is just what we want today," said the Countess, drawing back a little to make him understand that she had no wish for promises given under his breath. "So long as you satisfy Mme. de Senonches, you can count upon me," she added, with a royal movement of her fan.

Petit-Claud looked toward the door of the boudoir, and saw Cointet standing there. "Madame," he said, "Lucien is here, in Angouleme."

"Well, sir?" asked the Countess, in tones that would have put an end to all power of speech in an ordinary man.

"Mme. la Comtesse does not understand," returned Petit-Claud, bringing out that most respectful formula again. "How does Mme. la Comtesse wish that the great man of her making should be received in Angouleme? There is no middle course; he must be received or despised here."

This was a dilemma to which Louise de Negrepelisse had never given a thought; it touched her closely, yet rather for the sake of the past than of the future. And as for Petit-Claud, his plan for arresting David Sechard depended upon the lady's actual feelings towards Lucien. He waited.

"M. Petit-Claud," said the Countess, with haughty dignity, "you mean to be on the side of the Government. Learn that the first principle of government is this--never to have been in the wrong, and that the instinct of power and the sense of dignity is even stronger in women than in governments."

"That is just what I thought, madame," he answered quickly, observing the Countess meanwhile with attention the more profound because it was scarcely visible. "Lucien came here in the depths of misery. But if he must receive an ovation, I can compel him to leave Angouleme by the means of the ovation itself. His sister and brother-in-law, David Sechard, are hard pressed for debts."

In the Countess' haughty face there was a swift, barely perceptible change; it was not satisfaction, but the repression of satisfaction. Surprised that Petit-Claud should have guessed her wishes, she gave him a glance as she opened her fan, and Francoise de la Haye's entrance at that moment gave her time to find an answer.

"It will not be long before you are public prosecutor, monsieur," she said, with a significant smile. That speech did not commit her in any way, but it was explicit enough. Francoise had come in to thank the Countess.

"Oh! madame, then I shall owe the happiness of my life to you," she exclaimed, bending girlishly to add in the Countess' ear, "To marry a petty provincial attorney would be like being burned by slow fires."

It was Francis, with his knowledge of officialdom, who had prompted Zephirine to make this set upon Louise.

"In the very earliest days after promotion," so the ex-consul-general told his fair friend, "everybody, prefect, or monarch, or man of business, is burning to exert his influence for his friends; but a patron soon finds out the inconveniences of patronage, and then turns from fire to ice. Louise will do more now for Petit-Claud than she would do for her husband in three months'

time."

"Madame la Comtesse is thinking of all that our poet's triumph entails?" continued Petit-Claud. "She should receive Lucien before there is an end of the nine-days' wonder."

The Countess terminated the audience with a bow, and rose to speak with Mme. de Pimentel, who came to the boudoir. The news of old Negrepelisse's elevation to a marquisate had greatly impressed the Marquise; she judged it expedient to be amiable to a woman so clever as to rise the higher for an apparent fall.

"Do tell me, dear, why you took the trouble to put your father in the House of Peers?" said the Marquise, in the course of a little confidential conversation, in which she bent the knee before the superiority of "her dear Louise."

"They were all the more ready to grant the favor because my father has no son to succeed him, dear, and his vote will always be at the disposal of the Crown; but if we should have sons, I quite expect that my oldest will succeed to his grandfather's name, title, and peerage."

Mme. de Pimentel saw, to her annoyance, that it was idle to expect a mother ambitious for children not yet in existence to further her own private designs of raising M. de Pimentel to a peerage.

"I have the Countess," Petit-Claud told Cointet when they came away. "I can promise you your partnership. I shall be deputy prosecutor before the month is out, and Sechard will be in your power. Try to find a buyer for my connection; it has come to be the first in Angouleme in my hands during the last five months----"

"Once put you on the horse, and there is no need to do more," said Cointet, half jealous of his own work.

The causes of Lucien's triumphant reception in his native town must now be plain to everybody. Louise du Chatelet followed the example of that King of France who left the Duke of Orleans unavenged; she chose to forget the insults received in Paris by Mme. de Bargeton. She would patronize Lucien, and overwhelming him with her patronage, would completely crush him and get rid of him by fair means. Petit-Claud knew the whole tale of the cabals in Paris through town gossip, and shrewdly guessed how a woman must hate the man who would not love when she was fain of his love.

The ovation justified the past of Louise de Negrepelisse. The next day Petit-Claud appeared at Mme. Sechard's house, heading a deputation of six young men of the town, all of them Lucien's schoolfellows. He meant to finish his work, to intoxicate Lucien completely, and to have him in his power. Lucien's old schoolfellows at the Angouleme grammar-school wished to invite the author of the Marguerites and The Archer of Charles IX. to a banquet given in honor of the great man arisen from their ranks.

"Come, this is your doing, Petit-Claud!" exclaimed Lucien.

"Your return has stirred our conceit," said Petit-Claud; "we made it a point of honor to get up a subscription, and we will have a tremendous affair for you. The masters and the headmaster will be there, and, at the present rate, we shall, no doubt, have the authorities too."

"For what day?" asked Lucien.

"Sunday next."

"That is quite out of the question," said Lucien. "I cannot accept an invitation for the next ten days, but then I will gladly----"

"Very well," said Petit-Claud, "so be it then, in ten days' time."

Lucien behaved charmingly to his old schoolfellows, and they regarded him with almost respectful admiration. He talked away very wittily for half an hour; he had been set upon a pedestal, and wished to justify the opinion of his fellow-townsmen; so he stood with his hands thrust into his pockets, and held forth from the height to which he had been raised. He was modest and good-natured, as befitted genius in dressing-gown and slippers; he was the athlete, wearied by a wrestling bout with Paris, and disenchanted above all things; he congratulated the comrades who had never left the dear old province, and so

313

forth, and so forth. They were delighted with him. He took Petit-Claud aside, and asked him for the real truth about David's affairs, reproaching him for allowing his brother-in-law to go into hiding, and tried to match his wits against the little lawyer. Petit-Claud made an effort over himself, and gave his acquaintance to understand that he (Petit-Claud) was only an insignificant little country attorney, with no sort of craft nor subtlety.

The whole machinery of modern society is so infinitely more complex than in ancient times, that the subdivision of human faculty is the result. The great men of the days of old were perforce universal geniuses, appearing at rare intervals like lighted torches in an antique world. In the course of ages the intellect began to work on special lines, but the great man still could "take all knowledge for his province." A man "full cautelous," as was said of Louis XI., for instance, could apply that special faculty in every direction, but today the single quality is subdivided, and every profession has its special craft. A peasant or a pettifogging solicitor might very easily overreach an astute diplomate over a bargain in some remote country village; and the wiliest journalist may prove the veriest simpleton in a piece of business. Lucien could but be a puppet in the hands of Petit-Claud.

That guileful practitioner, as might have been expected, had written the article himself; Angouleme and L'Houmeau, thus put on their mettle, thought it incumbent upon them to pay honor to Lucien. His fellow-citizens, assembled in the Place du Murier, were Cointets' workpeople from the papermills and printing-house, with a sprinkling of Lucien's old schoolfellows and the clerks in the employ of Messieurs Petit-Claud and Cachan. As for the attorney himself, he was once more Lucien's chum of old days; and he thought, not without reason, that before very long he should learn David's whereabouts in some unguarded moment. And if David came to grief through Lucien's fault, the poet would find Angouleme too hot to hold him. Petit-Claud meant to secure his hold; he posed, therefore, as Lucien's inferior.

"What better could I have done?" he said accordingly. "My old chum's sister was involved, it is true, but there are some positions that simply cannot be maintained in a court of law. David asked me on the first of June to ensure him a quiet life for three months; he had a quiet life until September, and even so I have kept his property out of his creditors' power, for I shall gain my case in the Court-Royal; I contend that the wife is a privileged creditor, and her claim is absolute, unless there is evidence of intent to defraud. As for you, you have come back in misfortune, but you are a genius."--(Lucien turned about as if the incense were burned too close to his face.) --"Yes, my dear fellow, a genius. I have read your Archer of Charles IX.; it is more than a romance, it is literature. Only two living men could have written the preface--Chateaubriand and Lucien."

Lucien accepted that d'Arthez had written the preface. Ninety-nine writers out of a hundred would have done the same.

"Well, nobody here seemed to have heard of you!" Petit-Claud continued, with apparent indignation. "When I saw the general indifference, I made up my mind to change all that. I wrote that article in the paper----"

"What? did you write it?" exclaimed Lucien.

"I myself. Angouleme and L'Houmeau were stirred to rivalry; I arranged for a meeting of your old schoolfellows, and got up yesterday's serenade; and when once the enthusiasm began to grow, we started a committee for the dinner. 'If David is in hiding,' said I to myself, 'Lucien shall be crowned at any rate.' And I have done even better than that," continued Petit-Claud; "I have seen the Comtesse du Chatelet and made her understand that she owes it to herself to extricate David from his position; she can do it, and she ought to do it. If David had really discovered the secret of which he spoke to me, the Government ought to lend him a hand, it would not ruin the Government; and think what a fine thing for a prefect to have half the credit of the great invention for the well-timed help. It would set people talking about him as an enlightened administrator.--Your sister has taken fright at our musketry practice; she was scared of the smoke. A battle in the law-courts costs quite as much as a battle on the field; but David has held his ground, he has his secret. They cannot stop him, and they will not pull him up now."

"Thanks, my dear fellow; I see that I can take you into my confidence; you shall help me to carry out my plan."

Petit-Claud looked at Lucien, and his gimlet face was a point of interrogation.

"I intend to rescue Sechard," Lucien said, with a certain importance. "I brought his misfortunes upon him; I mean to make full reparation. . . . I have more influence over Louise----"

"Who is Louise?"

"The Comtesse du Chatelet!"

Petit-Claud started.

"I have more influence over her than she herself suspects," said Lucien; "only, my dear fellow, if I can do something with your authorities here, I have no decent clothes."--Petit-Claud made as though he would offer his purse.

"Thank you," said Lucien, grasping Petit-Claud's hand. "In ten days' time I will pay a visit to the Countess and return your call."

The shook hands like old comrades, and separated.

"He ought to be a poet" said Petit-Claud to himself; "he is quite mad."

"There are no friends like one's school friends; it is a true saying," Lucien thought at he went to find his sister.

"What can Petit-Claud have promised to do that you should be so friendly with him, my Lucien?" asked Eve. "Be on your guard with him."

"With him?" cried Lucien. "Listen, Eve," he continued, seeming to bethink himself; "you have no faith in me now; you do not trust me, so it is not likely you will trust Petit-Claud; but in ten or twelve days you will change your mind," he added, with a touch of fatuity. And he went to his room, and indited the following epistle to Lousteau:--

Lucien to Lousteau.

"MY FRIEND,--Of the pair of us, I alone can remember that bill for a thousand francs that I once lent you; and I know how things will be with you when you open this letter too well, alas! not to add immediately that I do not expect to be repaid in current coin of the realm; no, I will take it in credit from you, just as one would ask Florine for pleasure. We have the same tailor; therefore, you can order a complete outfit for me on the shortest possible notice. I am not precisely wearing Adam's costume, but I cannot show myself here. To my astonishment, the honors paid by the departments to a Parisian celebrity awaited me. I am the hero of a banquet, for all the world as if I were a Deputy of the Left. Now, after that, do you understand that I must have a black coat? Promise to pay; have it put down to your account, try the advertisement dodge, rehearse an unpublished scene between Don Juan and M. Dimanche, for I must have a gala suit at all costs. I have nothing, nothing but rags: start with that; it is August, the weather is magnificent, ergo see that I receive by the end of the week a charming morning suit, dark bronze-green jacket, and three waistcoats, one a brimstone yellow, one a plaid, and the third must be white; furthermore, let there be three pairs of trousers of the most fetching kind--one pair of white English stuff, one pair of nankeen, and a third of thin black kerseymere; lastly, send a black dress-coat and a black satin waistcoat. If you have picked up another Florine somewhere, I beg her good offices for two cravats. So far this is nothing; I count upon you and your skill in these matters; I am not much afraid of the tailor. But the ingenuity of poverty, assuredly the most active of all poisons at work in the system of man (id est the Parisian), an ingenuity that would catch Satan himself napping, has failed so far to discover a way to obtain a hat on credit!--How many a time, my dear friend, have we deplored this! When one of us shall bring a hat that costs one thousand francs into fashion, then, and not till then, can we afford to wear them; until that day comes we are bound to have cash enough in our pockets to pay for a hat. Ah! what an ill turn the Comedie-Francaise did us with, 'Lafleur, you will put gold in my pockets!'

"I write with a profound sense of all the difficulties involved by the demand. Enclose with the above a pair of boots, a pair of pumps, a hat, half a dozen pairs of gloves. 'Tis asking the impossible; I know it. But what is a literary life but a periodical

recurrence of the impossible? Work the miracle, write a long article, or play some small scurvy trick, and I will hold your debt as fully discharged--this is all I say to you. It is a debt of honor after all, my dear fellow, and due these twelve months; you ought to blush for yourself if you have any blushes left.

"Joking apart, my dear Lousteau, I am in serious difficulties, as you may judge for yourself when I tell you that Mme. de Bargeton has married Chatelet, and Chatelet is prefect of Angouleme. The precious pair can do a good deal for my brother-in-law; he is in hiding at this moment on account of that letter of exchange, and the horrid business is all my doing. So it is a question of appearing before Mme. la Prefete and regaining my influence at all costs. It is shocking, is it not, that David Sechard's fate should hang upon a neat pair of shoes, a pair of open-worked gray silk stockings (mind you, remember them), and a new hat? I shall give out that I am sick and ill, and take to my bed, like Duvicquet, to save the trouble of replying to the pressing invitations of my fellow-townsmen. My fellow-townsmen, dear boy, have treated me to a fine serenade. My fellow-townsmen, forsooth! I begin to wonder how many fools go to make up that word, since I learned that two or three of my old schoolfellows worked up the capital of the Angoumois to this pitch of enthusiasm.

"If you could contrive to slip a few lines as to my reception in among the news items, I should be several inches taller for it here; and besides, I should make Mme. la Prefete feel that, if I have not friends, I have some credit, at any rate, with the Parisian press. I give up none of my hopes, and I will return the compliment. If you want a good, solid, substantial article for some magazine or other, I have time enough now to think something out. I only say the word, my dear friend; I count upon you as you may count upon me, and I am yours sincerely.

"LUCIEN DE R.

"P. S.--Send the things to the coach office to wait until called for."

Lucien held up his head again. In this mood he wrote the letter, and as he wrote his thoughts went back to Paris. He had spent six days in the provinces, and the uneventful quietness of provincial life had already entered into his soul; his mind returned to those dear old miserable days with a vague sense of regret. The Comtesse du Chatelet filled his thoughts for a whole week; and at last he came to attach so much importance to his reappearance, that he hurried down to the coach office in L'Houmeau after nightfall in a perfect agony of suspense, like a woman who has set her last hopes upon a new dress, and waits in despair until it arrives.

"Ah! Lousteau, all your treasons are forgiven," he said to himself, as he eyed the packages, and knew from the shape of them that everything had been sent. Inside the hatbox he found a note from Lousteau:--

FLORINE'S DRAWING-ROOM.

"MY DEAR BOY,--The tailor behaved very well; but as thy profound retrospective glance led thee to forbode, the cravats, the hats, and the silk hosen perplexed our souls, for there was nothing in our purse to be perplexed thereby. As said Blondet, so say we; there is a fortune awaiting the establishment which will supply young men with inexpensive articles on credit; for when we do not pay in the beginning, we pay dear in the end. And by the by, did not the great Napoleon, who missed a voyage to the Indies for want of boots, say that, 'If a thing is easy, it is never done?' So everything went well--except the boots. I beheld a vision of thee, fully dressed, but without a hat! appareled in waistcoats, yet shoeless! and bethought me of sending a pair of moccasins given to Florine as a curiosity by an American. Florine offered the huge sum of forty francs, that we might try our luck at play for you. Nathan, Blondet, and I had such luck (as we were not playing for ourselves) that we were rich enough to ask La Torpille, des Lupeaulx's sometime 'rat,' to supper. Frascati certainly owed us that much. Florine undertook the shopping, and added three fine shirts to the purchases. Nathan sends you a cane. Blondet, who won three hundred francs, is sending you a gold chain; and the gold watch, the size of a forty-franc piece, is from La Torpille; some idiot gave the thing to her, and it will not go. 'Trumpery rubbish,' she says, 'like the man that owned it.' Bixiou, who came to find us up at the Rocher de Cancale, *wished to enclose a bottle of Portugal water in the package. Said our first comic man, 'If this can make him happy, let him have it!' growling it out in a deep bass voice with the* bourgeois *pomposity that he can act to the life. Which things, my dear boy, ought to prove to you how much we care for our friends in adversity. Florine, whom I have had the weakness to forgive, begs you to send us an article on Nathan's hat. Fare thee well, my son. I can only commiserate you on finding yourself back in the same box from which you emerged when you discovered your old comrade.*

"ETIENNE L."

"Poor fellows! They have been gambling for me," said Lucien; he was quite touched by the letter. A waft of the breeze from an unhealthy country, from the land where one has suffered most, may seem to bring the odors of Paradise; and in a dull life there is an indefinable sweetness in memories of past pain.

Eve was struck dumb with amazement when her brother came down in his new clothes. She did not recognize him.

"Now I can walk out in Beaulieu," he cried; "they shall not say it of me that I came back in rags. Look, here is a watch which I shall return to you, for it is mine; and, like its owner, it is erratic in its ways."

"What a child he is!" exclaimed Eve. "It is impossible to bear you any grudge."

"Then do you imagine, my dear girl, that I sent for all this with the silly idea of shining in Angouleme? I don't care that for Angouleme" (twirling his cane with the engraved gold knob). "I intend to repair the wrong I have done, and this is my battle array."

Lucien's success in this kind was his one real triumph; but the triumph, be it said, was immense. If admiration freezes some people's tongues, envy loosens at least as many more, and if women lost their heads over Lucien, men slandered him. He might have cried, in the words of the songwriter, "I thank thee, my coat!" He left two cards at the prefecture, and another upon Petit-Claud. The next day, the day of the banquet, the following paragraph appeared under the heading "Angouleme" in the Paris newspapers:--

"ANGOULEME.

"The return of the author of The Archer of Charles IX. *has been the signal for an ovation which does equal honor to the town and to M. Lucien de Rubempre, the young poet who has made so brilliant a beginning; the writer of the one French historical novel not written in the style of Scott, and of a preface which may be called a literary event. The town hastened to offer him a patriotic banquet on his return. The name of the recently-appointed prefect is associated with the public demonstration in honor of the author of the* Marguerites, *whose talent received such warm encouragement from Mme. du Chatelet at the outset of his career."*

In France, when once the impulse is given, nobody can stop. The colonel of the regiment offered to put his band at the disposal of the committee. The landlord of the Bell (renowned for truffled turkeys, despatched in the most wonderful porcelain jars to the uttermost parts of the earth), the famous innkeeper of L'Houmeau, would supply the repast. At five o'clock some forty persons, all in state and festival array, were assembled in his largest ball, decorated with hangings, crowns of laurel, and bouquets. The effect was superb. A crowd of onlookers, some hundred persons, attracted for the most part by the military band in the yard, represented the citizens of Angouleme.

Petit-Claud went to the window. "All Angouleme is here," he said, looking out.

"I can make nothing of this," remarked little Postel to his wife (they had come out to hear the band play). "Why, the prefect and the receiver-general, and the colonel and the superintendent of the powder factory, and our mayor and deputy, and the headmaster of the school, and the manager of the foundry at Ruelle, and the public prosecutor, M. Milaud, and all the authorities, have just gone in!"

317

The bank struck up as they sat down to table with variations on the air Vive le roy, vive la France, a melody which has never found popular favor. It was then five o'clock in the evening; it was eight o'clock before dessert was served. Conspicuous among the sixty-five dishes appeared an Olympus in confectionery, surmounted by a figure of France modeled in chocolate, to give the signal for toasts and speeches.

"Gentlemen," called the prefect, rising to his feet, "the King! the rightful ruler of France! To what do we owe the generation of poets and thinkers who maintain the sceptre of letters in the hands of France, if not to the peace which the Bourbons have restored----"

"Long live the King!" cried the assembled guests (ministerialists predominated).

The venerable headmaster rose.

"To the hero of the day," he said, "to the young poet who combines the gift of the prosateur with the charm and poetic faculty of Petrarch in that sonnet-form which Boileau declares to be so difficult."

Cheers.

The colonel rose next. "Gentlemen, to the Royalist! for the hero of this evening had the courage to fight for sound principles!"

"Bravo!" cried the prefect, leading the applause.

Then Petit-Claud called upon all Lucien's schoolfellows there present. "To the pride of the grammar-school of Angouleme! to the venerable headmaster so dear to us all, to whom the acknowledgment for some part of our triumph is due!"

The old headmaster dried his eyes; he had not expected this toast. Lucien rose to his feet, the whole room was suddenly silent, and the poet's face grew white. In that pause the old headmaster, who sat on his left, crowned him with a laurel wreath. A round of applause followed, and when Lucien spoke it was with tears in his eyes and a sob in his throat.

"He is drunk," remarked the attorney-general-designate to his neighbor, Petit-Claud.

"My dear fellow-countrymen, my dear comrades," Lucien said at last, "I could wish that all France might witness this scene; for thus men rise to their full stature, and in such ways as these our land demands great deeds and noble work of us. And when I think of the little that I have done, and of this great honor shown to me today, I can only feel confused and impose upon the future the task of justifying your reception of me. The recollection of this moment will give me renewed strength for efforts to come. Permit me to indicate for your homage my earliest muse and protectress, and to associate her name with that of my birthplace; so--to the Comtesse du Chatelet and the noble town of Angouleme!"

"He came out of that pretty well!" said the public prosecutor, nodding approval; "our speeches were all prepared, and his was improvised."

At ten o'clock the party began to break up, and little knots of guests went home together. David Sechard heard the unwonted music.

"What is going on in L'Houmeau?" he asked of Basine.

"They are giving a dinner to your brother-in-law, Lucien----"

"I know that he would feel sorry to miss me there," he said.

At midnight Petit-Claud walked home with Lucien. As they reached the Place du Murier, Lucien said, "Come life, come death, we are friends, my dear fellow."

"My marriage contract," said the lawyer, "with Mlle. Francoise de la Haye will be signed tomorrow at Mme. de Senonches' house; do me the pleasure of coming. Mme. de Senonches implored me to bring you, and you will meet Mme. du Chatelet; they are sure to tell her of your speech, and she will feel flattered by it."

"I knew what I was about," said Lucien.

"Oh! you will save David."

"I am sure I shall," the poet replied.

Just at that moment David appeared as if by magic in the Place du Murier. This was how it had come about. He felt that he was in a rather difficult position; his wife insisted that Lucien must neither go to David nor know of his hiding-place; and Lucien all the while was writing the most affectionate letters, saying that in a few days' time all should be set right; and even as Basine Clerget explained the reason why the band played, she put two letters into his hands. The first was from Eve.

"DEAREST," she wrote, "do as if Lucien were not here; do not trouble yourself in the least; our whole security depends upon the fact that your enemies cannot find you; get that idea firmly into your head. I have more confidence in Kolb and Marion and Basine than in my own brother; such is my misfortune. Alas! poor Lucien is not the ingenuous and tender-hearted poet whom we used to know; and it is simply because he is trying to interfere on your behalf, and because he imagines that he can discharge our debts (and this from pride, my David), that I am afraid of him. Some fine clothes have been sent from Paris for him, and five gold pieces in a pretty purse. He gave the money to me, and we are living on it.

"We have one enemy the less. Your father has gone, thanks to Petit-Claud. Petit-Claud unraveled his designs, and put an end to them at once by telling him that you would do nothing without consulting him, and that he (Petit-Claud) would not allow you to concede a single point in the matter of the invention until you had been promised an indemnity of thirty thousand francs; fifteen thousand to free you from embarrassment, and fifteen thousand more to be yours in any case, whether your invention succeeds or no. I cannot understand Petit-Claud. I embrace you, dear, a wife's kiss for her husband in trouble. Our little Lucien is well. How strange it is to watch him grow rosy and strong, like a flower, in these stormy days! Mother prays God for you now, as always, and sends love only less tender than mine.--Your "EVE."

As a matter of fact, Petit-Claud and the Cointets had taken fright at old Sechard's peasant shrewdness, and got rid of him so much the more easily because it was now vintage time at Marsac. Eve's letter enclosed another from Lucien:--

"MY DEAR DAVID,--Everything is going well. I am armed cap-a-pie; today I open the campaign, and in forty-eight hours I shall have made great progress. How glad I shall be to embrace you when you are free again and my debts are all paid! My mother and sister persist in mistrusting me; their suspicion wounds me to the quick. As if I did not know already that you are hiding with Basine, for every time that Basine comes to the house I hear news of you and receive answers to my letters; and besides, it is plain that my sister could not find any one else to trust. It hurts me cruelly to think that I shall be so near you today, and yet that you will not be present at this banquet in my honor. I owe my little triumph to the vainglory of Angouleme; in a few days it will be quite forgotten, and you alone would have taken a real pleasure in it. But, after all, in a little while you will pardon everything to one who counts it more than all the triumphs in the world to be your brother, "LUCIEN."

Two forces tugged sharply at David's heart; he adored his wife; and if he held Lucien in somewhat less esteem, his friendship was scarcely diminished. In solitude our feelings have unrestricted play; and a man preoccupied like David, with all-absorbing thoughts, will give way to impulses for which ordinary life would have provided a sufficient counterpoise. As he read Lucien's letter to the sound of military music, and heard of this unlooked-for recognition, he was deeply touched by that expression of regret. He had known how it would be. A very slight expression of feeling appeals irresistibly to a sensitive soul, for they are apt to credit others with like depths. How should the drop fall unless the cup were full to the brim?

So at midnight, in spite of all Basine's entreaties, David must go to see Lucien.

"Nobody will be out in the streets at this time of night," he said; "I shall not be seen, and they cannot arrest me. Even if I should meet people, I can make use of Kolb's way of going into hiding. And besides, it is so intolerably long since I saw my wife and child."

The reasoning was plausible enough; Basine gave way, and David went. Petit-Claud was just taking leave as he came up and at his cry of "Lucien!" the two brothers flung their arms about each other with tears in their eyes.

Life holds not many moments such as these. Lucien's heart went out in response to this friendship for its own sake. There was never question of debtor and creditor between them, and the offender met with no reproaches save his own. David, generous and noble that he was, was longing to bestow pardon; he meant first of all to read Lucien a lecture, and scatter the clouds that overspread the love of the brother and sister; and with these ends in view, the lack of money and its consequent dangers disappeared entirely from his mind.

"Go home," said Petit-Claud, addressing his client; "take advantage of your imprudence to see your wife and child again, at any rate; and you must not be seen, mind you!--How unlucky!" he added, when he was alone in the Place du Murier. "If only Cerizet were here----"

The buildings magniloquently styled the Angouleme Law Courts were then in process of construction. Petit-Claud muttered these words to himself as he passed by the hoardings, and heard a tap upon the boards, and a voice issuing from a crack between two planks.

"Here I am," said Cerizet; "I saw David coming out of L'Houmeau. I was beginning to have my suspicions about his retreat, and now I am sure; and I know where to have him. But I want to know something of Lucien's plans before I set the snare for David; and here are you sending him into the house! Find some excuse for stopping here, at least, and when David and Lucien come out, send them round this way; they will think they are quite alone, and I shall overhear their good-bye."

"You are a very devil," muttered Petit-Claud.

"Well, I'm blessed if a man wouldn't do anything for the thing you promised me."

Petit-Claud walked away from the hoarding, and paced up and down in the Place du Murier; he watched the windows of the room where the family sat together, and thought of his own prospects to keep up his courage. Cerizet's cleverness had given him the chance of striking the final blow. Petit-Claud was a double-dealer of the profoundly cautious stamp that is never caught by the bait of a present satisfaction, nor entangled by a personal attachment, after his first initiation into the strategy of self-seeking and the instability of the human heart. So, from the very first, he had put little trust in Cointet. He foresaw that his marriage negotiations might very easily be broken off, saw also that in that case he could not accuse Cointet of bad faith, and he had taken his measures accordingly. But since his success at the Hotel de Bargeton, Petit-Claud's game was above board. A certain under-plot of his was useless now, and even dangerous to a man with his political ambitions. He had laid the foundations of his future importance in the following manner:--

Gannerac and a few of the wealthy men of business in L'Houmeau formed a sort of Liberal clique in constant communication (through commercial channels) with the leaders of the Opposition. The Villele ministry, accepted by the dying Louis XVIII., gave the signal for a change of tactics in the Opposition camp; for, since the death of Napoleon, the liberals had ceased to resort to the dangerous expedient of conspiracy. They were busy organizing resistance by lawful means throughout the provinces, and aiming at securing control of the great bulk of electors by convincing the masses. Petit-Claud, a rabid Liberal, and a man of L'Houmeau, was the instigator, the secret counselor, and the very life of this movement in the lower town, which groaned under the tyranny of the aristocrats at the upper end. He was the first to see the danger of leaving the whole press of the department in the control of the Cointets; the Opposition must have its organ; it would not do to be behind other cities.

"If each one of us gives Gannerac a bill for five hundred francs, he would have some twenty thousand francs and more; we might buy up Sechard's printing-office, and we could do as we liked with the master-printer if we lent him the capital," Petit-Claud had said.

Others had taken up the idea, and in this way Petit-Claud strengthened his position with regard to David on the one side and the Cointets on the other. Casting about him for a tool for his party, he naturally thought that a rogue of Cerizet's calibre was the very man for the purpose.

"If you can find Sechard's hiding-place and put him in our hands, somebody will lend you twenty thousand francs to buy his business, and very likely there will be a newspaper to print. So, set about it," he had said.

Petit-Claud put more faith in Cerizet's activity than in all the Doublons in existence; and then it was that he promised Cointet that Sechard should be arrested. But now that the little lawyer cherished hopes of office, he saw that he must turn his back upon the Liberals; and, meanwhile, the amount for the printing-office had been subscribed in L'Houmeau. Petit-Claud decided to allow things to take their natural course.

"Pooh!" he thought, "Cerizet will get into trouble with his paper, and give me an opportunity of displaying my talents."

He walked up to the door of the printing-office and spoke to Kolb, the sentinel. "Go up and warn David that he had better go now," he said, "and take every precaution. I am going home; it is one o'clock."

Marion came to take Kolb's place. Lucien and David came down together and went out, Kolb a hundred paces ahead of them, and Marion at the same distance behind. The two friends walked past the hoarding, Lucien talking eagerly the while.

"My plan is extremely simple, David; but how could I tell you about it while Eve was there? She would never understand. I am quite sure that at the bottom of Louise's heart there is a feeling that I can rouse, and I should like to arouse it if it is only to avenge myself upon that idiot the prefect. If our love affair only lasts for a week, I will contrive to send an application through her for the subvention of twenty thousand francs for you. I am going to see her again tomorrow in the little boudoir where our old affair of the heart began; Petit-Claud says that the room is the same as ever; I shall play my part in the comedy; and I will send word by Basine tomorrow morning to tell you whether the actor was hissed. You may be at liberty by then, who knows?--Now do you understand how it was that I wanted clothes from Paris? One cannot act the lover's part in rags."

At six o'clock that morning Cerizet went to Petit-Claud.

"Doublon can be ready to take his man tomorrow at noon, I will answer for it," he said; "I know one of Mlle. Clerget's girls, do you understand?" Cerizet unfolded his plan, and Petit-Claud hurried to find Cointet.

"If M. Francis du Hautoy will settle his property on Francoise, you shall sign a deed of partnership with Sechard in two days. I shall not be married for a week after the contract is signed, so we shall both be within the terms of our little agreement, tit for tat. Tonight, however, we must keep a close watch over Lucien and Mme. la Comtesse du Chatelet, for the whole business lies in that. . . . If Lucien hopes to succeed through the Countess' influence, I have David safe----"

"You will be Keeper of the Seals yet, it is my belief," said Cointet.

"And why not? No one objects to M. de Peyronnet," said Petit-Claud. He had not altogether sloughed his skin of Liberalism.

Mlle. de la Haye's ambiguous position brought most of the upper town to the signing of the marriage contract. The comparative poverty of the young couple and the absence of a corbeille quickened the interest that people love to exhibit; for it is with beneficence as with ovations, we prefer the deeds of charity which gratify self-love. The Marquise de Pimentel, the Comtesse du Chatelet, M. de Senonches, and one or two frequenters of the house had given Francoise a few wedding presents, which made great talk in the city. These pretty trifles, together with the trousseau which Zephirine had been preparing for the past twelve months, the godfather's jewels, and the usual wedding gifts, consoled Francoise and roused the curiosity of some mothers of daughters.

Petit-Claud and Cointet had both remarked that their presence in the Angouleme Olympus was endured rather than courted. Cointet was Francoise's trustee and quasi-guardian; and if Petit-Claud was to sign the contract, Petit-Claud's presence was as necessary as the attendance of the man to be hanged at an execution; but though, once married, Mme. Petit-Claud might keep her right of entry to her godmother's house, Petit-Claud foresaw some difficulty on his own account, and resolved to be beforehand with these haughty personages.

He felt ashamed of his parents. He had sent his mother to stay at Mansle; now he begged her to say that she was out of health and to give her consent in writing. So humiliating was it to be without relations, protectors, or witnesses to his signature, that Petit-Claud thought himself in luck that he could bring a presentable friend at the Countess' request. He called to take up Lucien, and they drove to the Hotel de Bargeton.

On that memorable evening the poet dressed to outshine every man present. Mme. de Senonches had spoken of him as the hero of the hour, and a first interview between two estranged lovers is the kind of scene that provincials particularly love. Lucien had come to be the lion of the evening; he was said to be so handsome, so much changed, so wonderful, that every well-born woman in Angouleme was curious to see him again. Following the fashion of the transition period between the eighteenth century small clothes and the vulgar costume of the present day, he wore tight-fitting black trousers. Men still showed their figures in those days, to the utter despair of lean, clumsily-made mortals; and Lucien was an Apollo. The open-work gray silk stockings, the neat shoes, and the black satin waistcoat were scrupulously drawn over his person, and seemed to cling to him. His forehead looked the whiter by contrast with the thick, bright curls that rose above it with studied grace. The proud eyes were radiant. The hands, small as a woman's, never showed to better advantage than when gloved. He had modeled himself upon de Marsay, the famous Parisian dandy, holding his hat and cane in one hand, and keeping the other free for the very occasional gestures which illustrated his talk.

Lucien had quite intended to emulate the famous false modesty of those who bend their heads to pass beneath the Porte Saint-Denis, and to slip unobserved into the room; but Petit-Claud, having but one friend, made him useful. He brought Lucien almost pompously through a crowded room to Mme. de Senonches. The poet heard a murmur as he passed; not so very long ago that hum of voices would have turned his head, today he was quite different; he did not doubt that he himself was greater than the whole Olympus put together.

"Madame," he said, addressing Mme. de Senonches, "I have already congratulated my friend Petit-Claud (a man with the stuff in him of which Keepers of the Seals are made) on the honor of his approaching connection with you, slight as are the ties between godmother and goddaughter----" (this with the air of a man uttering an epigram, by no means lost upon any woman in the room, for every woman was listening without appearing to do so.) "And as for myself," he continued, "I am delighted to have the opportunity of paying my homage to you."

He spoke easily and fluently, as some great lord might speak under the roof of his inferiors; and as he listened to Zephirine's involved reply, he cast a glance over the room to consider the effect that he wished to make. The pause gave him time to discover Francis du Hautoy and the prefect; to bow gracefully to each with the proper shade of difference in his smile, and, finally, to approach Mme. du Chatelet as if he had just caught sight of her. That meeting was the real event of the evening. No one so much as thought of the marriage contract lying in the adjoining bedroom, whither Francoise and the notary led guest after guest to sign the document. Lucien made a step towards Louise de Negrepelisse, and then spoke with that grace of manner now associated, for her, with memories of Paris.

"Do I owe to you, madame, the pleasure of an invitation to dine at the Prefecture the day after tomorrow?" he said.

"You owe it solely to your fame, monsieur," Louise answered drily, somewhat taken aback by the turn of a phrase by which Lucien deliberately tried to wound her pride.

"Ah! Madame la Comtesse, I cannot bring you the guest if the man is in disgrace," said Lucien, and, without waiting for an answer, he turned and greeted the Bishop with stately grace.

"Your lordship's prophecy has been partially fulfilled," he said, and there was a winning charm in his tones; "I will endeavor to *fulfil it to the letter. I consider myself very fortunate since this evening brings me an opportunity of paying my respects to you."*

Lucien drew the Bishop into a conversation that lasted for ten minutes. The women looked on Lucien as a phenomenon. His unexpected insolence had struck Mme. du Chatelet dumb; she could not find an answer. Looking round the room, she saw that every woman admired Lucien; she watched group after group repeating the phrases by which Lucien crushed her with seeming disdain, and her heart contracted with a spasm of mortification.

"Suppose that he should not come to the Prefecture after this, what talk there would be!" she thought. "Where did he learn this pride? Can Mlle. des Touches have taken a fancy for him? . . . He is so handsome. They say that she hurried to see him in Paris the day after that actress died. . . . Perhaps he has come to the rescue of his brother-in-law, and happened to be behind our caleche at Mansle by accident. Lucien looked at us very strangely that morning."

A crowd of thoughts crossed Louise's brain, and unluckily for her, she continued to ponder visibly as she watched Lucien. He was talking with the Bishop as if he were the king of the room; making no effort to find any one out, waiting till others came to him, looking round about him with varying expression, and as much at his ease as his model de Marsay. M. de Senonches appeared at no great distance, but Lucien still stood beside the prelate.

At the end of ten minutes Louise could contain herself no longer. She rose and went over to the Bishop and said:

"What is being said, my lord, that you smile so often?"

Lucien drew back discreetly, and left Mme. du Chatelet with his lordship.

"Ah! Mme. la Comtesse, what a clever young fellow he is! He was explaining to me that he owed all he is to you----"

"I am not ungrateful, madame," said Lucien, with a reproachful glance that charmed the Countess.

"Let us have an understanding," she said, beckoning him with her fan. "Come into the boudoir. My Lord Bishop, you shall judge between us."

"She has found a funny task for his lordship," said one of the Chandour camp, sufficiently audibly.

"Judge between us!" repeated Lucien, looking from the prelate to the lady; "then, is one of us in fault?"

Louise de Negrepelisse sat down on the sofa in the familiar boudoir. She made the Bishop sit on one side and Lucien on the other, then she began to speak. But Lucien, to the joy and surprise of his old love, honored her with inattention; her words fell unheeded on his ears; he sat like Pasta in Tancredi, *with the words* O patria! *upon her lips, the music of the great cavatina* Dell Rizzo *might have passed into his face. Indeed, Coralie's pupil had contrived to bring the tears to his eyes.*

"Oh! Louise, how I loved you!" he murmured, careless of the Bishop's presence, heedless of the conversation, as soon as he knew that the Countess had seen the tears.

"Dry your eyes, or you will ruin me here a second time," she said in an aside that horrified the prelate.

"And once is enough," was Lucien's quick retort. "That speech from Mme. d'Espard's cousin would dry the eyes of a weeping Magdalene. Oh me! for a little moment old memories, and lost illusions, and my twentieth year came back to me, and you have----"

His lordship hastily retreated to the drawing-room at this; it seemed to him that his dignity was like to be compromised by this sentimental pair. Every one ostentatiously refrained from interrupting them, and a quarter of an hour went by; till at last Sixte du Chatelet, vexed by the laughter and talk, and excursions to the boudoir door, went in with a countenance distinctly overclouded, and found Louise and Lucien talking excitedly.

"Madame," said Sixte in his wife's ear, "you know Angouleme better than I do, and surely you should think of your position as Mme. la Prefete and of the Government?"

"My dear," said Louise, scanning her responsible editor with a haughtiness that made him quake, "I am talking with M. de

Rubempre of matters which interest you. It is a question of rescuing an inventor about to fall a victim to the basest machinations; you will help us. As to those ladies yonder, and their opinion of me, you shall see how I will freeze the venom of their tongues."

She came out of the boudoir on Lucien's arm, and drew him across to sign the contract with a great lady's audacity.

"Write your name after mine," she said, handing him the pen. And Lucien submissively signed in the place indicated beneath her name.

"M. de Senonches, would you have recognized M. de Rubempre?" she continued, and the insolent sportsman was compelled to greet Lucien.

She returned to the drawing-room on Lucien's arm, and seated him on the awe-inspiring central sofa between herself and Zephirine. There, enthroned like a queen, she began, at first in a low voice, a conversation in which epigram evidently was not wanting. Some of her old friends, and several women who paid court to her, came to join the group, and Lucien soon became the hero of the circle. The Countess drew him out on the subject of life in Paris; his satirical talk flowed with spontaneous and incredible spirit; he told anecdotes of celebrities, those conversational luxuries which the provincial devours with such avidity. His wit was as much admired as his good looks. And Mme. la Comtesse Sixte du Chatelet, preparing Lucien's triumph so patiently, sat like a player enraptured with the sound of his instrument; she gave him opportunities for a reply; she looked round the circle for applause so openly, that not a few of the women began to think that their return together was something more than a coincidence, and that Lucien and Louise, loving with all their hearts, had been separated by a double treason. Pique, very likely, had brought about this ill-starred match with Chatelet. And a reaction set in against the prefect.

Before the Countess rose to go at one o'clock in the morning, she turned to Lucien and said in a low voice, "Do me the pleasure of coming punctually tomorrow evening." Then, with the friendliest little nod, she went, saying a few words to Chatelet, who was looking for his hat.

"If Mme. du Chatelet has given me a correct idea of the state of affairs, count on me, my dear Lucien," said the prefect, preparing to hurry after his wife. She was going away without him, after the Paris fashion. "Your brother-in-law may consider that his troubles are at an end," he added as he went.

"M. le Comte surely owes me so much," smiled Lucien.

Cointet and Petit-Claud heard these farewell speeches.

"Well, well, we are done for now," Cointet muttered in his confederate's ear. Petit-Claud, thunderstruck by Lucien's success, amazed by his brilliant wit and varying charm, was gazing at Francoise de la Haye; the girl's whole face was full of admiration for Lucien. "Be like your friend," she seemed to say to her betrothed. A gleam of joy flitted over Petit-Claud's countenance.

"We still have a whole day before the prefect's dinner; I will answer for everything."

An hour later, as Petit-Claud and Lucien walked home together, Lucien talked of his success. "Well, my dear fellow, I came, I saw, I conquered! Sechard will be very happy in a few hours' time."

"Just what I wanted to know," thought Petit-Claud. Aloud he said--"I thought you were simply a poet, Lucien, but you are a Lauzun too, that is to say--twice a poet," and they shook hands--for the last time, as it proved.

"Good news, dear Eve," said Lucien, waking his sister, "David will have no debts in less than a month!"

"How is that?"

"Well, my Louise is still hidden by Mme. du Chatelet's petticoat. She loves me more than ever; she will send a favorable report of our discovery to the Minister of the Interior through her husband. So we have only to endure our troubles for one month, while I avenge myself on the prefect and complete the happiness of his married life."

Eve listened, and thought that she must be dreaming.

"I saw the little gray drawing-room where I trembled like a child two years ago; it seemed as if scales fell from my eyes when I saw the furniture and the pictures and the faces again. How Paris changes one's ideas!"

"Is that a good thing?" asked Eve, at last beginning to understand.

"Come, come; you are still asleep. We will talk about it tomorrow after breakfast."

Cerizet's plot was exceedingly simple, a commonplace stratagem familiar to the provincial bailiff. Its success entirely depends upon circumstances, and in this case it was certain, so intimate was Cerizet's knowledge of the characters and hopes of those concerned. Cerizet had been a kind of Don Juan among the young work-girls, ruling his victims by playing one off against another. Since he had been the Cointet's extra foreman, he had singled out one of Basine Clerget's assistants, a girl almost as handsome as Mme. Sechard. Henriette Signol's parents owned a small vineyard two leagues out of Angouleme, on the road to Saintes. The Signols, like everybody else in the country, could not afford to keep their only child at home; so they meant her to go out to service, in country phrase. The art of clear-starching is a part of every country housemaid's training; and so great was Mme. Prieur's reputation, that the Signols sent Henriette to her as apprentice, and paid for their daughter's board and lodging.

Mme. Prieur was one of the old-fashioned mistresses, who consider that they fill a parent's place towards their apprentices. They were part of the family; she took them with her to church, and looked scrupulously after them. Henriette Signol was a tall, fine-looking girl, with bold eyes, and long, thick, dark hair, and the pale, very fair complexion of girls in the South--white as a magnolia flower. For which reasons Henriette was one of the first on whom Cerizet cast his eyes; but Henriette came of "honest farmer folk," and only yielded at last to jealousy, to bad example, and the treacherous promise of subsequent marriage. By this time Cerizet was the Cointet's foreman. When he learned that the Signols owned a vineyard worth some ten or twelve thousand francs, and a tolerably comfortable cottage, he hastened to make it impossible for Henriette to marry any one else. Affairs had reached this point when Petit-Claud held out the prospect of a printing office and twenty thousand francs of borrowed capital, which was to prove a yoke upon the borrower's neck. Cerizet was dazzled, the offer turned his head; Henriette Signol was now only an obstacle in the way of his ambitions, and he neglected the poor girl. Henriette, in her despair, clung more closely to her seducer as he tried to shake her off. When Cerizet began to suspect that David was hiding in Basine's house, his views with regard to Henriette underwent another change, though he treated her as before. A kind of frenzy works in a girl's brain when she must marry her seducer to conceal her dishonor, and Cerizet was on the watch to turn this madness to his own account.

During the morning of the day when Lucien had set himself to reconquer his Louise, Cerizet told Basine's secret to Henriette, giving her to understand at the same time that their marriage and future prospects depended upon the discovery of David's hiding-place. Thus instructed, Henriette easily made certain of the fact that David was in Basine Clerget's inner room. It never occurred to the girl that she was doing wrong to act the spy, and Cerizet involved her in the guilt of betrayal by this first step.

Lucien was still sleeping while Cerizet, closeted with Petit-Claud, heard the history of the important trifles with which all Angouleme presently would ring.

The Cointets' foreman gave a satisfied nod as Petit-Claud came to an end. "Lucien surely has written you a line since he came back, has he not?" he asked.

"This is all that I have," answered the lawyer, and he held out a note on Mme. Sechard's writing-paper.

"Very well," said Cerizet, "let Doublon be in wait at the Palet Gate about ten minutes before sunset; tell him to post his gendarmes, and you shall have our man."

"Are you sure of your part of the business?" asked Petit-Claud, scanning Cerizet.

"I rely on chance," said the ex-street boy, "and she is a saucy huzzy; she does not like honest folk.

"You must succeed," said Cerizet. "You have pushed me into this dirty business; you may as well let me have a few banknotes to wipe off the stains."--Then detecting a look that he did not like in the attorney's face, he continued, with a deadly glance, "If you have cheated me, sir, if you don't buy the printing-office for me within a week--you will leave a young widow;" he lowered his voice.

"If we have David on the jail register at six o'clock, come round to M. Gannerac's at nine, and we will settle your business," said Petit-Claud peremptorily.

"Agreed. Your will shall be done, governor," said Cerizet.

Cerizet understood the art of washing paper, a dangerous art for the Treasury. He washed out Lucien's four lines and replaced them, imitating the handwriting with a dexterity which augured ill for his own future:--

"MY DEAR DAVID,--Your business is settled; you need not fear to go to the prefect. You can go out at sunset. I will come to meet you and tell you what to do at the prefecture.--Your brother, "LUCIEN."

At noon Lucien wrote to David, telling him of his evening's success. The prefect would be sure to lend his influence, he said; he was full of enthusiasm over the invention, and was drawing up a report that very day to send to the Government. Marion carried the letter to Basine, taking some of Lucien's linen to the laundry as a pretext for the errand.

Petit-Claud had told Cerizet that a letter would in all probability be sent. Cerizet called for Mlle. Signol, and the two walked by the Charente. Henriette's integrity must have held out for a long while, for the walk lasted for two hours. A whole future of happiness and ease and the interests of a child were at stake, and Cerizet asked a mere trifle of her. He was very careful besides to say nothing of the consequences of that trifle. She was only to carry a letter and a message, that was all; but it was the greatness of the reward for the trifling service that frightened Henriette. Nevertheless, Cerizet gained her consent at last; she would help him in his stratagem.

At five o'clock Henriette must go out and come in again, telling Basine Clerget that Mme. Sechard wanted to speak to her at once. Fifteen minutes after Basine's departure she must go upstairs, knock at the door of the inner room, and give David the forged note. That was all. Cerizet looked to chance to manage the rest.

For the first time in twelve months, Eve felt the iron grasp of necessity relax a little. She began at last to hope. She, too, would enjoy her brother's visit; she would show herself abroad on the arm of a man feted in his native town, adored by the women, beloved by the proud Comtesse du Chatelet. She dressed herself prettily, and proposed to walk out after dinner with her brother to Beaulieu. In September all Angouleme comes out at that hour to breathe the fresh air.

"Oh! that is the beautiful Mme. Sechard," voices said here and there.

"I should never have believed it of her," said a woman.

"The husband is in hiding, and the wife walks abroad," said Mme. Postel for young Mme. Sechard's benefit.

"Oh, let us go home," said poor Eve; "I have made a mistake."

A few minutes before sunset, the sound of a crowd rose from the steps that lead down to L'Houmeau. Apparently some crime had been committed, for persons coming from L'Houmeau were talking among themselves. Curiosity drew Lucien and Eve towards the steps.

"A thief has just been arrested no doubt, the man looks as pale as death," one of these passers-by said to the brother and sister. The crowd grew larger.

Lucien and Eve watched a group of some thirty children, old women and men, returning from work, clustering about the *gendarmes, whose gold-laced caps gleamed above the heads of the rest. About a hundred persons followed the procession, the crowd gathering like a storm cloud.*

"Oh! it is my husband!" Eve cried out.

"David!" exclaimed Lucien.

"It is his wife," said voices, and the crowd made way.

"What made you come out?" asked Lucien.

"Your letter," said David, haggard and white.

"I knew it!" said Eve, and she fainted away. Lucien raised his sister, and with the help of two strangers he carried her home; Marion laid her in bed, and Kolb rushed off for a doctor. Eve was still insensible when the doctor arrived; and Lucien was obliged to confess to his mother that he was the cause of David's arrest; for he, of course, knew nothing of the forged letter and Cerizet's stratagem. Then he went up to his room and locked himself in, struck dumb by the malediction in his mother's eyes.

In the dead of night he wrote one more letter amid constant interruptions; the reader can divine the agony of the writer's mind from those phrases, jerked out, as it were, one by one:--

"MY BELOVED SISTER,--We have seen each other for the last time. My resolution is final, and for this reason. In many families there is one unlucky member, a kind of disease in their midst. I am that unlucky one in our family. The observation is not mine; it was made at a friendly supper one evening at the Rocher de Cancale by a diplomate who has seen a great deal of the world. While we laughed and joked, he explained the reason why some young lady or some other remained unmarried, to the astonishment of the world --it was 'a touch of her father,' he said, and with that he unfolded his theory of inherited weaknesses. He told us how such and such a family would have flourished but for the mother; how it was that a son had ruined his father, or a father had stripped his children of prospects and respectability. It was said laughingly, but we thought of so many cases in point in ten minutes that I was struck with the theory. The amount of truth in it furnished all sorts of wild paradoxes, which journalists maintain cleverly enough for their own amusement when there is nobody else at hand to mystify. I bring bad luck to our family. My heart is full of love for you, yet I behave like an enemy. The blow dealt unintentionally is the cruelest blow of all. While I was leading a bohemian life in Paris, a life made up of pleasure and misery; taking good fellowship for friendship, forsaking my true friends for those who wished to exploit me, and succeeded; forgetful of you, or remembering you only to cause you trouble,--all that while you were walking in the humble path of hard work, making your way slowly but surely to the fortune which I tried so madly to snatch. While you grew better, I grew worse; a fatal element entered into my life through my own choice. Yes, unbounded ambition makes an obscure existence simply impossible for me. I have tastes and remembrances of past pleasures that poison the enjoyments within my reach; once I should have been satisfied with them, now it is too late. Oh, dear Eve, no one can think more hardly of me than I do myself; my condemnation is absolute and pitiless. The struggle in Paris demands steady effort; my will power is spasmodic, my brain works intermittently. The future is so appalling that I do not care to face it, and the present is intolerable.

"I wanted to see you again. I should have done better to stay in exile all my days. But exile without means of subsistence would be madness; I will not add another folly to the rest. Death is better than a maimed life; I cannot think of myself in any position in which my overweening vanity would not lead me into folly.

"Some human beings are like the figure 0, another must be put before it, and they acquire ten times their value. I am nothing unless a strong inexorable will is wedded to mine. Mme. de Bargeton was in truth my wife; when I refused to leave Coralie for her I spoiled my life. You and David might have been excellent pilots for me, but you are not strong enough to tame my weakness, which in some sort eludes control. I like an easy life, a life without cares; to clear an obstacle out of my way I can

descend to baseness that sticks at nothing. I was born a prince. I have more than the requisite intellectual dexterity for success, but only by moments; and the prizes of a career so crowded by ambitious competitors are to those who expend no more than the necessary strength, and retain a sufficient reserve when they reach the goal.

"I shall do harm again with the best intentions in the world. Some men are like oaks, I am a delicate shrub it may be, and I forsooth, must needs aspire to be a forest cedar.

"There you have my bankrupt's schedule. The disproportion between my powers and my desires, my want of balance, in short, will bring all my efforts to nothing. There are many such characters among men of letters, many men whose intellectual powers and character are always at variance, who will one thing and wish another. What would become of me? I can see it all beforehand, as I think of this and that great light that once shone on Paris, now utterly forgotten. On the threshold of old age I shall be a man older than my age, needy and without a name. My whole soul rises up against the thought of such a close; I will not be a social rag. Ah, dear sister, loved and worshiped at least as much for your severity at the last as for your tenderness at the first--if we have paid so dear for my joy at seeing you all once more, you and David may perhaps some day think that you could grudge no price however high for a little last happiness for an unhappy creature who loved you. Do not try to find me, Eve; do not seek to know what becomes of me. My intellect for once shall be backed by my will. Renunciation, my angel, is daily death of self; my renunciation will only last for one day; I will take advantage now of that day. . . .

'Two o'clock.

"Yes, I have quite made up my mind. Farewell for ever, dear Eve. There is something sweet in the thought that I shall live only in your hearts henceforth, and I wish no other burying place. Once more, farewell. . . . That is the last word from your brother

"LUCIEN."

Lucien read the letter over, crept noiselessly down stairs, and left it in the child's cradle; amid falling tears he set a last kiss on the forehead of his sleeping sister; then he went out. He put out his candle in the gray dusk, took a last look at the old house, stole softly along the passage, and opened the street door; but in spite of his caution, he awakened Kolb, who slept on a mattress on the workshop floor.

"Who goes there?" cried Kolb.

"It is I, Lucien; I am going away, Kolb."

"You vould haf done better gif you at nefer kom," Kolb muttered audibly.

"I should have done better still if I had never come into the world," Lucien answered. "Good-bye, Kolb; I don't bear you any grudge for thinking as I think myself. Tell David that I was sorry I could not bid him good-bye, and say that this was my last thought."

By the time the Alsacien was up and dressed, Lucien had shut the house door, and was on his way towards the Charente by the Promenade de Beaulieu. He might have been going to a festival, for he had put on his new clothes from Paris and his dandy's trinkets for a drowning shroud. Something in Lucien's tone had struck Kolb. At first the man thought of going to ask his mistress whether she knew that her brother had left the house; but as the deepest silence prevailed, he concluded that the departure had been arranged beforehand, and lay down again and slept.

Little, considering the gravity of the question, has been written on the subject of suicide; it has not been studied. Perhaps it is a disease that cannot be observed. Suicide is one effect of a sentiment which we will call self-esteem, if you will, to prevent confusion by using the word "honor." When a man despises himself, and sees that others despise him, when real life fails to fulfil his hopes, then comes the moment when he takes his life, and thereby does homage to society--shorn of his virtues or his splendor, he does not care to face his fellows. Among atheists--Christians being without the question of suicide--among

328

atheists, whatever may be said to the contrary, none but a base coward can take up a dishonored life.

There are three kinds of suicide--the first is only the last and acute stage of a long illness, and this kind belongs distinctly to pathology; the second is the suicide of despair; and the third the suicide based on logical argument. Despair and deductive reasoning had brought Lucien to this pass, but both varieties are curable; it is only the pathological suicide that is inevitable. Not infrequently you find all three causes combined, as in the case of Jean-Jacques Rousseau.

Lucien having made up his mind fell to considering methods. The poet would fain die as became a poet. At first he thought of throwing himself into the Charente and making an end then and there; but as he came down the steps from Beaulieu for the last time, he heard the whole town talking of his suicide; he saw the horrid sight of a drowned dead body, and thought of the recognition and the inquest; and, like some other suicides, felt that vanity reached beyond death.

He remembered the day spent at Courtois' mill, and his thoughts returned to the round pool among the willows that he saw as he came along by the little river, such a pool as you often find on small streams, with a still, smooth surface that conceals great depths beneath. The water is neither green nor blue nor white nor tawny; it is like a polished steel mirror. No sword-grass grows about the margin; there are no blue water forget-me-nots, nor broad lily leaves; the grass at the brim is short and thick, and the weeping willows that droop over the edge grow picturesquely enough. It is easy to imagine a sheer precipice beneath filled with water to the brim. Any man who should have the courage to fill his pockets with pebbles would not fail to find death, and never be seen thereafter.

At the time while he admired the lovely miniature of a landscape, the poet had thought to himself, "'Tis a spot to make your mouth water for a noyade."

He thought of it now as he went down into L'Houmeau; and when he took his way towards Marsac, with the last sombre thoughts gnawing at his heart, it was with the firm resolve to hide his death. There should be no inquest held over him, he would not be laid in earth; no one should see him in the hideous condition of the corpse that floats on the surface of the water. Before long he reached one of the slopes, common enough on all French highroads, and commonest of all between Angouleme and Poitiers. He saw the coach from Bordeaux to Paris coming up at full speed behind him, and knew that the passengers would probably alight to walk up the hill. He did not care to be seen just then. Turning off sharply into a beaten track, he began to pick the flowers in a vineyard hard by.

When Lucien came back to the road with a great bunch of the yellow stone-crop which grows everywhere upon the stony soil of the vineyards, he came out upon a traveler dressed in black from head to foot. The stranger wore powder, there were silver buckles on his shoes of Orleans leather, and his brown face was scarred and seamed as if he had fallen into the fire in infancy. The traveler, so obviously clerical in his dress, was walking slowly and smoking a cigar. He turned as Lucien jumped down from the vineyard into the road. The deep melancholy on the handsome young face, the poet's symbolical flowers, and his elegant dress seemed to strike the stranger. He looked at Lucien with something of the expression of a hunter that has found his quarry at last after long and fruitless search. He allowed Lucien to come alongside in nautical phrase; then he slackened his pace, and appeared to look along the road up the hill; Lucien, following the direction of his eyes, saw a light traveling carriage with two horses, and a post-boy standing beside it.

"You have allowed the coach to pass you, monsieur; you will lose your place unless you care to take a seat in my caleche and overtake the mail, for it is rather quicker traveling post than by the public conveyance." The traveler spoke with extreme politeness and a very marked Spanish accent.

Without waiting for an answer, he drew a cigar-case from his pocket, opened it, and held it out to Lucien.

"I am not on a journey," said Lucien, "and I am too near the end of my stage to indulge in the pleasure of smoking----"

"You are very severe with yourself," returned the Spaniard. "Though I am a canon of the cathedral of Toledo, I occasionally

329

smoke a cigarette. God gave us tobacco to allay our passions and our pains. You seem to be downcast, or at any rate, you carry the symbolical flower of sorrow in your hand, like the rueful god Hymen. Come! all your troubles will vanish away with the smoke," and again the ecclesiastic held out his little straw case; there was something fascinating in his manner, and kindliness towards Lucien lighted up his eyes.

"Forgive me, father" Lucien answered stiffly; "there is no cigar that can scatter my troubles." Tears came to his eyes at the words.

"It must surely be Divine Providence that prompted me to take a little exercise to shake off a traveler's morning drowsiness," said the churchman. "A divine prompting to fulfil my mission here on earth by consoling you.--What great trouble can you have at your age?"

"Your consolations, father, can do nothing for me. You are a Spaniard, I am a Frenchman; you believe in the commandments of the Church, I am an atheist."

"Santa Virgen del Pilar! you are an atheist!" cried the other, laying a hand on Lucien's arm with maternal solicitude. "Ah! here is one of the curious things I promised myself to see in Paris. We, in Spain, do not believe in atheists. There is no country but France where one can have such opinions at nineteen years."

"Oh! I am an atheist in the fullest sense of the word. I have no belief in God, in society, in happiness. Take a good look at me, father; for in a few hours' time life will be over for me. My last sun has risen," said Lucien; with a sort of rhetorical effect he waved his hand towards the sky.

"How so; what have you done that you must die? Who has condemned you to die?"

"A tribunal from which there is no appeal--I myself."

"You, child!" cried the priest. "Have you killed a man? Is the scaffold waiting for you? Let us reason together a little. If you are resolved, as you say, to return to nothingness, everything on earth is indifferent to you, is it not?"

Lucien bowed assent.

"Very well, then; can you not tell me about your troubles? Some little affair of the heart has taken a bad turn, no doubt?"

Lucien shrugged his shoulders very significantly.

"Are you resolved to kill yourself to escape dishonor, or do you despair of life? Very good. You can kill yourself at Poitiers quite as easily as at Angouleme, and at Tours it will be no harder than at Poitiers. The quicksands of the Loire never give up their prey----"

"No, father," said Lucien; "I have settled it all. Not three weeks ago I chanced upon the most charming raft that can ferry a man sick and tired of this life into the other world----"

"The other world? You are not an atheist."

"Oh! by another world I mean my next transformation, animal or plant."

"Have you some incurable disease?"

"Yes, father."

"Ah! now we come to the point. What is it?"

"Poverty."

The priest looked at Lucien. "The diamond does not know its own value," he said, and there was an inexpressible charm, and a touch of something like irony in his smile.

"None but a priest could flatter a poor man about to die," exclaimed Lucien.

"You are not going to die," the Spaniard returned authoritatively.

"I have heard many times of men that were robbed on the highroad, but I have never yet heard of one that found a fortune there," said Lucien.

"You will hear of one now," said the priest, glancing towards the carriage to measure the time still left for their walk together. "Listen to me," he continued, with his cigar between his teeth; "if you are poor, that is no reason why you should die. I need a secretary, for mine has just died at Barcelona. I am in the same position as the famous Baron Goertz, minister of Charles XII. He was traveling toward Sweden (just as I am going to Paris), and in some little town or other he chanced upon the son of a goldsmith, a young man of remarkable good looks, though they could scarcely equal yours. . . . Baron Goertz discerned intelligence in the young man (just as I see poetry on your brow); he took him into his traveling carriage, as I shall take you very shortly; and of a boy condemned to spend his days in burnishing spoons and forks and making trinkets in some little town like Angouleme, he made a favorite, as you shall be mine.

"Arrived at Stockholm, he installed his secretary and overwhelmed him with work. The young man spent his nights in writing, and, like all great workers, he contracted a bad habit, a trick--he took to chewing paper. The late M. de Malesherbes use to rap people over the knuckles; and he did this once, by the by, to somebody or other whose suit depended upon him. The handsome young secretary began by chewing blank paper, found it insipid for a while, and acquired a taste for manuscript as having more flavor. People did not smoke as yet in those days. At last, from flavor to flavor, he began to chew parchment and swallow it. Now, at that time a treaty was being negotiated between Russia and Sweden. The States-General insisted that Charles XII. should make peace (much as they tried in France to make Napoleon treat for peace in 1814) and the basis of these negotiations was the treaty between the two powers with regard to Finland. Goertz gave the original into his secretary's keeping; but when the time came for laying the draft before the States-General, a trifling difficulty arose; the treaty was not to be found. The States-General believed that the Minister, pandering to the King's wishes, had taken it into his head to get rid of the document. Baron Goertz was, in fact, accused of this, and the secretary owned that he had eaten the treaty. He was tried and convicted and condemned to death.--But you have not come to that yet, so take a cigar and smoke till we reach the caleche."

Lucien took a cigar and lit it, Spanish fashion, at the priest's cigar. "He is right," he thought; "I can take my life at any time."

"It often happens that a young man's fortunes take a turn when despair is darkest," the Spaniard continued. "That is what I wished to tell you, but I preferred to prove it by a case in point. Here was the handsome young secretary lying under sentence of death, and his case the more desperate because, as he had been condemned by the States-General, the King could not pardon him, but he connived at his escape. The secretary stole away in a fishing-boat with a few crowns in his pocket, and reached the court of Courland with a letter of introduction from Goertz, explaining his secretary's adventures and his craze for paper. The Duke of Courland was a spendthrift; he had a steward and a pretty wife--three several causes of ruin. He placed the charming young stranger with his steward.

"If you can imagine that the sometime secretary had been cured of his depraved taste by a sentence of death, you do not know the grip that a man's failings have upon him; let a man discover some satisfaction for himself, and the headsman will not keep him from it.--How is it that the vice has this power? Is it inherent strength in the vice, or inherent weakness in human nature? Are there certain tastes that should be regarded as verging on insanity? For myself, I cannot help laughing at the moralists who try to expel such diseases by fine phrases.--Well, it so fell out that the steward refused a demand for money; and the Duke taking fright at this, called for an audit. Sheer imbecility! Nothing easier than to make out a balance-sheet; the difficulty never lies there. The steward gave his secretary all the necessary documents for compiling a schedule of the civil list of Courland. He had nearly finished it when, in the dead of night, the unhappy paper-eater discovered that he was chewing up

one of the Duke's discharges for a considerable sum. He had eaten half the signature! Horror seized upon him; he fled to the Duchess, flung himself at her feet, told her of his craze, and implored the aid of his sovereign lady, implored her in the middle of the night. The handsome young face made such an impression on the Duchess that she married him as soon as she was left a widow. And so in the mid- eighteenth century, in a land where the king-at-arms is king, the goldsmith's son became a prince, and something more. On the death of Catherine I. he was regent; he ruled the Empress Anne, and tried to be the Richelieu of Russia. Very well, young man; now know this--if you are handsomer than Biron, I, simple canon that I am, am worth more than a Baron Goertz. So get in; we will find a duchy of Courland for you in Paris, or failing the duchy, we shall certainly find the duchess."

The Spanish priest laid a hand on Lucien's arm, and literally forced him into the traveling carriage. The postilion shut the door.

"Now speak; I am listening," said the canon of Toledo, to Lucien's bewilderment. "I am an old priest; you can tell me everything, there is nothing to fear. So far we have only run through our patrimony or squandered mamma's money. We have made a flitting from our creditors, and we are honor personified down to the tips of our elegant little boots. . . . Come, confess, boldly; it will be just as if you were talking to yourself."

Lucien felt like that hero of an Eastern tale, the fisher who tried to drown himself in mid-ocean, and sank down to find himself a king of countries under the sea. The Spanish priest seemed so really affectionate, that the poet hesitated no longer; between Angouleme and Ruffec he told the story of his whole life, omitting none of his misdeeds, and ended with the final catastrophe which he had brought about. The tale only gained in poetic charm because this was the third time he had told it in the past fortnight. Just as he made an end they passed the house of the Rastignac family.

"Young Rastignac left that place for Paris," said Lucien; "he is certainly not my equal, but he has had better luck."

The Spaniard started at the name. "Oh!" he said.

"Yes. That shy little place belongs to his father. As I was telling you just now, he was the lover of Mme. de Nucingen, the famous banker's wife. I drifted into poetry; he was cleverer, he took the practical side."

The priest stopped the caleche; and was so far curious as to walk down the little avenue that led to the house, showing more interest in the place than Lucien expected from a Spanish ecclesiastic.

"Then, do you know the Rastignacs?" asked Lucien.

"I know every one in Paris," said the Spaniard, taking his place again in the carriage. "And so for want of ten or twelve thousand francs, you were about to take your life; you are a child, you know neither men nor things. A man's future is worth the value that he chooses to set upon it, and you value yours at twelve thousand francs! Well, I will give more than that for you any time. As for your brother-in-law's imprisonment, it is the merest trifle. If this dear M. Sechard has made a discovery, he will be a rich man some day, and a rich man has never been imprisoned for debt. You do not seem to me to be strong in history. History is of two kinds--there is the official history taught in schools, a lying compilation ad usum delphini; and there is the secret history which deals with the real causes of events --a scandalous chronicle. Let me tell you briefly a little story which you have not heard. There was, once upon a time, a man, young and ambitious, and a priest to boot. He wanted to enter upon a political career, so he fawned on the Queen's favorite; the favorite took an interest in him, gave him the rank of minister, and a seat at the council board. One evening somebody wrote to the young aspirant, thinking to do him a service (never do a service, by the by, unless you are asked), and told him that his benefactor's life was in danger. The King's wrath was kindled against his rival; tomorrow, if the favorite went to the palace, he would certainly be stabbed; so said the letter. Well, now, young man, what would you have done?"

"I should have gone at once to warn my benefactor," Lucien exclaimed quickly.

"You are indeed the child which your story reveals!" said the priest. "Our man said to himself, 'If the King is resolved to go to

332

such lengths, it is all over with my benefactor; I must receive this letter too late;' so he slept on till the favorite was stabbed----"

"He was a monster!" said Lucien, suspecting that the priest meant to sound him.

"So are all great men; this one was the Cardinal de Richelieu, and his benefactor was the Marechal d'Ancre. You really do not know your history of France, you see. Was I not right when I told you that history as taught in schools is simply a collection of facts and dates, more than doubtful in the first place, and with no bearing whatever on the gist of the matter. You are told that such a person as Jeanne Darc once existed; where is the use of that? Have you never drawn your own conclusions from that fact? never seen that if France had accepted the Angevin dynasty of the Plantagenets, the two peoples thus reunited would be ruling the world today, and the islands that now brew political storms for the continent would be French provinces?. . . Why, have you so much as studied the means by which simple merchants like the Medicis became Grand Dukes of Tuscany?"

"A poet in France is not bound to be 'as learned as a Benedictine,'" said Lucien.

"Well, they became Grand-Dukes as Richelieu became a minister. If you had looked into history for the causes of events instead of getting the headings by heart, you would have found precepts for your guidance in this life. These real facts taken at random from among so many supply you with the axiom--'Look upon men, and on women most of all, as your instruments; but never let them see this.' If some one higher in place can be useful to you, worship him as your god; and never leave him until he has paid the price of your servility to the last farthing. In your intercourse with men, in short, be grasping and mean as a Jew; all that the Jew does for money, you must do for power. And besides all this, when a man has fallen from power, care no more for him than if he had ceased to exist. And do you ask why you must do these things? You mean to rule the world, do you not? You must begin by obeying and studying it. Scholars study books; politicians study men, and their interests and the springs of action. Society and mankind in masses are fatalists; they bow down and worship the accomplished fact. Do you know why I am giving you this little history lesson? It seems to me that your ambition is boundless----"

"Yes, father."

"I saw that myself," said the priest. "But at this moment you are thinking, 'Here is this Spanish canon inventing anecdotes and straining history to prove to me that I have too much virtue----'"

Lucien began to smile; his thoughts had been read so clearly.

"Very well, let us take facts that every schoolboy knows. One day France is almost entirely overrun by the English; the King has only a single province left. Two figures arise from among the people--a poor herd girl, that very Jeanne Darc of whom we were speaking, and a burgher named Jacques Coeur. The girl brings the power of virginity, the strength of her arm; the burgher gives his gold, and the kingdom is saved. The maid is taken prisoner, and the King, who could have ransomed her, leaves her to be burned alive. The King allows his courtier to accuse the great burgher of capital crime, and they rob him and divide all his wealth among themselves. The spoils of an innocent man, hunted down, brought to bay, and driven into exile by the Law, went to enrich five noble houses; and the father of the Archbishop of Bourges left the kingdom for ever without one sou of all his possessions in France, and no resource but moneys remitted to Arabs and Saracens in Egypt. It is open to you to say that these examples are out of date, that three centuries of public education have since elapsed, and that the outlines of those ages are more or less dim figures. Well, young man, do you believe in the last demi-god of France, in Napoleon? One of his generals was in disgrace all through his career; Napoleon made him a marshal grudgingly, and never sent him on service if he could help it. That marshal was Kellermann. Do you know the reason of the grudge? . . . Kellermann saved France and the First Consul at Marengo by a brilliant charge; the ranks applauded under fire and in the thick of the carnage. That heroic charge was not even mentioned in the bulletin. Napoleon's coolness toward Kellermann, Fouche's fall, and Talleyrand's disgrace were all attributable to the same cause; it is the ingratitude of a Charles VII., or a Richelieu, or ----"

"But, father," said Lucien, "suppose that you should save my life and make my fortune, you are making the ties of gratitude somewhat slight."

"Little rogue," said the Abbe, smiling as he pinched Lucien's ear with an almost royal familiarity. "If you are ungrateful to me, it will be because you are a strong man, and I shall bend before you. But you are not that just yet; as a simple 'prentice you have tried to be master too soon, the common fault of Frenchmen of your generation. Napoleon's example has spoiled them all. You send in your resignation because you have not the pair of epaulettes that you fancied. But have you attempted to bring the full force of your will and every action of your life to bear upon your one idea?"

"Alas! no."

"You have been inconsistent, as the English say," smiled the canon.

"What I have been matters nothing now," said Lucien, "if I can be nothing in the future."

"If at the back of all your good qualities there is power semper virens," continued the priest, not averse to show that he had a little Latin, "nothing in this world can resist you. I have taken enough of a liking for you already----"

Lucien smiled incredulously.

"Yes," said the priest, in answer to the smile, "you interest me as much as if you had been my son; and I am strong enough to afford to talk to you as openly as you have just done to me. Do you know what it is that I like about you?--This: you have made a sort of tabula rasa within yourself, and are ready to hear a sermon on morality that you will hear nowhere else; for mankind in the mass are even more consummate hypocrites than any one individual can be when his interests demand a piece of acting. Most of us spend a good part of our lives in clearing our minds of the notions that sprang up unchecked during our nonage. This is called 'getting our experience.'"

Lucien, listening, thought within himself, "Here is some old intriguer delighted with a chance of amusing himself on a journey. He is pleased with the idea of bringing about a change of opinion in a poor wretch on the brink of suicide; and when he is tired of his amusement, he will drop me. Still he understands paradox, and seems to be quite a match for Blondet or Lousteau."

But in spite of these sage reflections, the diplomate's poison had sunk deeply into Lucien's soul; the ground was ready to receive it, and the havoc wrought was the greater because such famous examples were cited. Lucien fell under the charm of his companion's cynical talk, and clung the more willingly to life because he felt that this arm which drew him up from the depths was a strong one.

In this respect the ecclesiastic had evidently won the day; and, indeed, from time to time a malicious smile bore his cynical anecdotes company.

"If your system of morality at all resembles your manner of regarding history," said Lucien, "I should dearly like to know the motive of your present act of charity, for such it seems to be."

"There, young man, I have come to the last head of my sermon; you will permit me to reserve it, for in that case we shall not part company today," said the canon, with the tact of the priest who sees that his guile has succeeded.

"Very well, talk morality," said Lucien. To himself he said, "I will draw him out."

"Morality begins with the law," said the priest. "If it were simply a question of religion, laws would be superfluous; religious peoples have few laws. The laws of statecraft are above civil law. Well, do you care to know the inscription which a politician can read, written at large over your nineteenth century? In 1793 the French invented the idea of the sovereignty of the people--and the sovereignty of the people came to an end under the absolute ruler in the Emperor. So much for your history as a nation. Now for your private manners. Mme. Tallien and Mme. Beauharnais both acted alike. Napoleon married the one, and made her your Empress; the other he would never receive at court, princess though she was. The sans-culotte of 1793 takes the Iron Crown in 1804. The fanatical lovers of Equality or Death conspire fourteen years afterwards with a Legitimist aristocracy to bring back Louis XVIII. And that same aristocracy, lording it today in the Faubourg Saint-Germain, has done worse--has been merchant, usurer, pastry-cook, farmer, and shepherd. So in France systems political and moral have started from one point and reached another diametrically opposed; and men have expressed one kind of opinion and acted on another. There has been no consistency in national policy, nor in the conduct of individuals. You cannot be said to have any morality left. Success is the supreme justification of all actions whatsoever. The fact in itself is nothing; the impression that it makes upon others is everything. Hence, please observe a second precept: Present a fair exterior to the world, keep the seamy side of life to yourself, and turn a resplendent countenance upon others. Discretion, the motto of every ambitious man, is the watchword of our Order; take it for your own. Great men are guilty of almost as many base deeds as poor outcasts; but they are careful to do these things in shadow and to parade their virtues in the light, or they would not be great men. Your insignificant man leaves his virtues in the shade; he publicly displays his pitiable side, and is despised accordingly. You, for instance, have hidden your titles to greatness and made a display of your worst failings. You openly took an actress for your mistress, lived with her and upon her; you were by no means to blame for this; everybody admitted that both of you were perfectly free to do as you liked; but you ran full tilt against the ideas of the world, and the world has not shown you the consideration that is shown to those who obey the rules of the game. If you had left Coralie to this M. Camusot, if you had hidden your relations with her, you might have married Mme. de Bargeton; you would now be prefect of Angouleme and Marquis de Rubempre.

"Change your tactics, bring your good looks, your charm, your wit, your poetry to the front. If you indulge in small discreditable courses, let it be within four walls, and you will never again be guilty of a blot on the decorations of this great theatrical scene called society. Napoleon called this 'washing dirty linen at home.' The corollary follows naturally on this second precept--Form is everything. Be careful to grasp the meaning of that word 'form.' There are people who, for want of knowing better, will help themselves to money under pressure of want, and take it by force. These people are called criminals; and, perforce, they square accounts with Justice. A poor man of genius discovers some secret, some invention as good as a treasure; you lend him three thousand francs (for that, practically, the Cointets have done; they hold your bills, and they are about to rob your brother-in-law); you torment him until he reveals or partly reveals his secret; you settle your accounts with your own conscience, and your conscience does not drag you into the assize court.

"The enemies of social order, beholding this contrast, take occasion to yap at justice, and wax wroth in the name of the people, because, forsooth, burglars and fowl-stealers are sent to the hulks, while a man who brings whole families to ruin by a fraudulent bankruptcy is let off with a few months' imprisonment. But these hypocrites know quite well that the judge who passes sentence on the thief is maintaining the barrier set between the poor and the rich, and that if that barrier were overturned, social chaos would ensue; while, in the case of the bankrupt, the man who steals an inheritance cleverly, and the banker who slaughters a business for his own benefit, money merely changes hands, that is all.

"Society, my son, is bound to draw those distinctions which I have pointed out for your benefit. The one great point is this--you must be a match for society. Napoleon, Richelieu, and the Medicis were a match for their generations. And as for you, you value yourself at twelve thousand francs! You of this generation in France worship the golden calf; what else is the religion of your Charter that will not recognize a man politically unless he owns property? What is this but the command, 'Strive to be rich?' Some day, when you shall have made a fortune without breaking the law, you will be rich; you will be the Marquis de Rubempre, and you can indulge in the luxury of honor. You will be so extremely sensitive on the point of honor that no one will dare to accuse you of past shortcomings if in the process of making your way you should happen to smirch it now and again, which I myself should never advise," he added, patting Lucien's hand.

"So what must you put in that comely head of yours? Simply this and nothing more--propose to yourself a brilliant and conspicuous goal, and go towards it secretly; let no one see your methods or your progress. You have behaved like a child; be a man, be a hunter, lie in wait for your quarry in the world of Paris, wait for your chance and your game; you need not be particular nor mindful of your dignity, as it is called; we are all of us slaves to something, to some failing of our own or to necessity; but keep that law of laws--secrecy."

"Father, you frighten me," said Lucien; "this seems to me to be a highwayman's theory."

"And you are right," said the canon, "but it is no invention of mine. All parvenus reason in this way--the house of Austria and the house of France alike. You have nothing, you say? The Medicis, Richelieu, and Napoleon started from precisely your standpoint; but they, my child, considered that their prospects were worth ingratitude, treachery, and the most glaring inconsistencies. You must dare all things to gain all things. Let us discuss it. Suppose that you sit down to a game of bouillotte, do you begin to argue over the rules of the game? There they are, you accept them."

"Come, now," thought Lucien, "he can play bouillotte."

"And what do you do?" continued the priest; "do you practise openness, that fairest of virtues? Not merely do you hide your tactics, but you do your best to make others believe that you are on the brink of ruin as soon as you are sure of winning the game. In short, you dissemble, do you not? You lie to win four or five louis d'or. What would you think of a player so generous as to proclaim that he held a hand full of trumps? Very well; the ambitious man who carries virtue's precepts into the arena when his antagonists have left them behind is behaving like a child. Old men of the world might say to him, as card-players would say to the man who declines to take advantage of his trumps, 'Monsieur, you ought not to play at bouillotte.'

"Did you make the rules of the game of ambition? Why did I tell you to be a match for society?--Because, in these days, society by degrees has usurped so many rights over the individual, that the individual is compelled to act in self-defence. There is no question of laws now, their place has been taken by custom, which is to say grimacings, and forms must always be observed."

Lucien started with surprise.

"Ah, my child!" said the priest, afraid that he had shocked Lucien's innocence; "did you expect to find the Angel Gabriel in an Abbe loaded with all the iniquities of the diplomacy and counter-diplomacy of two kings? I am an agent between Ferdinand VII. and Louis XVIII., two--kings who owe their crowns to profound--er--combinations, let us say. I believe in God, but I have a still greater belief in our Order, and our Order has no belief save in temporal power. In order to strengthen and consolidate the temporal power, our Order upholds the Catholic Apostolic and Roman Church, which is to say, the doctrines which dispose the world at large to obedience. We are the Templars of modern times; we have a doctrine of our own. Like the Templars, we have been dispersed, and for the same reasons; we are almost a match for the world. If you will enlist as a soldier, I will be your captain. Obey me as a wife obeys her husband, as a child obeys his mother, and I will guarantee that you shall be Marquis de Rubempre in less than six months; you shall marry into one of the proudest houses in the Faubourg Saint-Germain, and some day you shall sit on a bench with peers of France. What would you have been at this moment if I had not amused you by my conversation?--An undiscovered corpse in a deep bed of mud. Well and good, now for an effort of imagination----"

Lucien looked curiously at his protector.

"Here, in this caleche beside the Abbe Carlos Herrera, canon of Toledo, secret envoy from His Majesty Ferdinand VII. to his Majesty the King of France, bearer of a despatch thus worded it may be--'When you have delivered me, hang all those whom I favor at this moment, more especially the bearer of this despatch, for then he can tell no tales'--well, beside this envoy sits a young man who has nothing in common with that poet recently deceased. I have fished you out of the water, I have brought you to life again, you belong to me as the creature belongs to the creator, as the efrits of fairytales belong to the genii, as the janissary to the Sultan, as the soul to the body. I will sustain you in the way to power with a strong hand; and at the same time I promise that your life shall be a continual course of pleasure, honors, and enjoyment. You shall never want for money.

You shall shine, you shall go bravely in the eyes of the world; while I, crouching in the mud, will lay a firm foundation for the brilliant edifice of your fortunes. For I love power for its own sake. I shall always rejoice in your enjoyment, forbidden to me. In short, my self shall become your self! Well, if a day should come when this pact between man and the tempter, this agreement between the child and the diplomatist should no longer suit your ideas, you can still look about for some quiet spot, like that pool of which you were speaking, and drown yourself; you will only be as you are now, or a little more or a little less wretched and dishonored."

"This is not like the Archbishop of Granada's homily," said Lucien as they stopped to change horses.

"Call this concentrated education by what name you will, my son, for you are my son, I adopt you henceforth, and shall make you my heir; it is the Code of ambition. God's elect are few and far between. There is no choice, you must bury yourself in the cloister (and there you very often find the world again in miniature) or accept the Code."

"Perhaps it would be better not to be so wise," said Lucien, trying to fathom this terrible priest.

"What!" rejoined the canon. "You begin to play before you know the rules of the game, and now you throw it up just as your chances are best, and you have a substantial godfather to back you! And you do not even care to play a return match? You do not mean to say that you have no mind to be even with those who drove you from Paris?"

Lucien quivered; the sounds that rang through every nerve seemed to come from some bronze instrument, some Chinese gong.

"I am only a poor priest," returned his mentor, and a grim expression, dreadful to behold, appeared for a moment on a face burned to a copper-red by the sun of Spain, "I am only a poor priest; but if I had been humiliated, vexed, tormented, betrayed, and sold as you have been by the scoundrels of whom you have told me, I should do like an Arab of the desert--I would devote myself body and soul to vengeance. I might end by dangling from a gibbet, garroted, impaled, guillotined in your French fashion, I should not care a rap; but they should not have my head until I had crushed my enemies under my heel."

Lucien was silent; he had no wish to draw the priest out any further.

"Some are descended from Cain and some from Abel," the canon concluded; "I myself am of mixed blood--Cain for my enemies, Abel for my friends. Woe to him that shall awaken Cain! After all, you are a Frenchman; I am a Spaniard, and, what is more, a canon."

"What a Tartar!" thought Lucien, scanning the protector thus sent to him by Heaven.

There was no sign of the Jesuit, nor even of the ecclesiastic, about the Abbe Carlos Herrera. His hands were large, he was thick-set and broad-chested, evidently he possessed the strength of a Hercules; his terrific expression was softened by benignity assumed at will; but a complexion of impenetrable bronze inspired feelings of repulsion rather than attachment for the man.

The strange diplomatist looked somewhat like a bishop, for he wore powder on his long, thick hair, after the fashion of the Prince de Talleyrand; a gold cross, hanging from a strip of blue ribbon with a white border, indicated an ecclesiastical dignitary. The outlines beneath the black silk stockings would not have disgraced an athlete. The exquisite neatness of his clothes and person revealed an amount of care which a simple priest, and, above all, a Spanish priest, does not always take with his appearance. A three-cornered hat lay on the front seat of the carriage, which bore the arms of Spain.

In spite of the sense of repulsion, the effect made by the man's appearance was weakened by his manner, fierce and yet winning as it was; he evidently laid himself out to please Lucien, and the winning manner became almost coaxing. Yet Lucien noticed the smallest trifles uneasily. He felt that the moment of decision had come; they had reached the second stage beyond Ruffec, and the decision meant life or death.

The Spaniard's last words vibrated through many chords in his heart, and, to the shame of both, it must be said that all that was worst in Lucien responded to an appeal deliberately made to his evil impulses, and the eyes that studied the poet's beautiful face had read him very clearly. Lucien beheld Paris once more; in imagination he caught again at the reins of power let fall from his unskilled hands, and he avenged himself! The comparisons which he himself had drawn so lately between the life of Paris and life in the provinces faded from his mind with the more painful motives for suicide; he was about to return to his natural sphere, and this time with a protector, a political intriguer unscrupulous as Cromwell.

"I was alone, now there will be two of us," he told himself. And then this priest had been more and more interested as he told of his sins one after another. The man's charity had grown with the extent of his misdoings; nothing had astonished this confessor. And yet, what could be the motive of a mover in the intrigues of kings? Lucien at first was fain to be content with the banal answer--the Spanish are a generous race. The Spaniard is generous! even so the Italian is jealous and a poisoner, the Frenchman fickle, the German frank, the Jew ignoble, and the Englishman noble. Reverse these verdicts and you shall arrive within a reasonable distance of the truth! The Jews have monopolized the gold of the world; they compose Robert the Devil, act Phedre, sing William Tell, give commissions for pictures and build palaces, write Reisebilder and wonderful verse; they are more powerful than ever, their religion is accepted, they have lent money to the Holy Father himself! As for Germany, a foreigner is often asked whether he has a contract in writing, and this is in the smallest matters, so tricky are they in their dealings. In France the spectacle of national blunders has never lacked national applause for the past fifty years; we continue to wear hats which no mortal can explain, and every change of government is made on the express condition that things shall remain exactly as they were before. England flaunts her perfidy in the face of the world, and her abominable treachery is only equaled by her greed. All the gold of two Indies passed through the hands of Spain, and now she has nothing left. There is no country in the world where poison is so little in request as in Italy, no country where manners are easier or more gentle. As for the Spaniard, he has traded largely on the reputation of the Moor.

As the Canon of Toledo returned to the caleche, he had spoken a word to the post-boy. "Drive post-haste," he said, "and there will be three francs for drink-money for you." Then, seeing that Lucien hesitated, "Come! come!" he exclaimed, and Lucien took his place again, telling himself that he meant to try the effect of the argumentum ad hominem.

"Father," he began, "after pouring out, with all the coolness in the world, a series of maxims which the vulgar would consider profoundly immoral----"

"And so they are," said the priest; "that is why Jesus Christ said that it must needs be that offences come, my son; and that is why the world displays such horror of offences."

"A man of your stamp will not be surprised by the question which I am about to ask?"

"Indeed, my son, you do not know me," said Carlos Herrera. "Do you suppose that I should engage a secretary unless I knew that I could depend upon his principles sufficiently to be sure that he would not rob me? I like you. You are as innocent in every way as a twenty-year-old suicide. Your question?"

"Why do you take an interest in me? What price do you set on my obedience? Why should you give me everything? What is your share?"

The Spaniard looked at Lucien, and a smile came over his face.

"Let us wait till we come to the next hill; we can walk up and talk out in the open. The back seat of a traveling carriage is not the place for confidences."

They traveled in silence for sometime; the rapidity of the movement seemed to increase Lucien's moral intoxication.

"Here is a hill, father," he said at last awakening from a kind of dream.

"Very well, we will walk." The Abbe called to the postilion to stop, and the two sprang out upon the road.

338

"You child," said the Spaniard, taking Lucien by the arm, "have you ever thought over Otway's Venice Preserved? Did you understand the profound friendship between man and man which binds Pierre and Jaffier each to each so closely that a woman is as nothing in comparison, and all social conditions are changed?--Well, so much for the poet."

"So the canon knows something of the drama," thought Lucien. "Have you read Voltaire?" he asked.

"I have done better," said the other; "I put his doctrine in practice."

"You do not believe in God?"

"Come! it is I who am the atheist, is it?" the Abbe said, smiling. "Let us come to practical matters, my child," he added, putting an arm round Lucien's waist. "I am forty-six years old, I am the natural son of a great lord; consequently, I have no family, and I have a heart. But, learn this, carve it on that still so soft brain of yours--man dreads to be alone. And of all kinds of isolation, inward isolation is the most appalling. The early anchorite lived with God; he dwelt in the spirit world, the most populous world of all. The miser lives in a world of imagination and fruition; his whole life and all that he is, even his sex, lies in his brain. A man's first thought, be he leper or convict, hopelessly sick or degraded, is to find another with a like fate to share it with him. He will exert the utmost that is in him, every power, all his vital energy, to satisfy that craving; it is his very life. But for that tyrannous longing, would Satan have found companions? There is a whole poem yet to be written, a first part of Paradise Lost; Milton's poem is only the apology for the revolt."

"It would be the Iliad of Corruption," said Lucien.

"Well, I am alone, I live alone. If I wear the priest's habit, I have not a priest's heart. I like to devote myself to some one; that is my weakness. That is my life, that is how I came to be a priest. I am not afraid of ingratitude, and I am grateful. The Church is nothing to me; it is an idea. I am devoted to the King of Spain, but you cannot give affection to a King of Spain; he is my protector, he towers above me. I want to love my creature, to mould him, fashion him to my use, and love him as a father loves his child. I shall drive in your tilbury, my boy, enjoy your success with women, and say to myself, 'This fine young fellow, this Marquis de Rubempre, my creation whom I have brought into this great world, is my very Self; his greatness is my doing, he speaks or is silent with my voice, he consults me in everything.' The Abbe de Vermont felt thus for Marie-Antoinette."

"He led her to the scaffold."

"He did not love the Queen," said the priest. "HE only loved the Abbe de Vermont."

"Must I leave desolation behind me?"

"I have money, you shall draw on me."

"I would do a great deal just now to rescue David Sechard," said Lucien, in the tone of one who has given up all idea of suicide.

"Say but one word, my son, and by tomorrow morning he shall have money enough to set him free."

"What! Would you give me twelve thousand francs?"

"Ah! child, do you not see that we are traveling on at the rate of four leagues an hour? We shall dine at Poitiers before long, and there, if you decide to sign the pact, to give me a single proof of obedience, a great proof that I shall require, then the Bordeaux coach shall carry fifteen thousand francs to your sister----"

"Where is the money?"

The Spaniard made no answer, and Lucien said within himself, "There I had him; he was laughing at me."

In another moment they took their places. Neither of them said a word. Silently the Abbe groped in the pocket of the coach, and drew out a traveler's leather pouch with three divisions in it; thence he took a hundred Portuguese moidores, bringing out his large hand filled with gold three times.

"Father, I am yours," said Lucien, dazzled by the stream of gold.

"Child!" said the priest, and set a tender kiss on Lucien's forehead. "There is twice as much still left in the bag, besides the money for traveling expenses."

"And you are traveling alone!" cried Lucien.

"What is that?" asked the Spaniard. "I have more than a hundred thousand crowns in drafts on Paris. A diplomatist without money is in your position of this morning--a poet without a will of his own!"

As Lucien took his place in the caleche beside the so-called Spanish diplomatist, Eve rose to give her child a draught of milk, found the fatal letter in the cradle, and read it. A sudden cold chilled the damps of morning slumber, dizziness came over her, she could not see. She called aloud to Marion and Kolb.

"Has my brother gone out?" she asked, and Kolb answered at once with, "Yes, Montame, pefore tay."

"Keep this that I am going to tell you a profound secret," said Eve. "My brother has gone no doubt to make away with himself. Hurry, both of you, make inquiries cautiously, and look along the river."

Eve was left alone in a dull stupor, dreadful to see. Her trouble was at its height when Petit Claud came in at seven o'clock to talk over the steps to be taken in David's case. At such a time, any voice in the world may speak, and we let them speak.

"Our poor, dear David is in prison, madame," so began Petit-Claud. "I foresaw all along that it would end in this. I advised him at the time to go into partnership with his competitors the Cointets; for while your husband has simply the idea, they have the means of putting it into practical shape. So as soon as I heard of his arrest yesterday evening, what did I do but hurry away to find the Cointets and try to obtain such concessions as might satisfy you. If you try to keep the discovery to yourselves, you will continue to live a life of shifts and chicanery. You must give in, or else when you are exhausted and at the last gasp, you will end by making a bargain with some capitalist or other, and perhaps to your own detriment, whereas today I hope to see you make a good one with MM. Cointet. In this way you will save yourselves the hardships and the misery of the inventor's duel with the greed of the capitalist and the indifference of the public. Let us see! If the MM. Cointet should pay your debts--if, over and above your debts, they should pay you a further sum of money down, whether or no the invention succeeds; while at the same time it is thoroughly understood that if it succeeds a certain proportion of the profits of working the patent shall be yours, would you not be doing very well? --You yourself, madame, would then be the proprietor of the plant in the printing-office. You would sell the business, no doubt; it is quite worth twenty thousand francs. I will undertake to find you a buyer at that price.

"Now if you draw up a deed of partnership with the MM. Cointet, and receive fifteen thousand francs of capital; and if you invest it in the funds at the present moment, it will bring you in an income of two thousand francs. You can live on two thousand francs in the provinces. Bear in mind, too, madame, that, given certain contingencies, there will be yet further payments. I say 'contingencies,' because we must lay our accounts with failure.

"Very well," continued Petit-Claud, "now these things I am sure that I can obtain for you. First of all, David's release from prison; secondly, fifteen thousand francs, a premium paid on his discovery, whether the experiments fail or succeed; and lastly, a partnership between David and the MM. Cointet, to be taken out after private experiment made jointly. The deed of partnership for the working of the patent should be drawn up on the following basis: The MM. Cointet to bear all the expenses, the capital invested by David to be confined to the expenses of procuring the patent, and his share of the profits to be fixed at twenty-five per cent. You are a clear-headed and very sensible woman, qualities which are not often found combined with great beauty; think over these proposals, and you will see that they are very favorable."

Poor Eve in her despair burst into tears. "Ah, sir! why did you not come yesterday evening to tell me this? We should have been spared disgrace and--and something far worse----"

"I was talking with the Cointets until midnight. They are behind Metivier, as you must have suspected. But how has something worse than our poor David's arrest happened since yesterday evening?"

"Here is the awful news that I found when I awoke this morning," she said, holding out Lucien's letter. "You have just given me proof of your interest in us; you are David's friend and Lucien's; I need not ask you to keep the secret----"

"You need not feel the least anxiety," said Petit-Claud, as he returned the letter. "Lucien will not take his life. Your husband's arrest was his doing; he was obliged to find some excuse for leaving you, and this exit of his looks to me like a piece of stage business."

The Cointets had gained their ends. They had tormented the inventor and his family, until, worn out by the torture, the victims longed for a respite, and then seized their opportunity and made the offer. Not every inventor has the tenacity of the bull-dog that will perish with his teeth fast set in his capture; the Cointets had shrewdly estimated David's character. The tall Cointet looked upon David's imprisonment as the first scene of the first act of the drama. The second act opened with the proposal which Petit-Claud had just made. As arch-schemer, the attorney looked upon Lucien's frantic folly as a bit of unhoped-for luck, a chance that would finally decide the issues of the day.

Eve was completely prostrated by this event; Petit-Claud saw this, and meant to profit by her despair to win her confidence, for he saw at last how much she influenced her husband. So far from discouraging Eve, he tried to reassure her, and very cleverly diverted her thoughts to the prison. She should persuade David to take the Cointets into partnership.

"David told me, madame, that he only wished for a fortune for your sake and your brother's; but it should be clear to you by now that to try to make a rich man of Lucien would be madness. The youngster would run through three fortunes."

Eve's attitude told plainly enough that she had no more illusions left with regard to her brother. The lawyer waited a little so that her silence should have the weight of consent.

"Things being so, it is now a question of you and your child," he said. "It rests with you to decide whether an income of two thousand francs will be enough for your welfare, to say nothing of old Sechard's property. Your father-in-law's income has amounted to seven or eight thousand francs for a long time past, to say nothing of capital lying out at interest. So, after all, you have a good prospect before you. Why torment yourself?"

Petit-Claud left Eve Sechard to reflect upon this prospect. The whole scheme had been drawn up with no little skill by the tall Cointet the evening before.

"Give them the glimpse of a possibility of money In hand," the lynx had said, when Petit-Claud brought the news of the arrest; "once let them grow accustomed to that idea, and they are ours; we will drive a bargain, and little by little we shall bring them down to our price for the secret."

The argument of the second act of the commercial drama was in a manner summed up in that speech.

Mme. Sechard, heartbroken and full of dread for her brother's fate, dressed and came downstairs. An agony of terror seized her when she thought that she must cross Angouleme alone on the way to the prison. Petit-Claud gave little thought to his fair client's distress. When he came back to offer his arm, it was from a tolerably Machiavellian motive; but Eve gave him credit for delicate consideration, and he allowed her to thank him for it. The little attention, at such a moment, from so hard a man, modified Mme. Sechard's previous opinion of Petit-Claud.

"I am taking you round by the longest way," he said, "and we shall meet nobody."

"For the first time in my life, monsieur, I feel that I have no right to hold up my head before other people; I had a sharp lesson given to me last night----"

"It will be the first and the last."

"Oh! I certainly shall not stay in the town now----"

"Let me know if your husband consents to the proposals that are all but definitely offered by the Cointets," said Petit-Claud at the gate of the prison; "I will come at once with an order for David's release from Cachan, and in all likelihood he will not go back again to prison."

This suggestion, made on the very threshold of the jail, was a piece of cunning strategy--a combinazione, *as the Italians call an indefinable mixture of treachery and truth, a cunningly planned fraud which does not break the letter of the law, or a piece of deft trickery for which there is no legal remedy. St. Bartholomew's for instance, was a political combination.*

Imprisonment for debt, for reasons previously explained, is such a rare occurrence in the provinces, that there is no house of detention, and a debtor is perforce imprisoned with the accused, convicted, and condemned--the three graduated subdivisions of the class generically styled criminal. David was put for the time being in a cell on the ground floor from which some prisoner had probably been recently discharged at the end of his time. Once inscribed on the jailer's register, with the amount allowed by the law for a prisoner's board for one month, David confronted a big, stout man, more powerful than the King himself in a prisoner's eyes; this was the jailer.

An instance of a thin jailer is unknown in the provinces. The place, to begin with, is almost a sinecure, and a jailer is a kind of innkeeper who pays no rent and lives very well, while his prisoners fare very ill; for, like an innkeeper, he gives them rooms according to their payments. He knew David by name, and what was more, knew about David's father, and thought that he might venture to let the printer have a good room on credit for one night; for David was penniless.

The prison of Angouleme was built in the Middle Ages, and has no more changed than the old cathedral. It is built against the old presidial, *or ancient court of appeal, and people still call it the* maison de justice. *It boasts the conventional prison gateway, the solid-looking, nail-studded door, the low, worn archway which the better deserves the qualification "cyclopean," because the jailer's peephole or* judas *looks out like a single eye from the front of the building. As you enter you find yourself in a corridor which runs across the entire width of the building, with a row of doors of cells that give upon the prison yard and are lighted by high windows covered with a square iron grating. The jailer's house is separated from these cells by an archway in the middle, through which you catch a glimpse of the iron gate of the prison yard. The jailer installed David in a cell next to the archway, thinking that he would like to have a man of David's stamp as a near neighbor for the sake of company.*

"This is the best room," he said. David was struck dumb with amazement at the sight of it.

The stone walls were tolerably damp. The windows, set high in the wall, were heavily barred; the stone-paved floor was cold as ice, and from the corridor outside came the sound of the measured tramp of the warder, monotonous as waves on the beach. "You are a prisoner! you are watched and guarded!" said the footsteps at every moment of every hour. All these small things together produce a prodigious effect upon the minds of honest folk. David saw that the bed was execrable, but the first night in a prison is full of violent agitation, and only on the second night does the prisoner notice that his couch is hard. The jailer was graciously disposed; he naturally suggested that his prisoner should walk in the yard until nightfall.

David's hour of anguish only began when he was locked into his cell for the night. Lights are not allowed in the cells. A prisoner detained on arrest used to be subjected to rules devised for malefactors, unless he brought a special exemption signed by the public prosecutor. The jailer certainly might allow David to sit by his fire, but the prisoner must go back to his cell at locking-up time. Poor David learned the horrors of prison life by experience, the rough coarseness of the treatment revolted him. Yet a revulsion, familiar to those who live by thought, passed over him. He detached himself from his loneliness, and found a way of escape in a poet's waking dream.

At last the unhappy man's thoughts turned to his own affairs. The stimulating influence of a prison upon conscience and self-

scrutiny is immense. David asked himself whether he had done his duty as the head of a family. What despairing grief his wife must feel at this moment! Why had he not done as Marion had said, and earned money enough to pursue his investigations at leisure?

"How can I stay in Angouleme after such a disgrace? And when I come out of prison, what will become of us? Where shall we go?"

Doubts as to his process began to occur to him, and he passed through an agony which none save inventors can understand. Going from doubt to doubt, David began to see his real position more clearly; and to himself he said, as the Cointets had said to old Sechard, as Petit-Claud had just said to Eve, "Suppose that all should go well, what does it amount to in practice? The first thing to be done is to take out a patent, and money is needed for that--and experiments must be tried on a large scale in a paper-mill, which means that the discovery must pass into other hands. Oh! Petit-Claud was right!"

A very vivid light sometimes dawns in the darkest prison.

"Pshaw!" said David; "I shall see Petit-Claud tomorrow no doubt," and he turned and slept on the filthy mattress covered with coarse brown sacking.

So when Eve unconsciously played into the hands of the enemy that morning, she found her husband more than ready to listen to proposals. She put her arms about him and kissed him, and sat down on the edge of the bed (for there was but one chair of the poorest and commonest kind in the cell). Her eyes fell on the unsightly pail in a corner, and over the walls covered with inscriptions left by David's predecessors, and tears filled the eyes that were red with weeping. She had sobbed long and very bitterly, but the sight of her husband in a felon's cell drew fresh tears.

"And the desire of fame may lead one to this!" she cried. "Oh! my angel, give up your career. Let us walk together along the beaten track; we will not try to make haste to be rich, David. . . . I need very little to be very happy, especially now, after all that we have been through. . . . And if you only knew--the disgrace of arrest is not the worst. . . . Look."

She held out Lucien's letter, and when David had read it, she tried to comfort him by repeating Petit-Claud's bitter comment.

"If Lucien has taken his life, the thing is done by now," said David; "if he has not made away with himself by this time, he will not kill himself. As he himself says, 'his courage cannot last longer than a morning----'"

"But the suspense!" cried Eve, forgiving almost everything at the thought of death. Then she told her husband of the proposals which Petit-Claud professed to have received from the Cointets. David accepted them at once with manifest pleasure.

"We shall have enough to live upon in a village near L'Houmeau, where the Cointets' paper-mill stands. I want nothing now but a quiet life," said David. "If Lucien has punished himself by death, we can wait so long as father lives; and if Lucien is still living, poor fellow, he will learn to adapt himself to our narrow ways. The Cointets certainly will make money by my discovery; but, after all, what am I compared with our country? One man in it, that is all; and if the whole country is benefited, I shall be content. There! dear Eve, neither you nor I were meant to be successful in business. We do not care enough about making a profit; we have not the dogged objection to parting with our money, even when it is legally owing, which is a kind of virtue of the counting-house, for these two sorts of avarice are called prudence and a faculty of business."

Eve felt overjoyed; she and her husband held the same views, and this is one of the sweetest flowers of love; for two human beings who love each other may not be of the same mind, nor take the same view of their interests. She wrote to Petit-Claud telling him that they both consented to the general scheme, and asked him to release David. Then she begged the jailer to deliver the message.

Ten minutes later Petit-Claud entered the dismal place. "Go home, madame," he said, addressing Eve, "we will follow you.-- Well, my dear friend" (turning to David), "so you allowed them to catch you! Why did you come out? How came you to make *such a mistake?"*

"Eh! how could I do otherwise? Look at this letter that Lucien wrote."

David held out a sheet of paper. It was Cerizet's forged letter.

Petit-Claud read it, looked at it, fingered the paper as he talked, and still taking, presently, as if through absence of mind, folded it up and put it in his pocket. Then he linked his arm in David's, and they went out together, the order for release having come during the conversation.

It was like heaven to David to be at home again. He cried like a child when he took little Lucien in his arms and looked round his room after three weeks of imprisonment, and the disgrace, according to provincial notions, of the last few hours. Kolb and Marion had come back. Marion had heard in L'Houmeau that Lucien had been seen walking along on the Paris road, somewhere beyond Marsac. Some country folk, coming in to market, had noticed his fine clothes. Kolb, therefore, had set out on horseback along the highroad, and heard at last at Mansle that Lucien was traveling post in a caleche--M. Marron had recognized him as he passed.

"What did I tell you?" said Petit-Claud. "That fellow is not a poet; he is a romance in heaven knows how many chapters."

"Traveling post!" repeated Eve. "Where can he be going this time?"

"Now go to see the Cointets, they are expecting you," said Petit-Claud, turning to David.

"Ah, monsieur!" cried the beautiful Eve, "pray do your best for our interests; our whole future lies in your hands."

"If you prefer it, madame, the conference can be held here. I will leave David with you. The Cointets will come this evening, and you shall see if I can defend your interests."

"Ah! monsieur, I should be very glad," said Eve.

"Very well," said Petit-Claud; "this evening, at seven o'clock."

"Thank you," said Eve; and from her tone and glance Petit-Claud knew that he had made great progress in his fair client's confidence.

"You have nothing to fear; you see I was right," he added. "Your brother is a hundred miles away from suicide, and when all comes to all, perhaps you will have a little fortune this evening. A bona-fide purchaser for the business has turned up."

"If that is the case," said Eve, "why should we not wait awhile before binding ourselves to the Cointets?"

Petit-Claud saw the danger. "You are forgetting, madame," he said, "that you cannot sell your business until you have paid M. Metivier; for a distress warrant has been issued."

As soon as Petit-Claud reached home he sent for Cerizet, and when the printer's foreman appeared, drew him into the embrasure of the window.

"Tomorrow evening," he said, "you will be the proprietor of the Sechards' printing-office, and then there are those behind you who have influence enough to transfer the license;" (then in a lowered voice), "but you have no mind to end in the hulks, I suppose?"

"The hulks! What's that? What's that?"

"Your letter to David was a forgery. It is in my possession. What would Henriette say in a court of law? I do not want to ruin you," he added hastily, seeing how white Cerizet's face grew.

"You want something more of me?" cried Cerizet.

"Well, here it is," said Petit-Claud. "Follow me carefully. You will be a master printer in Angouleme in two months' time . . . but you will not have paid for your business--you will not pay for it in ten years. You will work a long while yet for those that have

lent you the money, and you will be the cat's-paw of the Liberal party. . . . Now I shall draw up your agreement with Gannerac, and I can draw it up in such a way that you will have the business in your own hands one of these days. But--if the Liberals start a paper, if you bring it out, and if I am deputy public prosecutor, then you will come to an understanding with the Cointets and publish articles of such a nature that they will have the paper suppressed. . . . The Cointets will pay you handsomely for that service. . . . I know, of course, that you will be a hero, a victim of persecution; you will be a personage among the Liberals--a Sergeant Mercier, a Paul-Louis Courier, a Manual on a small scale. I will take care that they leave you your license. In fact, on the day when the newspaper is suppressed, I will burn this letter before your eyes. . . . Your fortune will not cost you much."

A working man has the haziest notions as to the law with regard to forgery; and Cerizet, who beheld himself already in the dock, breathed again.

"In three years' time," continued Petit-Claud, "I shall be public prosecutor in Angouleme. You may have need of me some day; bear that in mind."

"It's agreed," said Cerizet, "but you don't know me. Burn that letter now and trust to my gratitude."

Petit-Claud looked Cerizet in the face. It was a duel in which one man's gaze is a scalpel with which he essays to probe the soul of another, and the eyes of that other are a theatre, as it were, to which all his virtue is summoned for display.

Petit-Claud did not utter a word. He lighted a taper and burned the letter. "He has his way to make," he said to himself.

"Here is one that will go through fire and water for you," said Cerizet.

David awaited the interview with the Cointets with a vague feeling of uneasiness; not, however, on account of the proposed partnership, nor for his own interests--he felt nervous as to their opinion of his work. He was in something the same position as a dramatic author before his judges. The inventor's pride in the discovery so nearly completed left no room for any other feelings.

At seven o'clock that evening, while Mme. du Chatelet, pleading a sick headache, had gone to her room in her unhappiness over the rumors of Lucien's departure; while M. de Comte, left to himself, was entertaining his guests at dinner--the tall Cointet and his stout brother, accompanied by Petit-Claud, opened negotiations with the competitor who had delivered himself up, bound hand and foot.

A difficulty awaited them at the outset. How was it possible to draw up a deed of partnership unless they knew David's secret? And if David divulged his secret, he would be at the mercy of the Cointets. Petit-Claud arranged that the deed of partnership should be the first drawn up. Thereupon the tall Cointet asked to see some specimens of David's work, and David brought out the last sheet that he had made, guaranteeing the price of production.

"Well," said Petit-Claud, "there you have the basis of the agreement ready made. You can go into partnership on the strength of those samples, inserting a clause to protect yourselves in case the conditions of the patent are not fulfilled in the manufacturing process."

"It is one thing to make samples of paper on a small scale in your own room with a small mould, monsieur, and another to turn out a quantity," said the tall Cointet, addressing David. "Quite another thing, as you may judge from this single fact. We manufacture colored papers. We buy parcels of coloring absolutely identical. Every cake of indigo used for 'blueing' our post-demy is taken from a batch supplied by the same maker. Well, we have never yet been able to obtain two batches of precisely the same shade. There are variations in the material which we cannot detect. The quantity and the quality of the pulp modify every question at once. Suppose that you have in a caldron a quantity of ingredients of some kind (I don't ask to know what

345

they are), you can do as you like with them, the treatment can be uniformly applied, you can manipulate, knead, and pestle the mass at your pleasure until you have a homogeneous substance. But who will guarantee that it will be the same with a batch of five hundred reams, and that your plan will succeed in bulk?"

David, Eve, and Petit-Claud looked at one another; their eyes said many things.

"Take a somewhat similar case," continued the tall Cointet after a pause. "You cut two or three trusses of meadow hay, and store it in a loft before 'the heat is out of the grass,' as the peasants say; the hay ferments, but no harm comes of it. You follow up your experiment by storing a couple of thousand trusses in a wooden barn--and, of course, the hay smoulders, and the barn blazes up like a lighted match. You are an educated man," continued Cointet; "you can see the application for yourself. So far, you have only cut your two trusses of hay; we are afraid of setting fire to our paper-mill by bringing in a couple of thousand trusses. In other words, we may spoil more than one batch, make heavy losses, and find ourselves none the better for laying out a good deal of money."

David was completely floored by this reasoning. Practical wisdom spoke in matter-of-fact language to theory, whose word is always for the future.

"Devil fetch me, if I'll sign such a deed of partnership!" the stout Cointet cried bluntly. "You may throw away your money if you like, Boniface; as for me, I shall keep mine. Here is my offer--to pay M. Sechard's debts and six thousand francs, and another three thousand francs in bills at twelve and fifteen months," he added. "That will be quite enough risk to run.--We have a balance of twelve thousand francs against Metivier. That will make fifteen thousand francs.--That is all that I would pay for the secret if I were going to exploit it for myself. So this is the great discovery that you were talking about, Boniface! Many thanks! I thought you had more sense. No, you can't call this business."

"The question for you," said Petit-Claud, undismayed by the explosion, "resolves itself into this: 'Do you care to risk twenty thousand francs to buy a secret that may make rich men of you?' Why, the risk usually is in proportion to the profit, gentlemen. You stake twenty thousand francs on your luck. A gambler puts down a louis at roulette for a chance of winning thirty-six, but he knows that the louis is lost. Do the same."

"I must have time to think it over," said the stout Cointet; "I am not so clever as my brother. I am a plain, straight-forward sort of chap, that only knows one thing--how to print prayer-books at twenty sous and sell them for two francs. Where I see an invention that has only been tried once, I see ruin. You succeed with the first batch, you spoil the next, you go on, and you are drawn in; for once put an arm into that machinery, the rest of you follows," and he related an anecdote very much to the point--how a Bordeaux merchant had ruined himself by following a scientific man's advice, and trying to bring the Landes into cultivation; and followed up the tale with half-a-dozen similar instances of agricultural and commercial failures nearer home in the departments of the Charente and Dordogne. He waxed warm over his recitals. He would not listen to another word. Petit-Claud's demurs, so far from soothing the stout Cointet, appeared to irritate him.

"I would rather give more for a certainty, if I made only a small profit on it," he said, looking at his brother. "It is my opinion that things have gone far enough for business," he concluded.

"Still you came here for something, didn't you?" asked Petit-Claud. "What is your offer?"

"I offer to release M. Sechard, and, if his plan succeeds, to give him thirty per cent of the profits," the stout Cointet answered briskly.

"But, monsieur," objected Eve, "how should we live while the experiments were being made? My husband has endured the disgrace of imprisonment already; he may as well go back to prison, it makes no difference now, and we will pay our debts ourselves----"

Petit-Claud laid a finger on his lips in warning.

346

"You are unreasonable," said he, addressing the brothers. "You have seen the paper; M. Sechard's father told you that he had shut his son up, and that he had made capital paper in a single night from materials that must have cost a mere nothing. You are here to make an offer. Are you purchasers, yes or no?"

"Stay," said the tall Cointet, "whether my brother is willing or no, I will risk this much myself. I will pay M. Sechard's debts, I will pay six thousand francs over and above the debts, and M. Sechard shall have thirty per cent of the profits. But mind this-- if in the space of one year he fails to carry out the undertakings which he himself will make in the deed of partnership, he must return the six thousand francs, and we shall keep the patent and extricate ourselves as best we may."

"Are you sure of yourself?" asked Petit-Claud, taking David aside.

"Yes," said David. He was deceived by the tactics of the brothers, and afraid lest the stout Cointet should break off the negotiations on which his future depended.

"Very well, I will draft the deed," said Petit-Claud, addressing the rest of the party. "Each of you shall have a copy tonight, and you will have all tomorrow morning in which to think it over. Tomorrow afternoon at four o'clock, when the court rises, you will sign the agreement. You, gentlemen, will withdraw Metivier's suit, and I, for my part, will write to stop proceedings in the Court-Royal; we will give notice on either side that the affair has been settled out of court."

David Sechard's undertakings were thus worded in the deed:--

"M. David Sechard, printer of Angouleme, affirming that he has discovered a method of sizing paper-pulp in the vat, and also a method of affecting a reduction of fifty per cent in the price of all kinds of manufactured papers, by introducing certain vegetable substances into the pulp, either by intermixture of such substances with the rags already in use, or by employing them solely without the addition of rags: a partnership for working the patent to be presently applied for is entered upon by M. David Sechard and the firm of Cointet Brothers, subject to the following conditional clauses and stipulations."

One of the clauses so drafted that David Sechard forfeited all his rights if he failed to fulfil his engagements within the year; the tall Cointet was particularly careful to insert that clause, and David Sechard allowed it to pass.

When Petit-Claud appeared with a copy of the agreement next morning at half-past seven o'clock, he brought news for David and his wife. Cerizet offered twenty-two thousand francs for the business. The whole affair could be signed and settled in the course of the evening. "But if the Cointets knew about it," he added, "they would be quite capable of refusing to sign the deed of partnership, of harassing you, and selling you up."

"Are you sure of payment?" asked Eve. She had thought It hopeless to try to sell the business; and now, to her astonishment, a bargain which would have been their salvation three months ago was concluded in this summary fashion.

"The money has been deposited with me," he answered succinctly.

"Why, here is magic at work!" said David, and he asked Petit-Claud for an explanation of this piece of luck.

"No," said Petit-Claud, "it is very simple. The merchants in L'Houmeau want a newspaper."

"But I am bound not to publish a paper," said David.

"Yes, you are bound, but is your successor?--However it is," he continued, "do not trouble yourself at all; sell the business, pocket the proceeds, and leave Cerizet to find his way through the conditions of the sale--he can take care of himself."

"Yes," said Eve.

"And if it turns out that you may not print a newspaper in Angouleme," said Petit-Claud, "those who are finding the capital for Cerizet will bring out the paper in L'Houmeau."

The prospect of twenty-two thousand francs, of want now at end, dazzled Eve. The partnership and its hopes took a second place. And, therefore, M. and Mme. Sechard gave way on a final point of dispute. The tall Cointet insisted that the patent should be taken out in the name of any one of the partners. What difference could it make? The stout Cointet said the last word.

"He is finding the money for the patent; he is bearing the expenses of the journey--another two thousand francs over and above the rest of the expenses. He must take it out in his own name, or we will not stir in the matter."

The lynx gained a victory at all points. The deed of partnership was signed that afternoon at half-past four.

The tall Cointet politely gave Mme. Sechard a dozen thread-pattern forks and spoons and a beautiful Ternaux shawl, by way of pin-money, said he, and to efface any unpleasant impression made in the heat of discussion. The copies of the draft had scarcely been made out, Cachan had barely had time to send the documents to Petit-Claud, together with the three unlucky forged bills, when the Sechards heard a deafening rumble in the street, a dray from the Messageries stopped before the door, and Kolb's voice made the staircase ring again.

"Montame! montame! vifteen tausend vrancs, vrom Boidiers" (Poitiers). "Goot money! vrom Monziere Lucien!"

"Fifteen thousand francs!" cried Eve, throwing up her arms.

"Yes, madame," said the carman in the doorway, "fifteen thousand francs, brought by the Bordeaux coach, and they didn't want any more neither! I have two men downstairs bringing up the bags. M. Lucien Chardon de Rubempre is the sender. I have brought up a little leather bag for you, containing five hundred francs in gold, and a letter it's likely."

Eve thought that she must be dreaming as she read:--

"MY DEAR SISTER,--Here are fifteen thousand francs. Instead of taking my life, I have sold it. I am no longer my own; I am only the secretary of a Spanish diplomatist; I am his creature. A new and dreadful life is beginning for me. Perhaps I should have done better to drown myself.

"Good-bye. David will be released, and with the four thousand francs he can buy a little paper-mill, no doubt, and make his fortune. Forget me, all of you. This is the wish of your unhappy brother. "LUCIEN."

"It is decreed that my poor boy should be unlucky in everything, and even when he does well, as he said himself," said Mme. Chardon, as she watched the men piling up the bags.

"We have had a narrow escape!" exclaimed the tall Cointet, when he was once more in the Place du Murier. "An hour later the glitter of the silver would have thrown a new light on the deed of partnership. Our man would have fought shy of it. We have his promise now, and in three months' time we shall know what to do."

That very evening, at seven o'clock, Cerizet bought the business, and the money was paid over, the purchaser undertaking to pay rent for the last quarter. The next day Eve sent forty thousand francs to the Receiver-General, and bought two thousand five hundred francs of rentes in her husband's name. Then she wrote to her father-in-law and asked him to find a small farm, worth about ten thousand francs, for her near Marsac. She meant to invest her own fortune in this way.

The tall Cointet's plot was formidably simple. From the very first he considered that the plan of sizing the pulp in the vat was impracticable. The real secret of fortune lay in the composition of the pulp, in the cheap vegetable fibre as a substitute for rags. He made up his mind, therefore, to lay immense stress on the secondary problem of sizing the pulp, and to pass over the discovery of cheap raw material, and for the following reasons:

The Angouleme paper-mills manufacture paper for stationers. Notepaper, foolscap, crown, and post-demy are all necessarily sized; and these papers have been the pride of the Angouleme mills for a long while past, stationery being the specialty of the Charente. This fact gave color to the Cointet's urgency upon the point of sizing in the pulping-trough; but, as a matter of fact, they cared nothing for this part of David's researches. The demand for writing-paper is exceedingly small compared with the almost unlimited demand for unsized paper for printers. As Boniface Cointet traveled to Paris to take out the patent in his own name, he was projecting plans that were like to work a revolution in his paper-mill. Arrived in Paris, he took up his quarters with Metivier, and gave his instructions to his agent. Metivier was to call upon the proprietors of newspapers, and offer to deliver paper at prices below those quoted by all other houses; he could guarantee in each case that the paper should be a better color, and in every way superior to the best kinds hitherto in use. Newspapers are always supplied by contract; there would be time before the present contracts expired to complete all the subterranean operations with buyers, and to obtain a monopoly of the trade. Cointet calculated that he could rid himself of Sechard while Metivier was taking orders from the principal Paris newspapers, which even then consumed two hundred reams daily. Cointet naturally offered Metivier a large commission on the contracts, for he wished to secure a clever representative on the spot, and to waste no time in traveling to and fro. And in this manner the fortunes of the firm of Metivier, one of the largest houses in the paper trade, were founded. The tall Cointet went back to Angouleme to be present at Petit-Claud's wedding, with a mind at rest as to the future.

Petit-Claud had sold his professional connection, and was only waiting for M. Milaud's promotion to take the public prosecutor's place, which had been promised to him by the Comtesse du Chatelet. The public prosecutor's second deputy was appointed first deputy to the Court of Limoges, the Keeper of the Seals sent a man of his own to Angouleme, and the post of first deputy was kept vacant for a couple of months. The interval was Petit-Claud's honeymoon.

While Boniface Cointet was in Paris, David made a first experimental batch of unsized paper far superior to that in common use for newspapers. He followed it up with a second batch of magnificent vellum paper for fine printing, and this the Cointets used for a new edition of their diocesan prayer-book. The material had been privately prepared by David himself; he would have no helpers but Kolb and Marion.

When Boniface came back the whole affair wore a different aspect; he looked at the samples, and was fairly satisfied.

"My good friend," he said, "the whole trade of Angouleme is in crown paper. We must make the best possible crown paper at half the present price; that is the first and foremost question for us."

Then David tried to size the pulp for the desired paper, and the result was a harsh surface with grains of size distributed all over it. On the day when the experiment was concluded and David held the sheets in his hand, he went away to find a spot where he could be alone and swallow his bitter disappointment. But Boniface Cointet went in search of him and comforted him. Boniface was delightfully amiable.

"Do not lose heart," he said; "go on! I am a good fellow, I understand you; I will stand by you to the end."

"Really," David said to his wife at dinner, "we are with good people; I should not have expected that the tall Cointet would be so generous." And he repeated his conversation with his wily partner.

Three months were spent in experiments. David slept at the mill; he noted the effects of various preparations upon the pulp. At one time he attributed his non-success to an admixture of rag-pulp with his own ingredients, and made a batch entirely composed of the new material; at another, he endeavored to size pulp made exclusively from rags; persevering in his experiments under the eyes of the tall Cointet, whom he had ceased to mistrust, until he had tried every possible combination of pulp and size. David lived in the paper-mill for the first six months of 1823--if it can be called living, to leave food untasted, and go in neglect of person and dress. He wrestled so desperately with the difficulties, that anybody but the Cointets would have seen the sublimity of the struggle, for the brave fellow was not thinking of his own interests. The moment had come when he cared for nothing but the victory. With marvelous sagacity he watched the unaccountable freaks of the semi-artificial substances called into existence by man for ends of his own; substances in which nature had been tamed, as it were, and her tacit resistance overcome; and from these observations drew great conclusions; finding, as he did, that such creations can only be obtained by following the laws of the more remote affinities of things, of "a second nature," as he called it, in substances.

Towards the end of August he succeeded to some extent in sizing the paper pulp in the vat; the result being a kind of paper identical with a make in use for printers' proofs at the present day--a kind of paper that cannot be depended upon, for the sizing itself is not always certain. This was a great result, considering the condition of the paper trade in 1823, and David hoped to solve the final difficulties of the problem, but--it had cost ten thousand francs.

Singular rumors were current at this time in Angouleme and L'Houmeau. It was said that David Sechard was ruining the firm of Cointet Brothers. Experiments had eaten up twenty thousand francs; and the result, said gossip, was wretchedly bad paper. Other manufacturers took fright at this, hugged themselves on their old-fashioned methods, and, being jealous of the Cointets, spread rumors of the approaching fall of that ambitious house. As for the tall Cointet, he set up the new machinery for making lengths of paper in a ribbon, and allowed people to believe that he was buying plant for David's experiments. Then the cunning Cointet used David's formula for pulp, while urging his partner to give his whole attention to the sizing process; and thousands of reams of the new paper were despatched to Metivier in Paris.

When September arrived, the tall Cointet took David aside, and, learning that the latter meditated a crowning experiment, dissuaded him from further attempts.

"Go to Marsac, my dear David, see your wife, and take a rest after your labors; we don't want to ruin ourselves," said Cointet in the friendliest way. "This great triumph of yours, after all, is only a starting-point. We shall wait now for awhile before trying any new experiments. To be fair! see what has come of them. We are not merely paper-makers, we are printers besides and bankers, and people say that you are ruining us."

David Sechard's gesture of protest on behalf of his good faith was sublime in its simplicity.

"Not that fifty thousand francs thrown into the Charente would ruin us," said Cointet, in reply to mute protest, "but we do not wish to be obliged to pay cash for everything in consequence of slanders that shake our credit; that would bring us to a standstill. We have reached the term fixed by our agreement, and we are bound on either side to think over our position."

"He is right," thought David. He had forgotten the routine work of the business, thoroughly absorbed as he had been in experiments on a large scale.

David went to Marsac. For the past six months he had gone over on Saturday evening, returning again to L'Houmeau on Tuesday morning. Eve, after much counsel from her father-in-law, had bought a house called the Verberie, with three acres of land and a croft planted with vines, which lay like a wedge in the old man's vineyard. Here, with her mother and Marion, she lived a very frugal life, for five thousand francs of the purchase money still remained unpaid. It was a charming little domain, the prettiest bit of property in Marsac. The house, with a garden before it and a yard at the back, was built of white tufa ornamented with carvings, cut without great expense in that easily wrought stone, and roofed with slate. The pretty furniture from the house in Angouleme looked prettier still at Marsac, for there was not the slightest attempt at comfort or luxury in the country in those days. A row of orange-trees, pomegranates, and rare plants stood before the house on the side of the garden, set there by the last owner, an old general who died under M. Marron's hands.

David was enjoying his holiday sitting under an orange-tree with his wife, and father, and little Lucien, when the bailiff from Mansle appeared. Cointet Brothers gave their partner formal notice to appoint an arbitrator to settle disputes, in accordance with a clause in the agreement. The Cointets demanded that the six thousand francs should be refunded, and the patent surrendered in consideration of the enormous outlay made to no purpose.

"People say that you are ruining them," said old Sechard. "Well, well, of all that you have done, that is the one thing that I am glad to know."

At nine o'clock the next morning Eve and David stood in Petit-Claud's waiting-room. The little lawyer was the guardian of the widow and orphan by virtue of his office, and it seemed to them that they could take no other advice. Petit-Claud was *delighted to see his clients, and insisted that M. and Mme. Sechard should do him the pleasure of breakfasting with him.*

"Do the Cointets want six thousand francs of you?" he asked, smiling. "How much is still owing of the purchase-money of the Verberie?"

"Five thousand francs, monsieur," said Eve, "but I have two thousand----"

"Keep your money," Petit-Claud broke in. "Let us see: five thousand--why, you want quite another ten thousand francs to settle yourselves comfortably down yonder. Very good, in two hours' time the Cointets shall bring you fifteen thousand francs----"

Eve started with surprise.

"If you will renounce all claims to the profits under the deed of partnership, and come to an amicable settlement," said Petit-Claud. "Does that suit you?"

"Will it really be lawfully ours?" asked Eve.

"Very much so," said the lawyer, smiling. "The Cointets have worked you trouble enough; I should like to make an end of their pretensions. Listen to me; I am a magistrate now, and it is my duty to tell you the truth. Very good. The Cointets are playing you false at this moment, but you are in their hands. If you accept battle, you might possibly gain the lawsuit which they will bring. Do you wish to be where you are now after ten years of litigation? Experts' fees and expenses of arbitration will be multiplied, the most contradictory opinions will be given, and you must take your chance. And," he added, smiling again, "there is no attorney here that can defend you, so far as I see. My successor has not much ability. There, a bad compromise is better than a successful lawsuit."

"Any arrangement that will give us a quiet life will do for me," said David.

Petit-Claud called to his servant.

"Paul! go and ask M. Segaud, my successor, to come here.--He shall go to see the Cointets while we breakfast" said Petit-Claud, addressing his former clients, "and in a few hours' time you will be on your way home to Marsac, ruined, but with minds at rest. Ten thousand francs will bring you in another five hundred francs of income, and you will live comfortably on your bit of property."

Two hours later, as Petit-Claud had prophesied, Maitre Segaud came back with an agreement duly drawn up and signed by the Cointets, and fifteen notes each for a thousand francs.

"We are much indebted to you," said Sechard, turning to Petit-Claud.

"Why, I have just this moment ruined you," said Petit-Claud, looking at his astonished former clients. "I tell you again, I have ruined you, as you will see as time goes on; but I know you, you would rather be ruined than wait for a fortune which perhaps might come too late."

"We are not mercenary, monsieur," said Madame Eve. "We thank you for giving us the means of happiness; we shall always feel grateful to you."

"Great heavens! don't call down blessings on me!" cried Petit-Claud. "It fills me with remorse; but today, I think, I have made full reparation. If I am a magistrate, it is entirely owing to you; and if anybody is to feel grateful, it is I. Good-bye."

As time went on, Kolb changed his opinion of Sechard senior; and as for the old man, he took a liking to Kolb when he found that, like himself, the Alsacien could neither write nor read a word, and that it was easy to make him tipsy. The old "bear" imparted his ideas on vine culture and the sale of a vintage to the ex-cuirassier, and trained him with a view to leaving a man with a head on his shoulders to look after his children when he should be gone; for he grew childish at the last, and great were his fears as to the fate of his property. He had chosen Courtois the miller as his confidant. "You will see how things will go with my children when I am under ground. Lord! it makes me shudder to think of it."

Old Sechard died in the month of March, 1929, leaving about two hundred thousand francs in land. His acres added to the Verberie made a fine property, which Kolb had managed to admiration for some two years.

David and his wife found nearly a hundred thousand crowns in gold in the house. The department of the Charente had valued old Sechard's money at a million; rumor, as usual, exaggerating the amount of a hoard. Eve and David had barely thirty thousand francs of income when they added their little fortune to the inheritance; they waited awhile, and so it fell out that they invested their capital in Government securities at the time of the Revolution of July.

Then, and not until then, could the department of the Charente and David Sechard form some idea of the wealth of the tall Cointet. Rich to the extent of several millions of francs, the elder Cointet became a deputy, and is at this day a peer of France. It is said that he will be Minister of Commerce in the next Government; for in 1842 he married Mlle. Popinot, daughter of M. Anselme Popinot, one of the most influential statesmen of the dynasty, deputy and mayor of an arrondissement in Paris.

David Sechard's discovery has been assimilated by the French manufacturing world, as food is assimilated by a living body. Thanks to the introduction of materials other than rags, France can produce paper more cheaply than any other European country. Dutch paper, as David foresaw, no longer exists. Sooner or later it will be necessary, no doubt, to establish a Royal Paper Manufactory; like the Gobelins, the Sevres porcelain works, the Savonnerie, and the Imprimerie royale, which so far have escaped the destruction threatened by bourgeoisvandalism.

David Sechard, beloved by his wife, father of two boys and a girl, has the good taste to make no allusion to his past efforts. Eve had the sense to dissuade him from following his terrible vocation; for the inventor like Moses on Mount Horeb, is consumed by the burning bush. He cultivates literature by way of recreation, and leads a comfortable life of leisure, befitting the landowner who lives on his own estate. He has bidden farewell for ever to glory, and bravely taken his place in the class of dreamers and collectors; for he dabbles in entomology, and is at present investigating the transformations of insects which science only knows in the final stage.

Everybody has heard of Petit-Claud's success as attorney-general; he is the rival of the great Vinet of Provins, and it is his ambition to be President of the Court-Royal of Poitiers.

Cerizet has been in trouble so frequently for political offences that he has been a good deal talked about; and as one of the boldest enfants perdus of the Liberal party he was nicknamed the "Brave Cerizet." When Petit-Claud's successor compelled him to sell his business in Angouleme, he found a fresh career on the provincial stage, where his talents as an actor were like to be turned to brilliant account. The chief stage heroine, however, obliged him to go to Paris to find a cure for love among the resources of science, and there he tried to curry favor with the Liberal party.

As for Lucien, the story of his return to Paris belongs to the Scenes of Parisian_ life.

ADDENDUM

The following personages appear in other stories of the Human Comedy.

Cerizet Two Poets A Man of Business Scenes from a Courtesan's Life The Middle Classes

Chardon, Madame (nee Rubempre) Two Poets Scenes from a Courtesan's Life

Chatelet, Sixte, Baron du Two Poets A Distinguished Provincial at Paris Scenes from a Courtesan's Life The Thirteen

Chatelet, Marie-Louise-Anais de Negrepelisse, Baronne du Two Poets A Distinguished Provincial at Paris The Government Clerks

Cointet, Boniface Two Poets The Firm of Nucingen The Member for Arcis

Cointet, Jean Two Poets

Collin, Jacques Father Goriot A Distinguished Provincial at Paris Scenes from a Courtesan's Life The Member for Arcis

Conti, Gennaro Beatrix

Courtois Two Poets

Courtois, Madame Two Poets

Hautoy, Francis du Two Poets

Herrera, Carlos Scenes from a Courtesan's Life

Marron Scenes from a Courtesan's Life

Marsay, Henri de The Thirteen The Unconscious Humorists Another Study of Woman The Lily of the Valley Father Goriot Jealousies of a Country Town Ursule Mirouet A Marriage Settlement A Distinguished Provincial at Paris Letters of Two Brides The Ball at Sceaux Modeste Mignon The Secrets of a Princess The Gondreville Mystery A Daughter of Eve

Metivier The Government Clerks The Middle Classes

Milaud The Muse of the Department

Nucingen, Baron Frederic de The Firm of Nucingen Father Goriot Pierrette Cesar Birotteau A Distinguished Provincial at Paris Scenes from a Courtesan's Life Another Study of Woman The Secrets of a Princess A Man of Business Cousin Betty The Muse of the Department The Unconscious Humorists

Nucingen, Baronne Delphine de Father Goriot The Thirteen Eugenie Grandet Cesar Birotteau Melmoth Reconciled A Distinguished Provincial at Paris The Commission in Lunacy Scenes from a Courtesan's Life Modeste Mignon The Firm of Nucingen Another Study of Woman A Daughter of Eve The Member for Arcis

Petit-Claud Two Poets

Pimentel, Marquis and Marquise de Two Poets

Postel Two Poets

Prieur, Madame Two Poets

Rastignac, Baron and Baronne de (Eugene's parents) Father Goriot Two Poets

Rastignac, Eugene de Father Goriot A Distinguished Provincial at Paris Scenes from a Courtesan's Life The Ball at Sceaux

Lightning Source UK Ltd.
Milton Keynes UK
UKHW030617060220
358273UK00005B/263